Decay

By D.C. Fortune

To request permissions, contact the author at authordcfortune@gmail.com

ISBN 979-8-218-20688-8 (ebook)
ISBN 979-8-218-22145-4 (paperback)
ISBN 979-8-218-22373-1 (hardcover)

First edition — August 2023

Cover art by Damonza

Published by D.C. Fortune

Table of Contents

Chapter 1...2

Chapter 2..14

Chapter 3..24

Chapter 4..40

Chapter 5..48

Chapter 6..59

Chapter 7..87

Chapter 8..92

Chapter 9...102

Chapter 10..119

Chapter 11..133

Chapter 12..151

Chapter 13..161

Chapter 14..181

Chapter 15..192

Chapter 16..203

Chapter 17..207

Chapter 18..216

Chapter 19..222

Chapter 20..235

Chapter 21..242

Chapter 22..248

Chapter 23..256

Chapter 24..260

Chapter 25..262

Chapter 26..268

Chapter 27...284

Chapter 28...302

Chapter 29...314

Chapter 30...317

Chapter 31...329

Chapter 32...332

Chapter 33...344

Chapter 34...371

Chapter 35...393

Chapter 36...418

Chapter 37...422

Chapter 38...430

Chapter 39...439

Chapter 40...442

Chapter 41...455

Chapter 42...460

Chapter 43...462

Chapter 44...465

Chapter 45...467

Chapter 46...477

Chapter 47...481

Chapter 48...493

Chapter 49...496

Chapter 50...503

Chapter 51...505

Chapter 52...511

Chapter 53...525

Chapter 54...533

Chapter 55...557

Chapter 56..583

Chapter 57..594

Chapter 58..620

Chapter 59..628

Chapter 60..631

Chapter 61..635

Chapter 62..649

Chapter 63..653

Chapter 64..664

Chapter 65..672

Chapter 66..674

Chapter 67..691

Chapter 68..709

Chapter 69..721

Chapter 70..723

Chapter 71..732

Chapter 72..739

Chapter 73..750

Chapter 74..762

Chapter 75..769

Chapter 76..770

Chapter 77..790

Chapter 1

Enslaved to a Nightmare

Every day that she wakes up, Maeva is shaken to her feet by a terrible menace, and sometimes by more than one. They speak with no voice of oppressive terror—their presence has enough power over her. Yesterday, the menace was Fatigue. The day before that was Hunger. Today, it is Hopelessness. She hates that vile feeling the most. It's the one thing that truly immobilizes her willpower to go forward and back and forward again the next day down one of the innumerable underground tunnels that she's forced herself to memorize.

The feeling of fatigue isn't lingering as long today, so maybe she *will* reach the end of the tunnel this time before she eventually collapses and has to crawl back to where she originally started, all while dragging her feet and pulling her heart by its non-elastic strings. A heart that has been tortured yesterday by Misery, whipped by Despair the day before, and scrounging for crumbs of Numbness today.

She's… getting into that unhealthy mindset again. And this frigid sensation *really* needs to stop biting at her swollen ankles. Goodness, does it all want to make her scream. Although, the cold is more severe than usual today. That can only mean one thing.

Nearly four years… has it really been that long? she wonders to herself. *I'm basically complaining about nothing but my own self at this point… I'm the only one who makes myself suffer like this.*

Maybe I'll grant myself permission today to finally say goodbye. I can tell I've been overstaying the welcome…

A few splashes of grime and sludge that precipitate from the jagged ceiling above interrupts her to help keep her senses in check. Naturally, she has to wipe her face off. She does appreciate the distraction, but there's no way she can get her baleful thoughts under control anymore.

A bloody tinge of scarlet light glows throughout the tunnel from an open maw in the distance as she nears. It overshadows the dark-red iris of Maeva's eyes and reveals the sunken creases in her skin and her soiled attire along with a sinister-looking black gauntlet on her right arm. She doesn't dare to look at herself anymore, using her gauntlet to block the light just to ensure it.

The discordant sounds of crashing waves, along with a thick and salty aroma, act as a greeting as she arrives at the tunnel's edge. Blood-colored water tickles her soles as she stares out into the ocean's great expanse. She then closes her eyes to bask in what little of the light that pierces the ominous clouds and nightmarish sky can hardly offer. Her moment of solace is disrupted as something damp and squishy brushes up against her feet.

She's half expecting it to be a sea creature, hopefully a deadly one to put her out of her misery. She opens her eyes, finding that it's a stranded and ocean-raped corpse instead. She crouches down next to the body—and examines it.

Let's see here… body mostly intact, a good chance of having its soul, and… no signs of infection?

Her gauntlet responds to her findings, opening its giant eye located at the backside of it. She gets hit with an idea—a distasteful one, but rationality hasn't been the reason she's been alive for so long. She grabs both of the corpse's arms—and pulls. The thrill of what she anticipates gives her the needed boost to drag the putrid flesh-bag through the caves, down into a new but much deeper path.

Her planned destination ends at the belly of the beast—a colossal cavern that provides undoubted shelter, a constant refreshment of peace and quiet, a home, and if this spell of hers works, and it's a major *if*, it'll become *their* home. She drops the corpse, making sure it's not too close to her bed as a safety measure in case an error on her part makes it explode or something.

Her gaze soon locks onto the ebony gauntlet that blinks alongside her. The gauntlet's gelatinous-like frame twists and coils around itself and sweats with a fine black substance, showing its eagerness, but only intimidating her more.

No time to rest, Maeva thinks, trying to overcome her reluctance.

She raises the gauntlet, aiming it at the corpse. She makes quick adjustments to pace her erratic breathing and attempts to focus every sliver of her leftover energy that was meant for the rest of the day into one single command.

"Restore!"

The gauntlet starts to glow a sickly shade of dull gray and shrieks out from its own uncontrollable surge of power, forcing the unprepared Maeva to struggle in maintaining her spell. The corpse's skin and organs begin to regenerate, causing the body to contort and thrash about wildly—a horrific and violent display of unholy reanimation. The performance finally ends, the gauntlet simmers down, and Maeva, takes a deep sigh of relief.

The body rises as if possessed and stands upright, albeit a little twitchy—must be a side effect. Its eyes open and it awakens with a scream. "Ah!"

"Gahh!" Maeva returns with a shriek.

The man, now reborn, looks at his hands in disbelief. "I-I'm alive?" He touches and caresses his nude and slightly blue body. "I can't believe this…"

Maeva gives a glint of a smile, believing that his expression is nothing more than contained elation. "Your welco—"

"Fuck! I'm alive!" He glares down at Maeva with a wicked type of fiery emotion born from his awoken soul. "Did you do this?"

"Ye-yeah?"

The man scrunches his face in disgust as he picks and scratches at his easy-to-peel skin. "Damn you! Look at me, what even am I?" he says, still ripping at his regenerating body. "You think you can just go shopping around for dead people and toy around with them just because you're depraved enough to do it?"

Maeva only stares at him in bewilderment. She cannot help but wonder if she somehow miscalculated the spell, or if she's *really that inept.* She ignores that slanderous thought and aims her gauntlet once again, hoping to use it to quell his anger, though the device only proves useless as it remains inactive and slumbers.

Instead of showing any signs of conforming, the man only looks at Maeva with increasing concern. And hatred. "The hell are you doing?" he asks.

"I'm trying to get you fully under my control… or at least get you to act right."

"Do those red eyes of yours mean that you're blind? I'm not some dumb beast or pet you can take advantage of."

Maeva chuckles. "A bonded undead is no different than a tamed beast. In other words, a petulant soul like you is naturally a subordinate to a necromancer like myself."

The man's eyes widen. "You look more like a swamp hag," he states, glossing over the various patches of caked filth all across her body "Who are you anyway?"

Maeva arranges herself into a more befitting position, seizing this opportunity to hopefully empower with brilliant dominance. "I am Maeva Solunn!" she proclaims. "The people of this land fear my title as one of the six Harbingers. But in regard to you, my slave, you may only refer to me as… master."

The 'slave' can only shake his head at her. "It still sounds like you're mistaking me for something like a dog. You think just because you revived me that I should just kneel and offer my services and gratitude?" He then directs a firm finger towards her, and almost snarls in his expression. "Who in their right mind would ever bark like a bitch for a bitch?"

Maeva cracks a weakened part of her bed with her tightening grip. "Did you not hear what I just said? I own you now. So just as I gave you life, I can also take it away!"

"Good!" the Slave responds with haste. "I never asked for this anyway…"

She can't really blame him for feeling the way he does—but she can shame him. "Then how about you ask for some attire. I'm tired of looking at your… I'm just tired of looking at you in general." She then points to a nearby pile of unwashed clothes and underwear.

The Slave scrounges through the dirty heap of hand-me-downs. Obviously nothing fits his size, or taste, but he does find something suitable enough to not be too embarrassed to wear. It's something stitched, from the leathery hide of an unknown beast. He does admire the detail, and how it scratches *jussst* right at the itches that cease to end.

"Alright," he begins to say. "So, you desire a mindless plaything. But what could you possibly need from someone like me? I'm no warrior so I can't slay your enemies, and I'm not sly so I can't poison any kings."

"That would've been too much to ask of you anyway," Maeva says. "With your stupidity, you seem like the type that would try to fistfight a dragon."

"Whatever. So, if it's not anything major then… why? Surely a wise necromancer such as yourself would have an understandable reason for not finding the nearest battlefield and raising someone more beneficial to your stupid cause."

"I have no desire to wreak any havoc, at least, no more than what has already passed… I just wanted a companion."

"A companion? So your first choice was a corpse instead of something normal like a bird or a horse? Hell, even a rock would have made more sense—there's plenty here."

Maeva can feel her heart swearing at her inability to muster more strength to properly explain. "Of course I didn't want to stoop to using the dead, but those other things you mentioned, there's no point in searching… They're probably long extinct by now."

She's really annoying, the Slave thinks. *But... it's getting harder to ignore her ramblings. They make so little sense.*

The Slave inhales and releases a breath of rancid air. "Listen, I have every right to be pissed right now because I'm positive that anyone who expects death one day shouldn't have to anticipate coming back to life, ever—but you're giving me the impression that there is something else than my current state I should be more concerned with, so I'm willing to give you a chance. For about five minutes."

He sits on Maeva's bed, it feels like heaven compared to the surrounding dense environment he's been standing on. "So tell me what's been troubling you… Master."

How silly to entertain her ridiculous command for calling her by title, but the air does feel lighter now. She smiles upon it.

In preparation, Maeva calms her beating heart and opens her mouth, readying to flash flood her temporary therapist with every detail she can think of that entails the definition of her hardships, but just as she does, footsteps are heard echoing deep from within the darkness, the type of sound that should be nigh impossible since this domain is only known and accessible to her alone—she's worked herself ragged to make sure of that.

There is little time to ponder the hows and whys though as danger nears.

"And here I thought you were some unfortunate hermit," the Slave says. "You should have told me there were more."

"You're wrong; I do live alone. Not as a hermit though, I want to make that clear."

"Then who's that?" he asks.

"An intruder obviously." Maeva rises from the bed. The pure determination and fearlessness that emanates from her face and commanding stance can rival the glory and regality of an empress. "To arms, slave! Defend your master!"

"…And you really have the gall to call me stupid. Didn't we just establish that I can't fight? Plus, you're a magic user, a dark one at that. Defend your own damn self."

"I've considered it, but I am feeling quite faint from dealing with all your constant horseshit today."

In the unbridled storm of aggressive back and forth that ensues amongst the work-in-progress duo, the mysterious intruder enters the main chamber. His clothes are dapper, but ragged and dirty enough to not be considered out of place.

As the enragement continues, the intruder can only stand from afar and enjoy the drama in merriment, although… *There's something about that woman.* The overuse of grim colors on her clothes along with the scarlet brightness in her eyes and hair that matches her fury looks extremely familiar.

"M-Maeva?" the intruder blurts.

Maeva jolts upon hearing her name. She spins around, searching for the source. As they both lock gazes, a warm and near forgotten feeling spreads inside them both evenly. "D-Draxis?" Maeva whimpers.

"Maeva!" Draxis says, elated. "I surely thought of you as dead! I'm glad those malicious thoughts were wrong but… how long have you been down here? You look disgraceful."

The Slave appears at Maeva's side, holding a splintered wooden beam. "So should I kill him or not?"

"What? N-No," she says, firmly. "Put that stick down before you hurt yourself, and where'd you get that from anyway?"

"I got it from over there," he responds, pointing at a now lopsided bed.

"What the hell, slave. That stick was meant to uphold the frame!"

"Don't yell at me! It's not like you have any weapons around here anyway."

A jovial chuckle comes from the one-man audience that is Draxis. "Still learning the art of Necromancy and soul-binding, I see? Otherwise, your wretched thrall there wouldn't act so rebellious."

"Wretched…?" the Slave mumbles.

"I hope you didn't come all this way to mock me," Maeva says.

"Hardly," Draxis responds. "This place was just a special location of interest I had in mind while on my travels."

"Travels? You mean, you've been exploring?"

"Well what else would I be doing? Praying? I don't do that."

"But where could you possibly want to go? There's nothing out there."

"I thought so as well seeing as how the majority of the places I've come across have been either hostile or near vacant. But Maeva—I've found it. I've finally found the epicenter of the world's collapse!"

"So? Who cares? It sounds like a breeding ground for the Decayed anyway."

"Hi, excuse me," the Slave interrupts. "I would like to know what the hell you two are talking about."

"He really is a rude one," Draxis says. "How about instead of stories, I just show you instead. To both of you."

"I'm not going out there," Maeva says. "I've already seen enough slaughter and carnage to the point where I've made up my mind to stay in here and here alone."

"Maeva… what happened to you? To think that *you* among the Harbingers would become so meek and feeble."

"I guess my eminence decayed away just like everything else."

"Was that meant to be a joke?" Draxis says. "Normally I would join your shallow levity, but not after hearing about you losing so much faith in our meaning."

"What meaning?" Maeva argues. "All is lost."

"Lost you say? You speak to me in the flesh, not as an old memory or a ghost. And I know the others who you claim to be lost are still out there fighting strong and hard."

"How can you be so sure?"

"Because we have unfinished business and unrequited justice that needs rectifying," Draxis says. "We must continue to stand insurmountable against the fears and subjugators that bring this world to its very knees, and that includes death itself. You believed in that truth once upon a time."

The Slave shuffles to Draxis, unable to avoid being entranced by his words of promise, and his own personal morbid curiosity.

"Wh-where are you going?" Maeva cries out to him.

"From what it sounds like, I'm about to venture into the unimaginable. I want to know what's been keeping you at bay all this time."

Draxis tags in to say, "Maeva, if there's a way to learn more of or somehow undo all of this destruction, then wouldn't you want to partake in it? Your help would be most… helpful."

"But we're not heroes, Draxis."

"You do realize that win or lose we're not going to be hailed as ones either way, right? But I still care enough about this world to want to *not* see it disappear forever." Draxis puts his hands in his pockets and turns his back towards her. "Maeva, it's been a miracle to see you alive and somewhat well, truly, but I'm not going to stay here forever with you. I have other places I seek to be. No matter what."

Maeva watches as they both disappear into the veil of the tunnel's darkness. Once again, she is in solitude. It's an aching feeling that resurfaces no matter how hard she tries to avoid it—just like the collapsing cold. Its encroaching grasp causes her teeth to chatter and break her enough to let those unwelcome thoughts of hunger, fatigue, and hopelessness invade her mind again. Corroding it, ever so slowly.

In an instant, she explodes into a mad sprint, barely avoiding crashing into the others as she catches up.

"Decided to join us?" Draxis asks.

"Just leave me be for now," Maeva says. "It's hard enough trying to build enough resolve to move."

Draxis grabs her shoulder, only offering mute consolation, and eventually letting go. He points to a nearby tunnel that inclines upward. "I broke in through here. It's a little steep, but thankfully it doesn't go too far up. Ready?"

Up-and-up they climb as their hearts beat rapidly at the sight of the approaching outdoors. Finally escaping the dreadful subterranean caverns and free to roam around on an overhang jutting out the mountainside, the trio scans the woodland landscape below and at the faraway horizon that bleeds into the sky. Draxis stands at the edge, unfazed by the twisted sight of decay and dead foliage. In a way, he admires it.

"What's… wrong with the sky?" the horrified Slave asks, staring at the rolling black clouds that complement the beauty of the world's despair.

"Oh, that?" Draxis says. "Honestly, I'm not too sure. No one else knows either. It happened a long while ago actually. You get used to it—especially if your favorite color is red."

Maeva takes a step back from the overwhelming sight and half-considers making a full retreat. "So, this is just how things are. I don't know why I kept trying to survive against a world that isn't going to change… Absolutely nothing has changed."

"Maybe not for you, but it has for me," the Slave says. "I feel like a fresh newborn here. What happened?"

Draxis does his best to put on a smile. "What you are looking at is the aftermath of a global pandemic. In other words, you were brought back to life in the middle of an apocalypse. Happy to have you here!"

Chapter 2

During Times of Despair

"Even with all those shortcuts, trekking down that mountain was still a pain in the ass," the Slave says while stretching his legs. "How much farther?"

"You asked that at the perfect time becaussse—" Draxis slaps away an obstruction of branches and leaves to reveal a small but humble campsite. "We've finally arrived at my camp! I know it's not much, but we can at least take refuge here."

Everyone strolls around the area, getting a feel for their temporary enclosed dwelling. Maeva sits on a boulder directly from Draxis, while the Slave takes his chosen seat at the outer rim of the camp, near the closest tree. Draxis begins to build a campfire, giving a tuneful hum as he does so.

Maeva squirms in place as she watches him work. "Won't starting a fire be dangerous?"

"I don't think there's anyone left that would care about wildfires."

"That's not what I meant…"

Draxis grabs a bulky pouch from within his coat. "I've scouted this area the best I could beforehand. Just try to relax. Or better yet, you could assist me?"

"I'll pass."

"Hmph." He then pulls out two stones, one orange and one red. He clicks them together and they both roar to life with blazing flames. He throws them into the pile of twigs and kindling, birthing a gentle fire that becomes a mesmerizing sight and an engine of security.

Draxis holds his hands near the fire's embrace. Its embers soothe away any personal discomforts, although the same cannot be said for the others who jump at every rustle and shadow that moves. "You two are shaking more than a fire kraken in the polar wind." He picks up a small gray pebble from nearby. "May I propose a short exercise that should put your minds at ease? We'll start with you, Maeva."

It's insisted, because he tosses the pebble to Maeva who reacts unprepared, pelting her in the head. She stares longingly at the rock that assaulted her as she picks it up and cradles it between her hands. "This used to be a game, right? Those little miscreants always loved doing these types of things."

"Yes, they did… and so much more as well."

"I suppose I'll play. What did you want to ask me?"

Draxis watches the sparkle of the campfire. He stutters to say the right words. "I–I really wasn't expecting to find you so far down in the depths of Mt. Everstone, so far away from the world's troubles. Your appearance, your stench, the protrusion of your bones… I want to know what happened to you and how you've managed to survive. To put it lightly, you look like you should be dead."

"That's the troubling part, isn't it? Well, I have died—countless times."

"What…?"

Maeva looks at him with a deflective smile. "As you might have already guessed, I'm absolutely terrified of the world we live in, so I stowed myself away within the mountain. Permanently if I could help it."

She then glides her hand across her gauntlet as she says, "I'm the Harbinger of Scourges. I'm not a specialist in necromancy and reanimation like Lord Suvius is, but when I found this armament, I learned that I could emulate a small portion of his power. And since I was too afraid to leave the comfort of safety, whenever I… perished, from either dehydration or starvation, I used this item to revive myself—over and over and over and over again."

Draxis feels the pain from clenching his fists for so long. "Maeva… there's no way you actually lived that way for all this time, right? Not even a bite out of any random insects or mice?"

"You don't think I've tried? I couldn't enjoy that luxury for too long anyway since they became so scarce just like everything else. There were times where I even debated using this thing to find… alternative ways to eat—but it all would have been so inhumane."

She curls and tucks her legs into her chest.

"Is what I had to go through really so hard to believe? If it meant that I never had to fear being eaten alive or encountering something worse from this hell, then I went with the only repulsive option that only a coward like me could possibly follow through with."

"Don't say things like that about yourself," Draxis urges. "I'm not trying to belittle your circumstance, I promise. We're not as powerful in this world as we were in the previous, so I understand that you had to do what it takes to survive."

"…I wouldn't call what I went through survival." Maeva looks over and waves at the Slave, then she says to him, "Your turn." She throws the pebble at him.

He catches the stone perfectly and examines it quizzically while saying, "Me? I wouldn't even know where to begin."

"Then allow me," Draxis interjects. "What's your actual name?"

The Slave ponders while looking into the fire. "I don't think I ever had a true name as far as I can remember—I think. I'm pretty sure the names that I'm thinking of aren't something I would appreciate being called."

"Or, there are some memories of yours that are tarnished and difficult to reproduce, which could be for a variety of reasons that I'm sure your master failed to prevent or delve into exactly why they are suppressed in the first place."

"Wha—what did I do wrong?" Maeva asks, bewildered.

"You didn't do the bare minimum," Draxis says. "No research, no planning, and no ambitions. You didn't even bother to give him a name."

"Oh… was I supposed to?"

Draxis lets out an exasperated sigh. "When resurrecting or binding a Soul you want to command, always designate a name or title to them for established dominance and ease of manipulation. It's a golden rule."

"Well the damn gauntlet didn't come with instructions."

"Just leave defilement to the professionals."

"Can I choose my own name?" the Slave asks.

"Yeah sure, go ahead," Maeva groans.

The Slave gives a smile of triumph. "Then I choose… Rend!"

"Rend? That's not even a real name."

"Sure it is," Rend says, "because I'm not going to respond to anything else."

"Well, Rend, do you have a story?" Draxis asks.

"I suppose, but if you're looking for tales of heroism and endless glory then you're looking at the wrong person—obviously. My past life was very similar to how it is now—a slave."

He leans his back against the lifeless tree, letting all of his energy and focus pump into his mind. "There isn't really much to say about it all. I was a simple commoner that dreamt of living in big and pretty castles like everyone else, but I had no hopes of ever reaching it because of my enslavement. I forgot that Asshole's name, but I will never forget the way he treated me…"

No words come to the minds or lips of Maeva and Draxis as Rend drifts on his words, so they wait.

"I bet you two feel a bit sorry for me," Rend continues. "Well, there's no need to, I can handle that myself. Anyway, my former master, he worked as a smuggler, and during the rare moments where I could rest after being overworked and or beaten, I got to see the most wondrous sights on our travels… but eventually it wasn't enough to satisfy me and stall the depression.

"It got to the point where I felt numb to everything except for my prayers and wishes for death. And so, one day, I managed to steal the bastard's boat, sailed to I Don't Care, and I drank the finest brew of wine and poison—it tasted so good. And now I'm here, to be a slave once again… It's funny how life works like that."

"You never really had the chance to live your lives the way you want to, have you?" Draxis says. "It's a tragedy, and I'm sorry to hear it."

"It wasn't all for the worse one hundred percent of the time though. I got to fuck his wife."

"Ooof course you did."

"Of course I did," Rend repeats after him.

"Well regardless, that story is a prime example on why you try to do a bit of research before you randomly revive unknown people—Maeva."

"…I was lonely," she responds.

"Well thankfully, not anymore." Draxis holds his hand up towards Rend while saying, "Hit me!" Rend chucks the pebble, hard. Draxis catches the rock and flips it in his hand like he's tossing a coin, while giving Rend a 'nice try' look. "Alright. Go ahead you two. Just be sure to keep the questions—"

Rend raises his hand. "How did this 'apocalypse' happen? I don't know how long I've been gone, but there's no way things turned this sour so fast. Didn't you say it was because of some pandemic? Where is everyone? Am I infected? Why is everything so quiet? Where is the sun and moon—"

"Could you slow down? Thanks," Draxis says. "Anyway, the pandemic—the *Decay* pandemic. It all happened three years ago, give or take. A mysterious virus swept across the planet, and when I say it affected everything—it affected *everything*.

"The bizarre thing is that the virus used to be something minor, something more containable… that was, until Blighted Day. Ever since that doomsday, pure chaos surged: kingdoms were left decimated, numerous races and monsters alike fell one by one, the Decayed—that's what we call the victims of the plague—kept growing exponentially in numbers, and as for any promises of hope… they all went extinct."

"No cure has ever been found?" Rend asks.

"There's a society of mages called the Arbiters. They once claimed to have found a cure, but if you know them like we do, then it was easy to tell it was all a big lie. I'm certain they are the catalyst for the end of the world."

"Those house curtain wearing idiots and their arrogance," Maeva comments. "Look at where it got them."

Draxis throws the pebble into the blazing fire, effectively ending the game. "Unfortunately, that's all the info I can give as a survivalist. I know nothing of the true nature about the contagion itself nor do I know of any solutions."

"Wow. Well, I sure am glad I killed myself before everything turned to shit," Rend says.

"You shouldn't say things like that," Maeva tells him.

"I'm just staying optimistic. And remember, I wouldn't be here if it wasn't for you… Master."

"You two are the type of treat that I needed for all these years," Draxis chimes in. "Is there anything you wish to add to the story, Maeva?"

"Yeah—the Arbiters, I've always wondered why they acted so secretive and exclusionist about the cure. You would think that with the world at the brink they would've wanted any help they could muster, even from us."

"That question is ringing in your head too as well, I see? Hopefully we'll find the truth one day, and luckily, that day may come very soon."

Draxis reaches for something within his coat, again. He pulls out a faded, torn map and displays its contents. Maeva and Rend study the map, recognizing some of the colorful and labeled geography, all except for one particular spot that's highlighted with a circle far away from the continent and inside the middle of Harmony Sea.

"Do you two see it?" he asks.

"I see the ocean but there's nothing else there," Rend replies.

"No, there *is* something there," Draxis says, tapping the highlighted area. "Every piece of info I could find about their meeting place for the cure-all leads to somewhere uncharted within this exact spot."

"Okay… but that's a lot of distance to travel."

"Indeed, but I'm willing to put up with it." Draxis stands up and returns the map inside his coat. "There is no fortune to be made from this and there is no sane reason for putting up with the number of risks, but I really am failing to see any alternatives."

Draxis leaves and scours the area for comfortable ground. He only finds a suitable, hardened mound of mud and lies his head down on it. "You two are free to stay or leave, but remember what I said about the dangers that linger out here. Something needs to be done about it." He then lets out a rumbling yawn and closes his eyes.

Rend gets up and sits next to Maeva. "Well, what do you want to do?" he asks.

"I'll let you decide."

"I kind of want to join and help him out. Plus, I've never been on a daring adventure before."

"Alright. Then we'll go with that."

"Are you sure? We don't have to if you don't want to."

"My preferences don't matter," she says. "It'll be a nightmare whichever path I choose, but I suppose staying here is where I would feel the most comfortable."

"Oh, by the way," Draxis interrupts. "Rend, I'm guessing you don't need to eat, but for you, Maeva, there's some snacks inside that bag over there near the fire."

"I'll fetch it," Rend says. He inspects the bag as he carries it—there's an assortment of meats inside. He isn't sure if it's a curse or a blessing to be immune to its scrumptious temptation. "Here you go," he says, handing the bag to Maeva.

Maeva grabs the bag and cracks open the floodgates. She almost gets into a coughing fit as her senses are blasted with divine scents and clashing spices from such a powerful strike. Her hand glides across each juicy morsel, but she gives up on making a first choice and begins to have at it—but before she can, she stops herself due to unwanted attention from a peeping tom.

"Don't watch me eat," she says, glaring at Rend.

"Eat? That looks more like stuffing."

"Just shut up and go away."

"Fine…" He then disappears to find his own spot to rest for the night.

Maeva chomps away mouthful after mouthful at her feast, as silently as her rumbling stomach can allow. The more she eats, the more she sprinkles her own special and moist ingredient that condenses and streams down her face, adding salt and zest onto every bite she takes.

Chapter 3

Our Lord and Savior

Ouch is the first word that springs from Draxis as he is zapped with the need to stretch and massage his aching body's critical points, while also suffering from disruptions of blindness as his eyes adjust to the grim lighting. It's a struggle to identify whether it is day or night from this accursed sky, but seeing as how Rend is active enough to give a friendly wave at him, there is only one clear assumption.

Draxis joins Rend at his favorite tree, but not without noticing an absentee for morning greetings. "Where's Maeva?" he asks.

"She took one of our water flasks to tidy herself up."

"That selfish beast," Draxis remarks. "We don't have enough supplies as is, she can't just consume an entire resource."

"Hey, don't disrespect my master like that. It's been a while for her, so let her be a little irresponsible."

"Rend, you do realize that she's not a true necromancer, right? You aren't bound by a contract or spell, so you don't have to follow her to the ends of the world."

"No, I don't, but I'm not entirely against it either. She treats me well enough… That's more than anything anyone else has ever done for me."

"Well at least you acknowledge your unused freedom," Draxis says as he plops down next to him. "You do seem to keep her occupied—she needs that. I'll leave it alone."

The forest intervenes in their abrupt silence with its natural reactions to the wind, while simultaneously playing its unnatural sound of lifelessness. They both give each other a few anxious glances.

"Sooo… did you sleep well?" Rend asks.

"I've slept in worse conditions, but mud feels like a soothing luxury. And you?"

"Hell no, can you believe it? I know it didn't seem like I was complaining before, but this 'Undead' nonsense is stupid. I can't sleep, I can barely eat—I wonder if I can even shit."

"That's… quite the predicament," Draxis says.

"Yep…"

They leave the conversation hanging, still amazed at how much their time is wasted away on waiting.

"Yesterday you mentioned about heading to sea," Rend says out of the blue, "but how are we supposed to get there given the world's condition?"

Draxis pulls out the map and slides his finger across it in a curved direction going northeast as he speaks—starting from their estimated location in a small forest near Mt. Everstone at the bottom of the labeled continent: Piorna.

"It should be a fairly straight path, assuming we don't need to rely on any detours," Draxis says. "The hard part is navigating through this forest, but the moment we find Lake Saventa then we will know we're going in the right direction towards the Vomenn Kingdom, and the roads past that should lead us directly to the sea."

"And then what? Swim?" Rend asks.

"If the kingdom still stands then they could potentially lend us a ship if we're lucky. And if not, then we'll have to go with my backup plan, and I sincerely hope our fate doesn't turn out that way."

Maeva arrives from a thicket behind Rend's tree. She looks a lot cleaner and practically glows from proper hydration, though some work still needs to be done.

"Were it another five minutes of waiting and we would have deserted you," Draxis says.

"You two should really stop doing that," Maeva gripes.

Draxis points over to what might as well be luggage. "Carry those bags for us, Rend. It has everything we need, so try not to damage it."

"Since when did I become a pack mule?"

"I offered you a chance at independence, so don't fall into dismay about it now."

"Come on, slave. We're burning nonexistent daylight," Maeva commands as she swings by him.

Rend equips the backbreaking satchels and sacks and holds tight to their straps as he struggles to march forward, but not without first grumbling, "Assholes…" under his breath.

***

It's easy to tell that they are deep within the inner depths of the forest—or whatever can be identified as part of the forest. The environment is beyond corrupted. It's sinister, and more ravaged than the demolished huts and festering corpses that lie abandoned all around, not to mention the violet-colored muck that bleeds and secretes into everything it can possibly smear and stain itself into. Rend is the first to acknowledge this—and poke at it.

"No! Bad slave! Don't touch that stuff!" Maeva yells.

"Why? It's not hurting anything," Rend says, still finding it fun to make the goop and fleshy growths jiggle.

"That's the Decay you're touching!"

Rend reels back in horror. "How about a warning next time?"

"It's a little hard to warn such a careless fool."

"…But you're walking around ignoring this stuff."

"Because we're already infected," Maeva states.

"Okay you seriously need to start telling me these things."

"Well the fact that I haven't tried to bite your head off yet should be telling enough. Just try to keep your senses with you—consider *that* your warning."

At the forefront of the hike, Draxis leads the trio, focusing on nothing but steady progression and ignoring any of the telltale warnings. A clawing sensation snaps him out of his trance. His vision begins to warp, causing him to stumble and hold his head to steady himself. Haunting flashes of blood-soaked teeth, along with reverberating sounds of violent tearing, ripple through his mind as he struggles internally.

"Hey, you alright?" Rend asks him, keeping his distance. "My senses are telling me that liar over there just lied to me about you two being okay."

"N-No. I'm fine, just a minor sting," Draxis affirms. "Your concern is rightfully warranted though, this exposure to all this excess isn't good for any of us. I should have noticed it sooner. We should turn back before—"

Something fast zips towards the ground and imbeds itself perfectly at its sharp tip. *An arrow?* they all think in unison. They look up, seeing a dark canopy ceiling painted with multiple pairs of glowing purple dots beaming down back at them.

"Maeva… that gauntlet… can it be used offensively?" Draxis asks, refusing to look away for even a second at the flickering dots.

"I-I don't know," she says. "I'm not even sure if it can. It has a mind of its own sometimes."

"Then here." Draxis pulls out a serpentine dagger—it looks like it's been needed for several altercations, but still offers a reliance on lethality.

"You're arming me?"

"For later, but for now…" Draxis takes small steps to get a head start, motioning to the others to do the same. "Run!"

They all run for their lives in a desperate attempt to escape the shadows that hop from branch to branch and tree to tree without missing a step or beat in following and shooting at their prey. There's no time to think, no time for fear. Dodge the trees, avoid any tripping hazards.

"Rend, stay behind us!" Draxis shouts.

"Are you fucking crazy!" Another blur of motion darts past, this time driving itself through Rend's arm, making him cry out in pain.

"That's why!" Draxis says.

"We're not outrunning them!" Maeva says, huffing and puffing from the exhausting rush.

Draxis takes in Maeva's words and sees that the current dangers has vastly multiplied since their initial start. *They're toying with us...*

Something tall falls from treetops and lands with grace onto the path in front of them. Its eyes look like portals from being so vacant and solid in purple color, and purple gunk runs like a waterfall from its mouth and jagged fangs. More of the despicable creatures fall like rain into the soon-to-be arena, with some crawling in from nearby hiding spots. All of them are holding weapons consisting of bows, claws, and insatiable hunger.

Rend recognizes the pointed ears of the assailants. He can hardly believe his eyes. "Are those… elves?"

"Not anymore. They're all Decayed now." Draxis raises his fists, readying himself for a brawl. "Be prepared to fight."

"You're going to fight in that human form?" Maeva says to Draxis.

"I don't have a choice. There's been a severe drought of souls as of late."

"You don't have anything? Not even a minor one?"

"This is all I can manage unfortunately, not unless… you're planning on offering yours."

The trio backs away and huddles together, anticipating for the worst from the enclosing horde that cackles from whatever scheme they plan amongst themselves. The horde stops however as the ground cracks and crunches beneath their prey. Then, it ruptures, and breaks away into a giant pit, sending the three of them screaming as their narrow fall darkens and deepens.

Their descent opens into a large catacomb where colossal spiderwebs and what looks like years of gross decomposition decorates the walls. The squishy and dead flesh from a mound of corpses breaks everyone's fall.

Rend gives a pained groan as he looks around, seeing all of the precious necessities from the bags spill out across the bloated corpses. "Well… we just lost our stuff," he says, finding a stable place to stand. "Sorry."

"No, it's my fault," Draxis corrects. "My mind and thoughts were elsewhere, and we accidentally stepped into their territory because of it. Now we're stuck in this trap."

Rend breaks off the arrows that lodge perfectly in his vitals—each wound automatically repairs, to his surprise. "This doesn't look like a trap; I'm seeing a severe lack of spikes and giant bats." He tilts his head upwards at the coffins and sepulchers that line up and down along the walls, with offerings and coins placed on a few of them. "This place looks more like a dungeon or a tomb of some kind. I have a bit of experience with these since I've had to raid a few just so that bastard could maintain a full inventory."

"A dungeon sounds even worse," Draxis says. "We need to leave."

Nearby, Maeva stumbles about, tripping over the backs and skulls of the carcasses. She finds a nearby wall for stability, shaking as she slides down against it.

"Can we at least get a timeout?" Rend says. "Maeva needs a break."

"I'm sorry, but we can't—not until we get to safety. And who knows what those elves are planning for us." Draxis hops down off the pile of bodies and scans the room for an exit.

"He's really persistent, I'll give him that," Rend says out loud. Still thinking about Maeva, he goes to her, and notices the dagger that she wields tightly in her clutches. "Maeva, it's just me, which doesn't really mean much… but try to calm down."

Eventually, Maeva lowers her weapon and gives up a shaky hand, connecting it with Rend's. "I hate elves," she says.

"Me too. Oh wait, that's not true. I met this one elf who was also a nurse and she was absolutely gorgeous and she was also *really* good at—"

"Hey, I found a door!" Draxis shouts from below.

"Oh, neat!" Rend exclaims, immediately dropping Maeva's hand and rushing down.

"Hey, wait—" Maeva cries out before losing her grip and footing, making her tumble all the way down to the bottom of the corpse mound.

Draxis peeks around the door, scouting ahead. "I can't see a thing. You said you've explored these types of places before, Rend? Perhaps you should lead us?"

"I'm not listening to you ever again. That's how I got shot in the back like thirteen times."

"Fine…"

The door grinds and croaks as Draxis pushes at it. They enter upon a large chamber where rows of colossal pillars and life-sized sculptures lead to an immaculate sarcophagus in the middle of the room that's illuminated by a few skylights.

"Look at this shit," Rend says, kicking a nearby sculpture. "It bothers me how some people get better treatment in death than others."

"Well breaking things isn't going to change that," Draxis scolds. "And stop violating that statue."

"Or what? You worried that these things will come to life?"

"It wouldn't be the first time. I'm offended because that image you're wrecking deserves more praise, for that man is none other than Malphunnos, the God of Death. We, the Harbingers, fight under his feared name."

"You fight… for Death?" Rend asks.

"We do, because the fear of death is an incentive to lead a better life," Draxis says.

"That doesn't sound like something that would really work."

"Sometimes the best therapy to realign a misbehaving world is with unshakeable threats and harsh truths. Everyone's final judgment is inescapable. It even works on the undead."

"Whatever. I'm going to go steal some stuff."

"Caution really isn't in your vocabulary today, is it?" Maeva scoffs.

Ignoring her, Rend rushes over to the sarcophagus. He lifts open the lid and looks inside, and quickly wipes his hands on his clothes after coming into contact with a black, viscous tar that bubbles within the sarcophagus as if it's still brewing.

"Well, what do you see?" Maeva asks.

"Nothing. There's nothing here. Just some gross—"

The black liquid begins to swirl. It spins faster and tightens its rotations, forcing Rend to nearly consider backflipping as a means of retreat.

A tall humanoid shape erupts from the depths within like a geyser. The tar drains and trickles from the being, revealing that it has no muscle, no skin, no hair—just bone. The skeleton is also encased in encumbering and mystic midnight-black armor that is etched with insignias, symbols, and inscriptions that only *it* would know the meaning of.

"Who dares awaken me from my slum—!"

"Lord Suvius!" Maeva and Draxis both interrupt, in extreme elation.

Suvius stands motionless as he works to remember the two who stare at him like children gleaming at a unicorn. "Ahhh, it's you two… How unfortunate."

"Don't be like that," Draxis begs. "I know we're your favorites… Or would you prefer it if we were the others?"

"…I would rather you didn't fill my head with unnecessary thoughts," Suvius says. "But I assume that means you have no word on their whereabouts?"

"Not ever since Blighted Day when the world crumbled around us and forced us all to divide."

"What a painful day that was. If it wasn't for Mixon's amulet that Aluna snatched during the World War, then we would all be…"

"You've gone silent," Draxis says to him. "Memories still too fresh?"

"A lot of things are still fresh on my mind. All the terror and the screaming… and the unimaginable chaos. What about the situation outside these halls? Has anything improved?"

"Not in the slightest."

Suvius has no muscles to form a smile, but his rise in tone reveals salient rejoice. "Then this only further proves that under the deceitful hands of the Arbiters just how doomed this world truly was. Have you both worked to continue spreading our truth?"

Draxis gives a slight bow. "I can promise you that I have personally made valiant efforts to the best of my ability, Lord. Maeva on the other hand…"

"Wait-wait-wait, that's not true, uhhh… here, look!" Maeva says, scrambling to drag Rend to her side.

"Hey!" Rend hisses.

"I-I've found my own way of staying active by practicing necromancy. Just like you can do." Maeva forces a grin, showing all teeth.

Suvius returns her gesture by giving her 'accomplishment' a cold and thorough stare. Whatever he's taking his time processing, it doesn't seem good. "Your minion lacks discipline along with respect. He barely wields any dignity as well."

"Well fuck you too," Rend says.

"As I have correctly analyzed. I am disappointed, Young Maeva."

"Sorry…"

"Do not apologize, only learn from this," Suvius consoles. "You have performed better than most. I can sense that much within him."

Maeva nods, still disheartened by the news.

Suvius steps out of his bath, flooding the immediate area. "I might have been out of commission for longer than what I anticipated, so I shall follow your lead for now, Sir Draxis."

"Then you'll be joining us on our uninvited visit to the Arbiters' lair," he responds.

"Ah, so you've found their little hideaway. How intriguing."

A nearby sculpture rumbles to life and marches to one of the many doors along the walls, highlighting the exit.

"Woah, they can move?" Rend says. "I was just joking before."

"Indeed," Suvius says. "They are old crypt keepers blessed with Light magic to guard this catacomb eternally. They have made this place the perfect resort for me."

Going through the predetermined exit leads them to an ascending staircase where Maeva and Draxis cry out in pain as each flight up becomes more and more grueling. This trial impacts Suvius as well as he staggers and nearly falls backwards. Maeva and Draxis leap in to assist.

"Forgive me," Suvius says. "I have not yet fully recharged my magic."

"We can tell," Draxis says. "Normally you would berate us so much worse."

"Jests like that are why I sought a hiatus from this world."

At the top of the stairs, they arrive face-to-face with a circular stone gate that has strange and near-alien glyphs painted around its outer rim.

"These glyphs have been tampered with," Suvius says, confused. "These used to be in the language of the local tribes. Judging from the overuse of these slashes and dots, I take it that elves have infiltrated this area?"

"Coincidentally, that's exactly what we're running from," Draxis says.

"Such a disruptive race…" Suvius extends his hand and begins to list off the symbols in clockwise order. "Hala. Ineres. Maniet. Vala."

Each letter hums and glows at each successful callout he makes. Speaking the final word, *Gala*, the door rings out a melodious tune, then rolls over to the side, forcing scarlet light to enter the room.

"The only positive note about Elves is that their main language is easy to learn, though I guess it's technically a dead language now," Suvius says. "Pitiful. Let's continue onward."

Suvius is first to exit the underground and enter the infected forest. He stands and surveys the area, becoming suspicious of the silence, and mumbles out loud, "There are multiple presences here…" Suvius holds his hand out in front of his chest plate, tapping lightly against the etched symbols on it. "Which one of you should I summon…? How about this one? It's been a while. You need to catch up on your debt to me like the others."

The chosen symbol on his armor vanishes as a refined and glorious golden blade manifests before him. He glides a bony hand across the sword as if relishing in its future destruction.

"Look at that," Rend says, amazed. "Got any spares for us?"

"Each of you already have your toys, you just need to learn how to utilize them," Suvius says.

They each look at themselves, with perplexed expressions.

"We don't need a damn lesson right now, we're about to die!" Rend shouts.

"Correction: *They* are about to die." With both hands, Suvius raises his sword high above his head, and impales the ground while shouting, "Grim Sanctuary!" with a thunderous echo that matches the powerful shockwave of his spell.

A transparent barrier constructed out of silver light surrounds the group. The alluring luminescence attracts a ravenous pack of elves who charge towards the shielded group at speeds that could rival the nimblest of beasts. They all disintegrate as they thrash themselves against the glorious ward.

Suvius points his sword forward. "This barrier will move wherever I go, so let us carry on lest we exhaust patience and precious time."

"Your strength seems to have held up well," Maeva says.

"As long as nothing tries to hold it down," Suvius responds. "This plague has been ruthless in that regard. Ironically, necromancy has now become a dying form of magic, but fortunately I have a premade arsenal of souls from our old journeys to help me get by. Is my influence of strength the reason you lowered your morals to practice manipulating death?"

"Let's just say that necromancy has saved my life—and restored Rend's." Maeva then shows her gauntlet to Suvius and says to him, "All of my efforts were because of this thing. It stopped working recently though."

"Ah, so that device is how you were able to raise a body. Rend is the boy's name… Hmm. I'm surprised you are so attached to him."

"It would feel wrong not to," Maeva says. "I wasn't thinking properly when I resurrected him into this abysmal world. I don't want him to suffer because of my lack of foresight."

"That's… surprisingly thoughtful of you. I can aid you later on this matter. My advice for now though is to focus on improving his sense of survival…" Suvius says, drifting off his words as he watches Rend goof around and mock the Decayed at the barrier's edge. "Maybe you can start by instilling discipline first."

After a few more worthless deaths, the Decayed elves lower their weapons and back away—ceasing their assault at the barricade while staring and snarling at their prey.

"My word… They've stopped," Draxis says.

"This is getting convoluted," Suvius blurts. "Even I am struggling to keep up. Either we are reaching the borderlands of their territory, or the Decayed may harbor greater intellect than previously imagined."

"But I've never experienced anything of the sort during my travels," Draxis says.

"Perhaps not against lesser Decayed such as humans or some accursed spiders, but have you encountered anything more heinous beyond that?"

Draxis's silence gives a golden answer.

"We need to keep our wits about us on this journey," Suvius continues. "I fear that this new discovery is only the least of our worries… and only the beginning."

Everyone hugs close to Suvius as they follow each step he takes on the path that they pray in silence will remain unopposed.

Chapter 4

The Nature of the Beast

Maeva walks in front of Suvius. The danger has passed for now, but her 'looking over the shoulder' technique begins to grind on Suvius's nerves. It might be less irritating if she would just *pick up the pace.*

"You seem distraught, Young Maeva," he says.

"What isn't there to be distraught about? But my primary concern is… Draxis. He keeps looking at me, weirdly."

Suvius glances back at Draxis, who is further behind than what would be considered a normal or safe distance. He can tell that Draxis is making small but poor adjustments to conceal his glares, almost like he's combating against himself with his own eyes. "I have seen this look of his before. This is urgent." Suvius turns and faces Draxis, startling him.

"What's wrong? Do you sense something?" Draxis asks.

"No, but something drastic has come up and I'll require your help with it."

"Okayyy…?"

"Golem hearts. Do you possess any?" Suvius asks.

"Not anymore. I used a few to make a fire, but the rest of them were lost during our struggle."

"I require them. Go fetch some."

"Seriously, right now? Just what do you—"

"I do believe I enunciated my demand properly, did I not?"

Draxis initiates a fierce staring competition with Suvius. The tension inevitably breaks however. Hard.

"Fine. It better be for good reason though." Draxis steps off the dirt path, stomping into the forest with no clear direction.

"You sent him out there alone?" Rend asks Suvius.

"It is necessary, otherwise we would all be at risk. Maeva, for how long have these episodes of his occurred?"

"He was fine originally, but then he started acting all antsy when we came into proximity of some Decay growths. He never mentioned anything about it afterwards though."

"It's just like him to place others ahead of himself," Suvius sighs. "I can only guess that this means his normal fits of hunger are conflicting with whatever side effect from the Decay he suffers from."

"Oh, so he's one of those people that get really upset when they're hungry?" Rend asks. "Well that's too bad, we don't have any more meat."

"Meat?" Suvius says in a tightened voice, glaring down at Rend.

"Yeah. You know, the stuff that you lack… Why aren't you saying anything?"

Maeva's heart plummets, down to the negatives, before she says, "It's because he doesn't even *need* anything like meat. I-I was so hungry, it never even once occurred to me. And seeing as how I'm the only person here that's not undead, he wants to eat… me."

"What the hell, he eats people?" Rend squeals.

"Worse. He devours souls—or at least, he's supposed to."

"Draxis is the Harbinger of Famine," Suvius adds. "Meaning that everything that exists will be consumed by him until only he remains, if left unchecked that is. That inborn trait of his is fearsome, loathsome, but it is the sole component where he derives his health and power from. I do not want to conspire, but if he is developing a taste for things that should be well inedible to him then… we need to determine if he's going to be a liability."

"How are we going to find out which one he likes?" Rend asks. "We have neither. Well, not entirely." He then smirks at Maeva. She rolls her eyes in response.

"It's a displeasing idea, but we might have to do something a bit risky to determine his needs. Hunting," Suvius says.

"I don't know much about souls, but I for sure have scored my fair share of exotic beasts before," Rend says. "Although, thinking about it now, I haven't seen any wild creatures so far. Not even a bird. Weird."

"I mentioned that to you before," Maeva says.

"Honestly, I ignore half the things you say. So which animals are still running around?"

"Very few," Suvius responds. "And we are not hunting for game, child—we're going to be hunting… monsters." Suvius already has an idea in mind as he stares off into the shrouded darkness that envelops the side of the dirt path.

***

A lone Decayed elf bites and scratches at an infected tree. It is currently being stalked and studied in the far distance.

"This plan is so stupid," Rend whispers. "We barely survived the elf assault from before."

"We do not need to lay siege to the entire area," Suvius says. "We just require enough soul fragments to equal a whole meal, if possible."

"I'm not sure if it's a good idea to feed people spoiled apples though," Maeva comments.

"Fair logic, but those who are truly sick can never tell the difference." Suvius then steps out of the shadows, sneaking up towards the oblivious elf.

"Hey, wait—we don't even have a battle plan!" Rend cries out.

I always have a plan. Suvius thinks to himself as he gets closer to his unsuspecting prey and aims his hand at it. "Wither…" he says, making the elf drop to the ground and scramble around as deterioration overtakes it. A tiny and pale bluish-white orb floats in its place. Suvius holds and dances the trophy between his hands.

"I have never seen anything like that before in my entire life," Rend whispers to Maeva. "Not even during the displays from the traveling Arcane Circuses. He's not even afraid. Just what is he?"

"One who should never be trifled with," Maeva whispers back. "You're better off asking him yourself though. He loves talking about himself."

Suvius returns, having a battle of balance with the soul between his hands. "Are you two done chittering? Maeva, extend your arm out, the one with the gauntlet, palm up."

As Maeva follows his instructions, Suvius leans in and offers the soul to the gauntlet, doing so about as cautious as a surgeon. A mouth forms in the middle of her palm and inhales the soul.

"Was that supposed to happen?" Maeva asks, wishing she could take the damn freaky thing off.

"Draxis has told me the details about your unfortunate circumstance, but what I found to be interesting was the subject regarding that gauntlet. Seeing as how it can bring a person back to life, I figured 'soul harvesting' would be befitting for such a device."

"Did he emphasize that I had to actually die in order for it to activate? Seems like death is all this thing is good for."

"I wouldn't rely on that assumption," Suvius says. "If I can find a use for it without ever seeing it in action, then you can do the same as well. Ultimately you must remember to stay creative. You act childish enough to where you should be nurturing *some* amount of that."

"Childish?" she snarls. "I should grab a branch and shove it up your—"

A group of elves drop from the trees above. They hiss as they move around in scouting formation.

"Ah, more willing participants. Wonderful," Suvius says before charging at his victims at ramming speed. After an impressive but sickening series of bloodlust and reaping, Suvius shows his unimpressive haul. "This is worse than I ever imagined; no wonder they act so beastly. It's like their souls have been completely ripped out. This is all I have. Three halves. The rest were nothing but empty husks."

"Is there anything we can do to get more?" Rend asks.

"Not without putting ourselves at more risk. It's harrowing that souls are becoming a finite resource. Our current offerings can hardly be considered a hoard, but it should be enough to stall Draxis's hunger—or at least prevent any needs for midnight snacking," Suvius says, eyeing Maeva.

The gauntlet once again opens to receive its rich nourishment. Suvius pours each soul individually, inserting his 'coins' into the machine. A prize is soon burped out, and a soul amalgamation hovers and moans above Maeva's hand.

"Woah… Maeva's hand gave birth!" Rend says.

"Shut up," she growls.

"It's been long enough," Suvius says. "Let us hope he is not waiting on us."

***

Returning minutes later, the forest still looks spooky—so nothing's changed. It's almost like they never left.

"Good," Suvius sighs with relief. "He hasn't returned yet."

"What's taking him so long anyway?" Rend asks,

"It's very simple actually. I didn't specify my request."

"That's… a damn harsh loophole."

Suvius lets out a rumbling chuckle. "You would be surprised at the damage one could cause if they ignore or don't disclose trivial details. I have been drunk with delight countless times watching armies buckle because of it."

Draxis darts through the bushes and crashes onto the ground, his clothes torn and scuffed. "Well… that was an adventure," he says under his breath. "I got your damn—I got your Hearts."

"Excellent," Suvius says. "Throw one." He catches the pitched emerald-green stone and grinds it into dust in his hand, drowning in ecstasy from the particles that shimmer across his body. "Ahhh, my favorite flavor. If only these were more common."

"You sincerely had me rush out there just so you could score a high? Well, at least it wasn't in vain, I guess. Wouldn't be the first time." Draxis takes a moment to lie on the ground, with his body outstretched like the letter X.

This is the perfect moment. Suvius proclaims with visual signals to the others. "You look a little worn out, Draxis. Are you perchance… hungry?"

"I'm guessing you're just going to ignore my injuries, are you? Such a bizarre question, of course I'm hungry! What difference does it even make? Aren't we all starving in one way or another?"

"Valid point…" Suvius grumbles. "Maeva?"

Upon hearing her cue, she opens her palm, and the soul amalgamation swirls upwards, shining like a lightbulb. A lightbulb that's impossible to miss, impossible to resist, is what goes through the subconscious of Draxis's mind as the treat figuratively calls his name, making him squirm.

"Go ahead, Draxis. Eat," Suvius welcomes in anticipation.

Draxis loses against the fragility of his temperance and darts to his lure.

"Oh shit! Not me!" Maeva screams as she hurls the soul at him. "Here, take it!"

Draxis secures his goal and vacuums it in one gulp. For the narrowest of seconds, his eyes have the glint of a suspicious and common color of danger. "Wait… why did you three have a Soul?" he asks with a mouthful, reverting back to his proper senses.

Suvius steps forward. "While waiting, we scouted ahead and stumbled across a lingering Wisp. I figured you wanted one. Consider it a bit of consolation."

"A Wisp? Well no wonder it tasted funny—hate those things. They don't even make for a good morning meal, but… do you have more?"

"Nay."

"I guess one is enough. Thanks for the generous gift, everyone. Now I don't feel as furious for risking my life." Draxis then walks past them, picking at his teeth as he starts his stroll.

Suvius leans in near the others, and whispers, "We can conclude that Draxis still hungers for his natural tastes, which means we can keep him in order. But we do not know what's truly going on with his other side. We should each keep an eye on him and report any abnormalities."

"Told you should have let me kill him," Rend says to Maeva.

"Can you please just shut up."

Chapter 5

This is Insanity

A new foe has decided to accompany and stir some trouble amongst the group with its intangible presence and relentless pestering, but they have no other option than to brave its attacks head on.

The weather. The havoc it brings is neither an enveloping storm nor a severe disaster, but with the wind bending anything that proves powerless against it and with the debris that whisks around freely and smacks into everyone's faces, the pleasant thought of shelter grows more desirable. There is a somber light at the end of the tunnel however, a clear point in the distance, over a hill.

"Is that the edge of the forest?" Rend asks.

"Looks like i–i-it," Maeva tries to say, jumbling her words as a leaf flies into her mouth.

Rend scurries off ahead, certainly being an energetic child.

Draxis and Suvius are walking together side-by-side, enjoying each other's company.

"I may have developed a phobia over woodlands—and things with slender ears—but overall, that wasn't too bad," Draxis says. "If you're an optimist that is."

"Then in the words of an optimist, I have faith that we will reach our destination," Suvius says.

"By the way," Draxis starts to say as he points to Suvius's left eye, "You have a leaf in your eye. Or, eye socket, I mean."

"I can see yet I cannot see. How droll. My gratitude." Brown grainy specks slides off the leaf as Suvius removes it, catching his attention. *Odd. This almost looks like... sand?*

"E-Everyone?" Rend calls out, meekly.

"Rend?" Maeva says. "Goodness, what did he find now?"

They all join up with Rend who stands at a precipice—and at the precipice of defeat.

"Draxis, does a valley of sand count as a lake?" Rend says.

"A desert… no, no, this *is* a lake, right?" Draxis says, panicking and whipping out the map in desperation. "This should be Lake Saventa. We hit all the right checkpoints, and we've certainly made no wrong turns unless… unless what we're looking at is just another fragment of the world's chaos. But to have an entire lake vanish, I-I just don't even know what to say."

The woes of it all, making Maeva nearly drop to her knees. "There's no way we can cross this. This is suicide! We don't even have proper supplies."

"We can't give up. We're so close to the kingdom," Draxis says. "Or at least *I* personally cannot give up. I have so many unanswered questions. So, so many."

"To hell with any questions!" Maeva snaps. "What is there to even wonder? So far all we've seen is our worst nightmares not even coming close to what we've actually encountered. We need to stop! You need to stop!"

"…I don't think you truly know what you're asking for. Maeva, what you're essentially begging me to do is to become disillusioned with what's left of my hopes, and to sacrifice my hope for the world. I will never do such a thing."

"Settle down, children," Suvius barges in. "Do not fret, Young Maeva, we're stumbling into the familiar corners of what was once my home. I faintly remember there being a secret somewhere within this area in case of war."

"So?"

"So there's a chance it could be a hidden passage. It should be an ease of effort to find since the lake is… no longer present."

"Can't we just go around?" Maeva asks.

"If you wish to continue the risk of getting eliminated by a stray arrow, then by all means. We must strive for efficiency."

"I'm glad *some* of us agree on doing something productive," Draxis says. He then takes a gander past the overhang. There's enough sand built up to reach the floor of the desert safely. Undaunted, he launches himself, and surfs the dune all the way down. Suvius follows after him, performing a series of sword tricks during his slow descent.

"Think you can ride the sands, Maeva?" Rend asks.

"It looks really steep…"

"Maeva, you can't be afraid of every little thing. Otherwise even I will start to overshadow you, and you know I would never live it down." Rend then offers her an empty hand. "Now here, we need to catch up."

She accepts and says to him, "Promise you won't drop me?"

"Promise you won't scream in my ear?" Rend pushes himself backwards, giving a devilish look as he slides back and tugs her along.

Maeva holds on to her lifeline with both hands, bracing herself. The thrill and rush fades, not that there was much to begin with.

She lurches, multiple times, for his other hand for additional support—an endeavor made even more unforgiving as Rend avoids her touch like the plague.

"Nope, we're one-handing this," he says as their speed accelerates. He digs his feet in even deeper, cascading heaps of sand on top of them. At the end of their surf, they both resemble sand monsters—or better yet, snowmen, but made out of sand.

"You all are having way too much fun with this," Draxis sighs.

"Ca-can someone help me? I can't see," Maeva pleads alone as everyone else leaves.

***

Is it possible for tears to boil? A recurring question met with numerous variables. The red light of the sky, the layers and coats of sweat, and the scorching heat that lashes and whips its searing chains during their trudge through the forsaken desert—this is their experience, and it only feels like it has been an hour. They dread the thought of what their already ravished bodies will feel like when the hour strikes two. The air shimmers no matter where they look, but not enough to distort perception.

"There's someone over there," Draxis says, pointing ahead.

That *someone* he sees wears a cloak, an ultramarine blue one in particular. Only an imbecile would wear such a thing and sit out in the open in such unbearable weather while meditating. There's only one person that fits that criteria.

"Is… is that Jellop?"

"No way… I think it is him," Maeva says, squinting. "I knew cutting through this desert was a mistake. Let's just go around."

"I second that," Suvius says.

"Oh come now," Draxis says. "Jellop isn't that bad, he's just a bit disturbed."

"He makes me queasy," Maeva says.

"I second that," Suvius repeats.

"Well we need all the help we can get, and I know he'll simply ooze with excitement to do so," Draxis says.

"He oozes other things as well."

"I… cautiously second that."

"We should at least let him know we're still alive," Draxis says. "And I'm not going to hear any more complaints about it!"

Maeva and Suvius groan, dragging their feet behind Draxis.

"Jellop!" Draxis shouts as he nears. "Jellop…?"

"Can he hear us?" Rend asks.

"He should. He always listens to us when we don't want him to. Jellop!"

"Shhh…" Jellop hushes. "I'm trying to listen."

"Listen for what?" Maeva asks.

"Shhh…" he repeats.

They all make an attempt to listen for something, anything. Nothing is heard but the whirring of the dry winds.

"Okay, all done."

"You… might have to help us out," Draxis says. "What exactly *were* we supposed to listen for?"

"Your heartbeats," Jellop responds. "The timing was short, but the vigor and volume was perfect. The heart is such a beautiful instrument."

"And there he goes acting like a psycho…" Maeva mutters.

"It is wise to practice the art of listening, otherwise you wouldn't be able to hear what normally goes unheard," Jellop says.

"Yeah… what language are you even speaking?" Rend asks.

"He claims himself to be a philosopher," Suvius says. "Though in truth, most of it is only rubbish."

"Ah, but you briefly implied that there is wisdom to be had from my moments of enlightenment, no?" Jellop says.

"…We have limited patience for your vague tricks today, Knave," Suvius says. "Step aside if you do not wish to aid us."

"No tricks, I only help."

"How so?"

"By distracting you all from the heat."

No more words are further exchanged as they all walk past Jellop, feeling too drained of energy to pursue dealing with his antics. If only it were just *his* antics they should be distraught over.

Laying next to Jellop is his trusty shepherd's crook that he uses to rush to his feet and get into action before the *real* action starts. "Draxis—stop!" he commands.

Draxis halts in place, not even being able to flinch an eyebrow—his frozen animation gives off secondhand embarrassment.

The foreseen threat reveals itself, a giant worm tunneling through the ground in the distance and spewing purple liquid that erodes the sands around it.

"Jellop!" Draxis screams. "Let me free!" Sweat drips into his eyes as he is forced to watch impending doom swim right towards him.

"No panic, I can handle this!" Jellop raises his staff at the creature. His aim is being delayed due to the torrent of rising sand making the perfect counter to his line of sight. Still, he finds the right time to strike, and shouts, "Suicide!"

The beast slows to a stop, then begins cannibalizing chunks out of itself with the rows of teeth that line around its ringed mouth. Guts and all are spilled until it collapses with a mighty thud.

"Maeva—take ten steps backwards!" Jellop shouts next.

Her body follows his command, just in time as another ravenous worm shoots upwards from where she once stood.

"Brain freeze!" Jellop shouts.

The worm spasms about uncontrollably until the life in its bulging eyes fades.

Jellop relaxes his arms, and his mental chains on the others. "The chaos, I no longer sense it. A wonderful victory, even if temporary."

"There was no need to turn us into puppets and bait," Draxis scolds. "Use your words next time. That's what a warning is."

"You all left in such a hurry, there was no time. Consider not abandoning the ones who care for you so quickly, no?"

They lower their heads after hearing those words, the words from someone they cannot truly hate, especially after it's been so long.

Jellop suddenly pops up in front of Rend, and looks deep into his eyes, or nose, or something. It's not apparent what Jellop is looking at as all Rend can see in return is a veil of black covered by a hood. "An outsider," Jellop murmurs, "but not an alien to our family. Welcome, friend Rend."

"Thanks?" I don't remember sharing my name with you though."

"Muhuhu!" Jellop gurgles.

"Is… is that your laugh?"

"Muhuhu!"

"S-Stop it!" Rend shouts.

"Muhu! I know everything about you, about everyone."

"Okay, so you know about our favorite colors. So what?"

"And all your special bathing preferences too," Jellop adds. "I tell you this because—muhuhu—all who deal with me are destined to collapse into true insanity for I am the Harbinger of Madness! Madness starts with the mind because it is only born from the mind. It is what I can sense and what I can manipulate. I can also read your thoughts too, so stop thinking of me as a weirdo!"

"I see… So, what am I thinking of right now?" Rend asks.

"Something defamatory and stupid, again. Maeva should have ended your second life ages ago, though she would vehemently disagree."

"Stop it, Jellop," Maeva says.

"Ah, sorry. I keep forgetting. *Privacy*," he sneers.

Suvius locks his hollow gaze towards a massive structure beyond the waves of heat and desert sands. "Jellop, we are seeking a hidden entrance to the kingdom over yonder. Have you found anything that could resemble one?"

"No entrances, no exits, but I did happen upon a monument of some kind earlier." Jellop points his staff, extending it in a direction that's a little off ways from the kingdom's castle. "I can retrace my steps, but there are many traps like before that clutter this wasteland, invisible to the eye and waiting to snare those most unfortunate. I know of their location. I shall guide. Follow."

Jellop begins his assigned duty as escort, swerving and leaping away from any premonitions of danger. At their current pace, either a heat stroke or boredom would end their journey before any 'trap' would, but their lives solely depend upon a riddle of a man, so they will happily play hopscotch if it meant to remain unscathed.

"I am deeply sorry to hear that, Maeva," Jellop whimpers beside her.

"About what? I didn't say anything," she responds.

"Your struggles. I hope you are finding peace now."

"I… Didn't I tell you to stop doing that?"

"Ah, right. Privacy."

"You've had an entire apocalypse to fix that habit," she says after giggling. "I'm finding out about a lot of things right now, but peace isn't one of them. Yet."

"Aren't you going to ask about us, Jellop?" Draxis says.

"You and Suvius, the struggles you both have are ones that I cannot relate to or speak properly of. They are unintelligible to me. I am no good at helping when situations like this arise, but I would still like to make all of your internal chaos go away if possible."

"That's all we can ever ask for."

"Muhuhu!"

"Shit!" Rend suddenly yells out as he trips, crashing head-first into the ground.

"Remember, Rend, it's left foot then right foot," Draxis says.

"Shut it! This stupid heat is making my body stiff. You try walking like this." Rend shakes his leg to loosen it up—there is an extra sensation present that feels different from his body's rigidity. "Hey, wait! Something's got my leg!"

Jellop springs to action and knocks away the hand that seized Rend. More hands begin to blossom through the ground all around, clawing their way up and swiping at everyone's feet. The Decayed rise, caked in sand and weighed down by ironclad armor long past its prime, along with their lack of coordination.

"This trap is too large!" Jellop says. "Can't escape, we must defend ourselves!" He raises his staff and strikes the ground with the flat bottom of it. "Hysteria!"

The Decayed lose control of themselves, swinging their broken swords aimlessly. Some even fall to their knees and drool, while others look like they're doing a circus act or a dance routine. Ultimately, it's a mishmash of turmoil—a favorable one.

"I sense a mass congregation nearby," Jellop says as the threat quells. "These knights must be being lured to something that resonates deeply with them. There is bottomless sorrow in their fragmented minds."

"I believe I know what it is that draws them," Suvius utters. "That pink light shining over there has my attention."

Suvius starts drifting towards the light. The only thing left to do now is to mimic what every moth does—go against reason and follow natural instincts. The others are subjected to gravitate and move along with the horde while trying to reach a certain skeleton who is locked into tunnel vision. At this moment, all manners of hostility have ceased—there is only harmony now, and the source of that scant illusion draws ever closer.

***

The pink glow emanates from a stone fountain in the middle of nowhere. It's been long stripped of its purity, worn down at its frame and design by harsh erosion and neglect. There is a mindless zombie crowd gathered around it.

"Annoying ants. Away!" Suvius says as he manifests a spectral blade, then wishes it away, all in a uniformed action—not even putting a stain on the fountain. He stands face-to-face with the fountain now, staring at the cracked, sculpted beauty of a crowned woman effortlessly holding up the thick skull of a giant beast.

"Suvius, where's the exit!" Maeva shouts.

Suvius breaks away from the woman's seduction and turns around to see an army of the dead hungry for a bloodbath. He gets into action, examining the fountain for anything conspicuous. "Defend me, I'll find something!" he says in a rush. "Damn this kingdom and their wasted architecture."

Rend put his fists up, getting on the defensive. "Stay behind me, Maeva!"

"No. *You* can stay behind me," she states, scavenging a rusted blade nearby. "I've been mulling over everyone's responses throughout this journey, more specifically with yours. You talk of overruling me soon, like that's even allowed. Having you gain self-worth and brag incessantly in my ear would send me into an utter frenzy. I'm going to see to it personally that you never earn that chance."

Rend gives that damned devilish smile again. "I'm already untamed, you just don't know it yet." He bends down and rips away an ax from the fingers of a buried hand and says to her, "And I'm going to prove it by getting way more kills than you."

Maeva two-hands her one-handed sword with confidence and says, "We'll see about that, slave."

Their attention is stolen as they watch Draxis hold his hand over his heart and mumble to himself.

"Wish I didn't have to use this so soon," he says. His body begins to glisten and morph into a familiar enemy—one with sharp ears, a slender physique, and pure anger.

"Draxis…?" Maeva says, puzzled.

"Don't 'Draxis' me," he snarls. "A Wisp? Really? I've tasted an elf's soul before. I know I was hungry, but I'm not stupid and blind. We don't need clashes of distrust within our team. If you all have something to say, then I suggest you say it directly. Now, let's focus on surviving—as a team."

Draxis performs a series of nimble flips towards a Decayed knight and perches his legs on its shoulders, following up with an attack of brutal decapitation with his bare hands. The same goes for the rest that stand in his way.

"Muhuhu!" Jellop laughs. "Even a gentle giant can become a juggernaut when wronged. His patience was tested."

"But we had reason to," Maeva says.

"Betrayal is never a good reason. It is a toxic excuse consisting of distrust, heartlessness, and corruption—also, take seven steps back."

Under the influence of Jellop's mind control, Maeva backs away just in time as a ravenous worm pops up from where she stood at. She starts frantically beating it with her sword, swearing in the process.

All Suvius can hear surrounding him is the common clash of war. No matter the opponent, it all sounds the same—and there are no cries of friendly casualties, so he doesn't look back. It allows him to focus, which leads to the discovery of a promising clue. A singular pink gem hidden within the sands.

Suvius unearths it and takes a closer look at the statue's top half, noticing that one of its eye sockets is missing the item that he holds. He pops the gem into the open slot. Now with two eyes made of bedazzling gemstones, the statue activates. The ground below it quakes as a form of extreme repercussion.

"Suvius, what did you do!" Maeva screams.

The ground breaks down even further, rapidly spiraling into an inescapable sinkhole.

"It appears I may have just flushed us," he says bleakly. "I can't even say that without questioning my life or this kingdom. This day is horrible."

Jellop digs through the turbulent sands to reach everyone else. "Friends! Cling to me!"

Saved one-by-one by Jellop, they huddle together as they spin around and around until they are buried under the dried ashes of the lake.

After what feels like an eternity, they are eventually spat out from underneath the lakebed and into a tunnel system that's dimly lit by colorful crystals embedded into the walls.

Suvius shakes out the sand in his innards and moves to drag everyone to their feet. "Keep moving! The roof is collapsing!

Faster than the destabilization of the tunnels around them, they run through the only one that is still accessible, which is forward. They collide and push against one another as they battle for first place to escape the cave-in.

***

Maeva has won the marathon sprint, seconds ahead of the others. She stops and rests her hands on her knees while gasping for air. "A-Are we safe? What if we're not even going the right way?"

"Only one way to find out," Suvius says. "Besides, I'm pretty sure we kept going straight after we got pulled in. I'm confident this the right path."

"That's… good. That's really—" Maeva collapses to the ground, without warning.

"Maeva?" Draxis says. "Are you—" He also gets struck with a similar case of weakness, zapping throughout his muscles as he stumbles to a kneel. "Well… that's not good."

"What's going on?" Rend asks.

"A perfect definition of exhaustion. I'm really starting to feel it now." Draxis crawls over to Maeva and places a hand on her forehead—the heat she gives off could melt ice. "We need to get her some aid."

"Then what are we waiting for?" Rend goes over and attempts to pick up Maeva's unconscious body, but with no avail. "Dammit! Aren't I supposed to have some hidden Undead strength or something?"

"Step aside," Suvius says. He has no trouble lifting Maeva up and cradling her.

Draxis reaches out to a disheartened Rend. "You can at least help me up," he says to him.

Rend hesitates, but soon obliges. Jellop joins in to assist in helping Draxis walk.

"I'm so disappointed right now," Rend says.

"Aww. Pep up," Draxis says. "If you ever need help practicing on how to carry a princess, I'll always be here for you."

"I don't know how to respond to that."

"How about a thank you."

"No."

"Muhuhu!" Jellop interjects with his usual laugh.

"S-Stop it," Rend tells him.

Chapter 6

The Last Kingdom

Despite being unburdened from carrying Maeva, Suvius moves ahead sluggishly, with hollow eyes that look occupied with internal ruminations.

"You look out of it, Lord," Draxis says.

"I have forsaken my loyalty towards this kingdom ages ago. But I cannot help but feel like… like I am home, after all this time." Suvius tilts his head away, facing the ground while muttering, "Must we be here?"

"I'm afraid so. The Arbiters' lair is in the heart of Harmony Sea. We're here to find the whereabouts of any functional ships, hopefully. I know this kingdom is unbearable to look at, but we'll have to try our best to put any personal histories aside."

"I feel like a child that's been away well past their curfew. But I will not apologize for any of it," Suvius says.

"That's the spirit," Draxis says. "If they want us to ask them for forgiveness, then we will demand the same—and we shall demand it first."

"Quit talking and pick your feet up," Rend says.

"Jellop agrees."

"Hey, be nice to the weak," Draxis whines.

Clank. Clink. Clank. Clink. Those metallic sounds mesh together, repeating and repeating, thumping louder and coming closer.

"Who's down here?" a commanding voice calls out. "Enam, is that you?"

The light from a lantern in the distance reveals the cracked helmet donned by a guard, exposing his worried eye.

"Th-the Harbingers?" the ironclad guard says, raising his blade. "St-stay away from our kingdom! I-I mean it!"

"Stand down," Suvius says. "We harbor no ill-will. We have injured people in need."

"I do not care for your sick and injured! What about the injuries you've inflicted upon all of us? You dare to sneak onto our lands, and now you beg for whatever you please whilst pretending that we are merciful towards sinners?"

"Well don't forget that together every saint and so-called 'sinner' is stuck in this twisted game of survival," Draxis says. "Goodness, we aren't asking for your women and children. We just want help… We promise we won't be long."

"And what if I choose to deny?" the guard asks.

"Then we'll continue to try and persuade you until it becomes nauseating. We mean what we say about pacifism. We just want a word with the king."

"The king…?" the guard mumbles. "I would have to refer you to the queen instead."

"It doesn't matter if it's a dog or a werewolf, anyone that's willing to listen would do," Draxis says.

The guard gives a silent look over at them. There's a sympathetic lapse in his heartbeat. "If that's all you Harbingers really need then… I'll take you."

"Our appreciation is immeasurable," Suvius says.

"I'm risking the lives of hundreds by doing this. Please do not let me bear the burdens of regret."

Traveling farther into the tunnel, the restrictions in breathing room and jagged hazards along the walls can make the inside of a throat look more appealing. The odd smell isn't too welcoming either.

"Here," the guard says, placing a hand against a part of the cave wall that's marked with a yellow capital 'V'. He lays against it and pushes with all his might, creating an unbearable grinding noise until there's enough room to wiggle out into an exposed and dilapidated corridor.

"This is so close to the people's supreme leader," Jellop says. "This seems like a security flaw, no?"

"It's an escape plan in case a breach occurs. We have an entire system in place," the guard says. He then sighs—and continues. "I remember a time when we never needed anything like backup plans. These halls were once so well guarded that even our own best assassins equipped with invisibility spells couldn't infiltrate our security. Sorry, the thought comes to me every time I enter this part of the castle."

"It can't be helped," Suvius says. "This nightmare wrought on these lands is difficult to accept."

"Shocking," the guard replies. "I had always assumed you wanted this to happen?"

"There are limits to my wrath."

"You? Limits? Not from what I've ever heard."

"We didn't cause this apocalypse if that's what you're implying," Suvius says.

"Then who did?"

"The world did as far as I'm aware. Don't pretend that the sword you keep close to you is only used against the guilty."

"A sword made out of dragon bone I might add," Draxis says.

"At least I keep it clean," the guard says.

"Did you at least remember to wash your conscience?" Draxis asks.

"I had enough of you all. Just follow me without uttering another word."

"…Okay."

"What did I just say!"

***

Nothing needs to be said about where exactly the two gargantuan doors that tower over them leads to. Although finely crafted, the doors themselves haven't escaped the omnipresent touch of ruin and collapse, but they still bring a sense of unworthiness to the unwelcome and unruly who gaze upon it. They hold their breaths as the guard once again uses all his might to push open the entrance to a new beginning.

They enter upon what should be the flawless, diamond heart of the kingdom—the Vomenn throne room. But with the tattered tapestry, the rotting tables cluttered with maps and spreadsheets, and the mounds of armor and other types of gear—it's been degraded to another storage room. The only thing that stands prominent is the woman sitting in one of the two ruined thrones, wearing a soiled gown along with a broken crown.

"Queen Ceranus," the guard pardons as he kneels. "I fully understand the myriad of difficulties with our enemies, but the Harbingers have come in peace and requested to speak with you." His words are met with silence as he watches her continue to play with her hands. "Umm, Lady Ceranus?"

"I heard you, Damel," she says. "Forgive my blatant ignorance…" She raises an arm towards him, like she's spiritually touching his heart. "Go replenish yourself with an early lunch today. You can even have extras if you wish."

"Thank you so much, Queen Ceranus!"

"My pleasure as always. I'll handle things from here." Ceranus watches Damel leave the room, all the way until the doors are sealed tight. She then crosses her arms and looks down on the five 'visitors' below the steps to her throne. "Well… we're alone now. Speak."

Draxis relinquishes himself free from his two supports. "We ask for a ship that's capable of voyage. Nothing more."

"Really? A ship?" Ceranus mocks. "Of all the priceless things you could demand from us: our resources, the kingdom itself—my decapitated head, with crown attached! Why choose something so meaningless?"

"We'll answer you only if you answer us," Draxis says.

"See, now that's the old Harbingers that I reprehensibly remember. Always scheming, always disturbing the peace, always barging into happenstances in which you've never belonged in!"

"Careful, Benevolent One. you're encroaching upon self-deprecation if I were to use your own words against you."

Ceranus reacts with a smirk, in its pure definition. "Such strong words. You gave me a fraction of whiplash there. To think it all spews from someone who's devolved into an elf. Though, I suppose it fits—a slippery tongue with a slippery mind."

"You mistake me for you diplomatic types. I only speak for our choir here. The words of retribution."

Maeva interrupts them both with a tiny sneeze.

"…You're missing some people, aren't you?" Ceranus asks.

"The same could be said about you," Draxis says. "Where's the king?"

"Answer my question before yours, wasn't it?"

"Well, you got me there."

"I… listen, this endless conflict between us, there's no place for it in current affairs," Ceranus says. "I cannot sustain its lust, and it'll only ruin what so little we have left."

"Are you proposing a truce?" Draxis asks.

"A truce only means that conflict will begin again after the tranquil state brought from a victory, and who's to say that the apocalypse will ever end through a victory? How about we start anew? Or at least ease our bickering and do more nurturing, like the troubled family that we are."

"Family might be a bit much," Draxis says. "We'll go with distant neighbors from down the road, and after a right turn or two."

"Well, whatever we are, I want to make a few things clear before our renewal. Don't steal our stuff—please. I'm offering you all only one chance to behave. Another thing, the survivors, they're scared enough as is, so don't give them any more fuel to add to that vicious fire. Just use your heads, that's all I ask."

Ceranus then takes the stairs that lead to her throne, avoiding the clutter of junk. "May I see her?" she asks, reaching for Maeva's forehead.

Maeva's chest heaves in shallow breaths, moving a growing collection of condensed beads of sweat that roll down across her face.

"We have a medical ward," Ceranus says. "I'll personally escort you there. In exchange, help us out, won't you?"

"Is that okay, Suvius?" Draxis asks.

"This will only make our intrusion longer than anticipated, but both parties do owe some semblances of repayment to one another for the expired costs of blood and money. I am willing to sacrifice our time."

"Then we're in agreement," Ceranus says. "We should move quickly now. I have a good ongoing streak of having the sick *not* die in the presence of my throne, and I would prefer to keep it that way."

Back outside the throne room, they pursue the promises from Ceranus's words as they follow her down the empty halls. The lasting silence is extreme enough to listen in to the castle's shallow breaths that moan through its crumbled walls.

"I-Is there a reason you all are so quiet?" Ceranus asks.

"Just staying on our best behavior," Draxis says.

"How colorful. Then what about you over there?" she says, giving Rend a watchful eye. "Are you a new member of theirs?"

"I'm just caught up in this loop of madness. My name's Rend, Your Majesty."

"So polite, but there's no need for formalities. I might be the last royal member of this house, but you should save it for when my position actually matters again. Anyway, I'm not going to ask about that rotting skin condition of yours, Rend. I like to think I have enough sense to at least tell the difference between a Decayed and a normal undead—but be wary of our people. They'll attack just about anything that moves funny."

"Doesn't sound too different from the times before," he responds.

"Eras change, but never society's hindrances," Jellop adds.

"How much farther, Ceranus?" Suvius asks.

"Just down these stairs actually."

"Doesn't this all lead to the dungeons?"

"It's been transformed into our medical ward. Nobody knew the subtle differences, so we didn't even need to waste any resources washing off any stains of blood or excrement." She then gives three solid knocks on a door at the bottom of the stairs—and waits.

A burly man opens the door, looking displeased. "For the last time, you filthy scroungers, you can't eat the rats! …Oh, Queen Ceranus!"

"Still dealing with the rat infestation I see?" she says.

"I'm dealing with a human infestation as well. People have been coming down here and offering to 'help me out' by trying to make a delicacy out of the vermin. Nobody listens to doctors on matters of obvious health hazards unfortunately. I'm afraid they might start turning to cannibalism soon."

"Just focus on your treatments for now. I already have some rough plans made on getting a handle for the famine situation. Anyway, take these two. The red-haired girl and the lanky elf. Make sure they receive the best of our best treatments—immediately preferably."

"Are you sure, Lady Ceranus? You're asking me to revive a pair of serpents in a chicken coop."

"I do not have a right answer for that, and neither do you. I relate to your worries, but I promise no harm will come to you, and it will be the same the other way around, understand?"

The burly man huffs as he takes Maeva in his arms, and Draxis limps right in behind him.

"Get well soon to you both!" Jellop shouts through the closing door.

"So… while we wait, do the rest of you want to join me for a leisurely stroll?" Ceranus asks.

***

Outside the castle's broken-down face, facing east, lies a dismal and makeshift town overshadowed by an encircling, massive stone wall that shields the inner sanctuary of what's left of the kingdom. In the near distance, west behind the castle and the massive wall, is the treacherous desert that is in the midst of a swirling sandstorm.

On top of the surrounding inner wall, groups of knights survey the perimeter with vigilant eyes, while down below in the town, there lies a decent-sized community of survivors. A few of them give Ceranus a friendly wave. She returns their gesture while she crosses a rickety skybridge with the others.

"Look how high up we are," Rend says in awe. "It's just like being on Mt. Everstone."

"To grapple on that verse," Suvius says. "I thought you and the Arbiters were going to bring the nations to new heights, Ceranus? This is the lowest point of descension."

"Well damn, I didn't know we were being graded on apocalyptic living conditions," she remarks. "I'm sorry this place isn't up to your standards. All of our servants are currently on an indefinite strike."

"Was there really any difference *before* Blighted Day and now?"

"You… Why are you always so serious? Did you leave your emotions behind when you renounced your knighthood?"

"No. I just left behind any strings of patience to be had."

Ceranus stops and turns towards him. She places a hand against his chest, feeling across his armor and digging into each groove and scar her finger can snag on. She stops at one symbol that brings a childlike smile upon her face—the symbol of a 'V' engraved in elegant penmanship.

"Well, Sir Patience, you claim to have disdain for our kingdom, but you still bear our mark of honor. And right next to your Harbinger tattoo as well. How adorable."

"That 'honor' is merely a stain that cannot be removed," Suvius says.

"Age really can sour a person's soul. I think I know what will take that grumpiness away. A game!"

Rend jolts. "A game? Can I join? What's it called?"

"All of you are welcome to join in," Ceranus giggles. "I call it: Monarch Hunt."

"That's a new one to me. How do you play?"

Ceranus guides them over to the edge of the wall that has the perfect overlook of what remains of a destroyed kingdom half the size of an empire. What lies below at the feet of the inner wall is a harrowing sight—it nearly makes them faint.

"See this endless horde of all the King's deceased horses and all the King's deceased men?" she says, tiptoeing and stretching her arms outward to show the world the drive of her merriment. "Well, the King himself is also somewhere in there, hiding away like a little fairy. Now, I don't like to brag, but I do hold the highest record currently. I think I'm sitting at fifteen wins or so."

"Ceranus… this isn't healthy," Suvius says.

"In a world like this, one would be mythically lucky to stay healthy."

"But you shouldn't— "

"Wait, is that him?" she interrupts, hunching over the wall. "It is! Another victory!" Her enthusiasm stands at an apex, but it is noncontagious. It only leaves them speechless. "S-Sorry… I guess I got a little competitive there."

"Do you have any more games?" Rend asks. "Something hopefully more kid-friendly?"

"On the holidays, we sometimes kidnap a random Decayed and watch people smack at it."

"How about we give up on playtime and continue our patrol," Suvius interjects.

"It's a stroll, not a patrol!" Ceranus says. "You people are no fun. Fine, I wanted to check up on the morning sermons anyway."

As they walk, Suvius takes another gander over the wall. Nothing of the kingdom on every side past the inner and outer walls is recognizable to him anymore, not even the armored knights below.

His moment of grief is disrupted by a nearby choir coming from the town, along with the words of prayer comes from an exuberant preacher who showers the people that kneel and pray with blisses of love and the needed strength to revere the many names of their faith.

"I sense a disconnect in your heart and mind, queen-lady," Jellop says. "Your heart watches in sympathy but your mind swears in disgust."

"Like a hawk, you target the cracks in my weakened state and strike my candid thoughts," Ceranus says. "I should have been more cautious around you, but yes, I have always found this kingdom's religious sphere to be one that's resourceful for the people but wasteful for where true progress lies: in the palms of government.

"I allow it, for I might as well—but I'd rather they spend their energy on making sure we don't get eaten alive instead of wasting words on the deaf ears of beings who are probably addicted to watching us suffer like this."

"A believer who exceeds faith shall be given a seat below the thousand golden thrones, but will be bereft of, and abjured, should the virtues of the pious turn to the sins of the unfaithful," Suvius delivers, without err.

Ceranus grabs Suvius's hands and connects her fingers in between his. Her smile shows peace, but her eyes mean war.

"A scripture can yield glorious truths and resolve, but it is deficient of persuasion and influence if sanctimony lies beneath its glossy surface. Did you hear all that? That's how you sound right now. Your words are empty because if any of what you said was true, then where are the gods?" She drops his hands from his lack of an answer. "That's going to conclude our tour for now. It's time you all pay your debts. Isn't that what we've agreed upon, Suvius?"

He still protests against responding.

"Or just stay moody and sit there," she continues. "You're not getting access to our ship if you don't help us. Anyway, just ask the knights what needs to be done—and try to stray away from any requests involving water resources if you can help it. The situation is fragile thanks to our only water supply magically disappearing. It happened around a month ago. According to the scouts, it was there one day, and then—poof."

"Poof?" Rend repeats.

"Yeah. Poof. I'm truly appalled that there is something out there that can disintegrate an entire lake like that. Or maybe the Water elementals went on strike."

"You make light of the disaster, but how dire is it?" Suvius asks.

"Well, even if purified with magic, ocean water still tastes like liquid crap—and for some reason also like blood. And piss is no better as an alternative, though it is useful as a dye. We do have plenty of water to spare for inhospitable guests however, and even enough to let them bathe fortunately. The other two smelled like they were raised in the back of a barn. Don't tell them I said that." Ceranus begins to take off, continuing her leisurely stroll alone.

Left on their own, Rend, Suvius, and Jellop team up and lend their able support in making the surrounding haven into a bastion, gaining positive rapport as they work—though their inhumane appearances deducts a few points towards their reputation. Their arduous tasks range from bolstering fortifications, passing out and delivering supplies, acting as temporary sentries, and burying the burnt ashes of the deceased.

Their work takes them all across the town and all throughout the day, to the evening, and until to where time is estimated to stand now—in the wake of twilight.

Suvius drops one final heap of dirt on top of a marked grave. "You boys work hard," he says, cracking and massaging his bones.

"Trust me when I say that I've worked even harder," Rend says. "I'm used to it. Plus… I don't like seeing these people live like this. For however long I've been alive both times, I've always dreamt about living in castles made of gold and being a part of the highest tiers of nobility one could reach. I'm finally here now after all this time. And seeing everything go to ruin… there's no magic to it. I should have just left it as a dream."

Suvius shakes his head. "You are too young to have already developed such a broken heart. Have you considered revising your dream instead of destroying it? This kingdom could still become like the one that you've always envisioned. You shouldn't give it up out of spite, not unlike…" Suvius pauses, before he plows his shovel into the ground, piercing it right through the grave. "Take rest for now you two. Our work here is technically perpetual, but we have done enough to fulfill our promise."

"Wait, are you leaving? Where are you going?" Rend asks.

"To revise a dream."

***

Maeva awakens. Her eyes dart around as she tries to ascertain the catharsis her body is experiencing. Her room is small, and chilled with a haunting of past horrors that she is desperately trying not to fathom. Aside from the gloom, she feels no doom. She feels cozy whenever her hand sinks into the plush fabric of the bed, and the cushion helps to ease her back pain.

There's a new pair of clothes sitting next to her on a wooden crate used as a table. *Oh!* she thinks as she fondles and smells the fabric. *These are soft, and it even matches my style.*

Past the cell's entrance where iron bars once blocked the freedom of countless unfortunate prisoners, a neighbor in a room on the opposite side of hers waves hello. He seems to be in the same condition as her, fresh and invigorated.

Maeva squints, trying to get a better look into the other room. "Draxis?"

"We meet again…" he says.

"Where are we?"

"Vomenn kingdom. I told you we could make it, you just needed to have faith."

"I had faith… it just only appeared now instead of earlier. I'm glad everyone's in good hands."

"You consider their hands good?" Draxis asks.

"Right, let me rephrase. Their intentions seem like they're good, but their hands remain the same."

"They're just doing this for us because they're desperate for help."

"Are we not the same way?" Maeva says.

"Of course not, they owe us for turning a blind eye towards the warnings we tried to give them. They deserve their suffering."

"Maybe, though I'm sure they feel the same way about us. We *did* take our constant rejections pretty harshly, you know."

"Well, you can only put up with an ignorant population for so long before becoming impatient. It's a shame we could never fix the miscommunication."

"Miscommunication… Draxis, can we talk about earlier?"

"Earlier? Oh, you mean back at the desert? I've already forgotten and moved past that."

"But I haven't," Maeva says. "We weren't trying to plot anything malicious; you were just scaring us is all."

"I suppose I tend to do that. It naturally runs in the family. I'm just fidgety about everything so far, and hunger accelerates it. Other than that though, I'm doing quite well."

"Are you sure?" Maeva asks.

"Positive. But… can I ask for a favor?" Draxis says.

"Always."

"The next time you all decide to go shopping, please take me with you. I never truly cared for spoiled apples."

"S-Sure. I'll… I'll keep that in mind."

***

If I'm remembering correctly, these are her bed chambers. I'll never understand why she has it so far away from everything else.

Suvius peeks around the door of interest. He sees Ceranus sitting at the foot of her bed. She stifles her cries as she rocks back and forth while clutching her chest—all while illuminated by a broken mosaic window depicting pairs of hands holding up a crown, bloodied by the outside light. He wants to retreat from the sight and never look back, but he cannot—*not this time.* He runs scenarios through his head, mentally yelling at himself not to just barge right in.

"Ceranus?" he calls out, entering her room with a bit too much force.

"Suvius?" She quickly wipes her flustered face. "How dare you! Go before I scream for the guards!"

"If you want to get technical, I am trained as one."

"Don't flatter yourself. You were so quick earlier to spat about your hatred for serving your home. Can't you see that I'm busy?"

"Yes, I can perfectly see that you're working yourself to the point of tears. May I come in or not?"

"Shouldn't you be helping out the community?" she asks.

"That's why I came here. I think having a proper discussion would be beneficial for the both of us."

"There's really no point in competing against your adamance… Fine. You may enter."

Suvius doesn't say anything as he sits next to her, and neither does she. It's been a while since he's seen the royal colors and the décor, even if faded. It brings out a special kind of peace within him, like a deep connection. His conscience mourns that he's going to have to break it.

"Between you and me, I am more than relieved to see such familiar faces," Ceranus says. "I would have never even fathomed that seeing your enemies could also have the same effect as seeing a loved one. I only say that because ever since Blighted Day, our people have been forced into this strict isolation. We have ways to escape and explore further out, but fear has always stalked us whenever we've tried.

"Suvius… where did everything go wrong? When did it get so wrong? I'm so tired… it feels like I'm at a point beyond despair."

"You should already know where I shift my blame," Suvius says.

"And you know where I shift mine," Ceranus responds.

"And that is why I want to alter this full circle of senseless conviction. But just like in all circles, there is an origin that creates the beginning."

"Don't try dragging us down with you. Things became like this because you Harbingers pushed the Arbiters over the edge. You ever think about that? For years, you and your posse have been nothing but warmongers and insurrectionists against our saviors."

"Saviors?" Suvius mocks. "You choose to deny religion, but you put the entire sum of your faith into false gods? Tell me, what makes them so worthy in the eyes of our Queen?"

"I've never claimed the Arbiters to be gods, but you can't deny their innovations and their remarkable feats. They demanded a lot, sure, but for certain they and I worked together harmoniously in tandem to see miracles unfold."

"And that's exactly all they ever wanted—your projects and theories. Your fierce determination and status were just additional boons to them."

"They wanted me because we were providing a foreseeable future. What's wrong with that?" Ceranus says. "Are you also against the idea of unifying countries? Or global security? How long are you planning on wielding your lies?"

"What is it that you deny?" Suvius asks. "Do you truly believe that everything the Harbingers have done against the Arbiters was just for the sake of evil?"

"Well I can't recall seeing any forms of prosperity from you monsters, it's quite the opposite. Suvius, you alone have slain hundreds—and don't get me started on the others. What about all those raids and regicides? What were those supposed to accomplish aside from a show-and-tell of ruthlessness? Do I even need to mention the World War over at Daison Peak?"

"Detestable, all of it," Suvius remarks. "This world only moves and responds when violence is involved, never peace, and make no mistake, different outcomes are preferred—but we were never and *still* aren't given the option for peace. I will never disagree that the Harbingers' values conflict drastically with our actions, but we do not know any other way because violence is all we have ever been tested with. And Ceranus, *you* are the same as us. Your values have never matched your actions."

"I don't know what you're talking about."

"I'm referring to your crimes, and the Arbiters'. You list our mistakes en masse, so should I start listing yours, Dragonslayer?"

"*Never* call me that again," she hisses.

"Ceranus, I don't say these things out of a pretense of winning, I'm saying it because I want you to finally acknowledge that you were a victim. I know you experienced the Arbiters' atrocities for yourself firsthand, but you were blinded by their gilded treasures and too wrapped up in all the glory. Look around you, Ceranus! Please! Your saviors are not here! There will be no cure to stop this plague!

They will remain absent while our nation bends their knees whilst engulfed in flames!"

Ceranus clutches her dress. "Suvius I— "

"No! I need to make this abundantly clear for you. Driving creatures to extinction for ingredients and inhumane experimentation, environmental destruction for the purpose of magical industry, the cruel enslavement and domestication of Dragons and all the other races in which they feared. In what hellish world would nightmares like that culminate into a brighter future? They have doomed this world."

"They… I never meant for…" She clutches her dress even tighter. "I want to hear more."

"No," Suvius says. "I have finally opened your eyes, so if you want more proof, then think for yourself. Take moments to relive every horrid experiment that you helped them with, every event that the Harbingers tried to prevent. You could even begin to ask your loyal citizens. I highly doubt they enjoyed being helpless sheep during the world's power struggles."

"…You came all this way up here just to make me feel worse about myself. Why?" Ceranus asks. "Do you honestly hate me that much?"

"I hate what you have become. I am a knight that is disgusted by the wickedness that has transformed my queen. Regardless, I believe things could get better for us now that we are free from outside politics and the bittersweet temptations of demons."

"She rests her back against the bed and says, "Wow… that's twice my world has been turned upside-down. I fell for it. I fell for it all… It's probably just what that bastard envisioned, and I fell for it."

"Which bastard?" Suvius asks.

"The biggest bastard that I know. King Laxan. He granted me paradise, but that was all he ever offered me. He rarely showed me love, and when he did, it was for entertaining his manias for war."

"Laxan…" Suvius repeats. "That man would send entire regiments to a single home in order to demonstrate his intolerance towards disrespect. I vividly remember being forced to take part in them. He got what he deserved. I wish I had this strength of mine beforehand, before he brought the both of us over the edge."

"That's what's scaring me, I don't think it was his power that enticed me—it was my own experiences that led to it all," Ceranus says. "The moment I first made summons for an execution was when I became just like him, and I think he saw that in me—why he even bothered to swoon a merchant's girl to become his queen and equal. But, with all this said, who is to blame for the end of the world?"

"We have all contributed to this fate one way or another, but I still believe that the Arbiters have caused the most impact. This is why we came here despite the risks. We have found a secret of theirs that may tell us what they have been doing all this time, and in order to find it, we need you to give us directions to any remaining ships. I know our ships are durable enough to last through an apocalypse if they were capable of enduring numerous wars consecutively."

"I'll have to ask our shipwrights and scouts for any information," Ceranus says. "Give me until morning, and I'll have an answer for you."

"That is good. I hope that we can salvage any truth the Arbiters kept secret."

"Maybe we should pray together to ensure fruition?"

"Huh? You've lost me somewhere," Suvius says.

"What do you mean? Surely you remember how to pray?"

"Ceranus, I barely have enough faith to sanctify a flea."

"Then what if the prayers of two faithless fools can create a sparkle of grace?"

"The two of us?"

"Absolutely!" Ceranus says as she sits up and snatches his hands, interlocking her fingers between the dry bones of his.

"I highly doubt that there is a god that would bless us," Suvius says.

"There's no need for a direct summoning. We're just doing a general one."

"Then what would you like to pray for?"

"Towards the restoration and the mending of the world's errors."

Suvius chuckles. "That's such an innocent request." He reaches for her face, accidentally moving a lock of her hair that reveals a minor aberration near her right ear. He hovers a finger over it, mistaking it for a streak of dirt.

"What?" Ceranus says, in an offended tone. "You never seen a scar before? I suppose not since you're skinless."

"I can still become scarred," he counters. "How did such an injury occur?"

"Would you believe it if I said that even I can be a hero? I took a slash attack from an infected knight to save someone."

"That's what I like to hear. Did you cherish that feeling?"

"It felt painful," Ceranus states.

"You know what I mean."

"Yes, Suvius, it felt appropriate to save a life. Now can you stop touching my hair?"

"It's not like I can feel it. Let me use my imagination."

"Right… Can I do the same with you then? Put my hands on your head?"

"If it'll get you to settle down and stop moving, then do it."

Ceranus mimics what Suvius is doing, much to his amusement. "I didn't mean to raise my temper at you earlier," he says. "I remain in grief that I wasn't persuasive enough in the previous world. So much could have been prevented."

"It's like you said, there were way too many factors that made things convoluted. I still have my doubts, but after remembering the sodden look upon your faces back at the throne room, those doubts are lessening."

"So what will you do now?" Suvius asks.

"My, what should I do indeed. There's a lot to atone for— but it's getting late."

"Should I leave to let you rest?"

"You're not dismissed. I still haven't shown you my appreciation…" Ceranus then slides over to him and sits on his lap. "Thanks for never truly giving up on this kingdom—or me. I know that doesn't mean much with everything you had to go through. I wish I could turn back time somehow and return the efforts of your perseverance—and maybe even return you back to your human state."

"You wouldn't want that," Suvius says. "I was hideous."

"It's been some years, but that's not what I remember." She rests against his chest and speaks softly. "Suvius, do… do you mind if I take this moment to repent for my sins?"

He wraps his arms around her, while saying, "It'll make this night longer."

"It will. Does that scare you?"

"Shouldn't I be the one asking you that?"

"I'm not the only one who's going to be punished…"

***

It's a new day, in a new room—the Great Hall. A silver card is slammed downward on a table, shaking a row of other glistening and colorful cards in front of it. There were no clear signs of any potential winner before that killing move.

"If currency ever becomes relevant again then you all owe me a hundred gems," Maeva says in a triumphant tone.

"Well I'll be," Draxis says. "Looks like we both fall tonight, Rend."

"What a load of crap. My hand was bullshit *and* horseshit!" Rend says, tossing his cards on the table. "Jellop, you rigged this game."

"…I'm not even playing."

"I bet you fed her information. Cheater!"

"How about you choke on the chaos of losing, loser!" Jellop ducks after saying that, having to dodge a card thrown at him.

Draxis rests his feet on the table. "Three losses in a row. How atrocious."

Suvius arrives out of nowhere. He takes an empty chair closest to the group and rests his head on the table.

"Suvius, where have you been last night? We figured you were mistaken for a pile of bone meal or something," Draxis says.

"…I thought I was incapable of experiencing back pain," he responds, groaning.

"Well, there is a saying about old bones—I think. Suvius?"

"Hello, everyone!" Ceranus greets. She bends down near Suvius to ensure he hears her next words. "Hello, Suvius Falacoster."

"Hold on, she can say your full name and we can't?"

"Jealousy doesn't win favors, Draxis; beauty does," Ceranus says.

"To hell with that. I'm attractive. Right, Maeva?"

"Maybe in the reflection of the smallest shard from a broken mirror."

Ceranus cannot help but laugh. "I like you people. I mean it. It's a shame we were all clouded by stupidity at one point."

"Stupidity still plagues us," Maeva says. "We're leaving soon."

"Damn, I forgot that you all needed a ship. Do you have to? The people really appreciate your help."

"We can't stay, Ceranus," Suvius says. "We have to go."

"But you all can live out your days here within the fortified walls of the kingdom."

"You're getting into that mindset again. Not everything that entertains you is yours to keep."

"But…" She attempts to cast away her frown and says, "Very well. Our scouts have informed me that there is indeed a ship you all can use. That is, if you all really insist on going back into that hellscape. Last chance to say no."

"Stop delaying us."

"Damn it all. Alright, well… I think Damel said that you all came here through one of our escape tunnels? He likes to guard them, so he shouldn't be too hard to find. He can show you the way to go."

***

Damel is resting his back against a statue near the original secret entrance. He stands like a statue himself, unmoving as he watches Ceranus and the others approach.

"Damel," Ceranus says.

"Ceranus," he says back.

"Mind doing me a favor?"

"I can already see where this is going. Talk to them first— I'll be listenin' in."

"Damel here will show you the tunnel that leads to our harbor," Ceranus says to the others. "Once you're outside the tunnel, go far left until you reach Ironside Bluffs. There's a path off to the edge somewhere that leads to a hidden opening. Past that, you should find Laxan and I's private ship. The Sora La Daellus."

"Sounds fancy," Rend says. "What does that mean?"

"It means 'path of one's breath'," Draxis says. "Stealing the Dragons' language now, Ceranus?"

"Didn't think there was permission required for that sort of thing?"

"Right, because as a Dragonslayer, your slaves don't deserve that respect."

"Draxis… I know, okay. I know. I'm reflecting heavily, but it's beyond too late to rectify anything. The only thing that's left within my power now is to help you all fulfill your mission—whether it's to save the world or give a good lashing to those responsible for this mess. The Vomenn kingdom is at your disposal, and I'm sorry that we weren't before."

"We want to say thank you, queen-lady," Jellop says.

"I know some of you do, but none of you should feel obligated to do so. I want to give my thanks instead—officially, because we owe you all so much for putting up with our ignorant nonsense, and I have a strange feeling that debt is only going to increase exponentially as time continues.

"This is a bit overdue but—as of today, all crimes and heresies conspired and executed by the Harbingers are hereby pardoned. This is the decree of Queen Ceranus of the Vomenn Kingdom, the last royal to stand indomitable."

***

And so, back into the claustrophobic nightmare in which they originally came from.

"These tunnels are like a riddle," Draxis says. "You sure do know your way around."

"It's what helped us maintain a steady hold on this side of the continent," Damel says. "And since it splits off in some areas, anyone that's ever tried to use these tunnels unauthorized would surely die due to becoming lost. Speaking of which…" He unsheathes and uses his sword to point further down. "This one leads to your destination. It stops at a dead end. Just push up at the ceiling to remove the camouflaged cover. And do make sure to put it back. We had a flooding incident once because of that."

"From this former knight to a loyal one, you are truly a blessed one," Suvius says.

"I just care for my birthplace, it's all I've ever done," Damel says. "But before I go—Suvius, may I take a moment to inquire about your loyalty?"

"If you insist."

"I'm only bringing it up because, illegally, I once took time to research into your old history, which led to even more questions than answers. And now that I'm seeing you in person, I can finally ask you: Why?"

"I'm assuming you're asking about my renegade acts? I cannot give a final answer that will ever suffice," Suvius says. "If I were to try, then the only reason I can give for everything I have ever done would be because I hate evil, whatever I label indiscriminately as such."

"I see. You just took a more direct and active approach to ac-complish that compared to the rest of us who refused to question our vows. From the way Ceranus is behaving, I take it we were all too hasty to sever your heroic legacy from our history?"

"I do not fight to become anyone's hero, or even villain," Suvius corrects. "I only work so that the sun may finally shine. For now, it still rains."

"The rain. It hits pretty hard, doesn't it?" Damel says.

"…It always does."

Chapter 7

Rising Tides

Maeva 'supervises' over Rend with her hands on her hips and says to him, "Make sure to put the cover back on properly, it's important to the Kingdom. And put some sand over it."

"Yeah, yeah," he groans.

Jellop squats near the ocean and dips his hand in the water. His hand is kissed with rust-colored stains as he pulls it out. "The queen-lady was right, the ocean is bleeding."

"This type of water reminds me of some of the carnage in the naval wars," Suvius comments.

"The only thing out of place here is the lack of partying and topless gorgons," Draxis says. "Oh the beach, how I do miss you."

"Well, we do have this one to ourselves," Rend says.

"Ah, I didn't think of that. Anyone up for a sand fight?"

"Don't even think about it," Maeva interjects. "I'll slay any-one who ruins my hair."

"None of you even have good aim," Suvius says.

"How would you know? You don't even use ranged gear," Draxis says.

"No, but you obviously have never seen me throw a blade."

"I'll believe it when I see it."

Jellop backs away from the ocean and retreats to the others while saying, "Something lurks in the water."

"Really?" Draxis says. "I swear, we can't go five seconds without having to draw someone's blood…"

The water begins to rise, and up with it is a bulbous-headed monster that stares at the group with its three globe-shaped eyes.

"What!" Draxis shouts. What is it that you want! Begone!"

The monster thrashes its tentacles against the ground and water repeatedly. It doesn't aim for anything in particular, like it's being destructive for the fun of it.

"Awww, I think it's a young water kraken!" Maeva says.

"Yeah, how sweet," Draxis groans, "This is *not* what we need right now."

A humongous serpent leaps out of the water and collapses its million-toothed jaws onto the kraken's back. The kraken is reeled down until its agonized shrieks and blood become nothing more than bubbles on the water's surface.

"No!" Maeva cries out. "Baby kraken!"

"Yeah…there's no way we're surviving through this," Rend says.

"Just don't fall overboard and you'll be fine," Suvius remarks.

***

Taking a far left and hiking up a miniature trail, they find a perilous natural path jutting out from the rocky edges of the bluffs. Maybe it's not too late to turn back? Though, Suvius won't let them… and it's not like they can fight their way past him. He gives them a warning look to thwart their foolhardy thoughts. Fortunately, the path turns out to be shorter than realized. It leads into the interior of a spacious cove. The cool air that breezes throughout is refreshing, thrilling. It makes them want to forget about the ship altogether and just dive straight into the water. That would also be foolhardy.

"Uhh, where's the thing we're supposed to be looking for?" Rend asks.

"Surely the scouts wouldn't fail their only job," Suvius says. "I wonder…" He picks up some loose gravel and throws it at the water below.

A hulking ship uncloaks before their very eyes.

"How clever. I suspected they would utilize something like this on more than just people when Damel mentioned the kingdom was using Invisibility magic."

"We didn't start encountering Mistrunners until the tail end of the decade, right?" Maeva asks. "I only assumed that they were just a rogue gang. Where did they even learn it?"

"I assume it's stolen arcana from the broken partnership with the Arbiters."

"Who cares," Draxis growls. "No amount of invisibility will hide any of the crimes they have committed." He gets a running start going and jumps off the overlook ledge, landing onto the ship's deck.

"Damn you! I wanted to jump first!" Maeva shouts, following after him.

"Ohhh… I hate jumping," Jellop groans.

"Here, Jellop," Suvius says. "You can climb on my back."

"Thank."

"Hey, what about me?" Rend asks. "C-Can I get a ride too? Suvius? Dammit…"

Walking around the ship, they marvel at their new and not so fresh vessel in all its splendor. The wooden boards are softened and moist, but they feel capable of supporting the extra weight—for now. The ship is of decent size and instills confidence in its potential speed. The only true negative quality is the lack of innovative design—it's too broad and imperial. Regardless, it will have to do.

"Now this, *this* is a ship," Suvius says, gliding his hand across the side railing. "It's worn, but it still has the form of something pristine, masterful. To show a vessel like this with so much neglect—it should be legalized as a crime."

"If you're driving then quit your drooling and get us out of here," Draxis says.

"A captain cannot sail the seas with their nautical stallion until they become linked as one."

"Captain? Nobody's going to call you that. Now hurry up before I set your beloved 'stallion' on fire."

"Insolence! Give me your map, then I'll go."

"So insufferable. Here!" Draxis shouts, shoving the item into Suvius's chest.

They both go their separate ways after an exchange of sharp glares, with Suvius manning the helm and Draxis keeping to himself at the railing. Jellop and Maeva watch from the sidelines, rooting for no one.

"I wonder if friends can make good enemies," Jellop says out loud.

"Then that would mean enemies could make good friends," Maeva says.

"Ah, but I counter by asking which relation is stronger?"

"I don't know. Conundrums don't usually have straight answers."

"They don't. But they are indeed fun to watch."

"We're departing!" Suvius warns. "And I recommend staying away from the edge. We've already seen how hostile these waters are." He grips the steering wheel of the ship and looks ahead at the crashing waves that taunt him from outside the drenched maw of the cove. "It's been a while since I've sailed. Much too long…"

"We can tell," Draxis says. "You forgot to open up the sails."

"I did? Maybe if you didn't act so needlessly combative and distract me, we would be halfway to our destination by now."

"Don't blame me for your shortcomings," Draxis responds. His attention leaps over to Maeva who seems to be struggling with bundles of rope. "Are you trying to hang yourself or hoist the sails?"

"Well, someone has to do it while you two work hard at doing nothing," she says.

"Thank you for your efforts, Young Maeva," Suvius says.

"There's no need to thank me. I just want you to shut up and drive so this sludge can stop dripping on me."

"Hmph."

Chapter 8

The Dead Sea

The world always seems so small and traversable on a map. Just how much distance have we covered so far? It seems like everywhere we go there's a graveyard, and this stupid ocean is just as large as all the other graveyards. It's like the whole world is nothing but one giant mausoleum, and we're its remaining keepers... Who am I even talking to?

Rend waves a hand in front of Maeva. "Hey, you listenin'?" he says. "You told me to keep you busy."

She sighs. "Try harder then."

"Alright, then how about this. I spy with my little eye, something big and demolished."

"A pirate ship," she responds.

"I spy with my little eye, something spooky and demolished."

"Pirate ship."

"Nope. A ghost ship."

"...This is so damn boring."

"I spy, with all my eyes, something blue," Jellop says from behind them.

"Is it my skin? It's sort of blue," Rend says.

"Lose. It's my robe."

"Jellop, don't you want to take that thing off and enjoy the air?" Rend asks.

"...You don't know what you're asking for."

"I'm a man of no regrets."

"Then you do not know what that word means. Maeva, are you prepared?"

She gives a half-nod in response.

Jellop grabs his hood. His fingers become more tense the farther he pulls it down. There is no summary for what Rend and Maeva behold, it's not possible. It is instead replaced with a twisting feeling in their stomachs and the strong desire to turn away.

"Unholy shit!" Rend shouts.

"I knew this idea was bad and not good," Jellop cries out.

"No-wait! I'm just confused is all. Why are you—"

"I don't know. I just don't…" Jellop responds as he pulls his hood back over.

"Rend, Jellop is… Jellop isn't from here, or anywhere for that matter," Maeva says. "The only thing he remembers of his past was that the Arbiters pulled him from somewhere. Somewhere that's beyond our perception."

"An accidental variable in their quest for knowledge," Jellop interjects. "My nebulous existence brings madness."

"Rend didn't mean to hurt you, Jellop."

"I know. I'm not angry, just given a sharp reminder. All is forgiven. friend Rend, but I must know, what did you see when you looked at me?"

"A mass of tentacles with eyes, I think? That's the best way to describe it."

"That's what many people see when they look at me. It's curious."

"I see him as a mass of fins and horns sometimes," Maeva says. "Draxis says he usually sees a tangle of wings, and Suvius says his perceived version is wholly indescribable."

"Is your staff special as well?" Rend asks.

"It is," Jellop says as he swings and spins it around. "I stole it from the Arbiters before I escaped."

"Oh… neat!"

"Hark! Man overboard!" Suvius shouts.

Everyone rushes over to the side of the ship for a better look. It's no man, but a woman! A woman covered in multi-colored scales and with a fish tail for legs. She sits on a rock with her back facing towards them. They all look at each other in confusion as their first reaction. For their second reaction, they scornfully eye one another to pressure someone to become a spokesperson to talk to the scary fish-lady.

"A-Ahoy!" Draxis says.

"Ahoy?" the woman questions before turning around with a scaled eyebrow raised. "Are you pirates? I don't want what you're selling. And I'm not for sale either."

"What? Nay! We be sailors!"

"Please forgive him, the waters just making him sick," Suvius barges in to say. "Do you need assistance?"

"Aye!" she shouts.

"Now she be speaking my language. Are ye a threat?" Draxis asks.

"Nay!"

"Then hop aboard! We leave no woman nor wench behind!"

"One more 'pirate-talk' like that and I'm tying you to an anchor," Suvius says.

"A mutiny it is then," Draxis remarks.

"We really need to get out of these waters before someone ends up murdered. I'm returning to my station."

The fish-woman dives into the water—and remerges a few seconds later, catapulting high into the air and landing onto the ship deck. "Yuck!" she says in disgust as she flops around. "Air always feels weird."

"Didn't think we would find any stragglers," Maeva says. "Where you from?"

"My name is Ronella and I'm not a straggler… I've just been ditched is all."

"For what reason?"

"Family. More specifically, a mishap involving family betrayal. They called me aggressive and acted like I'm a curse to their survival, but they fail to realize how good they had it. I'm positive that if it wasn't for me then they would have died from the very beginning in this deadly typhoon of pestilence. Though my love for them has darkened, I can't give up on returning to them."

"No offense, but they don't sound worthy of your kindness," Maeva says. "Do you know where they went?"

"To Meridian Subtropolis. It's where everyone flocked to when the apocalypse happened. You land folk wouldn't know where that is."

"No, I suppose we wouldn't. Is it far from here?" Maeva asks.

"It is. On the other side of the world to be exact."

"Well we're not traveling *that* far, but it is on the way. We could get you a bit closer if you like."

"Oh really?" Ronella says. "Thank you! It's been so long since I've interacted with any friendly land folk. You know, the ones who aren't Drowned."

"Drowned? Are you referring to the Decayed?" Maeva asks.

"It depends, are you referring to the Drowned?"

"We'… going in circles here. The ones with purple eyes and have a hankering for the flesh of the living? Here on the surface, we call them Decayed."

"Odd. Why?" Ronella asks.

"It stems from what we call the Virus, but it's mostly because of how the infected act and look. The surface isn't really creative with these sorts of things. But, Drowned, what's the reason for that?"

"Because the deeper you go the more treacherous the waters become. Anything that you may have seen here at sea level is incomparable to the trenches below—the sheer thought of it is suffocating. How about you folk? What's the worst up here?"

"Nothing but monsters and natives turning on you—the usual," Maeva responds. "We've been lucky so far, but it sounds like you've been through a lot unfortunately."

"I think I'd feel a lot safer at home. Even if I were to die, it'll be among my lovable and ungrateful family."

"Family's important. Mine is a bit on the rough side, but they also say the same thing about me," Maeva says as her eyes dart around towards the others. "Feel free to call this ship your home, and us, your family until you feel like departing. There's a long current ahead of us."

***

Draxis ascends from the lower decks in a groggy state. Nothing noteworthy is happening as he looks around while listening to the gentle crashing of the waves—it really does bring excitement with how much sound can be detected with his new elven ears. He does see Rend isolated however, sitting on a crate and minding his own business while being... *studious?*

"What are you reading, Rend?" Draxis asks.

"I thought you would have joked about me even being able to read."

"You think too lowly of me. Jokes should be challenging."

"Are you calling me an easy target?" Rend says.

"Well, you said it, not me. Anyway, where'd you get that pocketbook?"

"I stole it from the Kingdom's library. It's about Magic."

"You... want to learn magic?" Draxis asks.

"Hell yeah, you all get to do cool shit. I want to do the same."

"Just so you know, Magic isn't completely an automatic given. It requires effort."

"Well that was a quick shutdown," Rend remarks. "So... you can't teach me?"

"No, I can't teach you how to feel a tingly sensation," Draxis says as he sits next to Rend. "But we might as well try. Have you read about the fundamentals of Magic at least?"

"Yeah. Something about visualizations and natural-born connections. That's all I could gather from it."

"That would be a summarized version. I hate when books do that. From what I know, all Magic is linked to the two core foundations of the Natural Order: Life and Death. Almost everyone and any race has some form of connection to the major interconnecting branches of one of those two parent fundamentals, such as Light and Darkness or the basic world elements—and even those aspects have branches themselves. You still following?"

"Yes?" Rend says, meekly.

"Consider it as a hierarchical system," Draxis says.

"A what?"

"Hmm… Top to bottom? Most important to least important? A parent and offspring? A family tree even?"

"Oh."

"To further clarify, most people have only enough magical attunement to perform the bare minimum or possess enough prowess to aid in the military or agriculture or some other form of greater labor—making actual sorcerers somewhat rare. Special cases with users involve those who are more adaptable to multiple types of magic, and there are some who can escalate their specific magical ability to unfathomable heights. Then there are the anomalies…"

"Anomalies?" Rend asks.

"Someone that breaks the limits. The things I've seen some people do… it's unnatural. Calling down hails of meteorites and commanding the very seas, raising powerful undead armies and scorching entire forests. "Sometime in the past, the Natural Order as a whole became warped and unrecognizable to the point where it lies at currently—it's the only explanation I can think of. Your master is a decent example of harboring magic that shouldn't exist."

"You mean her necromancy?" Rend asks.

"That's not her true magic ability. Ah… perhaps I said too much. It's best not to talk about it—period. There are very few rules among us, and *that* is one you should never break unless she herself brings it up. I'm serious when I say this."

"I hear you…"

"Good," Draxis responds with a sigh of relief. "One thing I will say to ease your curious mind is that the magic that she used to be able to use is antithetical to other magic types, like Light."

"What do you mean by that?"

"Take your resurrection for example. Even if she had help from that bizarre gauntlet she wears, there are some quirks about you that makes your particular revival very unorthodox, like your enhanced rejuvenation. Even her own self-resurrections don't make complete sense. Maybe in your case it has to do something more with your soul? You might be undead, but you technically have the purest soul out of anyone. Finding a preserved corpse with a fully intact one is a diamond hunt nowadays."

"Yeah, we could tell with the way you were acting before," Rend says.

"I was nearly about to send you overboard for that comment," Draxis growls. "Anyway, do you have a preferred magic type?"

"I think… I think I want to make the ocean explode."

"I have a friend that thinks like that, if she's still around. The ocean is evidently still here, but it's been her lifelong dream. Are you sure you don't want to be more like us? We can raise up entire legions with our powers y'know."

"I thought about it but… maybe? I don't know. You people kind of scare me. You all don't even flinch at death, not that I'm one to talk."

"There are many reasons for our jaded outlooks and our signature titles—and most weren't by choice," Draxis says. "For example, with me, I was born with this ability to devour and manipulate any Soul I consume. It's made me an outcast—and a burden at times."

"Do you have to use them?"

"It's what we're good at," Draxis says. "Plus, these powers allowed us to even rival the greatest of the Arbiters."

"You all keep slandering their name, but I don't remember them ever doing anything horrific," Rend says.

"Ignorance, that's all there is to say. I don't mean that negatively, I promise. It would honestly be a feat to list everything they have done, that's if I even remember it all; but essentially, Magic is a gift upon this world, and the Arbiters took advantage of that by monopolizing it. When they started getting integrated into governments, their words became law. When the demand for miracles started to rise, their greed and prices did as well.

"Even us, the Harbingers, we are also broken products of their despicable and rising omnipotence. We've been experimented on, our lives and homes ruined, and what they did to my people… I'm getting myself all worked up over it."

"I had no idea," Rend says.

"They were masters of disguising their true intentions under plain sight. That's why everything negative was pinned on us instead, for we weren't as covert. Which is fine because we have the last hurrah—mostly." Draxis then snatches Rend's book and says to him, "Enough about them. We shall see what the Arbiters will have to say for themselves soon enough, but for now, let's at least experiment and see if you can prove that you have the blood of our nemeses within you."

Chapter 9

Promise

"So finally, when his adoptive parents went to sleep, the little sardine worked up the courage and took one. Small. Peek inside of the secret basement and saw a slaughterhouse completely decorated with…" Ronella stops herself as she bares her fangs and wiggles her fingers in preparation before she yells, "His family!"

Everyone jumps out of their seat all at once at their encircled camp in the middle of the ship.

"So not only can you do water tricks, but you also have way better stories than us," Rend says while panting, with his hand over his heart.

"I'm just talented is all," Ronella says.

"What else can you do?"

"I would love to sing a song, but my mother said to never do that. She always went on and on about how I kept accidentally luring land folks to their deaths at sea or something when I was younger. It's a shame really, being cursed with the inability to do something you love because it might inconveniently kill someone."

"Tell me about it," Jellop groans.

Suvius arrives late to the party—doesn't look like he's in the mood to share a drink. "We're here," he says.

They all rise up, pumped and overflowing with elation and eagerness to see their destination, but it soon falls faster than it climbed.

"Are you sure we're at the spot?" Draxis asks. "There's nothing here."

"We covered the appropriate distance. That I am certain of," Suvius says.

"What are you folk looking for?" Ronella asks.

"A building, a secret, anything really," Draxis responds.

"Sounds like an illusion. My sister always talked about some scary land folks that could partially bend reality. I don't quite understand it, but I do know how to break it. Stand back and cover your ears."

They all heed her warning as they watch her swallow impossible amounts of air for her size—and release it all into a piercing scream. The vast space in front of the ship begins to fluctuate and unravel into cracks and tears as she gives one hell of a performance. In place of the faux background is now a distant city on a sizable island.

"There you go," Ronella says, giving a darling's smile.

"That was incredible," Rend says.

"I know. What is this place?"

"It's a highly probable guess, but this should be the origin point that started it all—the day all of Allosha screamed," Suvius says.

"Wait, *this* is where the Drowned came from?" Ronella says.

"No, just the potential creators."

"Well now I feel conflicted on my priorities… naw, I have my own battles I need to fight. I can't join you all, but I do wish you boundless luck."

"We appreciate the help," Maeva says.

"No, thank *you* instead. You have *no* idea how badly I wanted this. Anyway, it's time for me to walk the plank. Bye!"

They all wave Ronella goodbye as she launches herself off the ship and performs a cannonball trick into the murky red depths.

"Well she was a lovely angel, wasn't she?" Draxis says.

"I feel bad for her," Meavs says.

"She seems capable," Suvius says. "And I think we need that inspiration. It's time to commune with our terrors."

***

Suvius anchors the ship. In order to reach and commune with their terrors, they first had to go through the lifeless, tropical outskirts of the island. Now, they walk close together through the desolate city, making sure nothing lurks around while also being extra watchful for any structural instability that decides *now* is the time to fall down.

If only there was more time to see all the wacky infrastructure and attractions throughout the metropolis. There are crosswalks, libraries, and skyscrapers all constructed and painted with a magical and mystical image in mind, but they barely hide the shame of their derelict state.

"This place is like a kingdom, no—something even grander," Suvius says, astounded.

"Their own personal utopia, now turned dystopia," Maeva says. "Where is everyone?"

"Anyone wanna bet someone is in that tower?" Rend says, pointing to a distant building at the epicenter of the city."

"The capital, a tower of power," Jellop says.

"Well said, Jellop," Draxis says. "Let's reintroduce ourselves. Surely they haven't forgotten their favorite people."

Traveling further through the city makes them feel like ants in a nation built for giants. No giant has yet to be found however, despite how easy it is to spot one. The next stage of the exotic hunt brings them inside the Tower. The interior and exterior are in an equal state just like the city, only with more debris of books and magic residue—so they move up, as high as the stairs can take them.

***

This is it—the apex of the Tower of Power. Inside, it smells like a bar that's been deprived of quality control, so they pinch their noses to stop the burning—the ones with the sense of smell look at their undead friends with envy. The odors become more potent as they explore the room, along with the sounds of mixing and pouring that come from the far back of the room.

There is a man dressed in an all-gray robe at a workbench, shuffling bottles and glass flasks containing a rainbow selection's worth of colors and liquids. He pours a potion into another one to create one final concoction and drinks the swill till its last drop.

He slams the flask down, slightly embiggening the crack on it, and gives a powerful exhale before saying, "It's been three years, Harbingers… What took you all so long?" He then turns around, showing himself. His hair is misty-gray, and his wizened skin is rolled into wrinkles upon wrinkles.

"Business has been a little slow," Draxis responds.

"Fair enough," the wrinkled man says. "Then how's the weather?"

"Bloody. Enough with the small talk, you know why we're here."

"Of course. You want to hear what comes from our mouths directly so you can validate your intuitions and justify your hatred. Well, you can't have that, because the rest of them are gone."

"Impossible," Suvius says. "You all hid like rats in your glorified safe haven in the middle of the ocean. It's even blocked off by mystical barriers and natural barricades. Where. Are. They!"

"Lord Suvius," Jellop interrupts. "H-He speaks the truth."

"I see. Then… who are you?"

"Klae," the wrinkled man says. "As far as I know, I'm the last of the Arbiters."

"That's good enough for us," Draxis says. "As long as one of you still remains then we can finally bring this rivalry to a rightful end. This is all you Arbiters doing, all the blood and all the chaos. For over more than a decade we have endured being vilified, battered, scarred, deprived, immortalized as beings of evil while you get to sit here in your shelter and mock the conditions that you brought upon us."

"I know," Klae says. "I've heard plenty about your infamous legacies. And as for the fabricated lies about you all, I had no power to stop them. I'm not as important as you think I am, but regardless, this is the final clash between the two dictating sides that even history itself fears because of the unforeseeable outcome. And now that we are finally here—what now?"

"What do you mean 'what now'?" Maeva says. "Answer for your crimes!"

"Is that all you people really desire? You want me to beg for mercy and fix all your problems?"

"Our problems are also the world's problems," Draxis says. "You would know that if you took even a second to go outside and look up."

"Blame, blame, blame, it's all you people were ever good for," Klae snaps. "Look at me, I have nothing left to fight with. If you feel so strongly against everything the Arbiters stood for, then kill me—right here, right now. But let me ask you something before you do. What are you going to do after you cleanse the world of your nemesis? What is your end goal? Because from my perspective, you've already won."

The more they listen to him, the more they are crushed. Tamed and quelled, like fire against ice.

"You all make for a great pack of hounds," Klae continues to berate, "but you never had intentions to bite, only to bark. I don't need to hear about our failures. The fact that I'm all alone here is enough anguish. Nevertheless, instead of bitching about the past, I am slaving away to find a solution or some temporary respite—not for me—but for the entire world because I recognize what needs to be done. It's time you all do the same."

Klae returns to blending and mixing his litter of random ingredients.

With no exchanged words, Suvius leaves, and the others follow him out to a nearby balcony where they congregate and overlook the entire city with a near bird's-eye view.

"I… hate being told off, and by our enemies no less, but they're right. All of them," Suvius starts to say. "Since the very beginning we have begged for the world to stop being so dependent on their oppressors, and we have done everything unspeakable to erase the Arbiters' existence and corruption. That's all we have ever done, but now, they are dead… and the world still remains the same. Our mission was incomplete. We never took the opportunities to figure out the rest of it."

"So what are you saying?" Maeva asks.

"I suppose an alliance—but should we really? This feeling of confliction would mean that I dragged you all down this fruitless descent with me."

"We joined you because we feel your pain, and we didn't want anyone else to feel *our* pain," Draxis says.

"And I am forever grateful. I would have none other stand by my side," Suvius says. "The four of us and our absent members have endured so much, been betrayed by so many, and now we are at the ultimate hour of justice. We can finally put an end to this long war, but once we do… what are we then?"

"Saviors?" Maeva suggests.

"We killed more than we saved on our decade-long journey. Scarcely have we provided inklings of mending and healing."

"Bringers of justice?" Draxis suggests.

"Under whose name? And for what crimes? Should we punish those who are more innocent than their evil predecessors? Would it be ironic to become arbiters?"

"Heroes?" Jellop suggests.

"Monsters are still at play. Villainy still lurks. The world is still on the verge of extinction. Heroes are there to remind you of hope. So far, we have only reminded those still alive about pain and despair."

"Harbingers," Rend states.

"Hm?" Suvius hums, cocking his head.

"I know that word has negative… cona… cono… connotations, but it doesn't have to. I've done a lot of observing so far—and I don't know anyone's personal histories, but that doesn't involve me. What does involve me however is seeing the world fall apart. There are people all around me that can potentially bring this hell to a swift end, but everyone's just been stuck on proving who's right and ignoring what the people actually need.

"I'll be the first one to admit that I hate the world, but I don't want to see it go away. I like you people, but this selfishness is becoming draining. You must understand that everyone's had it rough, not just you."

Suvius pats Rend's shoulder. "It's… a shame that it required one of our own to make that sin apparent, but we hear your desire for happiness, Rend. The Arbiters, the Harbingers, the entire world—we all share a common enemy amongst our enemies, and it's never going to leave us until we unify and purge it.

"As the founder of this team of misguided individuals, I would like to declare a brand-new objective for us: to cure our planet, Allosha, from this heinous plague and immediately abolishing our old causes, because whether we like it or not—*we* are in this together."

Maeva perks up, recognizing a verbal cue and says, "And it will never be for glory nor riches."

"It's for the pursuit of happiness for all," Jellop joins in to say.

"In the name of Death—for it's a swift and steadfast reminder—that all lives are weighed and judged for purity, by its harbingers," Draxis says, finishing their rally. "…When was the last time we said that together?"

Suvius lowers his head. "The fact that you have to ask that is disheartening. We should have never stopped."

***

"So… have you all decided?" Klae asks.

"We have," Suvius responds. "We wish to help you finally put an end to this nightmare."

"Good, I thought you all were going to make an old man fight his last." Klae says with a light chuckle. "Our interests are now aligned, but our knowledge isn't. It'll require a bit of told history, but the events won't be all the way exact and precise—they'll be limited, because despite the way I look, I'm technically nineteen years old."

"Karma's a bitch," Draxis blurts. "Oops, I mean… n-no, I meant what I said."

"This condition of mine isn't from karmic backlash or retribution, it's from my magic. I'm an apprentice of the Arbiters, particularly from a space and reality-bending one, and apparently messing with space-time can cause a whole myriad of complications. I already knew that however, but my lessons on how to negate it were cut short."

"We don't care," Maeva says.

"Listen people, I can get petty too," Klae snaps. "Anyway, earlier you all wanted to enact divine punishment on me for what the

Arbiters did, but I want to make it very clear that I wasn't a part of any of their schemes. I'm just like you all. I started to trust no one. When I was fourteen—"

"Ah damn, here we go…" Maeva sighs.

"…When I was fourteen, there was a massive uproar about a discovery made by the Elite Arbiters—one so vital that it caused a great division among them on how to handle its future and made them completely disregard the pandemic.

"I also remember when this strange… visitor, suddenly showed up sometime afterward. This visitor was of nothing I had ever seen before, but they had value. Value not in their being, but in what they could provide: a cure. That's when the deadliest of discoveries was made, and just like everything with the Arbiters, it quickly turned into greed."

"Over some medicine? Draxis asks. "What kind of cure was it?"

"Believe me, it was something divine," Klae says. "The Visitor's gift wasn't just a perfect cure-all; it was also an upgrade to the anatomical structure and more. You all might have felt a taste of that evolutionary power against non-Arbiters and Arbiters alike that had the luck to relish in their perfected state during the final years before the apocalypse."

"If the Arbiters already invented a cure, then our work here is finished before it even began," Draxis says. "Where is this cure? How can we obtain it?"

"You can't," Klae states. "It was only given to a select few anyway. I have been trying to replicate it from the random notes that I secured around here, but the ingredients and sources don't make any sense to me—they read like instructions for milking a cow instead of any generic formulas and recipes. Even if I could replicate it, the problem that surpasses everything is one that cannot be remedied through tangible means."

Klae then grabs a jar containing a conjoined mass of organic slime and tissue from a cabinet nearby and brings it to a large round device rooted in the middle of the room, using it as a table.

"Eww, what the hell is that?" Rend says.

"The Decay pathogen, in its fully-grown state. I've tested this particular specimen and many others like it by feeding it some loose Soul samples, and the results all come to the same conclusion. We've seen the end result of Decaying happen numerous times—how a man can be singing one minute and turn feral the next—but what causes it?

"Well, it's because of the rapid evolution of the parasitic virus within us all. If a victim isn't already soulless, in the literal sense, then the virus will make them so by eating away at them insatiably to feed and grow itself.

"And however much soul essence it takes to reach the final stage of Decay, the mature virus will then attain sapience and fully control the host's brain and husked body to use for its evil pleasures and thus repeating and accelerating the cycle if the virus affects another, which mostly happens through bite wounds."

Suvius inspects the sample closer. The pus and the overall gross-out factor don't even faze him. What does bother him is the hidden aura coming from the mass that only his trained eye would notice. "This specimen has been laced with something."

"Not just this one, all of them," Klae says. "Earlier you all asked me if a cure was possible… and it is… if there is anyone around that is capable of purifying the whole world from a universal hex. The Curse of Soul Decay. That's the premier reason why a cure can no longer be found."

"I tend to stray from curses," Suvius adds, "for that's the darkest form of magic that even I fear. But even for those who choose to peer deep into the abyss, it's a pact that severely harms both the user and their victim. So tell me, who would harbor this much incredible power and disdain for all life to enact something so irreversible?"

"I couldn't tell you," Klae says. "Maybe it was the Visitor, or maybe we were sabotaged. Either way, this damn curse has created a hyper-mutation and transformed what was once a minor epidemic into a manifestation of death itself. The extreme urges of cannibalism, the ravenous behavior, and the soul degradation were never a part of the original strain."

"This Decay inside our bodies, there are many that still maintain some, if not most, of their senses, but… I'm starting to see irregular signs from ones who have managed to linger thus far," Suvius says. "It's been three years. When will we finally succumb?"

"Impossible to calculate I'm afraid," Klae says. "My only working theory is that some people are just lucky to be born with more durable souls. Or maybe Magic plays a supporting role—it is all within us after all. Even the tiniest amount of it might be enough to stave off the infection speed from what I've been seeing.

"I also like to imagine that willpower might be helpful as well. Unlike the personality and spirit and magic made alive by our Souls, the memories and desires vaulted in our minds are not so easily consumed. It might be why some Decayed act territorial or intelligent, though it does make them more annoying to fight against. Ultimately, everything will decay given time."

"If the virus is gaining all of these extra properties through a curse, then can't we gather more info about such evil magic and reverse it?" Draxis asks.

"I've tried, but this particular curse goes beyond human or any other race's abilities to dispel it," Klae says. "Even if the other Arbiters were here with me now, we still wouldn't be able to crack it—it's that indecipherable. We would need the help of an ancient power to break it. That's where you all would come in."

"Ancient power? Us?" Rend says.

"None of *you* of course, but an outside source. This is my only solution, or something at least feasible. There are artifacts hidden all across our dying world of Allosha, but it would be safe to say that most of them are gone or depleted thanks to my predecessors."

"So you're having us go treasure hunting?" Draxis says. "It sounds like the scams of a convoluted heist."

"I would recommend remaining optimistic," Klae says. "A lot of the items you see around this room are what remains of the other groups before you who have also doubted."

"So you sent them to their death?"

"I sent them in hopes they could get the job done, and it'll be the exact same with you all. Like I said before, I only have one singular hope to dispel this curse. If any of you want to try breaking it yourselves then go ahead and test your limits, but you'll quickly find that you need intense magical proficiency and inhumane amounts of power. If it's a matter of trust, then we'll both compromise. How about you all hold on to some of the artifacts you find until we are completely ready to commence the curse-breaker ritual."

"These artifacts, how many would be required to attain a match for the curse?" Suvius asks.

"If it were just me—approximately thirty, but with the only group in the entire world that could match fire with fire against the most advanced of us mages, that number theoretically goes down to eleven, and perhaps even lower."

Klae grabs a potion nearby off the ground and pours it onto the high-tech device they converse over. The liquid flows throughout the grooves and canals of the device's design, converging and draining into the center of it to create a pool. Particles of light begin to funnel upwards and hug together to form a spherical and dense cloud above them. Protrusions both big and small take shape across the sphere's surface.

"This is a map," Klae says. "Isn't it impressive?"

"Somehow the Arbiters can even make cartography feel sinister…" Suvius says. "What kind of sorcery is this?"

"This room is the Arbiters' master observatory. It was originally meant for keeping an omniscient view over the entire planet, and as you can see, construction never finished, but I've managed to modify this console to instead act as a detection system to find and pinpoint magical anomalies.

"Some artifacts are more undetectable than others due to their sheer magical power that this crappy machine has a hard time detecting, so we will need to use the ones we are able to find to locate the rest."

"What's that swirl over the Nesolope continent?" Maeva asks.

"The only item I could detect within my limited power. I don't know which Artifact it is, but I do know where it's located. The Heaven Plains."

"It already took us an eternity just to get *here*," Draxis says. "Traveling to a whole other continent is just illogical."

"Then allow me," Klae says, lifting up his arms. He then shouts, "Gate!" and strains as an opposite force pushes back against his magnifying energy.

The vibrations shake the room so much. It feels like anything within the vicinity will tear apart, but regardless, an oval-shaped hole manifests through space itself nearby—forming a portal. An opaque fog surrounds the mouth of the portal, billowing and fuming out like from a chimney.

"I should have chosen a different Magic study," Klae says to himself while stretching his back. "Once you prepare yourselves then go through that nexus portal. And when you find the first Artifact, just activate it so the console here can detect it, and I'll bring you all back."

"So we can take some of this stuff that's lying around?" Rend asks.

"Some of you were doing that anyway, but now you have my permission."

A shopping spree commences in the emporium of goods, mostly of edibles and things to keep because they look cool. The wares would be enough to satiate most, but there is always one connoisseur whose needs have not been met.

"Klae," Draxis calls out to him. "This is a bizarre question but… do you have any souls?"

"And I have a more bizarre answer: I do." Klae then points while saying, "Look in that small cabinet near the window over there. There should be a jar with some inside."

Draxis finds the jar easily enough as it's the only one not broken or shattered. Soft blue orbs bounce off the glass and off each other inside it. One of them is smaller and cuter than the rest. "Is this… a child's soul?" he asks.

"It's not common, but some children can have strong spirits," Klae says. "That's all I'm going to say about the matter."

"Are we all ready?" Suvius says from near the portal.

Following him, the others proceed through it, without hesitation. Maeva hesitates however, her hand grazing the portal's lips. She furrows her brows and turns. "Hey! Mage!"

"Hm? Oh, it's you. The annoying red one," Klae says. "Got something to say?"

"This one-eyed gauntlet. Do you know anything about it? Or what could it be?"

"What am I, a blacksmith? Bring it over." He inspects the gauntlet around its base and finger guards, and even pokes the closed eye on its back. "This thing is definitely an Artifact. It seems to be deactivated, but I can tell it has immense power. I wonder if it's both Blessed and Cursed?"

"Blessed and Cursed?" Maeva repeats.

"Damn it all, I knew I forgot to tell them something. Don't worry about it for now, I'll explain it later. Do you know what this thing does?"

"It likes souls…?"

"So, something that is scarce. We might need its power later, but for now, don't try to fulfill its hunger. Not unless you're absolutely sure you know what you're doing."

"I see. Thanks, mage."

"It's Klae."

"I'd rather call you mage."

"…Get out of my sight."

"Alright."

Klae holds his breath as he waits for Maeva to leave. *Kids these days...*

Chapter 10

Disgraced

As the portal condenses and erases itself behind them, they look around at their new surroundings. They are standing in the middle of a valley. It's almost surreal going from one environment to another, from one continent to another.

High above them, there's a sea—not of clouds, but of islands and mountains all floating about in defiance to the land below. Some islands periodically lose their wings and hurtle towards the ground far off into the somber horizon.

Maeva erupts into a fierce coughing fit and plugs her nose. "Everywhere we go this stench of death intensifies. If my virus-parasite thing is listening, then you have my full blessing to cut off all my senses."

"That's the least of our concerns," Suvius says.

"Oh what would you know, you don't even have a…" Her voice trails, equally matching Suvius's tact for silence—along with his sudden restlessness.

On his knees, Draxis is completely immobilized in a lost and dazed trance. Everyone else is stunned as well. They all see exactly what he sees in all its sickening appeal.

"Draxis!" Maeva shouts as she rushes towards him and gets to eye-level with him. "Draxis… Draxis!"

"Mae… Maeva?" he says, letting her hug him close. "What am I supposed to make of all this? I can't accept it. Just… just give me a second to cool down."

"Are bones supposed to be this light?" Rend asks as he kicks and fumbles around a giant, hollow one.

"Rend, stop it," Maeva says. "You're being insensitive."

"You always say that. Why don't you try asking one of the skulls here if they're offended. I'm sure you'll get a response."

"She's not talking about them, Rend," Draxis says. "…She's talking about me."

"What about you?"

"These bones and bodies are… these are the remains of my people. The Dragons."

"Wait, you? No way… if you're a dragon then… then why the fuck have we been acting like we're defenseless? Transform, dammit!"

"So insufferable," Draxis says. "Do you only think of me and my kind as unstoppable beings of absolute destruction just like everyone else does?"

"No, I… It's just that having a dragon with us would have been pretty nice, don't you think?"

"Being a dragon is nothing but a damn burden. We are forced to act on our needs to survive and are destined at birth to be a victim."

"Draxis, you and your people aren't a burden," Maeva says.

"Then why is my entire family dead, Maeva? What did they do to deserve this!"

"Draxis, you have been pushing yourself physically a lot lately, and now you're about to push yourself to unimaginable lengths emotionally," Suvius says. "What I'm trying to say is that I want you to sit this out and we can go look for the Artifact."

"Ditching me again I see," Draxis says, rising to his feet. "Suvius, what emotions can I feel that I haven't already? I swear you get paranoid at the most bizarre moments. Listen to me closely: I'm *going* to explore this graveyard until I get my rightful answers… even if it strengthens my fear that I am the last of my kind."

Draxis stomps away and heads deeper into the valley of death.

"His mind is on a warpath with itself," Jellops states. "I never felt him get so upset before.

"I feel it too," Suvius says. "Whatever tragedy has occurred here is only going to break him further."

"Should we stop him?" Maeva asks.

"No. I owe him this much for not doing my part in stopping the kingdoms from oppressing his people."

"But you weren't even alive when those laws were signed."

"My death and legacy should still have provided an antagonistic voice worth adhering to. What happened at Isilios is a testament to what occurs when discrimination turns into extreme violence."

"It is apparent that this is a violent event, but it isn't from your doing," Jellop says. "You have always treated him more than what he *is* and more than what the world treated him *as*."

"Still, this shouldn't have happened," Suvius says. "This is too much."

"We should pursue Draxis before he gets too far away," Maeva says.

"Agreed. I would prefer it however if you stagger your involvement with this," Suvius says to her. "I don't want any hard feelings to be directed towards you."

"He knows better than to start yelling at me."

"There is hilarity in how stubborn both you and Draxis are. That backlash is meant for me as well."

***

Draxis touches a giant bone sticking out the ground in the middle of a field of rib cages and plunged swords. The bone partially disintegrates into dust from his touch, floating away wherever the harsh wind blows. "I can't be the last one," he says, looking at the white powder staining his palm. "There were so many of us…"

"Draxis the runaway!" Jellop calls out.

"…I thought you all wanted to look for the Artifact?"

"We have. You."

"And so you all attempt to defeat me with flattery yet again."

"We will find the artifact in due time," Suvius says. "But for now, how about we search for your answers?"

"I already found my answers," Draxis snarls. "This was a genocide. That wicked witch dared to look me in the eyes and tell me she's sorry."

"This has nothing to do with her. There aren't even any Vomenn insignias here."

"Now you're defending her? Tsk. It was a mistake to take you back to that temptress. I can't even tell which side you're on."

Jellop slides in between them. "Banters of resilience lead to assured dysfunction. To prevent any more, may I please act as a remedial agent and bridge both of your dying loves?"

"Brilliant lecture as always, Jellop. But we're not in the mood," Draxis says.

"Then are you just in the mood to complain?"

"If you're only going to patronize me then you can just…"

"…What?" Jellop says, questioning his sudden silence.

Draxis points. "Suvius, that rotting skull behind you…"

Suvius turns. He quickly identifies a dragon skull that is not only larger than the others found already, but it feels like it's staring back at him. The way the body is arranged indicates that two heads are missing. "How quaint," he says. "This one still has some life in it."

"Do you mean its soul?" Jellop asks.

"More than that it seems like. It has a story to tell."

"Can we uncover it somehow?" Maeva asks.

"Hmm…" Suvius touches the skull with both of his hands. "Its soul isn't vigorous enough for me to revive it whole—it will get disintegrated in the process, but it might last long enough to see a glimpse or two into its life. I would need a vessel to harness its memories since its body is unusable. Perhaps you can, Draxis?"

"I'm not hungry," he responds. "I will never be *that* hungry. Never again."

"I was just making a suggestion."

"Refrain from doing that."

"I will be the medium for these coveted memories," Jellop interrupts. "Shall we perform a séance?"

"A séance… That might work," Suvius says, thinking it over. "How determined are you to examine this corpse's memories, Draxis?"

"More than anything."

"Then let's see if we can make this work."

"Yay! Jellop cheers. "Let us three hold hands and connect our magic and abilities."

Suvius and Draxis offer their hands to him and to each other, locking the three of them into a triangle formation.

"This is so weird…" Draxis mumbles. "Did any of you wash your hands?"

"Muhuhu!" Jellop laughs.

"Gah. I hate it when you do that.

"Now, let us all close our eyes and focus on our roles," Suvius says.

They stand together in sync and lock themselves into a silent ritual. The skull resonates with their magic, shown by a faint black aura that surrounds it. From an outside perspective, the whole process looks boring.

Rend grabs Maeva's attention as they wait. "Hey… Master?" he says.

"Yes?"

"Draxis. Do you think he's mad at me?"

"He can forgive and forget easily, except when it comes to his personal circumstances. Oh… Well, now I actually don't know."

"So I messed up."

"Partially," Maeva says. "We can't expect you to know everything about us. We should have been more open."

"Even so, I want to do better. I should be better."

"You're already doing the best you can."

"Am I? I feel like I'm a… nuisance. And using these big words hurts," Rend says.

"Really? With everything you were complaining about you're worried about some vocabulary?"

"I was joking," he says. "I can use… humongous words just fine, like… apricot."

"That's a fruit. There's nothing special about that," Maeva says.

"Can't you just be proud of me?" Rend says.

"Why do you even need my validation? Or anyone else's?"

"I-I don't know. I guess it's just built into me."

"I'm not your old master, Rend. You can remove those chains of his."

"Then what about your chains on me?"

"It depends on how you view them. I might joke around about your enslavement, but the one chain I will never place on you is one that revokes your freedom. You are always free to become better."

"Yeah…"

Heavy panting is the first sign of error, followed by a breakup in the line of connection between the three in séance.

"That… was a lot to absorb," Draxis says, stumbling.

"A-Anything noteworthy?" Suvius asks.

"Y-Yeah, but I'll reserve any conclusions for now. I was unprepared for so much agony. Can we try it again?"

"Again?" Jellop groans. "Pain…"

"We have to, Jellop," Suvius says. "We need to know more of the Dragons' fate. Let's start it again."

Once again, the seance is performed, and flurries of animated images courses through Draxis's mind. He cannot hear the shouts of the soldiers that he sees through one of the eyes of the three-headed dragon, but their siege weapons are readied and aimed directly towards the viewer, and they strike—ending the vision.

Another scene plays—through the left head. The vision cuts off abruptly, just like the head. A final scene, through the eyes of the middle head. It is airborne, weaving through a dense precipitation of elemental breaths and spilled blood, and soaring above the brutality happening on the ground—eventually ending from an oncoming explosion.

"That's enough!" Draxis says, setting himself free and wiping his puffy eyes. "This battle was a massacre on every side. Human on human, human on dragon… dragon on dragon. I should have been here with them. I would have stopped all of this." He then reaches out and touches a cracked skull nearby. His hand is so miniscule in comparison. "So, this is how my race ends, isn't it? Unfulfilled dreams and nonexistent futures. We were never monsters—we just wanted freedom… Why did none of you ever see that?"

"But you're still alive, Draxis," Jellop says. "Their memories can still flourish."

"No, Jellop. My kind wouldn't have been driven this far if it wasn't for the Dragonslayer and her desire for control. Maybe in the end it doesn't even matter… just nothing but a damn burden."

"Hey, I think we found something!" Rend shouts from afar. His words are ignored.

"You only burn yourself when you tell yourself lies like that, Draxis," Suvius scolds.

"How kind, but you're only saying that because I'm no longer your main concern. Not ever since I've found some extra souls to satiate my needs. So now there's no need to come up with a contingency for me is there?"

"I would never… We'll talk about this later."

Maeva cradles a crystal half her size. She stands and holds it upright. "I think we found the Artifact."

Draxis can feel the erratic fog in his mind clear as he peers into the haze that flows within the stone. He takes it away from Maeva.

"H-Hey! I saw it first!" she snaps.

"Ah! Sorry!" he says, shaking his head to clear his mind and admit his fault. "This crystal is so enchanting for some reason."

"I hear that dragons like treasure," Rend says.

"Being forced to spend so much time with nobility will turn any man into an avaricious one." Draxis then lifts the crystal and twists and shakes it around. "I wonder if there's a command or something for this thing?"

"Just tap it a few times," Rend says. "That'll fix it."

"This is an artifact, not some…" Draxis gets interrupted by the crystal as its radiance becomes a beacon that's almost too blinding to look at, piercing even through closed eyelids. "Oh, that worked. Brilliant!"

"I told you it would. So… where's the portal that Klae promised us?"

"Hmm. Maybe poor reception?" Draxis wonders.

"We could stack on top of each other to get a better signal?" Rend suggests.

"Jellop disagrees. You all would break my back," he says.

"Those islands above us would be ideal," Maeva says.

"I'll take nothing short of a catapult to launch us up there, but the ones around here are a bit… rusty," Draxis says. "We'll find elevation eventually."

Finding higher ground proves more difficult than anticipated in the minutes spent searching. The soothing glow from the relic offsets the malignant atmosphere and turns time into an afterthought as they take turns on finding ways to amplify the crystal's resonance, even if the methods are silly like throwing it into the air or shouting profanities at it. The breezes of bliss are happening in small but impactful waves—just like the coming vortex of disaster.

A horrifying roar echoes across the valley. A few more gather in succession until an entire orchestration terrorizes everyone enough to freeze in place. The only way to find the source is to turn around.

Rend's head tilts higher and higher as he follows the rise of the towering skeletons. "Uhh… did we do that?"

"It must be the Artifact," Maeva says with urgency. "Draxis, turn it back off!"

"How!" he shouts back.

"Smack it or something!"

The Artifact's luminosity resonates brighter, akin to a star, and turning the dreadful battlefield into one that could outshine the heavens.

"It's not working!" Draxis shouts.

Slabs of thick flesh and fat begin to move and regenerate around the hundreds of corpses and bones across the valley. The blackest nights cannot even compare in resemblance to the current blotted sky as the shadows of each reanimated dragon envelops the land below.

"What can we do! What the hell can we do!" Rend screams.

"Hold on, stand back," Suvius says as he arches his back and raises his arms high. "Let me try something. Detain!"

"Well…?" Rend says.

"It's worthless, they answer to no one. What I'm about to say next is unpreferred but necessary. Run!"

As they try to flee, everything elemental and non-elemental is shot at them with cannon-like force—consisting of fire, electricity, earth, ice—all of which is born from the foaming jaws of the great flying beasts. Projectiles pound through and scoop up the ground, leaving behind widespread craters and deep pools of leftover magical residue.

"Keep running!" Suvius says.

"Brothers! Sisters! Please, stop!" Draxis shouts.

Fulfilling Draxis's wish, the sky illuminates in a warm amber light as if razed by the sun itself. Embers of scorched flesh litter the air in specks.

"Sorry for intervening!" a light voice says, coming from a small woman with insect-like wings who descends in front of them with crossed arms. "It was taking forever for someone to die for my amusement, so I took it upon myself to expedite the process. I'm still bored however."

"Aluna?" Maeva says.

"I know who I am," she snaps.

"Little Butterfly!" Jellop says.

Aluna squeals. "Jellop, you're alive!" She descends and hugs one of his hands with all her might.

"Your heart still remains hyperactive, Aluna," Jellop says. "I am thrilled, but I do still need this hand for hand-related uses. Don't hurt it."

She lets go—after another few seconds. She then looks at the others. She notices Rend cowering behind Maeva. "You got an overgrown tumor behind you, Maeva."

"Damn mosquito," Rend retaliates. "You have the same on your back."

"Bastard, you making fun of my wings?"

"You pixies make it easy whenever you try to start talking shit."

"Again, you're a bastard," Aluna says. "We *fairies* are much more advanced compared to those thuggish pixies. Though, people would say otherwise. Dumbasses."

"Never seen a fairy with six wings though."

"Hmph, it's because *I* am a princess."

"Since when?" Draxis remarks. "In which lifetime?"

"Shut up. I'm trying to assert my dominance here."

"You're trying to dominate my slave?" Maeva says.

"Uh, yeah, I am. So what?"

"I've been pretty tense lately, so I wouldn't mind relieving some stress by snapping apart something relatively small…"

"J-Jellop, help! They're bullying me!"

"Assailants are drawn to cowardice when served with justice and rebounded animosity," he says to Aluna.

"You know what, you're a bastard too. That's what all of you are."

"Children, please…" Suvius says after a deep sigh. "Focus on what is imminent."

"So damn bossy. Here, I'll handle it." Aluna flexes her wings and soars upwards. Each of her wings alternate in a variety of red and orange colors as she mixes and matches her elemental fire spells into a festival display's worth of explosions and mayhem. "Fucking dragons! Eat horseshit and die!"

"I'm standing right here you know!" Draxis shouts up at her.

"You look like you've already had your fill!"

"Impudent little—!"

"What?" she shouts. "I can't hear you over the sound of me fucking shit up!"

The ashes that continue to rain from her carnage are so plentiful and crisp. It almost becomes a choking hazard.

"How the hell did you all ever manage as a team?" Rend asks.

"Lots of miracles and glue," Draxis says." So, so, so much glue."

"I prefer tree sap," Jellop says.

"That's because you like eating it."

"Muhuhu!"

"Hey, get back here!" Aluna screams as the dragons begin to flee, all heading towards one direction in mass migration.

The Artifact's light dims to a soft glow.

"It's too late for that now you stupid thing," Draxis berates. "Thanks for that…"

"Draxis," Jellop begins to say. "I don't understand the chaos here, both the old and new. Was there purpose in their destruction?"

"They died trying to defend themselves. But now… there is only one purpose now that unifies the Dragons in their mindless states, and it's a deep sickness that even overrides the whims of the Decay: *Revenge*. There *will* be revenge against the ones who've blackened our magnificence. All of those defilers have already fallen on these bloodied grounds, but there is one place that still remains untouched and ripe for disaster. We have to go back."

***

"My apologies for the delay with the return portal," Klae says. "I couldn't detect a damn thing at first but whatever you all did made this map light up like a demon in pain. But welcome back nonetheless, how did finding the—"

"Take us to Vomenn Kingdom," Draxis orders.

"Actually, that's exactly where the next artifact is. A great coincidence, but why the urgency?"

"We'll explain later. Just take us there—now!"

Chapter 11

Repeat

"So let me see if I'm understanding this… dilemma," Ceranus says while pacing and forth in front of her throne. "Viruses and curses, all of that can wait. What I'm trying to grasp is how you all managed to royally damn this world even further. Why would you frolic around and touch an object that's beyond your comprehension in the first place?

"As a consequence for your stupidity, you all have accidentally revived those who should've remained slumbering, and now they are on an unstoppable warpath and will ravage all who stand in their way until their wrath can be stopped—but that's only *if* they can be stopped. And as additional mockery to our certain doom, you want me to relinquish the kingdom's secret weapon in our darkest hour?"

"That's right," Maeva states.

"So, war is coming…" Ceranus's own words bear too much weight, forcing her to sit down, with hands that feel the need to shake unceasingly. "That mass grave, I had no idea such a battle had even taken place. Who could have organized such an atrocity? Wait, where did you all say it happened at again?"

"Nesolope."

"Nesolope…?" Ceranus repeats. "It's far enough away, but with wishful thinking that only gives us a day to prepare if they attack from the east."

"Shouldn't we evacuate?" Rend asks. "Like right now?"

"Unless any of you know of a safe haven that can house and sustain more than half a thousand then I'll gladly let you lead the way, otherwise this might be our final stand… no—*my* final stand. If all you need is the Bloodheart Cuirass, then you are free to take it and leave. This overdue punishment is of my own, none of yours."

"It doesn't have to be," Suvius says. "We can protect you."

"No, we really don't," Draxis interjects. "We're not babysitters."

"I have to agree with him, Suvius," Ceranus says. "A knight shouldn't sacrifice their life for a soon nameless kingdom."

"But the people need a bastion, and a bastion needs a commander."

"Suvius, do you really want someone like me in charge of that bastion? Like I said before, I accept my punishment in full."

"Even so, Ceranus, accountability doesn't even fucking matter when what the world is essentially facing is a second apocalypse," Maeva says. "We need to unify and eradicate the enemy."

"The 'enemy' that you speak ill of is my family," Draxis snaps.

"And what about our families?" she lashes back. "Does no one else's matter to you? Your plight for your people isn't righteous, Draxis, it's foolish because the infected fangs that they bear are meant for everyone—which includes you. Obviously we don't want to hurt them or *you* any further, but our only option is self-defense to the highest degree."

"Don't speak to me like you're doing this for my sake. None of you will ever know what I'm going through. I'm not partaking in this holocaust, that much I stand firm by." He beelines for the exit, stopping just before coming into arms-reach of the door and looks back. "Ceranus, if there weren't any valid reasons for your protection… then I would personally seize my people's victory by devouring you myself."

"Draxis wait!" Jellop shouts. But it is too late as the door slams shut through a transference of raw emotion.

Little Nightwing... is all Ceranus can think of as a resurfaced memory pinches the back of her mind. "I-If the rest of you are serious about helping us prepare for war, then don't hesitate on utilizing this castle and her possessions however you please." She then rests her head on the armrest of her throne, her brooding attitude emanating. "I need to go order a council meeting with the Final Three, so whenever we come to a decision on our fated battle plan, I'll call for you all then."

In agreement, everyone nods their heads and leaves.

"I'll admit," Suvius says with a sigh as he gathers his thoughts and closes the throne room's doors behind him. "I have fought many foes in my dual lives: witches, serpents—all of them naturally a rival to my might, but never I'd have ever thought I would have to squeak a victory against a legion so monstrous that it far surpasses true horror. It… disturbs me."

"Well someone sure did lose their balls. Again," Aluna taunts. "What are you getting so scared for?"

"It's not just me I am worried about. And mind your little tongue, you miscreant."

"Make me!" Aluna flutters down the hall at breakneck speeds before he can respond.

"I swear… doesn't anyone listen to me anymore?" Suvius says.

"We're listening, grandpa," Rend says.

"Don't call me… Bah, all you people do is feast upon my patience. I'm going to go survey our battlegrounds. Alone."

"And there he goes…" Maeva says. "What are you going to do, Jellop?"

"To think—and eat. Everyone's emotions and thoughts are beginning to become incoherent and clouded. It's making it hard to help. It's like looking into darkness… I don't like the dark. Jellop then departs from the already diminished party.

"This is going to be a needlessly long day," Maeva grumbles. "We should do something productive while we prepare for tomorrow. What do you think, Rend?"

"You can do whatever you please with me," he says, winking. "I was wondering when you were going to ask."

"Goodness, you're such an idiot. Just follow me and don't say anything else."

He has no choice but to follow her as she grabs one of his arms and pulls him along. It's baffling to Rend just how large the castle is, but now he gets to see its hidden depths through every staircase Maeva guides him to. They're passing by so much unused space that is more dead and decrepit than the world outside. It's all haunting and ghastly. His wanderlust is bleeding out profusely, just like his dreams—again. They finally enter a room, somewhere beneath the castle's heart.

"This training room looks like it hasn't been used in centuries," Rend says, swiping away at the cobwebs and thick clouds of dust. "How did you know this was all here?"

"I found it back when we first came here," Maeva answers.

"What would ever make you want to venture so far down under the castle?"

"Didn't have a choice since they converted their dungeons into their infirmary. The dungeons here go farther down than you might think. I'm pretty good at navigating through those naturally."

"At what? Dungeons?"

"Yes…" she says grimly.

"Is that something you want to talk about?"

"I feel like I've already said enough."

Rend sighs. "Is that a second thing I'm not supposed to ask about? I was told to not ask about other stuff as well."

"I didn't know you started snooping around about my history," Maeva says.

"It just happened by chance."

"I see…"

"Err, but I'm still fascinated—about you."

"I know you are. I'm not worth the effort, Rend. It's better this way."

"Why?"

"…Stop pressing me about it."

"Why?"

"*Because I said so,*" Maeva says, grinding her teeth.

"Did you only bring me down here just to vent your frustration?"

"Where do you think some of my frustration comes from? Regardless, I want you here."

"Do I have the option to decline," Rend asks.

"Nope. You're stuck here with me."

"Then at least tell me what you plan on doing to me."

"Not *do* to you, do *with* you," Maeva corrects. "This is the perfect place to prevent us from getting disturbed. And yes, I know what that sounds like, but just hear me out."

"I'm listening…"

"A little dragon told me that you've been dabbling in magic."

"That snitch," Rend hisses. "Well, whatever he told you was probably exaggerated. Whenever I try anything, my hands only sparkle and the spell fizzles out."

"That's more promising than you might think," Maeva says.

"Neat. So now what?"

"We'll have to see if that promise is true. Show me what you can manage, and I'll figure out what comes after."

Rend aims his hands at one of the wooden dummies stationed around the room, completely focusing on attacking it. He feels a lumpy sensation trying to combine inside his body and burst out through his hands, but only a small cloud of glitter is made.

"Did you see that?" he says. "That big poof of nothing? I can't do this. I thought magic was as simple as pointing at the thing in front of you and watching it die—magically!"

"You have the right idea," Maeva responds. "But you might find it easier if you combine your imagination whilst channeling the magic essence within you instead of forcing it into existence. That's how most people do it anyway. It's a very popular practice to create personal incantations and patterns to help envision any desired spell effect, which can be further boosted by mastery level and natural attunement."

"I'm surprised you can act as my tutor. I don't think I've ever seen you use any of your own magic."

"And you won't," she says plainly.

"Why?"

"*Because* not all of us are happy that we can use magic. Now, as you were, slave. Continue practicing on creating a successful spell."

Rend tries his best for her—over and over again, being completely demoralized by the fifth attempt. "This sucks. Can you come give me a hands-on experience?"

"How pathetic. Most I can do for you is take away some of the workload." Maeva gets behind him and raises his arms at the dummy. "What form of magic are you trying to realize? Have you even thought of that?"

"Umm…"

"Goodness, you're so hopeless. We'll have to start with something numbingly easy then. Like fire. It's the most common type of bio-magical attunement, so try thinking of burning trees and volcanoes or something. That's about as basic as I can make it for you."

Rend closes his eyes and concentrates. "Hey… I feel something," he says, feeling something soft squish against his upper back."

"Is it a surge of magic power?" she asks.

"Sure… let's call it that."

Maeva squeezes his arms, making him flinch in pain. "If you keep acting like a damn fool then you'll never get anywhere."

"You're… right. I understand."

"I'm glad you're showing some initiative, but I know you can show me more than that. Don't be afraid of messing up. I'll guide you."

With Maeva guiding his movements to get his blood and magic flowing, Rend has complete freedom to picture his idealized spell. He imagines a simple and lone campfire, one that crackles passionately, but not too wildly either, in the middle of a barren snowfield.

Maeva feels his arms relaxing, and his heat rising. "Thattt's it," she whispers. "Take it slow."

"You're giving me mixed feelings here," Rend whispers back.

"Fire is a mix of emotions. Embrace it."

Tiny embers pepper Rend's palms. They then coalesce into buds of fire that populate the center of his hands. "Unholy shit! I really can use magic!"

"That's a good-looking flame as well," Maeva compliments as she lets him go.

"C-Can I blow things up now?" he asks.

"How about you don't do that. This room is too small for crap like that."

"Awww."

"Don't be sad, this is just the beginning. And be thankful that I'm here to make sure you don't set yourself on fire."

"I wonder if I could have always used magic…?" Rend says, staring at his ignited palms. He chuckles as he amuses himself with the possibilities he wish he could have done. "You don't know how much this means to me. Thanks, Master."

"See, isn't it great being under my servitude?"

"Ehh. Not enough benefits."

"You could get more benefits if you show me that you're worth my time."

"I'm taking that as a promise."

Maeva leaves Rend to his fun, and he's too preoccupied with his summoned flames to notice her disappearance.

Distracted by her own lone thoughts, Maeva doesn't see the towering shadow that lurks around the entrance and collides directly into it. She yelps as a shooting pain overtakes and dazes her completely. Whatever she just rammed full speed into is considerate enough to apologize. She cracks open her eyelids and fixates on the bony hands that reach out to nurture her face.

"What the actual hell, Suvius!" she says, plugging her nose. "I thought you left! Wait… were you stalking us?"

"That is not important," he says.

"I'll become important if I scream for help."

"…I was observing."

"Okay, so what did you 'observe'? See anything to your liking?"

"Indeed. You are growing, and it's showing."

"You and your poetry sometimes, I swear," Maeva responds.

"I mean it. I must say, it is an odd feeling, but I am quite entertained watching a novice work their way to become a master, but there are always details that books and even professionals do not reveal, so if you have any doubts then feel free to engage with me whenever."

"Well, there is one thing that I want some advice on."

"Certainly."

"I can't help but feel responsible for Rend," Maeva says. "I want to ensure that he improves."

"That he also doesn't leave you?" Suvius adds.

"I didn't say that."

"It's what you've been doing. Establishing a bond with him."

"Then, how would you determine the next step to make that bond stronger, if you were in my position?"

"It depends on the master's needs," Suvius says. "If you seek to turn him into a reliable knight that's fit to protect his queen, then let him be. But if you want a force that can rival against Light or Dark, then that would require more insidious training and desecration. You are not ready to make such dreadful commitments, so I would recommend *not* trespassing on that latter option."

"What do you mean?" Maeva asks.

"What I mean is that you're on the opposite side of the spectrum from where I sit. Necromancy is a dark art, but it isn't solely about abusing or defiling the dead if that's what the wielder chooses to do—it can also be about establishing or redefining a second life. Just now, I watched you unlock the opportunity to give him a chance at becoming something greater."

"Is that the best route?"

"You tell me. Would you prefer to treat him like how I treat my subordinates?"

"N-No."

"Then continue facilitating his growth. He's going to excel one way or another it seems. Look at him," Suvius says, gesturing towards a rambunctious Rend having the time of his life incinerating a defenseless dummy.

"That's another thing that's bothering me—his magic," Maeva says. "When he was able to concentrate, he had an aura to him that struck me. I didn't anticipate he would have so much over-flowing power within him. I don't know how to control something like that."

"Then don't. Unleash it," Suvius says.

"Isn't that what a master shouldn't do?"

"It's what *I* wouldn't do since I prefer to hold a suffocating leash that is made with no key over my subjects—but you're not me. You should instead cherish the bond you have created thus far, as it is better than a contractual or nonconsensual version, and let it flour-ish."

"Right. I'll have to think about all of this later, but I do appreciate your share of insight. It's a darn shame you don't listen to yourself," Maeva says.

"…This castle is already cold enough without you adding ice to it."

"Well, I'm sure the dragons will warm the place up nice and toasty for you… What the hell am I saying? I'm so sorry. I'm just tired and… I'm going to go get some sleep."

"There are times where I wish I could do the same. Until our next discussion, Young Maeva."

***

Aluna floats in front of the colossal doors to the throne room, looking down at her hands. She clenches them and pummels the door with every knock and kick she can muster as hard as she can. Ceranus opens the door, befuddled—until she sees the conductor of the ruckus.

"Ceranus… can we talk?" Aluna says in a near begging tone.

"My, it's been a while, Aluna. I wanted to say 'hello!' and 'how you been?' earlier, but you know, facing certain doom and all that. So, you too also wish to speak with me privately? I feel so important today."

"Oh?"

"Your fellow members came by before you… They're quick to relapse," Ceranus says.

"That doesn't surprise me, but it isn't fair that they treat you as a scapegoat."

"Well, I'm not the only topic of discussion, but it is what it is. I think this momentum of high stakes is just unveiling issues that nobody knows how to handle, or really dedicate the proper time *to* handle."

"You could make time, like right now. I'm listening," Aluna says.

"No, I really shouldn't," Ceranus says. "It'll just turn into rambling but… this whole situation is disgraceful and hopeless—to the point where sanity is an illusion. I'm trying to stay optimistic but no matter how many twists or turns or maybes and ifs, I keep thinking how it all links back to the day I made those laws, and with every nation following in ruthless stride. I shudder to think about which caused the most deaths—the Decay, or me.

"Ah, there I go with the rambling. Talking to you has always made me feel better and at peace. So far, you're the only one that's been pleasant to deal with."

"I'm not… pleasant," Aluna says. "I don't know why you would ever think that."

"You don't remember all the exhilarating escapades we shared during those high security escort missions?" Ceranus says. "I've always appreciated your company for helping me get through the voracious fog of subterfuge and secret ambushes."

"What if I told you that my hands have been drenched further in blood since those times? Would you still think of me as pleasant?"

"Spilled blood is as common as rainfall, Aluna—I would know—but it does matter where it comes from. Is that what you're worried about?"

"It is. I recently received word that all my contractors are dead. Personally, I'm ecstatic but… let's just say that there's a hanging contract that still needs to be fulfilled, and I desperately wish I could refuse it. This fate they have forced upon me, it's driving me fuc—freaking insane!"

"You can be informal here, Aluna," Ceranus says. "I like it when you're yourself anyway."

"It's not often I hear that. Cee-Cee, I'm at a loss here. I don't know what to do. I'm not good at fighting stuff that's immune to being blown up, and it's only going to get worse for me if I can't stop it."

"Sounds like we both share the same forms of decline, and our suffering is rapidly approaching. Even penance will not solve our errors."

"Stop talking like that. You are not forsaken."

"Are you playing the role of an ignorant fool just to make me feel better?" Ceranus asks.

"I just can't blame you for everything like everyone else does. My hatred goes to the King and the Arbiters."

"This is why I think you're pleasant, Aluna. But you shouldn't disagree with your allies' pain just because they are aimed at a friend. I caused them some of that pain. I'm also positive that I have affected you to some degree as well."

"But you're ignoring your own pain. You were being manipulated to become what you are now."

"No, I manipulated myself," Ceranus says. "I am seeing the world for what it really is. Too long I was stuck in a fantasy state of mind, until reality, in the form of five truths arriving before my throne, broke that fantasy. Everything around me is burning me to death, but what little of my purity I still have within me I will use to mitigate the fires I have caused."

"Uh-huh. And how's that been going for you?" Aluna asks.

"Well… some fires are hotter than others."

"I need actual advice here, Cee-Cee."

"I've already offered what I could, but I think what you need is undeniable truth: There's nothing you can do to reverse the past, secrets will never remain secret, and you're going to spend the rest of your miserable little life repenting and begging for innocence that you don't deserve."

"You're such a wicked bitch."

"Likewise," Ceranus says, smirking. She then grabs and brings the door closer to herself. "I don't wish to suddenly depart like this, but I need to return to drawing out our war plans, so I mustn't stay any longer. I can't tell an assassin like you *how* to kill their targets, but I *can* tell them who their priority target should be—in this case: you."

"Me?"

"Yes, you. All your imperfections and ill temptations. Just strangle and snuff them out or whatever."

"Only pussies do that. I prefer making them stare me down until their inevitable demise."

"Fascinating…" Ceranus says, rolling her eyes. "Just don't let me be a bad influence and have you take anything I say the wrong way. I'm sorry I couldn't be of much help."

"I don't really know what kind of help I wanted when I came here, but… I think I have some ideas," Aluna says.

"I would recommend pondering some more. Your ideas are usually extreme."

"Can't hear you! I'm flying away!"

***

Illuminated by a single candlelight next to her bed, Maeva can hardly contain the muffles of her screams with her palms. *It's so noisy! Can't a woman of darkness get some sleep?*

She drags her feet as she heads for the bedroom door to unlock it—and gives an audible yawn as she parades into the midst of a rising maelstrom occurring in the hallway. The yelling doesn't deescalate, even with her presence, so she does nothing more than rest her back against the wall to watch everything unfold—much to her dismay.

"You've been acting irrational and unpleasant ever since we first came here," Suvius says.

"And you've been pretending that you're some sort of misunderstood saint," Draxis attacks back. "Why are you going to such lengths for these people? Is it because of her that you're willing to sacrifice your life and ours? I owe you mine for being my guardian, but I *absolutely* will abolish my oaths if you think I'm going to remain a pawn just so you and her can have a happy ending."

"There's more to this at stake than what you're implying. The entire world is in danger."

"And where was all this righteousness before the apocalypse? Face it, Suvius, you've changed. To think *you*, a man who literally discarded his humanity just to spite Humanity would end up becoming their lap dog. You and I both know how this kingdom loves to ensnare and chain those dogs. So no matter how many times you may deny it, Ceranus has made you her bit—"

Suvius pins Draxis against a mosaic window, holding him in place with an arm across his chest, and with a fist clenched while saying, "You must really view me as something pitiful to assume I would even know what the definition of being tamed is. This misconception of yours; embodying humanity is not an inglorious sin as you see it to be, and not having it does not make someone exempt from experiencing it.

"Despite being reborn into an entity of darkness, even I can see the duality of it. I can see humanity in *her* because she is showing it, I see it in them because *we* are attempting it, whereas the only thing holding us all back from reclaiming it—is you. And as I recall, you're enamored with a lover as well."

"And? That 'lover' is my savior, not that you would know what that means," Draxis says. "She's the very same savior whose life was ruined by everybody just like me. And never jeer about Sadra. At least I have taste unlike that wretched witch you boned."

Maeva moves in to separate them. "Suvius. Draxis. Enough!"

"Out of the way, Maeva," Draxis says.

"Excuse me?"

"Y-You're interfering."

"If you would have chosen your words more wisely then you would be content with me remaining docile instead of basically begging for me to slap the horseshit out of both of you!

"Seriously, I understand your traumas—trust me," Maeva continues. "And I shouldn't have to say this, but we're saving this kingdom and the rest of the world because we're supposed to be different from the Arbiters, right? We don't abandon people in need, and we surely don't want any more cataclysms. The Arbiters were involved with the previous one, so let's not make this draconic one *ours*."

"But the dragons," Draxis whimpers. "I can't fight my family."

"Draxis, I honestly don't know what to tell you. They're already dead, get over it. This obsession with the corpses of beings who didn't even accept you isn't healthy, and no good is going to come from you driving yourself mad over it.

"And as for you, Lord Suvius—remember your priorities. Nobody's discounting your affections and your dreams, but if you truly care then you're going to have to do what you do best as the Harbinger of Sacrifice and abandon what's necessary so that a better future can come to pass. I know this isn't what you both want to hear—but if you two want more assistance, then talk to Jellop over there…"

Jellop waves from afar while holding a plate of something sloppy and unappetizing.

"Now either rest up or get back to work… idiots," Maeva says as she storms off, back into her room."

"Muhuhu!" Jellop laughs.

"Quiet, Knave," Suvius says.

Chapter 12

Blood, Sweat, and Tears

The War Room. It's where everyone is gathered—Ceranus, and two other knights that don protective gear so prestigious. There is history in this room, a bloodied timeline that has spanned many generations with weapons, trophies, and armor taken as spoils from every siege and from every successful defense. There's enough taxidermy mantled on the walls to fill at least three editions for a bestiary and the hearts of a hundred huntsmen. This is an exhibit, a culmination of a kingdom's pride and prime—and it'll be no different today.

The guests of honor finally arrive, escorted by Damel.

"Hello, everyone!" Ceranus shouts with added cheer. "Welcome to the Hall of Conquest! I'm so glad you all could… What's wrong? You all look so tired. Are you not excited for doomsday?"

"When you've seen an apocalypse once it sort of loses its charm," Maeva says. "Ignore our bleak attitudes, there were a few trials we had to champion through before this moment."

"Well, you weren't the only ones. I think we have finally compiled something that fairly resembles a strategy to get us through this, with the additional hands of these noble three."

The two knights beside Ceranus straighten themselves to a proper upright stance.

"Everyone, this is Enam, Borace, and of course, you already know Damel."

"So, these are the Harbingers up close and personal… Is it too late to switch sides?" Enam asks Ceranus.

"A kind greeting would have sufficed enough, Enam. Anyway, these three are the last of our elite knights. The rest you've seen out and about patrolling are just noble volunteers or have had some prior experience in our military."

"So… the Decayed outside these walls… are the rest of the elite?" Rend asks.

"Correct," Ceranus states.

"Damn."

"Correct again. But the thing is—we have you all here."

"But they have dragons," Rend says.

"We have an ancient Artifact."

"But they have an army."

"Well we have hope. Now let me finish." Ceranus takes a big breath before spreading a wrinkled map across a table. "So, what's the main idea here? Well, it's to have equilibrium between resistance and protection for both the sky and land, and to mitigate any structural damages and casualties—the usual annoyances of war.

"All of this will be maintained through an unbreakable defensive perimeter that concentrates around our advantage points around the inner wall and a preemptive strike strong enough to turn this fight over completely before it even begins. The skies are our biggest vulnerability that I'm still trying to figure out, so let's talk ground for now. Enam, you'll help cover the West side of town, near the castle," Ceranus says, drawing a marker on the map.

"Very well," Enam responds.

"Borace, the South side."

He nods, making the helmet that covers his head and face creak.

"Damel, are you okay with the North side?" Ceranus asks. "It's where most of the Decayed knights are congregated at, so if they breach it then you'll have to brave Hell's floodgates."

"I once showered in an eclipse of arrows," he says. "I would feel cheated if I didn't."

"So pompous and dramatic as always," Ceranus replies with a chuckle. "Now, the rest of you will have no requirements because I trust your teamwork, and I trust your leader, so do whatever makes you all feel the most comfortable in providing support on all fronts as best as you can."

"And what of the people?" Suvius asks.

The twinkle in Ceranus's eyes fades. "This is where things become contingent. Yesterday I brushed off the idea of evacuation, but after giving it more time and thought, I don't think we have a choice. No matter how many monsters we manage to kill, these walls will not protect our people for long. Our home no longer has that kind of strength."

"So where would they go?"

"We emigrate. About a month ago, we were auspiciously blessed by the good grace of a sky pigeon, the first bird to be seen in years. We captured and trained it to have it become our messenger. When it was ready, we attached a letter to it and sent it up north, to the fallen kingdom of Bruness."

"North?" Draxis says. "I've been up there—it's nothing but a ghost region now."

"One would think," Ceranus says. "But we received a letter back. Bruness—it's still alive and strong."

"That letter could have been tampered with."

"It's possible, but no one has time for pranks anymore. Plus, it's our only point of providence."

"What about Mt. Everstone?" Maeva asks. "I took refuge there and never had any problems."

"Sounds promising, but then we would have to deal with the neighboring elves. I like them, but not when they can flawlessly kill fifteen of us or more before they can be stopped permanently."

Ceranus and the others glance at Draxis.

"…Why are you all looking at me?" Draxis remarks.

"No reason in particular," Ceranus says as she looks away from his pointy ears. "I skipped over this part earlier but… does anyone know how to… how to…"

"Slay a dragon?" Draxis finishes for her.

"There was never a reason to ask that. I can handle them," Aluna offers.

"Allow me to handle the bulk of our defenses," Suvius joins in to say. "I have a particular Sacrifice meant exactly for this occasion. As for the ground, if it comes down to it… then I'll provide us with extra reinforcements."

"Fast targets hurt my head," Jellop says. "I decline aerial support."

"I recently learned that I can burn my hands, but that's about it," Rend says. "I guess I can punch them if they get too close."

"I knew you were the type to punch a dragon," Maeva scoffs.

"And you're the type that's about to get smacked," he remarks.

"Try me."

"Ceranus, I sure do hope you're not expecting us to be your sole champions and encumber all the weight?" Draxis says.

"Says who?" she responds, smirking. Ceranus grabs her soiled gown with both hands and tears it away with all her might—revealing a black and red cuirass that's grossly more eldritch than anything regal, alongside wearing thick plated pants and greaves.

Suvius's emotions jump. "This is my first time seeing you in battle-form. That armor suits you."

"Well, I mean… it is quite literally a suit of armor. Do you like it?"

"To the point where I wouldn't dare to scratch it with any blade or lecherous eyes."

"Stop inflating her head with stupid remarks will you," Enam says. "My Queen, with all due respect, you could stand to lose a little weight."

"Oh, Enam… nobody would miss you if you were to fail in battle."

"Pale words cannot pierce this armor or heart, My Queen."

"Whatever," Ceranus says, scrunching her face. "This assembly is adjourned. Let us all remember that if the war's situation even shows itself to be unfavorable in the slightest then all motion will need to go towards regrouping and or retreating, if possible."

"Understood," Damel says. "Final Three, let us prepare the troops for formation. For Kingdom's glory!"

"For Kingdom's glory!" the other two knights bellow.

"We should still have time left before we have to go to the eastern-side overlook, so don't exhaust yourselves before then,"

Ceranus says to the others. She then places a hand over her heart. "What I'm about to say I mean it a million times over. Thank you!"

Everyone chatters while they leave the room. Ceranus stops Suvius before he leaves by grabbing one of his hands.

"Yes, My Queen?" he says.

"Stop acting formal. There's… something I want to show you."

Suvius would be raising an eyebrow now if he could.

***

Ceranus and Suvius stand in an isolated part of town, in front of a blank building that rests behind the illuminated face of the castle.

"I'm sorry for what you're about to see, Suvius."

"I'll be holding my breath…" he responds.

She opens the door to the building for him, and silently awaits his reaction as he takes in the entire sight of the enormous room.

"What is all this?" Suvius asks. "Don't tell me that these are all… weapons?"

"That's right—each and every single one! A massive arsenal that is a generation ahead of current military power, and with enough potential to cause mass devastation never seen nor ever caused this side of history. Care to browse our armory?"

"I really shouldn't feed my old nature with these toys… but yes."

"I knew you would," Ceranus says, giving him a naughty smile.

Suvius gawks at each armament and siege weaponry beauti-fully displayed like in an exhibition. He starts with the smaller gadgets and works his way up to the big toys overtime. On a nearby table, he first picks up a pouch containing transparent orbs that glisten and rumble from the bubbling fluid inside. "What do these things do?" he asks, juggling one with one hand.

"Handheld explosives… so don't touch them."

Suvius nearly drops it as he panics.

Ceranus shakes her head, holding back a laugh. "They're like portable fire spells, without the extra effort of needing to know how to use magic."

"It's always the cutest things that are the most deadly," Suvius says.

"Uhh, thanks?"

"I suppose you are also relevant to that statement. Now tell me about those ballistae over there. And those ones over there. I don't understand their design at all."

"It's simple," she says. "As long as there is someone to feed them ammo and cool off that magic core you see underneath it before it overheats, then the device itself can handle the rest. The sigil stamped on it gives it a bit of intelligence, which makes it self-activating and auto-targeting. It's the same with those cannons over there too."

"What's a cannon?" he asks. "Where was all this weaponry when I was commander in charge?" Suvius then eyes a wall decorated with blades that even he wouldn't dare to touch. There is one that seems safe enough to wield for the curious, so he picks it up. He is perplexed at the tiny blades attached to the chain that is wrapped around the main blade of the exotic-looking sword. "Tell me about this tool. This one just looks barbaric."

"That one is my personal favorite. Try gripping the hand-guard and squeezing it tight."

Suvius grabs the curved handguard and puts little strength into squeezing it—and gives a sudden yelp at the results. "Woah!" he exclaims, quickly becoming mesmerized by the buzzing and speed of the racing blades."

"Are you impressed?" Ceranus asks. "We call it a Chainsaw. It tears through everything—even through some metals like they're made out of homemade butter."

"This is all beyond me. Just where did all this come from anyway?"

"Laxan had the connections, and I had the intuitive designs, but we both made it a reality. It wasn't cheap."

"Do the other knights know about all this?" Suvius asks.

"Yes. In fact, most of these were built by the very same knights who scratch at our walls now."

"And you want to use this fearsome power against the drag-ons?"

"I do," Ceranus says.

"Then do it. Why request for my opinion if you have already decided? You don't need my permission to kill."

"Because I can't bring myself to pull back the drawstring alone, so to speak. Not after I caused them so much anguish already."

"We don't have a choice," Suvius says. "I know you're upset with your past but you're going to have to kill it if you want to find the time to grieve."

"This isn't just about my past actions, this is also about sear-ing a permanent catastrophe into the fabric of the future."

"But this is mainly for survival towards *any* future if we can narrowly obtain it. War is war, Ceranus—even with pyrrhic gains."

"And it must be acquired through complete annihilation of another's future… Is there no other way around this?"

"Only if you're not planning on granting them the mercy we need to bring in order to set them free. It's sinful, but it will at least be your final sin against them."

"But there are so many dragons. That's going to be a lot of accrued sin."

"A whole feast of it," Suvius says. "Remember though that everyone who fights beside you is also going to be collecting their own fair share of sin. With that said, what do you wish to do now?"

"We kill," Ceranus says boldly. "I despise myself for even letting those words become a part of my vocabulary, but we are in agreement that eradication is a must." She turns her head and body slightly, looking behind herself. "Do you feel the same, Borace?"

Suvius turns his head as well. *How long has he been standing behind us?* he wonders.

"Prepare who you can to transport every bomb, glass shard, and dust speck they can carry out of here to the crank lifts for our mobilized forces," Ceranus commands. "We're using everything in our disposal, and we are not holding back for anything. I want there to be blood!"

Borace bows to her and runs off. Suvius notices that Ceranus's words are starting to shake, just like her body. He grabs her shoulder.

"You must be disgusted by me…" she says to him.

"I feel only pity. A woman like you could have done so much for this world if you didn't give in to pride and temptation… Why are you looking at me like that?"

"I thought you would say something better than that," Ceranus says.

"That was the nicest thing I could have said. I'm really trying here," Suvius responds.

"…Just go get situated at the east side of the wall. I'll be there eventually."

"Make sure not to dawdle. There are people here that need you."

"An unfortunate irony that is."

Chapter 13

Indomitable

The weather above surges with extreme fury, proving to be unfavorable and undesirable for the rows and rows of archers and their artillery as their eagerness and potential degrades against the harsh headwinds.

The Harbingers stand on the eastern side of the colossal inner wall that holds steady against the endless horde that claw and lick at it. Ceranus stands as the focal point in the exact middle of the group, with crossed arms and hair waving behind her. Even in her heroic pose, there is still a discrepancy that doesn't go unnoticed.

"Ceranus, you're slouching," Suvius says to her. "That is unladylike."

She moves quickly to fix herself, but stops before her instincts kick in. "Wait… you nearly made me forget where we were. Now I'm mourning over the antics during those old festivals and ballroom dances. I always had to prove myself to the other queens just who was the most gorgeous and illustrious—so many jealous women, and even more lovestruck men."

"I mean no harm, it's a force of habit," Suvius says. "I've always made my soldiers adhere to the mannerisms of proper appearance."

"Sounds like good practice, but one I can't fulfill because this armor is *stupidly* heavy. I don't see how you knights can carry this crap around all day."

He chuckles. "I can understand why you might think that as you sovereign types mainly shouldered the weight that comes with subversion and sleight of tongue. But to us knights, the armor will always be the lightest load we bear compared to the gravity from our burdens and extreme discipline. Today, you will soon experience that same sentiment through your first true tribulation of war."

"Right…"

A half-humanoid being that is engulfed in roaring and active flames arrives from the sidelines. The ground melts and liquifies wherever it walks.

Rend flinches. "Who are you?"

"It's me. Draxis. Don't you recognize my… Oh. I had a meal beforehand to switch fighting styles."

"I recognize the voice, but I've never seen anything like that. Are you some type of Elemental?"

"No, I'm a Demon. An Immolator to be more specific. Demons are kind of like Elementals if you think about it—some of them are imbued with Hellfire, Starfire, Fire-Fire."

"Fire-Fire?" Rend asks.

"It's a fire that is so hot that it burns itself."

"…What?"

"Look, I don't know, I just work here." Draxis glances over at Ceranus, who is trying her hardest to look anywhere else but directly at him. He chooses to get closer—much to her surprise.

"Draxis… you don't have to do this," she urges. "Please don't feel like you have to."

"I have to make a choice either way. If I stay idle, I'll lose everything. If I side with my people, then I'll keep them alive but everything else of value to me will be lost. But if I side with you all, then I might not lose as much as the other options. There's also this nagging voice from a younger me—I think it's Little Nightwing."

"You… you remember the name I gave you?" Ceranus says.

"How could I not? Despite your lies and sins, you were still my caretaker, and you've always fed me well—however you managed to do that."

"I'm glad you were able to become free from me."

"And yet, I'm back," Draxis says. "I'm still very cross with you, but we have a world to save, and that will always triumph over all. I blame myself for forgetting that."

"I wouldn't," Ceranus adds.

"Our Majestic Queen!" a soldier shouts from the courtyard behind them, below the wall. "Please give us the soothing silk of your blessings!"

"Yeah, Ceranus! Give us a speech!" another soldier shouts.

"What are they on about?" Ceranus says.

"It seems that they need a fount of inspiration," Suvius says.

"Me? What the hell do I look like preaching to a perceived army of the dead?" she snaps.

"People naturally seek comfort, and they see that in you. It's not like the rest of us can provide such a thing to them."

Grinding her heels, Ceranus stomps towards the other side of the wall and glares down at the hundreds of hopeful eyes and smiles that gleam at their icon. She has the look of the devil on her. "You—you… you fucking imbeciles!"

A hundred and more jaws drop, simultaneously.

"What do you people even want me to say?" she continues. "Remove your rusty helmets and take a *good* look around you. That'll bring you more morale than what a demoness like me would bring!

"You know what, I'll admit it—I *cry* my beating heart out every day! I sometimes wish I had been infected just like my stupid husband, and I sometimes steal food from you all because all I had to eat that day was a sliver of mutton! I don't even want to be up here right now because what the actual fuck am I going to do against a legion of some damn zombified dragons!"

She then somehow gets even louder than she already was.

"But you know what? Fuck being sorry for myself! Because when the other kings and queens abandoned their people or died a fool's death, at least I got up off my royal ass and made this place a bastion, a citadel, a stronghold where citizens and refugees could find sanctuary in this endless hell.

"And today, we, the Harbingers, and I will fight with all our collective hopes and overwhelming might to ensure that our kingdom and the entire world, with all its blemishes and beauty, will remain standing for the guaranteed generations that will come after us. So if any of you don't want your name swept into the rivers of blood that will flow today, then hold your head low and leave!" She crosses her arms and lets the silence ferment.

An uproar begins.

"We love you, Queen Ceranus!"

"Death to the old ways and long live the new and improved Vomenn Queendom!"

Suvius claps his bony hands together—slowly, but with genuine applause. "A brilliant performance," he says. "You even swayed my stubborn resolve. Long live the Vomenn name."

"I… I don't even remember what I said," Ceranus says.

"To summarize it in its entirety: it was hope."

"I feel so worn out… and nothing's even happened yet."

An earsplitting boom blasts through the air in three timed successions, indicating a cause for alarm.

Ceranus shakes her head. "I swear the world just hates me. Everyone, get ready!" She then grits her teeth and mutters to herself, "We *will* stand indomitable…"

The army works together as one unit, without saying a word. They arm and ready themselves and aim high towards the far-out approaching night, for there is no viewable horizon in the distance— there are only dragons, and they come in droves.

"**Fire!**" Ceranus commands.

A persistent stream consisting of barrage after barrage after volley after volley of countless projectiles soar across the lands and decorates the sky with an overcast of darkness. The onslaught continues to be unyielding no matter how much time passes.

Promise is beginning to show through the visible cracks that appear throughout the oncoming tempest of dragons, but it's going to take a lot more to make those cracks permanent.

"Well, it's a start at least," Ceranus says. "I want to say we struck down at least… three percent? Out of however many that makes up their infinite numbers. Suvius, would you mind doing that aerial defense thing? As soon as you can?"

"I'm on it." He then holds a hand over his chest plate. "Soul of Kylops, hear me and hear me well. I do not ask—I instead demand for your pinnacle technique. Grant me this, and you will be set free! I swear upon my name!"

A spirit escapes from a symbol on his armor and shapeshifts into a weapon. It continues to transmute into something taller, thicker, a more masterful variant than the spears and blades strapped to the backs of the soldiers—a halberd. It's fully built and ready for use. Suvius strikes the halberd's hefty handle into the ground, holding on to it and bellowing, "Ultimata Sanctura!"

A single beam of light shoots out of the tip of the halberd and reaches into the sky. A transparent barrier stretches around and across the entire castle and the inner wall. Suvius offers a slice of advice to the archers, notifying them that the barrier allows their retaliatory attacks to pass through, and they respond to it gleefully as they continue their strenuous labor just as the dragons begin to swarm and berate the dome with their searing elemental breaths and monstrous claws.

The unbreakable defense with an unrelenting offense is proving to be an effective strategy—*but for how long?* That harrowing thought is seeping into all of them as they can see Suvius starting to strain.

"Hang in there, Suvius," Ceranus cries out. "We only need to take down a couple hundred more."

He only grunts in response.

Ceranus's chest tightens. His pain is also hers, and she can't let it continue on. Ceranus hovers her left arm in front of her cuirass.

"Alright. It's now or never…" She hesitates a few seconds longer before uttering a keyword. "Submission!"

Tendrils dart out from the cuirass and inject themselves into her arm. She struggles to stand as the strings drain whatever they leech from her in hefty gulps. The tendrils then spit out black globules that coalesce and manifest into an ethereal bow between her hands. An arrow also manifests in her other hand each time she toys with the aim.

"What? What the hell is this? I thought I was more of a cloak and dagger type?"

"Nothing would please me more than to see a dumbass get pounded from trying to pickpocket a dragon," Aluna remarks.

"Hey!" Ceranus barks. "The only one who's going to get pounded are them!"

"Sounds hot. Keep talking…"

Ceranus rolls her eyes. "Don't you have somewhere you need to be?"

"Not yet. I don't want to get shot down by your lackeys."

"You'll be more useful out there, otherwise I might be the one to shoot you the longer you stay here."

"Thanks for the threat. I guess I'll see you in hell later then."

"Yeah…"

Ceranus watches Aluna zip through the barrier—and her hard work is instantly noticed in the form of reverberating shockwaves across the barrier's rim. Ceranus tenses at the thought of leaving her out there fighting for her life—so, she pulls back the drawstring of her ethereal bow, with a single arrow ready, and launches it sky high.

The perfect arrow burrows through the storm cloud of hardened scales and callused flesh with ease, causing massive collateral damage to the dragons. She continues to thin their numbers with no remorse, and even upgrades her potential to where she can shoot multiple arrows at once as she becomes more adept with her spirit weapon. The other archers join her as they rally from her brilliant rhapsody of ferocity and precision.

"Th-that cuirass…" Suvius says, straining. "I never knew the kingdom would keep such an unholy creation hidden underneath its gilded streets. Honestly, I thought it was for show."

Ceranus looks back at Suvius. "That's the funny part. This thing wasn't discovered by us. It *came* to us instead."

"I don't understand. That thing manifested here by itself?"

"It appeared sometime after we invaded Isilios. Its dark power has been fermenting for as long as we concealed it as a secret."

"So what you're saying is that once the kingdom started garnering the attention of unspeakable evils, you used that for an advantage despite knowing it will corrupt? Why am I not surprised."

"I admit that we deceived ourselves into thinking it was all for the better. In the Kingdom's defense, pursuing lawful faith and the glory of conquest at the same time doesn't really go together well—"

"Enough," Suvius says. "Speak no more or else my will to protect my home will be crushed. Just… get these damn dragons off of my barrier. Please."

"You are heard, Suvius. Continue to strike, everyone! Exhaust everything you have!"

Ceranus's command is heard as well, but it's becoming increasingly difficult to maintain both the speed and efficiency she demands, even when trying to be economical with the dwindling ammunition reserves by aiming specifically for weak points and searching for uncommon moments where kills can be doubled or more with a single deathblow. It's getting to the point where some stations have to be left unmanned just to make it all happen.

Their efforts have been valiant—that much cannot be denied or taken away by any source, but their limited time has been left unguarded for far too long. Suvius has been brought down to a kneeling position, almost like he was pushed. That's when they all remember that they're only untouchable because of his powerful bulwark. Even now, it's been shrinking without them being aware of it. Sections of the walls are exposed and unprotected, along with their fear.

Ceranus winces more at his pain and asks, "How much longer can you keep this up, Suvius?" He grips his weapon tighter in response to mitigate his trembling. She then looks towards a troubled Maeva. "We're going to need a commander for the ground troops. Maeva, would you like to become ours?"

"Me?"

"The Final Three are handling their own business, so we need someone else."

"I'd rather not," Maeva says.

"Odd. You've always given me the impression that you liked taking charge?"

"Presumptuous, are we? If you were to assume anything about me then assume that I would demand for such a role or any others like it whenever I see fit."

"Right, that's my fault. Then I suppose I'll have you go down and meet up with Damel at the North side. Tell him that his time is soon."

Maeva huffs as she takes Rend and Jellop with her.

"I just realized something," Ceranus blurts. "I don't know much about Maeva."

"How bizarre," Draxis says. "Surely the Arbiters told you some things?"

"No? Why would they?" Ceranus asks.

"I can't tell if you're being blissfully ignorant. Does the infamous name 'Prisoner Zero' activate any memories?"

"I wish it didn't. Is she that fabled prisoner?"

"The one and the same," Draxis answers.

"That would make sense. I wouldn't know anything specific about her arrest unfortunately. Our kingdom lost quite a few privileges and responsibilities for the security of Gravefall Penitentiary and more after our breakup with the Arbiters thanks to Laxan's temper. We couldn't intervene with whom they chose to imprison. Although… how did they capture her in the first place? And where did she originally come from?"

"I thought you would know," Draxis says.

Ceranus puts a finger on her lips. "I have heard accounts of how her wicked magic is highly undesirable, but still, I have never seen the Arbiters fear anything. So is that really enough extreme reasoning to have her abducted and confined to such a dreadful place eternally? Looks like a secret game was played behind the back of my oblivious shadow. That gives me chills. Damn do I miss the old world sometimes!"

***

"It's really nice to see you all," Damel says to Maeva and the rest. "We're all situated down here. How's the war up there?"

"The barrier is beginning to fail so we're down in case they breach it," Maeva says. "What's the plan for down here again?"

"To hold our ground and slay any and every bipedal Decayed that dares to shuffle past these gates with this fancy weaponry." As Damel finishes speaking, shards of light crash down from the shattered dome above. "There's just no hesitation in this war. Our bulwark is no more men, shields up! You three, get down!"

A curtain of metal and bone casts over their heads, forming an umbrella against the brutal downpour of solid light and stray fireballs.

"How are you all absorbing all this?" Rend asks.

"With dragon hide and scales," Damel answers.

"Attained from all the kingdoms' zoos, I presume?" Maeva says. "I suppose that's why you all are so good at fending off these dragons."

"Naturally," Damel responds in a dry tone. "I understand the irony of it. We all do."

"Sir Damel," a knight interrupts. "Something feels... off."

Damel heeds that suspicion. He takes a risk and slides his shield over just a little, enough to get a peek outside their defense. It's not only quiet down below, but above as well. *There's no point in wasting our energy,* he thinks to himself. "Everyone, retract!"

They withdraw the defense. It wouldn't surprise anyone if the silence was all an elaborate ruse—but still, nothing happens. The ambience is harrowing, distracting and disorienting. There's not even a scream. The respite gives them ample time to regulate their breathing, along with making their goosebumps rise.

And then it happens—a lightning-fast raid commences along all sides of the wall and marks the next phase of the battle.

"Seems like we just lost our air defenses permanently," Damel says, under a deep sigh of mourning. "I pray that they are alright." He catches a glimpse of Maeva's empty hands. "Being bait won't do you any good, ma'am. You should have told me you were unarmed." Damel unsheathes a sword from his belt and points the hilt towards Maeva. "Here. Take my regal sword, Inquestia. It was meant to be my backup, but you need it more."

The golden shine of the sword reflects Maeva's frown right back at her. "Yeah… I'm not about to face a million undead with this. I can barely scratch paper with a sword."

"Just swing the damn thing at their heads and you'll become a savant in no time. It's how I learned."

"You know, sometimes I wonder what you're good for," Rend says to Maeva.

"She'll take that personally, Rend," Jellop argues.

"She knows that I'm joking. Right, Master?"

"Let's just focus on what needs to be done… okay?" Maeva says, refusing to take her eyes off the frontline phalanx.

The army is preparing themselves, holding true to their grit and watching the dying symbol that has been paramount on warding off the nightmares that lie beyond its threshold. The main gate to the outer lands of the kingdom—it's nearing the end of its purpose, constantly strained against the battering from the enemy.

Then, it explodes inwards and topples. Ingress is now unrestricted to the shambling horde that pours in. The frontline marches forward to enforce the only law that shouldn't have been broken. Trespassing. The army brandishes their superior weaponry to resolve that transgression. For every ten Decayed that charge forward, they are evenly and fatally matched against a single armored rival.

The undead continue to spill into the town, uncaring about how many of their rank-and-file are mowed down as their forces keep increasing more and more, faster in production than the knights' slaying power. They could use some help.

Rend looks to Maeva for permission. She sees the hungry sensation for blood in his eyes and feels the pressure from him to obey. It's… intriguing to her. "I swear you're like a moth to danger," she says. "But I'll trust that you can remain safe. Just this once." Maeva watches him trip a few times as he charges into battle. She already regrets her decision as she realizes the idiot didn't even pick up a weapon to fight with.

As the war extends, the dragons gain an uncontested foothold and are free to set ablaze the town and blast away at the castle. The show of domination is empowered by the rivers of blood spilled by the wrath of the Decayed soldiers.

Jellop stands in a fresh pool of purple blood, spectating and listening to the world kill itself around him. An unknown voice suddenly speaks to Jellop, joining in on the mayhem.

"Long have I slumbered…" it says in a composed tone that could chill the soul.

"Who's there?" Jellop says back. He looks around, but Maeva is the only person nearby, and she doesn't seem to be in the mood to talk.

"Awakened... in the middle of war," the voice continues. *"Typical. Expected. Who is winning?"*

"D-Dragons," Jellop says out loud, still unsure as to who he's answering to.

"Interesting. Hmm... May I borrow your body?"

"Borrow…? My body?"

"I am not a fan of losing such easy battles. Let me finish this so I can do other things. It's not like you're doing much anyway."

"Can I trust you?" Jellop asks.

"I trust myself. Does my confidence not ease your needless worry?"

"What will you do with me?"

"You will become a messenger."

"Jellop, who are you talking to?" Maeva asks.

"Friend Maeva," he says. "I sense approaching demise. I have to be the one to prevent it."

"No. No riddles, Jellop, Tell me what's wrong!"

"I can't, too much time has already passed. It's now or never." He thrusts his staff into the ground and begins meditating.

"Wait—" She stops herself as Jellop has already locked himself into stasis. She stands completely perplexed as to what he is even doing in his statue-like state.

"W-Watch out!"

Maeva looks up to see Ceranus sliding down the roof of a house and jump off, landing on the head of a hapless Decayed with a stomp. "This Artifact is awesome!" she exclaims.

Suvius soon joins her. Draxis also arrives, floating down to the ground by expelling thick streams of fire from his hands and feet. "What's Jellop doing?" he asks.

"Channeling something messy I presume," Maeva remarks while poking Jellop's body.

"Then let him," Ceranus says while jogging in place to keep her speed and spirits up. "I have to go and continue rallying our soldiers. Good luck!"

A series of explosions detonates sporadically across the sky.

"The skies seem to be clearing up thanks to Aluna staying strong," Draxis says. "I think I'll put myself on crowd control duty. Seems like you all need it desperately down here." He carves a fiery path for himself through an oncoming horde like a living flamethrower, heading towards any nearby screams for help.

"You can go if you wish, Young Maeva," Suvius offers. "I'm sorry to say that I don't have much left in me, and nothing useful to help me recharge. I'll handle the grunt work."

Their eye contact breaks as a ruined corpse lands between the two of them from above—and many more pile on top of it, splattering the ground with their scorched and dismembered parts. The urge to hurl is strong. Maeva especially feels it.

"Or…" Suvius continues after a pause, "I guess I'll risk suicide and further expend my feeble energy. "Stand back, Maeva." Suvius kneels and lays his palms on the ground. A mystic pattern forms around him. "Men and women, linked in blood and tears to your throes and failures, a second chance is nigh, only if you will it. With my command, hear me now and continue to fight for your queen! Arise!"

The pattern sparkles and embiggens, then recedes inward without warning, and disappears.

Maeva looks aghast. "Suvius… you okay? I've never seen you fail a spell so miserably before."

"Me? Falter?" He doesn't hesitate to make another attempt, only this one fizzles out before it even manifests."

"I know this feeling all too well," Maeva says. "There was even a time where it consumed my entire being," She then sighs at his implied look of horror. "Lord Suvius, it's okay to be scared."

"Is that what attacks my mind?"

"Uncertainty begets fear, and it can strike anyone. Just like you, I needed, and still need to be reminded of ignoring both of those omnipresent monsters."

"Never fear, Fear. To think I needed to be reminded of such a thing…" Suvius conjures the spell one more time. Relief is felt as the deceased rise to the occasion in their mangled states and stumble their way onward to avenge themselves, with glowing white eyes to illuminate the way.

"Dammit, you two!" Aluna shouts at them from above. "Are you fucking or are you fighting?"

"Don't get your wings in a twist, little flea!" Maeva snaps. "We're just having a short recess!"

"Whatever!" Aluna scoffs, before zipping away.

"She's right though," Maeva says. "People are dying as we speak, and that disgrace is on our hands."

"Maeva—wait," Suvius says, stopping her dead in her tracks. "Forgive my outburst, but I need to have something clarified for me, and I only trust you to ask it. Are… are we doing the right thing?"

Maeva puckers her lips. "If you don't have the honest wisdom for that question, then what makes you think I would fare any better?"

"Then don't answer," he says.

"But I don't want to leave you alone like this. There is something I can say maybe. Draxis once told me this—he said that 'whether we are regarded as heroes or villains will be up to the survivors, win or lose.' I think the most important thing here is that we don't lose, otherwise there wouldn't be anyone left alive to complain. I'm heading off to do my part in this war. Stay safe."

I'll try... is what Suvius thinks to himself as his vigilance switches over to a motionless Jellop.

***

A sizable portion of the kingdom and its army has fallen already, and with some of the Fallen joining the ranks of the enemy—but the mightiest still maintain the core of the defensive line. Rend is blitzing through everything in his path with his self-taught brawling fighting style, and with a side technique of fire to back himself up. Ceranus and Draxis are fighting together, deep in the swamp that are the Decayed forces that have breached the eastern side of the wall.

"I can feel your flames from here!" Ceranus shouts to Draxis, keeping herself upbeat to the action and flow.

"Hell is hot," he says. "It's where these flames derive their intensity from."

"Guess I better get used to it then." She aims and launches a barrage of arrows that nail five undead in the head simultaneously."

Side-by side they work well together as a duo, matching each other's signals of flank-prevention and flashy combo moves. Nothing defeats teamwork—

"I could use a bit more wildfire over here!" Ceranus yells.

"Don't you think I'm trying!" Draxis shouts back.

Except for any overwhelming odds that pressures teamwork to the point of collapse.

Ceranus is staged directly in the center of an enclosing circle of livid monstrosities. She swings at them with her bow, repeatedly. "This is why I wanted a dagger you stupid—nooo!" "Get the hell away from me! Somebody!" Her wails diminish as she becomes submerged in the riptide that is the rushing horde."

Mentally, Draxis is blocked, but he swears at himself abusively to break free and *move!* He manages to spring to action. "Ceranus!" he calls out to her. As hot as his emotions, he cremates everything with a volcanic-like burst. "Ceranus!" he repeats. She stares up at Draxis, who crouches beside her. "Are you alright? I tried not to burn you."

"Yeah… just… let me lie here for a minute," she groans. "I've never seen so many teeth in my life. Funny how investing into dental care for our people would ever backfire on us."

"You and your jokes, and in the most inappropriate of time and manner… I swear sometimes."

"Sorry."

"Don't be. There's a guilty pleasure to them," Draxis says.

Ceranus looks side to side. "Wait, where's my bow?" She taps against her lifeless breastplate. "I think I took too much damage. It won't let me summon it."

"Even if your Artifact fails, your soldiers still need your presence to help them rally. Can you stand?"

"I might need some help. Or maybe you can carry me?"

"Ceranus, I'm too hot for you to handle. Besides, Suvius would have my head for it."

"And you said that I shouldn't be joking around."

"…I wasn't joking."

"Oh…"

***

Rend is left to fend for himself near one of the numerous holes in the southern side of the wall as the team he joined up with became free energy boosts for the Decayed. As nice as it would be to nab a sword off the ground to even out the battle for survival like his imagination is wanting him to do, he is forced to only use his wavering resolve that is hurled through each punch and kick he lands—until a clever surprise attack counters his brawn.

Shit! is the only swear that Rend can think of as he lifts his arm in an attempt to block, but the zombie stops—its chest is pierced clean through. It drops to the ground. Maeva is here, giving a nice and friendly smile while holding her murder weapon.

"Y-You saved me," Rend says, still in shock.

"I did, didn't I?" she says.

"Looks like I owe you my life again."

"Again?"

"Well, yeah. This second life's not so bad. Personally, this apocalypse doesn't feel too different from times before. Plus, I'm all magical and shit. But it could always use a bit more—watch out!" Rend pulls her away and sends a strong uppercut to her assailant, knocking off its head.

Maeva stands impressed. "I guess we're even now."

"We should keep it that way. Wanna stick together for now?"

"I think I'll take you up on that."

An arrow darts past them, barely missing their heads.

"Dammit!" Rend says. "That's seven times already! Hey, I'm not the enemy! How many times do I need to say it!"

Another shot skirts past them. A group of Decayed armed with bows pushes through a lumbering armored flock, drawing and readying their next arrows.

"No way… elves? Again?" Rend says.

"They must have followed us here," Maeva responds. "There's no escaping the Mark of the Hunt, I guess. I thought that was just a myth created by them." She gets an ominous but pressing urge to look around the area—seeing nothing but the lifeless bodies the Decayed feast on. "Hey… where is everybody? Are we the only ones left?"

Rend squints his eyes. "No. I see some people falling back to the castle."

"Already? Then we should do the same. I hope everyone's alright."

Another stray arrow zips past them.

Chapter 14

Pandemonium

An insignificant fraction of the resistance is left to hold their ground. Concentrated just within a leap's distance from the castle gates. They huddle close enough to each other to hear everyone's rapid breaths and stifled cries.

Maeva and Rend arrive moments later. Ceranus is the first to greet them. "Oh good, we're all here," she says, taking refuge in the middle of the pack.

"H-Hey!" Maeva says, huffing out of breath. "What's going on?"

"Improvisation. We can't advance, we can't retreat, and we're outmatched. What you see here is all that remains of what we can feasibly do."

"For some reason everyone flocked here like I'm a flagpole," Suvius interjects.

"And you make a good one at that," Draxis adds.

"What about the civilians?" Maeva asks.

"I've lost contact with the castle squad, but they should be deep within the escape tunnels by now. If we cannot escape, then they at least will," Ceranus says.

Aluna swoops down not too long after, tending to her own bloody wounds. Destruction just keeps raining down on the Vomenn kingdom. Everything is collapsing. Everything is burning—into a hellish coliseum.

"Our backs are against the walls of defeat, but there is no greater feeling of unity than a last stand," Suvius says. "If we all fall here, then I want to let it be known that it has been an unbelievable honor."

"Quiet, we don't need that idiocy right now," Draxis says. "Flagpoles aren't even supposed to talk."

Death is closing in fast, led by the hounds named Fear and Horror. Blood-soaked weapons that were used extensively snap in half from overuse. The sky grows darker with a thousand vengeful wings. This is it. Times up—and then it resets—through Jellop, who awakens silently.

He brushes past Maeva, startling her. "Jellop? He's finally awake!"

"You're a bit late to the party, but we can always use some additional dancers," Draxis says.

"So… noisy," Jellop mutters, his voice and tone: different. It's hard to pinpoint the exact undertone. Menacing would be too strong and eerie wouldn't do enough justice. Perhaps *fearless* would be it—and not the brave kind.

"This damn noise. What god in their right mind would ever use their divine birthrights to create such noisy beasts?" he says next. "I hate it. All of it."

Everyone watches and avoids Jellop as he walks through. He stands in front of everyone now, out in the open, and raises an open palm before uttering, "Silence."

The urgency of his command brings all incoming and planned attacks from the Decayed into complete submission.

"Woah," Rend says in awe. "Wait, Jellop! You forgot your staff!"

"I don't need it. But be a saint and hold it for me, would you? You'll only need to for a minute, and nothing more. Now, where was I?" Jellop then removes his hood.

All perspectives that can stomach it want to scream from his horrifying appearance.

"Who in their right mind would call this nonsense a situation of calamity? Just because this is war does not mean it is true destruction. If it was, then no living soul would be left standing to tell the tale. Let me grant you all a glimpse into the primal and true desire of life itself: Chaos!" Jellop then closes his palm into a fist, saying only one word. "Rupture…"

A thousand screams play across the battlefield, coming from every Decayed still standing or flying. He condenses his fist tighter. Tighter. Their wails soon turn to mush as their heads explode. *Pop, pop, pop.* The fountains of gore add wonderfully to the garden of death, chaotically cultivated as Jellop's massacre blooms.

"Thinking about it now, I don't know much about Jellop either."

"Okay, Ceranus…" Draxis says with a tired sigh.

"What? I'm just saying."

The entire sight is revolting, but everyone quickly gains immunity to the sickening feeling as their adrenaline pumps higher and higher over what looks to be like an assured victory—until Jellop faints. Draxis and Rend rush over to assist him.

"Jellop, talk to us!" Draxis says.

"What happened?" Jellop groans. "I-I can't hear anything, no more intrusive thoughts and emotions. I feel empty."

"Whatever you did just saved us all," Rend says.

"I felt… different. Like I was someone else, but myself at the same time."

"We'll think it over later," Draxis says. "Rend, help me lift him."

Damel launches his fist high, calling all attention towards him. "Our path is clear! Everyone, make haste to the tunnels! Now!"

"Hell yeah! We took out all the dragons!" a knight says. His rejoice strings to the other knights that join in his flaunting and tears of boundless joy.

Maeva walks over and wipes the liquid fire off of Draxis's cheeks, stinging her fingers despite the moistness of it. "Did you know that one of my favorite quotes Jellop has ever said to me is that 'water is the most powerful element because of the unlimited re-source of tears'? It took a while, but I truly understand the meaning of that now. We're so sorry, Draxis."

"It's… it's fine… it needed to be done. My people are free now. Finally, at long last."

Those who are miraculously unscathed or can put up with their injuries make it their solemn duty to make the evacuation swift. Even with the doors to paradise open, there is one soldier that seems unwilling to go.

"Damel, aren't you coming?" Ceranus asks.

"I see stragglers running about," he says. "I'll remain here to act as a gatekeeper and dispose of them."

"Alright. Just make sure you don't stay for too… long," she says, soon lingering on her words.

Damel is right, there does happen to be a straggler, one they both recognize in all his fallen majesty. Ceranus personally chooses herself to handle the sudden matter. Damel holds his breath as he watches her.

"There you are my sweet, sweet, dead husband," Ceranus says. "It's impressive how remarkable you are. I will never understand how you've always managed to avoid the laws of death, whether aimed directly for you or in between random crossfire. It's just… remarkable."

The King groans as he shuffles towards her.

"Are you proud of me, Laxan? Look at me. Look at what I have done. I became the general you always wanted, the monster you lustfully craved… your empress of conquest.

"Grrahhh," he growls.

"Cute," she remarks. Ceranus retrieves a broken sword from a half-eaten soldier. "It's time to end this charade through the only way I know how—with blood." She impales Laxan through his chest, making sure it's through the heart. Dark purple blood leaks onto her hands as she says, "I hate you, sincerely, but I would have greatly preferred to not have the world end just for you to finally meet yours. Farewell, Laxan, my terrible king."

She throws the tainted sword down onto his body, and walks away with clenched, bloody fists as she heads for the castle smothered in flames.

Suvius stands like a sentinel in the middle of the open gates, watching Ceranus approach him.

"Did… did you see all that?" she asks.

"Naturally. I have a keen eye for these exclusive events. I thoroughly enjoyed seeing your tempered strife, you handled it exquisitely. I'm only here because I wanted to see his death for myself. Alas, I don't feel any different."

"I feel the same way. It's weird, isn't it? I hated him so much, yet it feels like it's all beneath me."

"I guess we've moved on."

"Yeah, nothing holds us back anymore." She grabs his hands. "Now let us keep ascending—together."

***

"Damn meddlers. How'd you all survive his purge?" Damel says to himself, stomping down on a moving crawler.

"Oi!" a woman's voice shouts from behind him.

"Hmm? Oh, Enam! I'll be damned, you're still alive!" He looks down at her hands. "Oh no… your trident."

"No worries," she says. "I still have one prong left. See?"

"Just like your sanity."

"Careful, Damel. Wouldn't want to mistake you for an enemy…"

"It's happened before. Where's Borace?"

"He already left to go help with the retreat."

"And you didn't join him?"

"Not while there's time to say goodbye," Enam says while watching segments of stone, wood, and dying history crumble and collapse near and far throughout the kingdom. "Our home falls, Damel."

"Aye, it's a truly heartbreaking sight. You know, in the books of Reshod, he made a quote that has always stuck with me: 'Home is wherever the heart feels sheltered,' so while I am attached to this place, there is always a new one—even if you have to make the very soil around you yours to claim."

"I like that. Looking at this inferno does make my heart feel flighty. It's time we finally leave our cradle," Enam says.

"Just don't forget your toys," Damel remarks.

"Piss off!"

***

People from all different generations of life walk together without meaning on one muddy path towards the distant unknown. Their sanctuary, their home, their light—you could never tell it even existed as the great conflagration has completely taken over and consumed it. Consumed—just like the consumed friends and family that the teary-eyed majority express their sorrows and grievances over.

"Where to now, Ceranus?" Suvius asks.

"B-Bruness. It's… it's the only place I feel confident in… migrating to."

"Do you need a ride on the remaining livestock? You're sweating profusely."

"N-No, I'm just being cooked alive in this armor. I'll make it."

"I could cast a frost spell for you, Cee-Cee," Aluna says.

"Don't call me that in public you dummy."

"A what? Insult me like that again and you ain't going to be receiving shi—"

Something horrific interrupts her. It sounds abominable, whatever it is. Even the clouds themselves asunder, in fear of the serpentine behemoth of behemoths that descends. Heading straight for them with its hundred wings beating the winds into submission.

"A Godeater?" Draxis blurts out while trembling. Another thought enters him, this time internally. *Do the Heavens really exist...?*

"Draxis, you know that thing?" Ceranus asks.

"It's a far-reaching guess, but it looks exactly like one of the ancient beasts depicted in Draconic legends. Though, who even knows at this point."

"Well what the hell does it want with us?" Rend says.

"Believe it or not, but that thing is the closest thing we dragons have to a god. Seems like it heard their prayers."

"I-I can't handle this anymore!" a knight cries out. "I thought we had already overcome the worst, but there is always something more terrible! Always!"

"We can still turn back, can't we?" Maeva asks.

"Go back?" the knight shouts at her. "At this point I'd rather accept getting swallowed whole than bathe in the fire of my own home. At least it'll be quick and painless."

It only takes one to cause a stir, now everyone is bickering and delaying the fallback—that is, if they ever plan to. No one seems to want to retreat.

Aluna pays them no attention. Her wings buzz to life as she starts talking to herself. "This is my chance. Please let this be the end…" She ends her outspoken thoughts with a shout of assurance. "Leave it to me, everyone!"

"Aluna!" Maeva yells. "Don't do anything hasty!"

Aluna ignores her as she continues to ascend, faster than ever before.

"Butterfly…" That's the only word Jellop can announce as he tries to reach for her, before falling unconscious.

Aluna has now flown to a height that even she is terrified of reaching—but as of right now, she fears nothing. At her determined point for maximum effect, Aluna's six wings stand erect, with a vibrant rainbow pulsing through them and overflowing with volatile power.

The Godeater nears, close enough to get a whiff of its last meal. She is about to get devoured, a fact that she relishes in with a smile—until her wings become corrupted with black color.

"Shit! Not now!" she screams. "Stop! Why does this keep happening to meeeee—!"

Her magic is forced to expel from her body and wings, ending the crisis just as fast as it started. The sky suffers from the flash supernova of magical discharge by rippling across far and wide. For a split second, it was almost a sunny day.

"She… she actually did it," Damel says, shielding his eyes from the leftover residue of light.

"My enthusiasm will remain stifled until otherwise," Enam says. "Too many close calls."

Rend identifies a lone speck in freefall. *Aluna!* He's amazed at his heightened sight. He then says, "She's cool and all but did she have to summon her spell from so far away? Draxis, boost me."

"Huh?" he responds.

"I'm going to go catch her, so launch me up."

"Like with one of those controlled explosions from Fire magic users? That seems needlessly complicated. I'd argue that you still have suicidal tendencies, but I guess you can't really die easily so… sure? Here, Maeva. Take Jellop for us."

"Hold on, don't throw him at me! I can't—arrgh!"

"You wouldn't happen to know anything about aerodynamics, would you, Rend?" Draxis asks.

"Uhh…"

"Yeah, I don't know either. Just focus on maneuvering through the wind currents or something. And try not to crash into any birds up there. Wait… never mind. So how do you want to do this?"

"When I jump, I want you hit me with your best spell to propel me. We'll do it on the count of three. One…"

Draxis quickly kneads and compacts a singularity of fire between his hands.

"Two…" Rend says as he squats. "Three!" At the peak of Rend's jump, Draxis lets the spell go critical, and the eruption knocks him away. He's like a shooting star, only in reverse.

"You people are weird," Enam says as she watches Rend arc across the sky.

"There's no need to compliment us over our innovation," Draxis remarks.

In the air, Rend does his best to steer himself through the momentum. He finds the perfect angle. "I got you, Aluna!" He grabs her and tucks her inside his crossed arms, smiling with accomplishment.

On the ground, it's obvious Suvius also wants to smile. "I really do enjoy the delight I get from watching these little fruits of foolishness that blossom every now and again. You do realize that *both* of them are now falling, right?"

Draxis's pride is murdered by a dumbfounded expression. "Oh… oops. Maeva, do you want to go save them next?"

"Kill yourself," she hisses.

"Rude."

***

"I've seen boulders fall with more grace," Draxis mocks. "You two alright?"

Aluna is awake and responsive, but visibly drained. "No," she states.

"That's… unexpected. What's the matter? Was all that action not 'explosive' enough for you?"

She turns her head away, unamused.

"Aluna, I was joking. You're a heroine, and a god-slayer apparently."

"If there really was a god, then we all wouldn't be suffering like this. Especially me. Never mind, don't worry about it."

"…If that's what you want."

"Owww," Rend drones. "I think my spine is broken." He flails his arms around, trying to move the rest of his body.

Draxis shakes his head. "They're fine, everyone."

Chapter 15

Limbo

Like a final wish, the ashes of the kingdom help to guide the way on the open and epic trail to the northern half of the continent. But there's no rush to get there, not when they can finally experience tranquility—even if it's an unequal reward for what was lost. Overall, they still stand together as a nation, their pride still held close and neighbors closer, all the few hundred that remain. The flames are long behind them now.

Although, Suvius can't help but look towards the sky. *It still rains...* is what he's thinking.

"What's on your mind, Suvius?" Ceranus asks. "Am I getting too heavy for you?"

"I've dealt with heavier."

"It's the armor, I swear."

"I'm sure it is." He then hesitates on chatting further, before continuing on. "We've been through a lot together, haven't we, Ceranus?"

"Way more than any two people should."

"Sometimes… sometimes I wonder if I should make a prayer. But would anyone even hear it? I don't think the very few I've made have ever been answered."

"Ouch. Where's all this coming from? You're fantastic!"

"Those words mean nothing to me. If they were true, then so much could have been prevented… just like now." Suvius stops, then lowers her to the ground. "I want you to show it to me, Ceranus."

"What is there to show you?" she wonders. "Unless you mean 'that'. Wait until we get another bedroom together you silly dog."

"Enough. You know what I mean."

"…No. I'm not showing you."

"Do you not think it would be better to reveal it now… rather than by force later?"

"Hey slowpokes!" Aluna shouts. "What's the hold up?"

"Now look at what you did," Ceranus whispers. "They're coming over here."

"Good," Suvius responds.

"What's with all the disruption? Doesn't anyone get tired anymore?" Damel says from deep in the middle of the dawdling crowd. He forces his way through to the front, with anxiety rising. "Queen Ceranus? Suvius, what is the meaning of this?"

"Ask her yourself," he answers.

All curious eyes shift over to a reluctant Ceranus. She's cracking under the unwavering pressure. "I… I… dammit!" She pauses to hold back her emotions. "I've… I've been bitten."

"What?" Damel says, almost choking. "No, that can't be true. No! No, no! S-Somebody bring the doctor! Hold on, Ceranus, we'll get him. Doctor!"

"We have no doctor!" a random man says. "He's dead!"

"Him too?" Damel says. "Is there someone here who can replace him!"

"All of you stand down!" Ceranus shouts. "I swear, nothing can ever be done without uproar nowadays."

"There has to be something we can do!"

"There's only one treatment for something like this," Draxis says as he approaches Ceranus, making Suvius flinch and raise his guard. "Relax, I'm not going to hurt her. I just… I want to see her,"

Suvius eases, but he is still watchful.

Draxis crouches and tempers his flames to touch Ceranus's face. "Your eyes are starting to turn purple."

"I surely hope so," she says. "Purple is considered to be a royal color after all."

"Enough with the jokes."

"Well what do you want me to do! Ouch!" she yelps, rubbing her temples. "The real joke here is that stupid look you all are giving me. Isn't this what you Harbingers wanted? Isn't this what *you* wanted?"

"I never truly wanted your demise," Draxis defends. "I'll admit, I am quick with my words, and even quicker to kill, but it's not like your death will change anything—wait, that didn't come out right."

"Then how about you say what you really want to say. I want to hear it," Ceranus says.

"Surely the poignant wails of my people were loud enough to hear, even for those who are deaf. If only you made this type of effort all those years ago. Speaking of the past… I sometimes wish you had never found me all those years ago.

"There will never be any pain greater than knowing the person who gave me a home and such adoration is also the same reason why I'm even an orphan. And you want to know what's worse? We might have just killed my parents. Whoever they were."

"Little Nightwing…"

"Don't—don't touch me! I am not your pet anymore. I am Draxis, a free man… but what good is this freedom when I have no one else to share this with? I'm the last dragon in existence, Ceranus. Don't you understand how much it hurts to say that?"

"I won't even pretend to understand how much pain I caused you and everyone else."

"But you are finally aware of it. I want more justice than that, but instead you get the luxury of escaping your sins peacefully."

"This is *not* peaceful. I want to do more—but judgment has finally found me—and I accept it. You deserved better, Draxis."

"I suppose… but you were once all I had. That is all I will compliment you on." He retreats back to the others, trying to make his shaky hands undetectable, all while saying his final peace. "Goodbye… mother."

Suvius returns to Ceranus's side, remaining still as he watches over her.

"Why the sad face, Suvius?" she asks.

She receives no response.

"You're doing that silent treatment again. Come on, Suvius. Please. Talk to me. Let's just think about the now, forget the later."

"Why didn't you say anything?" he asks. "Why didn't you tell us about your affliction? I only noticed because of the way you're acting."

"…I didn't think anyone would care."

"If you're able, then take a look around you. These people are falling apart from hearing the heinous news. These valiant soldiers were united under your heartfelt speech. You brought us, your archenemies, to fight not against you, but beside you. You put too much blame on yourself." He looks into the vulnerability within her eyes and says to her, "Now you're the one staying silent."

Suvius grips one of her hands—they're easy to move, but he takes care not to apply pressure. "Do you remember the day I was knighted, Ceranus?"

She brightens. "Wow—that felt like so long ago. You were so young back then."

"As were you."

"Well damn, I'm still young. Just hand me some make-up and access to a bath, and you'll see eternal youth in the making."

"I already have, you looked your best that day. You… also waved at me."

"Did I? You sure I wasn't just wiping my face?"

"An outrageous claim," Suvius says. "If true, then you were wiping your face quite often." He grabs her other hand as he continues. "My Queen, when I saw you for the first time on that day I… I found my innate reason to become a loyal servant, to the very end if I could."

"I'm flattered. And here I thought most only choose that path to earn themselves inalienable rights. So then… why? Why did you leave us?"

"Because I lost my reason. The King, this Kingdom, the Blood—it all blackened me. But nothing drove me to darkness faster than watching my angel get dragged down by the tempting hands of those demons who sullied said angel, and the rest of her could-be paradise. I couldn't bear it. I couldn't understand it. I wanted so badly to bring you back. In my mind, in my dreams, I am instead king, with beloved friends, and a queen of queens beside me. A kingdom unrivaled in greatness."

"Such a wonderful dream—one that you should continue," Ceranus says. "Back then, you could have just told me what you wanted."

"I did. I've tried. The Arbiters made you their pawn and the King made you his bloodthirsty successor. I went to great lengths to make you see that, but it was for naught—the corruption and you were already intertwined consorts."

"I couldn't see it… but I did feel it, on that night when you finally came back to me. You're *really* good with your hands."

"As a master swordsman, it would be unjust if I wasn't," Suvius says.

She pauses, staring longingly into his missing eyes, before saying, "I want to experience that again."

"…I'm sorry."

Ceranus coughs up a puddle of grotesque phlegm in place of wanting to say more to him. The virulent infection brings her to the point of crying out for mercy. Her veins thicken across her body, specifically around her head and arms, pulsing with a deep violet color. "It—it hurts!" she screams.

"Fight through it, Ceranus!" Draxis shouts. "Never compel! We're stronger than it!"

"Argahhh!" She howls as she continues to writhe on the ground, subservient to the unrelenting agony as it escalates to the point of wishing for death.

"The people shouldn't have to see you decay like this, My Queen," Damel says. "Allow me to—"

His words bring the right dosage of insult to bring her back to sanity. "Don't you dare finish that sentence!" Ceranus cuts off. "I'd rather kill myself than to let that happen! Just forget about me." She lifts herself up to stand and gets into eye contact with everyone. "Suvius. Harbingers. I hereby nominate you, and only you, to take and bear our royal arm in my dying name. Final Three, make sure our kingdom and its people continue to thrive and live on. I know I asked for a lot, and I took even more, but can you all do this one act of mercy for me?"

Everyone summoned nods their heads, with the knights bowing, and the Harbingers giving their tactful silence.

The crowd shouts Ceranus's name, absolutely begging for her to do anything otherwise. So many voices, and all of them wanting the same thing. How often have they tried to reach her during her absolute rule? How many times has she ignored them? She can finally put an end to it. They'll no longer have to waste their breath. She's ready.

"Retribution," is the phrase Ceranus says to activate her Cuirass. She whines as something pricks her abdomen, then she shrieks as the puncturing turns into a series of stabs.

The Cuirass morphs and inches its way across every part of her flesh and body, soon encasing her in a red and black organic cocoon. The wriggling of the cocoon ceases after a minute or so and recedes back into its original form. Nothing is left behind, except for the armor itself.

Suvius hovers beside it, before picking it up, and staring at it with his hollow eyes—longingly.

"Come on, Suvius," Draxis says, grabbing his shoulder. "We got what we came here for. We have to go."

Inclined to agree, Suvius rises to his feet. Draxis doesn't leave his side.

The Harbingers huddle up. All attention is falling to them. The varied and hurt looks from the kingdom's survivors are both warranted and unwarranted. *We get it, we're all displeased, and we're all lost, so... so stop staring at us.* The Harbingers wish they could say that unanimous thought out loud. It looks like Damel wants to have a word with them. He's giving them mixed feelings from his cold expression.

Maeva makes the effort to make matters light. "Here's… here's your sword back, Damel."

"Appreciated. You sure you don't want to keep it?"

"Positive. I don't want to take anything else away from you."

Enam appears next to Damel. "It sounds like you all have to depart shortly."

"We do," Maeva responds. "Not to sound callous, but it'll take too long to explain everything. I promise it's not a secret agenda though. I can't even lie and say it's something that will bring hope— it's that uncanny of a scheme."

"No worries, nothing makes sense anymore. It'll be arduous, but we'll make it to Bruness. You can count on us!"

Damel chimes in by saying, "And we'll excuse the dragon incursion and the death of… And the *absence* of Ceranus, if you can give us a real reason to believe in her rising trust for you all."

"We will," Maeva says. "We promise."

"No promises, just do it. Now go."

***

The portal shrinks out of existence after everyone steps into Klae's lair. He's happy to see them. It's hard to believe how fast he can move given his age.

"You've returned, and with the Artifact I see," he says merrily. "You all had me worried when you coerced me to send you away. But then I saw them, and I sure as hell felt the heat from their vicious rage. But to behold a dragon for the first time in my life, let alone their entire population? Man, was that a legendary sight."

"Can we not talk about that accursed nightmare we just went through?" Draxis says. "Please?"

"I suppose I'm still jittery from such a paramount occurrence, forgive my insensitivity. I know this might not mean much coming from a lowly apprentice of your past enemy, but I want to offer my condolences to the dragons. I can't even imagine what *you* specifically had to go through."

"I'm surprised to hear you call me out," Draxis says. "Let me guess, the Arbiters knew of my true identity? I must have been careless somewhere along the way."

"They were bound to find out eventually," Klae says. "For years your deceptive Soul Inheritance ability gave them all quite the delirious spin. Naturally that angered them, and you should never anger a group of magical sociopaths. Queen Ceranus was also crafty in not exposing the truth, despite her obsession with hunting down every dragon to inflate her menagerie."

She did that for me? Draxis wonders to himself.

"Anyway, let's not discuss it further," Klae says. "If you want to then you all can tell me about what happened at Vomenn later. So right now, take a breather." Klae grabs a potion. It fizzles and bubbles as he chugs it down. "It seems like no matter what I do there's always destruction that follows. I suppose that's just how it is to be an Arbiter. I should have left the Artifacts alone and found a safer alternative."

"Safest doesn't always mean it's the best," Draxis says. "We're doing what we must. There's no going back with this. There was never the option."

"Y-You're right. But no doubt we will let the parasites within us know of the anguish they have brought upon us today."

Aluna is floating silently in the back, listening in. A thought occurs to her as she studies the room. *The ratio of emotions feels off around here.* She then grabs everyone's attention by saying, "Hey, where did Suvius sneak off to?"

***

Suvius is already standing outside on the balcony, dangerously close to the rickety railing. The others all approach him, but not too close. Klae is with them as well, unresisting his own curiosity.

"Sacrifice," Suvius says before anyone else can speak. "That is my meaning, that is my embodiment… that is my ongoing sin. I am reminded of it with each life I claim. My enemies, sacrificed. My own life and humanity, sacrificed. My future… sacrificed. Seeing all of you alive after all this time, it reminded me that I haven't lost everything.

"But in order to keep, I have to give. So much has been taken overall, and you would think I would be indifferent to it all, but alas, it still feels as fresh as the first, and I'm *deathly* afraid that it'll continue, with or without my consent. I have nothing else left to say… so, I think I'm going to go for a moonlight stroll," He then holds the Bloodheart Cuirass in front of himself and says, "And I think I'll take her with me."

Suvius leaves. The others do the same thing as well. Separately.

Chapter 16

Brotherhood

Suvius strolls along the bleak shoreline of the dilapidated Arbiter Capital. Not much is going on in his head. Not much is going on, period. Sacrifice, he is still reminded of it, just like he himself said. What good is wanderlust if he can't enjoy the touch of the tropical waters, or form any pleasant memories, or embrace a twinkling starry night if there ever was one—especially if he's all alone.

Suvius looks up from his sand-encrusted boots and stops, seeing something humanoid and incandescent up ahead. He wasn't expecting anyone to be out here, and so far away from the city too. He creeps in for a closer look. *Oh, it's just Draxis. I'll just leave him be and—*

"I already know you're there, Suvius. Come on back."

Draxis doesn't give him much of a choice. "Was I loud?" Suvius asks as he approaches.

"Quite the opposite actually. You give yourself too much praise—as if that armor and those rattling bones could possibly give you a dancer's grace. I only detected you because absolutely no one can escape my sense of smell."

"Death is a pungent odor."

"No, not your body odor, but your spirit. Its impurity makes it more revolting."

"I suppose that's why I'm here, to reflect on that. It is interesting how we both chose the same location."

"I feel like we think alike, and yet we don't," Draxis says.

"Until our worlds shattered and left us both with nothing left," Suvius says.

"Nothing but each other—and our mutual friends of course. I also see that you hold the relic of your home, and Ceranus, closer."

"To be used as my weapon… just like everyone else I've ever come across," Suvius says. "I don't want to use her like that—ever."

"I got the feeling from her that she wants you to use her leftover will in that manner. So she can be by your side and help pave the way to bring hope on your quest to restore the world; an atonement through death. I miss her."

"Really?"

Draxis pauses. *Should I tell him? What if he decides to… no… There needs to be more trust among all of us.* "Suvius, I shouldn't keep this a secret—it's about Ceranus—I feel responsible for her demise. She was surrounded by the Decayed and I just sat there… hesitating. I managed to save her, but I deeply regret not acting faster. Because of me, I failed her, and I failed the people that depended on her."

Suvius falls silent. The intensity is threatening. What else was Draxis expecting? He knew Suvius was going to be upset. He knew how harrowing the consequences of his inaction were going to be. He knows Suvius isn't the type to hold back when he feels wronged, he shouldn't have—

"You know, it takes someone incredible to recognize their flaws and be open about them, regardless of how others might react," Suvius starts to say, discontinuing Draxis's rambling thoughts. "Thank you for telling me. You are admirable, Sir Draxis."

"What? I fail to see what you mean. I'm foolish, and nothing more."

"You mistake my words with having undertones of perceived perfection. I know you are not perfect. But consider me inspired anyway."

"Truthfully, Suvius, I know I have always said a lot of harsh things about you, but I've always felt that you were more inspirational."

"I would agree if it was my past life, but now, I am not so sure. An apocalypse can really change a man."

"And in my case, a dragon—the very last one."

They stop talking. Something about this scene feels more blissful and ethereal than minutes prior, but they're still too stubborn to grasp the reason, or even admit it. It doesn't matter. What does matter is that they're both alive to bask in it. They continue doing so for another brief moment.

"I must say," Suvius says. "I don't think I've ever appreciated nature to this degree."

"It is something that is quite easy to take for granted. Oh, before I forget…" Draxis ejects a small colored stone from within the molten furnace that is his body and shows it to Suvius. "This is for you."

"A golem heart?" Suvius takes it in his hand. It's even in his favorite flavor.

"I should have given it to you during the war. That might have helped sustain your barrier… but I was being too bitter to give it to you. I just keep putting everyone at risk."

"Don't worry about it. I was fully aware that you wanted to preserve the lives of your people for as long as you could. After all, I don't think I ever saw you launch a single spell towards a dragon, but you seemed more than pleased to kill off the Decayed knights."

"That statement can also be inverted and applied to the butchers who exterminated my race," Draxis snarls.

"I wasn't meaning to lecture you. It was just to let you know that I do understand your actions. But of course, I had to make priorities for our survival, and so did they."

"All for a better future… By the way, you might want to savor that golem heart. I know you need periodic magic boosts to keep your soulless body moving, but Klae said to use those sparingly if possible. The Elementals and their kin are beginning to vanish faster nowadays than in previous years, so they might become scarce. Just a word of warning."

"I will try then," Suvius says. "Do you mind if I stay here? To also savor this scenery some more?"

"If I wanted to say no then you would have heard it loud and clear. Stay."

And stay he does.

Chapter 17

Sundown

"What is with you people?" Klae grumbles. "Did you all have to wake me up so early? It hasn't even been a full day since the incident. Are you all even sure you want to continue on? Please say no."

Maeva shifts around, anticipating for someone to answer like they usually do. She looks over at Suvius. *It seems best to leave him alone. What about Draxis? He doesn't seem to be holding up well either. Anyone...?* She feels that control of the conversation has fallen upon her.

"Klae, we'll be sitting here until the end of the century if we sit here wallowing. So we choose to make progress, while wallowing. Just make sure to give us salient details of any kind about the next artifact before we leave. You already know the reason why."

"I still need to get more accustomed to identifying and grading them, but I understand the complaint." Klae activates the world map. A pillar of light juts out from a landmass on the other side of the world from their location. "Looks like the next Artifact is… just below Excerina. On the subcontinent Isilios—in its heart."

Isilios? I remember hearing that name. Rend looks over to observe the rest of the team. He can tell he's not the only one affected by that word. It's always like this. He swears he could make a game out of it. *Oh, Klae's about to speak.*

"I'm not seeing any weird aberrations or anything else alarming on the map, so my only assumption is that it's a Blessed artifact. I wanted to mention this earlier, but so far, we… or rather you all, have collected two artifacts: that giant crystal over there and the Bloodheart Cuirass, which are both the same except for their opposing properties. One is Blessed and one is Cursed, in that respected order.

"The differences aren't too major. Blessed artifacts are supposedly created or touched by the Gods themselves whereas Cursed artifacts were once holy, but they are now dipped in and bleed with crippling Darkness, and that could happen for a variety of reasons—but the most common is through demonic interference."

Suvius perks up. "Demons?"

"Yes, that's right. Questions?"

"No."

Suvius takes a moment to revise his quick response. He thinks back on the few stories he's overheard of demons. Many of those stories include terrors of exorcisms, blood contracts, curses, and other things that ought to be left unspoken, but he's never come face-to-face with them personally or their lures. Although, that may not be necessarily true. A familiar lure is in front of him now actually, laying on the magical device that is projecting the world map.

"Actually… yes," he says. "I do have a question. Say I choose to wield the Bloodheart Cuirass—"

"Let me stop you right there," Klae interrupts. "Just how much do you actually know about Demonology?"

"Is that an Arbiter study? To be safe, not enough."

"Then that should be your approach the next time you ask about it so haphazardly. Weren't you the one who deemed curses as something to never be trifled with? It's worth noting that there were *very* few Arbiters that managed to successfully study Demonology and Darkness. Apostates we called them, and their capricious and often detrimental revelations have altered and shaped the delicate arcane seeds of magic for the worst. I can only hope that by telling you this I am altering your curiosity."

"Brilliant…" Suvius sneers. "You choose to chastise me over a mere question?"

"Yes, I proudly condemn errors. Now I know better than to try and stop you but remember we have already suffered a great catastrophe by meddling with the first Artifact. So spare us from your insanity and let evils rest."

"Fine, keep it. Just take us where we need to go. We're done here."

Begrudgingly, Klae gets into position to conjure up a portal—it's still as grueling to create as the first one. And just like the first, someone unexpected stays behind.

"Klae," Aluna calls out to him.

"First it was the annoying, red-eyed girl and now it's you," Klae snaps. "Why can none of you speak properly when we're all gathered? I'm not in the mood to be anyone's confessor."

"This is something you would want to hear."

"You don't make that judgment—I do. Go on, entertain me."

"It's about us, from one Arbiter to another. I think it's time I told them all who I really am."

"Forget them, how about telling *me*? I have never seen nor heard of you, ever."

"Oh, now you're interested?" Aluna wonders. "What's so hard to believe? There were plenty of Arbiters that were incognito or isolationists even. Just like Zazer."

"Zazer is different—*was* different," Klae says. "He was untouchable. Unreachable. No one saw the Paragon except for those in his inner circle. You boldly claim to be an Arbiter yourself, so tell me, what was your Arbiter status and title?"

Aluna flexes her wings high, and they glow with the sultry hue of a red rose as she speaks. "I am Aluna Quinfall, the Master Elementalist and the sole Arbiter of Judgment."

It's invisible, but Klae can feel the layers of her magical aura suffuse throughout the entire room. "Stop it," he commands, wiping the simmering sweat off his brow. "Nobody asked you to do that. *Excuse me* for asking for verification."

"It used to be my favorite way of introducing myself. It's an old habit," Aluna says.

"You do have their attitude. Causing structural damage was everyone's favorite pastime. So, little miss, you were our professional 'judge'?"

"Judge, executioner, cleanser, assassin, death-bringer, huntress, purifier, agent—the names always changed but the job remained the same."

"Then what responsibility do you hold now?" Klae asks.

"I can't disclose that."

"That excuse might have worked in the old world," he huffs, "but the others are dead, and we're all that remains. You don't have to abide by their policies anymore."

"Have you even confirmed that they're dead?" Aluna asks.

"N-No, I haven't. But even if they were somehow still around then what could they even do? Their reign has collapsed into nothing but ashes and incorrigible nightmares."

"But you admit that there's still chronic side effects."

"That's why we're trying to heal those scars," Klae says. "Or are you worried that you'll only create more scars by telling the others about your secret?"

"I guess I'm not so worried about having to tell them, but *how* I might have to tell them." She sees Klae's confused expression. "Do you know that *thing* you were yelling at Suvius about? Take a wild guess."

"Ah… so that's why you can't say much. How bad is it?" Klae asks.

"Enough to beg for any form of redemption, no matter how meager or impossible."

"Do you have any ideas on how to earn this 'redemption'?"

"Through the Harbingers," Aluna states.

"Not to ruin your faith, but they're not really the redemptive types."

"Exactly."

"Aluna!" a distorted voice echoes from the thin veil on the other side of the portal. "You're so tiny that we nearly forgot about you! Come on!"

Aluna gets the urge to slap whoever dares to harass her. She then waves and says, "Bye, Klae!"

"Yeah… bye."

***

Onward! Through the humid and overgrown jungle that tangles Isilios. In years prior, the only threats that were present were normally the wildest and the most exotic of beasts, the secluded tribes of hunters, or getting flattened by the great ancient trees that had a tendency to fall. Those threats seem so minor now.

Thankfully nothing like those has reared its head yet, probably because of how saturated the jungle is with the Decay. The smell of it is strong and heavy, and its purple muck has pretty much replaced any sources that would naturally be flourishing with a lush verdant green.

Maeva is trying to look away from it all, otherwise purple will become seared into her mind. She seeks to find comfort by distracting herself with something else, and it seems Suvius could also benefit from that. "By the way, Lord Suvius, what made you ask to wear Ceranus's armor? I thought that you would have wanted to keep it preserved to honor her."

"She may not be present, but I know that she would still want to fight. Aside from that, it's a really captivating item. I think I might chase after it if I ever feel it's worth the risk."

"What will you do about the souls inscribed in the chest piece you're wearing now?" Maeva asks.

"I'm planning on salvaging and transferring the ones that I want to keep—eventually. Some I will set free. Others still owe me a debt that can never be repaid."

She figured he would say something like that. "Remind me to never have you kill me."

"Worried that I would make you mine?" Suvius asks.

"Terrified of it."

He figured she would say something like that. "That brutal honesty will take some time to get used to. Others have already taken the liberty and expressed their criticisms towards me in my crippled state. It will be hard to balance our goal with adjustments to altering my old-fashioned ways. All I ask for is patience."

Maeva smiles and says to him, "That's good to hear. I'm sure your future victims will appreciate it."

"In a perfect world, there wouldn't be any," Suvius responds.

"At least you found new motivation. You made me worried."

"Hearing that will also take some getting used to."

Rend is watching the backs of Maeva and Suvius. He wants to join in on their conversation, but he has a more pressing issue he has to handle—the fairy that sits on his head. At first, he thought it was cute, but at this point she's just freeloading. "Is there a reason you're sitting on my head, Aluna?"

"Ignorant bastard. You try flying around in this jungle and tell me how well you can manage with these Wildbrood spiderwebs and this gooey purple shit."

"Then why not blast your way through?"

"Believe me, I would but… she'll get angry if I did," Aluna says.

"Who?"

"Sadra."

"Is she also a Harbinger?" Rend asks.

"One of the first among us."

"Oh, so she's a legend."

"Mmm… I guess—if you only go by first impressions," Aluna says. "She only encountered our leader because she's spent a long time hunting him down to enact her vengeance."

"Ah. How did that go?"

"It's like when an immovable object meets an unstoppable force. They are both too angry to die, so they had no choice but to team up and… become more productive?"

"Well how about you?" Rend says. "Are you excited to see her again?"

"The others might be, but not me. She acts like a know-it-all, and it pisses me off."

"What *doesn't* piss you off?"

"I know you're being a smartass, but truthfully, anything sweet," Aluna says. "I could really use something like that right about now."

"Sweets, huh? Desserts or something more savory?"

"Pure sugar all the way."

"Damn right!" Rend raises his hand, awaiting a hi-five. Aluna sighs and follows through with it.

At the rear of the group, Draxis is staggering, by his lonesome. Jellop slows down to equal Draxis's monotonous pace. "You seem more distant today, friend Draxis, which I can understand. Do you wish to speak about it?"

"There's quite a lot to sort through. Right now, I'm so nervous about… her."

"I'm sure she's here, Draxis."

"I already know that. She is more than capable of handling herself. I'm just wondering what she'll think of me after these three long years."

"The same as everyone else: happiness through reunion. Wouldn't you feel the same if your role and hers were flipped? Don't answer me, answer yourself." Jellop walks ahead, letting his question burn inside Draxis hotter than his demonic form.

Chapter 18

Twilight

"Aluna, what do you see!" Suvius shouts to her, looking towards the sky.

She swoops back down. "I'm not seeing anything that would do us harm. That woman really is like a guardian of this jungle, though it's not surprising given she's an Elemental. Speaking of Sadra, I think I saw her. She's just up ahead."

"Then we're only delaying destiny. Let us march."

***

A woman in black sits on top of a rock, facing away from the group and tending to her mystifying and long dark hair. It's not her clothes that are black, in fact, she's not even wearing any—it is the jet-black corporeal form that is her veiled skin. She's like a living shadow or darkness incarnate, one that is as mysterious and ominous as they come.

"Sadra," Suvius calls out to her.

She doesn't flinch or even gives a thought towards him.

"Sadra," he repeats. "I know you hear me."

Maeva shakes her head. "Some things just never change. We missed you, Sadra."

That comment gets Sadra to finally turn around. "Hi, Miss Maeva. I see everyone else is here as well…"

"Sadra Blessity," Suvius says as he confronts her.

Sadra meets his approach with scorn. "Hello… Nightmare."

Hold steady, Suvius. You knew this was coming, he thinks to himself. "I am glad to see you alive, Priestess. Though we were all forced to separate due to great peril, the six Harbingers are finally all reunited, with one promising addition to our ranks."

"I think our team would be better off if you were dead," Sadra remarks.

"I *am* dead."

"You know what I mean you stupid—you know what, I'm done talking to you." She directs her attention to a reclusive Draxis. "And why are you trying to hide from me? No matter your form, I'll always know it's you, Brightheart. It's been too long since you gave these sour eyes something sweet to look at, and just look at how lucent you are—simply scrumptious!"

"For some reason, when only *you* say things like that it sounds like harassment," he responds.

"I haven't seen you in three years. Plus, who wouldn't want to harass you? Or be the one harassed by you?"

"Just… go say hi to everyone else."

Sadra gives a retaliatory glare towards the others. Her first victim is the Knave. "Still alive, Jellop? Surely even you yourself are surprised by that miracle, yes?"

"I reluctantly bring chaos; therefore, I am absolved from it— even to yours."

She rolls her eyes, and then looks up. "And then there's *you,* Aluna."

"Whatever, you damn witch. Leave me alone."

"And who's this lost undead puppy?" Sadra asks, giving Rend a look over.

"Is that meant for me?" he says.

"Oh! It can speak. And who do you belong to Enslaved One?"

"He's mine," Maeva reacts.

"Undertaking lessons from Nightmare's sinful magic, are you? How shallow."

"Don't you think disrespecting the people you know and don't know is shallow in itself?" Rend defends.

"Sadra, take a second to calm down," Draxis says. "I know we all scattered on bitter and rushed terms, but please, show some concern."

"You're only going to hold us back if you continue to create fissures among us," Aluna adds.

"Oh that's rich coming from you," Sadra hisses. "If it only takes *me* to start a few tremors after all this time then maybe you all should reassess the lies you just told me. Now I'm wondering what's the lie you all have at the ready if I ask why I'm the last member found. Or did I just happen to be at the right place at the right time?"

"Sadra…" Draxis says.

"Let's not act like we're known for hospitality," she continues. "I highly doubt you are all here to check up on me or the ruins of my home. You all never cared about the devastation of this jungle before, so why now? Why are you here?"

Suvius intervenes to help absorb her verbal punches. "There is something deep within the heart of your home that we need, something powerful. It'll be used in conjunction with others like it to help rid the world of this pestilence once and for all. That's the condensed version."

"How ingenious," Sadra remarks. "But such a decisive plan could never have been manipulated by any of you, so tell me… under whose orders are you all following?"

She's met with defeated silence.

"Now this, *this* is comical, hysterical—a downright fucking fall from grace! What is it that struck you all? Is it fear? An infection in the head? Guilt? To think that *we* have lost everything to the point where an Arbiter decides who we are and what we do."

"We are not the same Harbingers you remember all those years ago," Suvius says.

"Clearly. But I'm not just talking about our public name and image, I'm also talking about the individuals before me. What even are we anymore?"

"We're harbingers," Rend says with a firm tone. "Harbingers of the Light."

"What? You again? The hell are you even—"

"I don't really appreciate being told that what we're doing is wasted. Why act so combative when you don't even know what we've been through?"

"I sympathize with that feeling. It's a shame that you cannot do the same." Sadra then attacks Rend by shooting a black disc from her hand that tethers him to her body.

The weight of her dark magic is monstrous, to the point where it feels like his gravity and sorrow are multiplied. Nobody steps in to stop her, not even… *Brightheart?* Who only gives her a disappointed look. She halts her attack.

Rend's body heals enough to let him stand again. "The pain that I just felt is nothing compared to what I've witnessed."

"Such a star pupil," Jellop compliments.

"Quiet, Jellop."

"Dammit, just shut up! All of you shut up!" Sadra wails. "I'm so confused. I don't know what to think anymore! You all say this shit like I'm supposed to accept that everything was a lie!"

"Make no mistake, Sadra, the Darkness we once faced as a team is still prevalent and far-reaching," Draxis says. "But we have the opportunity of a lifetime to rectify everything. That's why we are here—we haven't given up. It's just as Rend here says: the light is dawning, and we're bringing it."

"And if you can't find it, then perhaps take a closer look into what you believe to be is the darkest dark," Jellop interjects.

Sadra gives a thorough look at them, deep inside of them. Her unique vision allows her to see the bright and milky globules of light that battle against the smaller portions of dark blobs within them. "When… when did you all get so bright?"

"When we realized that the dark isn't so omnipotent," Draxis says. "Your own Darkness isn't omnipotent either, Sadra. Now I've never been one to preach, but we want you to join us, and please, show us the light as a Light elemental, before we become blinded by Darkness and evil once again."

Cracks are beginning to show in Sadra, both in her heart and across her body. The fissures part away and smooth over—and then, there is an eruption, a fountain of blinding light. A lucent woman floats where the entity of nightly shadow once stood, bedazzling her surroundings wherever she moves. She's the brightest thing they have ever seen, ever since the final dawn left and never came again on the first sunless morning.

Draxis surely is entranced. It's the same enchanting light that he's loved and adored for the longest time. "Feeling better?" he asks.

"I'd say half and half," she answers.

"You need to cull your shadows more often, Sadra," Maeva says. "I always forget how gorgeous your Diurnal side looks."

"No, you're gorgeous, Miss Maeva."

"No, you are," Maeva reflects.

"It sounds like things have finally dialed down," Suvius barges. "The amount of stress here could have killed an entire squad of cavalrymen. Priestess Sadra, we shan't force you to, but if you wish, then can you please aid this group of misguided neophytes?"

"Let me think… Maybe."

"That's good enough."

Chapter 19

Lights Out

"So… Sadra… how have you been?" Draxis asks.

"Why are you acting so weird? Are you experiencing the effects of Wild Haze? I always told you that you need to apply and ingest Isilium Sap before coming here."

"No, it's nothing like that. Thankfully. You could say that I'm feeling apologetic for breaking my promise to return."

"You said that you were feeling overwhelmed, and I can't really blame you for that. Has anything improved? It still looks to me that you're still whelmed," Sadra says.

"It's been an adventure, spent mostly looking for everyone else and ways to purge the Decay. How about you?"

"Stuck in a state of misery and wishing my little heart out every day for the sun to come back."

"Curse it all," Draxis says. "You should never have to endure that. I left you when you needed me the most."

"Brightheart, don't say that. You make it sound like you regret searching for hope."

"You're… you're right. I'm letting my emotions get the best of me, again. I just… hate to hear how much pain you're in."

"It's not so much as pain, it's just exhaustion," Sadra responds. "As much as I would love to leave Isilios behind and seek someplace better, I'm tied to being the tutelary beacon of this jungle because there's no one else left to do it. Yes, there is pain involved, but I proudly take it upon myself to continue to uphold the Natural

Order and to make sure that the infected here never escape into the outer wilds—there are enough monsters out there. Speaking of monsters, how's being a demon going for you?"

"You might be more lucent than I am, but it still has its bright sides—"

"Not funny," Sadra remarks.

"But overall," Draxis continues, "it's abhorrent. I scorch everything that I touch."

"Tsk. That's nothing. Before the apocalypse, I wasn't allowed to go anywhere where bright light was considered a nuisance—like hospices and places with small children."

"I wasn't making a competition out of this, Sadra."

"Too late. My body is hotter than yours by the way."

"I'm literally made out of hellfire."

"And? My light is capable of burning away all manner of blighted corruption and the unholy creatures of the night. That's way cooler."

"It's precious to see you two so close, but are we nearing the Artifact's location?" Suvius asks.

"Yes, Nightmare, we are." Sadra then points upwards. "Can't you see the dark fog above the canopy?"

Suvius sees it alright, and it's getting thicker the closer he gets. "What's causing it?"

"An untamable essence exuded by the Elementals here. It's been growing exponentially ever since Blighted Day. It might consume all of Isilios one day."

"And why are we approaching said untamable essence?"

"Because like it or not, that's where we need to be," Sadra says. "What's the problem? You all said that you wanted to steal the last vital organ of my home, correct? So that's what we're doing."

"You're misconstruing. We never said that."

"But that's basically what you all have been doing with the other Artifacts you've been stealing. Just because they exist doesn't mean that they are free to take. Why would you all even touch an object that's beyond your comprehension?"

"This lecture again…" Suvius says with a sigh.

"Why do you think there is calamity all around us, huh?" Sadra continues. "I don't know where you got your information from, but these Artifacts' sole existence is to maintain balance between the natural dynamics of the world. That's why guardians like the Isilians and other Elementals were created to protect them—but it's always impossible to stop covetous assholes like you from plundering our secrets! You're so fucking stupid!"

"Dammit, woman! I told you once before that we are going to use the Artifacts we can exhume to restore *balance* and dispel a worldwide curse. That's why we need them!"

"Even the Cursed ones?" Sadra asks.

"Whatever we can obtain."

"Gods, are you actually planning on using those cursed artifacts… to dispel a curse? Why do I even bother…"

***

It isn't too long until everything comes to a halt. It's not that they can't proceed forward, it's more like they don't *want* to proceed forward. There's an intense bubble of obsidian-black darkness erect-ed tall and extended wide across every cardinal direction wherever it originates from.

"This veil—do you recognize it, Nightmare?" Sadra asks.

"Would it kill you to call me by my birth name?" Suvius says.

"Not until I stop having nightmares about you. Anyway, answer my question."

"How am I supposed to guess when there's a wall of nothing in front of me?"

"*Try!*"

She's not going to give up, and Suvius knows that. He also knows that he has been here before, but it's been years. This scenery might as well be brand new to him. Judging from the look of intense hostility Sadra's been giving him—more so than usual—he knows there's only one conclusive guess he can give.

"Is… is this the Isilian capital?"

"Yep-yep!" Sadra cheers. "I knew you would recognize your handiwork."

"To put a city in ruin? Sure, I'll accept that villainous dishonor. But a half-continental quarantine zone? That's beyond me. This wasn't even here before."

"Well, it's here now and forever. And *we're* going to have to go inside it."

"I say we don't," Rend objects, still unnerved by a whip of motion he caught from the corner of his eye not too long ago. "There's something in there."

"That's just my people," Sadra states.

"Those shadow things? Aren't you a Light elemental though?"

"In my brightest days, yes. That changed during the First Night. The Isilians had never known darkness until those invaders arrived. I was one of the lucky few among us that could handle the Dark element and escape, so I'm more of a hybrid now."

"And from what she calls you, Suvius, you are to blame for that?" Rend says.

"…Yes. It's no secret that the Vomenn Kingdom was built over and painted with the cold blood of innocents, and while I try to distance myself from that past, I was still their pawn and the catalyst for their opulence. What was once here before was a paradise, one of a kind, and one that can never recover from the invasion that I led over a thousand on in the name of who was at the time my king."

"You know, you people make it really hard to even have a decent shred of good faith around here."

"Hey… your name is Rend, right?" Sadra asks.

Rend twists around. *When did she get behind me?*

"How would you like to be my volunteer for a quick demonstration?"

"Uh, no? For what even?" He swears he can see something evil resonating in her eyes for even questioning her. "Why are you being so creepy?"

"She likes to do that," Draxis says.

"That implies I should start running and screaming."

"It won't be that bad…" Sadra pushes with a tempting tone. "I promise." She then lunges at him and snatches his hand.

Rend tries to pull himself away, but her strength surprises him. It gives her enough time to shove his hand through the veil of the dark bubble. *This doesn't feel... natural,* he thinks to himself as he becomes mesmerized by the sensation. *Just what kind of darkness is this?*

"You want how much for him?" a woman's distorted and upbeat voice echoes.

What? Whose voice is that? Are these unknown voices... coming from inside his head?

"Mommy?" another unknown voice plays out, this one significantly younger.

"Look, Archias," the woman says. "Look at how many gems the nice man has. You're about to make mommy a rich mommy."

"Why do I have to go with him? I don't want to go with him."

"But *I* want you to. Just think of how happy I will be with the money I'm going to get in return. I can get a new home, a new man, a new everything! The gods truly do love me!"

"But… what about me?"

"Archias, there's a word for useless children like you—we call them bastards, and I never needed or wanted a bastard in my life."

"Stop calling me that!" the child shouts. "I don't understand, I've always been here for you, mom!"

"That's the problem right there, you little shit!"

"Listen, Ma'am, I need to wrap this deal up shortly. So is he for sale or not?" a gruff man asks.

"You can take him and anything else you want here, I don't care. I can finally live my youth again. Oooh! I'm so excited!"

"Alright boy, you're coming with me."

"No! Mommy, I'll do better, please! Make him stop! Mommyyy—"

Rend snatches his hand away, with so much force it's in a blur. His head is screaming in pain. He sinks towards the ground as he struggles to hold his composure.

"Rend!" Maeva shouts as she rushes over to him. "Sadra, what the fuck! Why did you do that!"

"Consider that to be a warning on what will happen if any one of us touches this darkness."

"So you do it by scarring people for life?"

"I know my words will not be heeded properly by any of you. I needed to provide something with a bit more… clarity."

"If attention is all you wanted then consider mine to be indivisible. What the hell even was that?" Maeva asks.

"Despair," Sadra states.

"What do you mean 'Despair'?"

"The forced remembrance of our sorrows and agony. Despair is one of Darkness's many horrific forms—sort of like me with my magical control over shadows, or Nightmare and his wicked Necromancy. There will be no escaping such horror once we enter inside the bubble."

"So we can't survive that?"

"Oh heavens no," Sadra says. "Our hearts and minds would get raped relentlessly. But luckily, as the Harbinger of Twilight, I can provide a proper safe passage for us. So allow me to become your guiding… dark? Light? Your shadow-light!

"Do we have to?" Maeva groans.

"Yep-yep!"

"Can't you just go fetch it for us?"

"I could, but I don't feel safe going in there by myself. A mission is better fulfilled with company after all."

"She's not going to offer us a choice," Draxis says. "Let's just get it done as quickly as possible."

Sadra's body dims. "Listen to Brightheart," she pleads. "And to say it for the last time. Do. Not. Touch. The. Darkness! Not even a Demon can handle the unbearable weight of Despair. Just stay near my luminous and sexy light and none of you will become driven to madness or get eaten alive by the Shades—that's what I call the Dark elementals here. Ready, everyone?"

"I don't want to do this anymore…" Rend croaks.

"That's good to hear!" Sadra cheers. "And remember, everyone—no potty breaks!"

***

Once inside, there is no turning back—and she meant it. Sadra's radiant sanctuary allows them to wade through the darkness completely unscathed, but it's still a *very* infinitesimal blip in the great void that expands as far as their eyes cannot see.

There's no indication of up or down and no indication of how far they have to travel. They can't even get a grasp on whose breathing is who's as there is the occasional whisper and hush that murmur much too close for comfort from outside the dome of light. Something wicked is walking alongside them, with purple eyes shifting and vanishing while watching their every move and craving for the impassable light to fade away.

Sadra chuckles to herself, hoping that no one has heard her uncontrolled glee. She has the uncanny insight to know that Darkness itself has countless talons, and the talon that is the sharpest of all, is Fear. The rising fear that she can see within everyone's hearts is her comedic relief, but she knows it won't do any good to let them continue to get harassed by the unknown.

"It should be a straight path as long as we find any notable landmarks on the way," Sadra says. "I've already seen a few, so we should be fine."

"Straight path my ass," Aluna remarks. "You keep moving like a succubus going through an exorcism."

"At least I have an excuse. You on the other hand keep fluttering around like one of those moth creatures that mindlessly ram themselves into shiny things."

"Ladies, be nice," Draxis warns. "It's too crowded for this."

"Sorry, Brightheart," Sadra says. "I might be able to stay more upbeat if you could… well, y'know."

"Want me to get closer?" he says.

She passionately nods her head up and down in response.

"Alright. Now, I can't get too close otherwise I'll—"

"Burn me alive?" she says, moving closer.

"Sadra, please."

"What? Fire isn't that bad. Ohhh, what if your hellfire can make my light shine brighter? Make me brighter, Draxis! Come on, burn me alive!"

"I don't think being in isolation for three years has been kind to you," he responds.

"I encountered a rabid Isilian squirrel a few months back."

"Splendid…"

Behind them, Suvius is forced to teeter and totter in an attempt to stay within the confines of the light due to his height. It's times like these where he's thankful for having unlimited stamina to move about. That stamina yields when he hears a distorted voice of jubilance.

"Ahahahaha! I'm surprised the Isillians were as weak as they were. I heard rumors that they could shoot light beams out of their eyes or some shit, but they can barely lift a finger or toe. What say you, Commander Suvius? You're guaranteed to go home a hero once we finish this up."

"A hero to whom?"

"Why, King Laxan, of course," the soldier says.

"If King Laxan was standing here at the foot of this burning altar as we are now, do you think he would still believe me to be a hero?"

"I wouldn't doubt it. He would have the best seat in this battlefield. He would probably even relinquish his crown to you personally he would be so overjoyed."

"Then the symbol of his crown has lost its meaning," Suvius says. "I've become a hero to a villain. What have I become…"

"You've lost me somewhere. I don't follow what you're saying."

"Forgive me…"

"S-Suvius, watch your blade! What are you—ackk!"

"I am sorry, Galvin. You are my best soldier, but this is the only crime I can think of to be granted a direct audience with His High Nobility—just to tell him that I forfeit my loyalty… That's if I survive his fury. I'll only be fair that he endures mine as well."

As that Nightmare ends, another one begins its inception, starting with his own voice in distress.

"They are using you, Ceranus!"

"They can use me however they damn well please! Just stop to think how far we have come with their technology and magic! Our kingdom's production has skyrocketed. We are achieving unparalleled advancements that the other rulers can't even fathom. Even the wild beasts and monsters that used to roam this region are nothing more but an afterthought now for our villages and local adventurers everywhere. Just think of what else we can do if this keeps up!"

"At the cost of how many lives?" Suvius asks.

"Significantly less than the bloodbaths you and your other rat friends like to commit."

"Because you people keep sending legion after legion after us when our only gripe is with the Arbiters. We are growing weary of the rest of the world's meddling, and we will not hesitate to let our exemptions turn into extreme prejudice."

"If the entire world is trying to stop you all from taking away our salvation, then consider rethinking who here exactly is actually the real threat," Ceranus says.

"Inequality is not salvation. You speak of salvation when you are doing everything within your growing power to enslave the dragons and more."

"They are dangerous!" Ceranus shouts.

"Plants are dangerous. Monsters are dangerous. Magic is dangerous. *Absolute power* is dangerous."

"I need such power. I'm trying to take out the threat before it even grows legs. It's happened with the Light elementals at Isilios, and it's going to happen with the Dragons."

"Unjust logic," Suvius says. "If you believe in it so strongly, then maybe to spare us all you should just kill yourself."

"Enough! Just… enough. You come into my castle and try to poison me, the queen, with your nasty words and expect me to believe them all from a traitor of the highest caliber? I do not know *what* in this godforsaken world would ever make you think you can take my patience for granted in any capacity, but I've had enough of it! I know that by the time I summon the guards you will be hundreds of fields away from here, but do know that I will do everything that's possible within my 'absolute power' to have you killed—for good this time."

"Ceranus, just listen to me!"

"**Leave**!"

The Nightmares are cut off. Suvius is lost to his surroundings for a few seconds, before becoming aware just how close his hand is to the outer rims of Sadra's aura.

Damn my lack of touch, he thinks. *I must have only grazed it. So... debilitating, that was. Was that my Despair? Why was there more than one?* He looks at Sadra, who is minding her own business and moseying. *How many of these has she endured? How many of them involve the Kingdom? Or... me?*

"Sadra," Suvius calls out to her with an increased tone, making sure to grab her attention. "It would serve you well to know that the Vomenn kingdom, and their leaders, have fallen."

She stops.

"Watch it!" Aluna shouts.

Sadra grits her teeth. It would serve *him* well to know that her light can make any evil lies or trickery transparent, so… why isn't she detecting anything? It puts her in a pensive mood. "You really aren't lying? Oh my, I… I really wasn't expecting to hear that. I mean, I don't really care—good riddance to them. But… how? They were the most powerful kingdom in the entire world. Not even our combined might could topple them."

"That kingdom prospered under the guise of its immortality," Suvius says. "But mortal reality and pride are exact opposites. We learned that the excruciating way."

"We?" she questions.

"I will not pretend that I am innocent in any capacity. My home's downfall was karmic, incurring the preordained. Draxis, are you well enough to speak on it?"

"I'd… rather we discuss it later," he says. "Let me rest."

Sadra can see the light within Draxis make a sharp decline, and Suvius's as well. She's never seen them so shaken up before, not even at their worst, and not even when they did their worst. She makes the assessment not to press them anymore and relights her aura as she continues on.

Chapter 20

Shackles

"We are too old for roll calls, but I shouldn't digress on this matter," Suvius says out loud. "Jellop, where's your partner?"

"Partner?"

"We should be sticking close with one another to ensure our safety, so where's Duchess Aluna? I thought she was with you?"

Jellop looks around. "Butterfly? It doesn't make sense. She would have normally announced her presence by now. She hates getting left behind. This is tragic. Everyone, cease movement! A butterfly is lost. Butterfly!"

Jellop's yelps are faint, but can be heard by the Butterfly, Aluna. She doesn't know when, and she doesn't know how, but somehow the darkness has captured her in its net. No matter how fast she flies towards the light, the darkness is always there, speaking to her and intercepting her berated and fragile mind. It starts with the distorted and hate-driven maledictions of countless voices that lash at her relentlessly.

"Kill her!"

"Leave us alone! Leave my family alone!"

"Go ahead, do it! But I know you'll never forget my face, that's why you're hesitating!"

"It burns!" a voice hollers out, which is then followed up with a myriad of screams melting together into a horrible chorus.

Then the noises cull to two voices in the middle of a conversation.

"She's obviously going to betray us. Just you wait and see."

"You've said that about everyone here."

"But she'll be the first."

"And why do you say that?"

"Because I see things that others don't."

"Like what? What is it that we're so blind to?"

"Something that is undetectable to the innocent, and something that is made blatant by the guilty. If you had my trained eyes, you would be able to detect each trace and strand of it, even in a roaring ocean of its own mass."

"This is the first time I'm hearing of such an otherworldly thing. What's it supposed to reveal?"

"Everything that can go wrong in a person."

The talon of Despair digs even deeper into Aluna.

"Just what are you saying?"

Who was that? Aluna wonders. *Was that... my own voice?*

"Your service is no longer required, Aluna. If the Arbiters request an inquiry for reparations, then tell them that there will be no need for any negotiations. All acquisitions lost have already been recovered and will be delivered right to their mountaintop doorstep by tomorrow's eve. It should be flying on a carrier dragon as we speak."

"King Laxan, you can't just—"

"This long-term agreement between the Arbiters and I was meant to include a cooperation of common interests and a sharing of intellectual and sovereign might to forge an unstoppable empire—but I do not tolerate suspicious behavior. If you wish to refute, then tell me, what opportunity is there to gain to deceive me about their involvement with those Harbingers?"

"We're merely determining on how to handle them. They're unlike anything we have ever dealt with before."

"What does that have to do with me?" he asks.

"Well, for starters, their leader *did* come to be from your lack of control," Aluna responds.

"I take no responsibility for men that can cheat death itself. He has disrespected the good and holy faith that this kingdom upholds. I want nothing more than to castrate his existence myself."

"Regardless, Laxan, you made a contract with us."

"A contract made either verbally or handwritten can be terminated by sword at any given time."

"Are you threatening us?" Aluna asks.

"I've only expressed my discontent with this whole situation. Any offenses taken by my words will only be reflected back to the accusers. Wrongdoers are always blind to their misdeeds, especially when they think they can get away with it."

"Laxan, please reconsider… I don't want to tell them. Don't do this to me!"

"Begone from my castle. And for further clarification, my command does extend beyond these walls and beyond this region, meaning that you *will* stay away from my wife. She is not to be distracted from her role in strengthening this nation. You do not want to disobey me."

Another painful transition occurs. The worst Nightmare of them all.

"Did you ask for me, Mixon?"

"I did… about thirty minutes ago, Aluna."

"It takes time to get over here."

"When we ask you to move, you move. When we ask you to strike, you strike. But when *I* ask for something, you better damn well answer with ungodly punctuality."

"I follow what you're saying but couldn't you have created one of your nexus portals if this matter was so urgent?"

"I am currently acting as a way of transit for over twenty-six Arbiters all across the globe as we speak," Mixon says. "I refuse to exhaust any more of my energy than I already am. You speak to me as if *you're* inconvenienced while I have to stand here and educate you on your ineptitude for the fourth time this week.

"Such utter nonsense. What have you done today so far aside from thinking that you have the right to freely address me however you please and failing to purge the target that we have specifically designated for you to handle? Remember that we own your entire being. You will never match us, and you will never *rebel* against us."

"…I'm just trying to be reasonable," Aluna says.

"Speaking out against any of us is beyond a condition of 'reason'. Come here…"

"Mixon, please, I didn't mean to—l-let go of my wings! Fucking let me go!"

The Nightmares fade as Maeva's voice drowns them out.

"Aluna! Aluna!"

"H-Huh?"

"Oh thank goodness we found you! You're outside the light! Come back!"

Aluna rushes over to Maeva and the others.

"Idiot moth," Sadra seethes. "Didn't I tell you not to touch the darkness?"

"Sadra, now's not the time," Jellop says. "Butterfly, you look distressed. Come rest over here."

Aluna flutters to him and sits on his shoulder. "Thanks…" she says.

"It's the best I can do for now unfortunately."

Aluna curls up, hiding herself from everyone else and muttering to herself alone. "Why do I have to suffer like this? I just want it to end. Somebody… make it end."

***

"Did you have a Nightmare, Brightheart?" Sadra asks him. "You look pale."

"Don't we all get nightmares?" Draxis says.

"You know what I mean."

"I didn't stay in the fog for too long, so my Nightmares were sporadic at best—some were about my encounters during my travels, most were during my time as a dragon. *And those visions of gnashing teeth again.* He keeps that last thought to himself.

"Will I ever see your true form again?" Sadra asks.

"Not if I can help it. Just… don't take that personally."

"I think I see what you mean. Are you still experiencing trauma?"

"Sure. Let's go with that."

"That's a shame. How about you two?" Sadra asks, looking at Jellop—and Aluna, who is still downtrodden. "Want to share your Nightmare experiences? Don't think I didn't see you stumbling around at the light's edge, Jellop."

"I've been seen, not good," he yelps. "It was an accident."

"The way you reacted was pretty funny."

"It hurt."

"Aww, that's not good," Sadra says. "I'm honestly surprised that you even have trauma. You seem too… gentle to bear a bad past."

"It wasn't my past. I heard voices instead, from a singular entity. It was overpowering, condescending, unfearful—unlike me."

"Just a single voice?"

"Yes."

"What do you make of that, Draxis? I mean, Brightheart," Sadra says.

"You're going to strain yourself if you try to keep calling me that," he says. "Jellop, does this have to do with what happened back at the kingdom? You complained about voices back then too."

"I believe it does."

"We were in such a rush, but I still shouldn't have brushed it off. Has anything significantly changed about you since that time?"

"Indeed," Jellop says. "My passive abilities, and my powers, are null and void now."

"Wait, do you mean… Can you not read our thoughts?"

"It is sublime, no? All is quiet now in this hellish hellscape."

"As reassuring for our sanity as that sounds, isn't that important to you?" Sadra asks. "Like for your health and such?"

"Incorrect," Jellop says. "That was my incurable sickness. Ever since I was plunged into this world it has been nothing but pure and utter discord in my head and having no choice but to expel that discord into physical being just to live another day. But, since it's disabled, I have never felt such peace. I never knew such a prosperous gift could exist; a pilgrimage I will embark on." The way Jellop jitters from his glee, it's almost contagious to the others.

"I'm still slightly worried for you, but I'm glad that you were given something nice for once," Draxis says.

"Muhuhu! May it extend to all of us."

Chapter 21

Suffocation

A glass monolith stands out in the open, surrounded by ruined toys and dried edibles from a decimated past. The structure is barely visible to the naked eye, but Maeva manages to see it just in time before ramming into an embarrassing situation. "Hey, Sadra, what's this?" she asks.

Sadra gasps. "It's one of our altars of prayer! In Isilian legends, our Light was bestowed to us by the God of the Sun, and in return, we serve to continue spreading his gift."

"It sure does look like something sacred," Maeva praises as she touches it to hopefully siphon any sensation of warmth from it. "Can we do anything special with this?"

"Not without some Isilium Sap and sunlight. The Artifact should still be near the Cathedral of Dawn, so if I'm remembering correctly then these altars should lead us directly to it. We can use this one as a landmark."

"That's reassuring. Keep up the good work."

"Yep-yep!"

***

Sadra is beginning to sway. Jellop launches himself and catches her before she drops.

"Whoops…" she says woozily. "This is… this is a longer journey than I thought." She plants herself on the ground to rest.

"Do we have time to turn around?" Maeva asks.

"To where?" Aluna says. "We don't even know where behind us *is*."

"Hey, not to trample our fun, but didn't we pass this glass altar already?" Draxis asks.

"What?" Sadra scoffs in disbelief. "But we've been walking forward all this time."

"How can you tell?"

"…I don't know. "

"W-We'll find our way. Don't worry."

***

"Nope…" Maeva groans. "Still the same altar."

"But—here, let me try something." Sadra picks up a random piece of ruined reflective material and imbues it with her light. She throws it forward as hard as she can, only to watch it get swallowed up in the blinding darkness. "That didn't show me anything…" She does it again and again in other directions, to no avail. "Forget it. Let's try going this way."

***

"Why'd we stop?" Maeva asks.

"Hold on. Bear with me…" Sadra says.

Sadra starts muttering to herself as they wait patiently. All they can overhear is her doubting and questioning herself over and over.

"Do you need aid?" Suvius asks.

"I just need to get out of here. Let's go this way."

***

"Seriously?" Draxis groans. "Did we really just loop around again?"

"I don't know what to do anymore…" Sadra mutters.

"Maybe we should we take a moment to rest and pray?"

"I'm going to make this entire world pray for mercy if we don't start seeing results."

"That's a horrible prayer."

***

"Grahh! Shut up!" Sadra shrieks.

"Woah!" Maeva yelps. "No one said anything!"

"Not you, it's these stupid Shades! They keep laughing at us! They won't shut the hell up!"

"Don't let them get to you. They're infected, they're just trying to lure us out."

"This is so irritating!"

***

"If I see this *fucking* altar one more time!"

"Sadra, calm down," Draxis says.

"I can't! I don't know where the fuck we are! It hurts to even move at this point! Fuck, fuck, fuck!"

"Draxis, get her to settle her temper!" Suvius yells.

"I know!"

A black blotch takes form on Sadra's back. More of them begin to appear, varying in sizes and turning her body polka dotted.

"She's going Nocturnal!" Maeva shouts.

"Sadra!" Draxis says. "It's going to be alright!

"It's dark! Everything's going dark!" Her falling tears, even those are becoming one with the night, corrupting her light even faster. The dark is seeping in, both outside, and even worse—inside.

"I don't think we can stop this," Maeva says as she looks around for ideas. "Wait, Suvius, you know some Light magic, right?"

"Only ones that can vanquish. I'll see what I can muster up for us." He claps his hands together—and spreads them apart to reveal a miniature orb of gray light.

"That's it?" she asks.

"Luminescence requires purity."

"Then start praying or something!"

"Oh Gods above, may you send your radiance down upon us and consecrate these unholy lands to save us from total annihilation—within the next minute preferably."

As Maeva watches Suvius continue to go unanswered, a faint voice mumbles to themself beside her, saying, "I don't want to…"

He spoke! Maeva shouts in her head. "Rend, have you finally come to?"

"Am I going to have to relive it all again?" he asks, looking in anguish at the thought. "I don't want to remember her again. I hate her."

Her? Maeva wonders to herself, before refocusing. "We're trying our best to not let that happen. I'll stay close to you. I'll even let you hold on to me—just this once." Both Maeva and Rend sit down together, anticipating a grim future as the light withers around them.

The bright hemisphere that has shielded everyone against the suffocating darkness has shrunken into the shape of a large cylinder. Any more shrinkage will result in the claustrophobic safe zone becoming a pillar, and anything else further than that will resemble an insignificant dot that *might* only last long enough to torture their dying hopes a bit more.

"Aluna, where are you going?" Jellop shouts. "Get away from there!"

"Look at her," Aluna says as her eyes guide over to Sadra. "She's not able to recover her light, so it's going to happen eventually. I'm just getting it over with early."

"No! Don't!" He is rendered helpless to stop her. Everyone is rendered helpless.

Draxis is the first to be touched by the darkness. His terror is muffled by the engulfing void.

Then Jellop, who holds on to his staff for dear life.

Then Suvius. He's already accepted his fate, standing tall with his chest puffed out.

Sadra is on the verge of doom as well. She crawls over to Maeva and Rend. "I'm so sorry, Miss Maeva. Everyone's going to die because of me! I can't stop it!"

"We tried, that's all that matters. And you tried really hard for us. You did great."

"I don't understand how you're so calm. Your friend over there looks dead inside."

Maeva rubs Rend's head. "I'm sure he has his reasons. Were this the old me all those weeks ago, I would have been the first one to succumb, easily. Things don't feel as harrowing now for some reason. It's like I can see the world in all its Light, just like how you can see all its Dark. And there are so many sources of light out there—and if there isn't, then just discover your own."

"My… own?" Those words linger as Sadra is finally absorbed by the darkness, and Maeva and Rend are met with the same fate."

Chapter 22

Midnight

It's been nothing but a frenzied whirlwind of dread the moment the darkness crushed Sadra's light. *I did this—I caused this,* is what goes through her mind. She bemoans at the ghastly sobs coming from the others, wherever they may be. She can overhear the heinous taunts from the shadows that thrive in this eternal night—she swears that they are even beginning to taste her.

Her one and only plan is to try and keep her mind in an exalted state, but she has vastly underestimated how deep the darkness can pull someone down. Her mind is fading. Failing. Her true nightmares will soon be unleashed.

But that doesn't happen, at least, not entirely. Being attuned with the Dark has its perks, many that she doesn't fully realize. She is able to see through the pitch-black veil itself. But what good is that perk if she can only use it to witness everyone else's writhing?

No! There are a million things that are weighing Sadra down, some even overpowering the darkness itself, but she has to save them! They entrusted her to be their light! She prepares to trudge into an impossible storm. Her first target to rescue is Maeva.

"Maeva!" Sadra calls out to her. "Maeva!"

"You can't call me a monster if you people have done worse!" Maeva screams as she rolls around on the ground. "I never asked for this! I don't even know what I am!"

"Poor Miss Maeva. She's hallucinating. How can I break her out of her trance? She'll have to forgive me for this…" Sadra runs up and slaps her, slightly enjoying it.

"Argh! Leave me alone!" Maeva then tries to retaliate by flailing her arms.

"Watch your swings! It's me! Sadra! I know you can't see me, but it's really me!"

"Sadra?" Maeva reaches out to confirm for herself.

Her hands become much too lecherous for Sadra's liking. "Stop touching me!" she yells, smacking Maeva's hands away.

"Do the Nightmares not affect you, Sadra?"

"Maybe I've grown used to them, or maybe there's a worst nightmare happening right in front of me. This darkness is mightier than my own, but I can still see. I can still guide us. We should collect everyone else and rally forward."

"Right. Let me just do something really quick." Maeva searches around for Rend on the ground. He's in the same spot she left him in, only that he's in a miserable stupor. "I'm here, Rend," she says, nudging his shoulder. "I didn't mean to be so selfish and leave you."

"Mother?" he says. "You came back? I thought you didn't want me?"

"No," Maeva says in a soothing tone. "I'm someone who's actually here for you. You can feel my presence, can't you?"

"I do."

"Then let's go. It won't be fast, but we're getting out of this."

***

They find Suvius standing tall while being heckled by a nasty swarm of Shades. Sadra jumps up and smacks him—and regrets it a little after realizing how much it stings.

Suvius doesn't even need to guess as to who would commit the atrocity. "Did you just hit me?" he growls.

"Yep-yep!"

"I think my urge to punish offenders is allowing me the strength to move."

"We'll need that energy," Sadra says. "Take someone's hand and follow."

"Hand holding? How embarrassing. I feel like a child."

They find Jellop next. He is wrestling with himself on the ground and howling at his own misery.

"Jellop!" Sadra shouts.

"I am not chaos! I am not you! Leave me alone!"

Sadra smacks him too.

"Somebody help! I'm being attacked!"

"It's just us, Jellop!"

"How dare you hurt a friend whoever you are!" He reaches for Sadra, accidentally touching her where he shouldn't.

"Dammit! New rule! The next person that touches me is getting their hand bitten!"

"The voices are getting weaker," Suvius says. "We need to continue our assembly."

Sadra drags the group over to Draxis. He's lying in a fetal position. "D-Draxis!" She hovers her palm over his face, before fully deciding to punch him in the noggin.

"Ow!" Draxis cries out. "What was that for?"

"Because I wanted to. And why the hell are you a dog? Why did you switch forms?"

"I'm a werewolf! I thought that because werewolves are nocturnal creatures then maybe I could survive this darkness?"

"This isn't your typical darkness, idiot!"

"You sure about that? Then why can't I see anything?"

Sadra punches him again before asking the others, "Do we have everybody here?"

"Butterfly," Jellop states.

"Oh, right. Her…"

***

"Aluna!" Sadra shouts.

"Hey," she responds, nonchalantly.

"You seem… casual," Sadra pokes. "Enjoying the weather that we're having? Soaking in the atmosphere? Playing with the neighbor's kids?"

"It's only because I have no choice but to smell the flowers since I can't rely on you at all to not get us killed. I'm not some agent of evil as you portray me as."

"But I can't skip over the fact that you're frolicking around in this darkness like you do it every day."

"Maybe I'm used to it from dealing with your crazy-ass all these years."

"Why are we dealing with a storm within a storm!" Suvius shouts. "Settle your matters later!"

"Then tell her to leave me alone!" Aluna yells.

"You first!" Sadra counters.

Their bickering and stalling has allowed the Shades to surround and trap everyone in an inescapable vortex that spins around faster and faster to form a kill zone. The Shades are trying desperately to break them, and it's working,

To assemble and strengthen their minds, everyone huddles together. "It feels like my skin is getting ripped apart!" someone cries out. Someone else shrieks soon after as a Shade bites and scratches at their skin and soul.

Such an overpowering night combined with the deepest roots of despair—but all it takes is a ray of hope to cleanse it all away.

A spotlight shines down on them from above, piercing through the void and saving them from a dark fate. More heavenly rays of light rain down and perforate the darkness further. The Shades react with their ghastly howls and are forced to scamper away to where the light doesn't blaze them. It all happens like an instantaneous shift from midnight to daybreak.

"Sadra, was that you?" Draxis asks.

"No?" She looks up at the radiant pink glow suspended above them, and she perks up with a bright smile. "It's Komet!"

"Who?"

"Komet, the Living Star. It was our most powerful guardian before the First Night snuffed out its power and forced it into slumber. I wouldn't be alive if it wasn't for Komet helping me with my escape. Maybe hearing and remembering my voice woke it up somehow?" Sadra then jumps up and down while waving her arms.

A geometric crystal, slightly larger than the size of an average human skull, descends in front of them. Its smooth and glasslike appearance shifts into a sunny yellow to match Sadra's positive turnaround.

"My word," Draxis gasps. "A Geshelon crystal? I thought they went extinct from being overhunted?"

Komet's crystalline body darkens into a deep ocean blue.

"Ah, I suppose that was rude of me to bring something like that up. I know the feeling. From a fellow victim of lonesomeness, welcome, Komet. I'm surprised we attracted something with so much brimming light."

The conversation is immediately dropped dead by Komet as it floats over to Jellop and glows a pure snow-white while circling around his head.

"M-Me?" Jellop squeaks. "Why me, little stone of hope?"

"That color you see can sometimes mean that it's detecting captivating power," Sadra says. "It likes you… for some reason."

"You're just jealous that someone here is brighter than you."

"I am not. Go get trampled or something."

"Sadra, is Komet really the Artifact that we need?" Draxis asks.

A portal suddenly manifests behind them.

"And never mind! For once, everything's coming together. We found the Artifact—" He then wraps his fluffy arms around Sadra. "*And* we found our shining star."

"Oh stop it you."

"We should keep this place in mind if this mission of ours succeeds," Maeva suggests. "I would like to restore this capital to what it was before. I bet it was truly something to behold."

"I appreciate the interest, but we should get Komet to a safe spot," Sadra says.

"Wait," Suvius says, with a raised hand. "There's something that I must do."

He walks up to a nearby altar and kneels, with his head down. He stays in that position for a long while, not saying a word. When he is ready to move, he heads straight for the portal. Sadra is standing in his way, as she was already there. He doesn't touch her. He instead walks around her, and leaves.

Sadra squints her eyes in suspicion. "Hey, Komet, don't leave with them yet. Follow me."

She takes Komet over to the altar and crouches down next to it. She finds a few unopened vials of syrupy liquid near the altar's base and takes a few with her as she thinks to herself out loud. "That numbskull. You're supposed to slather some Isilios Sap on your hands *before* a prayer, and then touch all four sides of the altar. But he made an attempt. That… surprised me.

"My friends… they really have seen the Light. I remember those days so vividly, when we used to slay any and all who stood against us. When we declared the world to be our enemy… back when things used to feel brighter than the darkness we face now."

Komet nudges Sadra's face, pushing her along to the shrinking portal.

"Sorry," she says as she starts to move. She returns to her thoughts, internally.

Times have changed. It's time to leave our shadows behind. I wonder what was with Aluna's...? Her own shadow doesn't seem quite ready to leave her alone. Then again, true evil never leaves the wicked...

Chapter 23

Morning

The high tower in the middle of the Arbiter's capital is significantly larger on the inside than it deceptively looks outside. Suvius has spent the early hours of the day messing with durable locks on doors and making sense of the scrambles of faded notes left on the ground.

It truly becomes a good morning when he finds himself in a room that would make every concurrent morning have meaning. There are shelves and rows of copious amounts of scrolls, grimoires, stone tablets and more in a galore of free-to-use knowledge. A library! He doesn't know where to even begin with it all.

There's an enormous wooden table in the center of the round room, and he is treated to a delightful surprise when he sees an uncommon friend reading the thickest book he has ever seen. Suvius claims a seat, a few chairs not too far away from Rend. "Good day, Squire Rend."

"Squire?" Rend huffs. "You're giving me honorifics now?"

"You are entitled to have one. And I wanted to offer *something* as a form of apology for Sadra's disgusting behavior,"

Rend flips to another page in response.

"Don't shelter yourself over Sadra taking advantage of you. I have thoroughly reprimanded her for it—as much as she was willing to put up with."

"It would only matter to me if she came here personally and looked me in the eyes to apologize," Rend says.

"She's not the type to kneel."

"I feel like that could be said about everyone else."

"More or less." Suvius leans forward to get a closer inspection of Rend's book. "I see that you're delving into the Arbiter's Mysticology. Mind if I ask if there's anything that interests you?"

"I'm just absorbing everything as a whole. Don't bother looking too much into it."

"So be it. I have my own studies anyhow." Suvius picks apart an unarranged pile of books in the middle of the table. He scopes out one particular book that is wrapped in velvet and has indecipherable lettering written on it. He doesn't examine the other books any further as he now holds the one that has piqued his interests.

An hour or so passes in silence. It's hardly noticed. Suvius peeks from over his book. His jaw nearly drops as he sees an orb of light bounce up and down on the table.

Rend smiles at the fact that he's gained an audience. "Hey, Suvius, is this what you were trying to do earlier?"

"That's a Skylight! How… It's so flawless and immaculate. Did you learn that just from reading a couple of pages?"

"You look jealous."

"Insolence. I'm struggling to ascertain where exactly your faith and purity lie, it's the primary way to create such a spell of radiance."

"I guess you can say that I'm putting my faith towards other things," Rend responds.

"The only other faith I can think of would be of the occult and sacrilegious kind."

"Not everyone resorts to the worst forms of faith when life gets abusive. I'm not like you."

Suvius slams his book shut. "If you have something to say to me or anyone else, then I suggest you speak."

"I have no quarrels with anyone. My life is too chaotic to maintain grudges—but that's exactly it. I recently realized that this chaos isn't going to be fixed anytime soon… not unless I make it so."

"You're planning on making yourself stronger?" Suvius asks.

"Not just stronger, but better. Reliable. In both of my lives, I have been trampled and dragged along through everyone's bullshit for far too long. I'm tired of being disappointed. My past nightmares were because of someone that ruined my first life with one single decision, and in this one, I'm watching the world itself try to ruin me. There needs to be an end to it."

"So, you choose to go the ways of magic to seek empowerment?"

"Absolutely," Rend says. "I didn't tell Master this, but I think she unlocked something within me when she helped me with my first taste of magic. I know I can do more. You already saw that with that Skylight spell."

"I only see your recklessness," Suvius corrects. "You do realize what the greed for magic is capable of doing to the mind, yes?"

"Again, I'm not like everyone else. I don't care what the Arbiters have done, and I don't care what *you* all have done. My faith and magic lie upon me to show the world some justice, and I'm the one that will make it a reality even if everyone else falls around me."

"You're deranged."

"We're deranged," Rend corrects.

"Mine is different from yours," Suvius says.

"But the feeling is the same, isn't it? You should understand."

"I… I do. But you don't want to accidentally step too far into the realms of madness."

"Are you leading that warning by example?" Rend says sarcastically. "I caught you reading something about Darkness and hearts of Malice earlier. I'm sure that goes against what Klae has told you."

"It does. I'm not saying all this to sound like a hypocrite, mind you. I just want you to take caution and to not let others' failures impact your decision-making."

"If you're going to shove a challenge in my face, then how about making it something less impossible? Listen, Lord Suvius, I don't think you need to worry your bald head about anything. If it really comes down to it where I am no longer myself, then I like to think that *she* would be able to bring me back."

"Such an odd bond you both have," Suvius chuckles. "This discussion has imposed a few challenges, many that my morbid curiosity would like to see the outcomes of their fruition. You're a man with your own path now—but you have been warned to not let it merge or conflict with any existing paths."

"And what if the existing paths start invading mine?" Rend asks.

"Then you better be proactive and become your own best gatekeeper," Suvius then stands and heads for the doors. "May your settled faith guide you in truth, Squire."

Chapter 24

Brittle

"So… you're a dog now?" Klae says to Draxis.

"Werewolf!"

"Ah yes—those things. I forgot what they were called. Werewolves haven't been threatening for quite some time now. I think even Arbiter Kalos had one as a pet."

"Okay, okay, I get it. But remember that these fangs will attack indiscriminately," Draxis remarks.

"Just keep barking at us, I'm sure you'll get us all to quiver eventually."

That gets a chuckle from everyone else.

"Today is a special day," Klae says. "The fruits of your hard labor are finally beginning to show. With the amassing of all this divine and malignant power, we can finally start detecting Artifacts that are higher in rank.

"And as a bonus, we even have two options to choose from today. You all can either go to the highest peaks at Bonamu Glaciers, or you can go locate—and I'm just reading from what these notes say—you can go find something called the Sunken Doll. Apparently, it's one of the few Artifacts that the Arbiters have blacklisted. If you choose to go after that one, then you'll have to take a dive into the unexplored depths of the sea."

"No! Maeva shouts. "No oceans, no lakes, not even a puddle."

"Water bad," Jellop says.

"Such strong reactions…" Klae questions out loud.

"We encountered a survivor and native of the waters before we came here," Draxis says. "She's terrified of her own dwelling, and so are we."

"I hadn't thought of what might be going on beneath the waters. I think I'll have to agree with that complaint. Off to the frigid icescapes it is then."

"From a hot-ass jungle to the freezing cold," Rend groans. "Damn, can't catch a break."

"Can't we find another artifact?" Aluna speaks out.

"Aluna, you can use Ice magic," Sadra says. "You shouldn't even be affected by the cold."

Aluna squirms in place in response.

"And that last Artifact you all found," Klae says. "I wasn't expecting it to be one of the Geshelons. I'm going to have to keep 'Komet' here for the time being. Having an energy producer among us could be absolutely vital for our operation."

Komet glows cherry-red in color.

"Umm… Komet says that it doesn't like that idea," Sadra says on its behalf.

"Oh—sounds like it's worried that I mean to exploit it like the other Arbiters did for its cousins. I'll get Komet up to speed. Just focus on treasure hunting and not dying."

"Yep-yep!"

Chapter 25

Evidence of Screams

In the span of one chaotic minute after exiting the portal, they all touch down on two feet, then they hop on one foot as their combined weight shifts the unstable igneous island beneath them, then they fall down as their balance is lost completely.

"Wahhhh!" most of them shout as they collide and slide into one another as the island tilts from side to side.

"Stop screaming and stabilize yourselves!" Suvius bellows. "Spread out!"

Everyone separates in opposite directions, forming the points of a heptagon.

"There. Equilibrium."

"Did I blink during the briefing?" Draxis asks. "I thought Klae said Bonamu *Glaciers*?"

"We see scenarios like these frequently," Maeva says. "How can you even be surprised anymore?"

"I just want something normal for once. Does anyone know if werewolves are capable of sweating?"

"Irrelevant question. We need to figure out how to climb this… volcano," Suvius says, looking up at the sinister, lava-saturated mountain surrounded by a thick overcast of soot that spreads across the region.

"Aluna, would you mind helping us out here?" Sadra says. "Freeze this lava or something."

"I'm not feeling so good," she responds.

"And yet, you can still fly…"

"There's no need to force her," Rend says. "I'll create a path for us."

Rend touches the ground before him and lets his mind clear. Gusts of cold air escape from the tips of his fingers and spreads across the lava around their island, turning a part of it frozen solid. He then looks back, long enough to see Suvius give him a quick nod of approval. He moves on to continue constructing a bridge for them.

"What a marvel," Draxis says. "I didn't think he was so serious about practicing magic. Have you been teaching him, Maeva?"

"I might have influenced his fascination, although… I know nothing about Ice magic, so I don't even know where he learned that fancy trick from. I can't help but feel like I might have blinked as well. Just not too long ago I was certain that me and him were growing up together. Did I do something wrong?"

"Do you feel like you did something wrong?" Suvius asks her.

That's a difficult question to answer, especially with the scalding heat starting to get to her. "Rend's getting too far ahead," she says, hoping to dodge a demand for an answer. "Let's catch up with him."

They now have a path forward and upward—a clean-cut ramp where every step made feels risky from the brittle ice, not to mention the slippery slope. They distract themselves by trying to piece together the still remains of the unlucky victims around them.

"This is an art show of horror," Sadra says, mourning. "Look at all these petrified natives. I feel bad for them."

"The death toll is becoming unbelievably scary," Draxis says. "Have we seen any major settlements aside from the ones at Vomenn?"

"I don't think we have," Maeva says. "Makes you wonder if there's anyone else left to save in the grand scale of things."

"Maybe some people just can't be helped," Sadra remarks. "Has anyone noticed the way these people are positioned? It doesn't look like that they were running away—it sort of looks like they were going *towards* the eruption instead."

"This group over here is pointing upwards," Rend says. "Something airborne must have terrorized them. Maybe a dragon passed through here on the way to Vomenn?"

"I might have to disagree," Draxis says. "We're too far up north from the battlefield where we found their mass gravesite. I do want to say that if a dragon *was* here then it should have been one of the boreal subspecies, not the volcanic or fire-type ones."

"If I may offer some inquisitive insight as well, the attack here looks to be more calculated than chaotic," Suvius says. "If a dragon attack were true, then I don't think it would focus this hard on the environment instead of the people."

"It could have been multiple dragons," Rend says.

"I do see multiple craters and holes on the volcano's side, but demolishing its integrity would take a massive effort—effort that I don't think a tag-team of undead dragons would have the patience for."

"What difference does all this make?" Aluna gripes. "We're here to retrieve the Artifact, not play inquisitor."

"Can't you have some fun for once?" Maeva says. "You should join in."

"None of this is fun!"

"Geez," Sadra remarks. "I would have figured the senseless calamity here would be a new playground of wonder and excitement for you, little miss 'Harbinger of Disaster'."

Aluna bites her own tongue, stopping herself from saying anything further. Her wings flutter into a flurry of motion, then she speeds ahead.

"You really need to stop taunting her," Draxis says to Sadra.

"There's nothing wrong with prodding things for fun. Besides, I have my own secret investigation that I want to start solving, sooner rather than later."

***

"Okay, seriously, what is even going on here?" Maeva says. "Did the entire town think you could acquire eternal youth from bathing in lava or something?"

"Something special must be at the peak if they went to this length just to try and reach the top," Suvius says.

"I'm more upset that I don't have a soul on me that can fly above this fire hazard like Aluna can," Draxis says. "But what I'm definitely not jealous about is her current standoffish attitude. My Beloved here isn't helping out with that unfortunately."

"Bite me!" Sadra hisses.

"I know you're not saying that figuratively."

"I would give up my peace, even if only temporarily, just to get a glimpse into what Aluna's thinking," Jellop says.

"I know it hurts to watch her act so distant, but we should give her some space," Draxis says. "Who knows what kind of nightmares she's had to endure back at Isilios."

"I can go talk to her to see what's up," Maeva offers. "Unless you think you should go, Jellop?"

"Hey, what did I just say?" Draxis snaps.

"I don't trust my words enough to… speak well, and with the necessary care needed," Jellop says. "I never knew how much I relied on telepathy to cheat socially."

"Take your time with everything," Maeva consoles. "I'll do my best to speak in your stead."

"Can somebody please just listen to me for once!"

Draxis's plea continues to go unheard as Maeva pumps her energy up enough to give off a contagious, cheerful aura and catch up to Aluna. "Hey, Aluna! Slow down!"

"What…?" she responds under a heavy sigh.

"I just wanted to see if you wanted to chat. Or it can wait until we get back to Klae's lair?"

"What could we even possibly talk about?"

"Umm. Boys?"

"Maeva… I know what you're trying to do… but you're only making this harder for me."

"Not as hard as a soldier fighting a gorgon," Maeva responds, waiting impatiently for any positive reaction from Aluna. "Come on, that was funny! You know it was."

"…Just go away," Aluna then flicks one of her hands, constructing a wall of ice that blocks the frozen bridge.

"Totally uncalled for!" Sadra shouts as she and the others finally catch up. "I knew she was lying about her health!"

"No success, Maeva?" Draxis asks.

"There wasn't even a chance," she responds, gloomily.

Rend knocks against the thick wall of ice to judge its density. He lays his hands against it—then, he engulfs them in fire. The wall falls victim to his incendiary touch. "I could really get used to this…" he says as he siphons the cold essence stolen from the melted ice and turns his left hand into a frosty resemblance. He stares at the duality of the elements he wields in both palms.

"Don't get ahead of yourself," Suvius snaps. "Your magic is barely in its infancy. You still need to suckle from the teat that your master provides you. Get out of the way."

"Hey! Don't push him!" Maeva shouts as she shoves Suvius.

"Insufferable wench! How dare you!" he shouts as he retaliates by pushing her back, harder. The conflict escalates into a classic tussle of Ring Out.

"Leave it to those two to have a clash above liquid death," Draxis says, shaking his head. "My bet is on Maeva."

"You're only kidding yourself," Sadra says. "As much as it hurts, I have to bet on Nightmare. He's got the height difference."

Draxis and Sadra bicker some more over their wagers while rooting for their chosen champions.

They're so silly…

Jellop's heart freezes. He knows he didn't just imagine that frail feminine voice that thinks out loud with such sincerity. The things he would do just to tell that little pitiful voice… that he is listening.

Chapter 26

Ashes

It's been an incredible ascent up the volcano, with the time it would have originally taken slashed in half thanks to Rend. The party stands on the rim of the volcano's summit. Looking back, they have a scenic view of what was once a thriving town, now sinking its way towards the territory of lost history. Looking forward, anxiety builds as they are daunted by the gaping caldera that dips farther down than ever anticipated.

Suvius points his gaze at the center of the caldera. Aluna can barely be seen buzzing around a dim light. "Ah, I see Duchess Aluna has already uncovered our treasure. I commend her work ethic. Squire Rend, bring us down, if you will."

***

The only thing that stands between them now: is patience. They take caution not to disturb any of the fragile, petrified remains of the villagers. Touching anything or even causing a small seismic disturbance results in feelings of sickness as the bodies crumble apart and release clouds of cinder and ashes that take up even more of their already-clotted vision from the present airborne soot.

They meet up with Aluna. She is flying over a heavy cube of ice that's covered in hoarfrost. It can be moved or lifted easily by the teamwork of two individuals, but that endeavor might have to be spaced out in intervals due to the Artifact's frigid power attacking their legs to the point of numbness.

"So, this must be what the townspeople were racing towards," Maeva says.

"I told you all that these artifacts were important," Sadra says, haughtily. "I bet all the gems in the world that this ice cube single-handedly made this volcano dormant—and someone tampered with that."

Suvius touches the cube of ice. "We should at least reactivate it," he says. "If we have the means to reverse any damages we come across, then we should do it more often. Would you know how to activate it, Sadra?"

Sadra grabs the opposite end of the block. "These things can be finicky, but this one shouldn't be too bad. Its purpose seems easy enough to figure out, so all you need to do is—"

A small but concentrated beam of magical fire pierces through the ice block, detonating it into a wild snowstorm. Suvius and Sadra both lie on the ground, reeling from the knockback.

Sadra coughs wildly trying to catch her breath and swipes away the cloud of icy dust. Somewhat recovering, she shouts, "T-The Artifact!"

"It wasn't you, Sadra."

She is unsure, but it sounds like Draxis said that. Sadra finds herself alone when the dust finally dissipates. She's surprised no one has rushed to her aid after such a violent explosion—but now, she can clearly see why. She stands and runs over to group up with everyone else.

Suvius is the last to stand—but the first to break the tension. He puts himself in front of everybody, with eyes glued to where everyone else looks. "You missed…" he says, directly to Aluna.

"Did I?" she defends. "I always strike what I want to kill."

"Aluna, seriously, what is going on with you!" Maeva shouts. "We had that thing in the palm of our hands!"

"Shut up!" Aluna cooks up a ball of fire between her hands and hurls it at Maeva.

Suvius intercepts the attack in full with his armor, then he brushes himself off. The others back away from him.

"Aluna!" he roars. "End this nonsense—now!"

Aluna slugs another fireball, directed towards Suvius this time.

Suvius bats the spell away with a quick swipe. He takes action and stomps his way towards her, all while sharing his words of controlled fury. "I was willing to give you the rarest of honors by allowing you a chance at providing an excuse, Aluna, but committing the same sin thrice is just asking for your villainy to be put to death."

"Go die again, old man!"

"Hmph." Suvius activates a symbol on his armor—summoning a black claymore with music notes etched along the front and back of the blade. He aims the hefty sword at Aluna. "The only reason you have the mental illness to speak such bravado is because you think I'm incapable of slaying the skies. You will fall, and you will die with your sins."

"Slaying the skies? Tsk. All you Vomenn knights sound the same. Is that what you *really* want to say right now? …Especially around Draxis?"

"*Enough*!" Suvius then taps a few music notes on his sword in a sequence, lighting them up. The sword sings a melody that harmonizes his bloodlust and wrath into a fighting will.

The battle song plays out and amplifies in accordance with each weighted swing Suvius makes—and whether it's upward thrusts, horizontal arcs, or vertical slashes, every attack launches projectiles made out of physical sound. He does this repeatedly in a berserker's rage as Aluna continues to dodge about and stay unharmed—aside from her hearing.

"You've gone soft, Lord Suvius," Aluna giggles as she dances around his attacks with a mischievous smile. "Such a tragedy for the famous one-knight army; the man that houses the world's arsenal and elites within his very own breast. I'm bored now." She flicks a speck of white dust at him that blossoms into a mystic pattern below his feet.

"Suvius, watch out!" Draxis yells.

It's too late. The space around Suvius detonates in a suffocating cloud of snow. He's frozen, deep inside a thick block of ice. As witnesses, they stand horrified.

Rend charges forward. "Stay back! I can handle her!"

Aluna ponders his intentions. She is surprised even further when her body is smacked with a snowball.

"You got her!" Maeva reacts.

Rend continues to pummel Aluna with an onslaught of snowballs. He is posing more of a threat to her than Suvius was, but it's not enough. She almost wants to tell him off for insulting her with his amateur spells. An idea comes to her as she goes nimble as a means of defense. Aluna summons up two blue orbs in each of her hands and corkscrews their travel as she aims them directly for Maeva.

"Maeva!" Rend shouts, running to push her out of the way. Aluna's spell splits off and homes in—one hitting Rend, and the other half drifting towards Maeva. Two more fatalities.

Jellop comes forward next. He doesn't raise his arms or weapon for battle. "Friend Sadra. Draxis. Forgive me, but I can't…"

"You know this makes you a coward, right?" Sadra bashes.

"You can't force a man to kill his angel," Draxis defends. "We'll make sure Aluna comes back to you—but I can't guarantee it'll be in one piece."

"I am humbled by your consideration," Jellop says. He stands firmly in place while looking up at Aluna. The only thing he says to her is, "Do what you will with me."

Aluna pauses. Longingly. Her next movements are the same as the summoned spell she sends towards him: slow and gentle. It coats Jellop in a speckled mist and leaves him frozen solid when it vanishes. Four down, two to go.

Sadra begins to laugh, soon turning hysterical. "See, I told you I was right, Draxis! All these years I knew it! We should have killed her from the very beginning! I knew I wasn't crazy!"

Draxis ignores her arrogance. His heart still isn't truly ready for his disbeliefs to be wrong. He might never be ready. He has to prevent a worst-case scenario by any means. "Aluna… are you really doing this to us? Even if you always wanted this, why would you choose this day, in the middle of an apocalypse, to betray us? You had over a whole decade to start acting goofy."

Aluna smirks at the sight of Draxis's puppy-dog eyes. "I can't take you seriously when you're like that, Draxis."

His eyes flash with a beast's ferocity. "Would you rather I turn into my true form then?"

Aluna retreats a little, then she returns to an undeterred state. "You nearly got me with that bluff. I don't know why you won't switch forms, unless… whatever. I know you won't do it. Nothing but all bark."

Sadra reacts for Draxis in his stead and shoots out a beam of light from her palms. Aluna dodges it. Sadra then shouts, "Why don't you come down here and say that shit to his face!"

An epic eruption is nigh, until Aluna makes war inevitable with a simple taunt.

"Make me…"

A clash of magical supremacy ensues. It is a dense and heavy conflict rife with old vendettas. While their spectacle is colorful and breathtaking, they are fully concentrated on not underestimating each other. They wield no blades, but everything else about them is sharper than anything ever forged: the dexterity of their single-shot and multi-shot spell summoning, their adaptable maneuverability, and their tight reflexes.

However, they could not have chosen a worst location to sprawl in despite how expansive and intense the battleground is. The unlucky, petrified remains of hundreds crumble against the vibrations and sheer output of the rampaging monsters, and chunks of the igneous ground begin to bleed pus of magma profusely.

Sadra and Aluna could go at it like this for centuries if they were gods. Draxis knows this. He also knows that their pain is also his, so he has to make them stop—it's the only way. He slams his paws down on the heated ground, and full sprints on all fours. He leaps high, and with an arm arching back, he brings it down with a force to cleave winds, declaring that there *will* be retribution and vengeance, even if he has to claw his way through Aluna to achieve that.

Aluna barely misses impending laceration from what might as well be serrated great swords to her in the form of his five vicious claws. Their rage means nothing to her, she knows that hers is stronger. All six of her wings are flexed to their limits, each radiating in a different color.

First, she unleashes Red and Orange, the elegance and fury of Fire. Sadra and Draxis are forced to predict and dodge accordingly as Aluna sends out erratic streams of serpentine fire trails that coil and whip through the air towards them.

Embers burn at the tips on the hairs of Draxis's body. "Damn you, Aluna!" he shouts in an attempt to distract her while he pats down his fur. "Has everything we have done together meant nothing to you?"

"Just keeping up the tradition of having everyone you know betray you at some point, Wolfie," Aluna responds.

"Don't listen to her, Brightheart," Sadra says. "Anyone that's ever betrayed us are just soulless dung piles." Sadra's light begins to shed away, her body transforming into a deep shade of midnight. She is Nocturnal, and her darkness is ravenous. She clenches her fists and says to Aluna, "Come embrace the night, bitch!"

"Are you talking to me or your pet?"

All that response does is make Sadra lick her lips as her adrenaline boils in an elevated rush. She crosses her arms, forming an

X, and fans them outward. All light is purged from a shroud of black miasma that covers the whole caldera. In other words—

"Nightfall!"

Somehow… this darkness feels worse than the one at Isilios. The jungle's darkness only induced nightmares, but this one is a signature of forthcoming death. Aluna, she hears something rushing up behind her, and once again feels the air splitting from a powerful swipe. *Dammit!* She thinks with agitated emotion. She has to apply more pressure, so she switches to the color Yellow, the energizing and golden empowerment of Electricity.

The air crackles with golden-bronze bolts and a heavily charged atmosphere in her proximity. It's keeping the dog away for now, but she still has to find and deal with—

"Argahh!" Aluna shrieks, brought down to the ground by an invisible attack to her face. Her fighting spirit is now halved, just like her vision and accuracy—so she doubles her destruction instead.

She now wields thunder along with her lightning. The volcanic floor splits as she pummels it with electric spears that blast away chunks of molten earth with explosive force, exposing pockets of noxious gas to vent and jet upwards.

A stray toxic blast dashes into Sadra's face, making her holler out in pain. Light returns to the caldera as she's forced to tend to her injuries.

"Aluna, th-this shit isn't funny anymore!" Sadra screams. "Ju-just stop! Look at what's happening! You're going to kill yourself too!"

"Sadra! Get out of there!" Draxis shouts.

Sadra tries, but she can only manage to crawl away. Draxis puts all power into his legs as he tries to reach her in time. As for Aluna, she has ample amounts of time to weave the perfect finishing spell between her fingers, and after a twirl, she throws a lightning javelin right onto Sadra.

In a spiritual sense, the lightning strike chains, zapping Draxis of everything. He only needed a few more seconds… just a few more. He arrives, and picks Sadra up. Her chest is still moving, even if it's shallow. Draxis tucks in his claws and cradles her in his arms as he sits down. He offers himself enough time to wipe the lucent blood that oozes from her open wounds, before clutching his chest and taking deep breaths.

"Don't even bother transforming," Aluna says. "This battle is over."

"All the more reason to go all out," Draxis says. "We're already at the point of no return. That is, if we weren't already there in the first place."

"You're still talking about our fight, right?"

"I don't know anymore. All I do know is that people like you gravitate us towards that edge."

"Since when have I ever made anything better? That's literally antithetical to my titles."

"Titles?" Draxis asks. "You said that in plural."

"That was a slip. But I guess what I say doesn't matter now—if I were to take your words from before to heart."

"Then say what you want and go ahead and finish the job. But please, leave the rest of them alone. Don't deny them the chance of saving lives…"

"Consider them already spared," Aluna states. "In fact, I don't even want anything from them. They have given me everything I could have ever wanted. I do need something from you though now that we're alone."

"What, you want my soul or something? I already said you can take anything from me, even if it's my life," Draxis says.

"How about we flip the deal?" Aluna says. "I never said that you weren't going to get anything out of this. Maybe acquiring even more—if you're hungry enough."

"…I don't like spoiled apples."

"From what I've heard that isn't exactly the case. And even then, that doesn't mean that I can't force you to eat."

"I'd like to see you try, traitor," Draxis says.

"You're still on about that? This goes beyond betrayal. This was always about devastation. It was what I was engineered to do, as a murderer, as a destroyer—as an Arbiter."

His heart is impaled. "You… you're not an Arbiter. You can't be one of them. We killed them together. I watched you liquefy their skulls and dance in their ashes. You're not an Arbiter!"

"I've slain a few, yes, but I have no control over who among us was chosen as a pawn. As much as I hated their ruthless methods, no one can ever deny the expanse of their hundred-layered plans and their roadmap of schemes. This was all planned before it even began. But you could always end it. Go on. Give in—give in to your hunger."

Draxis hyperventilates. His eyes turn bloodshot. He plugs his ears and bites at the air, but Aluna keeps repeating herself, and repeating herself. Sadra rolls off his lap and lands on the ground as he rises.

Aluna ceases her chanting. It's complete, the purple in his eyes says it all. He bolts at her, faster than anything possible by man or monster.

***

Rend has a quarter of his body sticking out of his frozen containment. He can barely move—but he can think, even if it's dulled. With little movement he can perform, he manages to extract and capture the rising heat from the seeping magma and convert it into particles of magical essence. He cooks his body from the inside. The ice is melting, but it feels like his body is too. Thankfully no one is around to smell his burnt flesh. He fans himself to cool off as he looks around.

"My wings!"

Wings...? There's no way he misheard that bloodcurdling scream. *Aluna! I have to stop her!* He wants to stop her, but he can't find her anywhere. He does see poor Sadra out of commission. And there's Draxis… doing nothing? At least they're alive.

Rend rushes over to him and says, "Draxis, is it over? What happened to Aluna? Hey, do you hear me?" The moment Draxis turns around, Rend scrambles backwards, and ends up falling down. He continues distancing himself as he stutters. "Spit… sp-spit her out!" He arms himself with a spell and aims it. "I said spit her out!"

Rend's voice tugs at Draxis—and soon, there's a lump of degrading flesh on the ground. He recognizes that lump. "Rend… I…"

"Stop talking! Just—just stay over there!"

Draxis obeys, giving Rend time to absorb the horror.

"…Focus on sorting yourself out, but don't say or do anything else. Shit…"

Rend travels over to his frozen comrades, taking caution on making sure not to leave his back too exposed. He starts freeing Suvius first.

"—And I will forever haunt your existence until the day you die! Oh? I'm free. Well, my head is at least. You should liberate someone who can put up more of a fight, Squire."

"The only reason I'm saving you first is because you are the closest," Rend says. "Bad joke, I know. I'm just trying to cope. I wish I was exaggerating when I say this, but *some* issues might be worse than we thought."

"An issue worse than Aluna?" Suvius asks.

"It's all horrible. There's no point in comparing."

"It was worth the ask. I'll go assess the damage. Continue as you were."

Rend goes to free Jellop next.

"I feel like a baby yeti being coddled by the snow," Jellop says, merrily. "Do you miss snow, Rend?"

"Snow? I haven't thought about it. Is it that time of year?"

"It nears. This time of year reminds me of Aluna… She likes the snow."

"Ah, is that what this is about?" Rend says.

"Take no offense, I do also want to know more about you. Think of my words as a trident used to kill multiple questions at once."

"After we get out of here, you're welcome to ask me anything whenever you want—or even rummage around inside my head when you get your abilities back. As for Aluna, I wasn't able to get a clear look at her. But I just freed your legs, so…"

"I'll prepare myself for the worst. Thank."

It's Maeva's turn next.

"Nice!" she cheers. "You're such a good slave."

"Not now, Maeva," Rend says.

"Why? What's going on—"

"Butterfly!" Jellop's horrified scream rings out.

"That's what's going on," Rend says. "And, no, I don't know how bad her condition is."

"Well, you're making my condition better at least. Just like you always do," Maeva says.

"What does that mean?"

"I'm not… too sure. I don't even know what compelled me to say that. Just get me out of here before I decide to speak again."

***

"My goodness. Look at them…" Those are the only words Maeva can say as she looks at Aluna's and Sadra's wounded bodies, otherwise she'll be speechless like the others. "How does it come to this? To the point where we're nearly killing each other? And it felt like we were finally beginning to act as one, like a… family almost. Sorry, I'm just thinking out loud." She scoops up an almost-wingless Aluna off the ground. Her hands become stained with her purple blood.

"Her infection is growing out of control," Jellop says. "It might be the reason she went rogue. If we stand idle, she'll become Decayed at this rate."

"I'm *not* allowing that to happen," Maeva says with a bit of bass. "If we lose her then it'll only be a downward spiral from here."

"But she's the one who started that spiral," Rend interjects. "Honestly, I blame Sadra more for pressuring her."

"You're only proving my point. Faulting blame is one of the freefalls of destabilization. Suvius, can we try to get Aluna some help? Maybe Klae can do something."

"I'd rather let her become a free sacrifice for this volcano," he responds.

"Ease up on Maeva," Draxis says. "I'm not trying to vouch for Aluna, but I think she wanted all of this to happen. It's hard for me to trust her words, but I did sense some sincerity behind them."

"I take it that freezing us was also meant to be a part of her sincerity?" Suvius questions. "The only thing she made outspoken was that she's definitely the type of person to go to such extremes— which is why I can't write off that she would use us for some idiotic plot."

"So… can we try to rescue her?" Maeva asks.

"If what Draxis says is true, then we would only be denying her dearest wish if we try to save her. Still, I'm the type that will usurp Death itself against those that still owe me an unpaid debt. Peace will not be granted so easily, not when there's work left to be done and hearts not yet ready to grieve."

"That's a cute way of saying that you won't even allow death to let us leave your side," Maeva says.

"Do not push my generosity."

"So, we're bringing Aluna back? I guess that's neat," Rend says. "As the voice of reason though, we can't even get back to the

Arbiter Capital. Remember that it was because of *her* that we failed our only objective here—"

The ground begins to rumble, violently.

"…And it's also because of her that we're about to get erased by this damn volcano."

"I'm sure we'll get out of this," Maeva assures.

"We probably will. It doesn't make it any less annoying though."

"Shield Aluna properly…" Jellop whimpers. A few muffled sniffles can be heard coming from him afterwards.

"Don't worry," Maeva says. "I have her nestled gently between my hands."

"Don't squish her!"

"Do *you* want to hold her since you won't stop instructing me?"

"I want to, but I'm a mess right now. Be careful where you place your fingers!"

Amid the entropy, Suvius feels something tug at his shoulder. "Ye-yes, Sir Draxis? You startled me."

"Can you carry Sadra for me? I'm not in the right state of mind to be responsible for her."

"You and I both. Whatever happened here, Draxis, I want you to know that no one here blames you. It's better knowing we can live another day rather than knowing how it happened, I think. Also… wipe the blood off your mouth."

A portal appears, interrupting everyone at once.

"Thank everything!" Maeva praises. "Everyone, hurry up! We have to save her before she turns!"

"*If* we can save her," Rend adds.

Chapter 27

Last Resort

Maeva is the first one to exit the portal, stumbling. All while shouting, "Klae! Help us!"

He groans. "How may I be of assistance…?"

"It's Aluna!" Maeva shows Aluna. Scabs of purple gunk have taken residence on parts of her body—and it's not stopping.

"Dear gods… what the hell were you people doing? How did this happen?"

Rend expresses to Draxis the strongest scowl he can possibly make. Draxis makes sure to take it in, before having to look away.

"I-I don't know!" Maeva screams. "She started acting ballistic and she started attacking us a-a-and I don't know! Just please say you can do something!"

"I don't think I can…"

"You have too!"

"I'm looking at her right now!" Klae shouts. "The infection is destroying her body entirely, there's nothing I can do!"

Maeva starts walking in place, nearly in full circles. "Dammit, Draxis! What did you and Sadra even do to her?"

"We defended ourselves properly, obviously. You shouldn't be this distraught over her anyway. She's not our ally. She told me this herself."

"Friend Maeva only speaks with a desire for truth," Jellop says. "Everything isn't as black and white as we keep thinking—there's gray involved too."

"Gray, huh?" Draxis says. "We were just in a life and death scenario, and you want to diagnose the situation as a weird case of colorblindness? Well, don't keep looking at me. Go ahead and try to play as a god and revive her."

Maeva lays Aluna down.

Jellop joins her, crouching on the opposite side from her at Aluna's body. "Allow me to assist," he says. "I don't know what I can do, but I want to be here regardless."

Maeva misses what he says as she is too preoccupied overclocking her brain. She has a couple of ideas that she can attempt, but they're all either too risky or too reliant on what ifs. At the same time, maybe she's been playing it too safe. Maybe it's time to add some 'gray'. Except… No… Now's not the time for thinking of the dreaded past.

"I think there's a chance I can heal her!" she proclaims.

"Heal the girl with what?" Suvius asks. "Necromancy? You might end up expediting her condition, or worse, you'll only guarantee that she is brought back as a mindless Decayed."

"Not with Necromancy—but with my Blood magic. It's time we bring it back!"

Her words bring upon a sinister echo that constricts around everyone's ears and chills their hearts to the core. She has no idea of the looming turmoil she just created.

"Just how far are we going to continue falling?" Draxis says in an uptick of aggression. "You're not really considering bringing *that* back, are you? It can't be done anyway. You had Suvius seal it away forever."

"Only partially," Suvius corrects. "I could barely get her power to cooperate even in that manner."

"I think it's what we need," Maeva says.

"What we need is anything *but*," Suvius corrects again. "Let's say we do entertain your psychotic noise—how would you go about saving her?"

"I've always used my magic to spread and inflict pain… but what if I did the opposite?"

"You plan on draining the girl of everything? Onto yourself? That's…"

"I know what it sounds like but if you really think about it, it's what I've always done. It's what my *magic* does."

"I seldom recall you doing anything of the sort whenever you tried to kill our enemies."

"Because I never tried *saving* anyone," Maeva says. "It's always been carnage after massacre with my magic. Even if there were good intentions."

"We've never been given the choice," Suvius says.

"Well, we have one now, meant for someone that was too afraid to ask for our help. For once, let me not be the monster."

"This persistence… You do realize what it is you are asking me to do, right? If we unleash your powers… we might lose you— for good this time."

"It might be different this time," Maeva says, glancing at Rend. "I have something that should keep my sanity anchored."

Suvius remains silent as he places Sadra down next to Aluna. Maeva is anxious at his stillness. "Come on, Suvius. Do it."

"I wonder if this is how pagans feel when bargaining with a devil…" he murmurs.

"Ah, but who is the devil in this case?" Jellop quizzes.

"Not now, Jellop," Suvius snaps. "Grab my hand, Young Maeva," After she does, he continues speaking. "In order to dissuade your old magic, I needed to apply a restriction around your heart."

"I think I remember you saying that the last time we did this," Maeva says.

"There is a reason. As far as I'm aware, a person's vitality and magic comes from their Soul. You however, your Heart is the source of your vitality. It is unorthodox, similar to how Jellop here has the power of the Mind under his command—when it works. Your soul is almost symbiotic in nature to your heart, hence why I had to spiritually unlink them both, thus restricting your magic. We made this pact together, but only I can dispel it. Are you sure you want your Heart's desires to establish dominance over you again?"

"I am," Maeva states.

Suvius nods. Gripping her hand tighter, he announces a phrase. "Temperance Removal."

Maeva's back arches into a crescent from the sudden reaction that ignites within her. Her heart punches against her chest. Her eyes flush in full with a deep sanguine color. Some of her teeth develop jagged points. Something ravenous is clawing within her. She is an animal—one with an unquenchable thirst.

"What did you all do to Maeva?" Rend says in distress. "She's frothing like a rabid fox."

"She's in an ugly trance," Suvius answers. "But she'll be right as rain once she—"

Maeva sinks her teeth into Suvius's arm and gnaws on it.

Suvius sighs. "I'm sorry you have to see your master this way, Squire Rend. I do request that you remain far away. Her relapse isn't going to be one for the faint of heart."

Suvius picks up Aluna with his free hand and brings her over to Maeva's mouth. Maeva reacts the same way with Aluna as she did with him and pierces the skin of Aluna's arm with her teeth. Restoration soon takes over Aluna completely, breaking away the hardened buildup of plaque and rebuilding her body.

Suvius pulls Aluna away before Maeva gets too carried away. "Are you finished?"

Maeva gives an exaggerated moan of pleasure in response.

"Great… wonderful," Suvius groans. "Now wipe the blood off your mouth. You people are persuading me to start carrying rags. Ridiculous."

"I've… forgotten how… how *tasty* people can be."

"Do you even hear what you're saying? Compose yourself."

Maeva's eyes return back to their normal state, staying red around the iris like before. "Don't worry. I'm here. What was I doing again?"

"Aluna…" Suvius states.

Maeva jolts. "Dammit—right! Did it work?"

Klae steps forward. "I don't get how licking people is supposed to avoid a future autopsy, but we'll see. Let me examine her." Klae raises his eyebrows higher and higher with each finding he comes across. "She looked like a plagued rat only mere seconds ago. Now her wings are so vibrant, and she suffers no physical injuries. She doesn't even have a trace of the infection on her. It's like… it's like she was completely… cured! Maeva, here, bite down on my arm."

"What?"

"Just do it!"

She opens wide—and jams her teeth down right into the gushing rivers in his veins, doing so for less than a minute. Klae sets himself free and flips his arm over to let his open wounds leak out blood onto the ground. After a few drops of violet, his blood turns crimson. "Incredible. Simply incredible! But we have to be absolutely certain of this miracle upon us. Go bite down on Sadra next."

Maeva looks back at Draxis. He gives her a nod of approval. Sadra's arm is impaled not too long after. The moment Sadra is reverted back into her Diurnal and healthy state is the moment Maeva collapses to the ground, shaking her head and muttering to herself. "By the gods, all this time… I was… I was… I was the cure. All this time I was the cure!"

Rend is approaching her, taking small steps not to escalate her panic. "Maeva, talk to me. It's okay."

She jumps back and shrinks herself into a defensive stance. Tears are flooding down her face.

"Maeva, take a moment to breathe and let the emotional stress die down," Draxis says gently.

"**No!**" she roars like she's spitting thunder. "Look at what I could do all this time! If only I wasn't so scared of everything, if only I wasn't so scared of myself! So many people died! I could have saved millions!"

"That's a tall order to claim," Draxis says. "There's no way you could have spread your harmony across the whole world unless you were the sky itself."

"But there were people out there who needed it most! I could have even saved Ceranus! I'm nothing but a monster!" She then bolts out of the room.

"Maeva!" Rend calls out.

"Let her go," Suvius says. "I don't want her in isolation either, but she's not safe to be around in her current state."

"Harbingers!" Klae interrupts. "Direct your attention over here, this is paramount!" He waits on them to make their approach. "I can't say anything without first mentioning that I'm positive Aluna here is going to pull through, though I would strongly recommend extreme convalescence until we can truly ascertain her health condition. But that's not what I want to talk about. I want to know more about that girl. What did you all say that magic of hers was? Blood magic?"

"It's what she calls it," Draxis says. "She's the only person we've ever seen that can do something like it."

"Same here. What does this 'Blood Magic' do?"

"She's sort of like an Elemental if I were to make an analogy. She can sense and manipulate blood—which allows her to harvest it, corrupt it, and spread it around like pestilence. That's a more basic explanation without getting into the gore. We've never seen it work this way in reverse."

"A type of magic that can either drain life… or give life," Klae ponders. "Interesting. What a wonderful development. I wish she didn't leave. I would love to know more about her. She might even be the answer to a question we didn't even know existed."

"Really?" Draxis asks.

"I might be getting ahead of myself, but there is a high possibility. The main issue that's prevalent is that she's only a one-person miracle. If we want to do a global cure-all, then we would still need to collect more power from the Artifacts for such a potent spell."

Suvius casts a spell on Aluna with the wave of his hand that scans her body for him. "Hm. That's what I was afraid of…"

"What did you find?" Klae asks.

"Aluna's constitution is in pristine condition, but her soul is still weak."

"So, body doesn't equal soul?" Rend says.

"I like that equation," Klae comments. "To extend that further, I will say that our Mind, Body, Heart, and more are all stabilized by the irreplaceable foundation of the Soul. Now I fully understand why the darker forms of magic are so frowned upon."

Aluna shortens their conversation with a few dry coughs.

"She's starting to wake up, so give her the situation delicately," Klae says. "I need to go run some laps in my head with some theories. Try not to break anything in the meantime."

Aluna holds her head as sits upright. "I'm alive? Why…?"

"Welcome to the club," Rend says.

"Wha—where am I?"

"One step from hell," Draxis snarls, revealing a few of his claws.

Aluna backs away, accidentally bumping into Jellop.

"You will not hurt her anymore. Otherwise, I will hurt you," Jellop says, raising his staff at the others.

"Fine, I'll let her be—as long as she can convince me otherwise," Draxis says.

"That makes the two of us," Suvius says as he steps forward.

"I wouldn't mind a little payback myself," Rend joins in.

"Impatient bears!" Jellop shouts. "You will not touch her!"

"Jellop, stop. It's okay," Aluna says as she stands up, though she wobbles a bit before gaining her footing.

She has the ordeal of using charisma to rekindle one the most fragile substances in the world: trust, without incurring the wrath of the towering gods in front of her who impatiently wait for the slightest reason to give her their absolute judgment.

She looks them in the eyes as she speaks. "I will not apologize. I know it will be nothing but dust in the wind, but I will say this: I wish you all would have let me die."

"You have that same energy just like from before," Draxis says. "Aluna, I want you to be absolutely honest with me—with us. Have you always wanted this? Did any of us drive you to it? Was it Sadra, perhaps?"

"No matter how frail our bonds become, I would *never, ever*, betray you all… but that was never up to me, it was what *they* imposed upon me. I never wanted to deceive any of you. I would have taken all this to the grave if I could—but here we are.

"Here's my truth!" she begins to announce. "My fate was stripped away from me the moment I was kidnapped from my home. And from there I was brainwashed, abused, and experimented on until I became what you see before you. I am Aluna Quinfall, the

Harbinger of Disaster, a biological weapon… and the Arbiter of Judgment."

"Seriously, what the hell?" Rend says, alarmed. "Hasn't she been with you all for years now? Surely that would have come up in basic conversation. I think this goes beyond colorblindness now."

"Halt," Suvius commands. "Slow it down. Just because she's an Arbiter does not mean she was their equal." He returns his focus back to Aluna. "Now, I don't know the inner workings of those mages and their occult culture, but I know I heard you make some claims about abuse. Tell us about it."

"Let's just say that magic can make anything possible, which also means it is an auspicious boon for the depraved. The most horrific thing they ever did to me was…" Aluna pauses, giving herself a few moments to think on how to say her next sentence. "Before we went into Isilios, we had that discussion about demons and curses. Klae also mentioned how some of the Arbiters studied Demonology and practiced Darkness. Do you see where I'm going with this?"

"That is just barbarism," Suvius remarks. "I can't even imagine what it would mean to be under their servitude. I do not mean to strain you, but if you can, I would like to know more about this Curse. I shall admit, I am afraid for you—a ferocious fighter who is hopeless and bruised to the point of doing the unthinkable. I want to know if there's anything we can do to ease the Curse's debt."

"You are gracious, Lord Suvius, but this is a debt that is insatiable and inescapable. It's practically seared into me. This Curse, its only demand is that I commit the sin of murder—over half a billion to be exact."

Draxis is stunned by her words. "Half a what? That's not even a massacre at that point, that's extinction. No one, not even the Demons, would go so far to satisfy such a cost."

"They knew that. They wanted to ensure that I would serve them until the day they no longer needed me, or I was somehow killed off. Is it bad that I once had a shred of hope of that happening…?"

"Aluna… how many people have you killed?" Rend asks.

"Rude," she snorts. "I don't go around asking about *your* kill tally." She shakes her head, knocking away any undesirable memories that spring up. "So those kraken-fuckers named this curse the Executioner's Pledge. I called it the Devil's Karma."

"A strong method of protest," Suvius says. "I hope you stood by it."

"The beatings were always worth it," Aluna boasts. "This Devil's Karma—I need to kill something, I *have* to kill something—always, otherwise my 'Karma' will begin to degrade overtime. If it dips low enough then I risk reaching a frenzied state, where I will then remain in until I return back to a neutral karmic state. It's happened more times than I can even keep up with. I like to blame it for my… irrational behavior at times."

"You have every right to be the embodiment of wrath," Rend chimes in. "They called you an Arbiter, but you were nothing but a slave. It's all clear to me why you wanted to kill yourself, but could there have been no other alternative?"

"You tell me. I heard you once killed yourself too."

"Unlike you though, I was alone in my suffering."

Aluna shakes her head. "Then we are more alike than you might think. This curse has a commandment: 'Thou will execute those who are judged to be Worthless, but none who are convicted as such, or thyself, shall execute the Judge of the Worthless.' From what I've experienced, anyone can harm me, but there is no one who roams that has lived after wishing death upon me—except for those Worthy."

"Are you saying we are Worthy?" Draxis asks.

"No one is worthy unless they manage to overwhelm my frenzy. I knew at least *one* of you wouldn't fail me."

"So you fucked around with the rules to shape things in your favor, and for what?" Rend says. "I know these guys are efficient at what they do, but to consider having your closest friends try to kill you is too far."

"But there is no hope for me," Aluna says. "I am beyond desperate! I—listen, it's not like I'm with the Harbingers for shits and giggles. Before the apocalypse, there was a chance we could have toppled the Arbiters' reign and killed the ones who placed this curse on me—but again, that was before the apocalypse.

"I've been out here all alone for so long, and it's been nothing but an endless cycle of killing and killing and killing just to prevent myself from succumbing to my frenzy or the Soul Decay. I can't even fathom what would happen if the virus took over my body. Ouch!" she yelps suddenly, running her hands across her chest—mostly near her heart. "I can't talk about this for too much longer. I can feel my psychic bonds becoming agitated."

"So the world itself is your prison," Suvius says. "This wave of destruction we've been seeing, like that village back at Bonamu Glaciers. Am I right to give you the honors?"

"Y-Yes, that disaster event was a result of my frenzy, about a year ago, I think? I've tried so many things to sate this curse and nothing's ever worked. I once tried killing the people of the Vomenn kingdom by destroying their water supply. I thought that would have been a good deed at least because of their history, but just like Cee-Cee—err, Ceranus, they are formidable.

"I also tried taking out the lingering Decayed, but I guess soulless bodies don't account for true murder—fucking oversights. I even tried to sacrifice myself to that Godeater, but this curse just loves to fuck me over!"

"Aluna," Draxis says. "What was with those little comments you made before I… uhh…"

"Before you ended the fight?" Rend interjects.

"Y-Yes, exactly. When you said all that stuff, was that to get me to… react?"

"I might have exaggerated a little," Aluna responds. "But I wasn't wrong when I said that there was something only you could give me: freedom. It would have benefitted you too."

"There is no benefit from betrayal," Draxis says.

"What I mean is that you would have had prevailing justice you never knew you deserved. Just—look over there, at that crystal. Not at Komet, but the larger one that came from the Heaven Plains. Do any of you know what it is? Or what it does?"

Not a clue, they say nonverbally as they shake their heads from side-to-side.

"Figures…" Aluna says after a sigh. "The Arbiters named it The Gift. When activated, it's supposed to only empower the Dragons to unfathomable heights. I think the Arbiters said it was a bestowment from some goddess to help them break free from their enslavement."

"But that never happened," Draxis interjects.

"That's because it was confiscated by the Arbiters once they found it. They always made sure that nothing good ever happened without their say-so."

"So how did it end up at the Heaven Plains?"

"My guess is that something went wrong when they were transporting it, and so they had to request help from some of the kingdoms nearby to make sure it arrived on time per behest of the Elite Arbiters."

"Well that's comical, because that would mean the kingdoms brought in their enslaved dragons to help guarantee protection."

"Oh shit," Aluna gasps. "You're right! That makes sense because if the dragons came into the vicinity of the Artifact… then they became invigorated from its power and used it to fight back!"

"Which caused a panic and forced the armies to summon reinforcements," Draxis says.

"The dragons must have done the same thing."

"This had to have happened near the dawn of Blighted Day," Draxis adds. "Otherwise, the Vomenn kingdom would have intervened directly and easily claimed a victory for Humanity—not to give them any praise."

"Agreed," Aluna says. "And even though I hate being associated with the Arbiters, once I found out about the war's history and aftermath, I felt it was my responsibility to keep checking up on the damn thing to ensure it stayed there. I couldn't really figure out what else to do with it. But who would have thought that the last dragon in the entire world would just so happen to reactivate it and resurrect the wrath of a condemned race and nearly cause a second apocalypse. Just my luck…"

"I wouldn't say you have all the worst luck," Draxis says. "Your near-death experience allowed Maeva to bring out her hidden potential in full bloom, making her invaluable to the world's future."

"Maeva? What does she have to do with me?" Aluna asks.

"Check your arm," Suvius says.

Aluna glances down, seeing the holes that spread across her arm. "You dumbasses! Why would you let her do this! Do you all know how dangerous she is now?"

"She chose this despite knowing the risks," Draxis says.

"But I don't like hearing that she would willingly jeopardize her health just for me. She shouldn't have done that! I don't give a damn how badly she would have missed me!"

"Eehhh, I'm sure she was also thinking about us. We're too hard-headed to admit that we would be screwed if we lost you. And I can't tell you how happy I am to know that you didn't try to kill us out of repressed anger for always calling you a flea. Overall, it's better knowing you can live for another day rather than complaining about how it happened. It's a weird quote I've learned recently, from a weirder person." Draxis overhears the low rumble of a groan next to him right after he says that.

"I still don't agree, but it does sound awesome to be the first of the Cured," Aluna says. "I couldn't ask for anything more."

"Cured—until reinfection happens," Klae says as he approaches.

"Wait… what?"

"Maeva can heal, but it's only temporary. There's still an extinction event going on out there."

"Nobody asked for your negative outlook, you fiend," Jellop complains.

"Jellop…?" Aluna says. He's been so silent that she's forgotten his presence. He starts sliding his hood down.

"Unholy shit, what is that?" Klae says, trying to swallow back his own nausea.

"Maeva's the best at explaining his circumstance," Rend says.

"I'm going back over there. Gods, you people are ugly on the inside and even uglier on the outside."

Ignoring Klae, Jellop says, "I want to share a story, if you all don't mind."

"Well this is a rare treat," Draxis says, giving a warm smile. "By all means, go ahead."

Jellop takes a deep breath—then starts. "Long ago, there was a winged woman that descended upon this world when we needed her the most. She didn't know that at the time, but that was because her torturers had placed a terrible, terrible, fragment of their evil onto her purity. But little did those torturers know that what they unleashed upon the world wasn't a weapon, but an angel.

"That angel, despite claiming to be no better than her tormentors, never did truly pay attention to all the good she's created— but the friends she made along the way always saw what she has done. Eventually, that good was overcome by the torturers' unstoppable evil that bleeds across the world and damned it to the point of no return. And soon, the angel was damned as well."

Jellop slides over closer to Aluna, never breaking his flow.

"But after finally finding a miracle of peace she begged relentlessly for the world to give her, through honesty and friendship and perhaps even love, it all became clear that she wasn't really an angel, but a phoenix. All phoenixes rise above what makes them weak, what prevents them from finding their true form.

"I know it feels awful, the weight of your agony, but you should realize that while ashes may always fall, once we remember that we are all born with wings, then we can all take flight and rise high, becoming unbeatable towards our ascension. I like phoenixes just as much as I like butterflies."

Jellop lends Aluna his left hand, and she accepts his gesture. It feels like he has his hand dipped into a planet's creation the tremors that ripple out from her heaving and beating chest are so seismic. He lets her hold onto his hand for as long as she has the strength to.

Rend tugs at his own clothes. "Wow… it's getting really hot in here."

"I'm glad Sadra isn't awake," Draxis says in relief. "She can get swooned fairly easily."

"I hope Aluna realizes that her actions will not be forgotten," Suvius says.

"The only thing more dead than this world are your emotions. Let the girl be happy for once you monster!"

"He's just grumpy that he took a major loss against her," Rend snarks.

"To hell with you two," Suvius says. "Seriously."

Chapter 28

Bittersweet

Rend pops in from another room, entering into the main room where most of the magic usually happens—figuratively anyway. He is forced to slink back and cower behind the room's threshold as he spies on Sadra and Aluna.

He doesn't mind one or the other, but it would be better if it wasn't both of them at the same time, or if there was a third party to offset their heckling tendencies—and no, he's not going to be that third party. From what he's overhearing, it might be safer to hang back for his own survival.

"I can't believe you!" Sadra screams. "Curse or no curse, you're a fucking monster! If you wanted to die so badly then why the hell did you fight like your life depended on it?"

"If I was going to die then I wanted to make sure to take you down screaming with me," Aluna says. "Anyone else's death would have been collateral damage."

"I… can't really dispute that, I would have done the same. You still disgust me."

"I disgust myself."

"Don't… say things like that. I don't want to be held responsible for your depression."

"You might as well get used to it. It's going to be like this for quite some time. I know Suvius isn't going to let me off so easily, just like you're not. And then there's the growing risk of me going into a frenzy again. I just don't know what to do."

"It be like that sometimes. Here, why don't you try looking out the window?" Sadra says.

"I mean, am I supposed to be looking for something?" Aluna asks.

"Yeah, something metaphorical. I read this book once that was written by the Great Wanderer Reshod, and he made a quote that said: 'An open door can still close, but an open window will always remain open.'"

"Uh-huh… He sounded high," Aluna says.

"Probably. But still—interpret it."

"I guess… freedom? I see it as a feeling of being relieved now that I can be honest with everyone from this point forward. But I am still burdened by my curse, so that quote doesn't even truly apply to me."

"Well, we're doing all we can to purify the world," Sadra says. "If we get to the point where we can finally do that super-cool mega spell, then maybe we can add you onto the dispelling list as well?"

"I don't know. You all shouldn't waste your magic on me."

"We already did technically. Was that too soon?"

"Waaay too soon," Aluna says.

"My fault. Let's start over. How are your wings?"

"My babies feel great. Maeva is one hell of a nurse."

"You also should also be thanking Malphunnos that you were spared. If you didn't get that one stupid shot in and knocked me out, then I totally would have blasted your ass to smithereens."

"Well that reconciliation didn't last long at all…" Aluna groans. "Sadra, I really don't care. I can't fathom why you're going after this so hard."

"Because you embarrassed me in front of my boyfriend!"

"But you embarrass yourself in front of him all the time."

"N-No I don't!" Sadra says.

"Yes you do."

"No I don't!"

"You call him that shitty nickname," Aluna says.

"He likes it. You're just jealous because it's sexier than yours. Jellop names you after a bug."

"*Insect*. There's a difference."

"No there isn't," Sadra remarks. "They're all as annoying as krakens."

"Are you trying to call me annoying?" Aluna huffs.

"I mean, why else do people swat at you?"

"Listen, we can tussle at any time."

Sadra massages her fist. "If you say things like that then I might get a little thirsty for some blood…"

Rend is enjoying eavesdropping on their riveting 'girl talk', if he can call it that, but he's going to have to stop this before fires arise. He barges into the room, saying, "Priestess Sadra. Duchess Aluna."

"Who gave you permission to use our honorifics, slave?" Aluna says.

"Yeah!" Sada tags in.

"I'm not having you two gang up on me just because the others are gone," Rend says.

"Oh? You think you stop us?" Aluna says.

"Yeah!" Sadra tags in again.

"For your sakes, he better," Klae interrupts from across the room. "But if he fails and I have to stop what I'm doing to become a pacifier, then count your lives as forfeit."

"Nobody's scared of you, old man," Sadra taunts.

"Nobody is afraid of me because there is nobody left around to fear me."

That sends a heavy chill down Aluna's spine. "You sound just like an Arbiter—like one of the Elites."

"I *was* training under one," Klae says. "You remember Mixon, don't you?"

"Don't bring up his name… please. It's bad enough that I can't forget him."

"He was indeed a man of impressions, but we can afford a breath knowing that he's finally gone. Now how about you idiots stop fighting for three seconds and get over here."

They meetup with Klae at a classic witch's cauldron that he's been messing with. Something is a brewin' and bubbling inside of its metallic belly. The lack of animal guts and maniacal cackling throws off their guesses as to what he's cooking up.

"What do you want?" Aluna says with impatience.

"May I interest you all in some candy?" Klae asks.

"Are you offering us drugs?" Rend says.

"No, that's Dark alchemy. This is the good kind—the tender kind. Magic can be fun, but have any of you seen the wonders it can do when merged with culinary arts? If you take a gemstone, any gemstone, and put it into a mixture filled with transmutation powder, a small cup of Slime Monster extract for texture, a few solid bolts of Living Lighting for boosted flavor, and add top it all off with a little bit of Lunar sugar…"

Klae stops himself, eagerly waiting for the bubbles to die down. Once the concoction solidifies, it crumbles apart into a buffet of bite-sized delicacies that are too miniature and colorful to not let the inner child within them take control. "You get candy! Anyone want to try some?"

"Me!" Sadra says, quickly pinching a nugget or two between her fingers and licking them. The taste makes her mouth pucker fiercely. "Ohh, damn. This is s-s-sour."

Aluna grabs hold of a milky-blue one and chomps into it. She drops it as she screams out, "Brain freeze!"

Klae gives a guttural laugh. "In my opinion, this is what Mysticology should have been used for. Talk about lost opportunities."

"Gods," Rend says in ecstasy. "When was the last time I had some candy? Can I have some more?"

"Of course. Grandpa Klae always provides."

"Is that what you're calling yourself now?"

"I probably shouldn't. I think I would cringe into a singularity if any of you started saying it."

"Thanks, Grandpa Klae!" Sadra shouts.

"Go to hell, Sadra."

"Which one? I like this one more because of the free stuff!" She scoops up a small pile of candy and shoves them into her mouth. "I should get some for Brightheart," she mumbles. "Or… maybe it'll just be his loss."

"Aren't you going to get some more, Rend?" Aluna asks.

"I'm only going to grab two more. One for me, and another for Master. I know how much you like sweets, so have at it."

She smiles. "I appreciate it, but you know I'm small. I can't have all of it."

"Ever heard of leftovers? By the way, do any of you know where Maeva is? Or anyone else for that matter?"

"Jellop's out looking for her himself," Sadra says, still with a mouth full of candy "I told him that he's only wasting his time since this island is so large. The rest of the boys are having their long-awaited alone time together."

"You… might want to change the way you said that," Rend says.

"Nope. It's kinda hot now that I think about it."

"I don't even know how that would work," Aluna says.

"Well… didn't Suvius spend some 'quality time' with the Queen?" Rend says. "I can take a few guesses on how his dexterity might be… resourceful, in the act."

"No way, he actually got to fool around with her?" Sadra says in awe. "Then does that mean she stopped being a dumbass and finally saw things from our perspective? Damn, I missed a lot of the action."

"They would kill us if they overheard us talking about them like this," Aluna says.

"Draxis nearly killed you," Sadra remarks. "Dammit, I did it again! Reconciliation is hard. I quit."

"But you barely started," Rend says." Keep trying."

"I don't need your encouragement," she responds.

"What you *do* need is to check that attitude."

"Go away before I wipe out your existence with a light beam."

"Fair enough. Klae, take care of these two for me. See ya."

"…Huh?"

Sadra and Aluna both look at Klae, with a mischievous fire in their eyes.

"P-Please have mercy, ladies. I… I'll make you some more candy if you behave?"

"We don't want a sugar daddy," Aluna says. "Especially an old one."

"Yeah!" Sadra tags in.

"Rend! Come back!" Klae shouts.

***

Maeva sits idle at the edge of the island's shoreline. *There she is...* Rend thinks, applauding that his intuition was correct. Now he's wondering how to approach her, and if he should even disturb her. He doesn't even know why he's debating it, of course he's going to bother her.

"It's a beautiful day at Hell's beach," he says to her. "You shouldn't be so worked up."

"Why did you even bother to look for me?" she asks after a strong pause. "Don't you know what I am? What I can do to you?"

"That's not even a concern of mine. I just wanted to make sure you didn't end up reenacting what I did at the end of my first life."

"I'm tired of your jokes," Maeva says.

"I'm tired of your sulking—so that makes us even."

"Rend, you saw what I did. So why won't you leave me alone?"

"I've seen worse. And I think you're overreacting."

"I'm not overreacting."

Rend sits down and exposes one of his arms in front of her. "Then show me what you can do. I want to see it up close and personal."

She turns her head away in refusal.

"In a way, Maeva, I think any fear I could have would be remedied if you show me your true self. I want to understand the person that I'm serving."

That loosens up her mood. She's convinced enough to grab hold and gently thrust her teeth right into the veins of his arm.

"Yep, this feels weird," Rend says. "But… you do look pretty hot sucking on me like that."

Her teeth become invisible as she amps up the pressure to drive them in further.

"Ouch! Shit! I deserve that… Hey, stop for a minute. I want to check something."

She's puzzled as to what could be so urgent to interrupt her feast, but then she realizes what she's been drinking. "This is bad… you're infected too."

"I've been traveling with carriers of the virus and inhaling this stuff wherever we go. It was bound to happen. Lucky for me, I'm also walking around with the cure itself."

"What good is being a cure though if it's only temporary?" Maeva says.

"That's why we're going to make it permanent. We can't do that without you."

"I wish that you could, or that there was some other way."

"You can't help what you are," Rend says.

"If I choose to believe that—then can I have some more of your blood? Pretty please?"

"You're acting like Draxis."

"Food is… going to be hard to come by," Maeva says. "I can relate to his struggle."

"But let's not resort to cannibalism, yeah? I'll let you munch on me for now."

"Thanks for being my enabler."

"…You're going to make me do this a lot, aren't you?"

"Mmhmm," she merrily hums while licking her bloodied lips.

"Maeva, I want to cheer you up, but I won't sit here and lie and say that I'm not… apprehensive about you. I'm surprised that Suvius would be so willing to limit you when here I thought that you all sought to be unrivaled. What's that about?"

"Try to think about what happens when someone is unrivaled among the unrivaled. This foul magic has destroyed my life and so many others, probably even more so before I was a prisoner. It's who I am."

"I know you spoke about dungeons before. Were you really a prisoner once upon a time?" he asks.

"In the technical sense, but it's nothing more than a generous word for how I was treated. The wardens called me Prisoner Zero. I was confined to my own fetid cell deep within the forgotten dungeons of Gravefall Penitentiary, a nightmarish place where the world banished their worst of the worst to rot with no remembrance. The reasons why I was held there are faint, and the reasons how are even fainter—just like the when. My mind becomes a void whenever I think back past a certain point in my life."

"Did the others break you out?" Rend asks.

"Them? They helped tremendously, but it was *I* who broke myself out with ease once I got my power rolling."

"When you say it like that, it keeps reminding me of the odd comments made by everyone else."

"Would those 'comments' happen to involve the word 'monster'?" Maeva says. "There's no need to dodge the word for my sake. It's a fallback term made by friends and foes alike, and myself as well."

"Is it because of something you did? Or is it because of what you can do?"

"Yes," she answers.

"I hate how that's a valid response," Rend says.

"I should give that answer more flexibility now that I've discovered that my magic is no longer purely meant for slaughter. Maybe I should have looked at it from a different perspective, kind of like how you do with your second life. You're taking what has been given to you and turning it into something that I or no one else can keep up with."

"I'm sorry if you think that I'm leaving you behind. I had an epiphany recently that made me want to pursue…"

"Independence?" Maeva finishes for him. "It's okay to say it. I would rather you detach yourself from me anyway."

"You're getting ahead of yourself. I value you. I don't think my mind would be here right now if you weren't here to… I guess be my light."

"Light? I think that's the first time I've been called that," Maeva says.

"I mean it. You pieced me back together when Isilios broke me."

"It wasn't the greatest feeling watching you suffer like that, I had to do something. May I ask you about your Nightmare? You accidentally called me… someone important to you."

Rend tenses up. "You can ask… but don't go too far. It's still a fresh memory I was forced to remember."

"I'll take caution. Are you stricken with mother issues?" she asks.

"You could have said that in any other way."

"It still will have the same impact if I say it any other way."

"That's another valid response…" Rend says.

"You were going back and forth with your mother in your dreams," Maeva continues. "Archias. I don't think I ever heard of such a name."

"I greatly prefer Rend."

"But would you mind if I called you by your real name though?"

"It'll be worth a try if you want to risk it. Just don't say it in front of the others."

"I know for sure Sadra wouldn't care for your wish if she got ahold of your true name," Maeva says. "Has she apologized to you yet?"

"Maybe in her own way? It's hard to tell with her," Rend says.

"Don't take it personally. She has a very sore spot for the undead."

"Do you think I could turn that into a soft spot?"

"I'm not saying this to deter you, but I think you're the one that's going to turn into jelly before she softens up. While it is unfortunate what the Dark element does to her psyche, I can never deny how tough it makes her."

"More like abusive," Rend argues.

"Assertive," Maeva argues back.

"Take out all the letters after the final S. Oh! I nearly forgot. Sweets!" He fishes through his pockets and reels out two little morsels. "Do you want some candy?"

"Candy? Where'd you get that?"

"Klae made some."

Maeva picks one up and slides it back and forth between her fingers. "Is this what candy looks like? I never had any before."

"Say what? How are you even alive right now?"

"I wonder that myself." She pops the candy piece into her mouth. "Goodness, this one has some strong spice to it—reminds me of stew. Do you have more?"

"If you come back to us, I do. That's if everyone hasn't vacuumed up the rest."

"Then you have a deal. You know, I think you pamper me too much, but I do thank you, Archias."

"Nope…" Rend says as he shakes his head. "Don't like it."

"It was worth a try."

Chapter 29

Enjoy it While it Lasts

"Rise and shine, Harbingers!" Klae yells.

"Damn you're loud…" Aluna groans.

"He's one of those elderly early bird types," Sadra says. "And he's elderly."

"Don't say it twice!" Klae says. "You people make me sick. You can't just lounge around and do nothing!"

"You told us we could," Rend says.

"Only until we make sure Aluna is stable and nothing else goes topsy-turvy. How many days do you all need?"

"All of them," Maeva says.

"I swear, only you all can find comfort during an apocalypse. There's more work ahead us now than ever before because you all can't even do one simple fetch quest without fucking something up. Are any of you listening?"

"I'm sure one of us is," Sadra says. "Keep going. Don't stop. But don't go too fast."

Klae activates the world map. "To whoever's listening, just know that this next Artifact is a Cursed one judging from how much magic power it's putting out. It's in Murgosh—the sister continent next to Excerina. Looks like it's somewhere deep in the extreme weather-battered lands of the Wania Swamps."

"Water isn't good for my wings," Aluna says.

"I don't care. You deserve it. Thankfully Komet here provided some extra juice to help me find this next artifact that *will* be recovered no matter what and *will* be hand-delivered to me personally with a bonus of rainbows and smiles. Now say thank you to Komet for preventing me from killing you out of rage."

"Thanks, Komet…"

Lying on the ground next to Sadra, Komet barely responds to everything by radiating a dim glow.

"If you all are lucky, you might be able to find some help locating the Artifact at the northern half of the swamp," Klae says. "I've heard tales of a group of survivors being able to—"

A jarring alarm sounds its high-pitched warning through the center machine, bringing everyone to their feet. A swirling mass overtakes the old markers on the world map, blocking out most of Wania.

"Okayyy… change of plans. Go investigate whatever the hell that is."

"Any guesses on what that could be?" Draxis asks.

"Something that wants to be found would be my guess," Klae says. "A surge of power that great doesn't just manifest out of nowhere—well, not without reason anyway. Depending on what you find at that new location of interest, I guess you can just proceed to the Artifact if nothing goes wrong. It's all in the same direction."

"This won't kill us, will it?" Rend asks.

"Don't worry, Komet and I will be here on standby."

Komet projects an image made out of split beams of light above its top half like a hologram, forming a cute smiling face.

"See, it's even been learning some new tricks under my guidance," Klae says.

"Komet could already do that," Sadra says. "You're nothing special."

"I cannot stand you. You remind me of a female werewolf."

"I don't get it."

"It's nothing…"

Chapter 30

Divine Intervention

"So what's our plan of action?" Rend asks Suvius.

"For those of us that were present during the misadventures in Evergreen Forest, we'll do the same thing here. Watch for shadows behind the trees. Vigilance along with diligence—minus the elves."

"This rain isn't going to help with that," Rend says as he shields himself.

"Or this infested water," Maeva adds. "I don't even want to think about what we're stepping in."

"Sadra, dear," Draxis calls out to her. "Could you give us some light?"

"Yep-yep!"

"Remember, everyone: unwavering attention," Suvius says.

***

"I've been holding my tongue on this, but there's still no sign of anything abnormal," Aluna says.

"I consider that to be good," Jellop states.

"I bet Klae made a mistake with that stupid machine," Sadra says.

"I think that's a good thing as well," Maeva says. "I was secretly praying that we weren't going to encounter some majestic beast or something."

"Well... I wouldn't necessarily call myself a beast, but I'll accept being called majestic!"

They all stop in place.

"Um, which one of you said that?" Draxis asks.

"I did."

"There it is again," Draxis says. "It's coming from the trees."

Sadra madly whips around her torched-up hand like a flashlight, still not finding a face to the voice that still pushes on with its verbal attack.

"The Lich. The Eclipse. The Chaos Twins. The World Eater. The Lifestealer, and an undefined Revenant. I've been waiting for this moment…"

The voice is found. All light and eyes fixate on the man perched on a tree. He returns the warranted exposure by flashing his garb that gives off an executioner's intimidation. It is as dismal as a starless night, with a few threads and stitching of gold that brightens that starless night, even if faded.

"You found me!" the man says in a childlike manner. "Congrats…"

"State your business with us!" Suvius says.

"I've already made an appointment. You all should have been expecting me—Malphunnos—the God of Death."

"Imposter! You're nothing but an imp that blasphemes his image!"

"Suvius, I'm hurt—I really am. You should recognize me. Weren't you the one who shed away his humanity in exchange for a taste of my power? I don't do that for just anyone you know."

"I have no reason to believe you. I was resurrected by my own will and my will alone!"

"Only a son of mine would be so defiant."

"Enough!" As fast as Suvius says that, two claymores are clutched in his hands. He points one directly at his opponent. "Have at you!"

"How about no?" Rend rejects. "If he really is the God of Death then he can just make us explode with his thoughts or something."

"I don't fear death," Suvius says.

"Well you shouldn't mock it either."

"You're startled by nothing but his false words. Just standby."

"Oh? You wish to duel me?" the man veiled in mystery eagerly says as he hops down to the ground. "Normally I would meet this with a minute of laughter and halving the opponent's lifespan, but I'll make an exception for my favorite follower. Don't disappoint me."

Suvius crosses his swords together in front of himself, forming a plus-sign.

"What am I looking at? Are you allowing me to go first? "

"This stance could mean anything," Suvius says. "Try me."

"Well that's a confusing invitation if I ever did see one. Guess I'll just do what I do best…"

The stranger starts moseying his way towards Suvius, with no weapons in his sleeves and no alteration in his movement—just a wide and bewitching grin. It's keeping Suvius on ultra-high alert.

"I'm getting closeeerrrr…" the man sings.

What a useless scare tactic. Nothing will deter Suvius, for he has already succeeded in manipulating the fight in his favor by initiating the bait. Now all that's needed is the final execution. He just needs to wait a few more seconds… *Now!*

Suvius makes his move, coming in hot with a forward swing after another forward swing and mixing them with wide, swift, and even wider arcs—a brutal technique meant to obliterate whoever dares to enter his close range.

Cheekily, the man smirks, and before it's even realized, he's reaching around from behind Suvius. The sleek curve of a perfect crescent comes into Suvius's view and presses against the ridges of his bony gullet.

"What's this around your neck?" the man says playfully. "Ooh, it's a sickle!"

"Urk!" Suvius cries out.

"Don't get so flustered. I won't end this bonding session so soon." He then removes the sickle, easing the tight space between life and death for Suvius. "Go on, be free!"

"Don't toy with me!" Suvius bellows. He whips his body around, bringing the weight of both swords with him. It's a direct hit—right into a trap. His blades are snagged inside the open curve of his opponent's sickle.

"My, this strength…" the man says calmly. "Not once have you ever made me regret transforming you into a monster among men, but you disregard one crucial detail: I'm the one who created the monster." He finishes his remark of triumph by cleaving through both of Suvius's blades with flawless effort.

Suvius is rendered paralyzed as he sees the pieces of metal scatter like dancing petals all around him and evaporate into ghostly dust and mist when they touch the ground.

"Oh, that's right! I forgot that the weapons you wield are manifestations of enslaved souls. I wonder how many of those you lost during battle. Have you even bothered to count?"

Suvius *is* bothered—but he isn't finished. He pulls out another deadly instrument—a dense war hammer meant for pure pulverizing.

"Suvius, seriously, I'm the Father of Necromancy! I know of every trick you can pull yet you still wish to go?" the mystery man argues, soon having to dodge every sluggish swing of Suvius's hammer. "See, look at you. You're fighting like a drunken barbarian now," he says under thick agitation. "I'm no god of war, but even I can sense the wild desperation from a cornered rat!"

The man then catches Suvius's swinging hammer at its head with one hand, and crushes into smithereens between his fingers. "Am I going to have to embarrass you further or are you finally recognizing your place? Go ahead. Say it!"

Suvius lowers himself to the ground to regain his strength, weighing his options thoroughly. "I declare… my defeat."

"Thought so. It only took a couple of hits to make you kneel. No fanatic of mine should be this weak—or maybe you've just gone soft."

"How dare you!" Maeva shouts.

"Take your rest, Suvius," Draxis says, with the others standing by him with their best spells armed and ready. "We'll take him down."

"You will not," Suvius says. "Stand down."

"But he can't take down all of us."

"I don't want *any* of you to be taken down—period."

Malphunnos lowers his weapon, and his guard. "Unwilling to finish a fight you started?" he says in a disappointed tone. "By my name, what a pitiful state you all are in. I'm glad that we have something in common."

"What would a god and a couple of mortals have in common?" Rend asks.

"Paradoxically: mortality. Ignore my godhood for a moment and look at me. Try to make a concentrated guess as to why I would even be down here. It should be obvious."

"To actually do your job properly and kill the Decayed?"

"…That's really funny. In the old world my power could have been considered that absolute, but as you already know, souls do matter—a lot. These lifeless beings that roam—I can barely track them, I can't control them, and I sure as hell cannot take the risk of having them infect me further."

"We take that risk with every moment of our lives," Draxis says.

"I know you all do. I've been observing periodically for quite some time now. It's all been very inspirational."

"So what changed your mindset? Really?" Maeva says. "Because everything has been going to shit since our team's origin— and now you want to show your face? It's too late to help. The whole world is on the verge of giving up! No matter how much devotion and faith people put in, they still end up dead with their unanswered hopes and prayers clutched in their bloody hands—!"

"Stop, don't go any further," Malphunnos interrupts. "Limitations and laws. We have those just like you mortals do—divine ones—and breaking said laws has and always will lead to calamity.

The Gods *did* hear your myriad of prayers, but the sole reason no one answers those prayers is because there isn't anyone left that *can* answer them."

"Surely there are other gods out there who are still alive, and some might be doing the same thing you're doing," Aluna says.

"And I wish they didn't. Or hadn't. This is the second time in history where the Gods chose to break Divine Law to prevent chaos, and because of that… Have you all ever sat down and thought about why everything is so screwed up? The oceans bleed red because the Water gods aren't here to purify it. The Sun is gone because the Celestial gods aren't here to call down its life-bringing radiance. Even the crimson skies, none of the Sky gods are here to cleanse the saturated stains of Immortal blood. As far as I know, I'm the last one to remain standing."

"The Gods have fallen," Suvius states. "To think that this pandemic can even reach the inaccessible realm of Birthplace. What about other higher beings? Does this chaos extend to the domain of the Demons?"

"As much as it pains me to say, the demons of Hell were smarter than us," Malphunnos says. "They have shut off all ingress and egress to their realm. Dare I say that it makes me want to go to Hell itself for protection."

"Me too…" Sadra says.

"Well, there has to be *some* god out there still unaffected?" Maeva says. "Time itself still functions, right? Winter still passes yearly. Umm… maybe even the Trickster gods?"

"Trickster gods?" Malphunnos scoffs. "Now you're just grasping at anything. You all have no idea just how fragile the global situation is."

"So why are you taking the risk of infection?" Draxis asks.

"Because contrary to what you mortals believe me to be, I'm actually a really nice guy, and I want to reverse this apocalypse just as badly as you all do. I know, I know, it's ironic for the God of Death to try and restore life."

"Where is Life?" Suvius asks. "Your counterpart. Can she do something about this?"

"Narisa… I wouldn't know if she could. I've lost hope that I will ever find her. It's like she's vanished off the face of the planet…"

"M-Mal…?" Rend whimpers. "You've stopped talking."

"Don't give me nicknames," Malphunnos growls.

"If you're planning on joining us then you're getting a nick-name."

"You're lucky that I'm so desperate. I do also owe you all my life, so there's that as well."

"What did we do?" Aluna asks.

"You know that Godeater that you all killed? Well, let's just say that because of your little 'distractions', I wasn't devoured on that day. Now, let's get to being heroes, shall we?"

"I feel like you're going to leech off of what we've already done," Sadra says.

"Not true. Not true at all," Malphunnos brushes off. "But hey, at least I am here. That has to account for something?" Before taking off, he catches a glimpse of the ebony item attached to Maeva's arm and moves closer to confirm his thoughts. "What in the… Hold on… is that my gauntlet?"

"Y-Yours?" Maeva whimpers.

"Yes. Mine. Why do you have it?"

"I found it underneath Mount Everstone."

"Is that where I left it? I'm telling you, the gods of debauchery really knew how to party. Drunken out of my mind I was. You do realize you're going to have to give it back?"

"I can't," she says.

"Mmhmm. Why is that?"

"It's grafted to me."

"Of course. Well—" Malphunnos starts to say, pausing as he raises his sickle overhead. "Hold still…"

Maeva retreats, shouting, "Hey!"

"Oh come now, you don't even know what that thing does. It's worthless to you," Malphunnos says.

"You're worthless!"

"Thanks for that come back, but I still want what's mine!"

"Why is it so important to you? You never even kept up with it."

"It's not *the* most valuable of my creations, no, but it has made my job easier. It's just a glorified portable storage device. Nothing more."

"What?" Maeva says. "Are you sure that's all it can do? I used it to resurrect myself numerous times before it stopped functioning."

"You said you did what with it? That's… not good. That's not good at all. That's downright terrible."

"Why…?"

"Just because you mortals *can* use Artifacts doesn't mean that you should," Malphunnos says. "With how you described it, it sounds like you depleted the souls that were contained within it to fuel your necromantic spells. I think those were the last pure souls in existence too… Damn."

"Are you telling me that I sacrificed hundreds of innocent souls just to cheat death—err—you?"

"While it is disgusting you would do such a thing, I don't shame mortals that overachieve to earn my eternal favor. Lucky you."

Maeva grabs her hair and yanks it as she lets out a berserker's roar. "Arrrggghh! You stupid waste of immortal skin! This wouldn't have even happened it you weren't so irresponsible!"

"Bite your tongue. I might have misplaced it, but who in their right mind would equip something that looks so egregiously uninviting? Would you do the same thing for a pair of unwashed dentures if they held magical power? Why would you even touch an object that's beyond your comprehension?"

"I'm not hearing this lecture again. The blood of the fallen is on your hands!"

Malphunnos rests his head against a tree to recollect himself. "Just take the damn item if you want it so badly. That gauntlet has served its purpose for me since I can barely find a usable soul nowadays. Maybe you can find more uses for it than either I or Narisa did."

"What would Narisa even need with this thing?"

"That 'thing' is named Samsara. It would be the name of the child that we could never… err, a-anyway, like I said before, that gauntlet is a glorified storage device. I mostly used it to collect lost Soul wisps or transport harvested ones. Narisa, however, liked to steal the gauntlet away from me and hoard my hard work—constantly."

"That's it? Did she have nothing better to do?" Maeva asks.

"It might sound simple-minded and mischievous, but in truth, any mother with a heart of love hates it when her children's lives are in danger."

Maeva holds her gauntlet close to her chest. "I know I haven't proved myself to be a good caretaker so far, but I'll take better care of Samsara—in homage to Narisa, and to the upsetting number of sacrificed souls that will traumatize me for the rest of my life."

"Sure. Just don't make it weird and start breastfeeding it or something," Malphunnos says. "Let's stop talking about it though. I want to keep moving forward so that no more tragedies like the ones discussed can continue to happen."

"No!" Sadra deflects. "You still haven't proved to us that you're a god. We can't trust you!"

Malphunnos rolls his eyes—then snaps his fingers. Sadra crumbles to the ground, and a small bluish-white orb floats above her body.

"Sadra!" Draxis shouts.

"Relax. Savor what you see before you because if I have to do this again, it's going to be permanent." Malphunnos snaps his fingers again.

The soul reenters Sadra. "I feel sick…" she groans as she struggles to rise to her feet.

"By the way, that little demonstration I had to do—your lifespan was decreased because of it," Malphunnos says.

"Asshole!"

"Want me to make it zero?"

She growls at him.

"Anyway, I'm joining this party whether you mortals like it or not. Now, lead the way! Well—go on!" Malphunnos says, shooing them forward. "I have no idea where you all are heading to."

Chapter 31

And Now for the Weather

"I know Klae said that the weather here is harsh, but this is ruthless!" Rend shouts. "This storm has a mind of its own!"

"Sometimes I wonder what sort of thoughts a storm would think of if it could," Jellop says.

"I would ask if it's upset because it's fatherless or something. This is ridiculous!"

"Always dress for every occasion," Malphunnos says.

"Screw off! It's too hot to wear a cloak," Rend says.

"But there's never too much style."

"Agreed," Jellop adds.

"Ugh!"

A brilliant flash erupts in front of Rend and the others, stopping them in their tracks.

"K-Komet!" Sadra says as she runs over to hug it. "Did Klae send you over to help us?"

Komet gleams a mellow shade of yellow in response.

"Is that a Geshelon?" Malphunnos asks.

"Yep-yep!" Sadra affirms.

"Hmm…"

"What?"

"It doesn't have eyes, but I can still sense the sorrow in it," Malphunnos says.

Komet lowers to the ground, with its crystal body turning midnight blue in color.

"Komet thanks you," Sadra says. "But it also says that you should turn that emotion into something else."

"Huh, I wasn't expecting a short lecture at this exact minute. What a productive day this has been."

"We're heading north, Komet," Sadra says. "Can you help guide us?"

Komet responds by lifting itself into the air and hover above them like a star, before shooting out rays of light above its top and expanding their width into a dome of physical light that shields the others from the torrential rain. The many thanks and praises Komet receives in return makes its illumination stronger.

***

Arriving at an odd spot somewhere deep within the swamp, Komet's light-based umbrella starts flickering on and off repeatedly—until it shuts down completely.

"Uh-oh," Sadra says. "What happened, Komet?" She keeps up with Komet's range of emotions and concerns by nodding her head repeatedly as she watches it periodically flash into different colors, consisting mostly of angry reds and apologetic grays. "What? But this was so short-lived! That's a shame. Thanks for the help so far though."

"What did it say?" Draxis asks her.

"Komet says that this is the end of the line for it because of those strange totems up ahead. Apparently, they're causing some type of interference."

"How so?"

"Some odd warding magic, I guess? Honestly, I've been feeling somewhat sick myself, but I thought it was because of that barely edible crap Klae keeps in his cupboards."

"Sounds like a fancy way of saying that you two are having an allergic reaction," Draxis jests. "Tell Klae he also has our thanks for the assistance, Komet."

Komet amplifies its light into a strong and blinding pure white color. A personal escape portal is made for it shortly after, and it leaves.

"Hmm. An allergic reaction…" Aluna ponders, kicking a totem nearby. She looks up at the sky. The rain curves erratically when it reaches a certain point in the air, like it's suddenly impacting a solid wall. "Jujus…? This type of black magic is more under Apostate territory. Why would something like this be here? No wonder Komet was feeling terrible. But how strong is this crap if it can disrupt the weather itself?"

"Leave other people's property alone," Suvius says. "A disruptive tourist is soon to be a dead one."

"Um, by the way," Sadra interrupts. "Komet also said to follow the totems' placement if we want to find our way out of the swamp."

"That Geshelon is a champion," Suvius says. "When we get back, I'm promoting it to a knight."

"A knight?" Rend questions. "Can I get promoted to?"

"…No."

Chapter 32

In Good Health

Past the low hanging vines and waist-high water, and at the edge of an elevated highway is a reinforced wall made up of segmented logs and rusted slag shaven into spiked points at their tip. The only thing that can be seen above the high wall are the unoccupied wooden watchtowers and the heights of the city within.

In front of the wall, there's a lone guard with forest-green skin standing out in front of the only gate. He wears nothing but a leather pelt and giant leaves that are fashioned together, and he also carries a small tree trunk as his weapon. "Halt!" he says to the party that cautiously approaches him. "Do not walk past the Blood Line." He points down at a dried-up red line that stretches horizontally far into either side of the swampland.

They all look down at their feet. Sweat rolls down their faces as their toes are a toenail away from ruining their day.

"You trespass on the consecrated blood-grounds of our people," the guard continues. "Either formally explain yourselves or informally fight me for entry. Or you can leave. Formally."

"The first option will suffice," Suvius says. "We are the infamous group known as the Harbingers, and we have come to ask for a precious item that might be present somewhere beyond these gates."

"Should you really say all that about us?" Aluna asks. "They might get the wrong idea."

"I'd rather let the truth of our legacy speak for itself. Lying about it will do more harm than good. Additionally, we are in no position to start any more skirmishes."

"Yaga," the orcish guard says. "The skinless man has chosen pacifism. Speak further about this 'precious item'."

"We do not know all the details, other than it's something seeping with darkness and brimming with power," Suvius answers.

"We do have something like that—but it is reserved only for those who can exhibit they are capable of slaying those who are undefeated, as well as slaying their own weaknesses. The Allmother will ascertain if outsiders such as yourself should gain passage to the Slaying Rite in which the item is held at." He then detaches a hollowed-out animal horn that hangs from his waist and blows at its tip, creating a low rumbling sound.

Soon, the gates crack open, and an elderly woman comes forward. She assists herself with a staff that's decorated with small skulls and even smaller talismans. "It's too early in the day for the horns," she says, pouting. "What is it, Head-Smasher?"

"Allmother Shiela," the guard greets, bowing his head. "The Harbingers are at our doorstep."

"Yaga," she responds. "It appears that the Whispers of the Dead were correct: our brightest future was going to visit this city today. Most of the time the Whispers moan about how much they miss drinking and pissing."

"Do I have your blessing to let these outsiders in?"

"Very much so. Do it with haste."

Shiela wanders over to the others as she waits for Head-Smasher to open the gates completely. "I do hope that none of you suffer from hemophobia."

"Is that a disease?" Sadra asks.

"Yes, it's a part of the common disease of Fear. More specifically, it is the absolute and crippling fear of blood."

"Is that meant to scare us?" Draxis asks.

"How bold to say such a thing. Be thankful I didn't mishear your passive tone."

"Don't get us banned, Draxis," Maeva says.

"I meant no ill will by it."

Shiela laughs. "Consider my false aggression a strict lesson on how to better assimilate yourselves into this city. Weapons aren't the only thing to be double-edged or sharp around here. The gates are open now, so why don't you all take a look at our city for yourselves?"

They follow through on Shiela's words. The intensity of the new scenery is incredible. It's a city! Full of lively people! And stuff! It's a refreshing sight that none of them can take their eyes off from.

"Oh wow!" Those words escape from Sadra as she admires the radiance coming from what feels like the life of the city itself. "Just… wow."

"Thank you for the kind reactions," Shiela says. "It was not the easiest feat to build this city when the Decay took everything from us. But now, all orcs, ogres, hobgoblins, trolls, gremlins, goblins, and more have come together to weather through this endless storm and live in harmony."

An ogre crashes through the window of a nearby shop and tumbles onto the street. "Arrrghhh!" he roars. "You bloody bastard! I'll rip your throat out!" He runs back into the store and raises hell, adding more excessive noise that distracts any nearby pedestrians walking about.

"That… was a part of our harmony," Shiela says after an aggravated sigh.

"That's some hardcore harmony," Aluna says. "It's pretty festive here, I must say. Did someone die?"

"Ah, you know of the shallow jokes of our people?"

"I'm a fan of Orcish culture."

"How serendipitous—it's rare to meet an admirer. Would that also mean that you all are here to participate in the Slaying Rite?"

"About that, I don't suppose we could opt out of it? Please?" Draxis asks.

"Adding manners won't exempt you from partaking in our traditions if fate deems it so," Shiela says. "Do not take my words as ignorance, your pleas are not drowned out by my old ears. I do comprehend the esoteric meaning behind your presences here. The Whispers have been very vocal lately about the sudden and shifting tides in the world scene. My words have power in this community, but not enough to convince handing over our secret prize without causing a massive rift—especially when it comes to outsiders. You all wouldn't turn down a fun tradition now, would you?"

"There aren't many cultures left," Suvius says. "So by principle, I suppose we must."

"Yaga. I do apologize for the inconvenience, but maybe there could be unforeseen fortune that you all may find beneficial for the cause?"

"We can only hope."

"Yaga!" Aluna shouts with added elation. "Sorry, the idea of spectating a death-game sounds incredibly thrilling! Am I doing it right though? With the whole 'Yaga' thing?"

"There's no way to do wrong, it is colloquial," Shiela says. "It has no true meaning, it's just something we like to shout for any occasion. We honor the word dearly for it embodies the long overdue unison of the Orcs and all other relative kin."

"So if I said 'I have to go use the Yaga' or 'I'm going to slice off your Yaga', that would be correct?"

"Yaga," Shiela says.

"Yaga…" Aluna repeats, sounding uncertain.

"You'll get the feel for it as you explore the city and interact with the locals. It's insisted that you do because the Slaying Rite won't start for another few hours. Before I let you all go free, I cannot stress enough to take great caution not to bump into or damage the totems strewn about. They are what keeps the ravenous eternal storm outside at bay, along with other nuisances such as the Decayed."

Shiela turns on her heels, preparing to leave. "Always remember this tidbit, outsiders: rise to legend. Now go have fun and enjoy your stay!"

"T-Thank!" Jellop says. "O-Oh… I don't think she heard me."

"This place is huge," Rend says. "What can we possibly do around here without getting lost?"

"You all can follow me," Maeva says.

"What's on your mind?"

"An idea struck me. I want to find their hospitals. I would like some support in case I go… overboard."

"What's she on about?" Malphunnos asks.

"Maeva here can cure people of the Decay," Aluna says. "You'll have to see it to believe it."

"That is indeed something I would love to see."

"Then let's ask for directions," Sadra says.

"What about that guy?" Draxis says, pointing to a lone cyclops hammering in a loose rivet sticking out the wall of a house. "He seems informative. I'll go make him our ally."

"Draxis… you're going to get yourself killed," Maeva says.

"Don't worry, it's all under control. My control." He ignores Maeva rolling her eyes at him before he approaches the cyclops, with his head held up high. "Excuse me, my good man."

"Hmmmm…" the cyclops rumbles deep in his throat, eyeing Draxis with a suspicious look.

"Draxis, you stupid dog! That's the complete opposite on how to act around these people!" Aluna scolds.

"Can I get a thumbs up for trying at least?"

"Move out of the way. Ahem—where's the location of your weakest brethren?"

The cyclops perks up. "What would outsiders like you care for our sick?"

"We might answer that, depending on if you know the way or not."

"You sure are quick to pin someone down to your whim," he compliments. "There's a facility not too far from here. I can escort you. It's a slow morning anyway."

"Yaga. Much appreciated. What's your name, stranger?" Aluna asks.

"Night-Drinker."

"That sounds like something Sadra could use."

"You know it!" Sadra chimes in.

"Strange," Night-Drinker responds. "Strange and weird. Now follow."

They are taken to the main streets where there is even more to admire of the city. The air is passionate and circulating with pride from the rapid downstream of bustling bodies that make it hard to navigate anywhere. The aesthetic is pleasing as well, showing off masterful resourcefulness through the random scraps and salvage that were put together to build the surrounding infrastructure.

Night-Drinker takes them through an alleyway, where it then leads to the backstreets of the backstreets. An unkempt building looms over the dead-end area, with an elongated line of people awaiting to enter.

"Is this the line?" Sadra groans "It wraps around the entire building…"

"It's all for visitation—and for the death shamans to bless those who have passed, before we burn the deceased," Night-Drinker adds. "It's like this at every hospice here."

"What's the general ratio between infected and non-infected?" Maeva asks.

"Staggeringly high for infected as of late… Why do you look so giddy?"

"Don't mind her," Aluna says. "She's a freak for those on their deathbed."

"Excuse me?" Maeva defends. "You people have done so much worse to the deceased. I bet it even keeps Malphunnos up at night."

"Why are you dragging me into this? She's not wrong though."

"Ignore them and focus on me," Maeva says to Night-Drinker. "I want to know if there's a way to get special priority around here. I have a certified method to cure your people."

"We don't take too kindly towards empty jokes about miracles."

"No-no, it's true!"

"Show me then, blood-haired girl. But be aware that your head looks very vulnerable and squishable."

"I don't think anyone has ever said such a thing to me."

"My patience wears…" Night-Drinker growls.

"I can see that. Hold out your arm and don't move—or squish my head."

Night-Drinker gives her full control of his arm. He turns resistant the moment he sees the fangs from her true smile form. Her strength doesn't allow him to leave. "What the hell are you doing?" Night-Drinker screams. "Stop it! I'm a married man!"

"Relax," Maeva says. "I can't do anything if you keep fidgeting!"

His panic tempers slightly. "People are starting to look at us. How long is this going to take…?"

"When I'm done," she responds, muffled by the girth of his arm. After a few more seconds, she yanks her mouth away. "There, all better. Take a look at the results."

"My blood… what did you do to it?" Night-Drinker asks.

"I sucked out the bad and purified the rest. You should be free of the Decay now."

"My mind does feel liberated. Just what kind of miracle are you?"

"What's the holdup?" a bystander yells. "Keep the line movin'!"

"Brother, take a look at this," Night-Drinker says.

"You're clean? Did these outsiders do it?" The bystander rushes and shoves his arm in front of Maeva, shouting, "Heal me! Heal me next!"

"Gladly," Maeva says. Just like with Night-Drinker, she heals the bystander with her uncanny blood medicine.

The bystander can barely see the results from all the crisp tears welling in his eyes. "Haha! I'm cured! Yagaaaa!"

"Brothers, sisters, did you hear that?" another bystander says to those next to them. "That blood-haired girl cured Glass-Breaker!"

As the good word spreads to the rest of the line, a hungry pack of desperation begins to surround Maeva and the others.

"Hold on, you brutes!" Maeva squeals. "I can't take on so many requests at once!"

"This attention is becoming infectious," Night-Drinker says. "This is about as good as it's going to get for that specialized priority you wanted. Brothers! Sisters! Clear the way! The people inside need her help the most!"

The lively and eager blockade that blocks the hospital entrance sunders for the miracle that they won't let leave their sight. Once inside, it is immediately felt that the day is going to be a long one. Rows of occupied beds line the walls, with not enough caretakers to even tend to a third of them—and that's just on the first floor.

The putrid smell of pestilence and unbridled suffering—it's almost all too perfect for Maeva. She licks her lips at the chance for an opportunity. "Oooo, that's a lot of bodies…"

Night-Drinker stands next her, pointing at the beds as he says, "There was a time when these people were fathers. Mothers. Warriors. Guardians. If you can save *any* of them—then the blessing that will be felt, even if it's only by one person, will be invigorating for our community. Please—save them."

Maeva nods, then she begins scoping out for her first participant. She doesn't give herself enough time to be a picky eater.

"Should we be feeding her this much?" Sadra asks the others as she grows weary from watching Maeva's gluttony. "You know what they say when a beast tastes blood…"

"I can see what you're saying, but just look at her," Draxis says. "I haven't seen her smile like that since forever."

"Yeah, she's really into it," Aluna adds.

"You're not afraid of her are you, Rend?" Sadra asks him. "I forgot that you were never a part of our original team. This all must be a major surprise to you."

"Not really."

"No need to act so tough. Or maybe that's just blissful ignorance."

"I don't fear good people," he says. "Or better yet, I don't fear those who try."

***

"I can't do this anymore," Maeva says plainly while massaging her face. "My jaw feels like it's locking up."

"You did a phenomenal job with what you could manage," Suvius compliments. "We've been chatting with the Cured and they say nothing but endless praise about you. I wish we had done more of these acts in the past. This is a good indicator that we are rising above our old cynical selves. Most of us anyway."

"Hey now, don't sell us so short," Draxis says.

"Rest assured, each of you are the exception."

"So, Ms. Solunn," Malphunnos says, approaching her. "That magic of yours—I dare say it has me stumped. Just what kind of power do you wield?"

"I don't believe it belongs to any form of power," Maeva says. "None that's known publicly anyway."

"You definitely showed that it's one of a kind. I never paid too much attention before, but I could have sworn that this nursing side of you never existed."

"Feels creepy to have a stalker."

"Stalking is an unwritten condition within my profession," Malphunnos says.

"That really doesn't help you if I were to report it."

"I dare you to do it. With the gods of justice at my beck and call, I am unstoppable in a court of law."

"You make me sick," Maeva says.

"Then I guess you should go bite yourself."

"Outsiders!" Night-Drinker interrupts.

"Oh hey," Aluna greets. "Where'd you run off to?"

"To revere your names. Gossip goes by faster than a throwing knife around here. The Ministers of Battle have accepted and invited you all into the Slaying Rite, if you wish to partake in our festivities."

"I didn't know we even had to prove ourselves just to be eligible."

"Permission is automatically granted for those who have or are willing to showcase the unbelievable," Night-Drinker says. "Or by cooking a good feast. Food is power."

"How much of that 'power' do you all have in stock?" Aluna asks.

"We always have enough to suffice for a last meal."

"At least we won't die hungry!" Sadra says.

"Speak for yourselves," Draxis mumbles.

Chapter 33

Harbinger of War

Past the city outskirts and around the ringed rim of a gaping crater about half the size of said city, thick and muscular hands pound away at the percussion that vibrate the hundreds of heartstrings who dance to the beat. Tribal hollers echo and loop throughout the blood-night's eve. There is fire, revelry, and rivalry. Blood is boiling—just as much as it spills from a contestant being eaten alive inside the crater's deepest point. Night-Drinker and the others arrive just in time to witness the mauling.

A voice booms over the dying man's screams, shouting, "Shame! Shame! Shame!" The upset voice comes from an announcer who dances around his raised platform. He shakes his fist high in the air as he relays his next message through a horn. "Let us all honor our first volunteer, Knuckle-Dragger, for giving us all a night to remember!"

"Yagaaaa!" the city's population roars in unison with thunderous ovations.

"Ah, but the beast who vanquished Knuckle-Dragger still hungers for a worthy opponent. Is there anyone out here who will take over and rise to legend? Come on, you savages! Don't let us go home disappointed!"

"I go!" someone shouts, waving his arms.

"Aha! Speak your war name, contestant!"

"I am Back-Scratcher!"

"Climb down those ropes, Back-Scratcher, and show us what a real legend looks like!"

Back-Scratcher takes one of the ropes that leads down into the pit, wielding his trusty wooden club and singing a war cry as he does so. This is a battle that he's been waiting for all his life—but there is an old saying about choosing battles wisely…

"Oooh!" the Announcer shouts like he's experiencing second-hand embarrassment. "He didn't even last five minutes! Talk about setting a new record!"

"So… how does this all work?" Aluna asks Night-Drinker. "Seems like your people are just feeding the animals."

"The flavor of the game changes monthly. Last month, it was under the theme of battle royale. This month, the theme is supremacy, where you must become and remain undefeated until there is no one left to challenge the titleholder. Right now, the champion is that chimera that is currently munching on the last two competitors."

"As entertaining as it is to watch people fail miserably, there has to be someone here who can give us a show!" the Announcer shouts. "Wait! Who is that way over at the opposite end? Ah, what about our newest guests…? Will any of you test your might in Slain's Pit and rise to legend? Outsiders are always welcome in my arena!"

"I want to smack him for calling us out," Sadra growls. "Well, everyone, it's now or never. So, who among us wants to earn some bragging rights?"

Sadra receives no immediate response.

"Anyone? Anyone at all…? I'm gonna start choosing people at random. Like… Aluna!"

"Hard decline," she responds swiftly.

"I know you weren't trying to, Aluna, but you single-handedly nearly brought upon the end of the Harbingers. You should be our champion."

"Choose a different candidate."

"Come on, we don't need a gallant champion. We just need someone who can rip through mountains and bend the oceans. We need your power."

"I don't feel comfortable representing anybody right now. Pick. Someone. Else!"

Sadra sighs. "Fine. How about you, Lord Suvius? I even said your stupid honorific for you."

"I'm not feeling much of a 'lord' of anything anymore. I'm only a figurehead now; therefore, choose someone more apt."

"What's with you people? Miss Maeva, would you want to give it a try?"

"After I just spent all my time saving their lives? Why won't you go?"

Sadra crosses her arms, lightly hugging herself. "How can I when I feel like a beaten-down pulp. I might be able to pull in a few victories, but what if they have something monstrous on their side? I'll lose for sure."

"Let me represent the Harbingers," Rend says.

"You…?"

"I said it respectfully, but I meant it to be the only option you all have. I'm going down there to score us an Artifact—and glory."

"I think you're getting cocky," Sadra says. "You have magic but it's nowhere near the level of ours."

"I took advantage of our days off. Enough to the point where I'm confident I can prove you wrong." He turns around and faces the proving ground below. "But just like you all showed me, actions are louder than words—and my fists have a whole serenade at the ready." Rend moves to the edge of the crater's lip—and raises a fist high.

The announcer, Slain, stomps his feet. "Someone has finally offered themselves up! Search for the pent-up barbarism within you and let us hear a voice that can pierce the heavens! Shout your war name, gladiator!"

"You will call me Rend! I will represent the Harbingers!"

"Let's give a deafening 'Yaga' for competitor Rend!"

"Yagaaaaa!" the rowdy crowd screams.

"Take a rope and climb down to your doom you bloodthirsty savage!"

"Rend… wait," Maeva says as she chases him.

"Yeah?"

She quickly shies away from his stare without saying anything.

"Well?" Rend says in a more aggravated tone. "What do you want? You're killing my adrenaline here."

"It's just… are you sure you're ready for something like this?"

"I've never felt more ready. I don't care who doubts this 'pitiful' slave, I know that I have something to prove. Will you allow me this?"

She looks at him while grabbing his hands. He is warm, as if heated up by the magic she senses within him. The only touch to him that is foreign to her is his slightly callused skin and tense muscles. "This vigor of yours feels different than the last time."

"Does that bother you?" Rend asks.

"More than it should."

"What can I say, survival is a cruel lesson in this world, and I never knew just how bad it could get. Either way, I need to test what I've learned."

"Rend… I feel like you've already done so much. But if you really feel like that it's not enough for you, then I will allow you to proceed."

"Thanks."

"But—don't get yourself killed," Maeva adds. "You're the type that needs to hear that."

"Hear what?"

"Don't make me push you into the crater."

"That sounds like a cool way to make an entrance." Rend grabs one of the comically long ropes that hang over the crater's edge and hops over. He lets gravity take control as he slides down the rope. He immediately screams out in agony as he experiences rope burn firsthand.

"Idiot…" Maeva mumbles.

Sadra peeks over the edge. "Is it really alright to let him go fight for us?"

"He took up our mantle when none of us wanted to," Draxis says. "I'd say that beckons our trust in him."

"I could have fought," Malphunnos pouts.

"Definitely not," Maeva says. "No offense, but you haven't really proven yourself to be reliable."

"But I'm a god. That should be more than enough to prove my mettle."

"Does it? I'm pretty sure I heard you beg specifically for our help despite the fact that we're 'mere mortals'."

"I know what I said but… never mind."

Rend makes it to the bottom of the crater. They really should consider cleaning up all the rotting remains he's stepping in. It looks like a cannibal's fantasy there's so many unmarked and unnamed victims.

The sound of bones clattering alerts the chimera. It was an accident, but now he has the beast's attention. It spits out its poison and snarls from all three of its animal heads at Rend as he approaches. It would be wise for him to strike first—and hard. That one phrase the Orkanians keep repeating… The one about rising to legend. It brings clarity on what he wants. He just never knew how to put it into words—or action.

The solution crackles between his fingers, and the moment he aims at the charging chimera, he launches a condensed beam of endless fire, fully dissipating it when he is certain that nothing remains in front of him.

Slain is blown away, as well as the audience who had their breaths held. "He… in one single attack, competitor Rend has taken the bloody crown!"

"Yagaaaaa!" the crowd roars.

"What the shit was that?" Aluna blurts. "Err—I mean, that highly concentrated output of pure magic was impressive and all, but explosions are way better."

"You don't sound too sure," Sadra mocks.

"Quiet! You can't do anything like that either."

"It'll still be larger and messier than anything you can put out."

"Settle down you two," Maeva says. "I'm sure if you ask him then he'll be willing to show you both a trick or two. That is, if you two can temper your pride…"

"Ohhhh but this game isn't over yet, you savages!" Slain shouts. "My dead grandfather could kill a chimera blindfolded while wielding nothing but his own tibia! Let's see if our rising champion can handle what comes next! Trappers! Bring in the Hydra!"

Hydra? Rend wonders. He looks up to see a heavily armored and weaponized transport team drag in a metallic crate that's nearly twice the size of the word gigantic.

"A chimera and a hydra are within the same category level of monstrosities, right?" Slain says. "No? Well, who cares! Moderation is overrated! Send it down!"

The oversized cage comes tumbling down. A hulking multi-headed serpent bursts through the damaged containment the moment it hits the ground. It's not hard to tell what each head is thinking as they flare their nostrils at Rend, but it is hard to predict which head is going to strike first. He doesn't give any of them time to decide by pummeling as many as he can with a barrage of orbs made of fire. The hydra only reacts by shaking off the flames and snapping at him in retaliation.

In theory, fire should have done the trick, but those thick scales are something else. Its impenetrable defense is only matched by its fury consisting of serrated teeth and earth-shattering quakes from the heads that hammer themselves into the ground. Rend remains quick-footed in not only his dodges but also with an adaptive strategy that requires him to switch up his elements—or rather, combine it. Fire in one hand and lighting in the other.

He tries to lure in only one of the heads and entice them to do another snap attack, hoping it's going to be the middlemost one—and his wish is granted. He grabs hold and rides on top of the head. The other heads of the hydra twist their necks and chomp at him, disregarding any preservation towards the head that Rend rides on. Perfect! He digs his hand into the open gashes made by the other heads and sends a fire and lightning combo that merge into a cataclysmic hell-storm, cooking the monster both inside and out.

Rend takes a moment to catch his breath—and admire his handiwork.

"Unbelievable!" Slain howls. "The infamous beast that terrorized our city for days before we could subdue it, and our champion here single-handedly brought it down within minutes! Minutes! Way to put us all to shame, outsider! Yaga!"

"Yagaaaa!"

"But we can't let the champion's bloodlust run dry. Trappers! Bring out…" Slain goes silent as he watches the audience part ways for the approaching elder that claims one of the few seats on his spectator platform. "What is this? What is this! Our very own wise and beloved Prime Minister has joined us on tonight's Slaying Rite! Is there anything you would like to say, Minister Shiela?"

"I just got here. There isn't anything to say."

"…A witty response from our glorious Prime Minister, everyone! Yaga!"

"Yagaaa!" the crowd cheers.

"It's obvious that she wants visual confirmation before she makes any conclusive judgments, so bring out the next threat! Come on! Move your asses!"

Another boxed containment is sent hurtling down. Is it good or bad that this one is considerably smaller than the first cage? It's almost the perfect size for a human. An aggravated screech comes from underneath the ruins of the broken cage. What comes crawling out is humanoid only in stature, unlike its avian wingspan and having an appearance that is both stoic and majestic than that of any bird.

"It's an Elder psiowl!" Slain shouts. "Did you know that their psychic abilities are so strong that they can infiltrate any location just by placing false images into the mind? A few wars have even arisen due to them impersonating as kings and queens! The only reason we caught *this* damn thing was because of the trails of bird droppings. Prepare to get mind-fucked, contestant!"

The psiowl stares at Rend—deep into his eyes. Rend returns the favor to psyche it out. He can feel an intrusive sensation trying to wiggle and pry into the vaults of his consciousness the longer he looks at it. Rend gives a devilish grin to show off his resilience.

"You seem to be having some trouble," he says to the Psiowl. "You're a little late buddy—I'm through dealing with any more mind games. Since you seem so determined to find secrets, how about I show you something that will really give you a sight to behold: the dark magic of Despair!"

The already large eyes of the Psiowl bulges further outward. It violently coughs up an eruption of bubbling froth as the spell destroys it from the inside. It soon tumbles to the ground and spazzes out until its life concedes while having the frozen stare of a witness that has seen true horror.

"Unholy shit!" Slain shouts. "He killed the damn thing with his brain! What kind of voodoo and juju do these Harbingers wield? This is the greatest night ever!"

That same reaction enters Suvius, who says, "Such dominance over his own power and his opponents. I miss having that feeling…"

"He does give off such a strong scent of raw strength," Maeva says. "I want some of that…"

"What do you mean by that?" Draxis asks. "M-Maeva…? You're looking a little starstruck."

"He's really, really, strong…"

"Ack!" Jellop spits. "I detected a naughty thought. This is a double offense because my mind's eye must be reopening. This world is pain."

"Are we really about to let an outsider upstage us all?" Slain says. "This will not stand! Tell you what, I think it's time I let someone from the audience join the fight this time. Isn't that right, World-Ripper?"

A part of the crowd separates to make an entrance for the one called World-Ripper. He is a living mountain that dons the heaviest armor that only he can bear. It's the same with his oversized great axe attached to his back. He wastes no time and leaps off the edge, staring hard at Rend as he falls. The moment he lands, the gargantuan man straightens and stands tall, unmoving, and squints at Rend from his only eye that's not wrapped up by a ripped cloth.

"He is our mightiest sentinel that has protected us for nearly three generations," Slain boasts. "The oldest survivalist and warlord from a long era that will never return. A living embodiment of Orkanian honor and bravery. I can't think of a better warrior to represent our races and protect our pride. Choose your first move wisely, champion."

Rend surveys the appraised warrior. "So… what's your story?" he asks.

"If you were more experienced, then you would know that anything on my person shares everything about me that my forgetful mind would leave unspoken," World-Ripper says. "When I look at you, I see multiple stories and fantasies. An Undead that looks so generic and yet they pack more lethality than an empire's arsenal. I appreciate that you seem to be capable of writing your own legacy."

"You gathered all that from looking at these ragged clothes and seeing a few sparks from my hands?"

"If you're being so modest about it then my eyes must not have deceived me." World-Ripper looks up towards the sky filled with eager eyes that look back at them, then he looks back at Rend. "The people aren't here to watch a debate. Raise your weapons—we fight!"

He barrels towards Rend like a hellbent leviathan, one that can overpower the offense and obliterate the defense. Still, the hastily summoned barriers and layers of parrying spells that warp and deflect his attacks provide Rend just enough shelter to whittle his opponent's stamina down. After enough missed swings and nullified attacks, World-Ripper backs away and stands down.

"You choose not to wage war," World-Ripper says. "Are you hesitating because I am old?"

"You figured me out. This doesn't feel right to me, there are way too many disadvantages against you," Rend says.

World-Ripper scoffs before saying, "Take off your crown; its shine is making you blind. This match is as even as it gets because you're dealing with someone who has honor they must uphold. This isn't just a fun pastime for us, this is what keeps us going. This is what it means to have devotion to something you believe in. I suggest you start respecting that."

Rend doesn't say anything after hearing that lecture. Instead, he presses his palms together. A one-handed spectral blade constructs within the space between his hands as he slowly separates them apart. He directs the pointed tip of the magical blade at World-Ripper.

A glint twinkles from World-Ripper's double-edged axe as he mimics Rend's taunt. Then, they reengage in combat. Their tussle is short and heavy, leading them into a stalemate with their weapons locked together, with one overlapping the other. They continue to struggle and push against one another like tectonic plates.

"There aren't many who can match my strength…" World-Ripper strains as his guard nears its limit.

"My crown makes me blind, not weak," Rend says.

"Durable it may be, but it will degrade eventually."

World-Ripper shifts his weight, enough to the point where Rend topples over and gets pinned to the ground. He's stuck in an airtight position where his arms have zero mobility. Breaking out would mean breaking a few bones, but that doesn't mean it has to be his own.

To make it happen, Rend wiggles his fingers by making spiral movements. The air around them is pulled into a dense bubble between him and World-Ripper that detonates it into a concussive shockwave and flips World-Ripper onto his back. It's not as effective due to his size and weight, but it staggers him long enough to allow Rend time to think of a follow-up.

A gamble has to be made. The only thing Rend can think of is to exploit his opponent's blind side—literally. It'll be risky, but he's done riskier. He takes a quick second to conjure up a spell and sprinkles his spectral weapon with a green snow-like powder of magic before World-Ripper can notice his scheme.

Rend stays on the successful path of trickery and charges straight at World-Ripper, surprising him. Still in the midst of confusion, World-Ripper has no choice but to defend himself. Rend slides underneath the mighty swing of his axe and nicks the flesh that gets exposed by a critical armor-piercing jab.

World-Ripper is brought down to a kneel from a sudden weakness enveloping him. He scrapes off the accumulating green goo that numbs his leg and sniffs it. "First magic, and now magical poison," he says with a gruff. "Quite a bag of tricks you hide underneath your skill. So, this was your plan all along… I can't say that I've ever fought under a time limit before." He plants a foot down and rises. "All this means is that there will be no more hesitation." World-Ripper inhales, then lets out the biggest roar he can give. "Worldbreaker!"

Rend can see the fury raging in his opponent's eyes. After a few stomps, World-Ripper abandons his warrior's grace. A berserker—now turned destroyer. Rend prepares for the worst by raising a protective barrier.

"Nothing is unbreakable!" World-Ripper bellows. He hammers the barrier with heavy overhead swings with his axe. The barrier tanks two strikes before it shatters. Rend switches spells and tries to hold him back with tidal waves of fire.

"Knock it off!" The force of Worldbreaker's roar sends the flames returning to sender.

Rend calls forth and excavates the earth around him to build a makeshift fortress. His miniature bastion is demolished swiftly by World-Ripper bulldozing into it. Every manner of magic at Rend's disposal is being put to full use in an attempt to keep up with the mountain he's fighting against. He can't freeze him, he can't electrify him, he can't burn him—he cannot stop him.

Rend can feel his impending doom approaching when World-Ripper lowers to the ground, preparing to make a tremendous leap with axe in hand. But in the last seconds of hope, luck prevails. The final stages of the poison kicks in, paralyzing World-Ripper down to his knees. His weapon tumbles out of his hands, and he is under complete submission to the poison's vicious bite.

The audience catches on to what's happening. "Finish him!" some of them demand. They start repeating themselves over and over.

"I see that you're hesitating again," World-Ripper says to Rend while breathing heavily.

"Sorry… It's the same feeling that I had before. I can't get over it."

"It's guilt, one of the most powerful spells to ever strike a man. I too have felt it enough times to drive a hundred men insane. You need to consider me to be an obstacle in your legacy, just like how you were mine. The difference being is that yours is much more prominent than the entire culmination of my life's journey. Gather your honor and send me away with whatever method you wish. And when you do—make sure that you go all the way. I don't want to end up like those mindless *things* that slaughter for no great cause."

"I got so caught up in the moment," Rend says. "I didn't want things to go this far. You don't deserve this."

"Some things aren't deserved, but rather earned. I chose to fight. You chose to fight. Ambition is a powerful drug, and its worst side effect is blindness. You're not just blind to what's in front of you, but you're also blind to what comes after. This is all on you."

"Why are you telling me this stuff? You should be more upset."

"I can't get upset when I have lived long enough," World-Ripper says. "I can tell when a grave premonition is underway. I had to share my aging wisdom with *someone* before I raised my weapon for the final time. Enough talk… you have a legend to be made."

Rend is slow with his movements—but he does what he has to do—and performs the fatal move to his opponent's head with his own weapon. Rend drops the axe and looks at his hands. His hands—his shaking hands just did something terrible. *He* did something terrible, and the crowd is congratulating him for it.

"Friend Rend doesn't look so good…" Jellop mutters.

"Jellop, can you get his attention for me?" Maeva says.

"I help." Jellop then focuses his gaze and thoughts and directs them towards Rend. *"Friend Rend, the signal is weak, but you must hear me! Look over here!"*

Rend hears Jellop's transmission. He looks up at the others. Maeva is waving at him. Everyone else soon copies her.

They're right... Rend thinks as he contemplates their weird method of showing support. *I shouldn't get so caught up in my guilt. After all, they did warn me about this. I understand why Magic is so tempting. To harbor this power makes it so easy to shape the world to your liking... and abuse it. That isn't what I want. I'm not like my abusers.* He then looks up over at Slain, who seems to have lost his jubilance.

"The boy is waiting, Slain," Shiela scolds. "Have you nothing to say?"

"We just lost a hero," he responds.

"What makes World-Ripper so special? You've been pitting gladiators like him against perilous challenges ever since you earned the keys to this glorified playground."

"Because there is an unfair exchange of blood that needs to be rectified. The time for challenges is over. This is war."

"You fool… must you feel personally attacked by anyone that overcomes your nonsense? I haven't seen you behave so energetically like this in quite some time. I was worried that the smile you try to put on for us was just to maintain a public image."

"Why would I show them any other face? You know I hate tears—especially theirs."

Slain readies himself before he speaks into the announcer's horn. "Sorry for the delay, everyone! As for you, contestant Rend, there will be *no* apologies! I want to propose a special challenge for you and *you* alone. This final opponent that you are about to face. It is one whose race was once considered sacred to our people, but with the way the world is now, everyone is forsaken. Found running amok in the Hagri Scarlands and decimating everything in its path, our trappers have found something so wicked that it has to be seen to be believed. Prepare yourself!"

The trappers arrive once again—in double the amount. Half of them are busy transporting and handling a containment that's more heavy-duty than the ones prior, and the other half seem to be there for the sole purpose of disaster prevention. In their favor, nothing adverse happens, so they do what they've been doing with all the other cages: Send it down!

An unsatisfactory amount of damage is made to the durable containment despite the great fall. It's up to Rend to unleash whatever the hell they have in store for him. As he starts to pry and bend at the metal crate, it's no monster inside that he's hearing.

"Let me out! Let me out!" a voice screams in pure distress.

It doesn't seem wise to assist the opponent you're about to fight, but maybe by showing his good side, he can avoid a fight altogether? The final locks and bolts are ripped off, and the hostage comes sliding out.

The once-imprisoned monster's skin is as red as the sky above it. It has two curved horns that protrude from its head just like a mighty bull, and its glorious leathery wings are large enough to eclipse its own body. The sight of such an out-of-place entity immediately captures the anticipation of the wanting audience.

"A demon!" Draxis gasps. "Malphunnos, I thought you said that Hell closed its gates?"

"I know it as fact. But closed doors do not help those that were left out."

"Then that means this one might have been wandering aimlessly and strayed too close to the Orkanian borders. Is that all this slaying game is? An easy means of pest control? I've been noticing that these wild monsters are all infected. Still, subjugation of any of them is a phenomenal accomplishment."

"It's because Orcs and their half-brothers are awesome and formidable," Aluna says. "I sometimes wish I was one."

"Really?" Draxis says. "How bizarre."

"Yeah, fuck that," Sadra interjects. "I'd rather have the flight of a fairy."

"Plus, have you seen how tall orcs can get?" Suvius adds. "I refuse to not be the tallest member here."

"I like your size, Aluna," Maeva says. "I also find it super cute when you sit on our heads like a lily pad."

"Jellop agrees."

"I thought you all found my buzzing annoying?" Aluna says.

"Only in the morning," Maeva answers.

"Agreed," Sadra says with a nod. "Now shut up and watch the fight. It's starting to get juicy!"

The demon whimpers as it crawls around on the ground. "My head itches so much," he says. He uses his hands to block off the excess light that affects his vision and sees Rend standing before him. "Wh-who are you? What do you people want from me?"

"I'm not divulging any of that," Rend answers. "You wouldn't like the answer."

"Then whatever you people want, do it fast. You shouldn't have brought me here."

"Do I even need to ask why?"

"Don't," the demon says. "You wouldn't like the answer—or the outcome."

"Figures. Just hold on, there is a way to help you out. I know of a cure—"

A sharp stake of intense pain drives itself through the demon, to the point where he grinds his teeth and snaps his head backwards like he's been pulled by the horns.

"This vessel will be denied from your prescriptions of torment!" the demon says in an offended tone. It is his voice that speaks, but not his own words. "You all cling on to life and breed with it every waking moment until you contract diseases like misery and evil and spread it anywhere you can touch.

"Existence itself is the ultimate mistake. What you propose as a cure is only an extension to that mistake, and what you call the Decay is only an end—a quietus, to what was once an irreversible mistake. This vessel will become free from that cycle, for he is undergoing a transcension: the salvation of finality."

The demon then shakes and contorts as it screams, "Get out of my head! Let me go!" He digs his jagged nails into the ground as he sobs. "Don't you see! It's too late for me!"

Rend is two steps ahead. He's already applied enough magic buffs and amplifiers on himself to drug a kraken—and he's not planning on stopping.

"I can feel it coming," the demon says, under intense pain. "I have to say this fast: everything that I may—no, that I will do to you isn't my choice. I can't stop this! My mind won't stop itching! I can only think about eating and destroying and eating! I don't know what to do! I'm so scared! We thought we were safe. We should have been safe from all this. None of us could escape… I don't want to be next! I don't want my mind to disappear! Please! You have to help me! You have to—arrghhhh!" His body jerks and twitches in place—until it inevitably stops.

It's a strange feeling to be felt when a person you've just spoken with becomes a stranger right before your very eyes. Rend isn't too terribly put off by it, but it does hurt to give it too much thought. "I'm not sure if there's anything left of you in there," he tells the demon, "but just in case you are still there, then I want you to know that I won't let that parasite use your body as a weapon. I swear to Malphunnos!"

"Ow!" Malphunnos blurts while rubbing his chest.

"What's wrong with you?" Aluna asks.

"A stupid somatic reflex for when mortals use my name too carelessly."

"Neither of them have yet to make a move!" Slain says, amping up the audience. "This back-and-forth exchange of tension is maddening! Who's going to strike first…!"

"He's… going to make it through this, right?" Maeva asks the others. "Can we intervene, Night-Drinker?"

"No you may not. He chose this risk."

"Forget that, let me switch out with him."

"Don't even think about it. Our rules are sacred. Respect them."

"But—"

"He's come this far without any issues," Night-Drinker says. "If it comes down to it, then I would prefer you let me join the fight instead. Just wait for now."

"The biggest battle of the year—no, the entire century has begun!" Slain says. "Look at them go straight into full force! Don't stand too close to this explosive battle, you savages! Keep in mind that we are not liable for any accidental mutations, dismemberments, decapitations, and… damn, this list gets longer and longer every month… Oh crap! I look away for one second and we already have a massive injury sustained on the battlefield! That's gotta hurt!"

Rend's arm, it's… He didn't see it coming. He couldn't see it coming. It wasn't from a bite, thankfully, but from a clean and powerful swipe—it still hurts like a bitch either way. Even with all his preparation, he's still outmatched. His arm is regenerating back to health, but he can't focus on that and think of a battle plan at the same time. Battle plan it is then. *But what would a demon even be weak to? Water? Air? No, those don't seem right...*

Rend's options aren't plenty, so he tries throwing a little bit of everything he knows how to do. Though, the more he tries, the more aggravating it becomes. Absolutely nothing he tries is working. He isn't too sure if it's because he's fighting one-handed, or if it's because his opponent could easily defeat *him* one-handed. It definitely feels like the latter as his other arm takes a brutal hit from the enraged demon—though, at least this one can still function.

That's twice now. Twice that Rend sees the wind-up, but not the motion of the attack. What hidden force is he not seeing? *Maybe it's hiding in plain sight?* he wonders. He thought that the blood loss was making him see double, but the only thing that *can* be perceived as such is the rising, orange shadow that outlines and surrounds the demon's whole body like a spiritual projection.

The phantom shows its full form, knowing it's been seen.

Oh, so that's how you damaged me! That extra reach should be considered a sin. Is there even a way to combat that sin? Nothing's worked before...

"You can do it, Rend!"

Was that Maeva? Of course it was. I get what she's trying to do but— Rend's internal thoughts get interrupted by a fuzzy glow emanating from his remaining hand. *Hold on, what is this light...? I really am an idiot. I need Light! I don't think hers is enough.* Rend kneels down and holds his illuminating fist close to his chest.

"What's he doing?" Aluna says. "Is that some type of guard?"

"Looks like he's taking a bathroom break," Sadra says. "Wish I could do the same."

"...Oh, I get it now!" Aluna exclaims. "He's praying to build up some Faith. See that white glow?"

"Ours won't be enough," Draxis says.

"Stand aside," Night-Drinker says. "I'll handle this." He cups his hands near his mouth to amplify his voice. "Hey! Everyone! If you keep cheering for Rend then I'll make sure the blood-haired girl gives you special treatment!"

His words are caught by the ears of people nearby. "What'd he say?" a male ogre says. "Is that true?"

"Well I'm not going to be the one left out if it is," a female troll says. "Kill that demon, Rend!"

"Y-Yeah! You better win!" another person says next to them.

It doesn't take long for the crowd's demands to grow into something massive.

"Fuck 'em up, Rend!" Aluna hollers. "Whoops—it's so easy to get carried away with all this…"

"You have an impressively sharp tongue, Night-Drinker," Suvius compliments.

"It was the first weapon I wielded; fell in love with it ever since. Your friend shouldn't have any trouble fighting now."

"Wouldn't this be considered cheating?" Aluna asks.

"I have no clue how bent the rules are right now," Night-Drinker says. "That's why I said if it came down to it that you should allow me to fight instead so none of you will get banned. None of it meant that I would get involved using my hands however."

"Scary…"

***

Faith. A power that cannot be learned, only felt. What Rend feels is a bastardized version, but there's so, so, so much of it. Possibilities: unlimited, from a wellspring that is all his to engorge in, and directly provided from a tumultuous audience that is stomping wildly with impatience.

To elevate himself to an even level with his foe, he capitalizes on the influx of power by transforming his own being. He conjures up two radiant wings made of pure light, an ever-reaching aura of inescapable purity, and a foresight of victory—and with a fully healed body that is raring to fight.

"Round two, motherfucker!" Rend shouts.

The demon charges, gaining extra speed from its arched wings. Rend does the same, and they connect fist to fist. It's all flurries of bloodied knuckles for the first few minutes, then the big guns start coming out. Spells—that are combined with enchantments of hallowing light that double their effectiveness.

Rend weaves a couple threads of fire and light and knits them together until they thicken into blazing ropes of golden holy fire. He uses his beautiful whips to thrash at and wear down the demon's phantom enough to where he can tear into the flesh of the puppeteer. The demon howls an otherworldly wail. The excessive lashing is too great to endure. It starts making its retreat into the air.

"I'm not letting you escape!" Rend bellows.

"Unholy shit!" Slain says. "This battle just went airborne! Remember what I said about no liability for injuries, you savages!"

The demon's flight is halted halfway up the crater from Rend grabbing onto its feet and pulling it down. Enraged, it belches out thick bursts of fire that pack enough intensity to linger and scorch the air.

That damn parasite is becoming more adept at using his body, Rend thinks to himself as he swings from side to side, dodging the flames. *I have to end this. Now!*

Rend charges through the oncoming torrent of the infernal flames and reaches for the demon's throat. He sends the dazed demon soaring high above him, then he cusps his hands together into the shape of a flower bud in half-bloom above his head. The position is made—now for the incantation, "**Smite!**" The absorption of everyone's faith is expelled into a humongous beam of tremendous power.

He lets his spell channel endlessly until every speck of light is exhausted.

With vanished wings, Rend slams ungracefully onto the ground. The pain is great. The sorrow still burns. But he knows he needs to regain his footing and declare his victory to end the blood festival once and for all. On two feet, and with a warrior's resolve, his next words makes everyone shudder in their skin. "I have presented to you all that anyone who dares to test me will be annihilated and sent to their dead god! For I am Archias Rend! The Harbinger of War!"

"Well said, champion!" Slain shouts. "While it truly is a heartbreak, for the first time ever, an outsider has beaten us at our own game and rose to legend! I don't know about you savages, but I think that deserves a special callouuuut! Yagaaaaa!"

"Yagaaaaa!" the crowd roars.

"Archias?" Draxis questions while plugging his ears. "Where'd he pull that one from?"

"That was his real name before he… you know," Maeva says.

"I don't get it," Sadra says.

"He committed suicide in his old life."

"He did…? Why would he do that?"

"Because he felt that it was his only way out," Aluna says. "I hate that the feeling is all too common."

"Miss Maeva, does he still feel like that?" Sadra asks.

"Not really. But that nightmare you forced him to remember didn't help to subside his pain."

Draxis moves closer to Sadra, concerned over her sudden silence. "Sadra dear, you're turning Nocturnal."

"I did something bad…"

"All right, you savages, settle down!" Slain says. "Now I know we all love a little bit of glory, but we all love riches more!"

Shiela gives a jewel-encrusted, round amulet to Slain.

"We have no idea what this thing really is," Slain says as he taps his finger on the amulet's face. "It's a mysterious and dark little surprise we uncovered in the far wilds while in search of the now fallen beasts. Normally we would keep such a profaned treasure to ourselves, but we find that it's too dangerous in our hands—so we're giving it to the most dangerous hands instead! Ahahaha! Take this grand prize and get the hell out of my arena! It's been an honor O legendary champion."

Rend barely catches the flung object. He takes special care not to drop it during his return ascent to the crater's top.

Maeva is the first to welcome him back. "You did it, Rend!"

"We did it," he corrects. "I might talk a lot of shit, but don't think that your cheers were unheard. It helped me push through to the very end."

"You didn't need us," Draxis jokes.

"Nonsense. I'll always need you all, because whether we like it or not—" Rend cuts himself off and extends his hand out, holding it in place and signaling for the others to do the same, and following up by saying, "We are in this together!"

Upon hearing his words, Sadra glows brighter and says, "And it will never been for glory nor riches!"

"It's for the pursuit of happiness for all!" Aluna tags in.

"In the name of Death," Suvius says.

"For it's a swift and steadfast reminder!" Jellop says.

"That all lives are weighed and judged for purity!" Maeva says.

"By its harbingers!" Draxis says.

"…What was all that?" Malphunnos asks.

"An old rally cry we used to shout in arms together," Draxis says. "This is what unifies us."

"Feeling left out, Mal?" Sadra teases.

"In more ways than one…"

"You are a welcomed friend," Jellop says to him. "We all can go back home together."

"Yeah," Rend says in agreement. "Let me just activate—"

"Don't activate the Artifact just yet!" Maeva shouts. "This is selfish, but I wanted to practice more of my magic on the people here. If that's okay with everyone?"

"I encourage that thought," Aluna says. "Can we please stay, Lord Suvius?"

"…We can stay."

Aluna squeals. "This is so great! I can't wait to browse their armories!"

"You kids have fun."

"You're not coming with us, Suvius?" Draxis asks. "I know you'll love it."

"In due time maybe. For now, I plan on acquiring a souvenir for myself before we leave. I wish to ask you to accompany me, Night-Drinker."

"Strange and weird," he responds. "If I must."

Chapter 34

Devilish

Suvius is joined by Night-Drinker at the foot of the capitol building of the city. Great care was taken to build such a marvelous monument for the common people. It's a long way up.

"You said you wanted to seek an audience with the Ministers of Battle, right?" Night-Drinker asks.

"That is correct," Suvius says.

"I indubitably believe you have earned the right to enter. Do note that any and all questions will be directed to Prime Minister Shiela unless told otherwise by them."

"Understood."

"Then follow."

These old footsteps that Suvius knows he's stepping over as they ascend up the wide stairs—his feet are so small in comparison. The sculpted warrior idols that look down at him from the sides of the stairs, it's like they are speaking to him and asking him why he dares to taint where they have once tread.

Suvius would only respond back to them with nothing. He tries to keep his head up about it. "Can I just say that you've surprised me today, both you and the people here."

"Oh? Were you that quick to judge us?" Night-Drinker says.

"It pains me to say that there were concerns."

"Trust me, we hear that a lot. You are entitled to your caution. On the surface, our way of life looks violent and self-destructive, but our fallen are forever honored and remembered, our sense of security and freedom is high, and we master the arts in which we are skilled at, which are then carried over by our future generations. It's all about encouraging growth and empowerment, not trashing and exploiting those below you."

"Consider my mind to be more opened," Suvius says.

"Keep it unlocked until you are dismissed from this place."

They arrive at the building's doorstep. Night-Drinker steps aside to allow Suvius to enter.

"Is there anything else I should keep in mind before I meet them?" Suvius asks.

"Be yourself," Night-Drinker says, giving a friendly nod as he closes the door behind Suvius.

Two painted, wooden totems belch flames from their gaping mouths and light up the darkness inside the building at the sides of the entrance. More totems ignite along the walls as Suvius walks into their vicinity and reveal to him the path that they have destined for him to go.

The path is winding and unnecessarily long, but he misses their comfort when they abruptly cease. In the far back of the last room he enters, only one totem lights up—then four more ignite one-by-one in a chain, starting from left to right.

Suvius takes the time to get a good look at the council members below each totem. He sees Shiela sitting upright in the middle of the five thrones, with her staff in hand. Slain is also a familiar face that's present. He doesn't know what to say about the third member who sits motionless with his eyes closed. There are also two vacant seats as well.

Shiela strikes the ground with her staff, creating a harsh echo. "The Harbingers have acquired what they wanted, and yet you all still seek more than what you need. This was all expected. Share to us, Harbinger Suvius, what it is that has agitated your greed so badly."

"Minister Shiela," he says after a bow. "I wish to negotiate or even barter with you for the grotesque but alluring trophy that you all have taken into possession from the carnage today. The demon's heart."

"Were we seen?" Shiela wonders out loud as she glances at Slain. "No matter, we don't care for the demon's heart. In fact, you would do us a great service to relieve us of its ominous lures. But we will not lend it to you."

"For what reason?"

"You are unfit."

"I will fight for it with blood if I must."

"There is no doubt about that, but the blood of others will not count. The Whispers that bemoan from your armor speak with ill-will and disgust for their captor, and they spit at his fraudulent legends and dying ambitions. Tell us something—without the talents and tools of others, what do *you* offer that would make you a standout in a king's personal army?"

"The power to make that army mine," Suvius states.

"Kill one, and the rest will fall," Shiela says. "An awe-inspiring and terrifying power that you wield indeed—but what if your opponent hasn't the need for their own army? The Whispers once again chastise about your overreliance on those dead or alive to make yourself appear stronger."

"And I wholeheartedly agree. The brutal challenges that I face are weighing on me more and more, overlapping well past my limits. I am a mere figurine of the monument that I once was."

"And how will the heart of a demon reverse your decline?" Shiela asks.

"To restore my body's prime—for I can no longer keep it intact in my current state. The slow devourment of my soul is softening this vessel of mine. I will exhaust every option of reinforcing my body before I am forced to lay myself to rest in a garden of unfulfilled promises."

"Noble—but very poorly thought out," Shiela says. "The heart is the solution, but you're ignoring the problems that surround the solution."

"Then educate me," Suvius says. "A long time ago, my king caught wind that there were multiple sects on this continent who frequently communed with demonkind. For what reason or more would the Orkanians have to involve themselves with them?"

"…Before I respond," Shiela says after an uncomfortably long pause, "what are your personal inclinations towards demons?"

"I once thought of them as polar opposites to Light and the Natural Order, but after everything I've heard and seen, they are just another race with their own societal structure that most would deem taboo and vile. I don't think I fear them—I just don't understand what their drive is."

"A good enough mindset. Our history with demonkind is not one to be revolted, there were mutual benefits between us and them. But we are not godless however—we communed with both the gods and demons equally. There is great knowledge to be gained from the magic the Dark gods and Demons offered us.

"You see, Suvius, their theories on Darkness are not about committing acts of corruption, it is instead the self-awareness and study of corruption itself and how it affects what the Light blesses. We took that knowledge and honed it into benefits like control over nature, medicine, and personal achievements of spiritual strength and enlightenment. In other words: duality."

"Balance. Does that really exist?" Suvius asks.

"I would think so. Before the apocalypse, you and your allies sought to prevent the Arbiters' rise to world domination. Would that not be an example of taking a stand against imbalance?"

"There were hefty costs…"

"And? Sometimes evil is born out of good intentions," Shiela says. "Think about these Decayed that you fight against. They were functional beings with beautiful lives once upon a time, but they will kill us all if we don't defend ourselves. Does that manner of killing make us evil? Arguments could be made but the results are what matters. The balance that you desire matters. Not only for yourself, but for those that root for you."

Suvius thinks, before saying, "I have to say that I intend to see my mission through to the end no matter what. In order to do so, I will need to play at my strengths. I shall accept that my greatest strength is the one thing that I thought made me wretched, and I want to delve further into that. How do I use my own 'darkness' to my advantage?"

"First, you must be aware that everything is a poison if you abuse it," Shiela says. "Darkness can be used as a tool just like any other aspect or division in the great Life and Death balance, but attuning with what can be derived from it will lead to unknown alterations in your physical and mental being. There is a way to mitigate it if you—"

"If I acquire a tool with the means to equalize said darkness," Suvius intrudes. "I've read it somewhere."

"Then you have a slight understanding of the Demons' heinous craft, but keep in mind that their Darkness is beyond the typical kind that us lower beings can fabricate—even during our darkest days."

"I have never been a stranger nor a timid fawn towards the scourges of virtue. There should not be any concern as I do have a tool in my possession that might temper any malignant overflow. It's called the Bloodheart Cuirass. Have you heard of it?"

"Minister Oppum, what do we know of such a cursed artifact?" Shiela asks.

The elder to her right opens his wizened eyes and speaks. "That ancient instrument is a living manifestation of collected agony and Malice," he says with a hoarse but ominous tone. "Darkness is a subsidiary of Death, and Malice is a subsidiary of Darkness, akin to Silence, Despair, Anti-light, and many others.

"Malice is a powerful tool for those unafraid to become a blight on creation, and the Cuirass itself can lend the wielder its copied malignant imprints that are siphoned from our world of dark desires. Its only limitation is the user themselves and their volition to commit sin. Beware of overindulgence and self-consumption." He then returns back to his slumber-like state.

"Thank you, Minister Oppum," Shiela says. "Sins are a product from Malice, and you, Harbinger Suvius, your own sins have left deepening scars on this world that will last for centuries. Even so, the combination of both a Cursed Artifact and the heart of a demon will still be overwhelmingly difficult to contain. In other words— you're crazy."

"What is there to lose otherwise?" Suvius asks. "No more will I remain incompetent in providing for what people need from me."

"You're risking everything to be akin to a demon."

"There is no difference as I am already impure. You really do not know who I am. I am Suvius Falacoster!" he shouts with thunderous pride. "The Harbinger of Sacrifice, the Lich, the Revenant! The noble who cursed his own king! And should I choose it, then I can even become the King of Demons! I demand the heart and I demand it now!" Just as fast as his temper rose, he rushes to the ground to kneel. "A-Apologies for my rant… I got carried away."

The Ministers start laughing, heartily.

"Bravo! Bravo!" Slain says. "I for one will stress that we should feed this starving beast his meal."

"I have no choice but to agree," Shiela says through her own chortle. "That was a victory made through only the ferocity of your self-confidence, and that was all we needed to hear. The Whispers speak better of you now, and so do we. Come…" she says as she shows a bizarre organic mass that she's somehow managed to keep hidden. "Come and claim your future."

Suvius walks closer. The heart is within his grasp. All he needs to do is just take it. Just… take it.

"You shouldn't hesitate on this," Shiela warns. "We all share the desire of becoming better than what we are now so that we can continue forward unopposed. You claim to be opposed on being the best version of yourself—someone that can do what's right."

Suvius takes the heart between his hands. He stares at it while holding back his nonexistent breath. He shoves the heart into his mouth, swallowing it whole.

"How intriguing," Shiela mutters. "You took it all in at once and are not screaming out in agony. What wonderful Malice you must have to be able to remain standing. Clearly, I have misjudged."

"I've had… over a decade… to build it up," Suvius says as he adjusts to the first thumps of his vigorous and fresh organ.

"And yet, some good will come out of it. We have faith in you."

A drawn-out blaring noise introduces itself and takes charge of the conversation. It startles everyone.

"What is that horrible sound?" Suvius asks.

"War horns," Shiela says with urgency. She rises from her throne. "We're under attack!"

"What? I must go. I'll help with the defense."

"Suvius!"

"Yes, what is it? The people are in danger!"

"I'm not sure if this will help to energize your alignment, but I wanted to let you know that there was a faint but hyperactive Whisper that spoke very highly of you. It's something I thought you would find interesting in case it was someone you are familiar with."

"…It sounds like something they would do."

***

Down a street, Maeva calls out, "Suvius!" as she runs over to him. "Thank goodness we found you! We—wait, what happened to you? You're making my skin crawl."

"I suppose that's my new aura. Let's just say that I underwent a spiritual journey. Anyway, what's the issue?"

Maeva turns and points upwards. Suvius follows her finger, looking higher and higher. He's at a loss for words for a few seconds. "Is that a person? Since when did people start flying?"

The others arrive, along with Night-Drinker.

"I said the same thing," Draxis says.

"That's not just any person," Malphunnos corrects. "That's Thurnos."

"What the fuck is a Thurnos?" Rend asks.

"The God of Thunder."

Gigantic bolts of lightning strike the entire city, with some hitting the ground and even more piercing through a few buildings.

"This isn't worth the risk of a massacre. We need to evacuate the town!" Night-Drinker demands.

"Allow me!" Jellop shouts. "I hope this works…" He raises his staff high and sends out a telepathic message. *"There is danger among us, look towards the skies and run away from it! Evacuate!"*

Soon, the streets begin to flood with wave after wave of people running for their lives after they verify the threat for themselves.

"This is why I shouldn't have taken the risk," Malphunnos whimpers to himself. "I open the gates for half a second and the rest of the gods take that as an invitation to bring their doom." He shakes his head, trying to steel his resolve. "I'll need you all to evacuate with the rest of the Orkanians."

"Hold on, we can help you," Rend says.

"Go! I'm not saying this to be a selfless hero, I'm saying it because I'm pretty sure none of you can withstand divine lightning!"

A terrible storm starts taking form, blocking out the entire sky. An absolute downpour of lightning darts everywhere, like it possesses intelligence, and shows it intent by striking and chaining between as many people as it can. The death toll is rising to a horrifying count. Everyone takes that sign as a true reason to make their escape.

Malphunnos takes a look around to ensure everyone has left. The charred streets are devoid of life—all except for one. "I thought I told you to leave!"

Suvius walks past Malphunnos and plants himself into the frontline. His armor clatters to the ground as he removes each piece individually. His skeletal body is fully nude, with a healthy heart beating right at his center.

"That heart," Malphunnos says, in full disbelief. "Suvius… you didn't…"

Suvius doesn't answer him. After a brief pause, he extends his right arm outward to his side, and straightens it. This marks his final destination at a point of divergence, with one future leading to the horizon of no return. There's time to walk away, but his decision was already made before he arrived at the crossroad of fate. His fate is sealed the moment he tightens his hand into a fist and shouts, "Bloodheart Cuirass! Come to me!"

A viscous pool of scarlet tar forms beneath his feet and he is soon enveloped inside a thick cocoon. It unravels, revealing a remodeled Suvius. He is covered from torso to feet in the eldritch design of the nightmare he summoned, and he has tiny flames swirling in a synchronized dance inside the void of his eye sockets.

Satisfied, he brushes himself off. "Well, how do I look?"

Malphunnos circles around Suvius as he inspects him. "You look like someone's worst nightmare, and I don't mean that as a compliment. Who the hell told you to go and rewrite your humanity for the second time?"

"I did."

"Only you would answer with something like that so quickly. Just because you have a higher being's power doesn't mean that you can go and fight one."

"You say that like I'm about to fight one by myself," Suvius says.

"Mortals are so stubborn…" Malphunnos sighs.

"Yes, they are. Now can we please go and save this city?"

"I feel like this is the only time I'm going to hear you say please."

"Don't be so sure. It's a new day—and a new me."

***

Trailing behind the rampage of Thurnos leads Suvius and Malphunnos into the heart of the city—at a barren plaza with a fractured fountain in the center. The Thunder god floats above the city high enough to cast his cataclysmic storm undisturbed. Even standing in the eye of the storm, the deafening wind is blasting away at them.

Malphunnos tries to overpower the noise with his voice, shouting, "Thurnos!"

"You know that's not Thurnos anymore, Mal," Suvius says.

"That doesn't mean he's dead to me."

"But you do know what we have to do."

"No I do not."

"Why do you say that?" Suvius asks.

"Divinity."

"That doesn't mean invincibility."

"But it does mean that his existence will be difficult to smite," Malphunnos says.

"Is it not possible to kill a god?"

"Depends on how 'dead' you want the god to be. I don't recommend doing anything permanent."

"What makes the hunt and execution so undesirable overall?"

"The consequences," Malphunnos states. "Let's say you find a golden egg, what would you do with it?"

"Is that a serious question?" Suvius says.

"It is. If you do *anything* regretful to such a one in a million item, whether you break it, eat it, or sell it—then you will live with the consequences forever. Primordial souls are the golden eggs of Life. Their existence stabilizes the world's foundations through the gods that are born out of them.

"But the gods are dying, Suvius, which means that we are losing those divine, golden eggs. Dozens of them. There's no mitigating it. You have already seen the global consequences when a divine creator or keeper manages to perish."

"But Thurnos is past that point of lifelessness. He is being controlled by the Decay."

"He's not a dragon, Suvius. You can't just mindlessly kill everything you don't like."

"I have also had to kill things that I love. I understand that you care for your family, but what if we need extreme insurance in case he's more determined to kill us first?"

"You can't afford that insurance. Not many can," Malphunnos says. "To kill a god requires specific types of magic to either suppress, wither, or erase their soul out of existence."

"Besides the Decay? I assume you're not going to reveal the info about these impossible forms of magic?"

"No I will not. There are enough Godslayers in this world."

"It might be what we need," Suvius says.

"We will do without it. Thurnos doesn't deserve that kind of harm."

"Then what's our actual option here, Malphunnos?"

"We'll have to delay his rampage and shove him back where he came from. That's the best idea I've got."

"Then we'll go with that. I'll let you handle the offense—just this once."

"Is that so you won't have to get struck by lightning?" Malphunnos says, snidely.

"Partially. I also don't want to overuse this dangerous power I do not understand."

"That's enough—no need to shower me with your excuses. Now stand back so I can call him over here. You better be ready."

Malphunnos casts a summoning to acquire his sickle and raises it high enough to make himself more prone to become bait for the lightning that hungers for the living. He staggers from the shock of being struck multiple times in a row—but it's going to be worth it.

Fighting lightning with lightning, Malphunnos brings his overcharged sickle behind his back like a baseball bat and swings it forward, launching a volatile arc right at Thurnos.

The electric jolt does nothing to harm the storm-bringer, but it does peeve him off enough to acknowledge Mal's presence. He starts descending. Then in a blinding flash, he is zapped away. Thurnos shouldn't have retreated too far away. In fact, threats are always closer than they appear to be.

Malphunnos steps to the side to dodge an incoming javelin of lightning that comes from behind. "I like how everyone thinks they can catch me off guard," he says as he turns to Thurnos, who seethes at him from a good distance away. "Death is always faster than lightning. I'm sure I've always told you that, cousin." As soon as Malphunnos finishes his sentence, Thurnos appears in front of him in a flash, and smacks the sickle out of his hands. "Well… maybe not always."

Thurnos's fists crackle with his full power. He raises them both with the intent to bring them back down like hammers.

"Malphunnos, get out of the way!" Suvius shouts, making a heroic dash towards him. As he nears, Malphunnos jumps out of the way just in time to avoid Suvius's brutal charge right into Thurnos, with enough knockback to send him flying into the plaza's fountain and causing his electric buildup to prematurely detonate, turning a portion of the plaza into rubble.

"Was that me?" Suvius says with a gasp. "I haven't even begun to tap into my demonic power."

"Relax," Malphunnos says. "The only thing you just did was piss him off more."

Thurnos blasts away the toppled rubble that has him pinned and brings his foot down with a crushing stomp, electrifying the plaza's ground.

Malphunnos can hold out against the staggering lightning and thunder, but he fears for his partner. "S-S-Suvius!"

"This is exhilarating!" Suvius shouts with glee, embracing electrocution. "My heart is pumping so much that it might even explode!"

"T-That's not a g-g-good thing!" Malphunnos shouts.

"I feel like I'm alive again! There's going to be a change of plans, I'm switching roles with you. Just regain your strength for when it's time to send Thurnos back to Birthplace."

"S-Sure, whatever! J-Just get him to stop s-s-shocking meee!"

"Gladly. Enough with the warm-up, God of Thunder! Let's get this over with!"

Thurnos doesn't take Suvius's invitation lightly, showing his rage through the blackened clouds and an electrifying air that would liquefy lungs.

Suvius inspects his cuirass. *Hmm. What was it that Ceranus said to activate this Artifact? Wasn't it... Submission?* He says the word again, only this time, it is out loud. He can tell the phrase is working as there is an agonizing pressure collapsing around his heart—but something's missing. *What? No weapons? Ah, I see. I am the weapon. My fingertips... it feels like I'm touching the gates of Hell.*

Thurnos constructs two perfected spears of lighting forged from his personal furnace in the sky and hurls them at Suvius.

Suvius is on a scenic route to reach Thurnos, as if he's walking on air in high spirits with a view of lofty clouds and basking in the euphoria of something unprecedented as the power within him expands past his body's shell into a controllable aura. "It all burns at my core with so much passion," he says. "All my hatred…"

Suvius catches both of Thurnos's thrown lighting spears and tosses them aside like discarded trash. He then prepares his own attack. Orange globs of spectral fire separate from his body's aura and hover around him.

"All my rage…" Suvius says next.

The swaying orbs turn ballistic and annihilate themselves by crashing into Thurnos like a point-blank meteor shower. After the barrage ends, Thurnos gets physical with his attacks and shapeshifts into a missile of lightning to launch himself at Suvius.

"All my sorrow…"

Thurnos is blocked by a summoned wall of hellfire that burns him completely out of his incorporeal form.

"All of my sins are as undying just as I am. Would you like to see it?"

Suvius takes hold of Thurnos's fists and drags him closer to his face, forcing him to peer into Suvius's fiery eyes and immobilizing him with a mental attack. Thurnos is soul-crushed and does not recover from whatever hell Suvius made him see or reflect on. He is brought down into total submission and gets slammed into the ground to make that message of subjugation even clearer.

Suvius powers himself down as he looks down on the motionless god. "The boy has told me something fascinating about the true motivations among you Decayed—that there is some sort of deeper plot. With that said, how is that working out for you? Are you feeling the weight of this Immortal's sins, parasite? The very same ones that you forced his mind and body to commit against countless innocents? All this damn preaching about how extinction is meant to be our salvation from ourselves. That is only cowardice. Do we look like cowards to you?"

Suvius lets his words ferment before he finally switches his focus over to Malphunnos. "Malphunnos, are you ready! I have him stalled!"

Malphunnos takes his sickle and makes a quick slash through the air, creating an open portal-like rift that splits apart space itself. Its stability begins to flicker and turn wavy. "You better bring him over here fast! This gateway isn't stable!"

Red-hot chains phase upwards through the ground and wrap themselves around Thurnos. He's a well-packaged god ready to be delivered by Suvius's hands.

"Just throw him in," Malphunnos says.

Thurnos is chucked into the portal, and the storm soon recedes and disperses from his absence.

"Short but eventful, just the way I like it. We make a good team, don't you think?" Malphunnos is met with no response from Suvius. "What's the matter?"

"I was only able to give a brief glance, but… your home… there wasn't a sliver of gold or light anywhere."

"Oh… I'm deeply sorry you had to see that," Malphunnos says. "No man of faith, even one who has renounced theirs, should have to see a fallen paradise."

"But I now know that it does exist. That makes me feel a bit more whole."

"Do you think things would be different for you if you saw it before you became the man you are now?"

"No," Suvius states. "My biggest faith wasn't towards the holy religions created to honor the gods—it was towards everyone else. This forbidden path of mine was made because I lost faith in the world."

"Will you ever go find that lost faith? You shouldn't remain faithless," Malphunnos says.

"I didn't need to search. That faith has come back to me instead. It now lies with us. All eight of us."

"Yagaaaa!" a familiar cry of rejoice echoes in the far distance behind them.

"You all should have been evacuated!" Malphunnos shouts. "Do the words from a god mean nothing to you people?"

"We really, really, love a good fight," Night-Drinker says. "Especially ones that are impactful. Let's not have any more at least for a week though, if this world can help it…"

Draxis barges his way over to Suvius. "What the hell is going on with everyone? And with you? I thought you said you wanted a souvenir, like a trinket or a pillow or something—not demonic power! How long have you been a demon?"

"Since the day this world turned me into one," Suvius responds.

"I don't want a hardcore response. I just want to know if you're going to be okay."

"Nothing's changed, but that's only a personal bias. These powers do not provide heightened introspection. Take that information for how you will."

"I'm not babysitting you," Draxis says.

"So shallow. I babysit you all the time."

"You're a bastard."

"Spoken like a child."

Draxis sighs. "Look, I'm sure you know what you're doing, but just don't do anything beyond common reason. Okay?"

Suvius responds with a light chuckle. "Why must you deny me of my fun?" He then turns to face Malphunnos.

"Yes? You need something?" he asks.

"Thurnos. He's not going to come back, is he?"

"I can't say for certain. If he was able to follow me outside of Birthplace, then I might have made things worse for us if the other gods start to follow by his example."

"Do not blame yourself," Suvius says. "Sometimes evil is born out of good intentions. A good portion of our actions these past few weeks have had similar repercussions."

"Still, I don't want to make it a habit." Malphunnos then lets out a sigh, before saying, "Why is it so easy to start a fire but never to quell it?"

"It be like that sometimes," Sadra says.

"Thank you, Sadra…"

"Yep-yep!"

"Wait. Where is the Artifact?" Suvius asks. "Is it secured?"

"I have it safe," Jellop says, pulling it out from within his cloak. "This shiny thing soothes my sanity like a kindred spirit. I want to keep it."

"I feel the same way with my Artifact," Suvius says. "Do us a favor then and signal us a way home."

Jellop links his mind with the amulet. It activates from his thoughts of home. A portal manifests shortly after.

"It's been an honor, Harbingers," Night-Drinker says. "Especially you, Minister Suvius."

"Don't. I don't deserve that title."

"You are free to decline, but we do have an empty seat that needs to be filled. You are welcome to claim it anytime."

"Lucky…" Aluna grumbles.

"Hmm. Then I will deeply consider it," Suvius says. "You remind me when I was a young and curious knight, Night-Drinker."

"Do I? If I'm considered a knight to our community, then maybe I should visit a human settlement just like you did with mine. It'll be a fresh learning experience."

"I don't think there are any human settlements remaining."

"That's fine, you seem capable of leading a new one."

"It is a common dream of mine." Suvius then bows to the Orkanian people that surround them in awe. "It's been a true pleasure, everyone. We'll be setting off." Suvius stands aside to let the others exit, only to block Aluna off when she approaches.

"Did I do something wrong?" she asks. "I'm so sorry if I did!"

"Slow down," he says gently. "You handled yourself justly today. I only wanted to know if later… would you mind filling me in about what you know about the Orkanians? I quite like it here."

"R-Really? That's so exciting!"

"I'm excited as well."

***

"Graaandpa!" Sadra yells. "We're baaack!"

"You all have been gone longer than usual. I hope that…" Klae's thoughts leave him as he notices the tall and menacing stranger approaching him. "Err… who might this be? A secret Harbinger?"

"Oh him?" Draxis says. "That's just Malphunnos. The God of Death himself."

"Eh?"

"Pleasure to see you in person, Klae Marriot," Malphunnos greets.

"Death is here… Does that mean that my time is up?"

"Wouldn't you like to know…"

"Stop scaring people, Mal," Maeva warns.

"But look at his face!" he says laughing. "It's priceless!"

"I'm prone to heart attacks y'know!" Klae says.

"It's not that bad, you only have a thirty-two percent chance on your worst days. You can lower that by limiting what you eat and exercising more."

"I just can't believe this. First dragons, and now gods. What's next? Demons?"

"Well…" Suvius says, with his words drifting off.

"There are way too many high-ranking players participating in this game," Klae says.

"Almost makes you want to bid against the world," Draxis says.

"Some people are crazy enough to do it. I'll analyze the newest Artifact you've acquired and pinpoint the next one. If it's any consolation, we might not need too many more. I think."

Chapter 35

Oasis

The sound of a portal phasing into reality breaks through the steady evening silence.

"Suvius!" Maeva says. "You're back!"

"I'm sorry I had to depart so suddenly without explaining myself. There were a lot of souls I had to go reclaim before we continued on. Primarily my own."

"Does that mean we can finally ask you where you hid it?" Draxis asks.

"Ooooh, I'm so excited," Sadra says, barely able to contain herself.

Suvius chuckles. "I didn't know you all cared so much about my soul."

"We made a game out of it," Draxis says. "My favorite guess was that you hid it somewhere in Vomenn. I suppose that would have been too obvious."

"I would say it's half and half, just like what my soul could have ended up as if Laxan beheaded me instead of sloppily dumping my body into Evergreen Catacombs."

"I feel like your haunting vengeance is the reason he started using dragons to cremate those he executed. I had to do it every now and again."

"And just like his madness, even that soon backfired on him," Suvius says. "Anyway, enough about that bastard. Does anyone else want to take a guess as to where my soul was?"

"What about me? I already knew of the location," Jellop says. "Does this make me the winner?"

"No, you cheater," Aluna says. "Disqualified!"

"Sadness…"

"I think we're through guessing, Suvius," Maeva says.

"Giving up already? I suppose I can't blame any of you. I had to think of every conceivable location across the globe before my struggles circled right back to my hometown, where I settled with burying my soul next to my parents' graves."

"That's sweet—and sad," Sadra says.

"I don't think about them too often. It bothers me to wonder what they would think of me if they saw me now."

"I like to think they would be happy that you still think about them, despite everything," Maeva says.

"You all are much too innocent for me," Suvius says. "That makes my next request even harder to ask for."

"Go ahead," Aluna says.

"I want to check up on the survivors from Vomenn. I consider it my responsibility to make sure they are well. Would you allow it, Klae?"

"Needy today, aren't we?" he responds. "Try to remember that these personal trips hurt the age of my body. I'm probably in my late 70s now, though it feels like I'm 90."

Malphunnos picks up an empty glass bottle. "Even without these side adventures, your death would be accelerated no faster than from you downing these 'potions'. You have a drinking problem."

"To think I would hear that from Death of all people."

"It shouldn't matter who says it. I need to know if you're going to stop. Children like you shouldn't even be drinking."

"Who are you calling a child?" Klae snaps.

"Just because you screwed up your age doesn't mean that you should be acting like a disgrace."

"Whatever."

"Don't 'whatever' me!" Malphunnos responds. "These flasks better be gone when we return!"

"Oh, would you look at that, my hand is moving on its own…"

The ground below them fractures into an inescapable, voracious void.

***

"Oof!" Malphunnos grunts, in shock from slamming down onto hardened soil. "That boy is so dead when we get back." Malphunnos staggers to his feet and looks around. He finds himself lucky that his face didn't connect with the old pieces of ruin that overtake his surroundings. "Wait, where the hell are we?"

"Bruness," Suvius says.

"Nonsense. This pile of rubble is a home for rats now. What survivor could possibly live in this?"

"All of them," Jellop answers. He moves his staff around from side to side. "My instrument is detecting presences, thoughts of serenity. We must descend."

"You mean like underground?" Malphunnos asks.

"Yes."

"These ruins are way too large to go around exploring."

"Why don't you use that new trick I showed you, Aluna?" Rend says. "It'll save us some time."

"Hell yeah!" She extends her arms out, with both hands connected to her thumbs and with her palms facing the ruins in front of her. Her wings are drained of their red and orange hue as she unleashes their color in the form of a ferocious beam of pure destruction that sweeps across the land and demolishes everything it touches.

"Well, that was overkill," Sadra mutters after the dust settles.

"And loud…" Jellop groans.

Near an excavated hole in the cobblestone, Maeva shouts, "There's something over here!" She waits for them to gather around before saying, "These stairs seem conspicuous."

"With how often we go underground we should become tomb raiders," Draxis says.

"Don't do that, you'll get dirty," Sadra says in disgust.

"Everyone, watch your step," Suvius says.

At the bottom of the muddy stairs lies a door, with a slip of paper attached to the front of it. Rend offers himself to examine it and read the paper out loud. "If you are not a filthy Decayed and, or, not illiterate, then knock twice. If no one answers by the third attempt, then try again later—if you're not dead by then. Huh… That seems simple enough." He then bangs on the door twice.

"Oi! Who's out there?"

"That sounds like Enam," Suvius says.

"It's us!" Rend says. "The Harbingers!"

"Oh yeah? Prove it!"

"Just open the damn door!"

The door opens slightly ajar. Enam peeks around it. "We are a peaceful community, so hostile guests are unwelcome. I'm surprised you all are even here."

"It would be a disservice to not be here," Suvius says.

Enam opens the door fully. "I really had you all wrong. I'm really thankful for that. May I ask why you all look so different? There's nothing wrong, it's just that you all are really going hard with that nightmare-inducing apparel style."

"We play at our strengths. You should try it."

"Me?" Enam asks. "I think it's healthier for me to stick with the holy faith. Darkness has its superior quirks yeah, but I'd much rather be able to see where I'm going."

"We're still talking about fashion, right?" Maeva asks.

"…Are we?"

"How about you move along and show us the way inside, miss 'guiding light'." Suvius says.

"H-Hey, don't be so mean. And don't push me!"

"You guys go on ahead," Draxis says. "I'm staying out here."

"I was going to say the same thing," Malphunnos comments. "I don't want to get a headache from answering a million questions about the other gods."

"Are you sure, Brightheart?" Sadra asks Draxis. "Are you still sensitive to humans?"

"I'm not. I just… don't want to put anyone in danger."

"Danger?"

"What I mean is… that I want to keep watch? Ye-yeah, that's what I meant. We did cause a major scene earlier, so I want to make sure we weren't followed by any Decayed. It'll be fine. I have Malphunnos to help out. Go and have some fun. You've earned it."

"O-Okay…"

Draxis watches Sadra and the others go further underground and makes sure that the door is sealed shut. He returns to the top of the stairs and looks around for something to rest against. His stomach rumbles as he reclines against a boulder.

Malphunnos plops down next to Draxis, forcing him to scooch over to make room. "Hungry, are we? How many 'soul snacks' do you have left anyway?"

"Two…" Draxis says.

"Bummer. Watching you shapeshift from a werewolf into a human earlier made me remember something about you. You're one of the few beings in existence that I know of who can eradicate souls completely."

"What about it?" Draxis asks.

"Nothing, it just makes me admire dragons more. Narisa created one hell of a race."

"Are dragons her method of destroying the life she creates? We *were* consumers of the world's elements after all."

"I never thought of it like that… and she would have never told me," Malphunnos says. "I guess she and I both tried our hands at each other's roles to some extent. Necromancy and Devourment. That's so crazy."

"Indeed…"

***

"Are you all ready?" Enam says to her tour group.

"What are we supposed to be ready for?" Maeva asks.

"To witness the joy of peace after so long. With that said…" Enam suddenly pauses her words and runs ahead, eventually turning around a corner.

Her action is disquieting, but they pursue her anyway. They are not prepared for what awaits them when they swerve around the corner.

"Welcome to New Bruness! The subterranean kingdom!" Enam cheers, while being outlined from the soft glow of countless candles and lanterns that illuminate the great cavern chamber behind her.

"H-How?" Suvius says. "There's no way this could have been made in any reasonable stretch of time."

"With just humans, yes. But there's Dwarves here too."

"Dwarves?"

"Heck yeah! Those guys are awesome at what they do."

"You shouldn't downplay humanity," a voice says, coming closer through the tunnel's blanketing light. "We have our own special form of manpower and talents that none can surpass. But yes, dwarves are indeed awesome." The voice comes from a man who stands tall and esteemed, along with the young woman who hugs his leg passionately.

"Are you two the king and queen here?" Suvius asks. "Didn't think we would have an encounter so suddenly."

"King Novair Bruness," he says before he bows. "And my crowning jewel, Damea Bruness."

"Happily married we are!" Damea says.

"Your eyes seem to be having a hard time adjusting to this serene place," Novair says to them. "I understand the disbelief. The history of New Bruness is quite a funny one."

Damea steps in to say, "Just as we were about to sink Old Bruness right from under the humans and seize a war victory, that scary day happened."

"Blighted Day," Novair adds. "Humanity and Dwarves in this region both suffered immense loss that day. And so, we merged our broken communities together to survive. Our coexistence has been a resounding success."

"That's so sweet," Sadra says.

"It's a shame the world had to end to change our beliefs, but hopefully something better can be made out of the ruins."

"Is that what you all are doing?" Damea asks.

"Slowly but surely," Suvius says.

"Then may you find something here to aid you," Novair says.

"Go around and show your faces!" Damea says with delight.

"And thanks for paying us a visit," King Novair says as he bows once again, before leaving with Damea.

***

"Ah…" Novair sighs as he identifies the pair of fiery eyes that sit idly in the corner of a bustling main area. "So, you're the spooky shadow that's been making everyone feel uneasy. You just got here and yet you choose to rest your hollow be-hind in this congested location."

"I'm only people-watching," Suvius responds, sounding slightly guilty.

"That won't do anyone any good. No one can see your intent of peace if you lurk in the shadows. Come, walk with me."

Suvius is coaxed to be taken on a tour while he listens to Novair talk.

"I'm more of the type of person that needs to keep moving in order to ponder what I can't solve. Right now, it's the conflict between my forgiveness and hatred. I would have never expected the proud people of Vomenn to come begging and crying at our doorstep. And you know what we would have done to them if this was the old world? We would have killed them. Something harrowing tells me that had I followed through with my grudges then my very own kingdom would have been next to fall if you would have found out."

"We aren't like that anymore," Suvius deflects.

"So some of the refugees say."

"Is that so?"

"In general, there's a wide variety of blame and praise aimed at numerous people of interest about this all-out dragon invasion that I missed out on. The gossip that I fancy however is about how the villains that were once believed to bring this world to ruin became the saviors that prevented a second doomsday."

"I wouldn't go that far about our efforts," Suvius says. "The Vomenn kingdom handled itself well enough on their own."

"That only makes them all the more impressive—and terrifying," Novair says. "Now, out of respect, I haven't brought it up with the surviving citizens and knights, but I wanted to know what became of Mad King Laxan and the Dragonslayer? Did they…"

"Laxan died as he lived—through spilling blood," Suvius says. "Queen Ceranus was different. She had remorse and wasn't afraid to admit that she herself was a catalyst for everyone's destruction as well as her own."

"That's a lot to take in. I can't lie to you and not say that I am thrilled that they are gone, but that shouldn't be directed towards those who are now bannerless and homeless beyond their control."

"You had every right to deny providing shelter for your life-long rivals—but you went against it. I want you to know that your willingness to provide such kindness is not going to go unnoticed."

"That is comforting," Novair says. "It's not easy to keep my hatred dormant, but what helps me keep my thoughts pure is believing in the faith that this good karma will amount to something. Maybe with enough of it I can start a new beginning, and it seems like everyone else is doing the same.

"Suvius, listen, I don't care who or what started this apocalypse. I just want it to finally be over so I can care for these people properly and venture out into the remains of the world with my wife. Of course, I'm not trying to propose that you fulfill that wish for me."

"There's no need to even if you were," Suvius says. "The Harbingers will always push back against the evils that make the world grieve."

"You all were so vocal about your heroic mission against injustice since the day the Arbiters declared the Harbingers as global terrorists. But alas, here we are, as the nonbelievers—reaping what we sowed every day and night. I must go now… but before I do, I have to say that I do like your armor. It's been distracting me for the longest time."

"Finally, someone does."

***

"Oop!" Maeva squeaks as she feels something lightweight plop down on her head. "For a second there I thought someone pelted me with a rock again. Hey, Aluna."

"Yeah… hi."

"What's wrong?" Maeva asks.

"I'm getting tired of these people swatting at me. It's like they've never seen a fairy before."

"Fairies weren't exactly super common in the old days. It's even worse now."

"So? Is common sense a rarity too?" Aluna says. "I'm starting to piss myself off the more I talk about it. Anyway, what's going on with you?"

"I'm hunting for children right now," Maeva says.

"Huh? We need to get you on a proper date or something. Your mind is starting to wander somewhere bad."

"N-No, no—what I mean is that we haven't come *across* any children, like at all. You ever notice that?"

"I hate that you're bringing something like that to my attention." Aluna then surveys the random citizens that move around each other like a swarm. "Well, I'm sure there are *some* kids around here, right?"

"Not from what I'm seeing. I hope that the lack of a new generation is out of choice rather than something else."

"Why are you thinking about children anyway? I thought you hated them?"

"A woman can change her mind," Maeva says, pouting.

"You're doing a complete flip though," Aluna says.

"Who asked you? Go away!"

"Agh! Now *you're* swatting at me!"

"I have found the source of distress," Jellop says, arriving just in time. "Do you need help, Aluna?"

"My hero!" Aluna cries out, rushing to her beacon of hope.

Maeva is no match for Aluna's determination to reach her awaiting checkpoint: Jellop's open palms.

"I think I know how you're feeling, Maeva," Aluna says while she rubs her hands against Jellop's palms. "Maybe creating a new generation isn't such a bad idea."

"I didn't say I wanted kids."

"For now. Take me away, Jellop!"

"Ughh…" Maeva groans.

***

Suvius finds himself in what he can only guess is a dining area. He surveys the stone tables, watching people as they eat and joke around. He sees a disgruntled and hardened woman sitting at a table in the far back. He can feel his heart beating faster as he thinks about how to approach her.

The targeted woman eyes Suvius up and down as she drinks her water and slams her tankard down on the table. "Get the hell away from us…"

"Just let him sit," a man says next to her.

"Hell no! I don't know why Novair let this bastard in! He's just causing a disruption!"

"You're the only one who's being loud," a woman says.

"If I may say something," Suvius intrudes as he takes an empty chair. "I came here with the intention of bringing peace, not breaking it."

The woman of interest brings a mighty fist down on the table, shouting, "It's too late for peace! Why am I the only one with the guts to say it around here? Some of us have never even felt peace—like my daughter! She was the best knight this kingdom's ever had, and she died years ago trying to protect good people from you Harbingers and all those other monsters who have slain other good people's daughters and sons. Is that peace to you?"

"You speak of Teresa," Suvius says.

"…How do you know her name? I bet you did something horrible to her."

"I have."

"That's all you have to say about it? Do you think of her death as meaningless trash? That's she's something beneath you?"

"On the contrary, she was always above me. I understood her brilliance the day I encountered her. I just never gave her the proper justice she deserves… until today." Suvius pulls out a large hidden crystal from within his hollow mouth and slides it across the table. "Your daughter's soul. I'm returning her to you."

The woman holds the crystal close to her face, watching the bluish-white soul inside clink against it towards her direction.

"I know this isn't how you want her to return to your arms," Suvius continues, "but this is the only thing a brute like me can do to return what shouldn't have been taken."

"You… I still want you out of my sight," the woman says, tightening her grip on the crystal and holding it to her lips. "Just… go away. Please."

"Of course. Hopefully you will never see or have to deal with me ever again." Suvius then exits the dining chamber swiftly.

After turning a few corners and straining to take another step, he holds his hand over his chest as he lays against a wall. "That took a lot out of me more than I thought it would. Still, this catharsis… I have so much more work to do."

"I saw what you did, Suvius. L-Lord Suvius."

"He looks to his side, locking eye socket to eye with Sadra. "My word, I think that's the first time you genuinely called me that without scorn. Are you unwell?"

"Don't push it, Nightmare. I'm only being polite because I'm acknowledging whatever it is you're doing. I've been watching you closely for some time now ever since you prayed at that altar back on Isilios."

"And people call *me* a stalker…" Suvius says.

"I was only in disbelief that you would even do such a thing. I don't understand you at all."

"I am growing to detest the man who viewed this world as unsalvageable. Isilios is a strong example of that old fool's unrighteous violence."

"He still looks like a fool to me," Sadra says, pointing at Suvius. "Take a look at what you're wearing. You'll never become a saint."

"Not if I had your attitude. You shouldn't treat Darkness as your enemy, but as a benefactor if you allow it."

"Darkness is only good for tearing this world apart! It used to be under strict supervision by the Isilians. You know, before our knowledge was destroyed and we were submerged into corruption…"

"A current age of darkness doesn't mean it can't be reversed."

"What do you mean?" she asks.

"By controlling it," Suvius says. "It's a lesson on Malice that I picked up from the Orkanians, who have learned it from the Demons. Darkness is an occult study that is harsh, but I am choosing to explore it because I believe it is a necessary tool that can allow fundamental change—just like Light can. Have you done anything to change yourself lately, Priestess?"

"Me? Change?"

"Yes. You. Take ideas from those you choose to critique. Maeva has turned her repulsive power into something attractive. Aluna has sinned greatly and bears a sadistic torment that should have descended her mind to high insanity, but she still fights continuously with maximum resistance. Draxis has lost practically everything in such a short amount of time, but he keeps his head high enough above the water to pursue a worthwhile goal.

"Jellop is a complete alien to our world and is constantly treated as such, but that doesn't stop him from being our true support in times of need. Even our newest member—Rend—he has been given a second chance in the worst possible timeline, but he is devoted to becoming a pillar of strength for himself and those he chooses to uplift around him."

"Sounds beautiful. But… I don't think I can raise myself to those standards that drive you all," Sadra responds.

"You're letting the darkness control what you say and allowing it to make you think that you're not worth it," Suvius says.

"Has it ever been wrong though?"

"Sadra…"

"Don't say my name like you're blameless, you're the one who did this to me! You're not worthy of preaching."

"And you're not saying anything new, but at this moment, I'm all you got, and I'm telling you that you need to have faith in yourself. Spread your blessings like a daughter of Light should be doing."

"Any blessing I could spare has already been forever lost."

"You sound just like I did before I renewed myself." Suvius then reaches for her shoulder. "Do you feel lost, Sadra?"

"I can't be lost if I never had anywhere to go. It's dark out there."

"Then think about the sun," Suvius says. "Isn't that the dominant symbol that defines your people?"

"But the sun is gone now. I forgot what it looks like."

"Then picture what it used to mean to you and become it. Become the one thing that you lost—whether it was innocence or hope or anything else in between—and let both your Light and Darkness manifest into an eclipse that is yours to command."

Sadra looks off to the side. "I remember seeing an eclipse once. It was… mesmerizing, like a reflection." Her body begins to dim. "Controlling my conflicting sides would be nice. But, umm… I'm struggling to think of a way how to."

"Start simple. You might have to learn more about yourself. Maybe even take a few risks. Since you seem to focus on trauma, maybe you could try alleviating others' traumas. Like apologizing to a certain someone that you have wronged."

"Wronged who?"

"Seriously?" Suvius sighs. "Just—just go and do something productive. I have more families I must reunite before today's end."

"I still don't really understand you," Sadra says.

"It keeps my enemies guessing."

***

The underground city is naturally filthy, muggy, and un-kempt—but someone has been going around and making it worse. Rend has been following that particular someone's trail of bad habits that litter the ground in the form of empty tankards and hazardous spills for a half hour. He's even stumbled upon Enam on the way, who is much too eager to go snooping around for troublemakers.

Their investigation is at its climax now, at a dead end near the outskirts of civilized territory. This isn't a moment of triumph. A friend is in dire need of help.

"Damel…" His name escapes from Enam's lips.

"Enam, is Damel here going to be okay?" Rend asks.

"Not when Novair finds out he's been skipping guard duty."

"What's the point anymore?" Damel muffles, sitting down with his face buried in his arms, and near a pint that could use a fresh refill. "Just let the dragons and Decayed and all the other horrors come in here and put me out of my misery."

"Wow, that's… really bad," Enam says, distraught. "Damel, we talked about this. Guard duty is supposed to help take your mind off things."

"What have we been guarding all this time anyway? When you think about it, I've been dedicating my life to protecting the guilty."

"Having them die horrifically would also make you guilty," Enam says.

"Regardless, if I couldn't guard my queen, then what makes you think I can guard these people?"

"You've already shielded them time and time again. They might not be here now if it wasn't for us being their trusted defenders. You have to understand that."

"It's only a matter of time before I fail to protect them as well. This isn't even our home to call our own," Damel says.

"Home is wherever the heart feels sheltered. You told me that, remember?" She wishes he would respond back to her with a yes. Enam takes a quick look around, frantically searching for aid. "Is that Borace?" she says, squinting. "He must have taken over for Damel. Oi! Borace! Get over here!"

He hears her plea and makes his way over, staying as silent as the night and with intentions shrouded by his dark helmet.

"Help us out here, will ya? Our captain here is sinking with the ship if you get what I mean," Enam says.

Borace is slow to approach Damel, like he's taking caution. He hunches over near him, startling Damel when he tries to reach for his drink. Damel takes a long look at Borace—then at his drink— then he rises from his seat. He doesn't speak as he leaves.

"What did you say to him, Borace?" Enam asks.

"Nothing," he responds. "He took one look at me and sprang to life."

"You do have such a way with nonverbal encouragement. Maybe he saw his reflection in that rusty tin-can you wear."

"My stillness inspires all, like a weathered statue enduring through a storm." He takes the closest chair and slumps down into it. "But no statue lasts forever, no matter the material…"

Enam pats Borace on the shoulder as she looks at Rend. "This may have been inadvertent, but regardless, thanks for bringing me here. Someone has to get these two moving along. It's getting harder, but we won't stop fighting!"

"I'm not sure if it's my place to say this, but don't be afraid to let the Harbingers help you out and carry you up high," Rend says.

"That sounds ironic seeing as we're underground, but I get what you mean."

***

How boring… Sadra thinks to herself. It isn't completely fair to think of the survivors as such as she watches them pass by, but they all move about aimlessly like they're just moving for the sake of doing something. She can change that. It's the best hour to strike.

Sadra has already picked out a good location to procure for herself the most influence inside one of the main junction chambers meant for traveling.

She scrambles and climbs on top of a stone table and makes her body shine as she yells out, "Everyone look at me and listen up!" She waits for their dulled attention to fall onto her. "The world may be going to shit but that doesn't mean that we should feel like shit! What you people need is sunlight, and I can provide more than you can ever dream of!"

She rubs her hands together and sends out a disk of light that spins on the tabletop, which then extends vertically into a skinny pole. "Behold and bear witness!"

Sadra grips the pole with both of her hands and latches her body onto it. Shimmering sparkles glitter the air as she dances and twirls around and around it. Her fluidlike performance has already lured in a large gathering that surrounds her on all sides to form a wild audience that demands more motion and hip swaying.

The thrilling excitement can be heard outside the chamber walls. Both Novair and Damea hear it loud and clear.

"This better not be another fight…" Novair groans. "Just how many more of these do I have to settle today?" Novair can't even get through the entrance without putting in some extra force. "Come on, people! Clear the way! Move!"

Novair finally arrives to the front—and is rewarded with a perfect, broad view of Sadra's performance. "Oh? Oooh! And here I thought these types of shows were a relic from good times. Fortune must be favoring my patience."

"Nooo!" Damea yells. "Don't look, my love!"

"Not even a peek?"

"No! Stop drooling and shield your eyes!"

Farther outside the party chamber, humans and dwarves are migrating in flocks. Maeva finds herself swept along with the pack after straying too close due to innocent curiosity. She has no choice but to go with the flow, but luckily, a human blockade is staged just up ahead. The jam gives her enough time to slither out and break free. Relief is achieved as she stays near the tunnel sidelines to get some breathing room.

"Maeva!" Aluna shouts, flying in from the opposite direction of everyone else.

"I'm glad to see a friendly face," Maeva says. "Did you happen to see what's causing this commotion?"

"It's not a what but a who. Sadra."

"Seriously?"

"Who else would it be?"

"I can't tell if I'm impressed or disappointed at her knack for mayhem. Go see if you can find Suvius, we'll need some major help. I'll be here for the time being… to avoid getting trampled."

Aluna flies away to look for Suvius. Luckily, he was already on the way. "Suvius, we have a problem."

"Who is it this time?"

"Our shining star."

Suvius doesn't say anything else. He nods to indicate that he's ready to execute some discipline. Aluna guides him—while he makes the path free of resistance for her by forcing the crowds to back away from him with his emanating dissatisfaction—all the way to center stage.

"What in the—n-no! Bad Sadra!" Suvius yells. "This isn't what I meant by spreading your light!"

"This is your fault?" Aluna shouts at him. "You dumbass, you know she easily misinterprets things!"

"Has she?" Jellop disputes as he joins the party, with Maeva stuck to his arm like a desperate squirrel. "To me, it seems like she has heard you, but was creative in interpretation. Look how happy everyone is at her splendid creativity."

"Couldn't she do something simpler and less… raunchy?" Aluna says. "Like arts and crafts? Ugh!"

Maeva is the only one not too terribly distracted to see the glaring fire hazard that Sadra is tiptoeing over. "Sadra!" she calls out. "Watch what you're doing!"

"I know! I'm pretty good at this!"

"No! Watch out for that lantern!"

"Lantern?" Before Sadra knows it, she's already kicked the lantern off the table, with all its combustible contents spilling over. "Oh shit!"

"I got it! I got it!" Aluna shouts. "Air magic, go!"

The cyclonic wind only aggravates the newborn fire more, forcing it to scatter across a wide area.

Rend arrives just in time to save a woman from incineration. "Idiot!" he screams. "Why didn't you use ice!"

"Fuck you! You try!"

Rend tries to do things his way, but he only gets mocked further by Aluna and the disobedient flames. "Seriously, what the hell is going on? Queen Damea, what kind of nightmarish fire is this?"

"I think you meant to say dreamy," she says. "The concentrated extract from golem hearts makes these eternal flames so pretty to watch before a good long nap."

The fire is fully developed at this point—and it's ready to produce some offspring. A few lanterns nearby get swallowed up by the sea of fire and regurgitate out little embers that start making their own families.

"For fuck's sake, how many lanterns do you people need!" Rend cries out.

"This place was so nice while it lasted…" Novair grumbles. "Everyone, abandon ship! Grab the essentials! Leave the booze! Save the children!"

"You're the only child here, Novair," Enam says.

"Then I guess I get to evacuate first. Let's go, Damea!"

"O-Okay!"

"H-Hey!" Enam shouts, "Wait for me!"

Outside the chaos happening underground, Malphunnos jolts awake, with a severe case of drowsiness. "So noisy. Did you say something, Draxis? Oh… you're asleep too. Never mind, I'm sure it was nothing."

***

"It's really… unfortunate, that you all were kicked out," Enam says.

"You don't sound too upset," Rend responds.

"I do have to clean up after your messes, so please understand why I'm a bit peeved. I will say that you reanimated all of us with that extravagant display today, Sadra. You have my thanks for that at least."

"Yep-yep! Just spreading my light!"

The door to the underground creaks as it opens, startling them. Damea shows her face. "Is it safe out here, Miss Enam?"

"It is, but what are you doing out here? The king will be worried sick."

"I wanted to say goo—" Damea interrupts herself mid-sentence by suffering from a sudden coughing fit. "I wanted to say goodbye to them."

"You should head back inside. You're making your illness worse by being so active."

"I already said what I wanted to do." Damea then looks up at the Harbingers with droopy eyes. "Will you all come back to us in the future?"

"In time," Suvius answers.

"I hope so, I really en-enjoyed—" She goes into a coughing fit again.

Maeva steps forward. "May I take your hand, Damea? I can help you with your sickness, but you may not like how I do it."

"It can't be any worse than this."

"That is true."

No hassle comes from Damea as Maeva gently bites into her wrist. The effects are immediately felt. "Look, Enam! I can move and scoot along faster now!"

"Yes, you really are," Enam says. "Though, I am confused by it. I have so many questions about you all, but I think the answers would only bother me more. I am happy to say that my hope is being restored incrementally the more I think about your actions, so just keep doing what you all are doing and I'm sure everyone else will say the same… Are any of you listening to me?"

Enam looks down to see what everyone is so fixated on. She grabs one of Damea's hands to stop her from dancing. "Don't exhaust yourself, silly. We still have a long day ahead of us—just like they do. Come on."

"Bye!" Damea says, waving back at the others.

Taking the stairs back up to surface level, they find Draxis and Malphunnos deep in their slumber, and even drooling a little. Nobody finds it cute.

"These slouchers…" Maeva grumbles. "Wake up!"

"Wh-huh?" Draxis then yawns as his vision focuses, before saying, "Oh? Back so soon?"

"Your girlfriend got us kicked out."

"As per usual," Aluna adds.

"*Sadra*..." Draxis growls.

"I don't care. I had fun!" she responds after giggling.

"I would have more fun if we could leave this rugged place," Malphunnos says. "Damn my back hurts!"

Chapter 36

Burdens

"Hey, look who's finally awake!" Rend shouts while lounging on a beanbag chair made from gelatinous slime.

"Huh?" Klae says, rubbing his temples as he finds the nearest chair.

"Feeling the irony, Klae?" Sadra sneers.

"Not really, though I do apologize for the delay. I had a rough night."

"Is the anxiety from our progress getting to you, friendly Arbiter?" Jellop asks.

"Worse. It feels like I'm being haunted. All around me are these disgruntled shadows who curse at me with scornful loathing because of my association with the Arbiters. I know I shouldn't be blaming myself for their actions, but I can't get this feeling to go away for some reason."

"A mark of shame," Aluna states.

"That must be what it is. You feel it too, don't you?" Klae asks.

"No matter how minor or major my part might have been, I know that I'm one of the reasons for something bad happening. I'm ashamed that I didn't use this power against them, I'm ashamed that I let them kill my hopes, and I'm ashamed that even in death they still claim a few victories over me. None of it means that my pride is shattered as a whole, only weakened."

"This shame of mine is unshakeable for now, but if you can fight against yours, then so can I. I won't let their evil shadows contaminate what we got going on here. Look at how far we have come," Klae exclaims as he admires the collected Artifacts and trinkets thus far. "I can't thank you all enough for working so hard."

"It's all for a better future," Draxis says.

Klae nods. "I'm too old to be getting worked up like this. I didn't mean to bring down the mood. How about you all? Are any of you ready for the next assignments?"

"You said that in plural," Suvius says.

"I did. Care to help me explain, Malphunnos?"

Malphunnos stands against a wall, resting his back with his head down like he's trying to be invisible. He remains that way as he says, "Summarized, there is something in Birthplace that will help accelerate this Artifact hunt you all are doing."

"Well, what is it?" Rend asks.

"The Eternal Flame. A primordial fire created by the God-Witch of Fire during her first ever moment of rage. It still should be burning intensely even without her supervision. I'm sure she won't miss it."

"If that's *his* task then what of us?" Suvius asks Klae.

"To find the artifact deep within the dungeons of Gravefall Penitentiary." Klae stops himself and rolls his eyes at their frozen faces of shock. "Oh come on, it's like I can't say one word around here without triggering a fight response."

"I-It's fine, Klae," Maeva winces. "Just keep briefing us."

"Are you sure?"

"Keep talking before I kill you."

"That's the normal response I was looking for. Now, this next Artifact is a peculiar case because not only are there two components that make up the artifact as a whole, but this one was stolen directly from the Arbiters' personal stash."

"That is both hilarious and scary at the same time," Aluna says, gleefully. "I wonder who could have done it?"

"My guess would be the same people who stole Mixon's amulet," Klae says. "Did he ever tell you about that?"

"Of course he did. He never stopped yelling and cursing at me after I plucked it from his stupid neck."

"That was you who stole it? Did you have a death wish?"

"Yes."

"Let me rephrase: *Why* would you do it?"

"Because he deserved it," Aluna says. "You don't understand how dangerous that thing was, or how many people he killed with it during the World War… and in general."

"It might be best that I don't—but still, I am ashamed that I understand what you mean. Thinking of it now, I suppose the only logical way an Artifact could have been stolen in the first place would be because of disobedient peers."

"It had to have been someone close to the higher-ups," Aluna says.

"It's likely," Klae says. "According to the Arbiters' unofficial list of 'things to worry about later', the return of the Braces of Symmetry wasn't that high on their priorities. Which is weird considering how potent the magical braces sound on paper. Something about the magics of Radiance and Shadow."

"If the Elites didn't care, then they knew exactly who stole it—and unfortunately, I think I do to…"

"Ah, I think I see whom you're referring to. These braces sound perfect for those two sadistic brothers. Err, who were they again…? Sylis and Crysis, right?"

"Don't say their names out loud!" Aluna cries out, glancing over at Maeva.

"Stop looking at me!" Maeva shouts at her. "I don't care where we have to go at this point. We are so close to the end goal that I can almost reach out to it and bite its scrawny neck. But when we finally succeed, I'm coming back and burning that bitch to the ground!"

"The penitentiary sounds like it suits you," Klae says.

"Shut up."

"Why don't you use that hostility for something productive. Anyways, it's time to send you all to prison!"

"You're having way too much fun with this," Draxis groans.

"There's a bit of morbid glee from sending such infamous criminals to their rightful place."

"We could always make you join us, Klae…" Suvius says, with hellfire taking form in his eye sockets,

"Eek!"

Chapter 37

Tartarus

"Get down, Rend!" Aluna whispers with aggression. "What the hell are you doing?"

"I need to get a good mental picture of the complex. You all have been here before, not I."

"Let the boy entertain his sense of suicidal wonder," Suvius says. "We should be far enough away to camouflage in with these boulders if we don't move too much."

Rend peeks from over their hiding place. As far as he can tell, it's a long. Long. Long way down if any of them were to slip on the labyrinth of metal bridges that connect the isolated smaller build-ings to the colossal main building of the sinister complex—all held in suspension above a great chasm by massive rusty chains that are rooted into the cliff sides.

Despair must be a never-ending feast in this place. Rend slides back down against the boulder with that final thought. He's seen enough. "By the balls of Malphunnos, what kind of place is this?"

"You rang?" Malphunnos says, popping up next to Rend.

"Huh? Oh… sorry."

"I don't understand you mortals sometimes. What do my balls have to do with anything? And what the hell does that even mean? Regardless, none of you are worthy of seeing my balls."

"Okay, end of conversation!" Maeva snaps. "Either help us think of a way to sneak in or piss off and do your own part of the fucking assignment!"

"Ooh! I just thought of something!" Sadra exclaims with cheer. "Malphunnos, why don't you do that soul purge thing to those guards down there like you did with me?"

"Why?"

"I dunno. Can't you kill everyone here all at once to save us the trouble?"

"That's not how… you know what, that's a fantastic idea. Let's see how that turns out."

Malphunnos sticks out around the corner of their hiding place and aims carefully at an unsuspecting guard patrolling on a bridge. Snapping his fingers, the guard crumbles to the ground like a toy doll.

Another patrolman notices the struggle and rushes in to aid. "Oi, Felban! You get drunk again? Don't make me walk out here alone! Again!"

"Nothing's happening, Mal," Sadra says.

"Wait for it…"

Felban starts to rise up, twitching unnaturally.

"It's 'bout time you got up, you slacker," the other guard says. "Wait, what the hell are you doing? Stay back! Arghh!"

His screams attract other patrolmen. "It's Felban!" one of them says. "He's Decaying! Kill him!"

"That was actually pretty funny," Sadra says, trying to stifle her laugh. "Poor guy."

"Yeah… that's why I don't do things like that," Malphunnos says. "My power is only good for expediting the Decay."

"How useless," Maeva says, scowling at him in disgust. "Have you considered *not* making this harder for us? We don't need more zombies in this world, you jackass."

"Sadra offered a genuine suggestion, so I gave her a satisfying answer."

"I suggest you go to Birthplace like you were told," Maeva growls.

"I suggest you go to Hell where you belong," Malphunnos responds.

"What was that?"

"Nothing… I'll meet you all back at the Capital when I'm done." He then cleaves through reality with his sickle and leaves through the created rift.

"Did you have to be so harsh to him, Master?" Rend says.

"You shut up and focus." Maeva then shifts to peek over the boulders. A small unit has formed around Felban's body. "I'm starting to worry if they might have multiplied their security since our last prison breakout."

"Damn that was a fun day," Aluna says, becoming giddy as she reminisces.

"And we're going to do it again," Suvius says. "Preferably without causing a massive riot. I want us to take a slower approach, if possible—"

"Wait a minute," Draxis says, stopping him. "Are you suggesting stealth?"

"I'll give it a solid five minutes before we somehow fuck it up," Sadra says.

Jellop claps his hands to break the tension. "Negativity leads to a lack of motivation and an unfair trial of effort."

"I take it that you have an idea, Knave Jellop?" Suvius asks.

Jellop pulls out a familiar amulet from underneath his cloak. Friend Klae and I have studied and uncovered the secrets of this Artifact we earned from the Orkanians back at Wania, saying that he is glad this one was kept far away from the clutches of the Arbiters. I have tested this 'Mesmerion' item and found that it compliments my chaos well, only now, there can be order added too. If pacifism is a must, then I believe that with this I can perform greater but also less harmful chaos."

"Which means…?"

"A theory of mass illusion. May I demonstrate?"

"Go for it. Just be careful, obviously," Suvius says.

"Yay! Come here, Aluna."

She hesitates. "What do you need me for?"

"No offense, but you are much too short for me to mask your true size."

"That's fine. I'll just kick your ass later to make myself feel better."

Jellop takes her in his hands and pockets her within the interior of his hood. He then goes out into the open and makes the descent down to the awaiting guards who spot him almost immediately. He staggers his movements with his staff, appearing to be frail.

"Hello, fellow survivors," Jellop greets.

"Sup," an eager patrolman says. "Did we send some scouts out looking for supplies or not? Guys?"

"Don't look at me," another guard says. "My memory is shot to hell."

"Yeah, same," another joins in.

"You people are hopeless," the first guard says. "Well, stranger, state your business here or whatever."

"I'm new here," Jellop says. "I'm only seeking refuge."

"Ah, a newcomer! It's been a bit since we've seen new blood."

Jellop combs through the guard's mind, evaluating his thoughts and emotional state. He seems casual. They all are. Casual enough for Jellop to prioritize not accidentally causing a panic by using deceptive tricks. Charisma will have to do, hopefully. "It's not just me alone," he says. "There are more survivors I brought with me. They hide away out of anxiety." Jellop then waves the others over to him.

"Six new survivors?" the eager guard says. "This is one hell of a haul! The Wardens will be pleased that there are new members to dine in their Radiance."

"Jellop, press him for more information," Aluna whispers in his ear. "These people might only be friendly on the *outside* if you get what I mean."

"Err, how *does* one become a member of this… community?" Jellop asks the eager guard.

"Oh, the process is very simple. You just need to go through a sacrament ritual and then you'll become a bonafide member that will be here to stay. There are more goodies in it for you if any of you pass and remain devout."

"Great…" Jellop groans.

"All of that might have to wait," a stuck-up guard says. "The Elimination Assembly is today."

"Didn't we just have one like four days ago?" the eager guard argues.

"Yep."

"I know I shouldn't speak out on it, but this paranoia is starting to become a bother."

"Then maybe you should do your job properly and prevent the psiowls from bypassing us," the stuck-up guard says. "Speaking of which, you six newbies aren't psiowls, are you?"

"I eat psiowls for breakfast," Jellop says.

"That's so crazy!" a hyperactive guard says. "I make that joke all the time! It's like you're reading my mind or something!"

"Haha…"

"Ignore him, he's dense," the eager guard says. "I can take you all inside without the Wardens approval, though we might have to detour if the assembly is starting soon. You all fine with that?"

They all nod their heads.

"Wonderful, or whatever. Hey!" he shouts to the other patrolmen. "Can I trust any of you to stay here and keep watch?"

One guard is busy kicking Felban's body around while the others watch him. "H-Huh?" he responds. "O-Oh yeah, sure! Definitely!"

"Whatever…"

The first sigh of relief is made when they realize they are being escorted to the Penitentiary's colossal metal portcullis of the main building, and the second sigh of relief is made when they earn the time to rest their aching feet after such a long and unbearable walk. They are told to wait as the guards on the other side of the lattice gate pull the heavy chains to lift it upward.

"Hello? Friends? This is Jellop, I speak through telepathy! Hellooooo!"

"We can hear you Jellop!" Draxis shouts in his head.

"Muhuhu! I know."

"This is an astounding development, Jellop," Suvius says. *"May I ask what you are making them see us as?"*

"Oh, that was the unimpressive part. I am a little uncreative, so we all just look like regular humans who could use some love and care—and a fresh home."

"Nothing wrong with going with the default. I approve."

"I must warn though," Jellop continues. *"Please try to stay close and avoid extreme interactions. I can handle my abilities for now, but I can't make this operation flawless."*

"I say we should make this operation more fun instead," Aluna says. *"If your illusions are this strong then I wonder if you can make them see us as monsters or other things too?"*

"You have a twisted idea of fun, Butterfly. But... muhuhu! To think I can already do this much with this Artifact. I could cause so much mischief with this power..."

"Steady, Jellop," Suvius warns.

"Sorry. I don't know where that heinous thought arose from. I must still be recovering slightly."

"Hey!" their eager escort hollers at them, making them all yelp in fear. "Did any of you hear what I said?"

"To be honest, no," Jellop says.

"Story of my life," the eager guard mutters. "I said that we *do* have to make that detour. They just told me that the assembly is starting now. We can make it if we start running."

"Hold on, what's this assembly about?" Rend asks.

"We have a growing infestation of psiowls. The one stupid creature that this world won't eradicate for us as a favor. The Divine Brothers—Sylis and Crysis—can sift through and detect who is real and who is false with their blessed power."

"So, they *are* alive…" Suvius says.

"Who? The Brothers? Oh, I see, you must have heard tales about their roles here in this prison as wardens before the apocalypse. Or did you all hear about their new endeavors from outside rumors?"

"Both."

"That's superb. You people are in good hands now."

"I beg to differ," Maeva blurts.

"Maeva… don't spoil this for us," Draxis whispers.

"What does she mean?" the eager guard asks.

"Ignore her. Just ignore her please."

"Well, maybe when you see them in action at the assembly later then you'll feel more at ease."

Maeva gets blocked from saying anything further by layers of hands that seal her mouth shut.

Chapter 38

A Shepardless Lamb

"G-Good!" the eager guard says. "We made it just in time! Listen to the Divine Brothers closely, newcomers, and their Radiance shall guide your future. I need to get to my post. Bye."

Well, they managed to infiltrate the penitentiary successfully. Now what? The deafening claps and hollers from the people nearby provide enough indication of what should come next in their operation.

Turning around, everyone is stunned as they look up and stare at the duo who stand on top of a catwalk from way across the other side of the overfilled room with exuberant people in prayer. The duo, two men—they are both opposites in appearance. One has a body and face of statuesque perfection, while the other one is less than ideal. The revolting one is supported by a cane, but they both wear a single arm brace that flashes as they wave at the people below them.

Maeva has her head down, as far down as she can flex her tightened neck.

"Master doesn't look so good, Draxis," Rend says. "What can we do?"

"Get out of this place as fast as we can. I don't know how we're going to steal those braces from Sylis and Crysis though. This day already sucks."

"Them? Aren't they the wardens?"

"Warden is the incorrect term. The only thing they 'warded' was Maeva herself from the outside world. They are nothing but tormentors."

"Shit!" Aluna cries out.

"What now?" Draxis asks.

"Didn't that guy say that this assembly was meant for eliminating imposters? We're going to get spotted!"

"I told you all we wouldn't last five minutes with stealth," Sadra remarks.

"It's been a fantastic effort though," Draxis says.

"And from the looks of it, we're stuck in this position," Rend says, glancing back at an approaching flood of people behind them.

"It's worse than that," Suvius says as he takes small glances around the room. "I see armed security posted around the perimeter. Not to mention that we're surrounded by crazed fanatics. I would also rather not sprawl with the Brothers since they wield the Artifacts we seek. I'm at a complete loss. We have to play along for now—but be prepared for a bloody war."

On the catwalk, the man with the golden radiance—Sylis, continues to wave both of his arms high, garnering the most popularity from the captivated crowd. "Thank you all for attending, my Divine Children!"

"Thank you for your radiance, Divine Brothers!" the crowd returns.

"I heard that we might have some new members today from our always-diligent paladins, so let's recap on a few things before we start today's elimination. But before we even get to that, today is my birthday!"

"Happy birthday, Brother Sylis!"

"Thank you! Thank you! Now, first, can we all agree that psiowls are the bane of our existence? That's why we do this so frequently, to eliminate them once and for all from this humble and holy haven!"

"You are always correct, Brother Sylis!"

"And lastly, tomorrow falls onto our bi-weekly house cleaning day. Make sure to properly burn the deceased, tidy your rooms, and in my name, *please* wash yourselves properly. My radiance can only purify so much."

"We'll do better for you, Brother Sylis!"

"I know you all will. Now, let's get this assembly started! Come, Brother Crysis. I have the feeling that today is going to be a blessed one."

The two brothers activate their braces. Sylis's gauntlet glows golden-bronze, and Crysis's brace glows raven-black. Together, they float upwards off the catwalk and descend to the ground while radiating their majesty. The crowd separates right down the middle for them. The light Sylis gives off infects and spreads to those nearby, highlighting to those affected that they are pure and true.

A woman reaches out to Sylis, overjoyed that she is close enough to touch him. "Your hands are so warm, Brother Sylis!"

"And who do you think is giving me such warmth?" he says to her, petting her face. "That's right, you are."

"Thank you for your radiance!" the woman says with teary eyes.

"These people are crazy…" Rend remarks.

"Well… this place was also an asylum," Draxis says.

Hoot! Hoot! the sound of a captured bird caws.

"Damn thing!" Crysis yells out. "Hold still!" Crysis manages to wrap his hands around the Psiowl's throat and vaporize it with the malignant mist that disperses out of his brace, leaving no trace behind.

"Brilliant demonstration, brother," Sylis says as he joins him. "Do you see why these assemblies are vital, Children? Just think of how many of these things would replace your neighbors if we let this get out of hand. I will hear no more complaints about these from this point forward, yes?"

"Yes, Brother Sylis!" the crowd shouts.

"Good. Let's continue."

Aluna whispers telepathically, *"He's getting closer..."*

"I still don't have an escape plan," Suvius responds.

"We could really use one!"

"Shit! Shit! Shit!" Sadra cries out. *"Maeva's not holding up!"*

They cut their thoughts off as Sylis parks himself in front of them. Right at the very spot they prayed he wouldn't start at.

"I don't think I've seen you before," Sylis says to Maeva. "You must be one of the newcomers. What's your name?"

"Uh… uh…" she stammers.

"Just make up something!" Aluna screams at her, telepathically.

"You must be too stunned at my radiance," Sylis says, grabbing Maeva's shoulder. "Don't worry, everyone has to go through this. Sorry. Now, let's see if… Hold on…"

"He's starting to notice!" Rend says.

"Don't move, Rend!" Suvius shouts.

Crysis pokes Sylis with his cane. "Hey, what's wrong? Why must you do this with every woman you come across?"

Sylis forms a perfect smile. "It's her…"

"Who's… her?"

"The only woman who matters. My precious lamb that left our flock so long ago. Maeva Solunn." Sylis relaxes a hand across her sweating forehead, traumatizing her even further. "I will remove this horrendous contamination off you, my little lamb. Purity…"

Maeva's illusion is silenced, and all attention falls to the red-haired, red-eyed girl that is reduced to a cowering victim on the ground.

"She was an imposter!" someone shouts. "Kill her!"

Sylis powers his brace, creating a shield of light around himself and Maeva. "Back away from her you damn—what I mean to say is that this 'imposter' doesn't concern any of you. In fact, this assembly is adjourned! Go!"

The room is cleared swiftly, like bright light startling a colony of scampering insects.

"Can a few guards come down to occupy me and Crysis please? Now!" Sylis then kneels down to Maeva while he waits for them to rush over.

He stares at her with eyes in disbelief, then speaks to her in a soothing tone. "You came back to give me seconds, little Sanguine Lamb, even though you cried otherwise. Why is that I wonder? Did you miss the delicate care I took to ripen your body into that of a woman? The passionate chains that I coiled around and around you to shape the perfect curves of your back, your breasts, and those luscious lips. Sometimes there are good days in an apocalypse, and now I can finally have mine." Sylis reaches out to her flailing arms.

"Stop touching me!" Maeva cries out. "Stop!"

"You've gotten so much stronger," he says. "I can feel it. You never kicked me this hard before, with all this vibrant ferocity."

"Let me go! Let me go! **Let me go**!"

"Don't damage her, brother," Crysis says.

"Correct as always," Sylis says. "Impatience will be the death of me one day. Would you mind binding her for me?"

Crysis hovers his brace over Maeva, and she is soon bound by restricting wraps made of physical darkness around her hands, legs, and even covering her eyes.

"Let's go, Maeva," Sylis says as he starts dragging her. "Who knows how long this apocalypse is going to last, so we mustn't waste the precious time we have until the cruel end—"

"Hey!"

Rend's shout makes Sylis jump. "Oh? It's the newcomers. I'm very certain that I dismissed everyone."

"That you did, brother," Crysis affirms.

"Why are you disobeying my direct order, newcomer?"

Rend abates his rage before he says anything else. "We understand that His Holy Radiance is busy, but you shouldn't let new acolytes become lost and misguided. Would it be below you to allow us a tour? Or perhaps something else to welcome us in?"

"You're needy, but I do like that initiative," Sylis says. "Brother Crysis. My calendar has already been cleared exclusively for my Lamb here, so handle this activity for me and entertain them for maybe an hour or so. I'll need your help after that hour has concluded."

"Of course."

"Great! I knew today was a blessed day."

A few guards arrive to assist Sylis in subjugating Maeva and transporting her off into an unlit path beyond the empty assembly room.

Crysis turns to look at his small group of awaiting tourists. "Is there a weird coincidence as to why that girl was with you all?"

"Honestly, fuck that question," Aluna says telepathically. *"How do we answer that?"*

"I just want him to stop staring at us," Sadra also thinks, looking away from Crysis. *"He's uglier than I remember..."*

"Is this coincidence a bad thing?" Rend speaks up. "Brother Sylis seemed to have taken it as a miracle."

"True," Crysis responds. "But miracles happen to him all the time."

"Then that only means that His Radiance truly is a wonder that surpasses the gods. Had we had known that she was a pretender all this time, then we would have delivered her here sooner."

"Yes… and only can Sylis attract such… devoted individuals to his humbling will and light and whatever other words fit in those pretentious categories. Let's just get this tour over with so I can get some sleep sometime today."

They let Crysis move on ahead before following him, taking extra care not to let him eavesdrop.

"Was charisma your choice there, Squire?" Suvius asks. "That was risky."

"It's my fault for raising my voice at Sylis and nearly breaking our stealth. The least I can do is turn it into a positive," Rend says.

"So, what now?" Sadra asks. "We just gonna follow this creeper around?"

"I'm building off of Suvius's idea of playing along and acting as the overzealous newcomers. Hopefully this won't take forever…"

"I'm pretty sure she'll be in the same place we found her last time," Draxis says. "Sylis is reckless, not methodical."

"We do still need to have a safe passage to get to her however," Suvius says. "This is a more welcome approach than the crawling pace we would be going in without Crysis to ferry us along."

"I concur," Aluna says. "Did you hear closely of our plan, Sadra?"

"I comprehend what we must do. I want nothing more than to save Maeva and corner these divine bastards like we should have done all those years ago."

"Muhuhu!" Jellop laughs. "Sadra is energized. We will not let this predicament dissuade us. Friend Maeva will be secured."

"Sylis isn't going to hurt her, is he?" Rend asks.

"He will try to," Suvius says. "That's the honest answer. But she's not the same woman from all those years ago. If he's wise, then he won't resummon the monster he's created."

"She doesn't like being called that."

"I'm not saying it as an insult."

***

Crysis slows down, stopping in the middle of a populated zone.

"Why are we stopping?" Jellop asks.

"Because I have a lot to think about. Which is why I'm leaving you all amongst these mindless—err, like-minded individuals. Don't mess anything up and you'll become Sylis's favorites in no time."

Crysis detaches himself from the group and becomes nearly unidentifiable among the surrounding ruination and fanatics that pray at him as he passes through.

"I wanted him to leave—but still, what an asshole!" Sadra says.

"An unplanned circumstance, but we'll have to adapt," Suvius says. "He got us in deep enough to get started so let's keep it moving."

"Wait for us, Maeva…" Rend mutters.

Chapter 39

Ravenous

Darkness and salty tears are the only thing Maeva can see and feel before she is roughed-up and thrown into a dank and cramped cellar. She whips around when she gains the strength to, only to find that she's locked in and mocked by her jailer with his inhuman grin.

"Even being at the peak of human physique thanks to this Artifact, you're still heavy," Sylis says. "It took three of us to lift you up. Have you picked up weight?"

Maeva looks away from him in disgust.

"I'm only caring for your health," he says.

"I'd rather you'd just kill me," she states. "Do that for me if you truly want to see me healthy and happy."

"You know I can't do that. This world would lose the last adhesive that holds it together."

"Spare me your horseshit," she says as she rolls her eyes.

"You're in there for your own safety, mind you," Sylis says. "Wouldn't want to indulge myself too early."

Maeva gets up and swipes at him through the small gaps between the metal bars.

"Look at you ram yourself into these bars to tear at me like a feral tigress. I could just watch you squirm and shake that gorgeous body of yours around until the world crumbles. Keep it up."

"Fuck you!"

"Careful, Lamb. These bars are also the only thing stopping me from feasting on you like a feral lion."

If only those metal bars could hold back words as well. Defeated, Maeva backs away into one of the filthy corners of the farthest wall and sits.

"Walls do provide great support during moments of intense pleasure," Sylis says. "You're just making it harder and harder for me to resist your charms."

Her tears from earlier surface back up, pouring down even more this time.

"And now you're crying… beautiful. I am so honored that you remembered all the little tricks that got me going. You really did miss my love."

"Fuck everything that you're saying!" Maeva shouts. "You don't need to treat me like this anymore, Sylis! The Arbiters are gone! What purpose is there!"

"That's perfect! That only makes this circumstance better. The one thing that ruined my perseverance was their pointless restrictions. Now I get to have you and your power all to myself. I bet the others are screaming in their graves right now."

"Just let me out!"

Sylis bends down over to the side of the cell door, away from her view—and rises back up to show off an unwashed, coiled snake of rope wrapped around his arms. "And let this rope go to waste?" he says. "Resources are scarce, Maevalina."

"Maevalina?"

"Oops… would you mind forgetting about that slip up for me? Actually, it doesn't matter. We can always make you forget again…" He starts to move, unraveling and tugging at the rope force-fully before unlocking the cell door.

Chapter 40

The Great Descent

First Level: Slums

The descent for Maeva's rescue begins. Their pace is purposefully slowed to ensure they avoid security's gazes and any civil instability they might cause if they garner attention from the deranged looks of the local inhabitants.

"So in order to go down where Maeva is detained," Rend starts to say, "we have to keep traveling down to each of the hanging buildings to reach the next level?"

"It adds extra security on all fronts against both the detained and detainees—and good exercise as well," Draxis says.

"I am certain there are shortcuts to bypass this nonsense," Suvius adds. "But most likely they are guarded by their most devout followers."

"Not unless we force our way in," Rend disputes.

"That'll just give them more time to prepare an impregnable wall to stop us by the time we make it to the Forbidden Level."

"Stay calm, Rend," Draxis says. "This will be quicker once we get away from the nosy masses."

"Speaking of nosy, there's a weirdo behind you, Jellop," Sadra warns.

"There is? Erk! Stranger danger!"

The decrepit stranger audibly inhales and gurgles from his own spit. "You people smell like kraken piss."

"Okay…?" Sadra says, puzzled.

"Arghh!" the man shouts, scurrying off to the nearest shrine of the Brothers' likenesses and kneels. "Cure this accursed pit-stain of this wicked stench Divine Brothers!" he prays. "Please!"

"That was incredibly rude," Draxis says. "But is it wrong to say that I'm relieved these former inmates have something to believe in? It always seemed like once someone was condemned to this place then they effectively became a memory to be forgotten."

"I say the relief should be half and half," Aluna says as she pokes her head out from inside Jellop's hood. "I know Sylis and Crysis are abusing these people's dependence. It's a damn shame we can't do anything about it though."

"Except hold our heads low and wade gently through these dormitories until we reach the next level," Draxis adds.

"Dorms, huh? I thought this level was where they threw away their trash."

"That is also incredibly rude."

"Let's stop joking around and keep it moving," Rend says, pushing forward in a huff."

"The least you can do is to stop stepping on these people's tributes!" Aluna shouts. "Look at how sad they look!"

"Fuck 'em!"

Some of the fanatics overhear their commentary and start moping and thrashing about in anger.

"Geez…" Sadra winces.

Second Level: Voracious

"You staying strong, Jellop?" Draxis asks.

"With unexpected regret, this amulet possesses power that my feeble mind is unable to savor," he responds.

"Which means…?"

"Our time to act is limited."

"And to think we have to go through four more levels," Draxis groans. "How about a snack boost to refresh?"

"Oh? Does that mean we've made it to the mess halls?" Aluna says.

"It's mostly just a 'mess', but yeah, it looks like it."

"There isn't a long line," Sadra says. "Should we?"

"No," Rend says.

"Let the Living have a quick bite," Suvius says. "Trust me, they'll need the nourishment."

Rend growls in response.

"Hey…" Draxis says, greeting a toothless individual at the lunch line. "What are they serving today?"

"Mystery meat."

"Mystery meat?" Draxis repeats.

"On every weekend,"

A bell rings, making a cute ding.

"Ah! It's my turn to eat!" the toothless man says.

Draxis looks back towards the others and says, "Mystery meat though?"

"Let's not judge it before we see it," Aluna says.

The bell dings once more.

"Well go ahead, Draxis. You're next in line."

He moves forward and greets one of the cooks with an eager smile, only to frown at the sloppy chunks that get splattered on a plate and given to him. He shows it to the others. "I just decided that I'm not hungry. And why is my meat moving? This is the worst."

"I wouldn't want that either," Sadra says. "I definitely prefer other types of meat."

"Hey wait a minute," Rend interrupts. "Is meat even a part of your diet, Draxis? Or did you say anything otherwise?"

"Umm…? I'm so hungry that I'll eat anything at this point?" He gives a mild chuckle after saying that.

"I don't get it," Sadra says.

"Don't worry about it," Suvius says. "He's just making light of a dark situation."

"Shame on you, Draxis," Sadra huffs.

"Shame on me indeed. Now before I throw this away, does anyone want it?"

"I do!" Jellop says. "Or as Sadra would say, 'yep-yep!'"

"Hey! He's right though. I don't know where I picked that up from."

"I think you appropriated it from those leprechauns at that one Arcane Circus we all went to," Draxis says.

"Yep-yep! I sure did!"

"We should probably have our food to-go," Suvius says. "Our Squire is becoming antsier."

"…It would really hurt my feelings if anything happens to her," Rend responds.

"We can respect that," Aluna says.

Third Level: Solitaire

Three levels deep, and they aren't even close to the bottom. If there is such a thing as radiance, then it has not ever reached such a hellacious level. The severity of the containment procedure inside each of the holding cells they walk past only grows more grotesque and rancid the farther they descend.

It's a free exhibition of torture devices, with pronounced imagery of past horror along with the constant sight of mangled bits and corpses fused into the decaying walls.

Despite the increasing demand to rush through such a dreadful place, Sadra brings their momentum to a halt. She finds herself attracted to a secluded room at the deepest part of the level. The cell in particular has no spaces or openings like the others, only a door with a tiny hole to allow anyone to peer inside the room.

Sadra's eyes widen in shock as she investigates. "There's a woman inside. How come she's in solitary confinement?"

"Does she look dangerous?" Jellop asks.

"She looks fine to me. Wait. She… she has a newborn."

"Let me see," Jellop says, squeezing in next to her to share the peephole. "Oh my! I'd never thought I would be so happy to see youth. What do you think about the woman, Sadra?"

"I can sense that she's angry and hurting—that makes up most of her Darkness. But I also see her Light, her determination to keep her child healthy and strong. I want to help her, but I know we also need to stay on track."

"We should definitely keep it moving," Rend says.

"Huh?"

"I said keep it moving! This woman and everyone else here seem content with living like this. Let them be."

"She can barely feed that child, Rend!"

"If she cared then she wouldn't even be here!"

"No extreme interactions!" Jellop buts in. "That includes arguing as well!"

"But we need to save Maeva!" Rend yells.

"And we will. Trust us."

"Fine. But may the gods help you if you're wrong…"

"Uncalled for, Rend," Aluna says.

"Shut up! I just… ughh!" He stomps away over to the opposite side away from them, looking for an exit.

"I'll go calm him down," Draxis says.

"The boy is impatient, but his impatience is just," Suvius says. "I personally do not mind you exercising your compassion, Sadra. So you may speak to this woman if you find this matter to be so urgent. But you should also understand that you're sacrificing our time and Maeva's safety in exchange for someone else."

"Yes. I understand the risks, and I apologize. I'll try my hardest to make this quick." Sadra turns around and fiddles with the flimsy lock to the door. It opens after a few tugs, and she enters the dull, compacted room.

The woman inside doesn't flinch at the fact that the door is wide open, or that there's another living soul she can talk to. She only hugs her baby closer to the ragged cloth that holds the child to her bosom. "What are you looking at, punk?"

"A good mother," Sadra states.

"G-Get out of my face before I do something bad to yours!"

"Don't you want to leave?"

"No!"

"It's dangerous for you and your child to remain here," Sadra says. "We know a place where you both can find the proper help."

"I know what I'm doing! In here, it's safe. I don't got to fear no child-eaters, and I don't have to deal with those brainwashing Brothers. Leave me be!"

"But—"

The woman pulls out a thick shard of glass from her pocket. "I said to get out of my face!"

"Okay… sorry to intrude." Sadra then leaves, making sure to close the door shut.

"Well?" Suvius asks.

"I have to respect her wish for being left alone. We can go now."

"I'm sure she appreciates the concern. You did great, Sadra."

"T-Thanks…"

Fourth Level: Below the Basement

Everyone bursts through the once-locked doors to the next level, out of breath and uncaring as to how noisy their grand entrance was. They are too fazed to even notice their teeth chattering in the frigid haze that surrounds them.

"Ar-are we safe?" Aluna asks.

"W-We did run pretty fast…" Sadra says. "What happened back there, Jellop? Why did we get spotted?"

"All these extreme interactions are making it harder to stabilize our illusions. I worry I might not be able to make the return trip free of danger if this keeps up."

"There might not *be* a safe return trip if those guards go back and notify the rest of the patrol," Draxis says."

"Just turn off the illusion for now until we reach the next level, Jellop," Suvius says. "We can at least take refuge here until the panic dies down a little."

"Wait!" Aluna intervenes. "Don't do it just yet! This place… I don't recognize this at all."

"Yeah, there's too many urns and cadavers around here," Draxis says. "Have they remodeled this level into a morgue?"

"That would be giving them too much doubt," Aluna says. "You guys aren't seeing what I'm seeing." She escapes from the confines of Jellop's hood and surveys the area as she flies around. "These cryogenic tubs and brimstone runes are unnerving. They are testing for something, and they have all the test subjects they could ever need or want."

"What does all that crap mean?" Sadra asks. "Are they practicing necromancy or something on these bodies?"

"No, nothing like that. This is way more advanced. To put it simply, this place isn't a morgue or a ritual site—it's a laboratory. It's a special word the Arbiters used to label these types of rooms that are meant exclusively for their diabolical experiments. The only thing I will say is that the Arbiters' science can be scarier than their magic."

"Ridiculous," Draxis hisses. "Even at the world's end, the Arbiters still persist in ruining lives by any means necessary. Just what else could they want from a demolished world?"

"Maybe they don't want anything, but instead they want to create something," Aluna says. "Look closely at these cadavers. They have jagged fangs, and some of them are being pumped with blood fed from those massive vats. Maeva comes to mind with the similarities…"

"So, they were trying to replace what they've lost, and we handed her right back to them," Suvius says. "We need to hurry."

Fifth Level: Crisis

Almost there. This building has felt like one giant obstacle course since the beginning—one that might soon be reaching an anti-climactic end. Security is at their maximum on this ballroom-sized floor, and all one hundred or more guards are staring them down—unmoving and aligned into two columns straight down all the way to the length it would take to reach the far exit from their location. There's no turning back, not that they dare to try.

"Uh-oh!" Aluna squeaks.

"They sure did mobilize fast," Draxis says.

"Should we keep walking?" Sadra asks, balling her fists in anticipation of a response of denial.

"I know of this stance," Suvius says as he studies the room. "They are ordered to not attack. We can proceed—for now."

Shifty eyes, like ones from a haunted painting, are following them as they each tread carefully down the aisle that is walled off by human flesh, armor, and withheld aggression. The dead stares from the guards are met with retaliatory middle fingers and hushed swearing. It is at the halfway point do they feel the need to stop and look up when they hear a pair of boots pounding on the catwalk above them.

"Newcomers!" Crysis shouts. "Or should I say—Harbingers! You worms should have stayed in your hole where you belong!"

"You have us mistaken!" Draxis shouts.

"Please don't even start with that horseshit. I knew it was you all from the beginning. I *was* hoping however you all took my feigned ignorance as permission to go away and never come back, but alas, history loves to repeat itself, doesn't it?"

"It wouldn't if you would just give us back Maeva!"

"Or, I can instead give you all what you truly want. This magical brace, along with my brother's," Crysis says.

"Are you bribing us?" Aluna asks, in an offended tone.

"If that's how you all want to interpret it as."

"You Arbiters will do anything for an advantage!" Jellop shouts.

"Whatever it takes!" Crysis says. "In this case however, my advantage is magnanimity. You all can be free of that wretched girl, *and* you can take this item from me and go save the world or whatever it is I keep hearing about from our scouts and devotees. I knew something was up when those Artifacts kept disappearing all over the world—and don't get me started on those damn dragons. It does feel good though to finally be rid of those things forever, so I'll take that mishap as a benefit."

Draxis steps forward. "You forgot about me!"

"I'd rather you didn't remind me."

Sadra blocks Draxis from doing anything bold by holding him back with a raised arm. "Brightheart… don't." She then glares at Crysis with rage. "If you know exactly what we're doing then why stop us at all? You're stupid!"

"Saving this world is pointless," Crysis says. "I personally think it's better to just reset it all."

"You can't reset anything if there's nothing left!"

"Not unless you have the tools necessary for rebirth. I have reaped all that I could to make that happen."

"We would rather let ourselves burn into ashes than to live in a world where any of you psychos rule like kings and queens!" Suvius shouts.

"Such shallow thinking. A monarch is one of the lowest echelons a mortal can ascend to," Crysis says.

"What does that mean?" Aluna asks.

"Interested?" Crysis says with a smirk.

"Insanity! Quit stalling us!" Suvius says.

"So, I'm going to assume that none of my offers will be taken?"

"Damn right we won't take it!" Draxis shouts.

"Ugh. Do you people hear yourselves? Nobody's impressed. That's why nobody cares about any of you or what you're doing!"

"We've dealt with worse!"

"Let me assure you that you haven't. Divine Children!" Crysis bellows. "These heathens threaten our Radiance! Kill them! With no mercy! They cannot be saved!"

"Yes, Divine Brother Crysis!" the guards shout together.

"Oh, and before I forget, I think it's time to finally activate the boons of your devotions…"

Crysis raises his right arm where his brace is equipped. A veil of black fog is produced from his brace and engulfs every guard in the room. Nobody can see what's going on, but the grotesque roars coming from within the dark miasma offer a few hints. The fog lifts; Crysis has vanished; and the entire room just became a cage—a cage where they are locked in with mutated abominations that don't even resemble their old human forms.

"And I repeat myself: Uh-oh!" Aluna yelps.

"We try to bring flowers and yet we are still threatened with torches," Jellop says. "These people deserve a fate worse than death, but I will not stoop to their level!" He raises his staff high, and with his amulet primed, he shouts. "Shutdown!" His spell deescalates the panic back into a state of peace as the mutants drop to the ground, resting in place like children in a daycare.

"Nice move there, Jellop," Draxis says. "But uhhh…"

"What? You think this is overkill? I do not care. I'm over this. What say you, Rend and Sadra? Do you both agree?"

"Oh?" Sadra says. "Is it that time already?"

"The speed of darkness is faster than the speed of light," Jellop responds. "Of course it's that time."

"Hold on, hold on," Draxis interrupts. "What's going on?"

"Have you three been scheming without us?" Suvius tags in.

"Mayyyybe," Sadra sings.

"Muhuhu!" Jellop laughs.

Draxis grabs one of Sadra's arms. "W-Wait a minute, Sadra. You're tuning Nocturnal!"

"No-no, it's fine. I'm in control this time. I'm just getting myself ready to play."

"O-Oh. Then, have fun?"

"T-Thanks! I will!"

"Enough!" Rend shouts. "They just declared war on us! I'm ending this, whether you people help me or not!"

"There he goes…" Aluna says.

"I guess we have no choice," Suvius says. "Everyone, let's go! Godspeed!"

Chapter 41

Innocence of the Guilty

Maeva squirms in place as her shoulder is caressed gently by one hand, and her hair combed through and separated into individual strands by Sylis's other hand. She is forced to accept his embrace as her own hands and legs are bound close together with rope, scrunching her body up.

"There is so much red in our world," Sylis begins to say while touching Maeva's face. "Even the sky and seas are flushed with its color, but nothing can ever hope to match the beautiful scarlet flames that paint your hair, your eyes, the blood that you spill."

Sylis then slides and gravitates his touch elsewhere. Lower. Only down to her lips and exploring the insides of her mouth.

"Have these fangs of yours become longer?" he asks. "Even after all these years without my apparatuses to maintain your biological tools, they are so sharp and ready to harvest anything they please." He inhales deeply, then says, "Oooh, the things I missed doing to you. It never felt the same with all the other Lambs here."

Maeva takes the chance to fight back and plunges her fangs right into his probing hand as deep as she can. He doesn't even utter a yelp. Maeva on the other hand snatches her head away and starts choking violently from what feels like a thousand suns scorching her tongue and throat. She spits out pools of a lucent, golden substance as she tries to recover.

"Look at what your playfulness has brought you," Sylis sneers. "Is the flavor of my blood too toxic for you? That sure puts a damper on things. I'm not one to give up though, so how about you and I have some more fun?"

She doesn't respond to him.

"Silence is still an answer. I know I taught you that lesson."

A knock at the cell gate interrupts Sylis.

"Ah, Crysis! Has an hour passed already?"

"Something problematic has arisen, Sylis. It requires your utmost attention."

"There's an astronomically high chance that I won't do anything about it."

"Sylis, I get that you're enjoying yourself, but you tend to forget the small things when you get like this," Crysis says. "Like how our Lamb was even able to find her way home in the first place."

"That's because she misses me."

"Sylis…"

"What? Are you talking about the Harbingers or something? I don't know why you always keep bringing them up, that jailbreak was years ago. There's no way they could have invaded our sanctum again. Besides, when we found her, she was alone, next to those… newcomers… Huh."

"That's all you have to say?" Crysis comments.

"I'll admit I was distracted at the time, so I didn't notice them."

"And you still are distracted."

"*Thank you* for your continued insight," Sylis growls. "Why don't you start a manhunt for the Harbingers then?"

"Because it took a really long time to get down here and I really don't want to make my way back upstairs."

"What makes you think that I should instead? You're the head of our security. Do your job."

"Sylis, I'm so tired already… please."

Sylis sighs. "You do realize your insubordination will be rectified later, yes?"

"At least I'll be somewhat rested before then."

"Hmph." Sylis trades his spot with Crysis and says to him, "Don't you dare touch her while I'm away. Have I made myself clear?"

"Yes, brother…" Crysis says, waiting for Sylis's mumbled swearing to grow faint before he does anything else. "Somehow, I got him to leave. Now, it's just you and me, Sanguine Lamb."

Crysis sits next to Maeva, who refuses to acknowledge him. "You refuse to speak, I see. 'Why are you here to begin with?' is what you want to ask me, I'm sure. I am seeking to find out the answer myself. Before I go on further, would you mind entertaining my irrational side for a while?"

She still gives him only distasteful silence.

"Just thought I should ask for permission first. 'I am not sorry for what I did, but for what I couldn't do.' That line resonates with me so much. I think it's my mind's only means of defense against my encroaching insanity. Seeing you come back must have triggered it."

Maeva only scowls at him.

"Learn to take a compliment," Crysis says.

"I will never accept anything from the monster who put me in here in the first place."

"Interesting… I thought I removed those memories?"

"You're not the only one whose mind is triggering something foul. You have no idea how badly I want you to disappear from my nightmares, but you can't even do *that* for me."

"Ha! But I was successful with removing everything else, so give me *some* credit. And give Sylis some credit as well—he's never been a slouch on disciplining you, nor has he neglected on developing and advancing your Lifeblood. That Sylis… you know, sometimes I think to myself if I am just like my brother, or has he become more like me? I am neither disappointed nor proud of him. I bet he feels the same way about me. What about you?"

Maeva shows her fangs in response.

"If it matters at all to you, we don't feel the same way—not in the slightest. We knew what we were doing when we were creating our perfected monster."

"You two keep saying crap like that with no meaning. You lock me up in here for years like I'm a world destroyer or something. As far as I'm aware, everyone else in this forsaken world should have taken my place instead."

Crysis massages his chin. "Should I bother telling you as to why? I'm thinking to myself if it will do any good."

Maeva looks at him with pleading eyes.

"Oh alright," he says, giving in to her charm. "Consider the duality of your existence that we made for you. You are a marvel who can bring vitality and rejuvenation, which is what we coined as Lifeblood, but you're also capable of forcibly taking away that vitality—which led to you taking the term 'monster' too close to heart.

"In other words, we didn't detain you here just because you were a life-ending predator, we kept you here because you are a life-giving prey. It's not our fault you didn't see it as such."

"But why me in the first place?" Maeva asks.

"Because of the power of discovery. We had our own moments, but the higher-ups were… fickle and reclusive with theirs, but they were very capable of foreseeing prosperity, so it wouldn't surprise me if everything is going according to plan. I wish I could snare even a fraction of that foresight. I'm clever—I'm just not *their* kind of clever."

Crysis stands up, with the aid of his cane, and heads for the cell door. He is hit with a sharp headache at the cell gate.

"Here comes that nauseating thought again: 'I am not sorry for what I did, but for what I couldn't do.' I swear it feels like my own memories are implanted sometimes. Even so, the more I ponder it, I don't know if I received what I wanted out of any of this. Somewhere along the way I lost my end of the bargain."

"How about you go feed the Decayed if you want to be productive with your life," Maeva snaps.

"I already did. Oh, you meant that as an insult. I like that one, it's clever enough." Crysis then locks the cell behind him. "The next time I see you, Sanguine Lamb, I wonder which side of the food chain you will be on, and whatever omens that side will bring."

Chapter 42

Godspeed

"Sadra!" Rend calls out to her. "There's a left and right turn up ahead! Which side you want!"

"I'll take left!"

"Sounds good enough to me!"

Both the left and right hallways ahead of them flood rapidly with murderous opposition.

"There they are!" one of the mutants says in a guttural tone.

"Get the hell out of our way!" Sadra shouts as she raises her hand and closes her fist.

The shadows beneath the mutants start to morph, entrapping them inside of an umbral pool and pinning them where they stand—while on the right—Rend gives a quick series of finger snaps, sending forth bolts of infectious frost that freezes and spreads to any enemies close to his original targets. They continue their unstoppable charge down the middle now that the side hallways are taken care of.

The others are having a hell of a time trying to catch up with such a breakneck pace, being slowed down even further by the duo's wake of destruction.

Aluna sure isn't having a good time with the bumpy ride, and the horror attractions aren't helping her out either. "I never knew you could be so scary, Rend."

"Then close your eyes if you don't want to look."

"We don't need an annoying conscience like you getting in our way," Sadra says.

"But look at all the bodies you two are leaving behind!" Aluna says.

"So? We didn't kill them or anything."

"They should be thankful we didn't," Rend joins in. "I still think that we're still going too slow because of it."

Even farther behind, Draxis stops to catch his breath. "Your children are starting to become too violent, Suvius."

"I see no immediate harm in it," he responds. "The less time we spend on the Forbidden Level, the better. Would you like to join them?"

"I'll have to pass. I only have two souls on me that should be saved for a 'rainy day' as you like to say. I'm trying to hold out for as long as I can, but this hunger is so unbearable."

"We could always go foraging for some souls. I don't want you to suffer," Suvius says.

"It wouldn't do anything. Tainted souls barely have any nutritional value."

"You speak of nutrition, but I haven't had any calcium in such a painful amount of time."

"Your jokes are painful," Draxis says.

"Better than yours," Suvius responds. "…We should go catch up with the others."

Chapter 43

Strength

Despair is crawling all along Maeva's back as if spiders were occupying the space with her, but she's unable to use her hands to brush off the growing accumulation of it. It's complete agony.

"Fuck!" she shouts to herself in anger. "I fuck up our stealth and now they have to come save me… What If they don't come? What will become of me if they don't show? What if something bad happened to them? I'm so scared… I'm scared, I'm scared, I'm scared!"

"And what is it that you are so scared of?" a distant voice in the back of her subconscious mind calls out, in all his crude manner. Rend. He would want her to get up. He would want her to strike back! He knows that she can—she knows that she can. Maeva relaxes her mind and thinks of a way how to—starting with her predicament of immobility.

"Hold on, didn't Draxis give me a dagger a long while back? I'm going to smack myself to death if I left it behind somehow…" She shuffles around from side to side, until the sound of clattering metal hits the ground. "Ah! He did! Bless him." It takes some time, but she manages to cut off her restraints.

"Well, now what?" Maeva says to herself.

"Save yourself, dumbass!" she imagines Rend would say.

"How?"

"I'm not always going to be there to save you. Do you remember in the very beginning, all those weeks ago, when you told me

that you were the Harbinger of Scourges? Care to finally show me why?"

"But I can't!" she says. "It's too dangerous! I'm too dangerous!"

"Is that what you think you are, or is that what everyone tells you? You're only dangerous to yourself if you keep staying dormant like this. Fight!"

"Fight…" Maeva repeats, letting that one word stick in her mind.

After that final thought, she notices her reflection in a nearby small puddle of yellow liquid, becoming disheartened by what she sees. She doesn't really understand why she's thinking about that idiot now or why she's imagining his usual crass vocabulary, but it's just another person to thank… and maybe even more, if she survives this. She shakes her head at that last thought.

Overall, the schizophrenia is annoying, but not as much as her own feeling of failure. There's no reason to hold back anymore. There never was a good reason to. It's everyone else who is the failure, and she's been constantly brainwashed to think otherwise. Well, not anymore. She can feel it now as she embodies all her rage. Her resurgence—it's nigh—and goodness, does it feel cathartic. Not too long after does she overhear the sounds of approaching footsteps.

Good...

***

"Is this the place?" Rend asks the others, standing on the first step that leads down to the darkest descent he's ever seen.

"Indeed," Suvius responds. "It doesn't go down further past this point."

"I hope we're not too late…"

***

"Maeva!" Draxis shouts.

"Miss Maeva!" Sadra shouts after him. "Can you hear us?"

The ambient silence arouses their fear. As they turn around the last corner, they find her—standing in the middle of a fresh pile of hollowed-out bodies.

"Hey, guys," Maeva says.

"Maeva…?" Draxis says, trying to hide his disgust. "We were about to come rescue you."

"I see that. I expect that from you all."

"Are you alright, Miss Maeva?" Sadra asks. "Are you hurting anywhere?"

"Not in the slightest. In fact, I've never felt better."

"Are you sure?"

"Yes," Maeva says. "Now get out of my way—and *stay* out of my way."

"H-Hey! Where are you going?"

"To burn this bitch to the ground…"

Rend tries to reach out to Maeva with a friendly wave and smile as she approaches, but he only gets ignored.

They all do.

Chapter 44

True Colors

"Ugh! More guards?" Sadra groans, directed at the reinforcements that hold a tight position at the first staircase towards freedom. "Hang back, Miss Maeva and we can—"

Her words are swallowed up when Maeva jolts forward and rips through the neck of a mutant with her teeth alone.

"You didn't need to do that, Maeva," Suvius bashes. "I get that you're angry, but we are starting to get things under control. Are you listening?"

"I don't think she is…" Aluna warns.

Jellop grabs one of Rend's arms. "Get back, Rend."

"W-Why?"

Some of the abominations backpedal to distance themselves, making close-quarters an issue—but not for long. Maeva's gauntlet, Samsara, tickles with a murmur of life. It hungers for the promise of sustenance. Maeva raises the gauntlet at the fearful pack of delicacies and plucks their life from within them, siphoning their blood into herself and into Samsara. She licks her lips to savor the assortments of flavor.

"Dammit, Maeva," Draxis says as he grips her unused arm. "This is going too far—!"

Maeva snatches her arm away and launches him back with a shove, sending him flying into Suvius, who staggers from catching him. *Barely* catching him.

Maeva looks at them unapologetically—and continues onward.

Rend comes over to help Draxis get on his feet. He notices that he's shaking a little.

They all are.

Chapter 45

Prisoner Zero

The main gate to the Fifth level is fully open. Maeva stands in the middle of it, bloodied, and looking hungrily at the palettes of fresh meat to devour. A few brave—and foolish—mutated guards brandish their fangs and strike first—but she gives the bigger bite. A few more bodies have just been added to her growing funds of blood.

She is not appeased. More. More, more, more! The more she consumes, the faster and more vicious she becomes. Killing ten becomes as swift as killing one, and the tallies multiply faster than anyone can count or predict.

Jellop takes action as soon as he connects mentally with his amulet, Mesmerion. *"M-Maeva!"* he calls out to her through his telepathy. *"Cease!"* He waits, but absolutely nothing happens. He even swears he hears maniacal laughter somewhere deep within her sadistic thoughts just to mock him.

"She's… she's not stopping? Is she immune?" Sadra asks.

"Not immune," Jellop says. "Inexorable."

"I don't get it."

"It means we are all powerless to stop her," Suvius says.

"I don't want to agree with that!" Aluna says, with clenched fists.

"Go ahead and be our guest if you seem so sure."

Aluna flies ahead and shouts Maeva's name. She then conjures up a fire spell once she is close enough to her and launches a non-lethal attack.

The attack crashes into Maeva's back, which gets her to turn around and show off the full flush of neon red her eyes glow in. The blood that soaks the ground beneath Maeva ascends and morphs into dagger-like spikes that soar towards the others, forcing them to dodge aimlessly.

"Fucking stop, Maeva!" Aluna then tries her spell again, adding more orbs to her assault. Her flames only get dissolved by a rising and falling wave of blood that shields Maeva.

Unamused, Maeva turns around and leaves them. They hesitate to chase after her.

Rend only grinds his teeth instead. "Suvius, how can we get her to stop?"

"I don't know," he responds.

"What do you mean you don't know!"

"This is a battlefield where everyone is blind. I wish I can tell you otherwise."

"You said this all happened before, didn't you? Just do it again!" Rend shouts.

"You mean with luck? That was the only thing we had that could be used against her."

"Are you that afraid of her?"

"Yes. I will never disrespect her power, and so should you," Suvius says.

"Time and time again I keep hearing about how much of a devil she is when it seems like she never had a choice but to go to the extreme. Why break her out of here in the first place all those years ago if you find her to be a liability?"

"Needs. Choices. Results," Suvius says. "We desperately needed someone of her caliber at the time, but those three actions failed to account how fragile her innocence was."

"What he's trying to say is that our need to succeed overtook our responsibility to heal a free but very broken woman," Draxis says. "We helped her escape this torment, but we never did anything to alleviate those lasting scars like we should have."

"Is that why Crysis tempted us with that shitty bargain?" Rend asks. "Because he knows that our side wouldn't be able to handle her if her patience fails?"

"It's not like that."

"But having to resort to sealing away her powers and tearing her down whenever she lifts a finger is supposed to be the best route for her health? I'm surprised you all didn't take his deal."

"Rend…"

"Don't 'Rend' me. Maeva always made it sound like you all were her heroic saviors. You people only ruined her further."

"We do love her, which is why it deeply hurts to see her like this," Jellop defends. "She shouldn't be like this, but it makes perfect sense as to why she is. Over the years, she has naturally adapted our ways. Our propaganda has sullied her with a cynic curse of hatred, misanthropy, and the ability to kill mercilessly. We struggle to help her because we don't have the goodwill to save her from this version of herself the world has created."

"Fine, give up then," Rend says, "but I'm not stopping until she returns to how she was before. She needs someone."

"You're going to get yourself killed," Aluna whines.

"If I have to die so she can have a second chance, then so be it. She needs to realize that she is not a monster. Only a true monster kills without reason, and right now, she has every reason to kill us."

"But not you," Suvius corrects. "You're the one who has given her everything she's never had. I won't deny our dependence on that."

"You should be the one to save her, Rend," Sadra adds. "We'll just end up failing her again."

Rend exhales a long sigh. "Stop acting like that. Do you people really think she would want to hear her friends say stupid shit like that? How they can so easily forswear making amends? Maeva knows exactly what this place means to her, and it seems like in hopes of trying to find closure or revenge, everything went back against her tenfold.

"My master, however, isn't as hopeless and disgraceful as you people seem to believe, because I refuse to think she would take such a great risk if she didn't have us as a backup plan. If she's absorbed this much cynicism from the world, then try to show some 'love' as well. It's never been too late. She can still be saved. Don't make me do this alone."

Rend waits on them to come closer before leading them onward.

Fourth Level

"Dammit!" Aluna shouts. "Where is she? We're never going to catch up with her at this rate!"

"Didn't one of you say there was an alternate route around here?" Rend asks. "There's no way it's still guarded with the current crisis happening."

"The Brothers always seemed to traverse this building faster than what should be humanly possible," Draxis says. "My guess would be stairs."

"Or like one of those magic jump pads at the Arcane Circuses," Sadra adds.

"That too."

"Let's go searching for it," Suvius says. "Don't split up too far."

Not much stands out as they search around for the elusive secret passage. Maeva has still been yet to be found, but they can identify her handiwork. Drained bodies, destruction of property, and the lingering scent of blood. They are glad to be late to the party—but it doesn't mean that it's over.

"Argh!" Rend hollers out. "Why does everything keep grabbing my legs?" He blasts away the unwanted pairs of rotted hands to dust with a quick fire spell. He overhears the others' struggles and turns around to save them from a similar fate—but they don't need his help.

The rest of the dormant test subjects and the freshly killed are starting to rise from the sounds of their friends' heads being crushed, adding more intensity to growing pandemonium.

"This floor is about to become a feeding ground for them if we don't go!" Draxis says.

Together they sprint between the rows of operating tables and around the giant pipes and tubes, and sometimes dodging and sliding underneath the many hands that swipe at them.

A pair of out-of-place metal doors grabs Aluna's attention as she scopes out ahead. "Hold on! Is this the exit?" She hovers closer to a panel with six buttons on it. "These buttons…"

"Just push one!" Sadra shouts.

Aluna slams her body into one of the buttons. After hearing a ding, the doors slide open horizontally. "Come on!" she yells.

They shove and crash into each other as they flood in through the small opening made by the unbearably slow doors, leading into a cramped room that's boxed-shaped but tall and wide enough for breathing and headroom.

Aluna rams into another button and the doors close, slicing off any Decayed hands and arms that have reached far too close inside. The boxed room begins to ascend. They take a few steady breaths to ease their beating hearts as they somewhat enjoy the ride.

"So, we're going up?" Rend asks. "Are we flying right now?"

"This is an elevator," Aluna says. "It's a type of machine that… elevates things inside it—upwards or downwards."

"Really? Using what?"

"Something with levitation and energy powered by electric-type Geshelons. You'd be surprised how much technology the Arbiters created using their dead bodies."

"Aluna, this form of 'technology' you describe that the Arbiters invented… I just don't know what to make of it," Suvius says. "Is this what their science is capable of? How far does it go?"

"To the stars if I had to compare it to something perceptible. Despite being one of the closest members to their council and having authorized access to some of their advancements, I still felt like I was a primitive animal in their presence. They always kept brainstorming new ideas and creating wonders that not even future generations will devise, but I *never* understood what their end goal was. I think Crysis revealed something he shouldn't have; he mentioned something that sounded like ascendancy. What do you think of it, Suvius?"

"Ascendancy? It puts things into perspective. We now know that gods do exist."

"And we've seen them fall," Aluna adds.

"And to some extent, we've seen them rise…" Suvius says. "I wonder what became of the Arbiters' apotheosis if they ever achieved it."

"…What kind of apotheosis?" she asks.

Suvius crosses his arms. "Do you think it's possible for a man… to become a—"

"Wait!" Sadra interrupts. "The baby! We have to stop! On the third floor!" She starts pressing random buttons on the panel.

"Stop it, dumbass!" Aluna says as she smacks Sadra's hands away. "We don't have time! The poor thing is probably already dead!"

"Please! We have to stop! It won't be long!"

Third Level

Ding!

Suvius pries open the elevator doors. "Stupid unreliable technology. We're here! Go!"

"Sadra, wait!" Draxis says. "I'm coming with you."

"Go you two!" Suvius says again. "We'll protect this elevator!"

Draxis grabs Sadra's arm and takes the lead, holding his elbow up to ram into the roaming packs of Decayed—at the cost of his visibility.

Sadra drags her feet. "Wait! That was the room! We just passed it up!"

"Sorry. I got a little caught up," he says, chuckling.

The backtrack is handled the same way until they reach their destination.

A lone Decayed twitches in front of the aforementioned room, appearing to not get the message that it's time for its lunch break. "Rarrrgh!" it growls at their oncoming approach.

"Enough with that," Draxis says, grabbing and lifting the Decayed up overhead. "Do what you need to do, Sadra. I'll make sure no one gets to you." He throws the zombie into the approaching horde, knocking them down like a house of cards.

Sadra quickly enters the room. She can hear the child bawling, but she hears nothing at all from the woman. Deeper into the room, she finds the baby in one of the corners, far enough away from a group of Decayed that are almost finished with its mother. She holds her hand over the child's eyes as she picks it up, and leaves.

Sadra scares Draxis a little with the way she forces the door open. "Where's the child's mother?" Draxis asks.

Sadra shakes her head as she wipes away the small tears rolling down the child's cheeks.

***

Aluna roars a cheer as she watches Jellop break a Decayed's neck with a perfect swing of his staff. "Nice hit, Jellop!"

"That person had a family here…" he says.

Rend pushes them both aside, waving over to Draxis and Sadra in the distance. "Come on!" As soon as they arrive, he smashes the button for the first floor.

"Good idea," Suvius says. "By the time we make it to the second floor, Maeva will have already cleared it."

Sadra sits down against a wall, holding the child close. Draxis joins her, saying, "I wish I could tell that woman that we're sorry."

Sadra sighs, before responding with, "She wouldn't be the only one I would say sorry to…"

Second Level

The elevator rocks back and forth, shaking them all off their feet. Red liquid is dripping from the roof of the elevator, burrowing through the thick metal and anything else it touches.

A stray drop lands on Rend's head. "Ow! Is this acid?"

"Enchanted blood," Suvius says. "She's getting stronger…"

The elevator rocks again.

"I don't think this thing is going to hold," Rend says.

Suvius forces the doors open and looks out. He sees the exit to the next level coming into view. "We'll have to jump!" He holds his hand to indicate for them to wait—then he brings it down, and shouts, "Now!"

They leap across after Suvius after he crashes through the metal doors to the next level with a powered-up punch. Behind them, the elevator creaks, and the cracked crystal on its roof shatters. They watch the elevator tumble into the dark below.

Draxis sings a drawn-out whistle before saying, "That's a long way down."

"To hell with everything right now," Suvius grunts. "Don't stop running!"

They were already expecting to see the worst as they run forward to reach the next level, but there is nothing quite like the hell they are witnessing. A hell where civilization is falling apart. A hell where heroes were never present, and all leaders have fled. It's reminiscent of Blighted Day—a history that feels like it's repeating endlessly.

Aluna blasts away a group of Decayed from surrounding a nearby couple. "I just can't stand seeing this carnage. It's too much…"

"I hope Sylis and Crysis are somewhere in this mess," Draxis says.

"She wouldn't stop even if they were…" Sadra says.

Chapter 46

Nadir

Whoever has managed to survive or run fast enough to escape the endless massacre has already alerted the survivors on the higher floors. But… Maeva—she's rapidly approaching, by flying. Despite how much blood she has stolen and pinched from an irreplaceable supply, none have yet to satisfy her starvation.

The amount she has collected so far is enough to be coalesced into a personal killing field where she can spread her bloody wrath ubiquitously. The puny lambs beneath her are nothing more than a thorn at her side as they prance around to defend themselves by hurling object after object and scream after scream. She laughs directly in their faces, only to melt them away a second later. She can only go up from here.

First Level

Sylis and Crysis both wait by the great metal gate that leads to freedom. So far, nobody has reached them yet—but they can hear them trying.

Crysis nudges Sylis with an elbow. "What are you thinking about, brother?"

"How terrible we are as wardens… and how we might die today."

"The door is right behind us. Feel free to leave."

"I can't. I'm just like you. I want to see for myself how much she's grown. Though I don't think we'll get to see her graceful side since you oversaturated her with your wickedness."

"You of all people are really blaming me?" Crysis snaps. "Whatever helps you die peacefully I suppose."

A sudden boom of tremendous sound echoes below them, and it is heard repeatedly until the final one spews a geyser of acidic blood that breaches through the floor. Rising out of the freshly-made hole in the distance is Maeva—and she's brought all of their followers with her.

"Go ahead and talk to her, Sylis," Crysis says.

Sylis shuffles towards Maeva with raised arms and speaks to her gently. "It hurts to see you like this, my Sanguine Lamb."

Her bloodied hands twitch in response to that pet name, making her crimson aura pulse with an unharmful, hurricane force that knocks him down.

"Y-You understand why I did all those things to you, don't you? The others all tried to turn you into something beastly, something unholy, but I convinced them that there's more to you than acting as their avatar of death. I spent so much excess time and energy uplifting your body to be able to withstand their experiments, to provide alternate applications to your potential. I made you an angel! You have to understand that!"

"Keep trying, Sylis. I'm sure she's listening."

"What is with you? I'm trying to—"

"Keep us alive?" Crysis says, finishing his words for him. "It's over, Sylis. We've been playing this dead game for years. What do we have to show for it? What have we gained? We are just chasing dreams in a nightmare."

"What are you even saying? Do you want all our work to be thrown away?" Sylis says.

"And yet, all our most promising specimens were eradicated in the blink of an eye thanks to our Number One over there. Just be thankful that not all our life's work will be thrown away completely into the ether. The Harbingers will have to continue what we started, as our successors."

"You can't be serious!"

"I'm always serious." Crysis then nods over to Maeva. "Maevalina Solunna... Kill him."

"What?" Sylis says, in shock.

"Gladly..." Maeva says, before driving a javelin of coagulated blood clean through Sylis's chest.

Sylis drops to the ground on his knees, failing to die from the massive wound. The golden brace he wears performs its restorative magic to negate the corrupting blight that rapidly attacks his body, but her power far exceeds it. He's stuck in a limbo state of liquefying and revival. He slithers his slug-like body over to Crysis, calling out to him in unbearable agony.

"Broootherrr! Heellpp!"

"Sure thing!" Crysis stands over Sylis and snatches off the bracelet from his gelatinous arm.

"Crysiiiiii—!" Sylis's words turn to mush, reduced into a fleshy puddle just like his body.

"Maeva!" Sadra calls out, running towards her with the others.

"Ah, it's the other Harbingers," Crysis says. "Well, Maeva... my work here is done. You are free to become your own person and start anew—"

Maeva has no reason to continue listening to his dribble. She points Samsara at his face, point-blank.

"Or…" Crysis continues. "I can give you back some of your memories. I'll even lend you some of mine."

"Don't listen to him, Maeva!" Draxis shouts.

"There they go again telling you how to live your life and holding you back. Don't you want to regain some control of that? Take my hand if you wish to rebel. Go on…"

There is a moment of hesitation. Should she do it? Yes? No? It's so hard to choose. Is a chronic liar even capable of making promises? For once, she decides to trust him. The moment Maeva touches Crysis's braced arm, everything in her mind goes to white.

Chapter 47

Fractured

Inside the ruined nave of a church, at the back of the building, there's a man ripping off a couple of black leaves from a potted plant nearby and mixing them into a bowl on top of the right side of a coffin, turning the concoction inside the bowl into the same color. Maeva sits on the other side of the coffin, watching another woman pace around the room and jump at every explosive noise and scream coming from outside.

"Maevalina!" the nervous woman yells out to her. "Can you tell Vale to hurry up? He listens to you more!"

"Nemi, if you rush me one more time then I'm going to send *you* away instead," Vale says.

"Do that, and you're not getting a farewell kiss."

"Good. Your mouth is too bloody anyway."

"So is yours!" Nemi shouts.

"My mouth is bloody from holding back my tongue so much."

Maeva chuckles at his remark.

"Look at that. Even in our doom, I still got it," Vale says,

"Fucking kill me now," Nemi groans. "Is this 'idea' even going to work?"

"Maybe."

"I don't want to hear a 'maybe'! I need affirmation! You're literally giving up our strongest person here when we could use her for the war effort instead of some bloody time capsule scheme!"

"Even if I said *yes* for an affirmation, you would still be nagging at me," Vale says.

"What do you think about all this, Maevalina?" Nemi asks. "Say something! This is something greater than a burden being placed upon you—this will be our people's entire future resting on your breasts and shoulders."

"So… just like any other day?" Maeva says.

"She does has a point," Vale remarks.

"So is that our verdict?" Nemi says. "To place a sleeping curse on her? What in the Ancient's name is that even supposed to accomplish?"

"To give our people another chance. A restart," Vale answers. "I'm as upset as you are about this, but you need to accept that monsterkind is not going to survive this. We just ain't."

"This is so… Why is this happening? This is insanity!"

"We've overstepped our boundaries according to the Gods."

"Us? But they literally killed their own to get to us. They killed our god!"

"We don't know that," Vale refutes.

"Then where is he?"

"Doing godly things probably."

"That's such a stupid response," Nemi says.

"I know I'm stupid…" Vale then pauses as he dips a glass vial into the mixing bowl, filling it up as much as he can before closing it off with a cap. He walks over and shows it to Maeva, letting her admire it despite her indifferent attitude, and saying to her, "That's why we're betting everything on my awesome sister. She is our only hope." before he secures the vial deep in his pocket.

A part of the ceiling collapses and crashes down nearby, making the mixing bowl fall off the coffin—which also makes Maeva snicker at Vale's misfortune.

"Maybe I should have considered making a backup dose…" Vale says. "Whatever. How's it looking out there, Nemi?"

She rushes to peek out of a broken window. "I can't tell if it's a sunny day or if that's the Sun god setting fire to our last city."

"Anything's better than Death hunting for us. Are you ready to move?"

"No."

"How about you, Maevalina?" Vale asks.

She only shrugs her shoulders in response.

"I really don't understand how you can be so casual. If you got so much energy, then would you mind helping me lift this coffin?"

"I don't want to," Maeva says.

"We are literally about to fucking die," Vale remarks.

"So? I'm not doing chores."

"I hate my spoiled family… Nemi!"

"I'm here! I'm here!" Struggling, Nemi helps lift the coffin up with Vale and they raise it together overhead, heading for the front doors.

"Yep… this is heavy," Vale grunts. "Alright, we're heading for the coastline. We got this!"

"No the fuck we do not!" Nemi cries out.

"We don't have a choice…"

"Breathe, brother," Maeva says, consoling him.

"I know. I know." Vale raises his leg and kicks open the doors. "Go… go, go, go!"

They flee right into the middle of a war zone. Every alley and roof of the gothic city is being buried under dead bodies and snow-white flames wrought from the divine invaders that fly above in search for more to kill while employing their scorched-earth tactic.

Thankfully the trio knows how to navigate through the shadows of every corner to remain unseen. Although, the city will most likely become a seared memory by the time they make any meaningful progress towards freedom.

"We've barely made it down three streets," Nemi whispers. "How the hell can we get out of here?"

In a morbidly serendipitous fashion, a body falls from the sky, far down past their view. They hear a splash not too long after, giving Vale an idea. "Aha! How about we use the canals to escape? We can use this coffin as a floatation device."

"That's a lot of unnecessary words," Nemi responds. "Let's just do it."

They hurl the coffin into the canal below and wait for a few moments after to see if they were heard. They jump into the water and climb atop the coffin, using their hands to paddle and steer.

"I don't remember there being so much blood in our waters," Nemi says.

"A bit of flavor for the sewer rats at least," Vale says.

They continue paddling in silence for a while. The water gets bloodier and more congested with debris of floating bodies as they head deeper into the city.

"I don't like how quiet everything is," Vale says. "It's like everyone's gone…"

"Hey, let's not think about that," Maeva says. "We need your leadership."

"Heh… leadership. I guess… we can try going into that sewer hole over there, to avoid all this clutter? It might even lead somewhere."

"Are we really entering into the sewers?" Nemi asks.

"Better hold your breath," Vale remarks.

"Fuck…"

Time elapses once again, significantly longer than before.

"My arms are starting to hurt," Nemi says as she stops paddling.

"Yeah… we can take a break here," Vale says.

Nemi turns to look at Maeva, who sits at the very back of the coffin. "Maevalina, why are you so silent about all this? Don't you care about what's happening?"

"Do you take my silence as an expression of apathy? It's hard to show any emotion when we are bereft of everything we once loved."

"Oh… I'm sorry. I shouldn't be assuming such horrible claims."

Maeva grabs her hands and says to her, "Just be thankful you still have enough cheerfulness to make me smile every now and again."

"Aww. You're a good person, Maevalina. Can we date?"

"Forgive her, sister," Vale says. "She's… you know."

"I can see why you love her," Maeva says.

Vale shakes his head. "Nah, I have horrible taste."

"I will kick you so hard off this thing," Nemi says to him.

Maeva chuckles at her aggravated response.

Their voyage continues onward without hassle, all the way until they reach a bright light at the end of the sewer tunnel. They are ejected out by the gushing water, crashing onto the wet sand below.

"Look at that!" Vale cheers. "We made it to the coast! I am on fire today! Even I'm surprised I got us this far."

"Quit jerking yourself off," Nemi says. "At least, don't do it in front of your sister."

"Can you focus on picking this thing up? Lift more!"

They stop bickering when they hear a feminine voice coming from the deep waters past the coastline, saying to them, "Where do you murderers think you're going?" A young woman rises through the water's surface, twirling around as she does so. She starts walking on the water, towards the trio. "Trying to escape your impending fates by using my domain?" she giggles. "My dad entrusted me to make sure none of you murderers leave."

"Ugh, a demigod," Vale groans.

"How about 'ugh, a daddy's girl'," Nemi says. "Can't you see that we're busy! What a bother…"

"Hopefully *this* isn't considered to be a chore for you, Mavealina," Vale says.

"Killing the weak is always a chore…"

The amphibious woman turns around when she senses the dark presence that insulted her. "Wh-when did you—" She is put to silence as her vocal cords are torn out and devoured, squirting blue blood everywhere.

Maeva wipes her mouth off. "Fucking gods!"

"That's what I like to see!" Vale cheers. "Now comes the hard part…"

"What are you talking about?" Nemi says. "We made it."

"I'm talking about saying goodbye."

"Bye, Maevalina! There, it's done."

"…Just help me get this thing near the water."

They both set the coffin down near the crystalline purity of the open waters. Vale opens it and shovels some sand into it. Maeva comes over to watch him. They both stare at each other.

"Maevalina…" Vale says, gently touching her cheek. "The next world… You will awaken in a world that has forgotten us. A world that may not even know what a Monster truly is."

"You worry too much, Vale," she says, removing his hand and stepping inside the coffin. "No matter the era, I will. Bring. Fear."

"That's my big sister. I… I love you. Just don't forget about us when you wake up in a thousand years or something."

"A thousand what? How potent is this curse potion?" Maeva asks.

"Shit, I don't know."

"I hate you."

The sky turns darker in shade, making Nemi react. "Vale! We need to do the thing! Like right now!"

Vale pushes the coffin forward, still talking as he does so. "I hope the future is kinder to you, Maevalina. And if it isn't, then burn the bitch down and start anew."

"Sounds like fun. I'm sure somebody will deserve it."

"The nasty cycle of justice, eh? Oh, do me a favor and find yourself a boyfriend, okay? Or better yet, a husband. You need someone who doesn't mind cleaning up your sloppy messes, 'cause I sure as hell got tired of it."

"Vale!" Nemi shouts.

"Damn you! I know!" He then grabs Maeva's hands. "Maybe we can fight them off with just the three of us?"

She shakes her head in response.

"But I can't let you go, Maevalina! I changed my mind!"

"Move out of the way!" Nemi says, pilfering the vial from Vale's pocket and pushing him away. "We love you, Maevalina, we're sorry, Maevalina, and don't forget to wake up kicking and fighting. Anyways, light's out!" Nemi then shoves the vial into Maeva's mouth, forcing her to drink its contents—then she closes the coffin's door.

Maeva feels the effects of the potion as she lies back, becoming drowsy and numb. She hears her containment being shoved into the water and sink. Her heart sinks even faster than the coffin from the depressing scuffle she hears happening topside.

"Vale! Above you! Look out!"

Thud. "Time's up…"

"Nemi, get behind—"

Shinnng! Thunk.

"**No**! Val—"

Shing-shing! Thunk.

The sounds diminish as Maeva's vision fades to black.

***

Click! Thud. Snap! Creak.

"Hmm… Sylis, come look at this."

"Crysis, I swear, it better not be another mummified—woah… shit! That's unreal. There really was something special underneath the Scarlands."

"I think we now know why this region is so contaminated with evil. Her emanating Darkness is… ungodly," Crysis says.

Maeva opens her eyes. "Where… w-where am I? Huh? Humans…?"

"And she seems functional," Crysis says. "Whatever she is."

"It hasn't been three minutes since she's awoken and you're already treating her like a toy," Sylis says after a sigh.

"She's a broken toy. This one looks like she is in dire need of some updates. Something with more modernity."

Maeva backs up and gets into a defensive stance, scraping her nails against the velvet linings of the coffin.

"What's your name, girl?" Crysis asks.

He receives a near-animalistic growl in return.

"Not answering? Unfortunate." Crysis motions to the other Arbiters nearby, saying to them, "Subdue her."

"But *don't* hurt her!" Sylis adds. "She's gorgeous."

An Arbiter in green snaps his fingers in Maeva's direction. She is stunned at the summoned ice that freezes her left arm, but she breaks it out free with ease and attacks the assailant by ripping through his throat with her teeth. The other Arbiters dash in to avenge the fallen sorcerer, but they lose their number advantage faster than anything they can react to.

"Ohohoho!" Crysis laughs in merriment as he watches the spectacle. "So, this is the power of ancient Darkness! She's going to be our best work yet, Sylis! Just wait until the Elites hear about this."

"She's… not stopping though," Sylis says. "We should have brought more people."

"Luckily we have a good amount of them already, enough to test and see what this monstrosity is capable of. I think I've seen enough for now."

Crysis starts moving towards the rampaging Maeva. She finds him to be her next victim and launches herself towards him. He captures her with a premade trap of malleable shadow that binds her to the ground, leaving only her head visible and free to move. He then crouches down and touches her forehead, while avoiding her snapping jaws.

"Blackout," Crysis says.

Maeva's eyes turn black—and return to their normal red shade moments later. "My… head," she mumbles. "W-Who are you?"

"I'm your master, and you're our pet," Crysis says. He unravels his binding spell on her. "Now… stand!"

"O-Okay…"

"Good. Now sit."

Maeva obeys him while saying, "Why are you having me do this?"

"Are you disobeying me?"

"N-No…"

"What's the point of this?" Sylis asks.

"A test on control," Crysis says. "We need to ensure everything henceforth will go correctly because the opportunity that sits obediently in front of us now will be the very thing that will bring us power. That blood dance she just performed is tantamount to that vision. Come now, Lamb. Follow your shepherd."

"Okay!" Maeva says.

"Good girl…"

***

Whriiilll. Whrilll. Whrilll, repeatedly goes the sounds of something mechanical and agonizing tearing into flesh.

"Stop! It hurts!" Maeva wails. She is chained, stretched out on a bloody operating table with syringes and drainage tubes sticking out across her body, and with floating crystal drills spinning and targeting random parts of her body as well. "Stop! Stop! Stop! Stop—!"

"Will you shut the fuck up!" Crysis says to her with a booming voice.

"Arrhaaa! Drahhgahh!"

"Stop the extraction, Sylis. I said stop it!"

"Alright, alright..." Sylis snaps his fingers, deactivating the drills and unhooking the tubes.

"Did we get enough of her blood for this to work?" Crysis asks him.

"Barely."

They both examine the mutilated cadaver that lays on another table next to Maeva as Sylis injects the severed body parts with a dosage of her blood.

"Look at his brain returning to normal…" Crysis says, yanking it out of the severed head and inspecting every fold and crease of it. "I think it's safe to say that this head is now cured of the Wild Haze."

"The rest of his body doesn't seem to agree with the transfusion," Sylis says, watching parts of the cadaver's body melt. "Not the torso, the arms, legs, not even a finger."

"Then we need better participants," Crysis responds. "Regardless, you were right. Her magic is an answer to the fragility of Life. If we can just get a *few* more practice sessions in, then we can confidently show off a live experiment in front of the Elites. Hopefully that will convince them enough to grant us more resources and control over this project. I'm not giving up on this. Alright, Maeva—you've had a long enough break. Sylis… start filling out some extra blood bags for us in the meantime."

"Haven't we harvested enough?"

"There's nothing wrong with having spares. Besides, it looks like half her body's healed itself already. Get to it."

"I'll try to make this short, Maeva," Sylis whispers to her, hesitating.

Whriiilll. Whrilll. Whrilll.

"Arrghaaaa!"

Every memory Maeva remembers thereafter, whether the distant past or near, hits her hard like the force from an iron mace. Every terrible emotion felt slices through her like with a serrated blade. And they're all coated with poison to make the hatred linger and sting ever deeper.

Chapter 48

Desolation

Maeva's mind has returned to reality—waking up to her staring at the abhorrent face of Crysis.

"Welcome back to hell," he snickers before letting go of her hand. "Do you remember what I said to you earlier? 'I am not sorry for what I did, but for what I couldn't do'? You are a legendary discovery that has given the Arbiters and I more than what our imagination holds. Just think if only we had more time. You are a fortune wrapped up in sanguine gold, and you paid all my blood debts handsomely. I cherished every moment with you."

Maeva backs away, gripping the skin on her face and screaming out as she cries.

"You are my angel of death. I have nothing left to offer towards your evolution. End me!" Crysis commands.

Maeva lashes at him with claws of hardened blood, cleaving off his head. His blood splatters, repainting her bloodied face. The pulses emitted from her aura are starting to grow in size and in frequency. The building's foundations start to rumble as the acidic blood she controls corrodes it, with the walls splitting apart and the floor becoming upended from the violent quakes.

"She's getting out of control!" Aluna cries out.

"Shit! Everyone, stay back!" Rend says. "I'm going in!"

"Rend!" they all call out.

The air is strong with a force of repulsion. Rend has no choice but to grip and crawl along the ground to resist the pressure while launching himself forward periodically in sync with the rest periods of the pulses. He finally makes it to her. He grabs onto her legs and continues moving up until he can fully embrace her in his arms.

"Maeva, it's okay! Everything's going to be okay!"

"Arghhhh!" she screams.

Rend's skin is melting faster that it can regenerate, but he sticks to her no matter how much it hurts. "Stoooppp!"

His wish is finally heard. She realizes what she's doing to them—to him. She *has* to stop. She has to calm down enough to… enough to stop… hurting them—then she passes out. The others rush over as the scene settles.

"I can hold Maeva!" Rend says, picking her up and cradling her. "Someone grab the braces!"

They are so close to the exit, only to be stalled by having to run slanted as the building starts tipping over diagonally and swings back and forth like a pendulum. The metal gate ahead has already been chewed through by the blood, so they continue running towards freedom, just barely outpacing the metal bridge that falls apart underneath them.

The final leap is made to reach stable ground. They look back at the enormous complex after they assess if everyone has made it to safety. Its supportive chains that hold it in suspension are snapping in half, all until one final thread is left—then at last, the last great chain: breaks. They stand at the very edge of the bottomless chasm to watch the entire penitentiary complex hurtle down to its doom.

"Looks like Gravefall finally lived up to its name," Draxis says after an extremely long pause.

Nobody responds. Not immediately anyway.

"Why does it always come to this…" Aluna mutters.

"And no survivors whatsoever…" Sadra says.

The baby Sadra holds starts laughing and flailing around joyfully in her arms. They all look at it with neutral expressions.

"I wonder how Malphunnos is doing…" Suvius says.

Chapter 49

Godless

I remember when being a god actually meant something. But now, I don't even know if it's worth being one. If I should have even been born one.

That is the first thing that comes to my mind the moment I return home, and after I was just humiliated by that stupid girl. First, she steals my gauntlet and dares to call me inept, and now, she's not afraid to look down on me. Maybe they all look down on me… like I disappointed them. Can't they see that I'm disappointed too…?

It's too early to start losing focus…

I'm finding it harder and harder to remind myself of the task at hand because of this sadistic fear that envelops around what's left of my courage as I tread carefully across this bloody trail left by a dead pantheon. It's suffocating me—to death. I am Death incarnate and yet I fear the very thought of it. Why do I fear what I am? Obviously no one else does. What am I rambling about? Again, I need to stay focused because all things will be restored soon. That's my belief anyway.

Where am I supposed to be going again? Why do I always feel so out of place?

What I was talking to no one else about earlier… Is that type of belief considered to be faith? Believing in something greater or what has a slim chance of becoming real? To think that I finally understand how mortals behave when they relinquish their lives and hopes into the hands of someone who declared that they would protect them in their times of need. When the moment of truth finally occurs, don't they pray? Can I even pray? As a god? What gods could I even pray to? How many are even left?

This is useless...

Even if one of my prayers does come true, would things even return to the way they were originally? Should it? Or… could it? If we reverse the curse of Soul Decay, then what will become of the minds of those who have already murdered and consumed their friends and families… and even their children? Will they automatically forget what they have done, or will they go mad from the unbearable guilt? What's stopping me from going mad?

That's enough rambling. I have a job to do.

I see the Houses of the other gods coming into view—nearly all of them are in a state of disrepair. Ever since Suvius expressed his pity, I can't stop thinking about how magnificent this paradise used to be and how it felt to breathe in the perfect air and dance underneath the soft blanket of the golden skies.

I also remember that fateful day when the heavens fell from grace and all that beauty was taken away from us. Blighted Day. Let me tell you, hearing the collective, endless screams of what sounded like damnation from both Mortal and Immortal kind alike is… quite the experience. We all scream equally, and so loudly too. I was forced to work overtime on that day. It shouldn't have been an issue since I've been doing this 'reaping' thing since the beginning of creation, but on that day, I wanted to quit.

But I won't quit. I know what I must do.

Now, this has been bothering me for a while, and I've been trying to ignore it, but I'm being pursued by some relentless degenerate.

Should I stop and say hi? Sure, why not.

So, I turn my entire head and body to say… hi, to the bottomless goddess who I once knew as the bodacious God-Witch of Fire. It's cute how she's trying to claw and bite at my ankles… and now it's not so cute anymore.

Why have so many of my almighty family members fallen? It's so quiet and barren here—not that I'm complaining. I couldn't imagine crossing paths with the Decayed versions of the Sisters of War or the Godfather of Hatred. Who gave them those nicknames anyway? Why can't I get a spooky title? I'm usually referred to as the 'Necrophiliac' or 'Day-ruiner'. You know, some gods even had the gall to tell me that death is overrated *and* exaggerated. Maybe they're right…

Or maybe not. They are dead after all. And look at who's still standing and not dead! Me!

I might be alive right now, but death is an inevitable event that even affects the very stars we once commanded. So when will it be my turn? I know that sounds grim—and trust me, I know what depravity is—but I am working blind out here. For the first time, in this eternity, I am almost left in total darkness towards the outcomes and fate of everyone everywhere. I can't tell anymore if it was better or worse to be able to predict the numbered heartbeats of everything that can breathe. All of this is sickening to me.

I'm more ill from these thoughts that keep plaguing my mind…

The House of Fire. I'm standing at the blazing foot of it. This building was always a major hotspot for the gods, but it had a more profound meaning for Life and Death, for Fire and its keepers once helped to serve us as our guides, trainers, and even parental guardians at times for this very reason: 'Fire is a paradox,' they would tell both Narisa and I, 'for it nurtures all life, but it can also bring death.' They are not wrong.

Fire does have its purpose. I know it has helped me claim many a life—and cook some *really* good dinners. Funnily enough, I can see my own House from here, far away from the warmth and glow of this place. I'm not surprised it's been untouched.

And to think I've always bothered myself to keep it tidy.

Walking through these molten halls makes me feel cozy inside. Death has a heartbeat, don't you know? Death has feelings as well. But Death is unwanted, whereas with Life, people can't get enough of it.

I'm not jealous of it, or of her. There's no reason to, because she is a good mother to all her creations, but it would be nice if someone thanked me for once, or at least honored my name… which is what *they* do isn't it? Both them and Life have thanked and honored me in their own way. Something about that makes me feel even cozier.

Death can also be thankful.

I finally find the Eternal Flame, stashed away in an urn within a giant crystal chest that was preserved within their treasure vault that was hidden behind a stumbled upon secret passage that is blocked by their beds which are located at the highest floor that can only be reached by ascending a scalding lava waterfall… lavafall.

So freaking needlessly complicated. They went through all that trouble but didn't even bother to install any chains or traps to protect their precious item. Realistically they could have left it out in the open and it still would have remained safe. Every god knew better than to try to steal from them—but then there's me. I take my leave after I bathe my sickle within the cerulean flames to soak it all up. Not to brag, but my weapon looks totally cool now… or totally hot rather.

Nobody's here to care.

Welp, I got what I came here for. I have completed my task flawlessly. But… I feel like I haven't actually triumphed or accomplished anything noteworthy. Why is that? Do I want an epic battle or something to ensue so I can brag about it to the others? I know better than to wish for that. I'm standing outside of the House of Fire with nothing else left to do, but I don't think I'm ready to leave Birthplace just yet. I think I want to go home first.

Home… how long has it been?

I can't stop thinking about how unimpressive this mission was. I bet those Harbingers are having the time of their lives right now. Harbingers… Such an idiotic name. I have watched those mortal fools carry out their rebellion against the world before the Decay and during. They fight under my name. It's cute, but I never gave them permission to use me like I'm some sort of mascot. They do have great heart though to continue sacrificing themselves just to save this ungrateful world from itself.

Say what you will about them, but that's more than anything most have done for the world, and I'm not afraid to admit that. I shouldn't stroke their ego too much however, the destruction and carnage they've caused over the years has made my life harder than it needs to be at times, but then again, some of the people they've killed—*really* needed to be killed.

Mmmh! I miss that rush of bloodlust...

I miss a lot of things. unsurprisingly. Today, I've been asking myself so much about this and that, and that and this, but it all comes back to one crucial detractor: Myself. It's almost hysterical the more I think about it all, how little credit I give myself.

The Harbingers wouldn't exist if I never accepted to resurrect their leader. This world would be overrun with monsters and even more monstrous people if I wasn't here to rid the world of them. Hell, I'm the one who is keeping the darkness of Silence at bay since only I can govern the shifting laws of Death and Oblivion itself. I am the final solution and the end.

Deep in the basement of this frigid place I call a home, my hands hover over an open chest that stores an endless void, and inside this void, is my ultimatum.

It's been far too long since I've been the Reaper...

This scythe that reflects my wicked smile right back to me, this was my old negotiator that made everyone obey my existence. A terror forged with pure abyssal matter from a period before time first ticked and creation was born. It is the type of physical silence where no gods of light can dispel or destroy it, a type of silence where no living thing can survive or escape it, a type of silence where not even *I* fully understand how deadly it is.

I no longer fear it. There was never anything to fear.

Each time I think about what those mortal fools imply to be a lesson, it gives me this longing sense of empowerment. Their mantra of never showing fear and never kneeling is one that I am willing to practice and master. Once this is all over, I will thank those mortal fools for teaching me that—but that will come much, much, later.

There is an ongoing task to complete that requires my utmost sovereign power, for I am Malphunnos, the God, and Harbinger, of Death. My will to be is the silence that I shall bring. It is coming for all of you. Apologies for the delay, it will *never* happen again.

None shall usurp the fate of Death.

Chapter 50

Unforgivable

"What is it, Damel?" Enam asks, joining him and Borace outside of Bruness's entrance. "Did they come back?"

"They *were* here," Damel says while handing her a paper note. "Take a look at this."

Her eyes tread carefully over each inked word as she reads the text:

Failure is never meant to be an option. This child was saved by us, but its family was not met with such equal mercy due to a reprehensible failure by all neglectful parties involved. We are in no excusable position to push the boundaries of our problems onto anyone else, but we will push our trust, even if we are undeserving to do so. Do not forgive us.

Signed,

Suvius Falacoster.

"He has really nice handwriting…" Enam says after reading the note over again. "I wonder what happened?"

"Something that they can't look us in the eye to say," Damel says.

"I wish they did. I would have listened."

"Do you want to hold this baby, Enam?" Borace asks. "It's starting to fidget."

"Yeah." She grabs and holds the child close, staring softly into its watering eyes. Her pleasant smile dissuades the child's fear.

"How come you never give me and Borace that face?" Damel asks.

"Because unlike this worthy young one, I have already disowned you both."

"I don't get how she can say that while looking so serene," Borace says.

"Aye," Damel replies. "Classic Enam."

Chapter 51

The Worst Century Ever

Klae steps into the main room of the tower's spire, breaking the silence. "So… I hate to be the bearer of bad news, but we don't have enough magic power to break the curse."

"What?" Sadra says. "But we have a whole bunch of these damn things now. What's the damage?"

"The damage? Well, that little mishap back at the Bornamu Glaciers did set us back quite aways."

They all look scornfully at Aluna.

"Uh… oops?" she squeaks.

"The fuck do you mean an 'oops'?" Sadra hisses. "We have to do extra work now!"

"Hold on," Aluna says while she avoids Sadra's sluggish swings. "We can still wait on Malphunnos, can't we?"

"I would feel more confident if we had one extra Artifact in our possession, even if he brings back his," Klae says. "Also, I don't think there are any more alternative Artifacts left in the world, not from what I'm seeing. So… you idiots know what this means, right?"

"We have to go to the blood-soaked depths of the ocean, don't we…" Draxis grumbles.

"I think it's the perfect temperature for a swim today. Have fun!"

"This is the worst century ever."

"The bottom of the ocean is where the Sunken Doll is, correct?" Suvius asks. "I thought it was blacklisted?"

"I burnt the list," Klae says.

"Well what are we supposed to do to navigate through the waters though?" Rend asks.

"I know some water-breathing spells," Aluna says.

"That's great, but the water pressure…"

Sadra nods her head as she follows along with the different expressions of colors Komet makes. "Komet here says he can be our vessel of submergence."

"It can do that?" Draxis asks.

"Geshelons can do anything. Komet's words, not mine."

"It'll have to do. By the way, Rend, is Maeva well enough to come along?"

"I am," she states, standing in one of the doorways. "There's no problem with that, is there?"

"Not if you keep acting like that," Sadra responds.

"I would rather have you stay rested, Master," Rend says.

"And to reflect," Sadra adds.

"Can you not, Sadra?" Maeva growls.

"Everyone, subside your tempers," Suvius pleads. "You are certain of coming along, Maeva?"

"I'm going to do what I want."

"Then it's settled."

"I feel like you're making a mistake," Sadra says.

"What's your problem?" Maeva asks her.

"This fucking world is my problem! You're my problem! You don't even care about all those people you murdered!"

"You're damn right I don't! Why should I?"

"Because there was a time when you would have cared! Don't you remember your own happiness when you found out you were the cure? You exhausted yourself ragged trying to heal everybody you could find."

"What good is this gift if people are so quick to use me and abuse me and then go right back into the world to cause more pain?" Maeva says. "Which side of me do you people want? The more I think about it all, nobody deserves my cure."

"Then why did you bother with Aluna when she was dying?" Sadra says. "Maybe this is my fault for not making it public, but you were starting to become my inspiration. When you told me to find my light, I took it to heart. Then everyone else started telling me the same thing. So I did. I tried to discover what it could be. Then you took away a chance for me to manifest it when you decided to act psycho and slaughter an innocent woman!"

"Are you still on about that?"

"I don't forget easily, Miss Maeva."

"So you say."

Sadra's hands turn black. "I will also say that you wouldn't be standing here right now if you killed her child."

"Child? There was a child there?" Maeva asks. "I don't remember seeing… don't tell me I…"

"No, you didn't. Thankfully," Suvius says. "We were as surprised as you are now that there was even an infant, let alone that it could still breathe."

"I wonder why I left it alone…?"

"Why do you think?" Rend says to Maeva. "You say all these horrible things, but you could have done a lot worse."

"What could be worse than a massacre?" Sadra asks him.

"I don't know. Let's be glad we were able to stop her before she reached beyond that point."

"Don't talk about me like I'm not standing right here!" Maeva snaps. "I didn't want any of that to happen. I had no choice but to defend myself!"

"Against the mutants and the Wardens, I can understand that," Rend says, "but I don't recall the other zealots doing anything cruel to you. Seems like they were defending themselves against you instead."

"So, what? You see me as a monster too because I show a little teeth? I thought you understood me."

"Yes, Maeva, I was *scared* of you. For the first time, I feared you. But I was more scared of losing you—and seeing you lose yourself. And I do understand your hatred. I hate this world too, both the old and this shittier one, but you six have taught me that there is a chance for a better future, and I want to make that happen.

"It's fine if you don't see it all the same way but remember that you are more important than you think you are. You are more *beloved* than you think you are. I don't care if you still want to punish the world, just take the time to think if it's something you really want to do."

With her secondary vision, Sadra sees the dying glow within Maeva brighten. Sadra herself mellows at the sight. "Err… yeah, what he's saying. I don't mean to yell so much, Maeva. I'm just really disappointed. I liked seeing you be so happy. Can you go back to being that?"

Maeva looks towards the ground as she crosses her arms and kicks the ground lightly, picking up a small cloud of dust. "Maybe…"

"…Are you all done?" Klae asks after the silence.

"We should be," Suvius says.

"Great. Go through that portal behind you."

"Huh? When did you—"

"That portal will take you all to the closest point of the Artifact's location. A place where land ends and water becomes the sole domain. Tearfallen Point."

"Never heard of it," Draxis says.

"Nobody speaks of it because there's nothing but sadness past that landmark," Klae says. "Not even the most suicidal of people would dare venture into that uncharted ocean."

"Wonderful…"

As Sadra leaves with the others, she stops as she notices the Braces of Symmetry lying on a display table. "Can I take these braces, Grandpa?"

"For?" Klae inquires.

"Fashion."

"You're literally a physical being made out of light."

"So?"

"And I've never seen you in any article of clothing. Listen, I'm fully aware that you all have been using these Artifacts to buff your shortcomings. I won't stop you."

"I wouldn't put it like that…" Sadra grumbles.

"Then why else would you want this Blessed and Cursed power?" Klae asks.

"Well, I'm also intrigued by the Light and Darkness these artifacts emit. I'm struggling to handle my own, so these might provide some aid for me."

"I'm no enlightened monk, but you may find that you won't even need those braces to find balance," Klae says.

"Really?"

"No. I'm just messing with you. Go ahead and take them."

"Wha—you suck!" Sadra yells.

"If you disagree, then prove me wrong."

"You know what, keep them! I don't need it!" Sadra says, hurrying through the portal.

"Heh. Too easy."

Chapter 52

Unholy Water

The wind—it doesn't howl, it instead feels like a whisper, telling them to turn back at once. Standing at the edge of the isle's overlook with the others, Draxis shares to them his sentiment. "I can't believe we have to dive into the depths of all… this. My heart's not ready."

"It's scary to think how much of this water might be mixed in with blood," Rend says.

"No one here asked you to say something like that," Draxis says.

"It's not like there's anything else to say."

"That's probably for the best."

"Ow!" Aluna yelps. The sharp pain in her chest is great enough to anchor her down towards the ground, where she then sits and rubs her chest.

"What's the matter?" Rend asks. "You alright?"

"Owww…"

"Hold on, this looks serious," Draxis says.

"I'm fine, I'm fine…" Aluna says, trying to shoo them away. "Just give me a second."

"Is it your curse, Butterfly?" Jellop asks. "We told you not to hold your pain in and let us know if something is awry with your health."

"But we're so close. It's bad enough that I fucked us over. I don't want you all to keep being held back because of me."

"You say that, but here we are tending to you, because you are a priority."

"Is there really no way we can stall or purify you of your Karma?" Sadra asks. "You can't keep going on like this."

"I am exhausted of any ideas," Aluna says.

"Lord Suvius," Draxis calls out to him, "you're studying Darkness and its morbid knowledge. Aren't curses a part of that?"

"Indeed," he answers.

"And?"

"The design of her curse is nigh unbreakable."

"Unsurprising," Aluna says.

"I said unbreakable, not that it is untouchable," Suvius says. "From what I could assume from the texts of the Apostates, there are a few options we could perform, but the severity of your curse hinders any easy attainment of your salvation."

"Let me hear the options anyway."

"Very well. How does Sacrificial Transference sound to you?"

"Detestable. Next!"

"Designer's Demise?" Suvius says next.

"Does that mean I would have to kill the one who placed this curse on me?" Aluna asks.

"Indeed."

"Wait… surely the motherfucker who did this to me isn't still alive? Right?"

"I would assume it's some random Decayed Apostate humping a dark corner somewhere."

"Then we'll never find them," Aluna says. "Just my luck. Next!"

"The last thing we could do, or… what could have been done once upon a time, is to bless you," Suvius says.

"Bless? Isn't that what priests do?"

"Their words are more like benedictions. True blessings are a step higher than the normal sanctity bestowed by the pious. They are the ultimate acts of absolution."

"Nice!" Aluna says. "How do we do it?"

"…I'm sorry."

"What are you sorry for? You didn't even say anything."

"But my actions already have," Suvius says. "Sadra would concur."

Aluna looks towards her with a worried look.

Sadra holds her head low as she speaks. "Unlike other aspects on the Life spectrum, like Radiance and Restoration and the natural elements, Blessings require a higher mastery of Light. You won't find anyone anymore who is capable of that kind of gift. It's futile to even talk about it."

"But you're an Isilian. Can't you try?"

"That's… I'm sorry. It's a sacred practice that died with my people. You think of me too highly, Aluna. My knowledge is too little, and my light is too corrupt to do anything that complicated—if I ever could."

"To go more into detail," Suvius joins in, "there is a high possibility that a curse of your status might only be absolved or redesigned by a Saint, the rarest attainment of Light or spiritual exaltation a person can reach. There were only thirty-one Saints in all of recorded history. Apparently the most recent one was the Arbiter of Light—Marcella.”

“Her?” Sadra questions in an offended tone. “That traitorous bitch left the Isilians to die!”

“Not to mention that she did try to kill us once upon a time,” Draxis adds.

“It does not matter if the magic of Light is used to harm or commit sin,” Suvius says. “The concept and power of Light is not about righteousness; it is but a tool just like Darkness is. We can’t deny how tactical she was with the duality of holy justice.”

“That’s such horseshit…” Sadra says.

“You’re telling me,” Aluna groans. “Is there nothing we can do?”

Suvius shakes his head. “While this conference has alluded to some possible theories of mine, they are not succinct. You’ll just have to hold on for as long as you can. We are almost at the end of our grueling journey.”

Aluna lets out a sigh of disappointment. “Okay…”

Suvius kneels down. “I don’t want you to move around too much for the time being, so I’ll let you rest on my shoulder.”

“Really?” she gasps.

He nods, confirming for her to climb on his shoulder. “Komet!” Suvius calls out to get its attention. “We are departing. It’s your time to shine.”

“That was a horrible joke,” Draxis says.

“I don’t know why I even bother if I’m just going to get ridiculed.”

Komet touches down on the ground and drags itself around, creating a big circle.

"What's it doing?" Rend asks.

"I think it… wants us to step inside the ring?" Sadra says, "Sometimes the translations aren't exactly clear."

"Thank you for your outstanding and continued support, Knight Komet," Suvius says. "You're a silent partner, but incredibly faithful."

Komet projects a glowing smiling face above itself.

Once they are all standing inside the circle, a bubble of solid light begins to take form, resonating with Komet's radiance as it secures its position as the core. Sadra rolls their hamster ball off the cliff, plunging them into the ominous waters below.

***

"Shit," Rend says as he squints. "We've barely descended and it's already pitch-black down here."

"I can provide some more light," Sadra says. "…As per usual."

"Wouldn't that attract monsters though?" Aluna asks. "I highly doubt this bubble could withstand one."

"We do need to see where we're going," Draxis says.

"Right…"

"Okay, everyone… be prepared." Sadra's hand flickers as she tries to be wary of awakening any slumbering shadows outside of the bubble. They seem to be alone, so she goes all in to illuminate herself. She shrieks as the massive body of a serpent passes by their view, thankfully uninterested by the lucent flash. They choose to wait it out after the immediate fear has passed.

"That is the largest fish I've ever seen," Draxis says. "It's still going…"

"Shouldn't something like that be farther down in an abyss or something?" Rend asks.

"Look around you. What's the difference?" Suvius says.

The tail of the serpent finally reveals itself, indicating that it's safe to leave.

"Alright, Komet," Sadra says to it. "Where to? Forward or down?"

Komet signals the way to go by displaying a directional arrow that points downward.

"I was hoping you would say the other direction…"

***

"Hey look, Maeva," Rend says, pointing towards a floating pile of wreckage. "A pirate ship!"

"Not this again…" she groans.

"Son of a witch," Sadra blurts. "This trip is going to take forever…"

At the edge of the bubble, away from the grumbles and groans of everyone else, Jellop helps Komet with the descent by guiding it on where to go as he tries to detect any roaming sea monsters. "Go left, there's a giant squid coming up. Now go right, there's a kraken battling an octolobster nearby. Now… stop. Just—stop."

"Are we taking a break?" Draxis asks.

"It seems so," Aluna says.

"We can take a short rest," Suvius says as he sits down. "Who knows how far we need to go."

Komet takes it upon itself to power down into a hibernation-like state.

Jellop rests his head against the bubble, taking time to rest his eyes. His solace is ruined by a familiar internal voice giving its 'humble' greetings.

"Hey... it's me again. The one who helped you end a war," the condescending voice that haunts Jellop says. *"Thinking about it now, you didn't even thank me."*

"Grrr… what do you want?" Jellop whispers.

"Don't sound so annoyed. I'm just curious as to how you're doing."

"Irritated."

"Irritated or upset? There is a difference."

"Who cares?" Jellop says.

"I care. If you're going to share your feelings at all, then do it right. Tell me what's bothering you," the Condescending Voice says.

"It's dark. Monsters lurk. Aluna…"

"Oh my, that is a lot to worry about. Sounds like you need my assistance again."

"No," Jellop says.

"Come on."

"Nay."

"Please?" the Condescending Voice says.

"Grrr…"

"Who are you talking to, Jellop?" Aluna asks.

"I'm… I-It's only a prayer."

"Aw, I could have joined you!"

"Maybe when there's less of an audience…" Jellop says, waiting for the intrusive voice to make its appearance again, but it seems that it has left him alone. He takes solace again as he lays his head against the bubble, tuning his ears to the ambience of the deep water—only to get disturbed once again, this time by his own senses. He has to act fast. "Sadra, could you do me a favor?"

She cocks her head to the side. "You sure have been quite demanding lately."

"I'll keep that complaint in mind. Anyway, can I have you aim your light this way? Over to where I'm facing?"

"S-Sure?" Her light shines clean through the opaque curtain of the deep, creating a bright tunnel through the sanguine darkness, and at the end of said tunnel, comes a shadow that has already noticed their presence. It roars the moment its face is revealed. "Um, Jellop," she squeaks, "there's an angry leviathan heading towards us."

"Pain," he groans. "I wish my premonitions were more of a fluke."

"Jellop, this isn't funny!"

"I'm not laughing either."

Those who are sitting down are forced to stand up and get involved.

"Tell Komet to wake up," Suvius says.

"Komet! We have to go!" Sadra yells.

Komet's center flashes a gloomy gray once it hears its name.

"What do you mean you're recharging! This isn't the time for that!"

"It's coming closer!" Rend says as he pushes against the bubble's walls to make it move. The others join in to help him.

The unsettling sight of a beast's ugly maw, a familiar and second occurrence for Aluna. In response, her wings are turning blacker than the fear that corrupts her as she realizes what's happening to her body.

Before it's too late, Aluna uses what control she has left and turns one of her wings Lapis lazuli blue in color and jerks her right arm to the side—hard, while screaming, "Get away from us!"

A whirlpool forms in front of the protective bubble and annihilates the serpentine leviathan as it charges into it, creating a chunky blend of blood and water. Aluna's wings then dim to their clear, default state.

"That was cool, Aluna," Rend says.

She barely hears him over her own rapid breaths as she retreats back to Suvius's shoulder and curls up.

"Aluna, I have never seen you so shaken up before," Suvius says. "You seem terrified of your own magic."

"I'm becoming a threat again! It's too dangerous for me to do anything," she says.

"Even though you just saved our lives? Stop beating yourself up over the past."

"I'm surprised you are willing to overlook that event so easily."

"There is always a time and place for atonement," Suvius says. "The monsters that surround us however do not possess a similar mindset, so it would be in your best interest to use your magic for something productive rather than stowing it away."

"Do you all trust me enough to use it? What if I do something bad?"

"Aluna, please. We need you more than anything right now," Draxis says.

"I trust you too," Rend says. He also lifts one of Maeva's arms to force her to show support.

"You will always have my vote," Jellop says.

"It was nothing but a damn water spell, Aluna," Sadra says with a sassy tone. "I've felt you do way worse than that."

"I'm not sure that's a good thing…" Aluna questions. "But that does mean a lot to me."

"Just don't let my words be in vain—or else."

"She means you're welcome," Draxis says.

"Quiet, you," Sadra responds.

All six of Aluna's wings become flush with a blue hue and bloom into a full spread. "I'll use my magic for a little while. I want to get out of here. Are you all ready?"

"Hold… hold on," Draxis says, trying to brace himself for the unpredictable. "Ready for what?"

"This." Aluna brings her arms up, causing the water around them to ripple, and forces her arms back down, propelling their bubble downward at a blinding speed, far surpassing any fathom reached by daring adventurers.

***

Komet emotes an exclamation point above its top—then it flashes in an alarming hue of red to notify the others. Aluna withdraws her movement spell, snickering as she watches the others recover from the sudden stop.

"Ow…" Jellop groans. "I miss the surface."

"I think Komet's saying that we're here. Look down." Sadra then switches off her body, allowing the luminous glow from the distant city below to become visible.

"So, this is what the civilization of the Meridians looks like in person," Suvius says. "Fallen civilization I mean."

"Meridian Subtropolis," Draxis says, staring in wonder. "This has to be the city Ronella said she was searching for."

"This city looks so… modern? I guess?" Aluna says. "It looks similar to the Arbiter capital."

"Sounds like stolen art," Rend adds.

"Ha!" Suvius laughs. "I like that jab. Say that is true, it makes me wonder how much Meridian 'art' was stolen by the Arbiters."

"And how much of it was converted to be used against the common people," Draxis says. "I'm not against advancement, but I know I sure as hell didn't feel my life improving."

"Same," Sadra adds.

"Show me where to go, Komet," Aluna says. "I'll push us forward."

***

Everyone is busy strolling around the bubble in circles, taking in the miserable sights of the underwater cityscape. The sea floor below is a trove of antiques, skeletal remains, and sunken ships lost to time. Off to the sides, there are bioluminescent coral signs on the corners and rooftops of any towering building fortunate enough to not be retaken by purple aquatic plants. They have never seen anything like it.

Some of the coral signs are designed to spell out words in an indecipherable language, which hinders the appeal, but that doesn't affect the signs that are fashioned to create an image. Fruits and fish to indicate stores, oyster beds and seashells to indicate housing and decorations, and then there's the more… suggestive signs.

Sadra directs her light through the broken windows on a few nearby buildings. "It's all so weird," she says. "Most of these ruins are preserved well enough to house survivors, so where are the Meridians?"

"Probably devoured by the sea life," Suvius says.

"I guess, but didn't you all mention that some fish-woman said that everyone flocked here? Where is 'here' exactly? This place looks like sunken crap."

"There might be a designated shelter somewhere," Aluna says.

"I hope there is."

Rend decides to disengage from everyone's group discussion and heads over to the less occupied part of the bubble, where Maeva is seated and keeping herself secluded. He patiently waits on her to acknowledge his arrival.

"Is it too late to ever say sorry?" she says, after a delay.

"To whom?" he asks.

"To anyone."

"Maybe? It would probably help to not stack up so much remorse in the first place."

"I only ask because I still feel some type of way about the inmates back at Gravefall. How far would I have gone if I wasn't stopped? I don't deserve this power."

"Honestly, it doesn't seem like anyone deserves power. I harbor some guilt because of mine, just like you do with yours," Rend says.

"You?" Maeva asks, looking up at him. "How much guilt? Do you feel that way over the Decayed?"

"I'm not the biggest enthusiast on killing them, but I'm mostly talking about that old warrior back at Wania."

"I didn't know that your victory affected you so badly…"

"Unlike the Decayed, he had a life—and I took that away," Rend says. "Then I started becoming hostile towards our friends when we were trying to save you. Guilt is a new feeling to me because I was always the victim, but now I have the power to make everyone else my victim. Regardless, this power of mine is only mine to wield. I want to do better with it. You should do better with your power too. I didn't like seeing you act the way you did. I refuse to serve another monster."

"But I am a monster," Maeva states.

"Even if you feel like one or were born one, that doesn't mean you should act like one—or even think like one. What are your thoughts when you look at these dilapidated ruins?"

"It makes me want to help, to heal back what was lost. But you must understand that I will not hesitate to remove those that disrupt what I want."

"Yeah… you and me both. You're a bad influence," Rend says.

"Ba-bad? That's such a strong word. Could… could you call me that again?"

"I don't know how to respond to you sometimes…"

"What are you two chatting about?" Draxis comes over to ask.

"Stay out of this," Maeva says.

"Make me."

She shows her fangs at him.

"That's more like it. I'm glad to see you talking again at least, Maeva."

"Thanks," she says, trying to hide her smile. "Dammit—don't look at me!"

Draxis chuckles at her.

Chapter 53

Even Angels Can Drown

A colossal underwater palace—the shining landmark of the Meridian city, wreathed with crystals and pearls bereft of their glamour. The palace is quite large indeed, but wholly insignificant and incomparable in size to the abyssal drop-off at the city's borders. The vast lightless trench does not bring despair, it *is* despair. Not even the pale illumination of the city can give it a heartbeat of life.

Stopping in a position to get a decent enough view of the palace, Komet shines its red indicator once again to alarm the others.

"The Artifact is in there somewhere," Sadra says, speaking for Komet.

"I see a windowed dome up top," Suvius says. "I think it's wise to catch a glimpse of the interior."

Komet takes them above the palace, stopping just a little above the dome to give them a bird's eye view.

"This is a pretty fancy place," Aluna says while admiring the interior. "Though I'm not sure how I feel about the decorations. It's too reminiscent of what you see topside. I was expecting more coral and taxidermized sea life or something."

"We're not meant to be window shopping," Suvius remarks.

"Guys, look!" Rend says, observing the lone woman lounging sideways from head to her fishtail lower half on a coral throne. "It's Ronella!"

"Heyyy!" Draxis cheers. "She made it! That's good. For once we get to see a friendly face."

"She'll definitely understand our plight," Rends says. "We should go down there."

Feeling suspiciously anxious, Maeva decides to look back—just in time to see her intuition unfold. "W-Wait. Come back over here!"

"What?" Draxis asks.

Maeva points downward, towards an entrance door where a group of crystal-armored soldiers drag in a young woman and an even younger boy. The soldiers throw the restrained duo in front of a smug Ronella. They look completely different compared to Ronella. They are more humanoid with a smooth and slippery texture for skin along with having webbing between their hands and feet.

"Well that's… that's probably a misunderstanding," Draxis says. "I refuse to say anything negative unless we get some context."

"Context. I wonder…" Jellop mumbles. He touches his amulet as he thinks. "New idea. I wonder if I can amplify my telepathy and transfer their spoken thoughts into our minds?"

"Jellop, just where do you keep getting these outrageous ideas?" Suvius asks.

"Imagination—and a deep study on psiowls. One contributor to my studies was Klae. He told me that there was a once an Elder psiowl that infiltrated the Arbiter hierarchy."

"An infiltration?" Aluna questions. "I never heard of such a thing, otherwise they would have had me exterminate it. What became of it?"

"It became the one of the first victims of Zoology," Jellop says.

"Hearing that doesn't make me feel good."

"Then I'll change the Brainwave Channel. That's an actual term in reference to what psiowls can see and detect."

"Hooray for science…" Aluna grumbles.

Jellop activates the Mesmerion and 'tunes in' to the hostile sea of brainwave frequencies that he can naturally perceive floating around the throne room below. The thoughts are muddled and unintelligible like static, but it soon clears up. "Do any of you hear anything?" he asks.

"Fuck you! You're nothing but full of kraken shit, Ronella!"

Mentally, they all feel a sharp neural response of pain and shock, along with a harsh thought that follows afterwards.

"Yeah… we can perceive the situation loud and clear," Aluna says, in a depressed tone.

"Shh! This is getting good!" Sadra says.

They all look at her in disbelief and disgust, then carry on with observing the drama playing out below them. They watch Ronella return to her throne, looking satisfied as she places both of her arms on the armrests.

"So many powerful swears. Is that any way to talk to your rightful queen, Beranda?"

"A queen, are you?" the young, captured woman, Beranda, scoffs. "I don't think we're *that* desperate yet."

"Shut up! I would have made a great queen!" Ronella shouts.

"I'm just saying that you never had the popular vote, not that there's anyone left to count the votes."

"I would have had something to rule if you all weren't so arrogant! But now it's too late! We both have to suffer with the consequences…"

"I don't know what is possessing you to say something so moronic," Beranda says. "Our people would still be dead even if you were in charge. You should be thankful that you weren't the one to have made the call to purge this city. I would rather have it be this way than to be led in circles by you."

"You know what I think, I think you're jealous," Ronella says. "You've always been that way."

"Hardly."

"But I'm smarter than you."

"Ambushing me in my sleep doesn't mean that you're clever," Beranda responds.

"I'm stronger than you," Ronella says.

"Have our soldiers unbind me if you're brave enough to test that lie."

"I'm better than you at everything!"

"And yet, even at world's end, nobody wants you as their queen. You make me yawn."

"Just admit that you're jealous!" Ronella screams.

"I will only admit my regrets for convincing mother and father to adopt you."

"Integrating me into the family to decrease the surrounding political drama. Yes, I know. Royals are always looking to only keep themselves afloat."

"At first it was like that, but we genuinely started to like you, Ronella. I admit we had our issues, but you're also…"

"I'm what? Say it!"

"You're a vicious threat," Beranda says.

"For so long I wanted to hear that. You all never wanted an outsider like me to have a voice! And now I'm the bad person because I'm taking what was supposed to be mine in the first place?"

"Yes, you're not Lagoonborn like us, you're Trenchborn. Call it discrimination if you must, but our distrust is warranted because nobody knows what goes on down there—but we could take a few guesses with you. Not just with you in general, but also with that stupid doll you had with you before we locked it away down in the treasury.

"These bad omens you brought upon us aren't a coincidence, Ronella. We didn't know we were inviting an accursed into our home all those years ago—and look at where our attempt at good karma is bringing us today. Think about how you're behaving right now!"

"Yeah, an outcome from betrayal," Ronella responds.

"There is nothing I can say that will alleviate your pain," Beranda says. "Believe me, it was either we banished for your own good or we would have resorted to doing something drastic. All that effort did though was delay this really annoying usurpation…"

"You can thank the surface folk for bringing me back."

"Damn it all, shouldn't those marauders be dead by now? Their ignorance is going to be the death of us all. More so than what's happened already—"

"I take great offense to that," Draxis whispers aggressively.

"Shhh!" Sadra hushes him.

"I still don't get why mother always told us to stay away from them," Ronella says. "They're colorful and capable of putting up a fight. Maybe we should ask her directly as to her reasons why. Soldiers, bring in the rest of the family! We have to make this a proper reunion before my accession!"

The sound of intense growling gets Beranda to turn around. She then quickly looks back the other way, trying to prevent herself from vomiting. "Ronella… what did you do to our parents?"

"Don't you mean *your* parents? I am adopted after all. They are Drowned now but I'm positive they are still capable of showing how much they love you both."

"W-Why would you do that to them? What the fuck is wrong with you!"

"Is this all it takes to remove that tough attitude of yours?" Ronella says, smirking. "How unsurprising."

"You're… not really going to kill us, are you?" Beranda asks. "Think about what you're doing! Please!"

"What else am I going to do with you and Mikola? Banish you both away like what you did with me? This family drama is going to end tonight!"

"Sister," the boy next to Bernada says with an innocent stare. "What's going to happen to us?"

"She's… Nothing's going to happen to us," Beranda says.

"You should make that a swear if you're so sure," Ronella says. She then snaps her fingers, motioning for the soldiers reining the chains on their parents to be released. They both rush towards Mikola first.

"No!" Beranda cries out. "Ronella! Stop them!"

"Mmm… Nope!"

"Mikolaaaaa!" Bernada tries to ram into the Decayed duo to push them off. She gets knocked back by a violent swipe towards her face that cuts through all the way up into her right eye.

"…That's enough," Ronella says to the soldiers after attaining enough satisfaction from the amount of blood filling the area. "Give Mother and Father their rest now."

One of the soldiers rushes in and executes the feasting Decayed by swift decapitation with a crystal sword.

"Hmm? You've gone silent, Beranda," Ronella says.

"Mikola…" Beranda sobs, staring at the mangled body parts beside her with her remaining eye. "Wh-why…! I didn't think you were actually this serious!"

"Nobody took me seriously! You all adopt me, then abandon me! Who wouldn't become wrathful after experiencing such everlasting pain?" Ronella then rises from her throne and swims towards Beranda.

"W-Wait! You can have the palace and the treasures and whatever else you want all to yourself! Just let me go!"

"I think you're forgetting something else that's precious…" Ronella says.

"W-What?"

"You forgot to include yourself."

"What—what do I have to do with anything?" Beranda says.

"Don't you think it would be unbecoming for the new queen to not have a royal pet?" Ronella grabs Beranda's chin and says to her, "The oceans are mine now, and so are you."

"Stay away from me!" Beranda shouts, trying to wrestle herself from Ronella's clutches.

Ronella goes into a laughing frenzy. "I'm so overjoyed right now! This power! This euphoria! It's making me feel so… *hungry*! I-I could just—" She forces her mouth onto Beranda's, eating through her face until nothing else left can be seen in the dense nebula of blood.

Suvius turns his head away. "Turn the connection off, Jellop. Now!"

"Y-Yes. Right away."

"Let's leave," Suvius says next after he waits for the lingering sounds to exit his mind. "It would behoove us to act now while she's… distracted."

"That bitch, she lied to us," Maeva says. "I can't believe we helped her enact her twisted revenge."

"And to think I once called her an angel out of respect," Draxis says. "I suppose even an angel can drown in insanity."

"That woman mentioned that the Doll was in a treasury of some sorts," Rend says. "Sounds like a fun heist."

"Oh no. Are we doing stealth again?" Aluna groans.

"Second times the charm," Rend answers.

"That's not how the saying goes."

"It's better than three."

Chapter 54

Saltwater

Starting from the top of the palace, they circle around to the front. On the way there, they stumble upon a gaping hole in the side of the palace, large enough to squeeze through. The consensus is made to take advantage of such a lucky find.

"It'll be impractical to search around like this," Suvius says as they park inside an unoccupied corridor. "Are you ready, Aluna?"

"Huh? Ready for what?"

"You mentioned you knew some water-breathing spells."

"Oh, that. I don't know if I should…"

"This will all be for nothing if you don't do it."

Aluna takes six deep breaths, flexing each of her wings in succession before she finally commits to a spell. Blue rings appear around everyone's necks, stamped on like a tattoo. "I did it? I did it!"

"Uhh, is this supposed to be spell working?" Maeva asks. "This makes it look like I have a choker on."

"Keep talking…" Rend pesters.

"Idiot…"

"As long as that 'choker' doesn't disappear, then none of us will die a horrific death by drowning and all the other million ways water can kill you," Aluna says.

"This thing feels weird. I don't even know how that's possible," Suvius says while scratching his neck. "Do I even need to have this?"

"Be careful what you wish for," Jellop says.

"I think a choker looks good on you, Suvius," Draxis says.

Suvius stares blankly at him, then he pops the bubble by smashing his fist through it, without looking.

Komet buzzes at him in an infuriated state, but it gets ignored.

"I was hoping that would kill you, Sir Draxis," Suvius says.

"Didn't you hear what Jellop said about wishes? If you would have succeeded, then I would have also taken you down with me."

"…Obviously this water is making everyone seasick. Move along."

They follow Komet deeper into the palace. It's like a bloodhound sniffing out the treasure they seek. It takes time to navigate around as they get adjusted to inhaling water and having to swim in order to move around. The corridor's exit leads out into an indoor ravine where many, many, open and closed pathways can be explored.

They stick close to their bloodhound, Komet, as it descends lower and lower into the palace depths. Komet blinks white in color in front of a gilded door at the very bottom of the palace grounds. They enter a rotunda, with a single straw doll lying on top of a pedestal in the center of the crystalline room.

"There it is," Aluna says. "This isn't much of a treasury if there's only one precious item here."

"Teehee! Yet everyone is tempted by my incredible value all the same!"

Aluna jolts. "Did you guys hear that?"

"Hm? Hear what?" Maeva asks.

"It was like a child's voice or something."

"Aside from yours? No."

"I don't have a—whatever. I could have sworn there was a voice."

They wait a while for the supposed voice to reappear.

"A new friend! Play with me! Play with me!"

"See!" Aluna shouts. "There it is! Did you hear it that time?"

"Uh, yeah, sure…" Sadra says. She then leans near the others and whispers. "I think she's going insane, just like Ronella."

"Must be something in the water," Draxis says.

"Assholes," Aluna remarks.

"This room is either a vault, or it is a prison for vessels of Darkness," Jellop says. "Should we be so willing to chase after the allure of loot?"

"We've already fallen into the trap of greed," Suvius responds. "If the doll does speak, then it seems aware of our needs. My greatest concern however is its own needs. Why would it insist on privately conversing with only one of us?"

"Depends on what Aluna here has that it wants," Maeva says.

"…Why are you all looking at me like that?" Aluna asks, terrified at their unwanted stares.

"Hmm…" Suvius hums while thinking. "If this item is sentient, then we would need to convince it to come along with us. That is to say that we'll be relying on you to entice it for us, Aluna."

"Do I have a choice?"

"I don't recall splitting your options."

"Erm… okay.

"Should we have someone to stay back here just in case the rest of us get cursed or somethin'?" Rend asks.

"It wouldn't hurt," Suvius says. "I myself am far too invested with this wicked item to be restrained. Who else wants to keep watch for us?"

"I volunteer," Draxis speaks up.

"Again?" Sadra groans. "Why do you keep holding yourself back? When did you get so lazy?"

"I'm not lazy. It's a matter of conservation," he says.

"And what are you conserving?"

"All the feeble energy that I have left in me. I always need a huge amount when I'm talking to you."

Sadra lightly punches him on the shoulder. "I'll ignore that derogatory comment if you don't recreate this stunt for a third time."

"It's hard to say no when you present me with a free getaway," Draxis says. "By the way, I think one of you lost the leash on that child over there."

"Child?" Maeva asks.

"Aluna."

"What the—Aluna! Get away from that!"

Over near the Doll, Aluna can't help but to be mesmerized by its stitched eyes. The doll isn't moving on its own, right? That's just the water making it so? She is not so sure as she hears a little girl's voice speak to her telepathically again.

"New friend! I knew you would come to me..."

"Are you actually getting brainwashed by that thing?" Rend asks Aluna.

"I'm trying to see what the fuck it wants. Stop interrupting me!"

"Let's just take it with us. Come on!"

While Aluna and Rend cause some waves with their bickering, Komet floats over towards Sadra and nudges her face, forcing her to look up at the ceiling.

"What has the crystal friend so spooked, friend Sadra?" Jellop asks.

"That's what I'm trying to decipher. Anyway, why are you asking about those giant pearls above us, Komet? Huh? What's so worrying about the way they're angled? Wh-what do you mean you think we're being watched…?"

Conch horns start to blare throughout the palace with deafening volume, unceasingly.

"Mayyybe we should have studied up on Meridian stuff before coming here," Sadra says as she huddles up with the others. "Aluna, have the Arbiters done any research that could help us out?"

"Hm? Why would I have access to forbidden information?"

Security bursts into the treasury through the gilded doors, flooding in fast and showing no signs of offering reprieve.

"We told you to watch the doors, Draxis!" Maeva shouts.

"What the—don't blame me because you're upset!" he argues while madly trying to swim away to safety. "How can I even watch something that's been obliterated! Do better!"

"Not now, children!" Suvius says. "We should have known that an Artifact like this in an uncharted world was going to be a difficult heist." He then activates his cuirass, and a manifested scimitar forged out of hellfire is wielded tight in his hands. The passionate flames boil the water to show off its dominance and immunity to underwater conditions. "To arms!" Suvius bellows, with the weapon raised high.

"Here we go!" Aluna roars with a pumped-up attitude.

"Hey! Wait for me!" Draxis shouts.

Everyone is barely given enough time to prepare against the proficient swimmers that torpedo straight towards them with their saw-toothed spears and pronged weapons pointed straight for their heads.

Suvius protects the others by engaging with any threat that gets too close and leaves them defenseless as he melts and cleaves through their weapons with his. Komet also helps to buy some time by diving into the middle of a group of attackers and unleashing an omnidirectional attack of blinding light.

A small device gets thrown in Rend's direction that ticks down before it explodes, smearing his face with an inky substance that blots out his vision. When he wipes it off, he is face-to-face with a guard who is already in a premade killing motion. Rend shoves his foot in the guard's face and launches himself away, putting some extra fire in his kick to maximize the damage. A crystalized helmet floats down to the ground, exposing the shark-toothed attacker and its cadaverous face.

"The hell?" Rend says in shock. "These soldiers are Decayed! Watch out!"

"They're fighting like this as zombies?" Aluna cries out.

"It doesn't matter, you are all granted permission to kill them," Suvius says as he swiftly impales one and slices it open. "They should have never shown their weakness!"

Reinforcements are showing up by the dozens, steadily bolstering the feeling of being outnumbered. Most soldiers that arrive are the same generic rank-and-file types, but they are also accompanied by a new type of foe.

There are odd shrimp-like entities that wield bedazzling crystal wands with a circular hole at their tip. The shrimps aim their wands towards their mouths and blow into them, launching a flurry of giant bubbles. The bubbles are near impossible to dodge due to their size and their bonus property of detonating when in proximity of enemies.

Despite trying to pop as many as she can with an offensive volley of spells, Aluna is the first to get hit. She takes no damage externally. Internally, however, she is reduced to staring at her hands in disbelief as she feels her magic leave her and make her disoriented. More bubbles are coming in hot to take advantage of her weakened state.

Suvius rushes over and shields her by fanning a wall of hellfire in front of them. Despite its potency, the fire shrinks rapidly against the harsh stream of bubbles.

"No way…" Aluna says in disbelief. "Why would the Meridians be using something so evil? No wonder this place was blacklisted. We're so screwed. They're using Anti-magic!"

"Anti-magic?" Suvius questions. "Didn't the Arbiters make that the highest capital offense?"

"I'm pretty sure that requires a functioning jurisdiction in places where it matters the most."

"Help!" Jellop screams. "This hurts!"

"No! Suvius, we have to get him!" Aluna shouts.

"Are you mad? We can't get to him like this!"

"Don't fall into despair, everyone!" Sadra yells, fully transforming her body into her Diurnal form. "No more will darkness trample us! The light of sunshine purges all evil!" With a luminous foot, she sends it down and emits a glare of golden light that consecrates the entire room. A coat of that resonating radiance covers their entire bodies, purifying them of any sustained negative effects.

"What kind of buff is this?" Rend asks.

"Isn't it super cool?" Sadra says, gleefully. "I think I might call it: Sunrise! If it works like how it's going in my head, then everyone should be granted resistance to stupid overpowered shit like Anti-magic."

"Look at you being resourceful. Good for you."

"Yay! I actually did something! I wanna do it again!"

Suvius takes account of the situation around them, finding that they are pinned down near the Doll, with no means of escape, and now having to shelter a vital boon that they can't afford to lose. "Is it possible to defend yourself in any way while you perform that constant cleanse, Sadra?"

"Um, I don't think so. I think I may have miscalculated this spell. I didn't think this would be so taxing on me…"

"Then we'll have to get organized to protect our last hope. Everyone, get into Circle formation!"

"Oooh, we haven't done that in an eternity it feels like," Aluna says.

"Hold on, a what formation?" Rend interrupts.

"Follow everyone else and form a circle pattern," Suvius says. "It's to cover our backsides—and to prevent ourselves from hitting friendly backsides."

"You can take over my spot, Archias," Sadra says. "I'm usually sandwiched between Miss Maeva and Jellop."

"For the last time, it's Rend!"

They then get into position to form a circle around their beacon of light, Sadra. Komet floats above her like a halo and creates a personal bubble for her.

"Komet, defend her at all costs!" Suvius commands.

"Good luck!" Sadra shouts just before the barrier is fully complete, sealing her off from the fight.

It's now up to everyone else to handle their designated point of the circle accordingly. Suvius stands at the point that faces the most retaliation—the main entrance. With a summoned sledgehammer, he bats at any oncoming chargers and pummels the earth before him, sending tremors that scald the water and explosively incinerate those he targets into blackened ash.

Maeva and her gauntlet, Samsara, are locked into each other's eyes, coming to an agreement. Using the massive reserves of blood she's amassed from events before, she kills all her victims in a series of horror. Her two favorite killing methods being corrupting their blood enough to mutate them into bloated meat-bombs or weaponizing her gauntlet with katana-sized crimson claws and slashing off their faces—all while committing the acts with an unhidden smile strewn across her face.

She takes a few glances at Rend as she becomes steadily bored. He's been doing nothing but creating spells of mass freezing and shattering. "You never struck me as a cold-hearted person," Maeva says to him.

"If you're going to make a joke like that then at least try to make it non-hypocritical. I've been trying out a little bit of everything with magic, but I've come to find that I really, really like freezing stuff. It feels natural to me."

Maeva gives a lukewarm chuckle. "No matter what I can never escape the cold it seems."

"Does it bother you? I can swap to something else."

"Goodness no. I want you to make me shiver."

"Once again, I don't know how to respond to you…"

"Tsunami!" Aluna bellows, interrupting Rend and Maeva's flow. They both look back to catch her warping the ocean itself, cycling multiple whirlpools that suck in entire groups. She even mixes in other elements with her attacks, from lightning to fire to ice, or everything at once.

Jellop stands amazed at the spectacle, along with another uninvited guest.

"You know what I noticed," the Condescending Voice says to him. *"You tend to think about her quite often. One could say it's unhealthy."*

"You again!" Jellop shouts.

"I wonder what about her you are so attracted to. Could it be she herself? Maybe the chaos she brings? Do you like destruction? Do you like destructive people?"

"You can say anything you want about me, but *never* slander her."

"Ooooh, is that a threat? That's not like you at all. You've been more... impatient as of late. It must be frustrating trying so hard to defend the world that is ever so quick to kill you. Look at how your sanctimony of pacifism turned out during the pandemonium at that failed asylum."

"The important thing is that we tried to make something out of it," Jellop says. "You only would have had me do the worst thing imaginable."

"It happened without my interference anyway, so it works out," the Condescending Voice says.

"What do you want from me!"

"Too many issues to pick between. An apology would satisfy most of them."

"What?"

"There's nothing worse than forgetting that you wronged someone. I'm referring to you when I say that. You may not remember, but I strongly remember warning you about how useless your 'peace' and 'order' are. It's just the world's nature to be this calamitous, a constant that will remain until the end of time itself. But you wouldn't, and still don't listen to reason."

"It only sounds like you've wronged yourself," Jellop says. "I don't care who or what I am, there is a world that needs to be restored, and it would be so much better if you weren't a part of it!"

"Hey… Jellop?" Aluna calls out to him.

"A-Aluna!"

"I've been watching you talking to yourself for some time. Later we should discuss about whatever, or whoever, has been bothering you. I understand if you don't want to, but I'm willing to listen if you do."

"I'm sorry it's been upsetting you to see this behavior. I accept your offer…"

"Whoopsie. I got you in trouble," the Condescending Voice mocks.

"Grr…" Jellop growls. Taking hold of his emotions from all the vitriolic feedback made against him, he converts it into a psychic lullaby that puts the parts of the room to sleep with a command from his amulet and executed into motion by his staff.

"You all are doing great but I would prefer it if you slaughtered a little faster!" Sadra shouts to the others, with her voice muffled from within her sanctuary. "This spell doesn't last forever! I swear, it's impossible to carry this team sometimes!"

"Don't get cocky!" Aluna shouts.

Sadra's body brightens as she laughs to herself. "Hehe. Cocky. That's a funny word!"

"Gods, I can't stand you…"

The tides are turning in the Harbingers' favor as the Meridian army thrashes themselves at them, leading only to their deaths. The Circle formation is infallible, worthy of being called unbeatable. It's so unrivaled that the soldiers cease their worthless advance, abruptly.

For a moment, they thought it was because the army retreated out of fright, but it is only because of the haunting melody that plays smoothly through their alerted ears—a woman's delicate song, coming from the entrance door this whole bloody battle originated from.

"My oh my…" Ronella says with slight appraisal as she surveys the destruction made. "Is it fate or a curse that we meet again, Harbingers? Are you all here to betray me too? Maybe *this* will get you all to reconsider your treason?" Ronella flaunts her 'object' of negotiation by his throat, making sure they can see him.

"Draxis!" they all cry out.

"Right, right!" Ronella says. "*That* was his name. I'm so horrible with names. It's downright embarrassing."

"I thought he made it over here?" Rend says. "Were we really not paying attention?"

"We would never treat him like that!" Sadra shouts. "L-Let him go!"

"Something about him always baited me in," Ronella continues, toying with Draxis's unconscious body. "I could barely contain my hunger at the time. I wonder if his taste is still fresh…"

"Don't you dare touch him!" Sadra screams at the top of her lungs. She pounds hard against the barrier, forcing Komet to tear it down.

"Wait, Sadra!" Maeva says, swimming after her.

A blockade of Anti-magic bubbles shuts down Sadra's heroic charge. She tumbles to the ground, barely able to move or breathe. Her support spell fades, leaving everyone else vulnerable.

Ronella is free to sink her teeth into Draxis. She glides her serpentine tongue across any unclothed areas to find the tastiest spot—soon settling for his neck. She makes contact with his flesh and pierces the skin with ease with her razor-sharp rows of teeth. Purple blood overfills her mouth, and she spits out the contents.

"Blech! He tastes horrible! He doesn't taste nearly as good as my sister."

"Fucking die!" Sadra screams.

"Weak words!" Ronella laughs. "You folk are nothing without your magic! I remember father telling me about those experienced wizards and witches who ruled and poisoned the Above world. They could never do anything to us however—only once have they made the mistake of trying."

Ronella sings her haunting tune once again to rally her army. The soldiers drop their weapons, turning more feral as the song lingers and slashing about like rabid sharks.

"Go, my royal army! Kill them all while I enjoy my—"

"Ah, ah, ah!" a divine echo speaks as a warning.

A crescent sickle swoops in and hooks Draxis by his clothes, reeling him to the others' care.

"H-Hey! That's mine!" Ronella shouts, trying to catch the elusive sickle.

"I got him!" Jellop cheers as he catches Draxis. He brings him over to Maeva. She crouches next to Draxis and administers what she can to heal him as fast as possible.

"How ungrateful," the majestic voice says. "Not even a thank you for me? Typical."

A tar-black rift opens up through the ground.

"Looks like I arrived just in time," Malphunnos says as he rises up through the rift. "On the contrary—time's up—for Death is here."

"Friendly god!" Jellop shouts.

"You rang?" Malphunnos then adjusts his positioning, standing with confidence and pride and staring down Ronella and her approaching army.

"Be careful, Mal," Aluna says. "They have Anti-magic!"

"Well, I have Anti-life."

"That's such a lame response."

"I'm going to add that comeback to the exceedingly long list of slick comments you all made to me before I left. Once I'm finished here… I'm coming for you all next."

Aluna quickly cowers behind Suvius.

"That's more like it," he says after a mischievous snicker. "Now… time to get to work."

Malphunnos fashions himself ready before clocking in—casually making his way forward to his next appointment and pulling out his brand-new investment from another summoned rift. His scythe, and his confidence, have already promoted him from someone menacing to someone scream-inducing—but the moment the blade of his scythe bursts into serene, cerulean flames from his eager touch, everyone in the room knows that he means business.

"W-Who the hell are you?" Ronella hisses. "What the hell are you!"

"Wouldn't you like to know…" Malphunnos responds.

She flinches at his wicked grin. "Forget them, kill that guy first!"

That's all Malphunnos was waiting to hear. She just initiated a death sentence. Blinded by the rush of his first kill on an armless Decayed, his wrath rolls into the momentum of a feeding frenzy as he carves his way flawlessly through the feral soldiers—syncing up perfectly with his sentient sickle to cause widespread havoc.

The floating severed heads and entrails are too much for Ronella to handle. "Stop it! Stop ruining my stuff!" The water around her starts convulsing and bubbling, compacting itself into an undulating mess of liquid tentacles that wrap around her and lash out at Malphunnos. "You dare to trifle with a queen! Die!"

Malphunnos's attacks are formless as he butchers the giant tentacles in half as if they were fresh meat. It doesn't matter how atrocious and furious she becomes, Malphunnos is incapable of stopping. Untouchable, like an epic hero in their prime and calling.

"Stay away from me!" Ronella cries out in a near pleading tone.

Coming in hot from her blind spot, the sneaky sickle strikes her in the back, giving Malphunnos enough time to run up and spring towards her—and slash her chest wide open. Ronella and every horror conjured and controlled by her is brought down—including what remains of her army. She is then cradled in merciful arms, by Malphunnos, as he lets the relaxing water send them downward gently.

"I can definitely see why sirens are considered to be the demons of the seas," Malphunnos says. "You're quite the fighter, Ronella. We could have used someone like you."

"It… hurts," she wheezes. "Why does this hot light hurt so much? What is this?"

"It's fire," Malphunnos says.

"Fi-fire?"

"A natural element, sort of like water—except way hotter. I hear it's good for cleansing the soul."

"Oh… that's nice." Her breaths are shortening more as she continues. "I-Is this why I'm feeling so calm? It's making me remember; I miss my family."

"And whose fault is that?" Malphunnos says.

"Theirs."

"Are you really going to put all your blame on them? With the way you've always acted, no sensible parent would ever love a child who brings discord. You disintegrated your own relationship with them."

"Who are you? How do you know all this?" Ronella asks.

"I am Malphunnos, the God of Death."

"Ah, I suppose that would make sense. Does that mean you saw everything I did?"

"Only the key moments in your life where you selfishly took away someone else's. Which does include your familicide. Impressive work."

"I was so angry at them that it drove me mad," Ronella says. "I just wanted them to care about me, to stop alienating me… s-so I took away what was super precious to them. I hold all of their crowns, but now I rule all alone."

"All of that is irrelevant to me," Malphunnos says. "Don't take that the wrong way. I want to make it clear that I am not primarily here to judge your actions. The main thing I care about with my job is to observe and scavenge those who need to pass on. If you think no one cares about you in life, then rest assured that *I* will care."

"Even for someone like me?" Ronella asks.

"Did I stutter?"

"Not at all. Then, I'm sorry you have to clean up after me."

"I don't mind housekeeping. Someone has to make sure this giant roof we all live under is well maintained. It's time for you to rest soundly, Ronella."

"I do feel… sleepy." She then closes her eyes, letting the cerulean flames finally consume her. She is gone, without even a remnant of soul or ash to remember her by.

Malphunnos finally touches down on the ground. He speaks softly to himself, still feeling the missing presence that was in his arms mere seconds ago. "Another soul gone. The world's population is such a mess now. I don't know how I'm going to restore it…"

"That was awesome, Mal!" Rend shouts.

Malphunnos swims back over to them. "Only you psychos would enjoy a bloodbath."

"That's horseshit. I'm pretty sure I saw you crack a smile too."

"Err… that wasn't me."

"Yeah, sure it wasn't."

Malphunnos cracks a smile, this time directly at Maeva, who is still offering intensive care to Draxis.

"What?" she says. "Why are you looking at me like that?"

"Aren't you impressed?" he asks. "You looked down on me before, but surely your mind has changed now?"

"…Why don't you take that scythe and shove it up your ass sideways."

"You're never going to get her to acknowledge you, Mal," Rend says.

"It's quite alright. I like a good challenge."

"Useless talk," Suvius interjects. "We should be securing the Sunken Doll. Speaking of which, where is it?" He looks back at the pedestal. "Aluna! Don't touch that!"

"Dammit, who was supposed to be keeping an eye on her?" Maeva says.

"If you want something done right, then do it yourself," Malphunnos says.

"You've been here for only a few minutes and you're already pissing me off immensely."

Aluna doesn't hear any of the bickering and complaining going on behind her. She is far too entranced by the eerie laughter of the doll.

"No more delays!" it says. *"You have something I want! Exchange!"*

"Exchange?" Aluna asks.

"Exchange with me! Give me!" the Doll shouts.

"What are we exchanging?"

"Whatever you want!"

"How vague," Aluna says. "What's the twist?"

"Whatever I want!"

"Who would ever agree to that?"

"Everyone has wished for something at some point," the Doll says. *"Everyone will do anything to fulfill a true wish. This is your moment! Abstinence is only virulence! Exchange now!"*

"You're not really going to mess with that thing, are you?" Malphunnos asks. "Just look at it, it's like one of those voodoo dolls those witch doctors back at Wania like to make."

"Yeah… but this doll talks like a merchant, and it's offering a deal that seems too good to be true," Aluna says.

"What does it want?"

"Anything. It's a purchase with an unlimited cost in accordance with the buyer's wish. If I handle my cards right, I might even be able to exchange or remove my curse with this thing."

"Are you serious?" Maeva jumps in to say. "That's great!"

Aluna thinks over what she just said previously—and gasps. "It's just now coming to me. I can't believe this! I can finally be free! I can—"

"Not so fast, Aluna," Suvius says.

"Wh-what's the problem? I'm positive that's what this thing does."

"I'm convinced. That's not what I want you to do with it though."

"Lord Suvius…" Maeva growls. "What are you planning?"

"Justice. I want you to use the doll, Aluna. But not to remove your curse—I want you to add another one."

"You can't be serious!" Maeva yells.

"This punishment is far more forgiving than all my other ideas. This is retribution for that stunt she pulled back at Bonamu Glaciers. Did you think I would forget?"

"That's so not fair!" Rend shouts.

"It's fine, everyone," Aluna says.

"No, it's not!"

"It is. I don't… completely agree with this either, but I understand where he's coming from. I nearly ruined everything for us."

The room feels like a pit of hellfire from the sheer intensity of everyone's glares towards Suvius.

"Don't be like that," he says in a reassuring tone. "Remember that we have enough Artifacts now to finally perform that ritual to break the Soul Decay curse. We can add Aluna's to it as well."

"You ever heard of cruel and unusual punishment?" Malphunnos says.

"I don't enforce dead laws. I only enforce mine."

Jellop goes over to Suvius and looks at him like he has something to say. He then bonks his chest plate with his staff, and tells him, "That's how I feel right now."

"Woah! He just hit Suvius…" Rend mutters.

"I wanna see him do it again," Maeva says.

"Sorry, Jellop. I will not budge on this however," Suvius tells him.

"We are not friends for right now."

"Alright, everyone. I'm activating the Artifact," Aluna says. "Here goes…"

The Doll animates, extending one of its plush arms out to her. Aluna grabs onto it, feeling a tingly sensation deep in her bones and blood.

"Ooh! So much naughty wealth you have for me!" the Doll praises. *"Your disgusting greed for the black arts far exceeds mortal capabilities. Your overspending shall instead be rewarded with your one true wish!"*

"Wish?" Aluna asks.

"A super rare purchase, fit for only the richest of patrons!"

"Sure? I accept."

"You, a tormented and fateless victim, shall be granted the holy Blessing: Truthseeker!" A white light, heavenly in its shine, envelops Aluna—and eventually fades away. The Doll returns to its slumbering state after saying, *"Exchange completed!"*

"Feeling alright, Aluna?" Jellop asks.

"It said that it couldn't handle the price of adding another Curse, and it gave me a Blessing to compensate. I don't understand why. Are my sins that hideous?"

"Seems like I was right," Suvius says.

"What do you mean?"

"Damnation Overflow. That was the fourth option for removing your curse that I kept secret. It's a simple equation. By forcing you to take on an extra curse that is equal to the fattened sins amassed by the Devil's Karma, your own accumulated Darkness overloaded, and thus, cancelling out the curses altogether and resetting your spiritual balance to zero. Seeing as you are not dead, the doll seemed to have helped ease the karmic whiplash, which is what I was betting on."

"I thought you were punishing me," Aluna says. "You could have just said that!"

"It was fun testing your loyalty. May that new Blessing serve your fate well."

"I utterly despise you."

"That hatred only feeds me." Suvius then goes over to check on Draxis. Sadra is sitting next to him, caressing his face and watching him breathe. "Sadra… how is he?"

"If Maeva wasn't here to save him, then he would be… Ca-can you carry him, Suvius? I don't think I have the strength to."

"Funny, he asked me to do that for you once," Suvius says.

"Did he? Aww, that's so—wait a minute. You touched me?"

"I had to."

"…I want to go home."

***

Klae barely gives the others any time to breathe the moment they step out of his portal. "Please tell me, in the name of Malphunnos, that you all didn't destroy this last Artifact!"

"We have it," Rend says, holding up the doll.

"Brilliant!"

"But we may or may not have disrupted foreign politics by killing a royal, and it may or may not lead to a war involving whatever remaining forces lie beneath the waters."

"Ah, so… it went well?"

"Are we just going to ignore that we might have set a future war in motion?"

"The sunken world is in complete disarray like the surface," Klae says. "If anything is going to occur then it won't happen until years from now. Maybe."

"Reassuring…"

"Have you all forgotten that I am here?" Malphunnos says. "I can negotiate with the Sea gods to convince their followers not to sink the lands into their domain."

"You sure?" Rend asks.

"For sure. Death is a key component for my negotiations. Plus, they will owe us once we restore the world. Guaranteed they'll be willing to excuse a regicide that was upholding the last bastion of an entire civilization."

"But—"

"Shut up!" they all shout at Rend.

Chapter 55

The House of God

A never-before-seen woman enters the usual meeting place in the Arbiter's tower, with her slender body and silvery hair stealing everyone's attention.

Malphunnos scrambles to get the first word in. "Excuse me, miss," he says, giving a courteous bow. "I don't believe we've met."

"Not in a million years," the woman responds.

"That doesn't affect me. I have all of eternity."

"Stop harassing people, Mal," Rend says, pushing Malphunnos away. "Did you arrive here by boat, ma'am? We can get you some proper care if you give us some time."

The woman squints her eyes in disbelief. "It's me. Draxis! Why do we go through this each time?"

"All this time you were a girl?"

"Stop acting like a 'you know you what'."

"You look gorgeous as a woman, my love," Sadra says.

"You say that about anything I shift into," Draxis responds.

"You're just that attractive. You even look better than Maeva."

"Why must you always compare my beauty?" Maeva says as she lifts her eyes from an open book. "Also, I hate you."

"Mohu—muhu—muhuhu! I can't do your laugh, Jellop," Sadra says to him.

"Muhuhu! Superiority is mine!"

Klae is the next one to enter the room, shuffling individual pieces of paper on top of one another continuously as he skims through them. "Everyone, I have something I need to share with you."

"What's with the ominous tone?" Malphunnos asks.

Klae finds the nearest chair, sighing as he sits down. "For— forgive me for my abnormal behavior," he says with shaky words. "It would be best to be blunt with this matter. But first, you have my thanks, Rend. I was inspired by your dungeon raiding stories and decided to try it out in the lower basements of the tower. I don't think rummaging around in forgotten areas is my style, but I did well enough to uncover a secret or two."

"Glad I could be helpful. I knew all my years of despoiling would be put to use someday. What did you find?"

"An underground bunker of some sorts. Normally a secret like that wouldn't bother me, that is, until I found these notes inside it. This one that I'm looking at right now provokes a call for action. There is only one word on it, in what I call only assume to be written in someone's blood. Eschaton."

"What does that mean?" Rend asks.

"The end. The *ultimate* end of the world. The significance is dire because these notes are left behind by the Paragon himself. Zazer Oakman."

"Him…" Aluna mumbles, with a hint of fright.

"Have any of you met him?" Klae asks.

"We had a face-to-face meeting with Mixon once, and he nearly killed us all in that short span of time," Suvius says. "We took an active approach to ensure we never encountered Zazer."

"Same here," Aluna adds. "It was torment enough for me to try to obey Mixon. I can't imagine what Zazer would have been like. Not like I had any permission to see him anyway."

"I see…" Klae says. "Then this will be an expedition into something that will put us all at an unknown risk."

"Why an expedition?" Draxis asks.

"For precaution. I might just be acting paranoid, but the symbols and numbers on these other notes must have some purpose. They might lead to somewhere of great importance to Zazer. I want to ask you all for your help on this matter."

Suvius nods. "We have our own suspicions about the Arbiters and their ultimate plans. A thread of investigation is crucial, even if it only leads to a dead end."

"You've already found some evidence?"

"Heard and seen evidence. The Arbiters desired something beyond their immediate reach."

"Something different than power and greed? That only deepens this issue…" Klae says. "If you all don't mind leaving as soon as possible, then we can follow the only starting place that I can gather from these scribbles about the Founder's home. Most of you know of that place as the old Arbiter Capital."

"Daison Peak…" Draxis says. "That's worse than the ocean."

"If it makes you feel better, I will be accompanying you on this expedition," Klae says. "We'll need all able hands for this."

"Let's get this over with…" Sadra groans.

"Komet, we're going to be gone for a while," Klae says. "Is it okay if we have you stand guard?"

Komet responds by twirling in place.

"Great. Make sure not to talk to any strangers and to lock the doors."

***

Rend kicks a skull off the nearest edge, watching it disappear into the shrouded fog below. "None of you said that this place was on top of the tallest mountain in the world."

"It's in the name," Draxis says.

"No it's not."

"I feel like it is. Don't tell me that you're afraid of heights?"

"I'm afraid of *this* height. I can't even see the ocean from up here."

In the distance, Suvius looks around at the old ruins of a once prestigious academy and archive fit for any scholar of sorcery. If he had any, his eyes would be closed shut to help ease his mind as the vivid and bloody memories of this place dwell on him.

Wild visions of nearly every nation, nearly every race, and nearly every Arbiter, bent on elevating the mountain's height with their own dead bodies—that was until the Paragon's second in command personally stepped in, arising like a god to his people and a devil to all the non-believers.

Very few survived and could tell the truth of the disaster— not that anyone ever believed Suvius and his allies at the time, or that Suvius would ever want to describe the horrible tale.

That's enough. To prevent insanity, Suvius goes over to Klae to take his mind off things. He finds him studying a premade square of four mysterious and alphabetic-like runes on the ground. "Do you need our help with anything, Klae?"

"This is a lot to decode but it looks simple enough to not require too much brainpower." Klae starts moving his free hand through the air as he follows along from what he can decipher from the list of symbols and numbers on his notes. "I never had to tear space itself apart down to the precise dimensions before, but if I'm reading these coordinates correctly then this should open up a gateway to—mlthbhbhb!"

He is drowned out by a great deluge brought forth from the bottom of the ocean. He scrambles to close off the portal.

"That… wasn't supposed to happen," Klae says after spitting out a mouthful of seawater.

"Dammit…" Sadra groans. "I'm all wet again."

"Again?" Aluna questions.

"Well, this page is completely ruined now," Klae grumbles. "Let me try this other one."

He rips off a piece from the soggy note that has a symbol in the form of a closed human eye and places it next to another page with its own set and list of esoteric symbols. He moves his finger over to a particular symbol that is highlighted by a red mark, this one displaying a full circle with a zig-zagged crack down its center. He makes another attempt at a spell.

A portal opens, and they are all blasted in the face by a breeze of fresh air and the intoxicating smell of lush gardens.

"What's this place?" Maeva asks.

"I'm… not quite sure. It looks unaffected by the Decay. But how?" Klae says.

A colorful flock of chirping birds fly out of the portal.

"Pretty!" Jellop says, trying to catch one.

"I think we just discovered a place that hasn't been touched by any civilization," Klae says. "Or… maybe it couldn't be touched, until now. How astonishing. If that's the case, then this first marked symbol must mean Blindness, and this other one must mean Shatter because we just broke into an inaccessible area somewhere beyond physical accessibility."

He points his finger at another marked symbol, this one showing an open human eye. "Alright. Here we go." Klae checks over the symbols one more time before he tries again.

Malphunnos walks over to the newly made portal. His hand reaches out to it on instinct, but he forces himself to pull it back.

"You know this place, God of Death?" Klae asks.

"This is… Birthplace. How…?"

"You mean the Realm of the Gods? That shouldn't be possible."

"The Arbiters breached my home. When? Why didn't I hear of this? Why haven't the other gods told me? Did those idiots not trust me with that knowledge?" Malphunnos then backs away and says, "Someone is *going* to answer for this atrocity!"

Klae closes the gateway, his heart and hands shaking from dread. "I understand this now. What I'm holding is a master spell, a cheat sheet capable of allowing anyone to bypass the boundaries of any reality. We can go anywhere and everywhere with this. If only I had more time to experiment…"

"One step at a time, Klae," Suvius says.

"Sorry." He looks back down at the note and takes a moment to breathe. "So, I figured out the other symbols, Blindness and Shatter. I need to be completely sure if this third symbol is Gate. Stand back."

The portal he conjures next is a nightmarish mix of red and black. The unbearable heat that emits from it is enough to liquefy the ground around it.

Through the red intensity of the portal, Klae hears his name being called out by a menacing voice, despite no one visible being inside it.

"Nope, nope, nope!" he screams as he waves his hands to wish the portal away.

Malphunnos gives a mild chuckle. "That was probably some infected demon trying to lure you into its lair. Glad to see that Hell hasn't changed one bit."

"Seems like an interesting place to visit in the future for a half-demon like me," Suvius says.

"…Moving on," Klae says. "This is so weird. Alright, we have Blindness for exploring the dimensions, Shatter for breaching the dimensions, and Gate for tethering the dimensions. But what the hell is this final marked symbol on the bottom? Aluna, could you come help me with this? I'm through with guessing."

"Really! Uh, I mean, sure." She glosses over the symbols with him, pursing her lips at the permutations. "Shit, this looks complicated. This last one at the far bottom right doesn't even connect with the other symbols. Maybe it's not supposed to? It could be a mixture of other symbols. Like combining the others to make a new one?"

"Of course! Damn I'm stupid."

"Not as much as me," Aluna says.

Klae laughs. "Nobody likes puzzles. If you're right however, then this symbol looks to be a merge between Vanish, Home, and Sealed. Say if the egomaniacal Zazer managed to create his own realm, then I think this symbol would mean… Throne?"

"Throne?"

"Let me show you. Blindness!" A rune on the ground synchronizes to his incantation by lighting up, as well as the other runes as he continues. "Shatter! Gate! Throne!"

All runes are pleased, displayed by their mass production of particles that have enough imbued power to flip gravity. Everyone is slightly touched by a sensation of weightlessness surrounding them, a feeling that reminds them of the ocean.

"This is it! His personal throne!" Klae shouts in eager anticipation.

The particles coalesce together into a singular oval-shaped entity, golden in color.

"Is it safe to go inside?" Sadra asks.

Klae sticks his hand in first, letting it stay inside for a few seconds, then he pulls it out. "There were about a million things that could have just happened, but my hand is unscathed. It's safe."

***

The ground beneath them looks endless like the cosmos they used to admire, yet tangible. So are the walls and sky above them, glistening in a royal purple color with specks of what looks like starlight embedded into the scenery. Tapping on the walls creates ringing ripples that outline the accessible areas. Watching the ripples scale up higher and higher shows that they are in the main hall of the largest mansion they have ever seen.

The ripples, however, do not show what's past any of the doors or whatever lies up the mystic stairs. Undeterred, everyone starts darting off on their own to start a fun adventure.

"Dammit, people! This isn't a playground!" Klae shouts with a swinging fist. He looks over to his side, noticing that Rend is the only one who hasn't moved yet. "Why are you still here?"

"I don't want to ruin anything."

"It might be too late for that already. You can go explore if you want. No need to tag along with me."

"Are we meeting back up anywhere?"

"I'll have to figure it out later. This is a horrible field trip."

Rend is left all alone as he looks around. *Where to even start?* he wonders. It's like being inside the head of a madman. He's met countless mad men, women, and beasts ever since his revival, so he should be an expert on their psychology at this point. He searches around for clues, only to find that the original portal where they came from has changed in color and shape.

He comes up with an idea. It might go horribly wrong, but his curiosity tells him otherwise. He turns around and exits the room through the origin portal, bracing himself to be ripped apart by some funky miscalculation or mishap due to the weirdness of reality warping.

Rend is ejected out and lands softly on a plush carpet floor. The portal on the ceiling should have taken him back outside of the dimensional mansion—but instead, he is here, in the middle of a pristine master bedroom.

"Can you even create traps out of portals?" Rend says to himself. "I should have thought about what I just did more carefully."

He decides to scold himself later because as he looks around, he finds that he might have hit the jackpot. He rummages through the bedroom, seeking out anything worthwhile.

So far, he's only found loose samples of alchemy ingredients and random clothes. Fishing underneath the bed, he pulls out a heavy notebook. Rend figures that they might be stuck in this place for a while, so he lets his head sink against the pillows on the bed and opens the book—starting with page one.

<u>Because I Was Told To</u>

I am not one to document my 'feelings' with every passing day, but I figured it would be beneficial to do this so they can get off my back about my tendency to—

Boring... Rend thinks.

He skips ahead a couple of pages.

<u>Fallen Stars</u>

Light and Darkness. I consider these two elements of the Life and Death magic hierarchy to be the most impactful on keeping a stable balance in this world. Every race and generation has a genius or two that can utilize Light or Dark to their full potential, but no one is more attuned to these two forces than the Isilians and their Light, and the Demons and their Dark. The Vomenn Kingdom, today, just obliterated the Isilian homeland, along with their archived traditions and knowledge of Light. We will have a meeting later this week to discuss this unacceptable matter with His Royal Highness… Damn him.

Sadra... Suvius... Light and Dark...

Rend flips through some more pages.

<u>Babysitting</u>

Why am I—the greatest Arbiter to ever have lived, aside from the late Founder, having to babysit people? Especially a queen! Damn royals. That so-called 'queen' is like an infant when she doesn't get what she wants. And because of her privileged mindset, guess what she feels entitled to. Dragons! Freaking! Dragons!

I am a man that looks for opportunity however, and she has the right amount of royal privilege and military might to handle their threatening existence for us. On top of that, she is unusually clever and inventive. It might be best if we let that child prodigy continue to play around and domesticate the dragons. It keeps them off our backs, and it helps stave away her curious side so that she can remain ignorant and never question us. Time to go get her milk… Damn her.

Is he talking about Ceranus? I should show Suvius this. Later...

Rend begins to divulge further, skimming through pages of diagrams, scribbles, and more enigmas. He then stops, flipping back to a few pages that he was too quick to gloss over.

<u>Nightfall</u>

There are three main passages that lead into the infernal core of the planet where the Demons thrive: the great chasm below Gravefall Penitentiary, the Black Maw Trench that is closely monitored by the Meridians, and a hidden gateway somewhere deep within the Lesion Bog in the heart of the Hagri Scarlands.

I'm jotting this information down because there's been major talk circulating around that we might need to switch our focus from Light over to Darkness and whatever else can be learned from it seeing as how one of those fundamentals is now in very short supply. We have already mastered what we could for now on Light, so why not the other?

We will have to create a new ancillary division to help establish a starting ground. I proposed for the division title to be Apostates as those who choose to volunteer will have to explore the opposites of our traditional studies. People seem to like the name enough. That makes me feel good. I wish I could say the same about my stomach—I hate Elven delicacies.

<u>A Bad Start</u>

Negotiations with the Meridians today were inspiring, but also unrewarding. We wanted to exchange with them about any experiences or secrets they might have had about Darkness since they live so close to one of its infernal faucets. The only thing they spoke about in depth were Curses. They proclaimed that they have accidentally cursed themselves from a seductive doll brought by some stupid little girl, and now they suffer from a rooted curse called All for One.

It was apparent that something was wrong with them as the entire royal family bloodline was falling apart at the seams trying to endure its effects and wipe it away from their fate. And here I thought that blood feuds were horrific enough on land. I partook in the vote to decide whether or not such an evil artifact was worth taking off of their hands and experimenting on it. While we might return back to the Subtropolis one day, we've concluded that some evils are better left unexplored for now, and some even blacklisted completely from life itself.

To think that one curse could cause so much hate and destruction. Ronella was the last person standing because of that curse. We are all cursed. Well, not for too much longer. Hopefully.

<u>Supernatural</u>

Bloodsingers. Tormentors. Vampires. The latter word being an ancient one spoken by the most ancient of all monsterkind: Demons. Sylis and Crysis, they have managed to find what might be the last descendant of the Vampires according to their latest tests. She is unique to us because her power is something which none of us can replicate or quite figure out. It's hard to describe. It heals like restorative magic, but its current output is double than what any cleric or potion can perform, and yet, she can also corrupt that healing should she deliberately choose to.

I should introduce the idea to the others that we should start categorizing these unnatural properties and elements of Life as… Supernatural, perhaps? Just like Soulpower, it seems like Blood is also a mutable essence that can be exploited to do the impossible, and we need that impossible power of hers. We have assigned Crysis and his brother to take over and oversee her growth and development for now as they are the only ones who are insane enough to… break apart and repurpose our newest 'Lamb' as they like to call her.

Maeva… how could they. It's amazing she's been able to push through this much. It does make me feel better to know that there is a proper definition for her condition. Vampire. I wonder if she's ever heard of them?

Rend skims through more of the book.

<u>Prosperity</u>

Marcella came to us with one hell of a proposal today. Interesting girl she is. I can see why Mixon was so adamant about letting her join our inner circle—ah, I'm starting to digress. According to Marcella, we are becoming too complacent and boring with our hegemony in the world's influential sphere. She believes we should strive for more, become something more. She reminded us about our recent projects to solidify her point.

I have no choice but to agree with her. Just this year alone we have artificially evolved many test subjects who couldn't perform Magic to now being able to use the highest tiers of it, and one of them is even our 'Executioner'. We also have unrestricted reign over some of the most powerful artifacts this side of history. And with the information we have gathered on Maevalina and her almost mythical healing capabilities, we might even have longer-lasting lives because of her Lifeblood. We will refrain from entertaining Marcella for now though until we come up with some fun ideas.

Rend takes a glimpse into the latter half of the book. He can tell the contents are getting juicier. He skips around, trying to find the most impactful bits of info.

A Point of Origin

It seems that immortality is a resurfacing topic amongst the betters here. I admit to myself that something like immortality and a 'higher purpose' isn't something that I comfortably deem to be possible, so I summoned for an all-day assembly today so that we can finalize on an idea once and for all. Sylis and Crysis were the focal point of this debate, along with their experimental Lamb whose power they claim is the ultimate answer to every problem.

Per the results of the discussion, if Soulpower is the gateway for the creation of Life, then Blood is the gateway to restoring and empowering it. Mortal blood alone is frail and incapable of being uplifted, but should it ever be mixed in or replaced entirely with blood from anything that is non-mortal, then certain… mutations start to occur. I never liked pirates, but the thought of plundering from the fabulously wealthy is a marvelous idea.

<u>Project Transmortality</u>

Success. I dislike that word. People use it too frequently. Success is meant for the full completion, not for any half-baked or minor milestones like a sparse chapter in some fledgling's book. All we did today was gather a talented team of top geniuses, nothing more, so does that even qualify as a success? Mixon won't give me an answer, he says that the results are all the responses he would ever need to give. Damn him—but I need him. He thinks he can spearhead this project just because he is the Head Arbiter of Metaphysics, specifically with Cosmology, so naturally this is where his years of expertise supersedes our criticisms.

Still, I can't believe we've come this far as sorcerers and scientists in this volatile era. This experiment is going to be our zenith if it magically 'succeeds'. Here's a cheer, to the end of mortality itself!

Transmortality? Rend wonders to himself. *I don't like the sound of that…*

<u>Project Transmortality—Experiment Nineteen</u>

Arithmetic formulas have never been my strongest skill, but even then, it should have worked… and it did, just not the way we envisioned. I cannot determine if we lack the magic power or the right dimensional coordinates. The coordinates we *have* solved led to a… let's say something that shouldn't exist. Just peering into the other side for even a fraction of a second rendered a portion of the team in a vegetative state.

Mixon pulled the summoning as fast as he could—and in a flash—it was over. An anomalous being sat in the middle of the room in place of the nexus portal. It was watching us, but we couldn't watch *it* for it was too imperceptible for our eyes to handle. It managed to run away. It doesn't matter. It'll probably get eaten alive by some ravenous fauna anyway, but we did send our Executioner to go dispose of it—for precaution. The only thing to take away from this is that reality-breaching is possible, so it is only through patience and time will we finish our objective.

A Critical Hit

We finally found Marcella today after… what? Two or more weeks of searching? Or more like we found her remains—butchered by those Harbingers. They are the only threat I can think of who are capable of bringing someone like her down. We always warned her *not* to engage with them alone. Damn her. She must have gotten too cocky because of her recent status update to the third rank and earning her stupid title of Arbiter of Light. Mixon is… not well, upon hearing the news.

There are a few harsh things I can say about Marcella, but she did make him happy, and she even made him smile once. I wish he would let me comfort him in his time of need, but I know I will only make his depression worse somehow. Those Harbingers… I hope Marcella did some damage to them.

A Hiatus

I write this passage on top of the crumbled statue of the late Founder with a question for myself as my thoughts leak: Is it wrong to respect your enemies? Daison Peak, our capital… or it was, before its fall. Apparently, a global revolution happened a few hours ago. What concerns me is that those Harbingers didn't even stage it, and I fail to comprehend why the rest of the world rebelled against us unless… unless our deep secrets were leaked somehow?

Referring back to my opening question, a lot of our best and wisest died today—and I have nothing but admiration and applause for that. Perhaps we offered the world too much of our knowledge and gifts if they can compete with us now—and as for those Harbingers, they have all of the remaining survivors here shaking in their silk robes. They even managed to steal Mixon's personal Artifact interestingly enough. Hilarious. Hysterical, even. But… I shouldn't be laughing at our misfortune. This event, along with the loss of his primary object of study has probably set us back by at least a year if we're lucky enough. Damn.

Speaking of Mixon, there he is now. He's staring at me from far down below. I can tell he's upset with me for not being here for the battle. He might be second to me, but he's still someone I would never trifle with. Today is a black day.

Restart

Mixon and I shook hands today in front of our new capital here in the middle of Harmony Sea. This is the first time I've seen some light in his eyes after the death of Marcella and the fall of our original home. Trying to make this project work has taken everything from us both, but as long as we still have his Master Dimensional Codes and my boundless knowledge of Mysticology, then divinity will be ours soon. We can't afford to lose this! We just can't…

Apotheosis

Finally, I can say the word for when there are no others that can dictate this moment: Successsss! We have finally opened the gates of the high heavens! Birthplace! If only I could somehow record the looks on the Gods' stupefied faces. I would watch that moment every day for the remainder of my life, but I won't need to worry about the rest of my life ever again for we have finally acquired our means of transcendence!

Overall, it was a surprisingly clean getaway too. All thanks to Head Zoologist Kalos and his 'flock' of pet psiowls that he unleashed to wreak pure havoc. Those weak-minded fools literally didn't know what hit them. Yesterday, we feared the gods—but tonight. We. Become. Gods!

<u>Divinity—Day Seventeen</u>

Can't anything ever go right? The Harbingers are the least of my concern now that we have achieved greatness, but now there's this rogue pestilence that's starting to run rampant. It has even affected a few of us despite being isolated in the middle of the sea, it's truly appalling. The deity that we took into our possession has been... quiet, ever since this infection sprung loose. But I can't focus on the Immortal right now. I need to reassure the people and their leaders that we have things under control before they grow restless and interfere with the infancy of our divinity.

I wonder what I was doing when all of this took place? Rend wonders. *Probably dead...*

He flips to one of the final pages. The rest of the book after that is nothing but scratches of incomprehensible letters and violent screams in written format.

<u>Suffering—Day???</u>

This will probably be my final log. They're dead, all of them—all except for me. And I wouldn't have it any other way! Who cares if the world dies! Once the Vampirism is complete then I'll achieve my godhood and restart this pitiful world from the ground up! Paradigms always shift, no doubt this is mine! I'll become almighty!

…And now my head hurts. I should consider leaving this diary back in my personal castle in case… in case somehow this is the true end of all history. At least *my* history will still exist somewhere. You know… thrones are built to be quite large. I absolutely would have shared this cushion with Mixon. Damn him…

***

"…What an avid reader you are," Klae whispers in Rend's ear.

Rend panics, accidentally falling off the bed.

Klae laughs as he stands over him. "Sorry, I couldn't help myself. How did you get here before me?"

"I don't think the space in this realm is the exact same wherever we go, or something like that. The entrance you made took me here."

"Did it now? That would explain why I couldn't find anyone else. Sounds like we're in a space conundrum where nothing is relative or adjacent to each other. I should have predicted this."

"I barely understood anything you just said. Can we get out of this?" Rend asks.

"I can create a forced loop that can override and reroute whatever machination Zazer has made here—that portal above us should suffice. Wait, what's that in your hands?"

Rend smacks the book. "This is Zazer's journal. It's pretty well intact."

"He thought of himself as legendary from what I've heard, it doesn't surprise me he would make a memoir."

"The stuff he mentions in this is incriminating. This is worth everything."

Klae takes the book from Rend. The way his eyebrows jump as he looks over the material is something to behold. "This is worse than I thought. They were in way over their heads."

"Do you think they survived somehow?" Rend says.

"Not if the Soul Decay got to them first."

"We can only hope so."

"And *we*…" Klae says while shutting the book closed. "Do not need to stay here any longer."

"But there could be more evidence here."

"You just found something that has the same value as a cure, and I'm not risking losing something this crucial. We're not giving Zazer the chance to ruin that. In fact—" Klae then conjures up a new portal inside of the one on the ceiling, doubling its size. Eventually, the others are summoned to the bedroom.

"Hey!" Sadra shrieks. "What's the damage?"

"We're leaving," Klae says.

"But this place is so cool!" Aluna whines.

"I found an Arbiter robe that can fit me," Jellop says as he holds and shows it off in front of his body. "How do I look?"

"Ugly," Klae responds. "Back to the capital!"

Chapter 56

Cursebreakers

Draxis twiddles her thumbs as she watches the clouds roll across the sky with the others at the spire's balcony, eventually saying, "This suspense is breaking me…"

"How much longer did he say we have to wait?" Maeva asks.

"Zero!" Klae shouts from the doorway threshold. "Congratulations to us! As of today, we have collected over eight Artifacts in total, with three being Cursed, three being Blessed, and two of them being an odd duality. It's a little less than what I originally planned, but certain unforeseen factors have alleviated every major concern…

"Over the course of a month and then some, we have survived impossible odds. We have inspired hope that can finally be realized and touched. Together we have become stronger. Together we have grown better. Together we have—"

"Shut the hell up so we can go save the world!" Maeva interrupts.

"Fuck it then! Let us begin the curse-breaker ritual posthaste! Everyone, to the main console!"

"Woooo!" Sadra cheers. "Let's go!"

Klae is shoved aside as they rush in. "I have everything already set up, so don't. Touch! *Anything*!"

***

At the center console, Klae lights up the final candle using another one. There are other similarly lit candles that go around in a circle behind everyone on the ground, setting a mood for something sinister. He holds the last candle close to his face. "We are gathered here today to—"

"Stop doing that," Maeva says to him.

Klae throws the candle at her, forcing her to dodge. "If this miraculously fails then I'm taking it as a blessing so I can finally stop dealing with you people. Anyway, do we have all the Artifacts? I got a list here to make sure. Call them out for me."

"Samsara," Maeva says, clenching her gloved hand into a fist.

"The Gift," Draxis says, struggling to find a way for the giant crystal to stand upright on its own.

Suvius's eye sockets ignite as he says, "The Bloodheart Cuirass."

"The *Mesmerion*," Jellop says, trying to sound creepy.

"The Sunken Doll…" Aluna says, watching it *very* closely.

"The Braces of Symmetry!" Sadra says, flaunting them on her wrists and clinking them together.

"The Eternal Flame," Malphunnos says, scratching his back with his flaming sickle.

"Me!" Rend says.

"You are most definitely not an Artifact," Maeva replies.

"I'm *your* Artifact."

Maeva responds to the sudden cacophony of giggles and snorts by giving them all a suspicious look. "What's so funny?"

"Oh nothing," Aluna says, still snickering. "Nothing at all."

"And we have Komet, the Living Star," Klae says. "Why is it called that anyway, Sadra?"

"Komet is a perfected Light Geshelon. Think of his rarity type as the same probability as getting struck by naturally occurring lighting—twice! That's why Komet is the best Artifact and we are best friends forever!"

In an amped state, Komet emits a single beam strong enough to escape through the ceiling.

"I should make you both pay for the roof," Klae berates. "By the way, Aluna, I've been doing the math and I'm happy to say that we have enough room to remove your Curse as well."

"That's unnecessary. I have a cool-ass Blessing now called Truthseeker, so leave it alone."

"That's the last thing I expected to hear. Blessings. Curses. Is there a difference? You really trust something with 'truth' in its name?"

"Wouldn't you? It's not that bad," Aluna says.

"I feel like you're underestimating the bluntness of candor." After Klae says that he gets a devilish grimace across his face. "Tell me something, Aluna. Was it you who made all our leftover candy 'mysteriously' disappear?"

Her eyes turn solid-green in color, and she speaks as if she is possessed by a robot. "Hell yeah it was me! Once I see an unsupervised or an unlabeled snack, I just can't help myself but to eat it all until it's gone. I even stole some from Sadra."

"Damn you!" Sadra says. "Those were meant for Draxis!"

"Wait…" Aluna says, shaking her head. "What just happened? I didn't want to say that!"

"As I figured. You're incapable of lying," Klae says. "Do you still want that curse-blessing now?"

"That really stings. But… it also gives me clairvoyance. Don't you know how good that is for winning card games?"

"You stupid cheating-ass flea," Maeva interjects. "So that's why you mysteriously started kicking my ass. You owe me my gems back!"

"Nobody gives a shit, Maeva," Klae remarks. "As for you, Aluna, you're literally going to hold on to a risk that might even ruin our *one* chance at restoring Allosha over some one second gratification?"

"Yeah…?"

"…Just go pick a spot so we can get this over with."

"So how is this going to work, Klae?" Suvius asks.

"There are three main components. These eight Artifacts and our combined magic power, which should be enough to help us maintain the entire duration and strength of this global panacea. As for the primary component—Harbinger Maeva."

"Yes?" she answers.

"We'll be relying exclusively on your Blood magic for this delicate operation. I know that might sound like the best thing ever for you since you get to be a legendary heroine, but the only thing that greatly bothers me about this is overusing your magic past your body's limits. With that last part said, are you still willing to listen to what I have to say?"

"Making sure this succeeds means everything to me. Even if I have to die for it."

"We'll see how far your tenacity goes. Now listen closely. What I need you to do is to prepare yourself to absorb the enormous amount of magic power we are going to pump into you. Once you get over the initial surge of feeling like a rising god, you will need to use your 'omnipotent' reach to extract *every* strand of the Decay you can possibly leech from across the globe.

"After you have internally siphoned and cleansed everything you can contain, you will then need to share that healing magic back to us, and we can handle the last part of manifesting your medicine into a singular spell gigantic and powerful enough to wipe this world clean of the Decay in one swift action."

"So a back and forth exchange?" Maeva says. "That doesn't sound so bad…?"

"That's because it gets worse," Klae states. "Hmm. How can I put this in the most horrific way possible just to fuck with you? Sooo… the one terrible drawback of this process is that because you are effectively curing every living and non-living thing all at once… it also means that you're going to experience what is essentially the collective agony of the world's population all at once."

"You're kidding me…"

"There is no form of modern technology or magic in our era that can house and deprecate the virus-curse like you can. You're our only hope."

Maeva breaks out into a cold sweat as she grips the edge of the center console, shuddering from her hostile imagination.

Rend taps Sadra on her shoulder. "Can we switch places?"

"Hm? I don't feel like moving."

"You get to be near Draxis."

"Kay."

"Grab my hand, Maeva," Rend says to her after switching spots with Sadra. "If it gets to be too much, then feel free to squeeze my hand to ease the pain."

"Then you'll be in pain too."

"It will be nothing compared to feeling the most indescribable pain never felt by any existence like your about to endure soon."

"Can I join in?" Malphunnos says, sliding in.

"No," Maeva replies.

"I meant what I said seriously. You won't be able to flatten my hand, so I can help alleviate the agony of withstanding the most indescribable pain never felt by any existence. Plus, I really want to know what that pain feels like."

"If I kick you in the balls then that can give you a close enough example—"

"Silence, everyone!" Klae commands. "We're going to start!"

Sadra raises her hand. "Grandpa, can I go to the bathroom?"

"I said **silence**!"

Everyone connects together to form a circle by placing one hand on their closest artifact and another hand connecting with someone else's.

"And whatever you do, do *not* break the chain under any circumstance," Klae says. "I have no idea what would occur if we disrupt the flow of a nation's worth of magic power."

"We hear you, Klae," Draxis says.

"I know I'm being annoying but I have to emphasize my warnings so we don't fail our lifetime opportunity. So, any final words before we start this? I encourage from the bottom of my heart to speak up now. Even if it's a plea to not participate."

Everyone looks at each other. They all shake their heads, showing that they are ready, albeit nervous.

"Komet, make your way over to the center of the console," Klae says. "As I finish the countdown, I want you to link yourself with the other Artifacts to get them activated. Your Light aura should be more than plenty to juice them to full capacity. As for everyone else, take the biggest breath you can suck in because we are about to start in three…!"

Komet lodges itself at its designated station. Its luminosity steadily builds up as it bedazzles the air. All the other Artifacts begin to illuminate under its rainbow light.

"Two…!" Klae continues to count.

Rend gets closer to Maeva. He locks his fingers in between hers, sealing their hands together.

"One… Zero!"

The spell of genesis commences, initiated by Klae and soon infecting the others, chaining clockwise around their circle until all power strikes the roaring engine. Maeva's screams, they are equal to nothing—not even something otherworldly. The veins in her body thicken and expand past their limits. She can't even fall unconscious as the pain keeps reawakening her in a vicious loop. Her gauntlet is going mad, bleeding out from its only eye in anguish.

Rend tries his damnedest to stifle her pain, but he has to substitute his aid by grabbing her arm instead of her hand as his own hand has already been crushed four times in such a meager length of time.

"I-It's *working*!" Malphunnos yelps out, barely keeping his strength afloat. "I can… feel… change! Keep going!"

So much overlap of concentrated energy alters the space itself around them, sending books and glass flasks flying around the room in turbulence. Outside on the island, the magical pulses are expanding past the trees, past the beaches, past the open waters, out into the farthest reaches of the world. The reward in exchange for their growing success is pain, which becomes doubled, tripled, quintupled—but it's working!

Maeva bites through the excruciating agony and initiates phase two, her eyes glowing a fierce scarlet red in both anger and power as she transfers the maximum buildup of her magical medicine. The others can feel her divine-like grace as their souls get a purifying makeover. It feels like nothing can stop them now.

If only that hope could last a minute longer.

Klae is fighting two wars simultaneously, unbeknownst to everyone else as they're barely withstanding their own. The physical side of him is pushing against the sheer strain of such an intense spell, but mentally, he is down to his last droplets of blood. It isn't the spell itself that wages a brutal war against him, it is an intruder that cackles their sinister laughter through a mental projection.

The vision Klae sees keeps stretching far across the known waters, towards the outermost edges of the world, in the heart of a necropolis plagued by dread, at the apex of a colossal mesa, flying sky-high and inside the middle of the moon's silvery gaze does he see a humanoid silhouette of pure darkness. The figure lifts its head up and looks right back at him in his mind's eye—and gives a perfect ear-to-ear grin. Klae jumps backwards and lands on the ground, breaking the immersive vision, along with the spell—to everyone's shock.

"No… no!" Draxis screams. "We were so close! What happened? What the hell happened!"

"I… I saw them," Klae whimpers, trembling on the ground.

"What?"

"I saw them! The one who plunged this world into decay! There is no mistaking such a malevolent evil…"

"We're all still standing, right?" Sadra says. "Can we try the spell again?"

"Not if that *thing* targets one of us again. Or worse, if it does something drastic." Klae then punches the ground, shouting, "Damn it all! If only I had stayed strong. What if I just doomed the world? I can't bear with that guilt."

"What should we do?" Aluna asks.

"We investigate," Suvius says. "Klae, did you happen to see where this evil was? Or who?"

"I don't even want to think about it. The menace was shrouded in its own evil, so I couldn't fully see what it looked like. As for its location, I've never seen such a despairing place in all my days. Not even the Hagri Scarlands looks like that. Whatever this place is, it was somewhere entire oceans away. Everything about that vision was wicked. So wicked that it sort of reminds of an old legend told by the Apostates. Wait a minute…"

Klae gets up and rushes over to a cabinet to find Zazer's journal. He flips through the pages wildly. "This! This is why we could never find the source of the Decay! Whoever has wrought this chaos lies in a place that has been forgotten and lost to time. The source of the Decay is somewhere on the lost continent of Calvrim!"

"Calvrim?" Suvius repeats. "Are you positive?"

"I thought it was a myth myself, but it's the only location left that would make sense. We have been nearly everywhere else across the globe, whether it was high or low, or too far or too small. There is one problem however…"

"It's a lost continent…" Suvius says for him.

"You would think something like that would be impossible nowadays. Even if it has been found by Zazer, that asshole didn't leave any clear directions."

"Maybe try using the Master Codes?" Draxis suggests.

"With how many combinations there are that would take ages. Maybe we *should* try the cure spell again so we can get a better picture of where to go. But I really don't want to anger that Dark Evil again."

"I… I have an idea," Aluna squeaks, "if you all want to hear me out."

"We'll take anything at this point," Klae says.

"I still don't know how this Blessing works entirely, but maybe it can reveal the path to Calvrim? Somehow?"

"That might just work. Try looking at these markings and loose directions. Maybe that can reveal the truth for us." Klae flips page after page, watching Aluna closely for any signs of triggering. "Come on, Aluna. We're running out of maps!"

"I'm trying! Ah…!" she yelps, cradling her head after a stab of pain. "It's working! Turn back to that last map!"

The page Klae flips over to is the closest thing to a functional world map. Her glowing leafy-green eyes show the path to her, highlighting from Harmony Sea all the way down to the middle of a blank space at the very bottom of the page.

Aluna points her finger. "It's that way. South, I believe? Extremely deep south."

"There is still a chance," Klae says. "There is still a chance! We have to go there!"

"How urgent?" Rend asks.

"Huh?"

Rend is sitting down, with Maeva breathing heavily in his lap. "We need one more day. *She* needs a day."

"Ah, I see. It would be best that way. We'll need everything in our arsenal before we tackle such a nightmarish environment. Very well, we shall take a day to cool off and form better ideas on what to do."

Chapter 57
Clair De Lune

A group discussion is taking place in the tower spire. Sadra gets up, rubbing her temples. "This is hurting my head. I'm going on a break…"

"Poor Sadra," Jellop says. "The information in the journal must be too much for her."

"I'll switch topics then," Rend says. "There are a few chapters in here about you, Maeva."

"What did you say? Damn my head hurts so much…"

"I said that there's a few chapters about you."

"Oh. I'm sure that bastard had plenty to say about me."

"You might be a part of an ancient bloodline. Does the name 'vampire' mean anything to you?"

"That does sound faintly familiar… Very familiar actually," Maeva says. "I do believe that I am one. I am Maevalina Solunna. That is my real name. I had a home somewhere in the world, but I think it was… destroyed? And then Crysis and Sylis found me and… and… they… Does Zazer explain why they abused me?"

"Your magic was like an endless feast for the Arbiters," Rend answers. "It was to the point where they overstuffed themselves and bit off more than they could chew. The merciful and restorative half of your magic has a name. Lifeblood. It was their greatest fountain of affluence."

"Lifeblood? That's a cute name. It's unfathomable how so much has happened because of my natural biology. Are there any more out there like me?"

"You're the last of your kind unfortunately."

"…My condolences, Maeva," Draxis says.

"I don't get you," she says to him. "How can you stand to say that to me with such sincerity? I said some horrible things to you back at Vomenn. Now I am feeling my own words tenfold."

"Your words were not perfect, but they kept my focus straight. You did your best."

"I… I am thankful for your kindness."

"This world doesn't have much left, and we're the last ones of our respective races. We have to make their legacy, and our own, last for as long as we can."

"Do you have any more questions, Master?" Rend asks her.

"It's already too much for me. I'm withdrawing," Maeva says.

"Let's move on to you then, Aluna."

"Not interested," she states.

"But it involves magic," Rend says.

"I already know enough. I was their Master Elementalist."

"Perhaps I'm not making myself clear enough. This is a new type of magic, created by *the* Paragon himself—with an extreme focus on explosions."

"An explosion spell? By Zazer? Tell… tell me more."

"Finale. That's the name of the spell. He calls it his greatest creation, just like everything else he's done. He could never perfect it, but he theorized that if he did then it would have had the destructive capabilities to level an empire in one use."

"Now that sounds super sexy! Mind if I take a gander?" Aluna says.

"Of course." Rend then holds the book up for her.

"Great magic power at the molecular level…?" she reads out loud. "Nuclear magic? It sounds right up my alley, but I don't quite understand the science and magic behind it."

"I don't think anyone can understand it," Rend says. "I feel like this apocalypse probably set the whole world back a couple of decades in regards to advancement. We lost a lot of good people."

"Not good people—smart people, with an extra side of cunning. They just lacked the human heart, so to speak."

"Yeah…"

"I do believe though that if you keep up with your studying then you might be able to regain some of that knowledge we lost. The more I listen to you talk about Magic, the more I want to call you a Neo-Arbiter just to mess with you. Were this the old world, there's a chance you could have even earned yourself a seat among the Elites with how fast you've been advancing. Oh, would you look at me rambling. I'm starting to sound like them."

"You're pretty smart too," Rend says. "You just don't give yourself enough credit. We should team up."

"You want to team up?" she says, eyes gleaming. "With our own personal mystic and science division? Alright. I accept your offer."

"Neat."

"Is there anything in that journal about Birthplace?" Malphunnos asks. "Anything at all? I need to know."

"Not really. I'm guessing anything substantial like that has already been ripped out. What about the word 'demigod'? I keep seeing that appear," Rend says.

"Is that so? That's… an ancient issue. How did they find all this out? Well, it does further add on where they got the idea of 'ascension' from."

"Does it? Who were they?"

"Children of the gods," Malphunnos says. "They were often the mixed offspring between Immortals and Mortals. It started as a promising way to see some new faces in Birthplace and could have even potentially retired some of the oldest gods… but then the honest acts soon turned into debauchery. None of the demigods exist anymore because that level of 'frolicking' was made illegal."

"Way to ruin people's fun," Rend remarks.

"Well it wasn't fun for me to enforce it. It had to be done anyway. An overabundance of godlike—and immature—entities leads to immense strain on the global balance, and *massive* family feuds."

"Did you have any offspring?"

"I can't. I've… tried. Are you still taking care of Samsara, Maeva?" Malphunnos asks.

"We take care of each other."

"I'm glad to hear it."

"Hey, everyone!" Sadra shouts. "Come look!"

They follow Sadra's voice out onto the tower's balcony.

A cold speck lands on Klae's forehead the moment he steps outside. He rubs the wet spot on his head and looks at the red liquid running down his fingers. "Blood? Blood rain?"

"No, Grandpa. It's snowing!"

"Snow? Is it the new year already? I haven't seen a sky like this in so long," Klae says.

A silver beam of light escapes past the thick blanket of storm clouds, shining down on the tower.

"Is that the Moon as well?"

"Moon!" Sadra yells out with excitement.

"Is that the Moon goddess, Malphunnos?" Suvius asks.

"I can't believe there's another god still alive," he says, basking in the moonlight. "We see you too, Selvita. Thanks for cheering us on."

"Come on, Draxis!" Sadra calls out to her. "Let's go play in the red snow!"

"How about we don't do that."

"But we can make blood snowmen!"

"That's the problem right there. I'm not rolling around in someone's blood."

Rend and Maeva arrive late to the gathering.

"Did someone say blood?" Maeva says before sticking out her tongue, letting the snow sprinkle it before ingesting them. Her body jitters. "Goodness! What kind of blood is this? This is like heaven!"

"That's the blood of the gods," Aluna says.

Maeva glances at Malphunnos while uttering, "A god's blood…?"

"D-Don't look at me like that. I *will* scream if you touch me."

"Don't tempt me."

"It seems everyone wants to pepper us with wishes of good luck," Klae says. "You all better make this a night to remember—because we're leaving at dawn."

"You're not coming down with us, Grandpa?" Sadra asks.

"I'm about to sail with you jackasses for Gods knows how many days, which is already more than what I want to endure. Plus, I still need to analyze Zazer's journal some more."

"You'll regret it."

"You will have to make it regrettable first. You kids have fun."

"That's my line…" Suvius groans.

***

Jellop meditates on one of the rooftops of the buildings that make up the general city skyline. He has his hood off to let the frigid chill of the night touch and embrace him directly. A detected presence brings him out of his zen state, forcing him to pull his hood back over.

"I find it odd that there is someone willing to stalk me," he says, "though I have the feeling that the culprit would still stalk me even in my most mundane moments. Yaga, friend Aluna."

She rises into his view, from below the building's vantage blind spot. "Y-Yaga…" she replies back.

"What brings you to this one particular spot in the middle of the city?"

"I get it, okay! I'm sorry for acting weird. I wanted to take advantage of this moonlit sky and use it to spend more time with you. If it goes well enough, then maybe we can—ahhh! This stupid Blessing!"

"Muhuhu!"

"Don't laugh at me!" Aluna shouts.

"I can't help it," he says. "Do not be ashamed, this is a beautiful bloody night. I am welcome to spend it with another."

"You're not mad at me?"

"I am no stranger to unwarranted intrusion. I am, however, such a stranger to Truth—I never thought truth would be such a blasphemous virtue. It helps separate the line between good and evil, but at what cost? I will ponder this later."

"Or we can ponder it together," Aluna says. "I want to hear the truth from you now, about why you keep yelling at yourself periodically."

"It's just self-dissatisfaction," Jellop says.

"I can tell when you're lying. Literally."

"You bind me with your words, but I am not comfortable going into exact details."

"I know the feeling. Curses aren't the easiest thing to share."

"That word itself is a curse, but it would be the most accurate label for how long this has been haunting me," Jellop says. "I am not cursed, but I feel like I am always being judged and attacked by an all-knowing witness. This witness has been criticizing me about these life-threatening situations we keep getting wedged into. I am worried that this witness isn't just a basic envoy of the Decay to get me to falter."

"Surely you don't believe a word spoken by this 'witness'?" Aluna says.

"It's hard to disagree with it when it knows more about me than I know myself."

"Do you feel like it's a part of you?"

"What if it is me?" Jellop says.

"Then tell yourself to fuck off," Aluna says. "It's okay to experience turmoil but it's never okay to feel like you're the one who causes it. You have never been that way."

Jellop touches his hood, holding it further down over his face. "Then why am I troubled to always mask my face? Why does the truth of me being an experiment accident hurt? Why does the wave of my hand bring utter chaos around me?"

"Listen, Jellop, you can't help what you are. You are the Harbinger of Madness, and we love you for that. What's not to love about keeping things fun around here? We're all freaks anyway."

"It oddly warms my heart to hear you say that. Is that why you stayed with us for so long? For years you had every opportunity to kill me and disappear into the night."

"I don't know what you're talking about," Aluna says.

"Should I retrieve the answer through a direct question then?" Jellop asks.

"You'll make me say something regrettable."

"There are no regrets or suppressed hatred here. I always knew about the secret mission devised by your masters that you willingly chose to disobey. You didn't know I could read minds back then."

"Well that's embarrassing. How come you never said anything?" Aluna asks.

"I noticed that over time you started to care less and less about finding the opportune moment to strike… You started to laugh and play more. You found hope. I will never take that away from you, and I will never let anyone else take that away from you."

Aluna's wings spasm into a flutter. "Why do you keep saying things like that!"

"Because I know what gets you flustered enough to bring out your truth, and you know what gets me timid enough to weaken my lies. It makes us even."

She flies over and sits on Jellop's left shoulder, reclining against the groove of his neck. "I wish I was human sized…"

"Wh—"

"Hush!" Aluna shouts, cutting him off. "If you ask me any more private questions then I'll blast your head off!"

"I would advise not doing that," Jellop says. "I would like to do this sort of thing more often… maybe where there's less snow— and not in public."

"Stop… you're going to make me say something regrettable."

***

Suvius is hunched over the railing on the balcony of the tower's spire, watching the snow fall steadily across the whole island. He stands upright and touches his cuirass. His heart is beating against it, unwilling to ease up on its harassment. He looks towards the moon as he talks to himself. "It is time for me to let go… not that any of you were mine to begin with. Let us begin."

The midsection of his cuirass opens and expands. The furnace that belches within waits for Suvius's commands.

"Soul of Ezkel, I release you."

A blue wisp zips out from the sizzling flames. It flies around, unsure of where to go before settling with circling in place high above the tower.

"Soul of Irona, I release you. Soul of Quim, I release you. Soul of Vicarion, I release you…" He continues the expulsion of the souls for however long he needs to. It's going to be a long night, with an even longer list of names that need to be sorted out and spoken.

Once every soul has been expelled, the Cuirass seizes control and shimmers down, closing up its midsection. Suvius observes the large party of playful souls in the air for a minute longer before turning around to leave.

Malphunnos stands in the doorway, blocking the exit. "Releasing doves, Suvius?"

"For once, yes."

"Those were the souls from your old armor, correct? Well, how does it feel?"

"Like a first breath," Suvius says.

"A breath, huh? Are you going to steal someone else's lungs now?"

"Recreating my body from scratch using desired organs and limbs from the deceased…? That is a peculiar idea."

"Only you would think of something so grotesque," Malphunnos says.

"It's a form of regret, for stripping myself away from what made me human. This beating heart reminds me of that lost appreciation."

"Would anything really change if you were still human?"

"I don't know how to answer that."

"What does humanity mean to you exactly, Suvius?"

"A strong body that can hold a willful spirit."

"Once again you mention a body," Malphunnos says. "I had no idea you wanted it back so badly. I mean, you *are* the one whose hatred was so strong that your burning soul refused to let me touch it. You demanded to be given a second chance. You didn't care what the consequences were."

"I know. It's a regret that will never end."

"Other revenant types would disagree with you," Malphunnos says. "Then again, they rarely lived as long as you have, if not greater. Why do you think that is? I'll answer for you. It's because your spirit is still strong, minus the body. I like to think that not being shackled to the limitations of the flesh makes you have such a strong spirit."

"It doesn't feel that way sometimes," Suvius states.

"So is what you feel about Ceranus not true then?"

"Don't bring her name into this."

"Why not?" Malphunnos asks. "Is she not the main reason for your stubborn ambitions? The anchor for your fighting spirit? You speak more about her than any of your kin, and even more than your fellow comrades. That woman, what was she to you?"

"She was the one thing I didn't want to lose. Some of my ambitions that you speak of revolved around avenging her fallen benevolence—and maybe even restoring her touch. There was a time when her hands caressed faces instead of skulls."

"Do you feel like you've failed her?"

"More than that," Suvius says. "During my final moments with Ceranus, I felt her warm touch, the kind that I would feel if I had a face to caress. Everything I did was for that one touch… and it wasn't worth it. I gave away everything for her. I killed everything that I believed was corrupting her. I spent so much of my time pursuing that touch that everything else was lost to me before I realized it.

"It affected what the Harbingers should have been. It affected what I should have been. Now, I'm trying to replace what was taken away from the both of us, and what was taken away *by* the both of us."

Malphunnos strides his way over to Suvius on the balcony, watching the souls bump about and chase after the falling snowflakes and each other. "You have a very long way to go before you can replace your sacrifices with redemption, but don't get stuck feeling like that day will never come to pass. I'm sure Ceranus wasn't like that."

"No, she wasn't. She fought through her guilt like a warrior," Suvius says.

"Then you should fight back like a demon. I feel like that matches you more than humanity ever will. Devils can cry too, so it's okay to let yourself feel burdened, son."

"I thought I told you to stop calling me that."

Malphunnos hugs Suvius, refusing to let himself be pushed away. "Death can also cry as well. I feel just as much as you mortals do. I wouldn't be here if there wasn't a particular group of mortals that shook my determination wide awake. I care for this team, and I do care for you, you know. Not once have I regretted sharing my power with you.”

Suvius attempts to reciprocate the sentiment by offering a loose hug.

“You’ve grown up so much,” Malphunnos says, patting him on the back.

“Don’t make this weird…”

***

This inn seems like a good spot,” Sadra says to Draxis as she peeks inside the building. “It should be far enough away from every-one else. Want to go inside?”

“If that’s what you want to do,” Draxis says.

“…Alright. Let’s go find a bedroom.” Stepping inside, Sadra picks up a dusty and festive banner off the glass-littered and cracked wooden flooring. She reads it out loud before folding it up to sweep the broken glass. “Happy Birthday? I never really thought about the Arbiters’ personal lives. I bet this building was used for all sorts of shenanigans.”

“Yep.”

“Brightheart, it feels like I’m talking to myself here.”

“Sorry.”

“You better be more energetic by the time we find a room.”

Sadra grabs Draxis’s hand as she clears the debris and helps Draxis hop over a series of tables that barricade the stairs. Sadra skips around the upstairs hallways to search for any bedrooms that don’t have any exposed walls or produce an eye-watering rancid odor that assaults the senses the moment they pass by.

She finds a bedroom that seems adequate enough, except for the clothed skeleton inside holding the door closed. She tosses it outside. Then, with the palm side facing up, she holds her hand out while waiting for Draxis to touch it. She brings it back down and sits on the bed, disappointed.

"Maybe you don't want to do anything with me," Sadra says.

"N-No, it's not like that," Draxis responds.

"Then come over here! Why are you being so distant? I've been trying to act respectful of your personal space, but how much longer are you going to make me wait?"

"Sadra, I'm not trying to hurt you—"

"It's already too late for that," she snaps as her mood flips to her Nocturnal state in an instant. "If you keep this up then we might as well become strangers. Is that what you want?"

"Never," Draxis says.

"Then tell me why you won't get close to me. You refuse to get close with the others as well. If this is about us failing to keep you safe back at the Subtropolis then I'm sorry! I'll say it as many times as I need to!"

"It might have been better if none of you saved me…"

"Don't tell me that you actually mean that? Draxis, you're the only one here who feels that way. And you know what, I'm sick of it!" Sadra grabs Draxis's wrist and wrestles her to the bed.

"Ge-get off of me, Sadra!"

"No! Don't you understand how much it hurts to hear you say things like that! Why won't you talk to me about anything? Is it my fault that you're like this?"

"N-No. It's never your fault. You've been doing a marvelous job. I've never been more proud of you. I just…"

"…You just what? I want you to talk to me. I've been keeping silent because I thought you needed proper time to grieve or whatever you need to do, but it's been long enough. Please just talk to me. At least tell me what happened at Vomenn. It seems like a sensitive subject around here."

"Death," Draxis states. "A *lot* of people died that day—all because of me. My entire existence leads only to death. I know you don't like me saying that, but it's true. Even something as basic as eating requires for someone else to die."

"But everyone eats something else in order to live," Sadra says.

"But a soul? The primordial essence that cradles life itself? Who else do you know that could eradicate all known life if given enough time… or enough hunger. You asked me what occurred at Vomenn. Well, I'll tell you. *I* was the one who caused that kingdom and its stronghold to fall.

"That one stupid artifact, if I didn't touch that stupid thing then nobody would have had to die. I wrought such a wicked form of destruction that my own people couldn't even enact their true vengeance—leaving me behind as the last of my kind. It also left countless people without a home, without a family. Without a ruler."

"Ceranus…" Sadra mumbles.

"Yes."

"I'm sorry. I thought you would be happier over her death."

"Not like this."

"This can't be the only thing bothering you," Sadra says. "I'm not stopping until I hear everything…"

Draxis gives in as Sadra starts tickling her stomach. "Is there anything that you fear, Sadra?" Draxis asks.

"Plenty."

"What about the Decay?"

"More than you might think. I choose to ignore it though. I'm aware of what it's capable of doing, and I've seen it turn the brightest of people into bloodthirsty monsters. Is that what's bothering you?"

"Hypothetically speaking, if I were to turn… would you ever…"

"Stop. I'm not answering that," Sadra says.

"But I'm so afraid that I'll… that I'll…"

"Are you that afraid of losing yourself? You can have Miss Maeva give you a temporary cure to help mitigate the pain at any time. Plus, we're going to eradicate the curse once and for all once we strike its heart. I promise you're going to be okay."

"Victory is the least of my concern…" Draxis says.

"All these issues that eat away at you, you should have told me sooner," Sadra says. "I don't want you to keep distancing yourself away from us. Like that time you abandoned me for years while I waited for you to come back. What were you doing all that time?"

"Distancing myself away like you said," Draxis answers. "I spent the first year in a psychosis of deep anxiety and fear. I spent the following year completely lost and buried in depression. Then finally, I managed to correct myself in the third year and started fighting back. I wanted answers for how the world came to an end, while searching for everyone else at the same time."

"You didn't come to me first?"

"I wouldn't have been able to stand it if I saw your face of hatred," Draxis says.

"But instead, I was overjoyed when I saw your handsome and gorgeous face after so long. I keep telling you all this stuff is in your head."

"I suppose so. You *are* in my head quite often."

"Oh?" Sadra says, blushing.

"Indeed. When the sun disappeared, your image gave me back my missing mornings."

"Stop it…"

"Along with every unforgettable memory we made together."

"*Stop* it."

"And let's not forget the times we used to—"

Sadra kisses Draxis to shut her up.

"…That's what I was waiting for," Draxis says.

Sadra touches her own lips. "It feels different kissing a girl. I don't think I mind having you be female."

Draxis pins Sadra down to the bed, reversing their positions. "Careful what you wish for."

"Oh no… Are you going to ravage me like a *dragon* would do to a castle?"

"That is so offensive."

Sadra licks her own lips after saying, "What are you going to do about it?"

Draxis hovers over Sadra's lips, pecking them, then fully intertwining both of their overheating passion. She slides down to her neck and salivates over the reactions Sadra's body makes as she nibbles. Overtime, that warm-up nibble turns into a pinch—then into intensifying chomps.

"H-Hey… stop," Sadra says. "Y-You're biting too hard! Stop!"

Draxis reels back, stepping off the bed and backing into the wall closest to the door.

Sadra pokes the bite marks left behind. "I like that energy, Brightheart, but start slower next time."

"I… I'm sorry, Sadra. I can't do this."

"But we're just getting started."

"I-I need to go!" Draxis swings open the door and dashes out.

"Draxis! …Come back…"

***

Sitting side-by-side at the trunk of a tree somewhere deep into the tropical woods of the island, Rend watches Maeva eat the snowflakes that fall into her mouth. "Do you ever stop eating?" he asks her.

"But it's so good!"

"We need to switch your diet."

"Rend, I am elated that I can even eat. I will scrounge for *anything* so I can never experience starvation again."

"Damn. I… I forgot about that. You eat really well. You look so filled-out and effervescent compared to when I first met you."

"Effervescent… I don't think I had anyone say that to me. Umm… what does that mean?"

"Lively," Rend says.

"Lively? Is that what this feeling is?" she asks, feeling around the smoothness and complexity of her skin. "Well if we're complimenting each other's bodies, then I have to say that you've gained some muscles."

"I'm just exercising the important ones."

"Your stomach looks a little flat however. Come drink some blood with me—I need you to stay big and strong."

"Yeah… no," Rend says.

"I *command* you to drink some."

"No," he repeats.

"Just do it."

"…This is gonna be so gross." Rend sticks his tongue out. He retracts it the moment his taste buds are assaulted by an acrid flavor.

"How is it?" Maeva asks.

Rend covers his mouth while shaking his head at her.

"More for me then... Can you stop looking at me like that? You must love watching me eat."

"That's about all I've seen you do. That and… killing."

"I did warn you that my magic wasn't pretty," Maeva says.

"I was warned that magic wasn't pretty in general."

"Yet you still pursued it."

"I only pursued it after you taught me how to use it," Rend says. "You turned me into this, so I'm blaming you for improper treatment and handling of me."

"What? I'm getting a bad rating?"

"You're lucky that's all I'm doing."

"You can't give me a bad rating. I own you!" Maeva yells.

"I can just get up and leave right now."

"Stop threatening me!"

"Maybe I'll forgive you if you give me what I'm owed," Rend says. "Don't you think I'm long overdue for those benefits we talked about so many weeks ago?"

"What kind of benefits?" she asks, with a raised eyebrow.

"Something that properly rewards my loyalty."

"I… I don't understand what you want from me," Maeva says.

"Oh really?" Rend says as he sneaks a hand underneath her shirt to lift it, stopping the moment he sees the capital version of the letter 'H' that sits in a sea of inked fire stamped just above her hip. "…Is that a tattoo?"

"Shit!" She smacks his hands away. "Don't look at me!"

"I already saw it—don't try to hide it. What's wrong with it?"

"Nothing much… it's just that I consider it to be a mistake from my younger years."

"When'd you get it?" Rend asks.

"A year after I was freed, and sometime before the first wave of the Decay scare. Sadra did this for me," Maeva says.

"Did she now?"

"She's actually really good at art. She says it's the one thing that helps her ease her mind. I can tell she's been aching to get back into it with all the doodles she makes in the sands."

"I never thought about you all having hobbies."

"Our infighting is the only relic of what we used to do every day together," Maeva starts to say. "We're people too, you know. We had so much fun together wrecking shit and terrorizing those stupid mages. It was bliss."

"What was your favorite hobby?" Rend asks.

"Everything that existed was my hobby. Finally seeing what the world looked like outside my four walls made me go through a period of wild overindulgence. Until it was all taken away from me and I was forced to retreat into a four-walled confinement again. You and Draxis broke me out of that confinement, but I stepped into a bigger one—and there's nowhere left to escape this time."

"You do know that *you* are our means of escape, right?"

"Hmm. I never thought of it like that."

"And you also have me as your backup key," Rend says.

"You're more than a backup key," Maeva says.

"So, I'm the 'master' key then?"

"Goodness. Normally I would reprimand you for making me cringe from such a stupid comment, but I can't. I didn't know what I was getting myself into, but reviving you was the best decision I think I will ever make. Is it wrong for me to say that you were worth all the souls that I unknowingly sacrificed?"

"About that… I don't think there's any higher being that can grant you forgiveness for that travesty."

"I don't care," Maeva states. "They'd have to kill me to pry you away from me. You're mine."

"I'm yours you say?"

"Y-You know what I mean."

"You call me an idiot more times than I can count," Rend says as he starts brushing his hand on her stomach and reaching lower, past the point where her tattoo lies. "So you might have to explain it to me. Thoroughly."

"Archias… mm-mmh! St… Stop!" Maeva says with a bit of urgency. "I get what you're trying to do. It's not that I don't want to… but I'm still… sensitive—to being touched."

He retracts his hand. "Sorry, sorry! I was just—"

"Don't bother explaining yourself, you'd just make up a shitty lie anyway." She then grabs and yanks his ear, making him yelp. "You should know by now that I will give you *clear* permission before I let you do anything to me. Understand?"

"Y-Yes…"

"I do love your tenacity and excitement, however. Keep it, for whenever I decide to summon you. For now, I'm feeling a little sleepy. Slave, be my pillow for me."

"But—"

"But what?" Maeva interrupts.

"Nothing. I thought I was going to sneeze."

"That's what I thought." She then lays against his shoulder—pinching his side each time he shifts around.

"You know, I can transform a log into a pillow for you," Rend says. "That'll be softer—"

"Shhh! You're being too noisy! Don't make me smack you."

Rend manages to stay still long enough for her to relax. He brushes her hair and face, scraping off the snow that dares defile his master's beauty.

"She cares for you greatly, Squire."

Rend tenses up, then relaxes while saying, "Oh… it's just our favorite stalker skulking about."

"I will ignore that insult," Suvius remarks. "Tell me, has been a good mistress to you?"

"She can be a bit bossy, but I guess that's the point. Why do you care?"

"I've been following the journey between you and Young Maeva because I can't help but to be interested in you both like a doting father."

"And what does our 'father' have to say about our development?" Rend asks.

"That I am a horrible parent, but I am also aware that I am no longer needed. There isn't much to say when maturity is shown."

"Can you two please keep it down?" Maeva hisses. "I *will* kill you both if I lose my beauty sleep."

"We should go, Squire…" Suvius says.

"I agree a thousand times over," Rend says.

***

At the highest point in the sky, at the zenith, the moon strikes the island with an ethereal glow. Maeva is strolling along the beach. She encounters Draxis on the return lap around the island.

"Go away," she says to Draxis. "This is my favorite spot to sulk. Not yours."

"You can't just charge in and make demands. Learn to share, woman."

"No. I do what I want."

"Is that going to be your life's mantra now?" Draxis asks.

"I will say whatever I want too."

"Then tell me why you are here."

"That's rude. What if I just wanted to say hi?" Maeva says.

"…Did Sadra send you over here?"

"No? I just wanted to come here and admire the scenery. Honest. Would Sadra have a reason to send me over here?"

"Potentially," Draxis responds.

"Is something bothering you?" Maeva asks.

"I already had this discussion with her. I'm fine. Okay?"

"If you say so. Then if you don't mind being a passive listener for a split second, I wanted to express my thanks to you."

"Huh? What for?" Draxis says.

"That moment when you showed up at Mt. Everstone—it was like staring at the gates of Birthplace. All of my pain was uprooted and disposed of in an instant."

"That's a huge compliment."

"To think I've come this far since my isolation. Now I have a purpose, and so much more. You really are a blessing. You know that, don't you, Draxis?"

"I have done some good things. I'm aware of that."

"Are you also aware that you haven't had your daily dose of medicine?" Maeva asks.

"What are you, a nurse?"

"Let me check your temperature."

"Don't you dare touch me!" Draxis shrieks. "I'm warning you!"

"Just—let me… Aha! Got you!"

"So bothersome. Well…?"

"According to your massive forehead, the results say that you need some immediate care," Maeva says.

"I demand a reanalysis."

"Nope. Now hold still…"

Draxis grunts as she feels the veins in her arm get pierced. "This feels so weird every time."

"Sorry," Maeva mumbles.

"Wait, can't you use Samsara to do this for you now?"

"Umm…"

"You just wanted a free snack!" Draxis snaps.

"Hey now. I got fed, and you are now cured. It's a win-win."

"More like ninety percent your win and the meager leftovers for me," Draxis says.

"It works out. Oops, I nearly forgot one part of the procedure."

"What?"

"This." Maeva snatches Draxis in for a hug.

"Maeva… Alright, alright. You win. This does make me feel better."

"What the fuck is this shit!" an enraged voice screams from over at the distant bushes.

Maeva and Draxis both look at the blurry motion of golden light sprinting towards them at an unbelievable speed.

"Sadra, no!" Draxis shouts. "You got the wrong idea!"

"Shut up! I'm coming for you last. But you—Maeva! You… you harlot!" Sadra starts turning Nocturnal. "You better hope the Decay kills me before I get to you!"

Maeva starts backpedaling in a panic. "Why is she so fast?"

"Die!" Sadra screams.

"Er, I gotta go. Bye, Draxis!"

"How dare you say bye to her! I'm going to rip your tongue out!"

Draxis can't help but laugh at their antics. The more she laughs however, the more a dense pressure envelops deep within her chest. She coughs into her hands, upheaving a nasty amount of purple splatter.

Her vomiting continues as she rushes over to the ocean to wash her hands and mouth. Finally gaining some stability, Draxis stares at her own muddled reflection in the water, saying to it, "Keep it steady, me. I have to hang in there. For them. For her…"

Chapter 58

The Last Voyage

"Is that the last box of supplies, Malphunnos?" Klae asks.

"I've already triple-checked."

"Extraordinary. Well, everyone—this is it. There is no turning back. Make sure you all have every trinket and Artifact you want to take with you. We'll need every pittance of power we can muster."

"We have everything that we need," Malphunnos says. "Let's do this."

"Alright. I'm really excited about this," Klae says, taking the ramp up to the ship's top deck with the others. "This is my first time being on a ship, and to think it will be on a royal one. It looks more like a warship though."

"Vomenn ingenuity," Suvius says. "They could even make a raft into a vessel of conquest."

"I'm not sure that's something to be proud of."

"At the time it was."

"With that confidence, I can only assume that you're going to be our captain?" Klae asks.

"Always. Welcome aboard to the Sora La Daellus."

"Sora La who? What language is that?"

"Draconic," Draxis says.

"Ohhhh? Now I'm interested. Could you perhaps share a few words?"

"The language can be a bit steep to learn, even for me, but one of the phrases that I know by heart is Aeros Wasate Bellum. That means 'flying clouds of rising thought'."

"I love hearing your language," Sadra says.

"I want to hear him swear at us with it," Rend says.

"Well… I can always say more. Let's get going first," Draxis says.

"Aluna!" Suvius shouts at her to get her to stop talking to Jellop and Maeva. "Get over here! I need your direction!"

"You could try saying please!" she shouts back.

"You could try not to waste any more time!"

"You sound so bitter, Lord Suvius. Are you still mad because no matter what you try to do to me it always ends up as a loss for you? You can't curse me, and you will never beat me."

"You just keep getting lucky," Suvius says.

"That beatdown back at Bonamu wasn't luck. That's my fifth win against you overall," Aluna says.

"Must you remind me of all those other lucky moments?"

"Quit being a bitch and rotate the wheel! You're turning it the wrong way!"

"Watch yourself when you sleep tonight, flea," he grumbles.

Only the glare of the full moon is present to bid them all farewell. The view of the Arbiter Capital soon disappears out of sight as they sail at a steady pace towards the unknown—the far unknown. Days pass without any errors. Games are played no matter how archaic the rules. Wishes are made with no one to directly grant them. Memories are forged, always to be remembered.

The fourth day on their journey is one such memory.

<u>Day 4</u>

Sadra finds Rend at the rear of the ship, entranced to his melancholy. "Archias," she calls out to him.

"I told you all not to use my real name," he says. "Don't you have anything else better to do?"

"Aw what? But you let Miss Maeva call you that some-times."

"Don't worry about her privileges," Rend says.

"I want to call you Archias."

"I want you to stop bothering me."

"But it's going to piss me off for the rest of the day knowing that I can't," Sadra says.

"At least you're honest. Tell you what, I might give you permission if you can give me a reason to smile."

"Why a smile?"

"I'm getting nervous about whatever lies ahead for us."

Sadra thinks to herself, putting in the extra thought. She smiles proudly as comes up with the perfect little plan. "I sincerely apologize for forcing you to remember your worst nightmares back at Isilios."

Rend chuckles. "It took you this long to say something? I don't even care about that anymore."

"Yeah… but I mean it. You didn't deserve that."

"Alright, that's enough. Nobody likes a kiss-ass."

"Really? Are you sure? Draxis used to love the way I made him feel," Sadra says.

"I'm not sure how to take that. Are we talking about the same thing?"

"…Are we?"

"Sadra!" Draxis shouts from afar. "Are you talking about me!"

"No!" She then looks back at Rend and whispers, "I totally was."

"I know. I was here for that."

"Hehe."

<u>Day 6</u>

There is a ferocious omen swirling around on the far horizon. A nefarious thundercloud, larger than any natural cumulonimbus, shrouds the entire sky with a nebulous darkness blacker and more harrowing than anything they have faced yet.

The titanic anathema of the sky periodically discharges menacing bolts of lightning that arcs throughout its body and strikes down at the very water it commands below. Every insidious hour that passes brings them closer to their destiny where they will have to face such an anomalous freak of evil.

Wanting a closer look for himself, Klae moves to the helm of the ship, swiveling his head every which way to try to comprehend the magnitude of the impossible storm. "Do any of you think this ship can survive that kind of doom?" Klae asks his stoic neighbors—Maeva and Suvius.

"Maybe if this ship was plated and in its prime," Suvius responds. "Can one of you ask Aluna if she can be on standby in case we need her magic to combat these hostile waters?"

"I can go," Maeva says.

"Much appreciated."

"Are you confident Aluna will be enough to overpower this peril?" Klae asks.

"Not at all," Suvius says.

"Then why aren't you raising any alarms? I sense no hesitation on your part to steer us to our deaths."

Before Suvius can say anything, he gets distracted by the others as he overhears them laughing. He lets go of the steering wheel and turns to watch them. He also turns Klae around by his shoulders while he asks him, "What do you think about this display of revelry, Klae?"

"That you people are blind to danger?"

"What it should be telling you is that we are determined despite anticipating the terror that is waiting for our arrival," Suvius says. "When we have a common purpose and surge of energy, we can't help but to feel jubilant at the predetermined victory we know we can either dictate or fulfill.

"We are not completely fearless, however. Admittedly, it is impossible to be immune to Fear—and especially towards Death— but remember that there is never any horror to fear if you fight back. Become terrifying to your enemies. I hope my message can still your young heart."

"Ha, what youth?" Klae says. "I had to abandon it to repair what my elders broke."

"And yet there is a certain childish innocence to you that makes you jump at the mere sight of a spooky cloud…"

"Th-that's not true!"

"That's what it looked like to me," Maeva says as she brings Aluna over, who sits on her head. "I'm surprised you're not freaking out more at the demonic skeleton right in front of you. And then there's also me."

"Don't say that, Maeva," Aluna says. "We wouldn't hurt you, Klae. Not unless you do something we don't like…"

"Maybe we should throw him overboard since we don't need him anymore," Maeva snarks.

"Feed the crabs! Feed the sharks!" Aluna yells out.

"Everyone, lay off!" Malphunnos shouts at them from the main deck. "Don't give the child a heart attack!"

"We're just messing with you, Klae," Aluna says. "Right, Maeva?"

"Hm? Is that a trick question?"

"Dealing with both of you at the same time is eternal suffering." Suvius interrupts. He looks back at Klae. "So, what do you think now? Have you gained some resolve?"

"I have no idea why, but this craziness puts me at ease. Maybe I'm the one not crazy enough."

"You're just the right amount. It takes someone special to be able to devise a plan that nearly saved the world. You might be the craziest person here."

"Um… thanks?"

"My pleasure."

<u>Day 9</u>

Arriving at an unnamed sea, it is now apparent where the dark eclipse of the thundercloud originates from. The continental land seen over yonder doubles down on the presage of their dreary future.

"There it is," Klae says. "Calvrim. The paintings and legends do not do this place justice."

"You alright, Jellop?" Rend asks him.

Jellop stops scratching his head, unaware he's been doing it unconsciously. "This place is making the back of my mind itch. Not in pain, but… something distant. I can tell there was great disorder here."

"Disorder…?" Malphunnos mutters to himself while putting a finger to his chin. "Aha! Order and Chaos! That rings up some memories. The Capital of Monsters… I remember Calvrim now."

"You do?" Klae says. "That's so good to hear. Could you tell us more about this place? "Like what can we expect?"

"There shouldn't be anything to expect. This continent shouldn't even be here."

"Clearly it is though."

"Let me tell you something that would make you wish otherwise," Malphunnos starts to say. "I was a late joiner, but I was here nonetheless when the Gods sank this continent to ensure the disaster here remained forgotten. The War on Horror. It was perhaps the greatest disaster in history, aside from our current era.

"That event was the first time the Gods had to break Divine Law and assist mortalkind to escape from an endless era of pure chaos. We lost some crucial gods during the war's long stretch and at the war's gruesome end. The primordial brothers: the God of Order and the God of Chaos are such victims."

"Order and Chaos?" Klae says. "Don't think I've heard of them? Is their absence why the world is in disarray? What happened to them?"

"What happened to them indeed. Chaos was the Father of Monsters, and he wanted to overrun the world with his insane creations, which soon led to him initiating the war—and Order was the one to finish it. Chaos was furious with his brother's 'betrayal', and he knew that his own defeat was fast approaching.

"Unfortunately, Chaos is a prime immortal. That is to say that the only thing the other gods could do to remove Chaos permanently was to banish him to an unknown realm where no corporeal key can be forged to set him free, but that also meant we had to make the ultimate sacrifice and banish Order as well—because he was devoured by Chaos."

"You mean that metaphorically, right?" Klae asks.

"If it makes you feel better, then yes—but actually no."

"That's a crazy story," Rend says.

"You had to be there," Malphunnos says, elevating the excitement in his voice. "But it was a pyrrhic victory at best. We're still reeling from the extreme repercussions it seems."

"Wooow!" Sadra says, amazed. "I couldn't imagine getting ate out by your own brother."

"Sadra, g-go back over there," Maeva says, directing a firm finger that points to the other side of the ship.

"Kay!"

Chapter 59

Serenity

The penultimate day. In an estimation of only a day and a half, they should touch down on the sands of a foreign and hostile land.

Before that impending day though, Suvius lays against the railing on the starboard side of the ship and plays a tune on a string instrument with the oceanic background behind him. He makes a call to gather everyone around for one last memory. They sit around in a circle, on top of their leftover empty boxes and crates of supplies.

"What instrument is that, Suvius?" Rend asks.

"It's a lute. I would prefer to have a proper performance for this song with better instruments and the supplementary heavenly voices of bards, but alas, I'm stuck with a crew like you."

"I call for a mutiny," Draxis says.

"At least allow me to indulge you all with a bit of history before you overthrow me. Back when I commanded my own fleet, there were superstitions made about the dead armies we buried at sea. They involve lingering specters that would drown an entire crew at any given moment when you least expected it. It's been so long since I've sailed—what I should have done prior to us departing was to play this lament in order to sanctify this ship and pacify any enraged spirit we might encounter."

After finishing adjusting the strings of the lute, Suvius gives it a test trial. He is met with agonized groans and ears plugged by hands.

"Damn this piece of garbage!" Suvius yells. "I'm sorry to say that I might have to cancel this event. I should have known this instrument is inadequate for such high-quality demands."

"That gives me an idea," Jellop says. "Do you remember how the melody sounds if played at perfection, Lord?"

"I will never forget it."

"Play your instrument then, and I shall link your memory of the song through everyone else."

"That sounds wonderful. Allow me to set the mood first. Bear with me."

The music starts out rough. Really rough. It soon smooths itself over, blending in with Suvius's determination to make lute function just enough to ease the transition into his old memory. They all close their eyes to help picture what they hear.

Soon, the percussive cracks of the overhead thunder subside into a serene harmony of strings. The harsh headwinds bend into breezes of calming delight. The bucking water that dashes into their faces turn into golden petals, descended from the heavens above. Such an embrace of passionate harmony has everyone conjoined in mind, heart, and spirit.

Maeva however has the strongest connection to the ongoing lament, with the rest of them empathizing with her melancholy. So many good moments, so many bad, but it all culminates into an epic of their journey.

It feels so long ago. In her eyes, it first started with miracles of salvation in a cavern deep beneath a mountain, to surviving a blighted forest overran by ravenous elves, to enduring the scorching desert of a once fabulous, crystal-clear lake, to withstanding the great fall of the mightiest kingdom, to venturing into the amalgamated hearts of darkness and despair, to rising above through the ashes of treachery, to proving their determination and honor against the most legendary of champions, to overcoming their worst enemies and own mental woes, to witnessing the tragic end of a foreign family long removed of their prestige, to uncovering the final secrets of a king of madmen, to now having to reclaim their prime victory that was despoiled by something spitefully baneful.

Such a surreal endeavor of peace this is. There must have been some incredible divine intervention and blessings involved for all of them to meet up again after being forcibly separated due to the nightmarish calamity years ago. Such generosity is unheard of. It always felt like the world has been against them—and they have always been against the world—but with this shining hour of bliss, now would be the most perfect time to reflect, to cherish, and most importantly, to finally let go of any withheld tears.

The future has never looked brighter—they just need to get through the present first…

Chapter 60

The Gravity of the Situation

Down in the cabins, in an empty hammock next to Maeva's, Rend juggles a coin between his hands as he watches everyone sleep in theirs. It feels wrong to keep watching them nap without their consent. It also feels wrong to exude so much envy at them. The only way to subside such raw jealousy is to appreciate that he can rest vicariously through them.

Every night, he's been watching Aluna's small frame move up and down to the rhythm of Jellop's breathing. Somehow, Sadra keeps convincing Draxis to sleep together in the same hammock. They look cramped in, but Draxis has always unconsciously hugged her closer, so it must be alright. Klae must be too old or something to not be bothered by the leak in the ceiling that keeps pelting him. There's also Malphunnos. Even Death itself can sleep, unlike him.

The coin slips out of Rend's clutches. Komet tries to catch it, but it only bumps into the coin and makes it roll into a hole in the floor. It wasn't clumsiness that made Rend drop the coin.

A second wakeup call is heard from above, louder than the first one that startled Rend, and awakening everyone else.

"I know you all hear me! Wake up!"

"Is that Suvius?" Maeva groans. "I never heard him sound so upset."

They all spring to their feet. With one foot out of the room, they can see what kind of emergency they are faced with. If there is already this much influx of water seeping down into the bottom of the ship, then they can only imagine what might be happening top-side.

The door to the top deck is snatched open by the wind before they even touch it, letting in a horrendous downpour that damn near blinds their vision.

Suvius is at his post, straining to steer through the maelstroms and hurricane winds. "Finally! You all had me worried! We need all hands on deck!"

They can barely hear him over the rising intensity of the storm.

"O-On it!" Aluna shouts. "Rend, come help me control these waves!"

"Aye-aye!"

Maeva shimmies over to the main mast of the ship, trying not to slip n' slide. "I'll help straighten our sails!"

"I can help!" Draxis says as she grabs Maeva to bolster their footing.

Sadra plants her feet down, and shouts, "Piss off, clouds!" Komet charges up and glows cherry red as if shouting in anger with her. They both fire thick streams of solid light at the sky.

The thundercloud is bruised by the assault, but it heals its wounds. It retaliates by sending a shower of lighting at the ship, tearing down some of its integrity. Komet swoops in to help absorb some of the damage with a hard-light barrier.

Jellop is busy scooping out the excess water as fast as he can off the ship. He realizes his efforts are about to be made futile as a tidal wave twice the size of their ship approaches from the Port side. "Suvius, a wave! It comes!"

Suvius fights hard to not yield to the opposing force that tries to commandeer his control. In the final tug, he loses the clash and the steering wheel spins out of control. Touching the wheel in its current fast rotation would mean losing a hand, but he tries anyway.

"Suvius?" Jellop says as he notices he has left his station. "What are you doing down here?"

Suvius shows him the broken steering wheel.

"O-Oh… But, the wave!"

Malphunnos skids over to Jellop and Suvius and says to them, "My, would you look at the size of that thing. Do any of you think it's possible to kill water?"

"What kind of brainless question is that?" Suvius says.

"One that I'm eager to figure out." Malphunnos's scythe turns raven-black, and he raises it overhead. He swings the scythe downward, shouting, "Hyahh!" and bisects the tsunami vertically with the dark energy produced by the scythe.

The ship successfully passes through the open gap, making Malphunnos shout, "Damn do I love this thing!" in glee.

Another giant wave is rolling in, rising up from the ocean and forming a complete circle that towers over them as it closes in from every side.

"Well, shit. That's outside of my league," Malphunnos says.

"Get away from the edges!" Klae shouts.

"Friend Klae, what are you doing!" Jellop says.

"I'm risking it all!"

Klae stands near the middle of the ship, using his hands to channel something special. He collapses the gray-colored energy he is churning up between his hands by closing them tighter and tighter—until the condensed energy reacts to the pressure and sheds away some of its concentrated power into a small blast.

The explosive shockwave tags everything in a sea monster sized radius, and its effects can be seen as anything that physically touches the gray deterrence field pauses and is abruptly lifted up into a state of suspension. The sky and sea around the ship is surrounded by massive globes of water and distorted lightning bolts.

Klae continues to channel the spell closely. "You all can have a seat while I take us to the front doorstep of Calvrim."

Malphunnos looks over the edge of the ship. There's a giant portion carved out of the ocean, and they are floating over it. "You gonna be alright maintaining such a master spell?" he asks.

Klae's nose starts to bleed. "No—but enough is enough, even if I have to use Mixon's spells to make it so." He alters the gray energy again, this time letting it stick out in front of him. The ship moves in whatever direction the spark goes, still warding off any danger. "We're not that far off," he strains. "We'll make it."

Chapter 61

Ground Zero

The ship dangles over the sandy outskirts of Calvrim—and gets dropped. The crash is enough to make the ship effectively unusable, but they're just happy enough to make it to the continent at all.

Klae shuts off his connection with the spell and lays on the floor. "Gods… this is too much."

"Need a pick-me-up?" Maeva asks him.

"Please."

As Maeva tends to Klae, the others take a look around. The thundercloud that's been antagonizing them billows high in the distance, cast from the peak of a distant citadel. It'll be hard to miss where they need to go.

"That's good enough," Klae says. "Thank you, red-haired girl."

"Excuse me? Call me that again, *mage*, and I'll break your neck."

Klae lets out a heavy sigh, unafraid of letting her hear all of it.

They all jump off the ship—some of them use their magic to break their fall. Suvius does a quick scan of the area, before leading them onward. The path to the citadel isn't openly clear as there's a gatekeeping, infected forest that blocks them. Peace is still not an option, far from it. The thundercloud is still miffed about being denied its food of spilled blood. Thunderbolts melt the ground where they impact, daring the group to get closer if they don't value their lives.

They do not heed. There *is* something to be aware of, however. All around them are stray pieces of fabric that stick up like weeds in a garden, revealed by the steady pouring of the rain and the periodic lighting strikes.

Klae rips off a piece of blue fabric that's attached to a hand sticking out of the ground. He holds it in front of his own gray robe before showing it to Aluna, without saying a word.

"No fucking way," she says, turning her head away. "It can't be…"

Curious at her outburst, Suvius finds a stray piece of cloth nearby and examines it. He incinerates it in the palm of his hands.

Jellop speaks out loud for them to deliver the unfortunate message, stating, "Arbiters."

"What?" Draxis says.

"We… we are not the first ones here. These remains are of dead Arbiters."

Rend kicks a skeleton's hand away. "They're not moving at least."

"I had anticipated that this might have been an outcome," Klae says, "but this is still a grim reality. I doubt they came here to stop the Decay from spreading. Now I want to know *how* this happened. This entire area, hell, this entire continent might be their graveyard—but what caused that?"

"Probably whatever's channeling that storm," Malphunnos says.

"I can't be disillusioned with this. We might have to accept that the Paragon is the malevolent evil behind the world's collapse."

"You really think Zazer has the power to curse the entire world? Or to take on every Arbiter at once and betray them?" Aluna says.

"He was our leader after all," Klae says.

"Even if they had Mixon helping them? What about the Head Apostate? The Eleven Sages? The Chronologist? The Sorceress of the Hunt? Or even the Mathematician?"

"Aluna, you can list off every legend you can think of, but if Zazer found a successful means of ascension then… anything might be possible. I would love to believe you, but there's no way of knowing unless we can peer into the past."

"We do actually have a way of doing that," Suvius says. "Draxis, would you be up for another séance?"

"No way!" she shouts. "Do you not remember what happened last time? In fact—" Draxis starts crushing any visible bones and half-rotten skulls beneath her boots. "We should start destroying these remains before they start rising!"

"Not even just once?" Jellop whines.

"No! I don't have time! For… this. I don't have time for *this*. Can we stop it with the delays?"

"If you want to rush in so badly, then shave off some time and transport us where we need to go—as a dragon," Suvius says.

"Hey, that's a good idea," Sadra chimes in.

"Why would you say that in front of her?" Draxis says. "I told you not to speak of it."

"Have you not told her anything yet?" Suvius asks. "Do you believe her innocence wouldn't be able to handle it?"

"I don't get it," Sadra says.

"…I shouldn't have told any of you," Draxis mutters.

"I would have revealed the truth anyway," Jellop says. "You have a lot to say but haven't spoken on any of it. You can either tell her here right now or have the truth scar her for life because of your inaction."

Sadra's wishful eyes are enough to make Draxis turn away from her gaze. She speaks after a deliberate pause. "Sadra… My soul… I wish it was as strong as all of yours."

"No matter how weak, surely you have enough to make it through one last trial?" Sadra says with an encouraging tone.

"That's one of my prayers. There's even a prayer of mine that involves you."

"What about me?"

"That no matter what you'll always keep the world bright," Draxis says.

"You know I always try. Why question it?"

"It's just something I needed to hear…"

In an instant, a bright flash disorients them all from close by, forcing them to look at the area of impact.

"Odd," Klae says. "I could have sworn that lightning bolt was purple."

"Purple?" Aluna asks.

"Y-Yeah. Over there…"

The location where the electric damage was dealt begins to form into a rising, small hump. The hand of a dead man punches through the sand and scratches around to find enough support to mantle up. The ground breaks apart, and a mutilated body crawls towards them. Other parts of the coastline are hit with the same purple lightning—as well as the rest of the continent.

"That's a loooot of bodies…" Maeva says.

"Did *every* Arbiter come here?" Rend says.

"Everyone!" Suvius starts to say, summoning for the group's undivided attention. "We are a hair's breadth away from bringing this world a type of miracle that only millions of dreams could conceive. I want you all to do your worst and to bring out your best! Even if we have to blow up half this damn continent!"

"I was already planning on it!" Aluna says. "This is going to be payback for them enslaving me!"

"This is payback for enslaving peoples' future!" Maeva says.

"This is payback for enslaving the world!" Rend screams with two raised fists.

An orb of lightning is shot from a Decayed Arbiter wearing a Blue robe, marking the first sin of the final war. The spell misses horribly and lands nowhere close to their location, making some of them chuckle. Their amusement stops when they see the growing army that they will have to slay.

The threat level of the Decayed can be easily distinguished by the color of their robes. The Blue robes, as they remember them, were merely trivial fiends and only threatening because they were always backed up by the superior Arbiters. It's the ones who wear Green and other colors of the rainbow spectrum that deserve to be exterminated on sight, mostly for the dangerous spells they boast that require quite the dastardly imagination along with murderous intent.

But the only colors that remain immediately absent are the prestigious ones who are outside the rainbow rank hierarchy. To see a Black robe at any point would spell disaster, and if they ever see a White robe—then all hope is lost.

Right now, there are a few rising Black robes that must be dealt with before anything else. Without any need for a command, Aluna launches into the air and sends down a scattered storm of fireballs.

Even with such a heavy strike, there were some Black robes hidden among a few stray packs. The remaining Black robe survivors perform their dark magic on their fallen brothers and sisters who can still be salvaged and revived. The other colorful Decayed migrate to the Black robes and start defending them with their own heavy spells.

Aluna dives back down for safety. "Apostates," she states. "We should have known this wouldn't have been easy."

Draxis touches her own chest and relaxes her body while responding with, "It never is. Though, I think this problem is enough to qualify as a rainy day." Draxis begins to morph using an already consumed soul. His hands grow into paws with beastly claws, his jaw extends outwards, feeling heavy and strong, and thick fur sprouts throughout his whole body. The transformation ends. "What the—am I a freaking bear!"

Rend bursts out into a fit of laughter—then gets launched airborne by an incoming boulder.

"That's what you get!" Draxis roars.

As everyone else warms up, Suvius meditates as fast as he can. It doesn't take long to feel the flames of his hatred burning passionately within his heart and armor.

His desires are shared with a whispering voice that speaks closely in his hearing range. "*Use me…*" it says with a delicate pitch.

"Bloodheart Cuirass," Suvius calls out. "I command you to summon forth the sacrificed Malice of Ceranus Vomenn." His wish is granted in full and a spectral bow manifests between his hands. He aims a magical arrow just like she once did, while also imbuing the tip of it with his own special enchantment of hellfire. "May your aim guide me, My Queen."

The one arrow he shoots zig-zags across the coast. It automatically dispels any enemy projectiles it comes into contact with, along with piercing through enemy heads until the arrow loses its strength. Pleased with the result, Suvius promises to the Whisper that he will impale every foe and blot out the sky majestically.

Everyone is making a steady push forward as they try to thin the growing herd. Klae is still in the far back, cowering somewhat near the ocean's embrace. Close by, an armless Decayed has marked him as its victim and starts howling its way towards him.

Klae wants to run away to the others for safety, but they are way too far away. Trembling, Klae aims his hands at the Decayed and shoots a dark gray orb that distorts the air around it. The spell impacts the Decayed and its chest starts caving in, imploding inwards until it's squished into a round bloody ball.

Rend comes flying in and slams into the ground next to Klae. "I'm really starting to hate Geo magic. Maybe I need to get better at defensive spells. What's going on with you, Klae?"

"I… I never killed anyone before. Is this what it feels like? I don't understand why anyone would want to do this." He starts rubbing and wiping his hands, as if cleaning them of filth. "I always hear that it gets easier with each successive kill. Is that true?"

"It depends," Rend says. "Are you okay enough to do it again?"

"I would say no if my hand wasn't forced. You'll see me out there eventually. Eventually…"

All across the coastline, the spells being thrown around in disarray has the layout of everyone's current position messy at best, but there is some semblance of a structured attack formation.

Forming the bulk of the backline is Suvius providing massive support on taking out and calling out any priority threats. Maeva shows nothing but fortitude as she holds her position tight as the immovable frontline. In a mixture between flanking and hunting for easy targets, Aluna rides on top of Draxis's head as her humiliated, furry steed and picks apart the incoming Decayed that spawn in from the dense forest that stretches inward across the coastline.

Forming the midline is Sadra and Komet, working in tandem to act as support and the corporeal body that connects the front and backlines. A lot of enemy spells would have hit their mark if it wasn't for them sweeping through and blinding the Decayed, and also ensuring Maeva doesn't become blind herself trying to feed her endless hunger. Ironically, Sadra gets targeted and blinded as well, by an isolated celestial spotlight that entrances her.

Malphunnos dashes in with godspeed and cuts the head off of a Decayed that is nearing too close for comfort towards Sadra. "Hyahh! Man, I love doing that. As for you, Sunshine, quit staring out into space!"

"But the Moon…" Sadra murmurs. "It's calling to me."

"Selvita?" Malphunnos looks up at the silver glow that is scarcely shone through the red velvet of the sky, wondering to himself in the process.

"Woah! Malphunnos! Look at me!" Sadra shouts.

He *is* looking at her, spellbound at her equal luminosity and color to the Moon's rich beauty. "It seems she's chosen you to be her champion," he says.

"Does that mean I'm a god?"

"Gahaha! No. Although, it seems like the boundaries between gods and mortals are more transparent nowadays than ever before. You are currently more of a god than your fellow mortals are."

Sadra studies her hands, picturing what she can possibly even do. She isn't given much time to think though due to the aching pain that's shooting throughout her body. The buildup needs to be expelled.

"You might want to get behind me, Komet," Malphunnos warns.

Sadra's body is too bloated with foreign power, so much so that everything she is unable to contain within her is gone in a megaton burst. Nothing of the excess is wasted, and anything that is not able to survive the wave of the divine power of the Moon is dissolved into sparkles of silver dust. If she were an actual bomb, half the coastline would have been gone. The pain subsides, and her body returns to its unpossessed state.

Komet peeks out from behind Malphunnos, making him chuckle. "You have just used illicit power from one of the Dark gods, which was Anti-light," he tells Sadra. "You should be familiar with the weaker version of it. I think you mortals usually refer to it as Shadow magic?"

"What…?" Sadra says, bewildered.

"Look at the terror in your eyes. You can thank the God of Chaos and his demonic children for turning Darkness into such an anathema… I get that you Isilians are afraid of the dark, but surely by this point your thoughts should have changed by now?"

"Are you trying to make me convert over to Darkness?" she asks.

"You say that like you haven't dabbled in it already. But, no, this was a rushed experiment for something Selvita and I have in mind for you later. This isn't the time to discuss it. Now turn around, put yourself to good use, and pay us back generously with some good offerings."

Over at the sidelines, Jellop has been manipulating the big baddies among the Decayed and disarming them of their will to fight. It's a slow process. It's probably more trouble than what it's worth, but he's been doing well for himself—or so he thinks.

"H-Hey, is this the best you can do?" the Condescending Voice comments. *"You're too gentle to handle the fate of the world upon your shoulders. Let me take over!"*

"No," Jellop says. "You'll just mess with my mind again, and I doubt you would even give it back this time."

"I'm honored you vilify me so much, but you're only talking about yourself. We are one in the same, you and I. I'm just here to pull the right muscle for you whenever you conveniently decide that war is necessary for peace."

"I've never summoned you for convenience."

"I can read your mind, see your actions, confess your sins. So don't lie to me."

The voice's pestering hammers at Jellop, enough for his mind control to slip. An unavoidable spell is sent his way and explodes at his feet. Jellop crawls around to recover, his skin snagging on elongated bits of splintered wood. His staff… it's broken. He picks up the pieces, then lets them slide off his hands and land back on the ground.

"All I want is for this world to stop hurting," Jellop says. "Do you think such a thing is possible?"

"I haven't seen it happen yet," the Voice responds.

"Neither have I. But I will show you what it looks like after we eradicate the root of this collapse."

"You have a plan?"

"Let's make a compromise," Jellop suggests. "You can take over my left side for a while."

"Now this is an idea I can work with. Let destruction rain!"

"And may it bring order!"

Jellop suddenly loses motor control on the left side of his body, then he watches it come to life despite not commanding it to. His left hand snaps two fingers. The Decayed afflicted by the action start turning on each other, slaughtering each other down to the last.

"See that!" the Condescending Voice shouts. *"The best method to win a war is to eliminate everyone at the same time!"*

"Or you can make it to where nobody has to fight at all." Jellop snaps his fingers with his right hand, making the Decayed run around in mass confusion.

"Are you just doing that to piss me off?" the Voice seethes.

"Muhuhu!"

So far, everything is completely within the Harbingers' control and well within order. They have to keep pushing forward. Leave no prisoners and leave no problems. It would be ideal if they were farther along into the assault towards the citadel, but the hot euphoria from smiting their lifelong enemies makes their patience and adrenaline unlimited.

At the intense zenith of the action, Draxis roars like the apex predator a mighty bear should be. The resonance of his rally would be admirable if it truly had the thrill of someone who is enthralled by the lust of battle. He starts flailing about like a feral hound, shaking Aluna off his head.

The deep purple in his eyes and dripping foam from his mouth brings Aluna to full alarm. That's when she says the unthinkable. "D-Draxis! No! He's Decaying!"

In no wasted time, Suvius runs over and tackles Draxis to pin him down, using all his strength to get him to stop snapping wildly at the air. "Get a hold of yourself!" he shouts.

Draxis bashes his head against the ground repeatedly, phasing in and out of the terminal stage while mumbling, "I was so close… to making it."

"I'm not listening to that! Is this how you want things to end! You *will* push through it!"

"Suvius… forgive me."

"Wait, Draxis! Don't—"

Suvius is blasted away by a blinding flash before he can take action. The others stand back as the bulbous mass in Draxis's place morphs and starts taking form. The size of it grows exponentially, matched with the formation of its tremendous claws and fangs. Thick muscles and blackened scales are next to form from head all the way to the beastly tail. And finally, gigantic wings that cast shadowy doom across the shoreline.

Draxis, in a tone of supreme power, speaks his mind. "So hungry. I must feast…" With nostrils flaring, he rises to stand upright and flexes his wings out. And with his head held high, he commits to a single word. "Rapture!"

Every Decayed that has even the smallest teardrop of a soul is ripped violently from their bodies and is pulled towards the black hole that is Draxis's mouth. His spell range is apocalyptic, and his gluttony is bottomless. With every consumed soul, he then regurgitates it all back at them, into a continuous breath of ephemeral, black and white flames.

His attack wanes as he cleans up the remaining stragglers that survived his initial blast. The coast is clear, and he sits down to rest while breathing heavily.

Sadra touches his side, feeling the smoothness of his scales and the roughness of his skin in between the slits. Her touch receives no feedback. "Come back to us, Brightheart," she says, sniffling.

"I never left," Draxis states.

"D-Draxis? Don't scare me like that! I thought… I thought the Decay took you away."

"I told you all that you worry too much. It was a gamble, but I should have enough souls now to stave off the Decay, and definitely enough to see the end of this era. Now get on my back! We're heading to the citadel!"

"Yay!" Sadra cheers in a near deafening pitch.

"I'm not super caught up with dragon ethics," Rend says. "Draxis, isn't it like super offensive or something to be riding one?"

"It's not like we ever had the option of consent. I like you guys though—you can ride me anytime. Wait… let me start that sentence over…"

"Too late!" Sadra yells as she starts climbing his tail.

"I'm open to new experiences," Rend says.

"As am I," Aluna jumps in to say. "I know the way Sadra always described it made it sound absolutely wild."

"No offense, but I'm not into dragons," Maeva says.

"Muhuhu!" Jellop laughs.

"Will you people *please* just get on!" Draxis roars. "And wipe your feet off first! Degenerates."

"Aren't you getting on, Suvius?" Sadra asks.

Suvius ignores her, still locking eyes with Draxis. "For once, can't you think about yourself? Do you even realize what you just did?"

"I'd rather focus on what I can do for the present," Draxis says. "As I said before, you're wasting my time. Get on."

"You better go fast."

"You must be getting old and forgetful. I never lose in a contest of speed when I'm the real me."

Chapter 62

Raindrops

"Woooo!" Rend hollers. "This is the best!"

"Go slower, Draxis!" Aluna screams at him as her little wings beat together as hard as they can. "I can't catch up!"

"You can eat my souldust!" he taunts as he arches his back and brings his titanic wings down, pushing him along even faster.

"Cheater!"

Draxis maniacally laughs. "It feels good to be the real me again!"

Bright glares appear in Maeva's peripheral vision. She looks off to the side, down at the forest flooring below. "We're about to get hit with some incoming fire!"

"…So are they," Draxis says. The others can feel his body rumbling and churning something vicious from within him. With his puffed-out cheeks, he razes the forest faster than any wildfire—not even the heavy rain can quell It. "Much better," he says next after attracting and devouring any vanquished souls.

Suvius smacks Draxis on the back. "Do try to remember that in the event of an emergency that we would actually *need* somewhere to land."

"You're very picky about how you want your life saved. Next you'll be complaining about how there's too much water in the ocean."

"I do not sound like that."

Sadra interrupts them both by saying, "Did you know you can force Draxis to spew if you touch his neck right here?"

"Sadra… what does that have to do with anything?" Suvius says.

"I don't know. Poke!"

"Gah!" Draxis cries out in shock, accidentally spitting out a weak cloud of fire. "Don't do that!"

"Hehe. I miss my big, strong dragon."

"…He missed you too."

"I want to get off this thing," Suvius groans.

***

The thrill of flying through the sky has lost its fun factor hours ago. This has been the bumpiest, most uncomfortable ride to ever be endured. There has not been a single moment of peace from the stabbing downpour of rain and hail and the constant jumping felt along Draxis's back each time he exercises his birthrights as a dragon against the foolish, grounded Arbiters that try to strike him down.

Regardless, the fortified citadel that once mocked them from beyond the shores is now near. The bulk of the citadel is embedded within the towering mesa that houses it—and guarded over by that damn storm.

It's just over past a deserted city that lies below. From what can be seen through the immense buildup of Decay plaque that infests the city, the towering structures and buildings are heavily gothic in design, with an emphasis on showcasing the depressing and unattractive side of creativity and architecture—all that's missing are deep rivers of blood and an ambience of howling from beyond any ancient graves.

"Malphunnos, when you said, 'capital of monsters', I wasn't expecting such elegance," Klae says. "Nothing here is formless or incoherent. You made it sound like the world at the time was nothing but infested with nightmares."

"And it was. The world was rendered uninhabitable for all living things except for monsterkind themselves. The monsters of today are vastly inferior compared to their cold-blooded and highly intelligent ancestors. No offense, Maeva."

"Hold on," she says. "Why do you say that so apologetically?"

"I… Hrm…"

Draxis suddenly dips downward, almost like he's nodding off, then realigns himself back upright. "I think my body is telling me to stop…" he says.

"It's fine, Draxis," Suvius says. "Get us as close to the citadel as you can and bring us down."

Another few minutes pass until Draxis soars down and drops them off at one of the central streets, halfway to the mesa.

"I swear that citadel keeps moving back farther and farther," Draxis says. "And look at how high up I need to go!"

"No, I think that's just you becoming delusional," Aluna says.

"This back pain says otherwise."

"Great chaos is imminent," Jellop interrupts, shivering as he looks around. "I sense an army coming this way."

"I love you, Jellop, but you really need to stop doing that," Aluna says.

"Pain…"

"Ridiculous. This place is so evil," Draxis says. "You guys can handle the rest of the way, can't you?" He extends his body to stretch his limbs before launching back into the air. "I'm going to circle around the area and purge these grounds."

"Come back down here, Draxis!" Aluna demands. "I can handle the cleaning sweep!"

"I'm considering this to be my lunch break," he says. "Plus, I don't think this place was designed well for people like me to roam around."

"That is true. You have put on some weight recently."

"Ridiculous. See you all up top!"

"So… castle raid time?" Rend says, filling in for the awkward silence.

"Castle raid!" Sadra says.

"Castle raid!" they all shout together—except for Suvius. They stare him down, with a strong hint of loathing.

"Err… castle raid," Suvius groans. "Yay…"

"You're so dead inside," Sadra pouts.

"Because you people are killing me here." Hellfire starts blasting out of his eyes. "Now go!"

"Wahhh!" they wail.

"Go!" Suvius shouts again, chasing them down the street.

Chapter 63

Teardrops

"Did something get in your eye, Maeva?" Rend asks.

"No?"

"Oh. Well, it's just… you're crying."

Maeva wipes her face—there's more liquid streaming down than she's realized. "I don't know what this is, I'm not sad. It's probably just irritation from the infected air."

"You sure?"

"Of course. I'm more pumped than anything with how close we are."

"So am I," Rend says.

***

A gelatinous roadblock overtakes the streets ahead. Jellop throws a rock at it, making some of the others chuckle.

"Aluna," Suvius calls out to her, "do us a favor and search around for alternate routes."

"On it!"

Suvius then walks over and grabs one of Malphunnos's shoulders, and asks him, "Do you wish to wait for her here?"

"Why ask for my needs?"

"To give you some time to concentrate. You possess the look of a man who needs the world to pause for only a minute."

"Yes… that might be exactly what I need."

Malphunnos looks around for an uninfected area to sit at. There's an open spot at a street corner near a small, demolished building. They all sit next to him, wrapping around the corner.

"Do you want to say anything, Malphunnos?" Sadra asks. "We're listening."

"Not to any of you. None of you have done anything wrong. This city is placing a heavy mark on me for my sins, and they are mine alone."

"All sins have a story. Tell us one. It might alleviate something."

"I am not a storyteller."

"Have you ever told one?" Sadra asks.

"None of them are good," he responds.

"Neither are ours."

They can tell from his silence just how hard he is weighing his decision. Malphunnos then grabs Komet and starts petting it, much to Komet's dismay as it tries to pull itself away.

"I'm trying to figure out how exactly a story works," Malphunnos says. "I am always the end of all things. I am never the beginning, the origin that is rocked in a cradle or the young heart of curiosity that runs towards a lifetime of destiny. Don't stories with a purpose usually have a title? Something to help them stay remembered? We'll call this short detachment of my history: The First Murder. It's about the first time I wrongfully killed someone."

"Umm, Malphunnos, don't you do that on a daily basis?" Sadra says.

"According to the unwritten and enigmatic laws of Death that I myself created, it's all determined by intent. That's what I keep telling myself at least. Deep down, I know I committed a crime—one that Narisa never forgave me for."

"You seem to hold her opinion high," Suvius says.

"It's hard to argue or disagree with your other half, especially when they are an eyewitness to the slaying of two innocent souls. It happened during the final hours of the War on Horror when Narisa approached me with a look that I will never forget… It was like getting disowned by your own mother. She didn't say a word to me or waste a breath, she only took the souls from the two bodies and left me alone, soaked in their blood.

"…That's when I realized the severity of the tragedy and the mess the gods left behind. Narisa was the only one who never lifted a finger against the people here, but she still had the bloodiest hands and the dirtiest job to complete—because she was on cleanup duty."

"But you did what you had to do," Sadra refutes. "It was to save the defenseless against the Monsters' regime."

"Sometime during the war, the Monsters stopped fighting back," Malphunnos says. "We knew that, but we didn't care."

"Was there not a general who commanded and rallied the gods?" Suvius asks. "Could anyone convince them to lower their weapons and prejudice?"

"There was a general, yes," Malphunnos says. "One could even consider him to be a king, back when his power and intolerance were more absolute. When the king moved, everyone followed. When the king spoke, everyone listened. When the king declared war, victory was to be expected by tomorrow's eve."

"How did this 'king' respond when he learned of the war's conclusion?"

"He took out and stared into his favorite mirror like always. It was always kept clean and polished to pristine condition—but not on that day. What he saw back in the reflection was regret and disgust. So, he apologized to the blood stains on his reflection and followed up by renouncing his rule. That was the second worst decision he made."

"Why?" Suvius asks.

"Because when a seat of power is made available, and depending on its symbolism, people will do anything to take hold and never relinquish it."

"What did this seat symbolize?"

"It took many forms, but now it represents anarchy because no one is capable of retaining its former prestige of leadership for as long as I have."

"Mal…" Sadra says.

"I am a humiliated king who is a servant to my regrets. My actions nearly costed the world everything. The concept of Divine Law isn't put in place for control or oppression, it's to prevent us from overstepping our boundaries and causing irreparable damage to our creations. The other gods stood beside me when I chose to go to war against Chaos and his monsters, but it only led to mass extinction and a world that was more chaotic than before the war, just like Chaos himself foretold.

"It also doesn't help that my choice to strip myself of power and responsibility might be why the dark crippling call of Silence looms so heavily across the world. People are so quick to commit sins against Life like murder and the slow suffocation of anything they touch until it dies, all until there is nothing but complete silence."

"The world is still here breathing," Sadra says.

"Is it really? I only hear its dying screams," Malphunnos says.

"You're still here."

"Hm. That I am, Sunshine."

"Malphunnos… excuse my intrusive curiosity, but did Narisa ever forgive you?" Suvius asks.

"What, does Narisa remind you of a particular someone?" he chuckles. "But yes, she has a heart of gold—of course she forgave me. There was a world to rebuild, and she held my bloodied, weakened hands up while she herself never stopped moving. That's where my idea of Necromancy came from, a way to help ease her burdens…

"I wish I didn't take her aid for granted and took any time at all to thank her when I had the chance. If she was here, I can promise you that she would be saying that I need to get up and work harder while there are still things to do. She really likes to overwork people. Damn do I need her right now…"

"I'm back!" Aluna shouts. "There's an empty canal system just below us we can use."

Malphunnos stands up while saying, "Well would you look at that. I'm impressed that I not only passed the time, but I've also managed to say a couple of sentences that somehow were cohesive enough to form a story. The only error is that it's a snippet of *my* lowly and terrible experience. There are significantly more tragic stories here that will never be remembered or recalled. I think that is the one thing that bothers me the most. And above everything, I am currently waiting for the most important story to be told—but it shan't be told by me. It is not my story to tell…"

***

They detour through the empty canals of the ancient city, avoiding the bubbling purple puddles and anything that might lurk in the drainage tunnels.

Sadra is keeping a close eye on Maeva, more surprised at her than anything else. "Is there a reason you're so silent, Miss Maeva? You were so hyper back at the coastline."

"What a weird thing to be observing."

"When Draxis isn't here to pleasure my eyes, I like to look at you as an alternative."

"Ugh."

"I'm only joking—mostly. Are you feeling alright?"

"I'm feeling alright to move, isn't that enough?" Maeva answers. "Do you take my silence to be an expression of… apathy? Nemi…?"

"Who? No, I'm Sadra."

"You… you sounded like…" Maeva loses her thoughts when, overhead, Draxis zooms across the sky while dodging a bombardment of elemental fireworks that chase after him.

"Wooo!" Sadra cheers. "Look at Draxis go! He really does try his best to protect us."

"He does give off that brotherly aura," Rend says.

"Brother…?" Maeva mumbles to herself. "Vale…"

***

"I wanted to give you this, Master," Rend says, holding a plant in his hands.

"A flower?" Maeva asks. "Why is it black?"

"I don't know. I just thought it looked neat."

"Where'd you get it?"

"There were others like it growing outside of some church-looking place."

"Dammit…"

"What?" Rend asks, curious at her outburst.

Maeva doesn't respond as she runs off.

"Hey, watch it!" Klae shouts. "Where the hell are you going!"

"Follow her," Malphunnos says. "She'll take us where we need to go."

***

Drenched from the unstoppable rain and completely out of breath, Maeva collapses down to her knees at the great obsidian-black doors that lead to whatever lies inside the skyscraping mesa. She caresses the doors and winces as a distant memory overwhelms her every time she touches it. There's fury boiling inside of her.

"Malphunnos!" she calls out.

"Ye-yes…?" he says, holding his breath after.

"You said that there was a war here that devastated this continent… I want you to know that I remember that war!"

"Excuse me?" Klae interrupts. "You're telling me that you were here? That's impossible."

"For years it felt like I was experiencing life with one eye closed," Maeva starts to say. "When Crysis restored my memories, I saw parts of my past. I could finally see who I really am—a life that has seen two eras rise and collapse. I escaped the first collapse because I voluntarily accepted being put under a curse of Eternal Sleep and was sunken beneath the gods' omniscient eyes. That's why you were never able to find me! Malphunnos!"

"Maeva…"

"Don't say my name like you're innocent!" she yells while scraping her nails against the doors. "H-How dare you do this to me! The emblem on this gate is my family crest, this was our estate! But now it means nothing! Why did you destroy my home? How many of us did you personally kill? Why did you kill my brother! I want you to answer me, Malphunnos!"

"I have already given you my best answers," he says. "You don't remember how archaic the old world was. You don't realize how long you've been *away* from that world. It is my right as one of the war's veterans to leave that horrible past buried. I didn't choose to limit my words out of disrespect for the murdered—this just isn't a part of history that I wanted to recall."

"I don't give a damn about how you feel! What about me? Were you never going to tell me that I was here?"

"I don't know *what* to tell you, Maevalina! The Vampires, the Demons, the Arachnid queens, the Lycan overlords, the Titans, the Leviathans along with alllll the other Monsters had to be stopped. I had to even try to stop *you*!"

"Me?" Maeva questions.

"And as forgetful as you are, you obviously don't remember how vicious you were," Malphunnos says. "You just never. Stop. Consuming! The number of cities and mortals that were laid to waste because of you is just… Maeva, once I remembered who you were, I pretended to be unaware of your past because I didn't want you to return back to your primal state of bloodlust."

"You could have at least told me about my restorative power!"

"How in the hell could I have told you about something that is the exact opposite of the one power that I am still fearful of today? Whenever I saw anyone get bitten by a vampire, there was no coming back. But not with you it seems. You're better than your ancestors."

"Ancestors… I can't even remember them," Maeva says. "My mind is still trying to catch up."

"Sylis and Crysis fucked with your head too much," Aluna says. "Don't blame yourself."

"I can't even remember my parents," Maeva continues.

"But I do," Malphunnos says. "The Solunna Dynasty. They were… fearsome—but highly revered by all of monsterkind. They were Godslayers."

"Godslayers?"

"A rare term that I do not use lightly. That's what they were capable of. I've lost many people here too, Maeva…"

"Then tell me this one last thing: Do you think my parents would accept what I'm doing?"

"Hahaha…! Not even a little bit. Their rage and misanthropy were unbearable. That's why I killed them."

"You piece of shit—"

"Nope! I will not hear of any more complaints," Malphunnos says. "Earlier you scolded me for withholding information, so if you want to haggle me for anything else, then prepare to hear things that may reduce your sanity. Shall I continue?"

"You've said enough. I will not forgive you for what happened here."

"There are plenty of people, both past and present, that will never forgive you either. I'm sure that orphan Sadra saved a while back would vouch for me if it could."

"B-But…"

"But what?" Malphunnos says.

"…Nothing. As you were."

Maeva turns to face the obsidian-like doors, staring at the carved, giant capital S that curves through both doors. At a second glance, she notices the grooves that outline the letter are carved in much deeper than she realized—especially the extra lines that create the design of a bat's wings that split off from the giant letter. A flying S; her forgotten family crest.

Maeva follows the downward curves of the bat wings with her eyes. The end lines of both the left and right wings lead into the ground and travel into the tails of two gargoyle statues that each hold up an empty stone bowl that sits atop their heads.

Maeva inspects the bowl of the left gargoyle at the left door. There's a hole at the bottom of it. She looks up to see what substance the bowl needs to collect. The branches from a tree nearby are extended out to her location and are wrapped up by ropes and nooses that are suspended above the gargoyles, and it's the same on the other side as well.

"Did you find a way in?" Rend asks.

"I can't tell if my people were a bunch of masochists or sadists," Maeva says. "Would anyone want to volunteer some of their blood to help me open this?"

"Do you mind if I lend some of mine?" Malphunnos asks. "Consider it to be a blood tax for the family."

"I should make your ass pay extra."

"And where would those extra funds go towards? Think about that the next time you try to extort someone."

Malphunnos walks over to the right gargoyle and summons his sickle to cut into his wrist and let his blood drain into the bowl. Maeva does the same by biting into her arm.

The mechanism reacts positively to the fresh supply of the unsightly lubricant by pushing their blood up and through the thirsty veins of the door's structure until every line and crevice fills with their discolored blood. The doors creak as they open outwards, letting a rolling black fog escape from whatever ancient and foul air it held back. A terrible type of cold also stirs from within, almost like a whisper from the deceased.

"After an eternity, I am home," Maeva says, wiping her moist eyes. "Your sister has finally returned… brother."

Chapter 64

Final Breaths

Anyone with a working sense of touch rubs their hands together while shaking uncontrollably from the cold as they enter the disintegrating and macabre house of dark nobility. An extremely faded and ripped painting, larger than what their eyes can take in, fills out the far back wall that overlooks the main entrance and the maze of stairs and connecting halls that lead deeper into the manor.

"Is that your father, Maeva?" Rend asks.

"I don't think my father was that narcissistic. I think."

"That was more on her mother's side," Malphunnos interjects.

"Please die," Maeva remarks.

"I'm mostly sure that painting is portraying a depiction of the God of Chaos," Malphunnos continues. "He was definitely pompous like that, even in artwork. By my name did I hate that man."

"I don't recall worshiping him," Maeva says.

"Keep it that way."

"Maevalina," Klae calls out to her.

"Don't… don't call me by that name."

"Now you know how it feels," Rend says.

"Silence," she tells Rend. "What do you want, Klae?"

"I was hoping that, since this your home, maybe you could escort us?"

"You're asking for too much already. I do remember that there was something special at the top of this mesa. I spent a lot of my youth up there. That's all I got. Sorry."

"Don't pressure yourself. Up it is then."

***

The soft blend of silver moonlight and the scarlet light of the sky, along with the periodic echoes of Draxis's rampage, passes through the gaps of the broken windows as they speedwalk through the vacant interior of the grim manor.

"It's quiet in here," Sadra says, with her breath turning into mist from the dropping temperature.

"Don't question it," Klae says. "It's whatever that awaits at the top we need to worry about the most."

"I have to disagree," Suvius says. "Take care of where you step. There's tangles of thorns and caltrops at every crevice here."

"Too late for the warning," Jellop states. "Earlier I brushed up against a patch of nasties, and now Maeva won't stop licking my wound."

"Stop licking people, Maeva," Aluna snaps.

"Calm down. I'm just refueling."

"Tsk. Whore."

"Hold your tongues, everyone!" Klae says with a raised hand.

They remain silent, hearing the faint sounds of thumping coming from a room nearby.

"That almost sounds like a… heartbeat? Hmm." Klae grabs the handle to the door, finding that it doesn't budge. "Something's blocking it."

Suvius grabs Klae and moves him aside. "Allow me," he says. He then uses his shoulder to ram into the door until it breaks open.

They take a quick peek inside—and leave the room almost instantly.

"Hell no!" Sadra cries out. "Do we have to go this way?"

"It might be promising," Klae says.

"No, I'm with Sadra on this," Suvius says. "This room is far too contaminated."

"But I see stairs. They don't appear to be blocked off like everywhere else."

"This is the weirdest thing to remain persistent on. All right, let me see what I can do. Stand back." Suvius belches out a wave of fire across the room, flooding it. The walls shift and morph against the repeated lashing of his flames. He does it again, and eventually stops when he thinks the room has had enough.

"That was flashy, but the growth seems to be too thick to burn," Maeva says.

"Immunity to hellfire…" Suvius groans. "That doesn't sit right in my mind."

Klae crouches down, examining the flesh of the flooring. "These veins that run across the walls and up past the stairs… If we consider this to be the body of the Decay, then there should be a heart or brain somewhere. We should follow them."

"Gah, this sucks!" Sadra cries out. "I hope you didn't piss off the House too much, Suvius!"

"You say that like it's a living thing," he responds. "What kind of abomination are we dealing with…"

The hunt begins to either look for a safe way up top or to find out what makes the insides of this sentient beast live and breathe. The stairs leading upwards do not creak; they squelch on every step made. The halls beyond the stairs are melded together brick-by-brick with decaying flesh-like growths.

Still following the pumping veins of the manor, the next level above the bottom floor seems to be where decadence and leisure was commonplace for a people long gone. The dining area is avoided entirely due to the low growling and constant gnashing sounds that terrify their imagination, and the same can be said for the torture rooms. Even one of the washrooms is made impassable due to festering blisters that cover the area and squeeze themselves tight to pop open and splatter the ground with purple gunk if anyone gets into their proximity.

A cave-in through to the upper heights of the manor provides a way up, but it's worse than the lower levels. Most of the floor is overtaken by pools of violet acid and palisades made of thorns and pikes of callused Decay growths, so they are forced to be crafty with how they maneuver—whether it's by using stone columns and gargoyle statues as steppingstones or climbing along on the rickety rafters. Aside from the bubbling acid and the heartbeat of the castle, all is silent.

"It sounds like Draxis is finished on his end," Klae says as he and the others shimmy across to the far end of the attic.

"Just in time," Suvius says. "This is the end of the road."

"Maeva, you are the one who started this, so you should be the one to finish it," Rend says."

"You're just scared of opening that trapdoor ahead, aren't you?"

"You know me well."

"She might not be able to," Klae says. "There's a magic seal stamped on it, a powerful one." His hand is zapped each time he touches the trapdoor. "This thing is too ancient. It doesn't want to accept anything I do."

"Stop," Jellop intervenes. "I can remove it."

"Can you?"

Jellop touches the seal, feeling the magic dust run across his fingers.

"It seems someone has been divulging into the history of this forgotten land," the Condescending Voice says. *"To think that there is someone who can master my ancient language and make use of it..."*

"What must I do to dispel it?" Jellop asks.

"You must use a bypass phrase. You need only to speak my name. My real name..."

"What is it?"

"Seriously? You've been saying it this entire time," the Condescending Voice says.

"I have? No…"

"Say it. Make it fast, it's cold in here."

After an uncomfortable pause, the bypass phrase, "Jellop," is uttered. The magical seal disappears, and the trapdoor swings open, letting cool air gently blow in.

"Jellop?" Malphunnos repeats. "Is your name all it took to open it? Odd… Why does that word sound so familiar now? Or was it always something more?"

"What are you talking about?" Jellop asks.

"Your… The… I—I don't remember. What are we doing here? What just happened?"

"My head feels fuzzy too…" Sadra whimpers.

"Let us all rush outside," Jellop suggests. "This haunted place is ruining your minds."

"Is that really what happened?" Suvius says. "It's all a blank. Maybe I'm getting old."

"Not as old as me," Klae adds. "I'm used to this. Wait, has this trapdoor always been open?"

"I just said that this haunted place is ruining your minds," Jellop says, agitated.

"Listen, I need a nap, okay? Move out of the way."

Jellop stands back to watch everyone else exit—mostly everyone. He can feel the scornful intensity of a witness's judgment buzzing next to his ear, one that he cannot ignore. He doesn't look at her as he speaks out. "You're giving me those perspicacious eyes again, Butterfly."

"Never do what you just did to them ever again, Jellop," Aluna berates. "Actually, how many times *have* you done something like this?"

"This was the second time. Honest."

"Second…?"

"Y-Yes," he responds. "A long time ago, to staunch something undesirable. It was to protect you."

"Protect me from what?" Aluna asks.

"From a doomsday that I wish never happened. Everyone wanted to hurt you—just like at Bonamu."

"So, this has all happened before? I betrayed them… twice."

"Subtract your guilt, it was the Arbiters who betrayed you. The World War at Daison Peak exposed everyone's lies all at once, but you still stood by us and helped us survive. It was your best moment of bravery and rebellion. But most importantly: freedom." Jellop reaches into his hood and pulls out a cracked, chained item. Not the Mesmerion, but instead—

"Mixon's amulet?" Aluna gasps. "You kept it? After all this time?"

"Symbols of pain can motivate us to attain peace," he responds. "This once ruinous item is like Truth. It can be a gateway for interconnection, but more often than not does it sever. The harsh truth of your Arbiter affiliation was too unbearable for our friends. So I had to… sever. It was to protect you."

"Jellop, as… *refreshing* that is to hear, I can't fully appreciate it. This memory deletion incident is still one too many and too soon. I'm willing to keep this a secret for you—but remember that you're making me suffer with the knowledge of your actions. I will hate you if you make this a habit."

"It was a sudden impulse… I'm ashamed I let myself hurt my friends so easily. Forgive."

"We've both hurt our friends," Aluna says. She then pauses. She flies over to him and suddenly tugs at his hood.

Jellop lets her struggle for a few moments, hoping that she will give up. He concedes and helps her pull it down, letting her see the face behind the veil. Whatever she's seeing, it brings her a calming sense of delight.

"To say it again, we have *both* hurt our friends, Jellop—which is why I believe the sincerity of your apology. Not because of what this Blessing reveals to me, but because of what my heart can sense. Don't be so afraid of the truth that is making you lie so much, Jellop. I know what I just said isn't ideal, but I for one would know that some lies just aren't worth it. It would make me feel better if you believed in that truth as well."

Jellop looks at her directly in her eyes, and tells her, "Yes…"

Chapter 65

Spring

Finally back outside, everyone stands on the flattened top of the mesa, where they experience the first moment of serenity ever since arriving on this dreadful continent. Their feet and hearts are hugged and nurtured by a botanical meadow of flowers and grass that covers every surface area. The tickling wind sways the gorgeous meadow, encouraging the variety of plants to release their harmless pollen and spores that sprinkle the air.

The Decay's corruption still overtakes such a surreal Eden however, in the form of the ever-constant color that will never leave them alone. Purple. Even still, the flowers retain every part of their beauty and opportunity for life.

"It's… it's beautiful," Klae says, finally coming out of a trance.

Malphunnos bends down and picks up a particular purple flower from among the rest, immediately recognizing its shape. "Roses…" he mumbles after smelling it. "This little one seems to be far from home."

"I think my mother loved roses," Maeva says.

"So did Narisa…"

There is one final purple thunderbolt from the great storm cloud that strikes the ground, impacting a massive structure in the distance.

Maeva holds her hands out, like she's anticipating to catch something from above. "Huh… the rain stopped."

"Looks like it finally gave up on trying to kill us," Aluna says.

"I still don't like how this continent exhibits sentience," Suvius comments.

The harsh wind responds to him by whirling around and navigating through his hollow skull, before departing.

"You oughtta limit your words around those who can hear you," Sadra remarks.

"Hmph. Then I'll speak of my complaints directly to the chief. Onward!"

Chapter 66

Eschaton

The storm has a heartbeat. The ancient city has a heartbeat. The garden that they step over has a heartbeat. The Decay—has a heartbeat, coming from a colossal and festering tumor at the very center of the surreal meadow. The amalgamated growth resembles the shape of a human heart, and the booming thumps from within resemble the real conditions and throes of the entire world. Strained. Helpless. Dying.

Rend is the first to say anything, and his words matches what everyone else is thinking. "What. The. Fuck is that thing?"

"Jellop wants to poke it!"

"Jellop will not be poking anything," Suvius says.

"Sad…"

"And what's with those Apostates?" Aluna says as she watches a group of them congregate around the slender pea pods that are hooked up to the tumor. "They seem to be… worshiping it?"

"So is this the main source of the Decay or what?" Maeva asks.

"How about we set fire to everything and ask questions later?" Klae says.

"For once, we can agree on things," Suvius joins in. "Does everyone have a spell ready?"

Draxis comes in hot from above like a descending arrow and slams down with a grand entrance. "Ready!" he shouts.

"Then—fire! Aim for center mass!"

The Apostates are erased instantly as all hell is unleashed at the colossal heart. Everyone's fury is pouring down hard to ensure that the heart-shaped tumor dies horribly and mercilessly. Suvius eventually makes the command to halt, to reveal the fruits of their hard work.

"Damn, no damage," Sadra says. "What are we supposed to do?"

"It's only a condensed blob of Decay, right?" Aluna says. "Maeva—do you think you could…"

"I am *not* putting my mouth on that."

"You put your mouth on Jellop without hesitating though."

"Will you get over that!"

Their arguing is cut off as the storm begins to collapse in on itself and is sucked downward, funneling through the open valves of the Decay mass. The Heart stops beating as one of the connected pea pods—the only one that isn't crushed or completely empty—shakes.

"Oh gods…" Aluna says, gagging. "It's moving!"

Something inside the pod is kicking from within and wants to be let out. Those who cannot stomach the sight look away, still being forced to hear the sloshing of slime and grease from the birthing process.

A man dressed in a faded all-white robe and stained with purple blotches, bursts through and slides out from the pod. He helps himself to his feet while ripping off the organic cords and spiked tendrils attached to him. He wipes off his face, revealing that half of it is scarred.

"I estimate another week or two," the revolting man says to himself. "Another week or two of incubation and I would have succeeded with this lifelong experiment. Why must everything go wrong? No… there is still time. I will make the time."

"Zazer…" Suvius mutters, clenching his bony fists.

Zazer laughs at his name being uttered. "You… *all* of you… What will it take to kill you people? You are worse than this virus, than any curse, worse than any nightmare the horrors of this world can ever create! We are nearing the end of history itself and you worms still will not succumb to defeat!"

"We are the Harbingers. Only we get to dictate finality."

"What kind of shitty—you know what—I respect that. You are the only people who have the iron to look me in the eye and say that kind of conviction like it's fact. Still, my divinity will not be made perishable by this interference."

"A god of what?" Suvius sneers. "You serve no purpose."

"When I cleanse Allosha of all of its scum, only then will this world have no choice but to call me almighty!" Zazer yells. "Kneel before me now, for when I take hold and reshape this world into what it should have been, I might be merciful enough to grant you all a free rebirth."

"You'll just have us kneel to you in the new world. It's always the same with you power-hungry psychos."

"Funny you should mention power as there is *no* manner of power or creation that can stop me," Zazer says. "You *are* welcome to try. I never had the luxury to relish in what makes the Harbingers so monstrous. Go on. Entertain your new god."

"Harbingers!" Suvius shouts. "Bring forth our reckoning!"

Zazer snickers. "A reckoning he says."

"Fucking bastard!" Aluna screams.

Just like with the Heart, they use everything to strike Zazer down, only this time they extend their fury for double the length of time.

Zazer repeatedly claps his hands as the smoke clears after they exhaust themselves. "Ow," he says after a scoff. "That almost felt just as painful as this damn scar—but this was an *insignificant* price to pay. I still remember that day when my supremacy was achieved. I am alone because they are weak! They couldn't handle a god's wrath! Only I am destined to ascend! Let me show you all what I mean…"

"Jellop, behind you!" Aluna shouts.

Jellop turns around just in time to see Zazer come out of a portal, and his left side reacts immediately to catch Zazer's swung fist. There is a struggle to keep him at bay.

"Ah, the runaway mistake," Zazer says to him. "You've killed so many Arbiters with just your presence alone."

"Seems I missed the important one!" Jellop retorts.

Aluna hurls a colorful flurry of spells at Zazer, shouting, "Hands off of him!"

"You have the will to fight against your masters? It seems someone has finally severed your impossible contract, hm? Impressive." Zazer then freezes her incoming projectiles in place, without looking or moving a muscle. "You remember this spell, don't you, Executioner? This was Mixon's favorite. Astral Reflection."

Aluna's spells are redirected back at her, going as fast as rockets in full boost. She only manages to dodge due to her size. Her own spell is hunting for her, orbiting and striking at her like an angry insect swarm as she tries to defend herself.

Jellop continues to try and resist Zazer with physical strength, but he can tell that Zazer is holding back on him. He makes a swift choice to cheat and weaken Zazer through a barrage of mental debilitations, forcing a ruthless clash inside Zazer's own mind. The decisive siege ends when both sides of Jellop scream out in agony, before going limp in Zazer's grasp.

"Oops," Zazer says as he holds Jellop up and tosses him aside. "Looks like he saw something that his feeble mind couldn't comprehend. What a shame."

Suvius bull-rushes towards Zazer, holding up a manifested great shield and bashing him in the face. Not even a flinch is made. Suvius raises his shield to prepare for a retaliatory attack, but his shield and guard gets punched through, and Zazer's fist connects perfectly with his skull, cracking it above his right eye. Suvius is hurtled through the air from the impact.

"Did you feel that?" Zazer says while rubbing his fist and reimagining the damage he caused. "That was for what you lucky bastards did to Marcella."

Rend comes to the rescue by throwing a few icicles at Zazer and following up with a targeted hailstorm.

Zazer accepts the icy pummeling, not even worrying about the accumulating snow and frost. "I don't know you," he grunts, "but you already piss me off."

"Likewise, asshole!"

"Great… They recruited another child. Why do I even bother." A pair of serpents made up of coalesced fire appear and coil around Zazer's arms before detaching themselves and slithering towards Rend.

Rend puts up an ice barrier around himself to shield against them while praying that they don't burrow through before they dissipate.

"That spell reminds me of one of master Daison's," Zazer says, admiring the framework of Rend's defensive spell. "I hate that. Away with you, pretender!"

With haste, Suvius flings a manifested dagger that travels and impacts Zazer's hand to divert his attention.

"Gah!" Zazer cries out, despite only receiving a scratch. "Damn you!"

"I told you I could throw a blade, Draxis," Suvius says.

Draxis appears behind Zazer, casting his great towering presence over him before saying, "I stand corrected." He then swipes at Zazer. Each swipe he makes gets blocked and parried by Zazer's inhuman strength. Draxis switches up his attacks and breathes his black and white fire at him.

"My, what a thrill this is!" Zazer says while bathing in the pain. He then collects the stream of fire in his palms and redirects it back, uppercutting Draxis with it to send his head reeling and dazing him enough to topple him over.

A beam of light strikes Zazer in the eyes, then the quickest sucker-punch ever made brings him down to the ground. Sadra flashes bright as she darts around him with incredible speed and kicks him incessantly while he's down—never giving him the chance to get back up. Zazer pounds the ground with his fist and the immediate area freezes over, tripping Sadra. She lands on her hands and recovers to her feet with a flip.

"Stupid Isilian!" Zazer yells.

"Stupid human!" Sadra yells back.

"I'm a god!" He aims his hands at her, towards her feet. Her shadow begins to wiggle and jut upwards. The shadow latches on to her and wraps around her from head to toe, encasing her.

Zazer wipes his nose as he watches Sadra squirm about, feeling something leak from his nostrils. "Blood? Oh…" he sighs, turning around. "I nearly forgot about you, Sanguine Lamb."

"*Don't* call me that," Maeva growls.

"Well it's not like I remember your stupid name! Isn't it Beatrice or something?"

Maeva dashes at him instantly and fires condensed bullets of blood from her gauntlet, aiming them at his head. Zazer blocks her bullets with his arms to protect his face. As she nears, she doesn't trust the way his hands twitch in place—it moves like he's preparing a heinous trick.

Maeva's intuition saves her life as the moment she gets close enough her only choice is to duck and slide underneath the swipe of his blood sword. She twirls back around while simultaneously casting her own lethal blade to use—then they both clash together, grinding their crimson blades against one another.

"It's all thanks to your magic that any of this was possible," Zazer says to her with a wicked grin. "Remember that."

"In an indirect sort of way, sure," Maeva says. "But all this ruination? Now is that my doing… or is it all yours?"

Before he even dares to come up with a bullshit excuse, she kicks him in his side with a spiked shin guard made out of hardened blood, making an audible crack. Zazer fails to recover from her strike and attempts to distance himself from her, but he collides with a wall of solid light made behind him, constructed by Komet.

"End it, Malphunnos!" Maeva yells.

"Y-You know," Zazer starts to say while breathing heavily against the wall, "it's blasphemy to speak a god's name in another's god's presence."

"Don't sound so jealous of my eminence!" Malphunnos says as he rushes in with his sickle. "Hyahh!" he shouts, just before his attack whiffs and scrapes the wall. Dammit, that shouldn't have been a miss. Malphunnos looks around, wondering where that slippery magician disappeared to.

Zazer reappears, through teleportation. near the Heart. He slumps over the pod he arose out of. "Unfathomable," he says to himself. "I didn't think you all would be so... heh. I still need more time. More... power."

He picks up one of the tendrils from the pod and injects the spiked end into his arm. He connects even more tendrils throughout his body, each one boosting his magic stamina further. "This should be enough..." Still hooked up to the pod, he begins to incant a phrase. "Underworld! Shatter! Gate! Duplicate!"

Scarlet portals start occupying and multiplying across the meadow. Magma and molten rock spews out from them, along with horned humanoid and non-human monstrosities that crawl out while howling out in pain incessantly.

"Army of Hell! Attack!" Zazer shouts.

"Is this man serious?" Rend says. "Demons? Just how much magic does he know!"

Maeva rushes over and pokes the black cocoon that enveloped Sadra earlier. "Sadra! You alive in there?" the cocoon shuffles in response. Maeva starts tugging at the skin of the cocoon, helping Sadra break free from within. The cocoon bursts and travels back to its original shadow form. "Thank goodness," Maeva says. "I thought Zazer put you in a body bag for a second."

Sadra rolls her eyes at her.

"Oohh, my head," Jellop whimpers. "Your head doesn't look too good either, Lord Suvius."

Suvius rubs his hand along the thick crack in his skull. "I'm woozy, but I'll manage. How's everyone else?"

"I need a good massage from a slime monster," Sadra says.

"That would be something nice to look forward to after this battle," Draxis says, stumbling to his feet.

"And I look forward to claiming this first blood!" Aluna shouts. Her wings turn emerald-green, and she targets the ground she hovers over. She is surprised to discover that she can manipulate parts of the Decay meadow to her control. She combines the abundance of grass and flowers together to create thorny vines to ensnare and thrash at the demons.

Jellop steps in to add his own attack to support. He raises his hands in the air and claps them together, shouting, "Temporal Deception!"

The demons' movements and thoughts are slowed down to half-speed, buying everyone some time to whittle them down further.

"Wha—Jellop!" Sadra yells. "You accidentally hit Maeva!"

Maeva curses vehemently with slurred speech as she jogs towards him with a raised fist.

"O-Oops!" Jellop says, innocently. "She must have blended in."

"We can't get to Zazer if we don't close those rifts!" Malphunnos says.

"Sounds like a job for you, Suvius," Rend says.

"Don't give me commands. I don't even know if it's possible for me to do that."

"Don't think, just do!"

"…Fine. Bloodheart Cuirass, bring forth the Malice of… the Malice of… the Monarchs." Hellfire appears in front of him, stretching across horizontally. After completion, a physical weapon forms through the flames. Suvius catches it and checks it for authentication. He nods his head, appeased.

Rend stares at the four-barreled heft of Suvius's new sinister weapon and asks, "What's that?"

"This is a dark wish made physical. A firearm, in its finished state," Suvius says. "Before the Dragon War, Ceranus showed me a secret schematic devised in a massive cross-kingdom project that was proposed exclusively for nothing but destruction without the need for spells or lumbering war machines, though it was quickly shot down due to explosive complications and the general favoritism and resource-efficiency of Magic. It's suitable because if portals are nothing more than glorified gates, then why not destroy them from within like one?"

"A big toy like that needs to have a name," Rend says.

"As it should. A few were tossed around. Castle-Buster, Downpour, Hailstorm, but none of them had any bearing. What do you propose?"

"…Hellbreaker!" Rend shouts with glee.

"Perfection."

Suvius grips both of the handles along the spine of the firearm, aching to pull the front handle back to let the weapon create some lasting nightmares. The weapon cranks as he tugs the front handle, then he pulls it backwards until it cannot move any further.

It takes two hands and some muscle to wield the burly behemoth, but even that isn't enough to restrain the raw force of the recoil that makes his aim wildly unsteady and unpredictable. Suvius has no intention of yielding to his own creation. He begs the cuirass to extract his own malignant imprint to let all of his hatred bloom unrestricted. His true inner demon is unleashed, taking over his skeletal body as it evolves.

The evolution turns his once hollow eyes into a fiery furnace. The top of his head is encumbered with two ever-growing horns, and his body combusts into a scarlet mist that darkens the longer he taps into his own fury. With so much brimming power, he can finally hold the Hellbreaker in place.

All four barrels spin clockwise at blinding speeds, steadily spitting out bullets made from the purest form of sin and hellfire. The demons are shredded and utterly left decimated, and the portals implode from within and vaporize from being unable to handle so much direct overflow. So much is burning in front of him from his incendiary firepower—even Suvius himself.

His body is experiencing a total meltdown. Despite his demonic heart pumping furiously, he refuses to cease until the Cuirass activates itself as a failsafe, forcing him to stop by jamming his weapon and his body. Suvius kneels down as he cools off. "Zazer… he's exposed! Hit him!"

In a panic, Zazer yanks a few tendrils from other pods nearby and stabs himself repeatedly like a lunatic. "I need more time! I need more fucking time!"

The purple blood that pours out from his wounds, along with the vast sea of demonic blood, floats towards Zazer and congeals together into multiple blobs around him, each shifting into a humanoid shape.

"I bet you never knew you could do this with Blood magic, did you, Beatrice? That's why I reign supreme! This is why I will not fail! Go and kill them, my clones!"

Draxis pounds at the ground while yelling, "Nraxe Sel Gono!" and rockets into the air.

"Oooh!" Sadra says in a childlike manner. "Draxis said a swear."

The fragmented souls of the dead are rising across the meadow and are whisked away into the air. An army of souls orbit around Draxis, waiting for their commander's order to strike. Draxis roars, ordering his personal army to attack. Zazer's clones try to repel the coming phantasmal storm with a sporadic barrage of explosive spells, but there's no stopping the wrath of the undead. The clones are all swarmed and devoured within seconds.

"My clones!" Zazer shouts. "Damn you!" He attempts to recreate his clones just like before, but his hands freeze up midway through his casting. The ground and air around him are hazy blue in color. He can't move his eyes, but he can scarcely see that the cause is because of Rend, who gives Zazer a devilish smile. "You… you can even freeze time?" Zazer winces as his body locks in place. "Perhaps you are not a pretender. Remarkable…"

Malphunnos has his scythe and sickle ready in his hands—both wreathed in a pitch-black aura. "Time's up!" he bellows. "And for the record, I don't miss twice!" He crosses his tools overhead, letting their dark energy corrupt the air above him to form a thick nebula in the shape of a ginormous human skull. He fans the weapons out and downward, sending the omen of doom directly towards Zazer.

Zazer—he has the desire to close his eyes, but even that is taken away from him. The dire skull makes contact, exploding into a devastating burst of darkness that blinds the skies and suffocates the senses of anything nearby.

The darkness fades—and Zazer—still remains. He gives a sinister grin as he looks at their faces of pure despair. "I just saw Oblivion firsthand, and yet I still stand. I have transcended Death. It is complete. *I* am complete." He raises an open palm at them and says, "Fate Reversal."

A halo appears above everyone's head and engulfs them in a thick pillar of white light. They are smitten with a horrific agony that they can only equate to what Zazer should have felt from the touch of Death. Zazer's body passively heals away his life-threatening injuries the more they scream and cry. The spell ends, and they all collapse to the ground.

"That spell was weaker than I imagined," Zazer grumbles to himself. "But—I did it. Yes… Yes! A Divine spell! Success!" Zazer starts rising into the air as he continues to express his euphoria. "The winds—they are changing!" He raises his arms high into the air.

Scarlet-colored particles manifest above him, doubling by the second and coalescing together. "Witness the omnipotence of the new demiurge!"

Aluna cranes her neck, even though it hurts to do so. "Oh my gods… Rend!"

"W-What?"

"That spell—he's conjuring up the Finale spell! This world is fucked if he unleashes that in his current state!"

"You know of this spell?" Zazer snarls. "You invaded my home! Why must I be so careless? Then your doom shall be expedited! Begone!" Zazer sends down his incomplete ball of annihilation at their helpless bodies.

Komet constructs a protective dome of light, making it as thick and large as it can get before the spell reaches them. The eruptive impact instantly shatters the barrier. Komet then swoops in to absorb the remaining bulk of the massive discharge, suffering a deep wound that cracks along its body from the reverberating shock of the spell, but everyone else is left unharmed thanks to its shield.

"You stupid animals!" Zazer howls. "Just let me kill you all!"

"Kill yourself!" Maeva counters."

"Foolish Mortal immaturity. Stay like that then! No amount of praying will spare you all from armageddon!" Zazer restarts the spell, focusing all of his magic into it. The size of the spell is exponential. It's like staring into the sun, a supergiant star.

Sadra takes a few potshots at Zazer. "He's still not taking any damage!"

"This is so bad," Rend says. "What can we do!"

Malphunnos throws his sickle. It disintegrates before it even gets close to Zazer. "Dammit, that thing was a birthday present. Welp, I'm out of options."

Klae then arrives to the scene, through his iconic portal spell.

"Oi, where the hell have you been?" Aluna asks.

"Thinking. Practicing. Preparing." He then sighs before saying, "I see Zazer has finally done the impossible."

"More or less," Suvius says.

"Then there's no other choice," Klae says, walking towards Zazer. "Thank you all for giving this foolish child a chance to do something great. It's time to use the Magic of the Arbiters for good for once."

"Klae, what the hell are you talking about?" Maeva asks.

"I have one string of the Master Dimensional Codes memorized by heart in preparation for something like this. I'm sending Zazer somewhere far beyond the known reaches of the accessible realms.

"He'll just negate it."

"Not if I do it point-blank."

"W-Wait!" Aluna says. "This isn't your typical magic! We don't know what's going to happen to you!"

"He's almost done with the Finale spell, there's no time! Forget about me…" Klae says. The space around Klae reverses in gravity, allowing him to soar through the air. He bends the space and light around himself to remain undetectable, until he latches on to Zazer's back.

"Eh—what?" Zazer says as he looks around in confusion. "Who the hell are you? Freaking imp, get off of me!"

"Tell Mixon that he's a horrible teacher," Klae says.

"Get his name out of… your mouth… Klae? Impossible. Is that really you? Y-You shouldn't be doing this! Don't you dare ruin this for me! For Mixon! You should be joining me!"

"Join you? I'm not making two life mistakes in a row."

"Get away from me!"

"…Blindness!" Klae shouts.

"Th-think about what you're doing!" Zazer cries out.

"Eternity!"

"Another minute is all I ask!"

"Gate!"

"S-s-somebody stop him! I'll give you anything you want! Infinite wealth! Infinite power! *Infinite* worlds! I have the means to grant you all godhood! Save me!"

Klae finishes his incantation with one final word. "Exile!"

A giant hole—a black hole, sunders reality apart to manifest. The singularity has enough suction to even affect the others down below as they try to run away from its inescapable pull.

Zazer is deep inside the event horizon, with nowhere to go and no spell that can save him. His body, spell, and words, undergo spaghettification as he is dragged into the infinite void along with Klae. But not before screaming, "Damn youuuu—"

The black hole crunches itself into a tiny blip and vanishes, finally silencing Zazer's existence.

"G-Grandpa!" Sadra cries out.

"He… he saved us," Aluna says.

"No… he saved the world," Draxis says. "We can't let that go to waste."

"Malphunnos," Suvius calls out to him, "can you feel any change across Allosha? Is the pandemic over?"

Malphunnos gives him a troubled look, only shaking his head from side to side.

"There's still this gross tumor thing that we haven't dealt with yet," Rend says.

"I'm still not putting my mouth on that," Maeva chimes in.

Aluna flies over and touches the ragged skin of the heart. Her eyes glow a vibrant lime-green and she clutches her head as she howls out in pain.

"Shit!" Sadra winces while plugging her ears. "Why are you screaming?"

Aluna points at the Heart and stumbles on her words. "Something… s-something wicked is coming!"

That's when the Heart begins to beat again.

Chapter 67

The Mother of All Decay

Aluna rolls around in Jellop's palms, screaming her lungs out. "Make the visions stop! Make them stop!"

"I-I'll see what I can do," Jellops responds as he attempts to settle her mind.

The Heart turns pale as it pumps its body furiously, like it's having the deadliest heart attack imaginable. Its terminal condition rages on until it bursts open, with something both equally elegant and hideous speeding out through the top.

Infected blood and gunk drains off the feminine entity and her two angelic-like wings made out of amalgamated Decay growths. The silver light of the moon illuminates behind the entity as she stares down at them, curiously.

With his mouth agape and losing all his strength, Malphunnos drops his scythe. "No—this isn't real. Narisa…"

"Her?" Rend says. "That *thing* is the Goddess of Life?"

"She's… she's the deity the Arbiters kidnapped," Malphunnos says, still bewildered. "Why… why did it have to be her? I'm going to go talk to her."

Suvius grabs his shoulder. "Are you sure, Malphunnos? She doesn't appear to be the same woman you knew."

"She needs to hear my voice."

"Then… be careful. Please."

Narisa locks eyes with Malphunnos as he approaches her. She descends, keeping her distance. Malphunnos keeps his distance as well. He covers his mouth to muffle a cry as he gets close enough to take a good, long look at her: staring at every scar, gazing at every gash, and glancing at every sore that looks to have been healed and reopened countless times.

"Narisa… what have they done to you?"

She covers her body with her wings and backs away slightly.

"Say something to me," he says, pressuring her further.

She hesitates, eventually responding back to him with non-foreign but cryptic words. "Uoy tn'dluohs evah emoc ereh."

"Narisa, I don't understand what you're saying. What are you trying to tell me?"

"Siht dlrow tsum eid. Neve uoy…" Narisa lowers her wings, revealing her left hand, with her fingers stretched out and curled like a bird's claws. "m'I yrros," she says before dashing at Malphunnos, with wings aflutter, and rams her hand through his chest. He clutches her arm as he staggers and collapses. Narisa pulls her arm out of his chest cavity, staring at the dripping blood on her hand.

"Malphunnos!" the others shout.

Draxis spits out a fireball, forcing Narisa to jump out of the way.

Aluna manipulates the plants to drag Malphunnos away from Narisa. "I got him!"

They circle around Malphunnos to examine the damage around his chest as it pools with purple blood.

"This is bad," Rend says. "If he becomes Decayed, then life as we know will come to an end."

"Have you all forgotten that I'm here?" Maeva says. She crouches next to Malphunnos and grabs one of his arms to bite it.

"Hold still, you worthless god. You're an idiot for even getting near her."

"Narisa… is hurting," he says with a weakened voice. "Her unending rage has corrupted the world, but I know that this isn't what she truly wants."

They all hear a sadistic laugh taunting them in the distance.

"Like I'll believe what a god says," Maeva retorts while standing back up. "Don't you hear her? We should just kill her before she makes things worse."

"I know how you feel, but every death has a consequence," Malphunnos says. "If she goes, then I am nothing without her. This world is nothing without her. Please… save her."

"Save her? After all the innocents she's killed?"

"Your friends did the same thing for you."

"I… that was different."

"It was because you were hurting. She is hurting just like you were. I know you understand what I'm saying…"

"If Narisa is completely corrupted by her own blight," Suvius starts to say, "then do you believe you are capable of curing her, Young Maeva?"

"These fangs have never failed me."

"Understood. Everyone, our mission is to subjugate or distract Narisa long enough for Maeva to inject her Lifeblood. We are beaten down and have very little on our side. Needless to say, try not to die."

"No promises," Aluna refutes as she watches Narisa twitch her way towards them. "Look at that walking disaster."

"She seems terrified of my Soulfire," Draxis says. "I can try to lure her into a trap."

"And I can try to try!" Rend shouts.

"How inspirational…" Sadra groans.

They all turn to face their newest opponent: Narisa, the Goddess of Life. She is giving them the described grin that is undoubtedly the one that terrified Klae.

"Tsk. Gods," Suvius scoffs, wishing he could roll his eyes at her. "Everyone, attack! Free-for-all formation!"

Aluna zips towards Narisa head on. Narisa aims her hands at the ground, bringing the meadow to life. A small jungle of carnivorous plants with thorns for teeth snap at Aluna, forcing her to alter her path constantly.

All of Aluna's wings turn plum purple as she spins through the air like a drill, summoning a small field of tornadoes and solidified blades of sharpened air that follows her warpath through the garden. Narisa directly fights back with a tangled mess of vines, coiling them around Aluna's, who had the foresight to plan for and summon her own wild vines to defend herself and engage in a tug-of-war stalemate.

"I guess I'm stupid for trying to fuck with the mother of veganism," Aluna says, straining. "How about this then!" Her wings flash red and orange as she sends forth a torrent of fire across the length of the vines.

Narisa wails as her plants are scorched alive.

"You almost make me feel sorry for you. Almost." With blue wings, Aluna casts a sigil underneath Narisa and cages her inside a thick block of ice. "I got her—!" she shouts, but she is interrupted as

Narisa breaks out of the spell completely due to the mass production of acidic Decay slime oozing out from her hands and wings.

Narisa rockets upwards and divebombs towards Aluna, making her squeak, "Uh-oh!" and flee for her life.

"Bring her over here!" Rend shouts. "Come closer! Now… go up!"

Aluna does as Rend says and makes a sharp vertical turn. Narisa howls, failing to react in time to avoid a sudden portal made in her flight path.

"No shit. I can really do that? Fuck yeah! I-I did it!" Rend cheers.

"Excellent!" Suvius says. "Bring Narisa to me! Get ready, Maeva!"

"Let me know when!" Rend says.

Suvius holds his right hand up, waiting to make a catch. "I'm ready! Do it!" A portal appears in front of Suvius, with Narisa tumbling out of it. He immediately grabs her by the throat and slams her down headfirst. He then makes the summons for a blade and starts chopping off her left wing.

Narisa beats against his chest and skull as she flails around and screams. "Pots gnitruh em!" With purple slime oozing out of her hands, she grabs the mighty arm that has her pinned down and corrodes it with her touch.

"Suvius!" Maeva shouts. "Your hand!"

"Shut the hell up and get over here!" His arm melts faster than Maeva can run. Suvius is forced to retreat to avoid Narisa's deadly reach for his other vitals.

Now freed, Narisa attempts to escape with her remaining wing.

"Nay!" Jellop says. He targets her and assaults her mind, forcing her to stay grounded. She runs and trips all over the place trying to make sense of the pandemonium.

Aluna dives back in for a second attempt. "Come on, Sadra! Let's do our secret spell!"

"What? You mean the one from Zazer's journal? But we haven't even practiced it!"

"We're about to practice right now!"

"O-Okay!"

"Follow my lead!" Aluna shouts as she alters the colors of her wings, turning their color into one never seen before—a pure brightness of white.

"Aluna!" Sadra says in awe. "You're using Light!"

"Join in!"

"Right!"

Side-by-side, they both aim their hands at an unsuspecting Narisa, and in tandem they both shout, "Come embrace the light, bitch!" Their two great beams of golden and white light merge together into a unified source of trust and power.

"Now this is how you do a L.A.S.E.R!" Aluna shouts. "I am *so* patenting this spell!"

Narisa uses her remaining wing to shield herself. The light isn't just tunneling through her defenses, it's also burrowing through the evils within her.

"Mind if I join in, ladies?" Draxis says, swooping down and soon unleashing everything he has previously devoured into the ultimate rain of fire.

There is an enormous wall of flames made behind Narisa, one that is much too tall to fly over and too thick to jump through. From her perspective, it's like the world itself is on fire. The fire starters are closing in on her.

Jellop begins to lose his strength and lowers to the ground. "Her mind is so chaotic… please hurry!"

Draxis descends like a meteorite and slams his foot down on Narisa. Her head and neck are the only things fully exposed between his claws. "Now, Maeva!" he roars.

Maeva was already on the way. She kneels down and picks up Narisa's bloodied chin while staring into her teary eyes.

"Esoht sgnaf… Yats yawa morf em!" Narisa cries out.

Maeva shows off her moistening fangs and says, "I'm going to make you feel what the entire world has felt—just like I did!"

Narisa cries out in a shrill wail as Maeva sinks every jagged tooth into her trembling neck. The remaining Decayed wing of Narisa's soon disintegrates, along with the purple in her eyes. Draxis removes his foot, letting her free.

"St-stop it!" Narisa screams. "Stop hurting me! STOP HURTING ME! I can't *take* this anymore!"

"Then how about you stop hurting us first?" Malphunnos says, limping along as he clutches his chest and holds his scythe close like a walking stick.

"…Me?" she says.

"Are your eyes damaged? You have to fix this, Narisa! Heal the world!"

She looks at him with disgust. "Why should I?"

"What?"

"I should have never made this world! This world is a mistake! I am a mistake!"

"Then you're calling me a mistake as well," Maphunnos says. "There was a time when you would have never conceived to denounce any lifeform to be a curse or a scourge. I know some of your children have wronged you, but this retaliation is automatically worse than all of history's greatest evils combined.

"Look at what you're doing! Look at what you *have* done already!" Malphunnos points at the others. "Look at them. Even if you don't care about them or anyone else… then take a look at what you did to me. Is this what you want?"

"No… this isn't me," Narisa says. "But look at what mortalkind has done! They used me! They abused me! I give them the Blessing of Life to be used however they please and this is what they do with it? They defy their own mother? To ruin the world in which we have worked so hard to make them happy and thrive in? This is agony! I can't stand to live anymore!"

"…Then would you have me kill you?"

"What? Mal-Malphunnos?"

He seizes the back of Narisa's head and pulls her forward, pressing her neck against the long blade of his scythe as he says, "You have the final say on whether or not existence lives or dies. So tell me how much you hate yourself. If you truly want life as a whole to end by my hand, then tell me right now, and I shall bring upon the era of Oblivion."

"I… I… Malphunnos!"

"It's a yes or a no, Narisa. There is no in-between. If life is a mistake, then which option will you choose to become your solution? Be wise and thorough with your final decision."

She can barely swallow a gulp due to the cold metal threatening her. "I want… to live. I want to live! Don't… don't hurt me! Don't hurt them! I don't want anyone else to become hurt!"

Malphunnos chuckles as he backs away. "You are not as far gone as you think you are if you can still express empathy. Go and walk around for a bit. Get acquainted with the world you destroyed. Stand up. I said—**stand**!"

She listens. Her chest feels heavy as she reaches out towards the sky, sensing something only she can detect. "What is this universal pain? My children… they are screaming. The whole world is screaming. I can't fathom the suffering I have caused them. How could I become so… monstrous. I became chaos. What have I done?"

"Then become order," Malphunnos says.

"But I am *still* soooo angry," Narisa states, running her fingers across her facial scars. "I want them to suffer longer…"

"That would only make *your* suffering longer. I can't allow this type of agony to continue. It will end today, one way or another."

Narisa touches the ground with both hands. She runs a finger through the dirt, searching for an invisible vein that interconnects the biosphere. She winces at the faintness of the thumping. "Have I become so corrupted that I am incapable of showing even a blink of true love anymore? I don't have the strength to make things right."

"Yes you do," Mavea says, picking out the blood stains from between her teeth."

"You… you are the one who cleansed my mind," Narisa says. "A vampire still exists… The last daughter of those violent people."

"We were the violent ones? Sweetheart, that war was nothing but monster-on-monster crimes. I don't like you."

"Yes, I really do have the bloodiest hands. I am unfit to exist."

"I agree," Maeva says, "but I really want to know what you are going to do now. I'm talking about the future, dammit!"

"The future?" Narisa asks.

"Anyone that fucking mattered, good or bad, has been devoured twice by your vengeance. There's nothing else to do but to go up from here."

"But what if this happens again? No, it will happen again!"

"I'm sure there are preventive measures that could be put in place. There are enough people remaining out there who are more than happy to tell you what needs to be fixed. Plus, it's not like *we're* going anywhere," Maeva says, turning to point at the others. "You'll be fine."

"You have a lot to say," Narisa says. "Just who are you?"

"I am the Harbinger of Scourges, the Last of the Vampires, a Godslayer, and an *extremely* tired woman. I am Maevalina Solunna, your savior. Never forget that. Take that last statement seriously; the mind is disgustingly fragile."

"I see," Narisa starts to say. "Then, as you all have tried to do, I will reset this. It's my duty as the Goddess of Life. It is as you said, Maevalina, the real filth of this world has been removed, but at a hefty cost. Hopefully this catastrophe will remind myself and others to never take life for granted and abuse it."

"I am not here for your speech! Just hurry up and heal the world so we can get off this cold-ass rock!"

"You are unpleasant," Narisa grumbles.

"I am also beyond royally pissed right now. There's only one thing you can do to appease me…" Maeva then points at the ground, aiming specifically at a Decayed rose.

With hesitation, Narisa hovers her hands around the rose, using it as a catalyst as she incants a spell, "Heal! Heal, my beautiful children! Heal, my beautiful world!" She leans in near the rose, and whispers to it. "Rebirth…"

Her breath purifies the rose, receding the Decayed growths and purple leakage down into its roots. Her grandiose wish still reverberates far and deep—a blinding tidal wave of purification that erases the Curse of Decay once and for all as far as they can see and feel.

Standing in a now green and lush field of merry flowers, Malphunnos feels across his chest and watches the gaping hole repair itself. "I can feel your hope, Narisa. Thank you."

"You will only receive a partial thanks from me, Goddess…" Suvius says, touching the space where his right arm used to be.

"You're pretty," Sadra says.

"Pretty god-lady!" Jellop says.

"I can't believe I got to see an actual goddess," Rend says.

"We should spar again one day, Narisa," Aluna says.

"I promise you the pain will heal, Narisa," Maeva says while picking up one of Narisa's hands to help her stand. "If you want, we can work on that together."

"It might be too early to try to recall what caused the scars, but… thank you," Narisa says. "You all are much too kind for me. I wish my apologies had any power."

"You and me both."

Draxis's legs give out, forcing him to lay down. "We did it. It's finally over…"

"Hey, why are you laying down like that?" Sadra says, shoving his side to get him to move. "G-Get up!"

"I don't think I can stand anymore…" Draxis says.

"Yes you can!"

"My spirit is standing. Does that count?"

"I don't understand why this is happening! You're stronger than this! We stopped the Decay! So why…!"

"Sadra… there's a reason why I couldn't tell you about my grave condition, to any of you. This goes all the way back to the day I left you alone. It was for your protection. The Decay was already ravaging my mind and body to where manic episodes were frequent. More… lasting. More violent."

"But… but you're here. You're still you."

"I don't even know how much of myself is the real me anymore," Draxis says. "The only reason I'm holding up now is because of my Second Heart, a barrier that I made out of any of the Souls I could salvage from this famine to protect my very own. I'm surprised it lasted this long."

"A second heart?" Sadra turns to look back at the others. "Di-did you all know about this?"

Maeva shakes her head. "He spun me a different story. That jackass told me that my Lifeblood was enough to stop the Decay. Jackass…"

"Consider me fooled as well," Aluna says. "I knew there was something off, I just… didn't think it would be this bad. Shit… I'm so stupid."

"I must have been the only person he was truly honest with," Suvius says. "Typical. He told me that if it ever came down to returning to his original form, it would act as a final desperate measure to slow down the Decay. This was all under borrowed time."

"My soul was already frail," Draxis comments, "but every hiccup I suffered diminished it into a teardrop—and that teardrop was getting closer to the ground. A compromise had to be made. A sacrificial one."

"You… you ate your own soul?" Sadra says.

"As much as I could, yes. My time was already slated, so I exchanged it with the future. I say it was a fair trade."

"Fuck that! Narisa, do something to save him!"

"…I can't."

"To hell with you! This wouldn't be happening if you weren't such a stupid god!"

Narisa's eyes turn violet.

"Narisa, settle down," Malphunnos says. "This world is unable to handle any more of your wrath."

"I'm more angry with myself…"

Malphunnos grabs her shoulder, slightly tugging her. "We should let them be and not take away any more of their time. Harbingers, if you need us, then we'll be close by, looking at the metaphorical sunset. And… Draxis… rest easy. You did good."

"Thank you, Death."

Maeva stomps her way towards Draxis, glaring at him—before softening her demeanor.

"Ah… you look like you have something to say," Draxis says to her.

"…I had a brother.

"So I've heard. Was he as charming as you?"

"He was better than me. You are better than me."

"Nonsense. We are both the best."

"I can't thank you enough for being here," Maeva says. "Why do I have to lose two brothers who mean so much to me? Shit…! I can't handle this!" She runs away, keeping her distance from the group while trembling.

Suvius walks over to Draxis. Draxis chuckles as he skims over Suvius's injuries. "Look at you. Always pushing yourself."

"Sir Draxis… this is my fault."

"Oh stop that. I was dead before you even took notice."

"This world wouldn't be standing if you weren't here. You mean everything to me. I can't—this is breaking me."

"I'm bringing everyone so much grief," Draxis says. "I tried everything in my power to not let this happen. I could have been more selfish and stole some souls from isolated innocents, but that would go against what we are trying to do and what we are trying to become. I wish I could be here longer."

"May you find rest wherever your people have gone. I trust they will welcome you home," Suvius says.

"I don't think they have a choice… Hey! Rend! Get over here! Don't make me say it again! It hurts to yell…" Draxis waits for Rend to arrive, before asking him, "Did you have fun?"

"Fun?"

"You struck me as someone who wants to live life to the fullest. I'm glad Maeva was able to resurrect you to tag along for this journey. You might be a late joiner to our bizarre group of misfits, but you're great."

"You're even more bizarre."

"Can't even make a good comeback, huh? You sound like Sadra," Draxis says.

"…You're leaving a lot of things behind," Rend says.

"Hopefully nothing bad. You know, I'm jealous of you, Archias. I want a second life too."

"Then you'll have to be enslaved to either Maeva or Suvius here."

"Good point. I think I'll take the loss."

"I can't blame you. I'll see you later, Draxis."

"Wouldn't that be nice, though I'd rather you all don't chase after me too soon. Take care of Maeva for me. She's prone to night terrors."

"Really?"

"She holds a lot within her. You make her feel better."

Rend nods. He switches places with Aluna, while taking Suvius with him.

"You should do some spiritual exercises, Aluna," Draxis says. "Your soul tasted foul, worse than even the tainted ones from the Decayed."

She responds by hugging his snout, as tight as she can.

"Now, now. It's alright. I forgive you."

"Why would you ever forgive me?" Aluna says. "I took advantage of you. You should finish the job."

Draxis only sighs at her. "I have never met anyone with a worse vore fetish than you."

"Please don't say that. You're making me sound like a degenerate."

"I know you always mean well. Just… do yourself a favor and make sure that you take control of your fate now that you are truly free."

Jellop arrives to lend Aluna a resting spot. He looks at Draxis next. "I had never thought I would encounter this type of pain, friend Draxis."

"Oh come now, you've been through worse."

"We were supposed to be invincible," Jellop says.

"We still are, that's what legacies are meant for."

"An invincible legacy. I appreciate the share of wisdom."

"I have my moments," Draxis says. "By the way, that fancy Arbiter robe you stole from Zazer's home—it looks nice on you."

"Thank…" Jellop then steps aside to let a distraught Sadra take over, bringing Aluna with him.

Sadra stares at Draxis, blinking periodically. Draxis stares at her, blinking periodically. She moves in closer to hug and cuddle his giant head. Draxis closes his eyes, embracing her perfect touch for as long as he can. He eventually breaks the silence by shouting, "Ah, I almost forgot! I still have a soul left!" His body then morphs and shrinks, shapeshifting into the form of a young boy.

"Don't you want to be in your real form?" Sadra asks.

"Dragons aren't easy to transport—or hug."

"It is your choice. I love you no matter what, Brightheart."

"Maybe I should have stayed in my true form before you said that…"

"Draxis… don't go. Don't leave me again…"

"I hate how often I make you cry," Draxis says, touching her face. "Sadra… forgive me. "

"I will never despise you. You make me so happy."

"I've always tried to. Keep that happiness close, just like your light. There's a whole new bright age approaching, Sadra. A world where people are now free. They will… need… you…"

She waits for Draxis to continue speaking; for his hand to return to her dampening cheek; for his eyes to return to life instead of turning blank. She even calls his name to let him know that she's still listening. That wait is made eternal.

"Umm… Sadra?" Rend says, slowly approaching her.

She looks at him with her eyes drowning in her lucent tears.

"This is… we…"

"What's that you're holding?" she asks.

Rend shows her the colorless and lightless crystal shards between his hands. "We found Komet…"

Sadra reaches out and touches the shards, then she collapses to the ground, near Draxis. Suvius walks over and sits next to her unconscious body.

"S-Sorry!" Rend says. "I didn't know she would react like that!"

"It's to be expected," Suvius responds. "I want to do the same."

"…What should we do now?"

"We are depleted and are in dire need of help. Summon us a portal for Bruness."

"On it…"

Chapter 68

Glimpse

Deep inside New Bruness, Maeva enters an empty chamber and finds Sadra in her Nocturnal form, sitting at a stone table while playing with and pinching the soft skin of a baby. "You're up early, Sadra."

"…I never went to sleep."

"You want me to rock you to bed?"

"That does sound cozy."

Maeva takes a seat next to her and grabs her shoulders, rocking her gently, which moves the baby as well.

"Miss Maeva… if Draxis and I had a child, what do you think it would look like?"

"Either an Isilian with giant-ass dragon wings or a giant-ass dragon made out of light. I think the second option would look more fabulous, but I think your body is much too small to give birth to that kind of creature."

"What is childbirth like?" Sadra asks.

"What's with that question? And how the hell would I know?"

"I don't know… I just want to talk—about anything."

"And that's the first thing that comes to your mind?" Maeva questions. "I didn't know you had such love for children. Was having one… something you wanted to do?"

"I guess it could have been a possibility. Although the world never slowed down enough for us to even consider a time or place or thought—not even enough time to decide upon a cute little name. I like to think we would have shown that child all the love and care that we wished we had received when we were young ones ourselves. It should have happened…"

Sadra starts playing with the baby's arms again, making it giggle. "I know why you're here, Maeva. You don't have to mash your brain to come up with the appropriate thing to say—just tell me. When are we having Draxis's funeral?"

"Expect the summon in a couple of weeks or so. Malphunnos is handling everything, so if you find him then tell him of anything you would like to see or bring to the memorial. He's even generous to allow us to pick the burial spot."

"Okay…"

"Hey, ladies!" Aluna says, swooping into the discussion.

"Hey…" Sadra says, softly.

"My heart goes out to you, Sadra. Do you need anything? Don't hesitate to ask."

"Hearing other people talk and laugh is enough for now."

"So what I just heard is that you want gossip?" Aluna says.

"What—no. Gossip is bad."

"I hear that Enam likes Rend."

"That's not true," Maeva interjects.

"She's with him right now."

"…I'll be right back."

"Is that even true, Aluna?" Sadra asks.

"It is. The Blessing of the Truthseeker never lies. It's super easy to eavesdrop in here when you're small."

"I really shouldn't encourage your naughtiness…"

"But…?" Aluna says, enticing her.

"What else you got? I'm curious."

"Beware the internal depths of New Bruness," Aluna states.

"Oh great, a ghost story…"

"I'm actually serious about this one. Whatever happens down there is not meant for anyone to discover. The dwarves themselves beg for anyone not to go down there."

"What do you think it could be?" Sadra asks.

"A kitchen. There's been a scare going around for years now about a secret society of cannibals. And according to a few, they have already mastered their vile techniques on the abundance of Decayed flesh and mass produced it."

"I don't believe that is true," Sadra says. "Yes, supplies might be scarce, but there are a few spells capable of making foods and drinkables replenishable, and I think they can even work on animal meat too. There's no need to resort to such horrific depravity."

"You might not agree, but your opinion doesn't help feed desperate mouths. There's no trustworthy reason or excuse as to why some of these settlements have had a roaring populace like this one to last so long."

"I haven't seen anyone go missing," Sadra says.

"Not yet," Aluna adds.

"Now I feel like you're just trying to scare me. Got another rumor?"

"Do you remember that sign on the front entrance about knocking in a specific order to gain entry? Apparently, a disgruntled witch in disguise placed an evil Juju spell on it in response to her forced exile after she was found out. So now there is a rare chance you will hear someone knock back whenever anyone knocks on the door first, regardless if they mess up the entry sequence or not.

"If that happens, and the person opens the door anyway, then the entrance will instead lead to someplace that Novair seems strict on never letting anyone find out about. It's why security is so tight around there."

"You make me not want to live here," Sadra says.

"It doesn't hurt to be alert. I don't really think anything truly heinous is happening… but I've been wrong before."

"I want to start snooping around too now. It might take my mind off things."

"We can totally do that together later," Aluna says.

"I would love that."

"I'm back," Maeva says, returning to her original seat.

"Odd, there's no blood on you?" Sadra says.

"Haha…" Maeva says sarcastically. "I'm not a murderer."

"You might want to try that sentence again."

"Goodness… What I mean is that I didn't touch or harm Enam. All I did was offer my concerns."

"Did you intimidate her? That's not any better," Sadra says.

"Whaaat? Reallly? I never would have guessed. Tsk. We'll call this situation an unforeseeable mistake that I will absolutely learn from and never let happen again. Absolutely."

The baby starts to giggle.

"Why do I get the feeling that this baby is evil?" Aluna says.

"Aww, don't listen to them," Sadra says in a cute tone. "You're the best little nugget in the entire world! Aren't you a cutie! Yes you are!"

"Ugh…" Maeva groans.

***

In the deeper caverns of Bruness, Novair finds Suvius at his usual lurking spot. "You really adore dark corners, don't you?"

"I find peace within them," Suvius responds.

"I suppose that is common seeing as the sun remains absent."

"Malphunnos said that it'll remain that way for a long while until the remaining gods can fix our broken world."

"Is that the same dark individual everyone keeps raving about?" Novair asks. "I have a few choice words I would like to say to him."

"He is already aware of what us mortals want to complain about," Suvius says.

"I want to make sure that mine are heard as well." Novair rests his back on the wall, copying Suvius. "So, is the world finally saved?"

"The world is freed, not saved. The existing damages are…"

"…You seem to be trailing your words. I won't make you speak further on it. I'm only thankful that I can now fulfill my hastily made promise to Damea."

"Promises are a good source of motivation," Suvius says.

"Agreed, but don't be like me and make one that at the time seemed impossible. I have a nasty habit of doing that."

"Remind me of what your promise to her was."

"A world tour," Novair says. "We want to see what became of the ruins and see if there are any survivors we can convince to come with us."

"I would advise against that. It's still a cesspool of death and emptiness out there."

"We're going to do it anyway. I need to do it more than anything right now. I'm aware that it is my duty to lead the remnants of the world's populations, but it also comes with warring against the world population's despair—and I'm on the verge of defeat. The issue with my decision is that I do not have an heir to take over my collapsed throne. There is one candidate however…"

"Turn your hopeful eyes away from me," Suvius says.

"Your words put us both at an impasse. I know I am selfish with this, I'm self-aware of it, but if I don't escape this heartache soon then I fear I might become a mad king. Surely you wouldn't want another 'Laxan Vomenn' on your hands."

"You won't persuade me, Novair."

"Can you at least entertain me as to the reason why?"

"Ending an apocalypse does not automatically make me suitable for kingship. Leadership must be a stable position. So much about me and my future is disconnected and aimless, like my sources of strength. These injuries of mine do not inspire a show of power and competence."

"I was wanting to ask what happened to you."

"It's just a recent sacrifice," Suvius responds. "Well worth all the pain, the hardship, the betrayal, the loathing, the despair, the rage, the… I'm slinging my insidious thoughts around. Apologies."

"You sound like me after a savored pint," Novair says. "What an empty world we made for ourselves. What are we to do, my skeletal friend?"

"Kings. Queens. Lords. Bishops. Gods…" Enam lists off as she approaches them. "Why have any of that in the first place? We've been thinking about this for quite some time."

"We, Enam?" Novair asks.

"Damel and Borace, and myself of course. The world has been divided and ravished by the madness and greed of the individual for far too long. The idea is to expand upon Bruness's success of co-existence. We think it would be better to strive for something differ-ent, a government designed to unify everyone under one banner with multiple leaders and advocates acting under one covenant."

"A global nation? Were this the old world, I would have tried you for lunacy and a treasonous threat."

"It was just an idea—"

"*But* I didn't say that it's a bad one," Novair says. "I was merely implying that your unorthodox ideas are what we need for the new age. It couldn't have come sooner."

"I will directly aspire for such an act of cooperation," Suvius says. "As I have seen throughout this journey, power needs to be di-vided or at least have the superior holder limited. I think it's best if we introduce the voices of the common people to this new govern-ment as well. As a former knight, it was suffering to punish the inno-cent for speaking out when all they want is happiness and security. The world's power struggles have made them all weary and distrust-ful.

"I'm really enjoying this discussion," Novair says. "Hell, I say we should break this crown atop my head right now and share it with everyone."

"Ah! I'm happy that you two like our proposal!" Enam says, with a gleaming smile. "I was afraid we were stepping out of line."

"That type of mentality needs to be eradicated," Suvius says.

Novair nods his head in agreement. "The more we talk, the more convinced I am. Very well, I shall stay here in New Bruness until we fully establish the foundation of a council of world powers." Novair then laughs, before saying, "I can't believe I was being so close-minded. I hope you will pardon me for trying to pressure you, Suvius."

"Perish the thought. If things were more bleak, then I would consider the leadership position more. We have good people around us who are capable of making a new world order function. I would recommend starting an accord with the Orcs and their kin first."

"Really? Those brutes?" Novair asks.

"Trust me when I say that they are more level-headed than any kingdom of era's past."

"Then I trust your word on that. Sometime this week I will send forth a group of envoys to hopefully convince them of opening their borders to us."

"I can lead the negotiations if you grant me the honor," Suvius says.

"Consider the action already in motion." Novair then sits down on the ground and says, "My heart feels as light as a feather now. I thank you all so, so much for your patience and foresight. I feel a smile coming on."

"Don't. We've seen enough horror," Enam says.

"Hm-hm…" Suvius chuckles.

"Did you just laugh?" Novair asks.

"Erm, it was just my bones creaking."

***

Malphunnos ascends the stairs that lead to the entrance of New Bruness. He sees Narisa sitting on the ground, with her clothes and hair swaying against the wind. "There you are," he says.

"You found me…" she responds in a fake, surprised tone.

"What are you doing out here?"

"I'm trying to recreate life."

"By picking at your scabs?" Malphunnos asks.

"…I hate looking at my scarred skin—it reminds me of this world."

"Narisa… why don't you come on down with everyone else? Come on."

"I'm up here to limit my contact with people until I can control these… homicidal impulses. How did you know I would be up here anyway?"

"It wasn't hard to find you," Malphunnos says. "All I needed to do was to follow the lingering smell of death and destruction."

"…You've never been this angry with me before."

"I'm doing everything within my divine power to not let my 'anger' escalate any higher."

"I know. It hurts to hear," Narisa says.

"It hurts me too."

"It feels so backwards, I used to be worshiped and adored by just about everyone. Now I'm the most hated person on the planet. It… hurts."

"Now you understand how it feels," Malphunnos says.

"About being a person?"

"N-No, about being—why are you like this?"

She attempts to smile, barely making a curve. "I hate myself so much. I wish I could just erase myself."

"Then I would erase myself too," Malphunnos speaks out. "You know I'm nothing without you, both literally… and everything else that affects my heart. I will be with you until we set the world right again, just as I have since time immemorial."

"Can I help with anything?" a woman's voice says, startling both of them.

Narisa looks back, then scampers over to Malphunnos.

"What's her problem?" Maeva asks.

"You scared her quite a bit when you… you know…" Malphunnos says.

"Neat, a pathetic god fears me. That's what I like to hear."

"Can you not belittle us?"

"Why shouldn't I? You gods love to do it to us."

"You can say whatever you want about me but ease up on Narisa."

"She has the right to speak about our injustice," Narisa says. "We should aim to bridge the meaningless abyss between mortal and immortalkind. No good has come out of upholding Divine Law and no good has come out of mortalkind rebelling against us to have their voices heard. I welcome your help, Maevalina."

"How mature," Maeva says. "Tell me something, Goddess of Life, have you ever heard of Lifeblood?"

"Can't say that I have. Despite the name, it sounds off-putting coming from a vampire. Are you suggesting that blood has a benefit for Creation?"

"More than you might think," Maeva says. "I'm confident that it's superior to the Soulpower that you wield. But first, I need to know how Souls are made in the first place."

"Oh… well, it takes two to make one. New souls are generally created by the splitting of two existing souls that are then exchanged and combined through the act of copulation.

"It's a self-sustaining process, so ironically, my involvement of any kind usually comes after a living body dies. Once a soul is harvested by Malphunnos, we would then judge the purity of it and decide to either let him toss it into realm of Oblivion or have me recycle it back into the world so I can transform the soul into a new creature, or something organic to help restore the ecosystems—like golems and elementals and plants."

"Are you saying that trees and other crap used to be people?" Maeva says.

"Everything's made up of a little bit of everything," Narisa says. "Isn't life beautiful?"

"More like horrifying."

"Yet we all try to extend and pursue it."

"That we do. Is it still possible to create those new souls?"

"I don't think so," Narisa answers. "My Curse may have been lifted but I can sense how frail it has made everyone."

"Perhaps Blood might be the best substitute to birth new souls," Maeva says.

"How so?"

"We'll have to see. You've given me enough information to have my top geniuses ready to test that theory. It's just Rend and Aluna. Those two are eager to make some new revelations happen."

"But blood is so icky and unsightly," Narisa says.

"And delicious," Maeva adds.

"So, we're combining a Monster's dark magic with our divine and sacred arcana? Ludicrous," Malphunnos says.

"We accept this opportunity for harmony," Narisa says to Maeva.

"Don't volunteer me…" Malphunnos groans.

"Some prep work needs to be done first," Maeva says. "One of us will contact you two when we're ready."

"I'm not going to be on standby," Malphunnos says. "To hell with you."

"Then I guess we all die—which means significantly more work for you."

"Let's do it, Malphunnos," Narisa says. "It's not like I can make things worse for the world."

"I don't know… Is it alright if we think about it some more?" Malphunnos asks.

"Sure," Maeva says.

"That's it? …No snarky comeback?"

"Nope. You two already know that I hate you. I don't like being redundant."

"Okay. Go away then."

"Alright."

"…I feel like she wants to eat us," Narisa whispers.

"No, she's not that senseless," Malphunnos says. "Just be careful not to bleed around her though. She's already re-tasted our kin's blood once already."

Narisa cowers behind him even more.

Chapter 69

Aftermath

Malphunnos rushes the others along into an empty cavern by batting his scythe at them, as if he wants his swings to connect with their heads and necks. He looks back to ensure that they weren't followed.

"What's the damage, Mal?" Sadra says. "You brute!"

"Settle down, Sunshine. We all need to have a private conversation."

They all give him a suspicious look—especially Maeva.

Malphunnos targets her stare as he continues. "You brought something to my attention yesterday. I decided to do some similar… assessments over the new fate of our world. And I want to say that while I'm impressed with how smoothly things are going, there are certain matters that need to be addressed."

"What kind of work are you having us do?" Aluna asks.

"Here is an example of the difficulty and expectations of the challenges we will be facing: As we speak, Birthplace is being swallowed up by primordial monsters. I need everyone's help on exterminating the infestation before my home is completely consumed."

"Are those monsters the Godeaters?" Rend asks. "Draxis said that his people worshiped them."

"Hm… I can see why the Dragons would do that—they are both distant relatives with similarities after all. I do hear the disapproval in your tone, Rend, but there's no need to feel guilty about slaughtering these types of 'dragons'. Narisa's curse has already turned a lot of her creations feral beyond curing. Just think of the Godeaters as mere divine rats."

"Divine vermin? I'm not touching that mission," Maeva says.

"You all are not meant to pick and choose these threats like they are skippable," Malphunnos says. "This is serious! I need the help of the world's champions!"

"Icky vermin," Jellop says. "What's next?"

"Wow. Just… wow. If you all want to treat these situations as low-reward quests, then screw it. Other side objectives include fixing my sleep over why the Thrones of Hell are currently unoccupied, leading a crusade into Isilios to restore the sanctuary of all Light back to its former glory, and helping Maevalina with a Soul project proposal."

"They all sound like fun," Aluna says.

"Sure, because that is a natural thing to say…" Malphunnos ridicules.

"I'm not surprised the aftermath of our work has led to even more work," Suvius says. "No matter. We have always performed our best when staying within the world's shadow, so let us enact these secret missions to ensure we start the new age right."

Chapter 70

All Hell Breaks Loose.

Rend, Maeva, and Suvius step out a portal—their feet touching down on the black and red sand that take up the region as far as they can see past the dunes and bleak landscape.

"So… this is the Hagri Scarlands?" Rend says. He then casts a spell over his body, coating himself in a thin, cool mist. "This air fucking burns."

"Does anyone else feel a low rumbling?" Maeva says as she touches the loose ground.

"Tremors?" Suvius questions. "I can't feel them. How bad is it?"

"It's minor, but noticeable."

"Minor or not, there is strange activity happening in what should be an uninhabitable region."

"Actually, there *is* something special and hidden in this region," Rend starts to say. "I remember in Zazer's journal that he mentioned there is a landmark here that leads to Hell. I think it's called the Lesion Bog or something?"

"And he made no indication or map I presume? I swear, why wasn't there an Arbiter of Cartography?" Suvius takes another step forward to look around. His cuirass activates on its own and lashes out at the air with tentacles coming from its opened midsection.

"That's new," Rend says.

"Hmm, I have never seen it react like this before," Suvius says. "It's salivating for something malicious in this direction. We must make haste. Bloodheart Cuirass, summon the Malice of a great warhorse."

A viscous red puddle swallows the sand beside them. An eldritch neigh booms from the puddle's depths, and the summoned beast scrapes its hooves against the edges to worm its way out. Ironclad and sinister stands the horse, huffing out its noxious breath and creating hoofprints that melt the ground as it stomps with one of its front legs.

"Oooh…" Maeva says in awe. "What type of Darkness did you say the demons specialized in again?"

"Malice," Suvius states.

"I might look into it myself after this."

"I'll be more than happy to become your tutor again." Suvius then pets the hellish steed before he reins control over it. "Now get on. We ride!"

***

Forming a blazing trail that lingers across the desert long after they have passed, they race towards a half-sunken temple sticking out of the flooded and soggy lands in the distance.

Suvius's cuirass lashes out more the closer they near. "Urk!" he cries out.

"Damn! Are you having a heart attack?" Rend asks.

"That's what it feels like!"

The earth beneath them quakes, soon splitting away in all eight directions.

Suvius steers the horse away and over the bottomless fissures that deter them. "Faster steed! Go!"

"You should have summoned one with wings!" Rend shouts.

"Do I look like a damn princess to you?"

A scarlet tornado erupts through the roof of the distant temple, fattening and spiraling higher into a cyclone and making the ground tremble even more intensely.

"That smell…" Maeva says as her hunger tingles. "That's blood!"

"That's way too much!" Rend says.

Water splashes on the horse's hooves as it enters and gallops through the nasty bog where the temple resides.

"Rend!" Suvius calls out. "How good did you say were at Cosmology?"

"I'm decent enough at the basics. Don't expect anything spectacular though."

"That's good enough. Make some hoops for us."

"Hoops? Oh, I get what you mean! Gate!"

A portal appears in front of them, teleporting them in the middle of a molten sea at the base of a volcano.

"Why are we back at Bonamu Glaciers?" Maeva says. "Archias!"

"Ahhh! Stop yelling at me! Gate! Reverse!"

"We're back!" Suvius shouts.

"How the hell did Klae make this look so easy?" Rend says. "Let me try again. Gate!"

The splashing of water turns into the clinks and metallic sounds of coins, gems, and other valuables that are trampled over as the horse charges forth and endures the changes in scenery. They have a lot of ground to cover in the underground world of treasure.

"Money!" Rend says with glee, catching the coins that hit him in the face. "Maeva, help me collect some of this!"

"It holds no value. This is all worthless now," she says.

"Really? Ughh! Then what was the point of owning all this shit in the first place?"

"Materialism is a curse."

"Says the person who owns a slave."

"And a shitty one at that. Get us out of here!"

"Hold on," Suvius interrupts. "Can we take a moment to learn more of the riches here? History has value too."

"This slowness is why we shouldn't be protectors of the world…" Maeva groans. "Go on with your research, grandpa."

"It won't be long. I want to see if my guess is correct if this is the lost tomb of Onnic the Collector. I wish there was some way to tell where this hoard is located so I can come back later…"

"Treasure hunters!" an angry voice bellows. "Get out! This is my stash! **Mine**!" A gigantic hand that is covered in dirty rags punches through a mountain of coins. Suvius steers the horse to evade getting smashed. Another gigantic hand punches through at the opposite side of the city-sized cavern and does the same thing. "Thieves!" the voice screams. An even more gigantic head rises up and stares them down with its bulging eyes.

"I didn't know mummies could get so big," Maeva says.

"I'm not interested in history anymore," Suvius says. "Save us, Rend."

"G-Gate! Reverse!"

"Yay… we're back," Maeva says.

"Can I do my spell again?" Rend asks.

"No."

"But he did bring us somewhat closer to the temple," Suvius says. "Do it again."

"Gate!"

The horse's momentum stops abruptly. It still tries to run forward despite remaining in place in an endless black void. The same application of weightlessness affects the others. They all hold on to each other to prevent themselves from floating off.

"Great, now we are literally nowhere!" Maeva screams. "I am *this* close to kicking you both off the horse!"

"Sorry, horse…" Rend says.

The horse neighs in response.

"Gate. Reverse."

The horse neighs again, informing them that they have returned to the bog.

"Oh wait a minute, how about I add some direction?" Rend says. "Uhh, Gate! Forward? Duplicate!"

A series of portals and rifts randomly appear throughout the scenery and paints the entire bog in a scattered jigsaw, with no semblance of comprehension or flow.

"My goodness, Rend…" Maeva sighs.

"Whatever! Either we take one or we don't!"

"Suvius, ask the horse what we should do," Maeva says.

"Show us your wisdom, steed!"

The horse takes the initiative and speeds towards a particular portal that is yellow in color around its rim. They are teleported high above the desired temple the moment they exit it.

"This horse is trying to kill us!" Maeva screams.

"Have faith!" Suvius shouts.

The horse breathes a stream of fire through its nostrils and creates a frontal flame shield. It crashes through the roof and skids across the stone floor once it lands. The whole room is cast in the thick shadow of the blood tornado that rises from a gaping vortex in the center of the floor.

There are four summoners standing at the four corners of the vortex that are doing weird movements with their hands and bodies. Two of them are masculine with curved horns sticking out from their hoods, and another two are feminine with pointed horns.

"Do not disturb our ritual!" one of the summoners with curved horns bellows. "We will prosper! We will prevail! We will—"

An open tear is made through reality, slashed open by the blade of a scythe. Malphunnos comes running out of it. "Thank goodness I found you all! What the fuck is going on here? The whole world is shaking around like a damn child in a haunted castle!"

"We don't know!" Maeva cries out.

"Fools!" the summoner insults. "It is too late! The new, new era begins…! In a few more seconds!"

Red lighting and hellfire spew out from the vortex as it also spits out a humanoid entity. The vortex collapses and repairs the gaping hole made by going back to its original stone brick flooring. Blood rains down on everyone as they stare at the robed figure where the vortex used to be.

"Huh?" the mysterious figure says, perplexed. "How did I get here?"

Suvius steps in closer for a better look. "Jellop?"

"Hi, friends!"

"Who the bloody hell is this?" one of the Pointed horns shouts.

"You're not our Dark Lord! Imposter!" the other Pointed horn shouts.

"Wahh! Danger!" Jellop cries out, folding himself inward and cowering.

"Hold on, everyone. Slow down!" Malphunnos says. "Why are you doing a sacrificial ritual in a time of peace? Are you four the leaders of Hell's factions?"

"We were… before Hell fell," one of the Curved horns says.

"Heh, that was a nice rhyme," a Pointed horn compliments.

"And whose blood is this?" Malphunnos asks.

"Our followers." the second Pointed horn says.

"…How many followers?"

"Quite a bit actually. To the point where even our smartest over there refused to count."

"Why would you sacrifice half of Hell?"

"We wanted our Dark Lord back," the first Pointed horn says. "You see, in a world where Malice, Anti-light, Silence, Despair—"

"Skip the speech," Malphunnos sighs.

"Aww. I was about to say that this new age would be the perfect time for Darkness to reign supreme and rule everlasting once again. Down with the Light!"

"Are we in trouble, mister God of Death?" one of the Curved horns asks.

"Uhh…"

"Mal, what's happening here?" Rend asks.

"Seems like they're zealots. What actually happened to the four faction leaders?" Malphunnos asks the demons. "Be honest before I lose my temper."

"Our parents didn't live to see this day," a Curved horn says.

"Civil wars aren't fun nor productive," a Pointed horn says.

"Then that Soul Decay curse finally breached our magic barriers… which led to an even worse war," the second Curved horn says.

"We thought it would be resourceful to make use of all the body pits along with the veil of darkness that engulfs the world and assemble all that crap into this ritual thing," the second Pointed horn says.

"It's what our parents would have wanted—to uphold the Old Order and all that," the first Curved horn says. "It sucks that we really messed things up. I blame the Eastern faction for everything."

"We kept you heart-eaters alive!" the first Pointed-horn woman shouts.

"Is that meant to be a slur? Say that to my face!"

"By my name," Malphunnos groans. "They're… teenagers."

"Oh gods…" Maeva says, gagging in horror.

"So… should we not worry about demonkind and Hell?" Rend asks.

"Hard to say," Malphunnos says, "On one hand, there seems to be a lack of higher authority amongst the Demons, which could mean more isolated incidents like this one. On the other hand, however… this is a stupid joke."

"Very unsatisfying," Suvius comments.

"At least no one got hurt. Err… none of us were hurt," Rend says.

"You all can go. I'll clean up the mess here," Malphunnos says. "Thank you for your help."

"On to the next challenge then," Suvius says, saddling up on the warhorse. "Come on, Dark Lord!"

"C-Coming!" Jellop shouts.

Chapter 71
Reclamation

Sadra touches the viscous skin of the ever-expanding black bubble that shrouds the deeper jungles of Isilios and listens closely to the weeping and wails from behind its veil.

"Have patience, Sunshine," Malphunnos says. "We're going to liberate them from this corruption soon."

"What are we waiting on?"

"Selvita. She's finishing up the night cycle on the other side of the world."

"Does a night cycle matter when there is no sun?" Sadra asks.

"Well, technically, the Sun isn't gone, there's just no one to equalize and spread its radiance and warmth. She took me up to the cosmos to show me. It's very complicated up there. She's had to separate herself into multiple aspects to even the cycles out. It's why we're stuck in this permanent twilight."

"That must be hard on her," Sadra says.

"She's been getting assistance from some of the other gods."

"Oh? There are more?"

"There's a small hamlet on the Moon apparently," Malphunnos says. "They're doing alright. It's mostly 'lesser' gods, but there are a few notable figures too."

"Anyone that you care about?"

"I saw the Sisters of War. I also met Senturas, one of the surviving Keepers of Time. There was also Chromas, the God of Color."

"Excuse me? A god of color?" Sadra says.

"Someone has to pay attention to the minor things in life."

A pillar of platinum-colored light appears next to them. It recedes, revealing a ghostly being that makes the air twinkle from her silver beauty as she floats towards them. Selvita grabs Sadra's hands, delicately, and gives her a smile that could calm a rampaging beast.

"H-Hi?" Sadra squeaks.

"That's her way of greeting her favorite people," Malphunnos says. "Selvita tends to be silent and reserved… despite how loud she can be in bed."

The silver sprites floating around Selvita spin around her violently as she gestures her middle finger at him.

"I'm just repeating what your husband has told me."

She shows him a second middle finger.

"Oh? You have a husband?" Sadra asks Selvita.

"Wrong type of tense used, Sunshine," Malphunnos says.

"Oops. I got too excited. You seem like a loving person, Selvie. I lost someone very close to me too."

"Did you just give her a nickname? Stop giving us nicknames!"

"Did you say something, Mal? Anyway, how are we going to bring this gargantuan blight down?"

"…The four of us are going to use and combine our dark arts to leech this continental corruption together and then let Selvita properly absorb and dispose of it. That's pretty much it."

"Four of us?" Sadra asks.

"Crap. I'm terrible with surprises…" Malphunnos says.

Selvita nods her head in agreement.

"I didn't ask for feedback. Just… just come on out 'surprise' guest!"

Suvius steps out into view from behind a dead tree. He walks over to Sadra, making sure not to stray too close to her.

"Nightmare?" Sadra gasps.

"There you go calling me that again…"

"It's a reflex. You're too close to my home."

"I know. This is my bad memory as well, which is why I want us to heal it together."

"I don't know what to say."

"It's best not to prematurely show appreciation or a twinge of hope," Suvius says. "We have to see if this evil fortress can even be eradicated."

"Right..."

"Are you still up for this, Sadra?" Malphunnos asks. "I know you hold the Dark element within you, but this blight is not comparable."

Her body turns Nocturnal. "If Miss Maeva can take in the entire world's sickness within her bosom, then I can take in a continent's darkness within *my* bosom. Ehh… that doesn't sound all that appealing out loud. I don't care. I'm thankful to have you all here to help me."

"That's why I call you Sunshine," Malphunnos says. "Everyone, link up! We're going to walk side-by-side and vacuum the night around us once we step through this bubble. I don't know what will become of the people inside, but I'm hoping we can drain the corruption from them too."

Selvita extends her arms out to her sides, with her palms up. Malphunnos and Sadra each grab one of her hands.

An extra hand comes into Sadra's view.

"Are you okay with holding my hand?" Suvius asks her.

"I am. There's only one to choose from anyway."

"So many people have been making snide comments about my missing appendage. I was hoping you were better than that."

"Um… nah!"

Suvius chuckles. He then nods to Selvita. "You may lead us, Goddess of the Moon."

Selvita takes them to the front of the black bubble. Her silver light orbits and showers around everyone else as she takes a deep breath. The others copy her meditation before they enter the blight.

"Urgh! Fuck!" Sadra cries out as she struggles to step inside the Corruption.

"Hold it steady," Suvius says.

"Damn these Nightmares!" Malphunnos growls. "This is not the type of therapy I needed today!"

"I said hold it steady, people!"

"Do not surrender to evil thoughts," Selvita says.

"Never thought I would get to hear you use your tongue again. It's been a while," Malphunnos says to her.

"I don't like to use weapons often."

"You might have to make an exception."

Selvita glances at the others. The way Suvius and Sadra shudder implies that she will have more bodies to de-corrupt soon if they stay any longer. She drops the hands that hold on to her as their lifeline and glides forward without them.

"Selvita!" Sadra shouts. "You're breaking the connection!"

"It's intentional," Selvita responds. "I'll handle this myself— trust me. Follow Malphunnos."

Trusting her persuasive and delicate tone, they abandon the push, and retreat.

"Why'd she tell us to leave?" Sadra asks while panting. "What's she about to do?"

"I tried to make this reclamation a special moment for you," Malphunnos says, "but I for one should have known that it's better to leave things to the professionals. Look up."

Suvius and Sadra crane their necks upwards, all the way up to look at the moon that shines through the crimson color of the cloudless sky like a star. The platinum light that is swallowing up the Moon's face grows brighter as it expands, then it shrinks to a dot. In a blink, the dot twinkles, and it fires—sending its omnipotent power at the entirety of the massive black blight. Suvius pulls Sadra back as they cower away from the sky-piercing beam.

The attack ends—and Selvita, the army of Shades, and the glass and crystalline ruins of the Isilian homeland, are left intact.

"Now that is a score for Team Divinity!" Malphunnos cheers while clapping his hands. "Way to represent us, Selvita!"

"The Shades are still aggressive," Suvius warns. "Tell her to get back!"

"She's not in danger," Sadra says. "She's just waiting on me…" Sadra switches to her Diurnal form and lifts her foot up—and she brings it back down with a mighty stomp that reverberates the shock of the force back into herself. She transforms the pain into a powerful shout. "Sunrise!"

The mass holy exorcism that takes over the Shades is not as painless as Sadra wished for. She winces at their morbid wails, but she smiles at the results. She can finally see their faces. She can feel the return of their light and purity.

Selvita goes around and collects the dark refuse that is separated from the Isilian people by using her silver sprites.

An Isilian woman wobbles as she stands up. "My body…" she whines.

"Who are they?" another person says.

"Hello," Selvita says, greeting them both as she passes by.

Suvius ganders at all the confused entities that glow in a golden light. "I'm surprised they don't recognize me…"

Sadra shakes her head. "You don't look anything like your human self."

"Should I tell them?"

"Suvius, we *just* liberated them. Can you not?"

"My inconsideration knows no bounds apparently. This sight is enough for me. I will leave this place, for good this time."

"…Wait!" Sadra says, running over and hugging him from behind.

"S-Sadra!"

"You have no idea how badly I wanted to see my home shine again…" Sadra says, with lucent tears streaming down and illuminating the backside of his cuirass wherever they fall. "Everyone is still here… I'm so happy!"

Suvius twists around and grabs her to help her stand, and slowly brings her down to the ground while holding her tight.

"…I wish Komet was here," Sadra says, sniffling.

Selvita finds Malphunnos chatting with a few Isilians. "Malphunnos," she calls out to him.

"Yes, hero of the day?"

"How is Narisa doing?"

"About the same as us—trying to make something function out of all the pain," Malphunnos says.

"Is she recovering at least?"

"In her own way. She's stronger than she looks."

"Clearly…"

Chapter 72

Genesis

Inside the spire of the tower at the Arbiter Capital, Rend is at the center console, looking closely at the contents written inside of a scroll.

"How we looking, Archias?" Aluna asks.

"I'm trying to figure out why I'm doing all the hard work."

"If you're planning on becoming an Arbiter then you're going to have to do some heavy mathematics and master your skills on weaving complicated forms of Magic."

"Yeah, yeah," Rend huffs. "Here, check and see if this is correct."

She skims over his work. "Nice! You even remembered to carry the two."

"And why is it so important to carry the two?" Rend asks.

"No reason at all. I just wanted to make you practice something until Narisa gets here."

"You and I are going to have a looong discussion after this if we are going to make our partnership work."

"You better make that crap short. I get bored easily," Aluna says.

A pair of voices are heard shouting from the spiraling staircase below.

"Come on, Narisa! The Arbiters are officially gone now! You have friends here!"

"No! No! I don't want to be here! I'll bite your hand!"

"Ouch, dammit! Stop being feisty! Come onnnn!"

"No! You tricked me! I—wahh!"

Narisa and Malphunnos tumble through the doorway, piling on each other. They awkwardly stare up at Rend and Aluna from the ground.

"Umm. Hey, you two?" Rend says.

"Good morning," Malphunnos responds. "Or afternoon… Or night… Did you bring Maevalina?"

"She's here. She's just using the restroom," Aluna says.

"This place has a washroom?"

"Yeah…?"

"What? How come no one told me?"

"Did you bother to check? Did you go outside like a damn animal?"

"I don't need to explain myself."

Maeva appears through the doorway. "Did they show up yet?" She asks. She then looks down.

"I hope you wiped your hands," Malphunnos says, looking up at her.

"Ugh… Let's just get this done."

Everyone meets up at the center console. Maeva looks away each time Narisa glances at her.

"Come on, you two," Malphunnos says. "Collaborate."

"Your pet is very noisy," Maeva says, which makes Narisa chuckle.

"I don't mean that kind of collaboration! By my name, this week has been utterly unbearable. You two! What do we need to do?"

Aluna volunteers to speak first. "This is going to be a lot, but bear with us. So… using the information Maeva told us, along with everything we can physically compile from the Arbiters' research, this entire experiment is going to be what Rend and I call: Fusion. We will only be fusing the *known* Supernatural elements of Life—Maeva and her Blood magic, and Narisa and her Soulpower.

"To create a new, functional soul, our theory is to have Blood act as the body and vessel to hold any Soul essences we fuse with it, which should then bring that blood formation to life. Now, because there are too many variables and mutations at play here, more than likely the original soul we test on will completely lose its old personality and other qualities."

"If this works, then there is a strong chance that a new generation of souls can be made," Rend says. "But… that's the only positive."

"What do you mean?" Narisa asks.

"There can only *be* a new generation. For four years, we, the old generation, have been suffering from soul deterioration because of your curse. As it stands, the leftover atrophy severely hinders the reproduction process between two souls. In other words, every attempted pregnancy automatically results in stillbirths or miscarriages due to the incomplete component of Life."

"The world is on a time limit," Aluna says. "While that time limit does differ between everyone, it will all lead to the same result. This project *has* to work."

"Then, how was that one child born?" Maeva asks. "Is it a rare exception?"

"With Sadra's permission, we… experimented on that child we saved."

Maeva shakes her head and says, "Typical Arbiters."

"That… stings," Rend says, with a brooding expression.

"We didn't hurt it," Aluna defends. "We just drew a little blood from it."

"They don't care," Rend states.

"Fuck. Well… regardless, we reverse-engineered some things with its blood and we discovered that the child is a prototype of the new generation of Souls. It has a fully matured Blood-Soul that functions just as well as any soul did before the Decay. Essentially what Crysis and Sylis were working on was their own method for immortality. Reincarnation."

"Reincarnation?" Narisa asks.

"That's what they called it," Aluna says. "There was a major divergence sometime during the Transmortality Project that led to two opposing sides. While Zazer and the other Elites mutated themselves with the blood of the Gods to attain ascension—which they called Vampirism. The Apostate brothers, however, sought to manually die and transplant their souls to start anew in a fresh, modified body and take over from there. It is unknown the extent of progress the Brothers made, let alone if there were other Arbiters who sided with them."

"So that's why Crysis said to me that we were going to have to succeed them and finish what they started," Maeva says. "Those bastards…"

"We have the two supreme masters of Blood and Soulpower with us right now," Rend says. "We can make this work!"

Maeva looks at Narisa. They both nod at each other.

"Alright," Aluna says. "Maeva, please create a coagulated orb of blood. That will be the 'vessel' we will use."

"Does the size matter?"

"I want to say that the Vessel will turn into a floating wisp anyway just like normal souls do, but just in case, make it edible-sized if you can."

"Also, it shouldn't matter whose blood you use since most of it will be unwritten anyway," Rend adds.

"And what of the side effects?" Narisa asks.

"A complete mystery, but we don't have much of a choice," Rend says. "At that point, I think it will mostly be the challenge of the designer's choice since you're the one who creates life out of souls in the first place."

"This seems so extreme…"

"You can do it, Narisa," Malphunnos says. "I'm here with you."

"Yeah, don't be nervous," Maeva joins in. "I want this as badly as you do."

"Y-Yes."

Maeva activates Samsara and lets the stored blood within pour out. She controls the flow with her other hand and winds the liquid down into a ball the size of an apple. "Your turn, Narisa."

"Darn. I think we came unprepared. We don't have a—"

"Hold on!" Malphunnos interrupts, running out onto the balcony. He comes back a few seconds later with a soul between his hands that's slightly smaller than Maeva's creation.

"Suvius isn't going to be happy that you're sacrificing a soul he freed," Aluna says.

"Well if you two can do horrible things to a child then I can do my own thing as well."

"We just took some of its blood!"

Malphunnos rolls his eyes at Aluna and offers the soul to Narisa. "Here you are."

Narisa controls the soul with her hands, placing it in front of Maeva's blood rock. "Now what?" she asks.

"Smash that shit together!" Aluna says with glee.

"Say that differently!" Rend nags.

"No. Smash!"

"Ready? I guess?" Maeva asks Narisa.

"Are we counting down?"

"No, I'm kinda lazy. Zero!" Maeva rams the Blood Vessel into the awaiting Soul, making a flurry of red and bluish-white sparks discharge from the collision. Narisa copies Maeva after the initial shock from the sudden start."

"Just like that!" Aluna shouts.

"Why is it rejecting it?" Maeva grunts.

"It's like a wall!" Narisa says. "It's conflicting because of my Light and your Dark! Push harder! You're almost there!"

"We're not giving birth! Stop making it weird!"

"Harder!"

"Mal!" Rend shouts. "Help Narisa stand still! I'll do the same with Maeva!"

"Come on, ladies!" Malphunnos says. "A sea hag can give birth better than the both of you!"

"You're not helping!" Maeva screams.

Through enough force, the Soul pierces and slips through the womb of the Vessel. The Vessel then transforms into a misty and gaseous state as it accepts the transplant.

Narisa trembles as she touches the ruby-colored orb that floats closer to her out of curiosity. "Look at how healthy it is. I can hear its breath, its humming. It seeks to be given life. It seeks to create life. This is so beautiful!"

"Damn," Maeva blurts, "Does this mean that I have to follow you around each time you want to create a soul? Welp, there goes the rest of my life. Shit…"

"Come on, Master. Be happy," Rend says.

"I am happy. I can be annoyed too though."

"You don't look as impressed, Aluna," Malphunnos says.

"I'm more focused on the other half of our problem. The future is promising, which is great—but this doesn't help the old generation. We could try to replace everyone's souls with the new Blood ones maybe, but then they would lose their original individuality. We've already lost so much knowledge and beauty in our world already. I'm not comfortable with losing myself—not after I have fought for so long to stay alive."

"Then we've failed," Narisa says. "No, I've failed. I'm not letting any of you die!"

"But you've already killed us all. The only thing we can do is pray."

Rend gazes upon the floating Blood-Soul. He sees his reflection in it, a glimpse of his own bluish, undead skin and his pensive expression. "Malphunnos, I have a suggestion."

"I don't think my dark services can do much, but I'm listening," he responds.

"I think it might. How about Necromancy?"

"That's a… stupid but curious option. All Necromancy does though is steal souls from my clutches and return them back into the original body, regardless of the state of decay of said body."

"Where do you put souls that aren't stolen?" Rend asks.

"If I don't hand them off to Narisa, then I throw them into Oblivion. Nothing can survive that abyssal realm, but things can still linger before their deprecation."

"I think I accidentally went inside that realm not too long ago—it's a long story. But that word you said. 'Linger'. That's what I was looking for. None of us wants to die or be replaced, there's too much left to do and not enough time. So what if we pause our lives? Or suspend it? We take a small portion of our souls and put that piece into Oblivion while the majority half stays here in the Mortal Realm. Would that cause a disruption in the life-death process?"

"That's… cheating," Malphunnos says. "You're encouraging that the whole world cheats me, and Narisa."

"It's no different than cheating with Necromancy."

"This will be completely different to Necromancy," Malphunnos corrects. "This might potentially put people in a stage between life and death instead of reversing their deaths outright. This is beyond my understanding."

"I need to know if you're willing to do this," Rend says.

"Are you volunteering?"

"I am."

"No!" Maeva interjects. "I forbid you!"

"Please, Maeva," Rend says. "This might be a chance. I'm already used to being resurrected."

"If I lose you…"

"I have the largest soul out of anyone here, I'm the most capable. I want to go."

Maeva grabs his shirt and looks into his eyes.

"You're pretty close to my face…" he says, staring right back at her.

"Forget it," she says, shoving him backwards. "I'm not giving you the satisfaction."

"That's fine. It only means that you're confident I won't die."

Maeva raises a clenched fist as she stammers. "You…You… Come here." She yanks him closer and gives him a half-baked kiss.

Aluna's wings flutter as she watches the sight. Narisa only blushes with her hand over her mouth. Malphunnos gives a single nod of approval.

Rend feels his lips after Maeva pushes him back again. "Neat! I can die happy now."

"Please do," Maeva remarks.

"Alright, Mal. End me."

"Hm. Reaping. It feels different this time than all the others. Hold still…" Malphunnos snaps his fingers, severing Rend's soul from his body. Malphunnos then aims his scythe, and with a perfect swing, Rend's soul is bisected.

"What have I told you about being rough with souls!" Narisa says. "Be careful with him!"

"Make yourself useful and help me control it."

Malphunnos slices open a rift to the void of nothingness that is Oblivion. Not a sound or sign of life is made from the realm within. They both deliver one half of Rend's soul inside it. Malphunnos then snaps his fingers again, rejoining Rend with the remaining half of his soul.

Rend twitches as he rises up. He takes a huge gasp of air, and after recovering, he says, "That felt fast. Di-did it work?"

"I mean, you're moving," Malphunnos says.

"Yeah… I am. Is this considered to be my third life? Neat! That's so freaking—" Rend stops talking and holds his hands over his stomach. With a mouthful, he vomits out black sludge that disgusts everyone else and forces them to back away.

"Are you dying?" Maeva cries out. "Stop dying!"

"My stomach hurts…"

"Well, it's like he's alive. I can sense that much," Narisa says.

"But he's also not really setting off of my senses either," Malphunnos says. "Does this make him Un-undead or something? Why can't my job be simple for once…"

"Am I immortal now?" Rend asks.

"Hahaha!"

"It was a genuine question!"

"Hilarious. Your soul is still mine whenever I want it, just like everyone else's. I don't think we can realistically pause your natural lifespan, but this treatment seems to have extended things to an acceptable degree. I hope we can replicate that."

"You're better at my job than I am," Narisa says to Malphunnos.

"Likewise…" he responds.

"What do we do with this Blood-Soul?" Maeva asks. "Do you want it, Narisa?"

"Me?"

"Mm-hmm. I trust you enough."

"O-Oh, well… I'll do my best? I'll think of something I can do with this."

"Would you mind telling me the results if you do?" Aluna says. "Having more data would help me figure out how to make the Fusion process more streamlined."

"I will."

"Thanks in advance. Also, Rend, did you write any of this down?"

"Was I supposed to?"

"…You are the worst partner ever."

Chapter 73

United We Stand

Under the mild tapping of a steady drizzle, Suvius, Aluna, and Jellop stand on the stairs of the Orkanian capitol building, welcoming the various and diverse guests that pass by. Only a few more are left.

"I feel like having us act as security is a bit too much," Aluna says.

"I agree," Jellop says. "If fear is present, then peace is not."

"I understand both of your concerns," Suvius says. "I too would prefer to doubt these visitors, but an event this delicate needs to have every contingency covered. You both are chosen because you two are the best at concealing your powers and not provoking any potential threats."

"And what about you?" Aluna says. "Do you feel that you are capable of making the world indivisible?"

"Not at all. However, I have learned that the sharpness of the tongue is a skill that I need to hone more into."

A cyclops starts walking up the stairs towards them, saying, "I don't suppose I had any influence with that revelation?"

"Night-Drinker!" Aluna shouts.

"Yaga, Aluna. And a similar greeting to you as well, Suvius and Jaundice."

"It's Jellop…"

"A small hint of insight for you, Suvius," Night-Drinker starts to say. "Minister Shiela has already voted to become an ally for your cause—but she will test your mettle anyway."

"I fully expect to be put under the executioner's blade today. All one hundred of them."

"Is that the estimate of people attending this assembly?"

"It's a full exaggeration. But if there are enough people here willing to spread the word then this movement will be declared to be a massive success," Suvius says.

"A robust Yaga to that. May I stay here to help 'keep the peace'?"

"You know this city better than us. With that said, I must depart."

"Good luck, Lord Suvius!" Aluna shouts.

"Remind the world that survival isn't just based on luck!" Jellop shouts.

The gaping mouths of the decoration totems ignite once Suvius enters the capitol building, showing him where to go to seek his destiny just like once before. In front of Suvius at the long trail's end to the center of the building is the gateway to the future, calling him to open it and step through. He grips the handles and swings the doors open. Shiela stands in his way, to his surprise.

"Oh, you startled me," she says. "It is good that you have made it, I was just about to come find you. This is your first time being in this debate chamber. The center of the ringed arena behind me is where you will take your place to let your voice be heard."

"How uncomfortable," he responds.

"Hoho!" she laughs. "You will not find any mercy here, but this should not be an issue for one of our finest." She leaves him to return to a seat that Ministers Slain and Oppum stand next to.

Suvius recognizes a few faces that sit around the enormous ringed table. There is Sadra, Damea, Selvita, Malphunnos, and of course, Shiela. In spirit, they are with him—but in reality, he is alone. Outnumbered in an unsettling and strict environment. Thankfully he has no sweat to produce, no breath to hold in, no body parts that can tremble, but he does have a heart that beats—and it's not stopping anytime soon.

He opens the small gate that leads to the inner space of the debate circle. So many eyes are staring at him. They are all colorful. Emotional. Judgmental. He puts those impatient stares to rest.

"I believe the best way to ease into this rushed and crude assembly of fragmented minds and make it feel more organic is to introduce with a proper expression of thanks. I, Suvius Falacoster, an undead delegate of the human race, offer my sincerest thanks to everyone who is present here, and to those who would be here if the world had more of its stingy mercy to give.

"As you can see, many of these seats are vacant, which makes morale feel incomplete. Imagine if the Elven races, the Meridians, the Demons, the Dragons, and more were here to improve that morale. It truly is heartbreaking. The world has shrunken greatly… but our hope will not.

"Even now, there are numerous search parties en route to any accessible part of the world to look for hidden settlements or isolated parties and individuals. I have been on a few of them myself. That Half-giant that you see over there…"

The half-giant raises his hand, letting everyone know he is the subject of the topic.

"His name is Bregor," Suvius continues. "He, along with his wife and parents, have emigrated to this city after being recovered by one of those search parties. There are many other success stories like Bregor's.

"I say this not to brag, but to inspire. The act of unity and cooperation is considered taboo by most, but that old history no longer matters… only the future does. We cannot aspire for such a future if there are any ongoing pains and distrust. I will not pressure any of you to make pledges to waste or share your precious resources, your people, or any other valuables to unknown strangers.

"I will however make a suggestion to think about it. No one is better or happier than the other in this after stage of the apocalypse. We have all lost something, and I know we all want some of that back."

Suvius pauses to look around before he continues on. "I think I have said all that I could for an introduction. Does anyone have any questions? Or any pleas for help? All comments or criticisms will be accepted. Please feel encouraged to make any."

A tiny, winged woman, who hovers above an unused chair, raises her hand and speaks as loudly as she can muster. "I am Ting-Ting, a chosen representative for the Pixies! When the Decay receded back to wherever it came from, it left some of our previously infected weak. We do not have enough hands to nurse them and distribute our supplies. I want to ask for help!"

"Then you have found it," Suvius responds. "Once again, I cannot speak for everyone here, but the human communities are willing to provide aid to anyone that needs it. We have enough supplies to spare, and even more kingdom ruins to disassemble and salvage to provide even more."

"You have my appreciation!"

"Typical," a man made of frost and ice scoffs. "It's always typical how Humanity always have enough resources to overstuff themselves."

"I hear your complaint," Suvius says. "You are free to make even more that are similar to it but do know that you are entitled to our share. I want to make it clear that what I just said is meant for all of you. If you want reconstruction, then practice the art of sharing. Use one hand to feed yourself and use the other hand to feed another. Tragically however…" he starts to say as he raises up what remains of his right arm. "That has not been so easy for me to do as of late."

A few people around the room laugh.

"So, any more questions? Statements?"

Malphunnos raises his hand. "Oi! Tag me in!"

"Go for it."

"Everyone! Yes, I'm over here! Do I look out of place? Well, I should, for I am Malphunnos—the God of Death!"

Whispers of the skeptics start to pollute the room with a constant buzz.

"I… I can't hear any of you, but I already know the type of common upsets you all are saying. I've been hearing them for… I guess my entire life. The Gods do exist. I am here, along with a few others that are watching us from above and below. We are doing everything in our failing powers to restore what was lost. We are even going as far as sharing our ancient secrets and Divine magic to tighten the gap between us and all of mortalkind.

"This is our oath, our new Divine Law. Keep in mind that it does not mean that all future prayers will be guaranteed to be answered. I'm not sure if we ever had that type of unlimited power before, but we sure as hell don't have that capability now.

"Regardless, this world is not godless. It *is* imperfect because of us, but not godless. Despite being a god, you all should put more of your faith and trust in the Speaker who preaches to you today. There's a reason he is standing there instead of I." Malphunnos then gives a slight nod towards Suvius.

The chatter erupts again. Louder, but with less venom and scrutiny. They all stop when Shiela raises her hand.

"Let this elder speak. I am Prime Minister Shiela, the chief leader of this city and a beloved mother who has made coexistence possible between so many clashing clans and warlords. My people, conjoined in blood and honor, are now known as one: the Orkanians.

"I volunteer my people as an example to strengthen this righteous cause for unity. The Orkanians have survived because we understand each other. No matter who you are, suffering feels the same. No matter where you are from, we all need a place to call home. No matter what you are, we all bleed the same.

"The apocalypse has challenged the Orkanians to honor those truths. Our culture has not been tainted by the great merging of diverse societies—it has only expanded; ideas and generations made enlightened and eternal. I implore you all to not fear those who have wielded a blade against you in the past—a smart person wouldn't do it twice. As we have done before, the Orkanians will continue to welcome those who are open to accepting the truths we have discovered. My argument is finished.”

Sadra raises her hand next.

“You may speak,” Suvius says.

She lowers her hand as everyone looks at her, shrinking down in her chair. At Sadra's side, Selvita whispers to her, “Don't be nervous.”

Sadra straightens herself. “I-I am Sadra Blessity!”

“I didn't say to shout either…” Selvita groans.

“Just let me speak! What was I saying? I-I am an Isilian! I used to be one of the last Light elementals. My people's history ended years ago when my home was decimated from a violent and unjust invasion that submerged most of Isilios and my people in a state of perpetual darkness and despair. Recently, with the help of Suvius and the gods, my home has been cleansed and is experiencing a steady recovery. I wanted to bring some of them here to solidify my claims but… they are not quite ready yet for social contact.

“Can you imagine being stuck in your own mental state of insanity and then waking up to a world that is significantly more destroyed than when you left it? They are now freed from their torment. They are also thankful that the world is somewhat restored, and they are even more thankful that the world hasn't forgotten about them. They want to return that favor one day. We all could use a miracle like that.”

“Are there any more questions or statements?” Suvius asks everyone.

No responses are given despite the ample time allowed to do so.

"Then I suppose this will act as the conclusion. There are no future dates planned for another conference. If, however, there are enough votes, then we shall schedule another meeting. I can—"

The abrasive man wreathed in ice raises his hand, interrupting Suvius and asking him, "What did you say your name was?"

"It… It's Suvius Falacoster."

"That name. Where have I heard that particular name…?"

"Depends on who or where you've heard it from."

"Oh I've heard many things about your name the more I think about it. A powerful name that has many horrors and myths attached to or surrounding it. Specifically, ones about a skeletal boogeyman who would steal the souls of anyone who crossed the deadly paths of him and his loyal dark servants. Suvius… are you a Harbinger?"

"…I am."

"I'm a Harbinger too!" Sadra yells as she stands up.

"As well as I!" Malphunnos says, copying her. "Take a moment to disregard the negative stigma surrounding us. The world was healed through our efforts."

"I was here for a small slice of the Harbingers' journey to restore our world," Shiela interjects. "Now that it is brought up, I would like to ask you all about what became of the help I have offered?"

"Your help has been bountiful," Suvius states.

"If only we knew what we were getting ourselves into after we left…" Sadra adds.

"There are a lot of details," Malphunnos says. "To put some concerns at ease, just know that the Arbiters are responsible for the kraken's share of this apocalypse. They have overstepped well past the point of evil to fulfill their atrocities and sins against nature and Life until it escalated to the point where they dared and succeeded in abducting a goddess, which caused the horrible and adverse effects you all see today. The Arbiters are all dead from their madness. I just wish it didn't bleed onto the rest of us."

"That's horrible!" Ting-Ting cries out.

"Oh trust me, we've seen the worst of it all. We're still resolving the aftermath of their lunacy. These last few weeks have been full of such endeavors."

"I wish to add some additional commentary—about the Harbingers," Suvius says. "I intend to tell no lies today or any other day. We have not been the best warriors in the past when it came to stopping the oppression from the Arbiters and the kingdoms and races that cooperated with them. We have our own terrible sins that prospected this apocalypse, but that doesn't mean that we are going to let the world suffer because of us and them. We don't want anyone to make the same mistakes as we have."

"You seem less cold-hearted than I imagined," the Ice elemental says.

"Is that meant to be some Elemental pun?" Suvius says.

"People like my jokes enough."

"I don't."

"Ha! I'm really attached to your honesty. Tell you what, before I consult with the other Ice elementals about this alliance, I would like to personally see this long list of evils the Arbiters have committed."

"I want to join in on that," Bregor says.

"I too as well!" Damea says. "Can we add a few world locations to that as well? I want to know what became of the Dwarven Nosha Empire. Novair and I sent a party out years ago to hopefully gain a strong ally, but the exploration proved to be too treacherous. I still worry about them."

"Very well," Suvius says. "We can add in a few expeditions if everyone is interested—there will be security added as well. Are there any final questions or comments…? No? Then—this assembly is adjourned. I will visit each of you in the coming weeks to gather your votes and show you our terrible discoveries. Speak to the undead boy near the entrance for a personalized transport back home."

"I'm not a boy!" Rend shouts.

As everyone talks amongst each other and leaves through either nexus portal or the main exit, Suvius's allies slide across the ringed table and rush over to speak with him.

"That was intense," Sadra says, equalizing her breathing while holding a hand over her chest. Selvita nods at her statement.

"I'm usually the one who does the judging, not *be* judged," Malphunnos says. "You mortals are ruthless. I love that!"

"Do I even need to say how thankful I am for you all?" Suvius asks.

"Spare us. My ears are too heavy from all the exchanged words today," Malphunnos says.

"I do not envy you. You all can be dismissed. I need to stay behind and consult with Shiela since she might become our first member of this council. I also need to check up on our security…"

***

"Minister Suvius has returned," Night-Drinker says, grabbing Aluna's and Jellop's attention.

"How have things been out here?" Suvius asks.

"Gentle as a breeze!" Aluna says.

"Wonderful."

"Lord Suvius, I do not know if you know, but you brought a stranger with you," Jellop warns.

Suvius turns around, then up, and left and right, then he turns around again—still not finding the supposed meddler.

Ting-Ting pops up from Suvius's right eye socket. "Hiya!"

"Gah! How did you get inside me?" Suvius says in a panic. "Get out of there!"

"I was doing some sleuthing," she says. "My verdict is that you're legit."

"I also feel violated."

"So sorry."

"Who the hell is this?" Aluna asks.

Ting-Ting flies out of Suvius and circles around and around Aluna while saying, "Oh my goodness… a fairy?"

"That's me…"

"Are there more of you?" Ting-Ting asks. "We couldn't find any of you when we checked the inner parts of the Mystic Groves. We thought you were all wiped out."

"I wouldn't know anything about that," Aluna says. "I have no connections with my people."

"Were you banished? I hear that's a thing with fairies."

"It would make things easier to explain if I was."

"If you need a temporary home, you can stay with us."

"I already have one," Aluna states.

"You seem standoffish," Ting-Ting says. "Sorry for the rude observation."

"It's not because of you if that's what you're worried about. There's just more to me than some useless feud I'm not even involved in."

"Definitely! It's good to know that I'm not the only one who feels that way. I wish everything would go back to the way it was. Well, way before the Arbiters made their impact I mean."

"…I'm sorry," Aluna says.

"What for?"

"Nothing. What's your name?"

"Ting-Ting."

"I'm Aluna. You're surprisingly patient with me. I guess what I'm trying to say—or rather ask—is if you would like to talk some more?"

"That sounds great!"

"Let's fly around the area to get out of this rain. Bye, everyone!"

Suvius notices that Jellop isn't waving goodbye alongside him and Night-Drinker. "I'm surprised you didn't exercise your manners, Jellop. Does her disappearance upset you?"

"…I am happy she can make new friends."

"I can tell when you're jealous. How about the three of us go cause some ruckus too? We might see them while we're passing by."

The condescending voice within Jellop awakens. *"Did someone say ruckus? Make this party a four-way! I want in!"*

"Grr…" Jellop growls.

Chapter 74

Redemption

"Hey! I know you're not dead!" the Condescending Voice says. *"Get up! We've been abducted!"*

"Why does this keep happening to me?" Jellop groans. "I was walking with Suvius and Night-Drinker, and then…"

"Take it easy—I know it's all tiresome. It's not your fault…"

Jellop stands up from the cracked street he woke up on, finding that he's been dropped at the middle of a crossroad. As far as he can tell, it seems like this intersection isn't the only one around as there are similar ones down the road behind him that branch off into even more streets and turns.

Whatever those roads lead towards is unfortunately blocked from view by derelict ruins of houses, temples, and manors that are of no mortal or earthly design. Even farther down the main street behind Jellop is a faraway city-like paradise that barely retains some of its luminosity.

Above the grim ambience and surrounding false grandeur is a hellish red sky that is cloudy with pale and abhorrent winged abominations. He needs to escape before the prowling monsters know of his vulnerable presence. The closest safe spot that is readily available are the houses at the cul-de-sac ahead of him.

Jellop runs to the unkempt mansion at the furthest point of the dead-end, lured in by the dim light that comes from the sculpted, marble-like material of the building that glows pure white as if irradiated.

"Hello?" Jellop says meekly as he peers inside the building.

"Over here!" a woman's voice calls out to him.

"God-lady?"

"Welcome to my home, Jellop," Narisa says. "Join me."

He takes caution as he steps inside. The satisfying plushiness of the carpet that takes up the flooring is inviting to step on, until he realizes that it's layers of dead grass—dead and decaying just like the other flora that decorates the walls.

He joins Narisa at the centerpiece of the room—a girthy tree with branches and roots that upholds a part of the building's structure. Both of them watch the falling leaves of the mystic tree pile up more and more on the ground.

"I'm surprised you're not making up a lecture or some platitude about the state of my home," Narisa says to him.

"…Some things don't need to be said," Jellop responds.

"I suppose not. But some things do need to be addressed no matter what."

"Like what?"

"Retribution," she says. "Selvita, take off his hood."

Jellop's hood is snatched down in an instant from a pair of hands that reach from behind him. "Wah! No!" he cries as he tries to cover up his face.

"Look at me, Jellop!" Narisa says. He lowers his hands after she says it again, more politely. "Darn… your face doesn't tell us anything. What about *our* faces? Don't you recognize us?"

"She has no right to ambush you like this just to get to me," the Condescending Voice says. *"Hey, let me take over completely. You don't need to get involved with this."*

"…I trust you," Jellop murmurs.

Almost without pause, Jellop's whole demeanor changes, voice and all. "Yes! For once I get to have a voice! Hear me, world!"

"Stop shouting! I heard you after the first hurrah!" Narisa says, plugging her ears. "What are you screaming about anyway? Who was I talking to before?"

"My brother. But now you answer to me! Chaos! The one you want to prove guilty! Anyway, what was your first question? Do I recognize you? My brother does not *obviously*, and barely can I. The Narisa I knew had flawless skin, a touch that could bring dead men back to life in more ways than one, and a type of patience that could outlast the Keepers of Time themselves. You've seen better days."

"I don't remember those days, Chaos."

"Well, there's definitely not going to be any more for a long while. Why is *he* not here with you?"

"Because he would kill you," Narisa answers.

"But why aren't you two? I know you two love to hold grudges. Here I am! You found me!"

"Because you always make yourself nigh impossible to strike down. Why are you hiding in your brother's body?"

"How do you know it isn't the opposite?" Chaos deflects. "I can't tell my ass from my head in this duplicate body of ours. Or is the correct thing to say is that we're conjoined? Melded together? Whatever, I'm not trying to give myself a double headache today."

"Stop being difficult with us," Narisa hisses.

"I'm being defensive. You forced me out of hiding, what did you expect?"

"We want to know what you are planning."

"I'm planning on getting some sleep after this. Can't a man change? Is he never allowed to once he has sinned in the beholder's eyes?"

"You will never change," Narisa says.

"So you can change for the worst, but I'm not allowed to change for the better?" Chaos questions. "How long should I remain hated? I just thought that I might as well try something zany since everyone else is doing my timeless work for me. There will always be chaos in this world—and it sure as shit does not matter who causes it, only that it *will* happen.

"I will say however that you disappoint me, Lady of Omnibenevolence. If anyone was going to 'teach me the errors of my viewpoints', then there should have been no doubt it was going to be you. Your falsehood actually disgusts me."

"You have no idea the pain I went through."

"Don't even contest with me about pain," Chaos says. "Last I remember, I was banished into a lifeless realm by my entire family. I stayed in that realm for *so* long that the reality there started to devolve and become an infinite reflection of my mental state. Then one day I suddenly woke up in the middle of a war in the middle of an apocalypse with no body or soul to call my own and scream out of. And now I'm being held here at spellpoint like I'm a wanted man of every state. I know what madness is like—yours is not special. And what of you, Selvita? You're not too far off from a dark descent like Narisa over here."

Selvita pinches his arm.

"Ow. I really don't know what you harlots want me to say. I haven't even done anything, and I'm still being treated like I'm some mastermind above masterminds. I'm literally a hero! I helped my brother dispel your ugly curse. I also created the Vampires, that you all *slaughtered* without remorse I might add, and the last one in existence brought your sorry ass back into the Light. I demand praise! Where are my riches? My bedrooms full of women? My golden throne for such flawless valor!"

"Knock-knock!" Malphunnos yells, using the backside of his hand to tap against the entrance door frame. "Why do I always have to keep the peace around here? Can I not get a break?"

"Stop following me, Malphunnos!" Narisa shouts.

"Then stop playing with fire!"

"Says you. Didn't you steal the Eternal Flame?"

"I gave it back! …Mostly."

"This is so cute," Chaos says. "It takes a special kind of man to still care about his beloved given everything they have done… It's not like I'm getting that type of love around here."

"It's because you're a tricky bastard," Malphunnos snaps. "You know that, right? And I know you've been jumbling up my memories. Stop it!"

"I only did it once, the rest is on you. It's not hard to fool a fool. You understand me?"

Malphunnos moves in closer, but he gets stopped by Selvita as she raises an open palm and shakes her head at him. He then looks at Narisa and says to her, "Why did you entice this man to show himself?"

"I guess… I thought I still had something to prove—but deep down, I know I caused more injustice than he ever did. It's just so hard to accept."

"We really have lost our majesty, haven't we?" Chaos says. "Especially you, Overlord."

"Don't call me that…" Malphunnos says. "That's not me anymore."

"Sorry could you say that again? I keep getting distracted by that glint reflecting off your scythe."

"I could add some of your blood to it to stifle the polish."

"You flatter me. May I go back into hiding now? Let my brother handle things like he has already been doing. It's been a treat watching him play around and try to create Order out of whatever the hell this world is supposed to be now."

"So you're really not going to do anything?" Malphunnos asks. "Nothing at all?"

"Ehhh, I don't have the desire to live out my wish list right now," Chaos says. "Narisa's already outplayed and surpassed me without even trying—that really kills my motivation. There is nothing to fear about me. I'm not the most dangerous 'monster' on this planet anymore." Chaos then yawns, before saying his final thoughts. "I really do wish this family reunion was much larger. Welp, I'm leaving now. But remember—I'll be watching you…"

Jellop returns, in full control of his mind and body. He looks around in confusion. "Mal? When did you get here? Why does everyone look so angry?"

"At this point, it's just how we look naturally." Malphunnos then pulls Jellop's hood over for him and says to him, "Let's get you home…"

Chapter 75

Time's Up

At a carved stone table in a dining area, there's a small party happening among the Harbingers and some of New Bruness's residents.

"That is so not true, Novair!" a man shouts.

"It is! Laxan couldn't kill anyone with a sword even if the damn thing was his own hand! That's why none of you ever saw him in battle after that war. That man was all talk until he was bested by me."

"Isn't your kingdom known for its poisons though?" Damel asks.

"The gall! The audacity! Who brings poison to a sword-fight?"

Rend slurs on his soup.

"You got something to say, Rend?" Aluna asks.

"Naw. Nothing whatsoever. But I don't exactly discourage that particular fighting style…"

"So that's how you defeated World-Ripper. You fucking cheater!"

Rend slurps on his soup even louder, making everyone laugh. They cease little by little after they notice Suvius approaching them.

"Everyone…" he says after a brief pause. "It's time…"

Chapter 76

The World's Grave

"Should we really be burying Draxis here at Vomenn?" Rend asks.

"This is where the Dragons fought their last," Suvius says. "I would greatly prefer to give him the true respect he deserves and honor his burial at his birthplace, but alas, the Dragons made sure to keep their secret homeland only known to them. I'm thankful they were successful in doing so."

Malphunnos arrives to join everyone, rushing out from a black rift. "Sorry, sorry! I know I'm late! I was working overtime today. My best estimates didn't even come close to how many victims were under the full control of the Decay. There are just too many bodies out there and too many people who are… violently depressed about those dead bodies."

"Does that include the former Decayed who made those dead bodies?" Rend asks.

"It does, if they even still have a shred of their mind or soul left to remember their suffering."

"We appreciate you joining us despite the tremendous task set for you," Suvius says.

"This might sound callous of me, and I never thought I would say this, but it feels nice to get back to work," Malphunnos says. "It feels like a real start of forward motion after being lost and unmotivated for so long. Honestly, I wouldn't be here to work at all if it wasn't for the magnificence of mortalkind, so I want nothing more than to pay my due respects. Plus, it's my job to oversee funerals. This is automatically my least favorite one."

"You have a favorite?" Aluna asks, with an eyebrow raised.

"You ever seen a leprechaun funeral?"

"Not at all."

"You're missing out." Malphunnos then goes over and takes time to console all the dismal faces that stare at the ground. He visits Sadra first, and asks her, "How you holdin' up, Sunshine?"

She sniffles and wipes away her lucent tears.

"Aww… come here," he says, hugging her. "You're nothing but full of happiness and starlight. You know that, don't you?"

She nods at him.

"That's what I like to hear. Stay strong, for him." Malphunnos visits Jellop next and says to him, "You're a good person, Jellop."

"I like compliments. But… why?"

"I said it because it's a sentiment people need to hear more of."

"Thank. I-I think you're a good person too!"

"You say that so innocently. Everyday you're starting to sound more like…"

"Like who?" Jellop asks.

"Like yourself," Malphunnos states.

"I don't get it."

"Hmph. You've been hanging around Sadra too much."

"Stop being mean," Sadra remarks.

"Sorry, Sunshine," he says to her. His apology doesn't seem to lighten her mood. Now would be a good time to go to the next person to avoid feeling guilty. Aluna is up next. "What are your thoughts on me?" Malphunnos asks her.

"Umm, I don't know. Realistically I'm still in shock that gods exist."

"I'm planning on changing that common notion very soon. Looking back at your prayer history, I'm certain that you had an unfortunately lengthy list for us. I hope your wishes were finally answered somewhat."

"They are not perfect answers, but I can at least move forward now. I have no quarrel with you," Aluna says.

"I am pleased. I wish I was the type of god that could do more than just count dead bodies."

"I, for one, appreciate what you do."

"And I appreciate all of you."

After Aluna, the next person to visit is Rend. Malphunnos inspects Rend up and down, a scene almost reminiscent of the harsh scrutiny Suvius put Rend through when he first met him.

"Hmm. Aside from you being my most difficult hunt, Archias, I don't think we've spoken to each other much."

"Not really," Rend says.

"Do you have any curiosities or questions, perhaps?" You defied Death—twice. Surely you must be wondering about something?"

"Actually, there is one thing. I would like to know who my father was."

"Your father was human."

"That's not what I meant…" Rend says.

"You should have been clearer then. Next question."

"You sound like my mom. Can you give me a straight answer?"

"Gah… this is what I get for being nice," Malphunnos groans. "Let's just say that your father is writhing in the darkest nether regions of Oblivion. I'm not having you repeat his mistakes—not unless you want to join him. That magic of yours is already bothering me enough."

"So wouldn't it make sense if you tell me anyway to *avoid* any mistakes in the first place?" Rend asks. "You failed to do the same thing with Maeva."

"How dare you speak your logic to me. Why don't you use that cranium for your own damn question then, huh? To hell with you!"

"W-Wait! Dammit…"

In a huff, Malphunnos goes to visit the next person in line, with whom he engages in strict eye-contact with. "Maevalina," he says.

"Death," she responds, crossing her arms.

"…We have history together."

"Unfortunately."

"Would you care to start over with me? I'm not trying to trouble you, I just want to make amends," Malphunnos says.

"I've noticed your efforts, so I'll acknowledge your existence… But I still want my brother and best friend back."

"Vale and Nemi, correct? Narisa told me their names. I would change everything if I could."

"I'm glad you mean that, but don't do it for my sake alone," Maeva says. "I'm not the only person you've wronged."

"Of course, but you are the most ancient of my debts I need to pay off."

"I'm not that old."

"A thousand years or more is still a thousand years or more," Malphunnos says. "I'm surprised your servant here loves women who are older than most civilizations combined. I'm not up to date with people's kinks."

"Please go away and die," Maeva snarls.

"I agree," Rend tags in.

"Damn. Guess I'll go bother my son then. Suvius!"

"I am not your son! I am so tired of telling you that!"

"I swear this type of family dysfunction happens at every funeral I go to…" Malphunnos sighs. "How about we start this ceremony! Yeah!"

"This world is so noisy with you in it," Maeva remarks.

"Shut up, I'm talking!" Malphunnos then relocates himself to the front of the group, forcing everyone to focus on him. "So, the end of an apocalypse," he says, with a single clap of his hands. "Not too many people can say that. It's quite an accomplishment—far out-rivaling the spectacle of the birth of creation itself. For every fallen hero who has been struck down and to those who continue to fight now, we have all made this grand experience possible… but not without suffering and nefarious payback from this brutal reality we all try to make peace with."

Malphunnos walks over to Suvius and rips open reality with his bare hands, creating a small rift pocket that he can control and move around.

"You're getting better at manipulating Oblivion, Malphun-nos," Suvius says.

"See, the fact that you know what this dark matter is terrifies me."

"I'm an erudite of Darkness."

"I'm disowning you." Malphunnos then reaches inside the rift and pulls out a ceremonial, gilded sword with the inscription 'Piorna' written down its blade. "Here's one of the swords you requested from the Dwarves."

"Wonderful," Suvius says. Malphunnos tries to give another sword to him. Suvius only stares at it while mumbling, "Um…"

"What the matter, amputee? Need a han—"

"Do *not* finish that joke. Just go down the line."

Dragging his pocket portal, Malphunnos hands a sword off to Maeva, then two swords to Rend, and one to both Jellop and Sadra. Aluna requests for Jellop to hold her sword for her.

"Does everyone have a sword?" Suvius asks.

"What are these for?" Maeva asks.

"Do any of you know how we Vomenn knights honor those we wish to remember? We impale swords like these into the ground firmly and say our final sentiments. The Dwarves showed their sympathies and had some of their best forge these perfected blades for this… funeral. I asked them to inscribe the name of all seven continents on them. Let me show you all how it's done."

Suvius raises his blade and plunges it into the scorched wasteland of what used to be the makeshift refugee town of Vomenn. "I place this sword in honor of Vomenn, a kingdom that should have become utopian. I will also honor the glory of Bruness along with the rest of this continent—Piorna, my decadent home."

"That was beautiful," Sadra says. "Ah, so my sword says Excerina for a reason. I place this sword in honor of my homeland: Excerina, the first continent of civilization, and Isilios, the birthplace of Light. May true sunlight return to that lush paradise someday." She slams down the sword next to Suvius's. He helps her drive it in further.

Jellop and Aluna step forward next.

"You can go first, Jellop," she says.

"Err… I place this blade, to injure this ground, in the name of Nesolope, the continent where I was originally found and welcomed into this chaotic world by my friends for life. I will also honor the Heaven Plains where great tragedy fell and retribution rose. I also honor my trusty staff… I miss it."

Jellop then plunges Aluna's sword for her. She flies over and touches the hilt. "My tiny body, with a giant spirit, places this blade in honor of Murgosh, the best continent ever—despite it being a region where nightmares have nightmares. I will also honor the Orkanians for remaining strong through such a harsh period of time and helping us succeed. Yaga!"

"I guess I'll go next," Maeva says. "I place this blade in honor of Calvrim, the Monster Capital, and apparently the prolific epicenter of all chaos. I love my dark and ancient home. I wish to return there and rebuild its glory someday."

Rend is the last one to go. "I place this sword in honor of Terica. I didn't know my home continent had such a depressing gorge that housed a creepy cult's lair, but what can you do?" He raises the

other sword that was given to him. "I will also honor Bornamu for…
having a cool-ass volcano? I feel like I got the worst swords of the
bunch…"

Malphunnos shoves two hands into the rift-pocket that follows him. He pulls out another sword—a gargantuan one. "Okay.
Wh-which of you want this claymore? Speak fast, this thing is killing
me!"

"Hand it here," Suvius says. He grabs and inspects the hefty
blade that has 'Allosha' inscribed deep into it. He moves to stand behind the seven planted swords, in the exact middle of them. "Before
we say our departing words for… for Sir Draxis, I want to take this
moment to honor the fallen of our world."

"Just with one sword?" Maeva asks.

"It would take most of the continent to cover the appropriate
space to individually honor every victim and Decayed. This supreme
sword is meant to symbolize and represent the world across all
stretches of history, blood, honor, and eternity."

"I can feel its staggering gravity from here. You may continue."

With his left and only hand, Suvius marks the location of the
grave, using a bit of his demonic power to seal the sword deep into
the ground. He holds his hand on the hilt, letting the winds of emotion help navigate his next words.

"A second chance. There are so many lives that deserve a
second chance. Too many innocents, families, fighters… and an unfortunate number of heroes. Heroism is a rare word. A good word
that can protect countless innocents, but it can sometimes lead to an
ultimate sacrifice. None of us truly understand its impact until the

heroes that walk with us fall… or until we step close to the edge our-selves. Some falls are greater than others. Some falls are singular acts of redemption… And some falls are too emotionally painful to stom-ach their recent impression. With the few heroes we have been blessed to walk with, just like with the innocents we fight for, we have to ensure that we remember their sacrifice. Like… Klae."

"…I miss yelling at him," Maeva grumbles.

"Komet," Suvius says next, after a pause.

"…Thank you so much for illuminating our lives and fu-tures, Komet," Sadra murmurs to herself.

"Ceranus," Suvius says after another pause.

"I don't feel like that woman's name belongs here," Maeva comments.

"She does," Aluna speaks up. "At least… to me she does. As the Arbiter of Judgment, I was also their soldier, and I remember dur-ing some of those long nights when I lied to you all so I could sneak out to go rush and fulfill an escort contract, sometimes it was Ceranus who I was assigned to. She made those particular nights not so bloody. Though, maybe it's because we both shared that bloodshed. We shared a lot together. Our wishes. Pains. Our secret passions—err, not like that. She was my best friend—a wicked one—but she was my Cee-Cee. She had her decent moments. She… also liked to talk about you, Suvius."

"…Positive things?"

"Depends on what news she's heard about us—which was usually about how badly we fucked things up."

"Sounds appropriate," Suvius says. "Maybe one day we can all gather and drink together and recount our misdeeds. I really do miss our old adventures. The anarchy was… fun sometimes."

"So mischievous," Aluna remarks.

"Hmhm," he chuckles. "But, um, to continue on with this, there's also the fallen, valiant knights who fought for the Vomenn survivors. There is also anyone who was wrongfully slain by our hands. To make things simpler and broader, the whole world of Allosha and everything that it cradles is to mourn—with the exception of those who desired to bring true evil and despair upon it."

"Well said," Malphunnos says. "…Shall I bring him in now, Suvius?"

"…It is time."

Malphunnos pulls on the edges of his pet portal to embiggen it, allowing a familiar helmet-wearing knight from within to step out.

"Borace?" Rend says.

"That reaction is the story of my life," he responds. "Before I dedicated my life to living the lie of serving a perfect society, I was a simple undertaker for a small church in the far countryside." He then extends his arms out more, showing more of the child's lifeless body that was once known as Draxis. "As you can see, I'm here to return to that role under Death's orders. Don't pay me any attention."

"It would still be appropriate to show our gratitude," Suvius says.

"It is heard. I just wish I was deserving of it." Borace places Draxis down close enough to the eight grave-swords and removes the shovel strapped to his back. He starts digging in front of the swords at a steady and slow pace.

"Who wants to go first?" Malphunnos asks.

"We should let his fair lady speak her eulogy first," Suvius says as he goes to pat Sadra's shoulders. "After her, it'll be whoever chooses to stand before his greatness."

Sadra drags her feet as she approaches Draxis's body. She drops to her knees when she arrives—staying silent as she holds his hands. She speaks when she feels she is ready to.

"Brightheart… Draxis… my darling sun in this sunless world. Whenever I wanted to touch the skies and get closer to the heavenly dawn, you always took me up there to give me an experience that I will always cherish.

"Whenever I felt like I was losing a war against myself, you always stood by me and raised me up so we could repel the darkness together—and sometimes, I had to be the one to lift you up, like on that day when we saved you after raiding Vomenn to liberate as many of their enslaved dragons as we could; I had never heard a queen swear as much as Ceranus did as she chased after us. The way you smiled at the brand-new lands beneath you during the first time you experienced freedom—I fell in love with that.

"This world, if this *fucking* world wasn't so cruel, then I know you would have made me the happiest wife… maybe even a mother. I would have loved that so much because I love you so much. So often did we try to talk about our futures together, and now… and now… I'm going to miss your scales—they were so warm and smooth, just like your touch. Why did you have to go so soon? This world will be darker without you, but I will always stay bright just like you told me to. I will!"

Jellop walks over to Sadra. "Do you need some help getting up, friend Sadra?"

"Please…" she responds, letting him guide her back to the group.

Aluna flies over to Draxis, descending and resting on the ground next to him. "I don't deserve to be here. I'm so fucking stupid that I'm surprised I even have the mental capacity to fly. I just don't deserve to be here—but I can't help it! You are a master of forgiveness, even towards someone like me. And if you were here now, you would tell me to stop bitching and get up off the ground—in your usual polite manner as always.

"You had a bewitching spirit to you that somehow made me keep going—and it will forever haunt me that I tried to exploit that with my one. Stupid! Moment of betrayal. But you want to know something? This world is filled with curses and blessings, and not once have I ever felt that you were a curse. I have never met a blessing as powerful and as illuminating as you, and I hope I can reach such an exalted state just as you did. One day I'll forgive myself, just like you told me to."

Jellop is next to step forward. He cusps his hands together in front of himself, below his waist, while looking down. "My fallen friend… Draxis. It is appropriate now to say that I did hear your whispers about doing the unthinkable. You had many wishes, but none that I would ever choose to fulfill—"

"Damn, Jellop," Rend says.

"Pause—you misunderstand. You do not know the things he said to me in secrecy. He once wanted me to erase everyone's memories of him and to have me snuff him out to be left forgotten. He also once wanted me to accelerate his Decay before we even reunited with Sadra. He wanted so many things, but I always told him in return to live through it and push forward because we have never, should not, and will never tarnish and sever our love for him.

"I know you were in deep pain, Draxis, but ours would have been tripled if this world wasn't merciful enough to have you stay with us for as long as you did. A true friend is lost today, a heroic one, but we will never lose the memory. May my falling tears turn this aging battleground into a garden so that you may continue to support life even in death. Friend…"

"I shall be next," Suvius says. He kneels next to Draxis while plotting his next words. "…And so it rains. My presence here is empty like my body and soul. I can drown the world in its own blood, but I can't even add a single tear of my own to that sea of blood despite how desperately I want to.

"I lost my truest friend, a man that deserved better than following around this failure of an undead dreamer. You have done *so* much for me. My stubbornness may have made us fight like childhood rivals countless times, but I always took your candor and bravery as reliable criticism. I would have sent this team spiraling down to their deaths long ago if not for your advice.

"You did not fear anything, Sir Draxis—not even death. The only thing you were fearful of was not being your best—but let me assure you here and now—you were never, *ever*, worthless. You were never a sacrificial pawn to me. You are my brother in arms, and it will be impossible to fight evil the same way now that our paragon has respectfully returned his dulled blade and retired. I should have been better to you. Please… please forgive my imperfections and forgive the innumerable imperfections of humanity—and Humanity."

Suvius remains kneeling, longer than what Maeva has the patience to wait for. "You planning on getting up anytime soon?" she asks him. "Some of us still need to share."

"…Must I have to?"

"Not if you want me sitting on your lap. Scoot over."

"Could you choose your words more wisely? I'm trying to grieve, not be tempted by your dark desires."

"Here I come…"

"Alright, alright. I'll 'scoot' over."

Suvius wraps an arm around Maeva the moment she sits down, consoling her as she speaks.

"Draxis… I'm sorry for not saying goodbye to you properly back at Calvrim. I don't do well with seeing my savior die before my very eyes. You have no idea how thankful I am that you existed. You brought me back up from a type of despair that I didn't think was possible—and now I'm here, acting as a glorified and bipedal apothecary. 'How bizarre' as you liked to say.

"But that's enough with the stupid compliments. You're lucky you're dead now so I can't slap the shit out of you for lying to me. You stupid idiot… Why couldn't you have been stronger! What kind of dragon has a weak soul anyway, huh? A child has a stronger soul than you! You hear that! A child! Was it so hard to stay alive so we wouldn't have to be in this situation? Dammit…!"

"What she's trying to say is that we will greatly miss you and that she's sorry she couldn't have been of more help," Suvius says. "You already know this, Draxis. You and I both know how fickle she can be."

"…Go to hell," Maeva says,

"Hmph. Another day perhaps."

"I hate everything."

"I do too. I think it's time we let Archias have a word in—if he wants. Let's move."

Rend pats Maeva's shoulder as he passes by. He shakes his head while he looking down at Draxis's body. "Well… damn. What do I even say? I feel like my farewell from before was decent enough… maybe. It's obvious everyone here cares for you, and I wish I was here at the start of the Harbingers' crusade so I could enjoy our friendship longer. I do want to express my thanks to you. 'For what?' you might be wondering. It's for showing me the awesome glory of Magic.

"Thinking of it now, I might've never pursued magic if you hadn't been one of my best mentors. Umm… I also think dragons are cool. Like, really cool. I never saw one up close before, and I never thought I would get to ride one. That was neat. You're neat. Shit, I wish I had more to say. Overall, I consider these people behind me to be my bestest friends, so thanks for taking care of them. I'll be sure to do the same. Rest easy."

"You can say something if you want to, Malphunnos," Maeva says after wiping her eyes. "You don't have to remain invisible behind us."

"I appreciate the invitation. I'll try to say… something. One would think that I would have the proper words to say in moments like these. I think the clear reason why I don't is because I don't want this adventure to end. This adventure and its many misadventures have all been an eye-opener for me, and I know I have you to thank for it, Draxis. As a god, I feel helpless that I can't do anything to bring you back. You're truly one-of-a-kind to make the gods themselves feel powerless.

"Honestly, someone like you is more than a god. You knew what was happening to you, and yet, you looked me right in the eyes and showed no fear, like Suvius said. Truly beyond godlike behavior. I know you were ashamed of who you were, but if you would allow me to speak your true name to honor dragonkind, then let me, Malphunnos, the God of Death, say that I acknowledge and venerate Draxsi Novebellum, the Souleater. A majestic and marvelous race the Dragons were, one that has put the gods to shame. May you and your kind find everlasting peace."

"Thank you, Malphunnos," Sadra says.

"Should I really be thanked? The Gods have watched what transpired to their kind, but the majority of us were too afraid of breaking Divine Law to offer help."

"Not all of them. You're here after all."

"A little too late… but I am here. Yes, I am. I appreciate the constant reminder."

"And I too am here as well!" a new voice says from behind them.

Malphunnos makes no hesitation to recognize the voice and turns his head. "Narisa? Why are you here? I thought I told you to get some sleep."

"I haven't slept in years," Narisa responds. "The pain wouldn't let me."

"Why didn't you say something? I could've had Selvita help you. She's literally night incarnate."

"I feel perfectly fine as is. And I get to be more productive now."

"We need to rehabilitate you," Malphunnos says.

"Can I perform my elegy first? Don't let it go to waste."

"You made one in less than a day?"

"See? That's impressive, isn't it? It's good to be sleepless," Narisa says.

"You *do* need to sleep!" Malphunnos shouts. "Whatever, just do your thing."

"Do what thing?"

"Your elegy!"

"Right! Am I allowed to sing it?" Narisa asks. "Will you all allow me to?"

The others look at each other. They look towards Sadra next as she speaks up, with her words matching her scorn. "Draxis exhausted his life away so that you and everyone else can still breathe. Do you understand that?"

"I will never forget it. That's why I want to immortalize him," Narisa says in a pleading tone. "A melody from a graceless witch such as I is ultimately a pittance, but I have nothing else to offer. I really want to show that I am in misery for any of this happening."

"Are you only here for Draxis? You don't seem too concerned about the rest of the world," Sadra says,

"I am extremely biased for those who have faced enslavement rather than those who have not."

"Were you close with the Dragons?"

"I tried to be," Narisa says. "I sent them something special before I was rudely abducted to help unify them. Do you know if they found it?"

"The Gift," Sadra states. "That's the untrue and improper name given to your misbegotten act of support. Draxis told me that the Artifact blessed his people and resurrected them from their graves, but with your curse and their rage combined, it led to them nearly toppling the entire world. Draxis here was the very last dragon to survive up until now."

"What? No! Why does everything I do lead to destruction? Oh, Sadra… I had no idea. I just wanted them to be free, not to become killers!"

"Intentions can be double-edged, just like your presence here. Right now, you risk angering us, but I know what you desire above everything else is pacifism and to rectify indirectly killing our closest friend. I appreciate that. You can go ahead and sing your song. It's a tiny step forward."

"Am I allowed to thank you for your kindness?" Narisa asks.

"That would be bargaining for too much."

"Am I allowed to apologize for bargaining for too much?"

"For fuck's sake, Narisa…" Malphunnos says with a tired sigh.

"I'll… I'll just start singing then. Oh gosh, why am I so nervous? Are any of you nervous?"

"No!" they all shout at her.

"Eek! Just say no next time!" Narisa screams.

"We just did!" Malphunnos shouts. "Go to sleep!"

"No!"

"Then sing!"

"Okay!" Narisa starts humming to herself out of spite, soothing her way into a perfect tune.

"There she goes. Sometimes you have to demotivate her anxiety. You mortals should take this moment and engrave it into your minds and souls. She rarely sings to the public—but when she does, it's truly the real meaning of life."

"Hush, Malphunnos!" Narisa complains. "I'm starting."

She continues to hum, soon escalating her intro into a full-blown performance and a powerful inspiration of peace. Her perfect song commands them to listen and for their aching hearts to abide in the moment of solace.

The weight of their sorrow is ultimately too heavy to be completely lifted, but the sincerity and genuine love molded into her lullaby-like pitch provides help for most of that lifting.

As her song lingers, the ground rejoices in sync. A small garden patch surrounds them and the eight swords behind them, growing with thick and verdant abundance the longer and louder she sings.

Sadra is quick to brush her hands through the miniature meadow. "Look! Flowers! They're so cute! Come touch one, Borace!"

"Eh? But I'm almost done with—err… I might as well before I have to dig them up. Although… doing that might be shortsighted. Heh. It's been so long since I've seen the lushness of nature that I have forgotten that… that it is what makes our world so beautiful. This is really nice."

Narisa pauses, stunned at the grass that tickles her feet. "Did… did I do this?"

"Of course you did," Malphunnos says. "You still got the green touch."

She drops to the ground and brushes her hands through the grass like a playful child. She waters the plants with her tears as her felicity overwhelms her. "I can't believe this… I'm so thankful that I can! I'm so, so, thankful! Thank you so much, Draxis! Though your passing is a great blow to the glory of this world, your lasting heroism will lead us to a brand-new age full of life and serenity! Thank you!"

"Thank you, Draxis," the others repeat together.

Chapter 77

Petrichor

At the highest peak in the world, the remaining six Harbingers: Maeva, Rend, Suvius, Jellop, Aluna, and Sadra, are gathered together.

"What are we doing here?" Aluna asks Suvius.

"I was thinking that Daison Peak would be a good base to build the World Council. The name isn't finalized, and neither is this location, but I wanted to see what all your thoughts were."

"I don't know about that… this place is too elevated," Aluna says. "No one wants to climb upwards for a hundred years for a five-minute meeting, and then climb back down for another hundred years."

"Ah, I sometimes forget that stamina is a mortal problem. I'll decide on someplace else later then."

"You really didn't need us *all* here for that."

"No, but I do appreciate the feedback nonetheless," Suvius says. "We're here because we need to have a private discussion about our future. The future of the Harbingers."

"You're not planning on disbanding us, are you?" Sadra asks, with a minor shift towards fear in her voice.

"I just assumed that now that we have finally achieved the peace we have fought so long for that we would all want to remove ourselves from our dark past. Our futures are brighter, but also divergent. Duchess Aluna and Squire Archias are restarting and reforming the schools of Mysticology. Young Maeva has a sacred quest that will take her years to master. You, Priestess Sadra, have the world's Light to restore, and I myself have to convince a scattered world to unite and rebuild. And Jellop is Jellop."

"Disrespectful!" Jellop shouts.

"Oh he's more than disrespectful," Aluna remarks. "You're free to quit, Lord Suvius, but I'm staying with everyone else."

"Yeah!" Sadra tags in. "I've known you all for so long that life would feel empty without everyone."

Suvius chuckles. "I suppose that answers that. It's just… this new age is a stark contrast to what we have been doing for fourteen years now. Our dark powers and cynicism will have to be culled because there isn't any world-ending threat that requires such offensive might."

"Oh, Suvius, you're much too hopeful," Maeva says.

"Hey! Jackasses!" Malphunnos yells with additional spite as he steps out of a rift. "Are you not going to include me in this discussion?"

"Well… you're not an original member," Aluna says.

Malphunnos points at Rend. "Neither is he!"

"Umm, he's been here longer?"

"That is such horseshit. Your little party here wouldn't even exist without me! I should make you all kneel…"

"We don't kneel to anyone!" Sadra shouts.

"And *that* is the exact reason why this world is still somehow standing," Malphunnos says. "Suvius, there will always be a reason for the Harbingers to exist. I guarantee you that there is someone out there plotting or misbehaving in the most inconceivable way imaginable."

"I understand my foolishness," Suvius says. "I just wish for everlasting peace."

"Who says there can't be? Are we not going to be the official enforcers of that peace? I surely would hope so—because whether we like it or not…" Malphunnos extends his arm, with the back of his hand facing up. He waits on someone, anyone, to join him. "I said—*whether we like it or not…!*"

Suvius places his hand on top of Malphunnos's and shouts, "We are in this together!"

"And it will never be for glory nor riches!" Aluna says.

"It's for the pursuit of happiness for all!" Jellop says.

"In the name of Death!" Sadra says.

"For it's a swift and steadfast reminder!" Rend says.

"That all lives are weighed and judged for purity!" Maeva says.

Their pause is abrupt. They look at each other, disheartened by the unbearable silence.

"…Draxis," Sadra mumbles. "He isn't here to finish this…"

"Then we all say it together so that he may hear us from whatever empyrean beyond he is resting in," Suvius says. "On the count of three! One! Two! Three!"

"By its harbingers!" they all roar in unison, with their hands and pride raised high.

"That felt good," Malphunnos says after the adrenaline dampens.

"Truly," Suvius says.

"Friends, look!" Jellop says as he points upwards. "The sky!"

They all turn around, only to get blinded by the unmistakable marvel that scrubs the sky clean of its deep crimson hue.

"It's… it's the Sun!" Sadra cries out. She jumps up and down as if she's trying to catch it for herself. "It's the Sun!"

"Damn that bitch is bright!" Rend says with his hand hovering over his eyes.

"How is this possible…?" Suvius wonders out loud.

"*Freaking* Narisa ruined my surprise…" Malphunnos growls.

"What does she have to do with anything?" Maeva asks.

"Let's just say that she figured out a use for that Blood-Soul you two created."

"She revived the Sun god?"

"Not exactly," Malphunnos says. "It hurts to say this, but the Sun god everyone once knew him as is officially dead. He didn't even have a face to remember him by. Seeing him in that state… it damn near broke me. As for Narisa, she is technically already broken, so in her eyes, his death was only seen as an 'opportunity'."

"An opportunity…? What does that mean?"

"I think she's been going through a revelation, and I sort of understand her morbid philosophy. Now that we know that Blood is essentially the Dark version of Soulpower, the only way to learn more about its benefits is to utilize it ourselves. You're a big influence on her."

"…Is that good?" Maeva asks.

"Hell no. She is already prone enough to danger, and now she's starting to mess with sharp objects for some reason. I even caught her running around with my scythe once." Malphunnos then sighs and says, "I really need to get her some mental help."

"I can help with that!" Jellop says.

"Appreciated—but we're not that desperate yet."

"Malphunnos, can you tell me more about the Blood-Soul? I need the info for my research," Aluna says.

"Oh, sure. So, the good news is that Reincarnation seems like another decent option on relieving this Soul famine situation until we get the Natural Order stabilized, and there are some people out there who are willing enough to donate their failing bodies for… 'science', I suppose.

"We asked around and found an Isilian male who was one such volunteer. The soul transplant worked, but… I'd rather avoid doing it too often. And you were right about the potential loss of identity; he's basically a stranger in a stranger's body now."

"But why an Isilian?" Aluna asks.

"It was mostly for their particularly high resonance with Light. You mortals have shown me that you are indisputably strong and adaptable, and that potential gave us an idea—a dark one. Do you remember what I said about Narisa and sharp objects?"

"Sharp… objects? Don't me that she actually—"

"She sure did, and we all know what happens when you combine the blood of a god and mortal through Vampirism. Because when you do, you get…! Err… pretend that this is the moment when the Sun first appears. Anyways, you get… him! Behold! This is all thanks to you, Maevalina!"

She lowers her head, her expression darkening despite being shown in the surrounding light.

"Oh shit, I didn't mean it like that," Malphunnos says, panicking.

"I know you didn't," Maeva says. "I'm already painfully aware of my indirect sins—but I am thrilled that my magic still has some good purpose in this world."

"And because I like seeing you be so thoughtful and happy, let's hope things *stay* good," Malphunnos says. "To ensure that, I am keeping a very close eye on this new 'Demigod' in case he becomes greedy. You mortals have shown me your strength, but rarely any temperance."

"If you're that worried, then why not just separate and distribute his power among others?" Suvius asks. "Like what the World Council is doing with the remaining populations and leaders?"

"Be… because that would make too much sense obviously. By my name, I really should have thought of that. I'm just so… jumbled; uncertain of this uncertain future."

"We'll always be here to assist you, Malphunnos," Maeva says. "Never fear, Fear."

The sun radiates its almighty light some more, blanketing the world in an overpowering golden shine.

"He really is trying his hardest to brighten our lives, isn't he?" Malphunnos says after a chuckle. "Maybe we're all just being paranoid. The Sun is showing us that genesis is occurring. Our better future is finally here. All thanks to our victories, and that Blood-Soul that can now create new memories, new creations, and even a new generation. I have never felt so passionate towards all of life like this moment now. What a beautiful day this is."

"Wait, what's going on with the Moon? Is there about to be an eclipse?" Rend asks.

"Oh no…" Malphunnos says, letting out a heavy sigh. "Are they actually serious right now? It seems like Selvita has introduced herself to her new 'husband'. I don't know what she did or what she could have said to him, but that woman needs to learn some damn chastity. The man isn't even a week old! He was just fucking born yesterday! I wish they didn't do that in front of us…"

"Do what in front of us?" Sadra asks. "What's Selvita doing?"

"Well, when the Sun and Moon get into that position, it usually means that they're about to… Actually, I'll spare your innocence."

"I don't get it."

"I wish I didn't either. I walked in on them once. That wasn't a good day."

"I think I've seen enough," Suvius says.

"You and I both," Malphunnos says. "Now, who wants to help me exterminate some divine rats in Birthplace?"

"Can't you clear them out yourself?" Aluna asks. "You're Death."

"I mean, I can. But… I, for one, always enjoy monster hunting with others. I'll even let you all take some souvenirs from our fallen houses and pantheons as compensation."

"I'm in!"

Suvius chuckles. "Consider *all* of us to be in on this."

Malphunnos raises his scythe overhead while saying, "Then let's…" and brings it back down and shouts, "Go!"

They all rush into the fresh portal, with spells and swears blazing. Sounds of monstrous howling and victorious cheers echo out, lasting until the portal eventually snaps shut.

Dedications

So… you've made it. Welcome! This is the part where I express my thanks. Do people even read these? I sure hope so because I have quite a bit to say. It all started back when I was… No… that's not right. Since the dawn of creation, mankind has… Actually, let's not do anything flashy or bombastic.

What I really want to say is that creating this story has been an incredible journey. I believe overall this took me around… three years? With lots and lots of revisions and long nights. Though I might be acting somewhat dramatic, this adventure has been the greatest accomplishment I have done thus far, and I say thus far because this is only the beginning.

Now comes the praises! Infinite praises to my family for helping me stay on track and lifting me up over the hurdles when real life wanted to intervene and delay my progress for weeks sometimes. A high-five, a fist bump, and a gold star to a special someone for also keeping me focused. And a head pat for my pet rabbit Nova.

Also, a huge and special thanks to the wonderful team at Damonza @https://damonza.com who have helped me make my book cover look spectacular. They are masters at transmuting iron into gold.

But the most important "thank you" goes to you, reader! Thank you for reading and thank you for everything else in between!

About Me

A classic tale of being born and raised in Missouri. I used to write a lot when I was in elementary school, but I have now rediscovered my true passion once again and it will stay with me until the very end. My secondary passions include gaming and reading, with a side of music appreciation and good ole television watching. As for what I like to write, it's anything and everything in every genre as long as I have the perfect idea and vision to make something truly wonderful, so you can expect plenty more out of me that will hopefully entertain you to your heart's desires.

The best way to contact me for anything business related, or other, is to email me at: authordcfortune@gmail.com

Also, if you want to see what I'm up to next or for any other miscellaneous reason, then please check out my website!

Website: https://dcfortuneauthor.com